READER'S DIGEST

CONDENSED BOOKS

FIRST EDITION

THE READER'S DIGEST ASSOCIATION LIMITED
25 Berkeley Square, London W1X 6AB

**THE READER'S DIGEST ASSOCIATION
SOUTH AFRICA (PTY) LTD**
Nedbank Centre, Strand Street, Cape Town

Printed in Great Britain by Petty & Sons Ltd, Leeds

Original cover design by Jeffrey Matthews F.S.I.A.D.

For information as to ownership
of copyright in the material in this book see last page

ISBN 0 340 28392 0

Reader's Digest
CONDENSED BOOKS

ALONE
AGAINST THE ATLANTIC
Gerry Spiess with Marlin Bree

GILDED SPLENDOUR
Rosalind Laker

THE DAM
Robert Byrne

STALKING POINT
Duncan Kyle

COLLECTOR'S LIBRARY
EDITION

In this Volume:

ALONE AGAINST THE ATLANTIC

by Gerry Spiess
with Marlin Bree   (p.11)

Yankee Girl was tiny: only ten feet long. But Gerry Spiess, her American designer and builder, was convinced she could sail the Atlantic, and set out on an epic voyage to England. Here he tells the story of 54 days at sea, of battles with raging storms, loneliness and pain, and of his ultimate triumph. An inspiring story of how one man pitted his courage against the elements and conquered them.

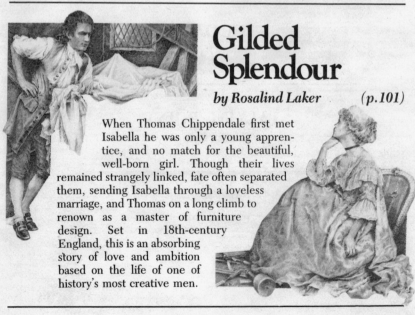

Gilded Splendour

by Rosalind Laker   (p.101)

When Thomas Chippendale first met Isabella he was only a young apprentice, and no match for the beautiful, well-born girl. Though their lives remained strangely linked, fate often separated them, sending Isabella through a loveless marriage, and Thomas on a long climb to renown as a master of furniture design. Set in 18th-century England, this is an absorbing story of love and ambition based on the life of one of history's most creative men.

THE DAM

by Robert Byrne   *(p.259)*

Above the little town of Sutterton in California towers the massive Sierra Canyon Dam. An engineering marvel, it is widely acclaimed as the safest dam ever built, but Phil Kramer, a young, inexperienced engineer, does not agree. According to his computer calculations the dam is fatally flawed: slowly, inexorably, it is disintegrating. But no one believes him except his girl friend Janet, and their frantic warnings go unheeded. How soon will the dam unleash its fury? Who will save the people downstream? A hair-raisingly tense and powerful novel.

STALKING POINT

by Duncan Kyle   *(p.385)*

It is 1941 and, in deadly secret, a meeting is planned between Churchill and Roosevelt: the whole future course of the war depends on its conclusion. In Washington, a German diplomat has discovered where the meeting will take place, and swiftly plans a daring airborne mission. Success depends on the reluctant cooperation of a disgraced German pilot, Ernie Miller, but when his wife intervenes, the picture changes dramatically . . .

ALONE
AGAINST THE ATLANTIC
Gerry Spiess with Marlin Bree

ALONE AGAINST THE ATLANTIC

A CONDENSATION OF THE BOOK BY

GERRY SPIESS WITH MARLIN BREE

PUBLISHED BY SOUVENIR PRESS

TITLE-PAGE ILLUSTRATION BY CHRISTOPHER BLOSSOM

Gerry Spiess, an American schoolteacher, had a
dream: to build the smallest, practical-sized
sailboat capable of surviving on the open seas.
After seven years of planning and construction
he set forth in his tiny *Yankee Girl* from
Chesapeake Bay in Virginia—his destination
England, the far side of the wide Atlantic.

   This is the inspiring account of Gerry Spiess's
amazing voyage and his extraordinary preparation
for it. It is the story of a man who dared to dream
and to make his dream come true.

CHAPTER 1

STORM OVER WHITE BEAR: JULY 1978

Purple clouds towered over the western horizon as I hurried toward White Bear Lake. Trouble clouds. Out of the blustery darkness could come the bane of all inland sailors: a tornado.

I shivered as I reached the dock at Tally's Anchor Inn. At the water's edge two teenage boys, hastily dragging Tally's rental fishing boats onto shore, had stopped to watch a fisherman race his boat at full throttle toward the dock. "That's the last of them," said one of the boys, sounding relieved.

"All right, you two, don't just stand there," barked a gruff female voice behind us. "Get those boats put away." The boys jumped, and so did I.

I turned to face Millie, Tally's manager, bait seller, and all-around boss. She frowned when she saw me. "Gerry, don't you know there's a tornado watch on tonight?"

"Sure," I replied. "It's a good night to do some real testing."

"Not if there's a tornado on the way." Millie's tone surprised me. Usually she joked about my being White Bear's resident "foul-weather sailor," always heading out onto the lake while other sailors were hurrying in. But not tonight.

"We're closing," Millie snapped. "The boys won't be here to help you." My boat was moored about a hundred and seventy-five feet out, and a dockboy usually shuttled me to and fro in one of Millie's rental rowboats.

"That's okay," I said. "I'll just tie the rowboat to the mooring."

Millie studied the sky. "Well, at least you won't be able to stay out long." She turned abruptly and marched toward shelter.

The boat carrying the fisherman bumped into the dock. As the man climbed out, I clambered in, and one of the boys helped me lift off the motor. Then I threw my weight hard against the oars and, fighting the wind, headed out to my own boat.

Yankee Girl was a stubby little craft only ten feet long. Because of her size, I often had to endure teasing comments, like "Where's the rest of it?" But *Yankee Girl*, in my eyes at least, was the most beautiful boat in the world. I knew every inch of her—from the tip of her mast to the bottom of her keel. I had designed her, built her in my own "boatyard"—my garage—and tested her every motion in wind and water. I knew the secret she carried: my dream of a solo Atlantic crossing.

Now, tugging at her mooring, she seemed anxious to get under way. The purple-black wall of clouds was closing in fast. If I didn't set sail immediately I would be stranded, unable either to row back to shore or hoist the sails.

I climbed aboard, slipped off the sail covers, unlocked the hatch, and dropped inside the quiet familiar cabin, where the pleasant aromas of plywood, paint, and beef jerky greeted me. I reached down into the footwell for my four-horsepower Evinrude motor. Hefting its forty pounds over the stern, I secured it tightly to its aluminum bracket, so it couldn't shake loose. My safety depended on that motor. Then I wormed my way into the forepeak to screw the mushroom-shaped ventilator shut. Now the main hatch behind me was the only opening that could let in water.

Lifting a locker cover on a floorboard, I peered down into *Yankee Girl's* bilge. It was filled with ballast—seven hundred and twenty pounds of water in plastic jugs. Sometimes the caps on the jugs came loose, leaving the bilge sloshing with water. At the moment, though, everything looked secure and dry.

It was time to set *Yankee Girl* free. I crawled to the bow, untied the mooring rope, then scrambled back to the stern and started the Evinrude. *Yankee Girl* began to move obediently out toward the center of the lake. As soon as we were clear of the shore and buoys, I turned off the motor and hoisted the sails.

Suddenly the first gust of gale-force wind hit us broadside, and *Yankee Girl* reeled under the blow. I gritted my teeth. I knew I could not turn back. I had something to prove—if only to myself.

Advance winds from the onrushing storm now pushed against *Yankee Girl's* white dacron sails until they were as stiff as iron. I secured the mainsheet (the line that holds the mainsail taut against the wind) and braced my knee against the stubby tiller. Ahead stretched open water. There, with room to maneuver, *Yankee Girl* should be able to take anything the weather threw at her.

Beginning to enjoy the ride, I settled back on my special "tiller seat", a sort of saddle I had attached to the top of the transom (the planking across the boat's stern) just above the tiller. From there I had a splendid view of sails, sky, and water, but my boat was so small that part of my posterior hung out over the edge.

The first drops of rain splattered loudly on *Yankee Girl's* cabin. I reached for my worn Minnesota Twins baseball cap and jammed it on my head; over it I pulled the hood of my foul-weather jacket. The test had begun.

My goal was simple: I wanted to keep *Yankee Girl's* sails up as long as I could. I wanted to learn, first, how much wind she could take before heeling over on her side. Second, I had to know whether I had the strength during a major storm to get the sails down before the boat capsized or her rig was damaged.

Already, in the gale's increasing fury, *Yankee Girl* had begun to heel sharply. Water was rushing over her port rail. The mainsheet was vibrating violently in its cleat. I yanked it out, loosening the tension on the mainsail. Immediately *Yankee Girl* fought her way upright and surged forward. From now on, I would have to sail with one hand holding the mainsheet, ready to let go in an instant, and the other gripping the windward rail for balance.

I glanced at *Yankee Girl's* aluminum mast to see whether it, too, was vibrating. That—or a humming sound—would signal that it was being forced out of its column by the wind. If the pressure kept up, the mast could even snap in two and come crashing down on me, shrouds, sails, and all.

Yankee Girl's mast was in good shape, but now the wind was

13

playing alarming games with her and she was heeling more than ever. Cautiously I headed the boat's bow directly into the wind. Suddenly freed of the tremendous pressure, the sails cracked with the sound of whips above my head. I lashed the tiller. It was time to get the sails down—if I could.

I wrenched free the halyard (the line used to raise and lower the sail). But nothing happened. The wind had jammed the sail in its slot. To loosen it I would have to go out on deck. Too late I remembered that I had foolishly left my safety harness at home.

I had no choice, though; that sail must come down. I pulled myself forward. The wind screamed around me; the rain was falling so heavily that I could barely see. Above me swung the heavy wooden boom, missing my head by inches. Clinging with one hand to the mast, I reached high and grabbed a handful of slippery dacron. With a yank, I pulled down the sail. But the task I dreaded most still lay ahead: the jib had to be secured. I inched forward on my knees. Under my weight, the boat plunged into the waves, wetting me to the waist.

As *Yankee Girl* fought to regain her balance, I was thrown against the forestay (the stainless-steel rigging that runs from the bow to the top of the mast). Desperately I caught the sharp wire in the crook of one arm to keep from being thrown back against the mast. Then, with my free hand, I gathered in the jib and lashed it down.

My work done, I scrambled into the cabin and slammed the hatch shut above me. I sighed in relief. Never again, I promised myself, would I be caught in a storm without my safety harness.

Crouched down in *Yankee Girl*'s belly, I could not see now what lay ahead. I could only estimate my position, hold my compass course, and hope for the best. But I needed power to stay in the center of the lake, or the wind would drive me back to shore. One quick tug brought the Evinrude back to life. Working the tiller from inside the cabin, I headed directly into the jaws of the wind and turned the throttle up to three-quarter power. Even then, *Yankee Girl* made barely enough speed to let me steer her. Still, she was holding her own.

"We'll just sit here until the storm ends," I told myself. All things considered, I was pretty satisfied. We were in the midst of the worst weather *Yankee Girl* had ever experienced, and I was in no

14

real danger—as long as I held my compass course, kept the motor running, and maintained my mid-lake position.

I glanced at my waterproof watch; it was six thirty-seven pm. By now my wife, Sally, would be home from work, even though it was a long drive from her office south of Minneapolis to our house in White Bear Lake, a northern suburb of St. Paul. Lately her workload as a manager for a computer consulting firm had been heavier than usual, and on a night like this it was good to know she was safe and warm inside, instead of out waiting for me on the shore as she often did. I was glad I'd left that note for her on the kitchen table:

Gone sailing. Probably be back late, don't wait for me.

Love, Ger.

I had no way of knowing it, but even as I was comforting myself with these thoughts of Sally, she was frantic with worry. She had first heard the weather bureau's storm warning on her car radio. Arriving home at five forty-five and finding my note, she thought perhaps I hadn't heard the news of the tornado watch. She had hurriedly changed into her jeans, grabbed some dry clothes for me, and driven down to Tally's intending to tell me about the storm and to help me secure *Yankee Girl* against it. But Tally's was dark when she got there, and *Yankee Girl* and I were nowhere to be seen.

Sally had rushed back to her car then and started circling the lake looking for us. By this time the rain was falling in thick sheets, and soon the weather announcer was reporting winds of over sixty miles per hour. Several times Sally stopped the car and ran down to the water's edge to look for us. Each time she returned to her car, drenched to the skin and increasingly fearful that *Yankee Girl* was somewhere in the middle of the lake—bottom-up with me trapped inside.

THE STORM WAS worsening. Gale-force winds shrieked in the rigging, and rain thundered on *Yankee Girl's* cabin roof. Over all the noise I could barely hear the rasp of the outboard motor. We plowed on through the black water.

Now lightning crackled around me. *Yankee Girl's* aluminum mast was a perfect lightning rod, so I was glad her mast tip was connected by a heavy wire to a six-inch-square copper plate on her bottom. That plate, I hoped, would protect us in the event of a strike. But another thought came to mind. In the bilge, in addition to the water jugs, I had stowed three hundred pounds of steel weights and lead castings for ballast. If one of those weights had snapped a lightning connector when I had shoved them around to make them fit into the tiny space, then lightning could sizzle downward, jump the wire, and burn a hole right through the bottom of the boat. . . .

I shook my head. I *had* to think positively. I had to keep trusting in *Yankee Girl*—in myself, really, for I had designed her, built her, cared for her. If I ever lost confidence in *Yankee Girl*, I would lose confidence in myself. So all I had to do now was sit tight in *Yankee Girl*'s cabin and ride out this storm.

THE WIND HAD diminished to a whisper and the lake now displayed only a few gentle ripples. The storm—and the test—were over. *Yankee Girl* and I had both passed.

As we headed toward shore under the outboard's power, I could see two stranded boats that had been torn from their moorings and tossed up onto the beach. Higher up the hill, Tally's was dark. I decided to steer *Yankee Girl* to the deserted dock. It was the perfect time and place to find out one more thing: how much force it would take to knock her on her side. She was buoyant enough in most weather conditions. But what if she were suddenly hit by a violent squall with all her sails standing? Would she be able to right herself then?

With a light bump, we arrived at the dock and I stepped off carefully. Stretching up high, I got a firm grip on *Yankee Girl*'s port shroud, the one-eighth-inch stainless-steel wire leading to the top of her mast. Pulling hard on the shroud wire, I tried to bring *Yankee Girl* down on her side. But like an eager puppy she only came closer to me, nudging against the dock.

I *had* to find out what her righting moment was. I climbed onto her cabin top, again grasped the port shroud, then jumped and swung like Tarzan toward the dock. As soon as I landed, I quickly grabbed for *Yankee Girl*'s mast tip and pulled on it with all my weight until her spar was horizontal with the lake's surface.

16

She was down, her bottom jutting out of the water, her port side partially submerged. I looked about for a way to hold her in this position—a halyard, perhaps, that I could hook under a plank of the dock—so I could inspect her more closely. But I didn't dare move. The thousand pounds of ballast in her bilge were trying to force the mast back into the air—and me with it.

Suddenly I felt more than saw something move on the steps leading up to Tally's. Peering in the dim light, I could barely make out the shape—but I knew it was Sally.

Then the realization hit me: all Sally could see was *Yankee Girl's* upturned bottom.

"Sal, I'm here!" I shouted.

She ran down the remaining steps, raced across the dock, and threw her arms around my neck.

"I'm doing some testing," I said, still hanging on to the mast. "I want to check *Yankee Girl's* righting ability."

"I thought she had capsized and washed up on the dock," Sally said, her voice trembling.

Abruptly I released the mast, and it soared into the murky sky. I put my arms around Sally and held her tight.

"I drove all around the lake looking for you," she said. "Didn't you hear the tornado warnings? I was so worried!"

"I was watching the sky the whole time," I replied. "I'm sorry." But I knew an apology wasn't enough. She was still upset. Suddenly I decided to turn her attention to *Yankee Girl*.

"Want to give me a hand?" I asked. "Help me hold her down. I want to make a quick inspection of the bottom."

Sally hesitated. Then she followed me over to the boat, whose tiny portholes were dimly illuminated by the soft glow of the cabin lights. "Won't the water come in through the hatch when she's on her side?" she finally asked. "Is everything inside secure?"

"She'll be all right, and everything is strapped down."

We stood for a moment, studying *Yankee Girl*. When I had managed to pull her down the first time, I had estimated the lift of her mast tip to be about a hundred pounds. Sally weighed about a hundred and ten.

"Okay," I said. "You hold her off while I pull her down."

With one foot Sally shoved *Yankee Girl* away from the dock. I jumped up and clutched the shroud. Once more *Yankee Girl* fought back on her way down. Sally grabbed the tip of the mast.

"Have you got her?" I asked.

"Either I've got her or she's got me." Sally was lying nearly horizontal on the dock as she hung on to the mast.

Yankee Girl was now far over on her side. Inspecting her, I found she had come through the storm unscathed. And in spite of the load she was carrying, the lip of her open hatch was still at least six inches above the waterline.

"Isn't she fantastic, Sally?" I asked proudly.

"Unbelievable. Now let's put her away and go home."

Working together, Sally and I eased up on *Yankee Girl's* mast and let her go upright. Then we climbed on board and shoved off from the dock. Above us the stars came out, and lights on the shore twinkled on the smooth surface of White Bear Lake.

"I really *was* worried about you," Sally said softly.

"I'm sorry about that," I answered. "But you know, Sal, that I don't take chances."

It took only moments for the two of us to secure *Yankee Girl* to her mooring. Afterward we rowed back to the shore, watching *Yankee Girl* recede into the freshly washed night. I was convinced that she was now ready for deeper waters—and for her true destiny.

CHAPTER 2
THE BIRTH OF YANKEE GIRL

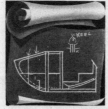

The idea for the boat had first begun to take shape a year and a half earlier—in January 1977.

About two thirty one bitterly cold Minnesota night, I had awakened with a start and stolen out of bed. Sally didn't even stir. After fifteen years of marriage, she was used to my getting up at odd hours. I padded down the hall to my study, turned on the light, and began sorting through the piles of papers on my drawing board.

At first glance they seemed a hodgepodge: sketches made while waiting in doctors' offices, notes scribbled during university lectures, scraps on which I had written sudden inspirations while traveling. But my collection made sense to me. Every piece of paper bore a variation on a single theme: boat building.

I had been fascinated by boats for more than seventeen years. I loved what they could do and what I could do with them. To me, sailing was the closest a person could come to complete freedom.

Looking through my papers brought back a flood of memories. During the early 1960s, while I was in the Air Force, I had sailed whenever and wherever I could, from reservoirs in Colorado and Kansas to minuscule prairie lakes in Nebraska. The first boat I built by myself had come out of a kit; a fifteen-and-a-half-foot Snipe, she was a delight to sail. The first boat I designed was a seventeen-foot miniature cruiser that I christened *Yankee Doodle*. In 1969 and 1970 she made it possible for me to live out one of my biggest fantasies: sailing down the Mississippi River from St. Paul to New Orleans, then through the Caribbean and on to Panama. By the time I arrived at the Canal, I was so lonely for Sally that I asked her to join me. Together we sailed from Panama to Ecuador.

During that voyage I discovered that Sally was a great ocean sailor. However, that was very nearly the last major trip either of us ever made. One day, while we were cruising off the coast of South America, a pod of whales suddenly appeared about a mile in the distance. One eighty-foot giant broke away from the group and charged our little boat. When he was only a hundred feet away, he dived.

Sally and I held our breaths and prayed that he would not decide to surface beneath us. If that happened, it would be all over. Moments later the whale erupted out of the sea in front of us and rose straight into the air. When he fell back into the water, the noise and the turbulence were devastating.

We got the message. As soon as we could, we put into port and sold *Yankee Doodle*. Back in Minnesota, I was so relieved to be safe at home that I vowed never again to undertake such a trip.

But a few years later I was at it again, this time in a fifteen-foot boat of my own design. In November 1974 I set sail out of Miami on the first leg of a two-year solo voyage around the world. Two days later I was back in Miami. I had sailed nonstop for thirty-three hours battling adverse winds and waves. I was exhausted, hallucinating, and close to a complete collapse. The sea had taught me that I was neither physically nor psychologically prepared to meet its challenge head-on.

As years went by, I thought about these "failures". Twice I had set out to conquer the oceans—and twice I had been the one conquered. I began to understand that the only sensible way to cross any sea was by cooperating with it.

And that was what I fully intended to do on my next voyage. For there would, of course, be a next voyage. Only this time I would build, in my garage, a special kind of boat—one I would design myself, using everything I had learned from my previous experiences. It would be radically different from any boat that had ever been built before.

As I now looked over the three years' worth of notes and sketches spread out before me, I realized that what I must come up with was a radically different type of sailboat, one that would carry very little ballast. Ballast is what pulls a sailboat upright again if a high wave or strong wind pushes it over on its side. But it can also drag a damaged boat to the bottom. I wanted my boat to float no matter what happened.

Though the boat would be incredibly small, it would have to be large enough to carry sufficient supplies for months at sea. Though its sail area would be limited, it would nevertheless have to be speedy and maneuverable. And, finally, it would have to protect its pilot—me—from the raging elements, while still providing some degree of comfort. In short, I wanted a boat whose priorities would be safety and reliability. A work boat—not a beauty queen.

I reached for a clean sheet of graph paper and marked off forty squares. On the scale I was accustomed to using, four squares represented one foot. My boat, I had decided, would be no more than ten feet long. That, I felt, was as small as I could go and still end up with one capable of carrying a normal complement of sails, tacking into the wind, and navigating the high seas.

Next I had to settle on the boat's width. If I followed the conventional rule of thumb and made the beam one third as wide as the boat was long, I'd end up with a craft only three feet four inches across. That would give me a faster boat, but not a very stable one, and it would never be able to carry the enormous load of supplies I'd need.

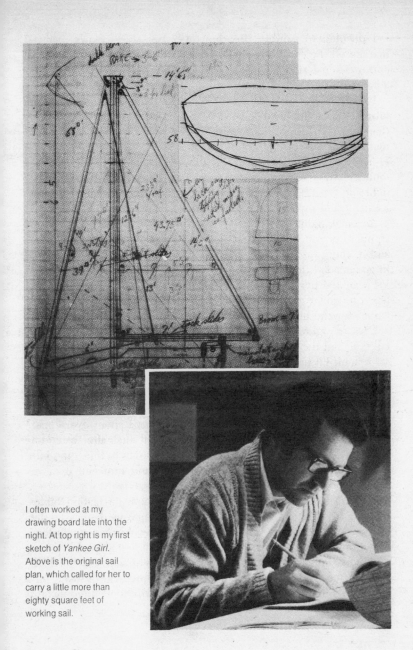

I often worked at my drawing board late into the night. At top right is my first sketch of *Yankee Girl*. Above is the original sail plan, which called for her to carry a little more than eighty square feet of working sail.

I decided to gamble. Bending over my graph paper again, I marked off the equivalent of five feet six inches and penciled in the curve. Then I stared at what I had just drawn. It didn't look like a boat at all; it looked like a sawed-off pumpkin seed.

I was a little surprised at what I had come up with, because my ultimate goal had not been to design a boat that would be smaller than anyone else's. All I cared about was building a compact, manageable vessel that could survive a journey across the treacherous North Atlantic. Still, I felt an enormous sense of relief. After months of doubt, I was on my way. Satisfied, I turned off my study light and went back to bed, knowing that in the middle of the night I had turned my life around.

As usual, Sally was up before I was the next morning and already sipping her coffee at the kitchen table. I sat down across from her and, without preliminaries, made my announcement. "I've decided to go ahead with my plan."

I watched her face closely as I waited for her response. She set her cup down carefully on its saucer and said, "There goes the garage for the next six months. When are you planning to sail?"

I was delighted. "I'll build the boat this summer, test it in the fall, and sail the Atlantic next summer."

"I think I'll have that second cup of coffee now," Sally said.

AS IT TURNED OUT, I had underestimated my departure date by a full year, for I had no notion of how much planning, building, and testing lay ahead. For the next three months I spent every spare moment completing my design. That meant that after attending classes at the University of Minnesota every day to finish my education degree, I came home every night and hunched over my drawing board.

I sent off countless requests for information: navigation tables, pilot charts, sailing directions, Gulf Stream surveys. I amassed data on wave heights, wind directions, atmospheric pressure, precipitation, fog, traffic, currents, and even icebergs. I haunted libraries, seeking accounts of single-handers who had braved the North Atlantic before me. Although none had attempted the crossing in a boat as small as the one I envisioned, their experiences and insights would, I knew, prove invaluable.

Then, late one night, I realized something that nearly put me into a panic. My boat would weigh about seven hundred pounds—but it would have to carry more than a thousand pounds of supplies, plus everything I could possibly need for the voyage, from a first-aid kit to a portable head. I'd have to have a galley for cooking, and a radio to maintain contact with passing ships. And I'd need a motor to maneuver in port, to stay out of the way of ships, and to push me along during periods of calm. That, of course, meant that I'd have to carry gasoline. And I hadn't even considered my own one hundred and fifty-five pounds!

I stared at my figures in disbelief. Could a ten-foot boat really bear such a load? Or would it sit so low in the water that it would be in constant danger of swamping? "Gerry, old buddy," I said to myself, "maybe you'd better stick to teaching."

I *had* set impossible standards for myself. The more I thought about them, the less sleep I got. And by the middle of May, my stomach was beginning to hurt. This was a warning; I had a history of ulcers, and I knew that I had to slow down. But how? I had only one short summer to build my boat, for in the fall I had to begin student teaching at Mariner High School in White Bear Lake.

I began the actual construction at the beginning of June. At first everything went smoothly. To keep costs down, I planned to use plywood wherever possible—for the keel, the frame, the outer skin. A few of my money worries were solved when the neighborhood kids told me about a hardware store that was going out of business. We all piled into my old station wagon, rushed to the store, and found quantities of plywood sheets that had been used as shelves and partitions. I got the whole lot, along with some used two-by-fours, for twenty dollars—a real bargain. Some of the lumber was still full of nails, and some of the kids made a few dollars pulling them out.

The first step in construction involved laminating the elements of the boat's "backbone": the keel, the stem (the upward-curving extension of the keel at the bow), and the transom knee (the piece used to reinforce the stern end of the keel). In most boats these elements are made up of many sections, but I wanted to make mine in one piece. I began by glueing and screwing two plywood sheets together. Then I added two more pieces to either side. The finished keel structure was four and a half inches thick. My little boat would have an enormously strong backbone. And I had done it all in twenty hours of work.

I wondered whether the frame construction would go as easily. According to my design, the boat would have only four ribs, each cut from a single sheet of plywood, incorporating the deck cross-beams, the starboard bunk support, and the port storage area. This would give my little boat great strength. I zipped out the parts in just a few minutes with my electric saber saw, but as I worked I started worrying again about the boat's size. It was going to be awfully small, and I wondered whether I'd be able to fit myself inside when it was finished. I decided to find out. After cutting the fourth rib, I laid it on the floor and tried to curl myself along the top of it, approximating the sitting position I'd take inside the boat.

That was when Sally chose to come looking for me. "What's going on?" she asked. "Something's definitely wrong," I answered. I kept trying to squeeze my body into the frame's contours. But no matter how much I turned and twisted, some part of me still hung out over the edge. I lay there a moment with my feet in the air, feeling foolish, then sat up. "Well, I just hope I'll fit when I'm done."

During the next few weeks the pain in my stomach intensified, and finally I went to see my doctor. It turned out I did have an ulcer. "We'd better operate," my doctor advised. A surgeon seconded his opinion. I was horrified. Surgery now would mean the end of my dreams. So, disregarding the doctors' advice, I decided to follow a regimen that had helped me in the past: frequent meals of fresh foods, and vitamins. I drank gallons of milk, consumed dozens of eggs, and ate six meals a day. I felt so terrible I could work only four hours at a time.

My little boat's ribs and frame now rested upside down on an old kitchen chair, and I was about to lay the stringers (long thin pieces of wood that run the length of the boat along its frame). But the stringers refused to bend to the extreme curve of the bow. They kept breaking. I finally succeeded in fitting two stringers to the bow, glueing them, and screwing them in place. Thinking I had the problem solved, I was walking wearily toward the doorway when, with a loud cracking noise, they broke. The pain in my stomach intensified.

For a while I considered reducing the thickness of the stringers. But I couldn't afford to sacrifice any of the hull's strength. I started having nightmares—of enormous waves rolling over my boat, of the hull breaking in two, of me being washed overboard.

One evening, after cleaning up the garage, I sat down on an old chair, rested my head in my hands, and just stared at the few stringers that had not yet cracked. I tried to imagine a way of making them fit around the bow. All I could think was, It can't be done. After five months of planning and nearly a month of building, I had reached an impasse. I would have to burn everything and start over again.

Filled with deep sadness, I dragged myself to bed. Sally rolled over and looked at me questioningly.

"It isn't going to work, Sal," I said.

"Get some sleep," she recommended. "It'll look different in the morning."

But the problem remained unsolved, and by the Fourth of July my ulcer was unbearable. Sally and I had driven up to the north woods to spend the holiday with my parents. I had hoped that the change of scenery would help, but I was so ill that I stayed inside the cabin while Sally and my parents went fishing. I wondered whether I would ever again be well enough to undertake *any* voyage.

One evening Sally and I took a walk through the pines along the lakeshore. "You've had ulcers before," Sally remarked, "and you've always gotten over them."

"When I get this sick, I lose my strength," I said. "If the ulcer doesn't go away, I'll just have to give up."

"The first thing you need to do is to get your construction problems squared away," she said.

"I know, but I'm running out of time. In six weeks I'll have to start getting ready for my student teaching."

She stopped and turned to face me. "Listen, Ger," she said, her voice firm. "It's mostly a matter of psychological outlook."

Her words rang true. *I was doing all this to myself.* No one else was responsible for my unresolved fears, my impossible schedule, my inner conflicts. I would have to straighten myself out inside— or forget my dream.

Sally took my arm and we began walking back to the cabin. "You've reached your low point," she said gently. "You're on your way up now."

She was right again. As had happened so many times in the past, her help and insight filled me with hope and courage. I took a deep breath of the pine-scented air. I could do anything I wanted to do.

ON OUR FIRST MORNING back in White Bear, I pulled on my old work clothes and went to the garage. Somehow I knew I would solve the problem of the stringers that day. I picked up a very thin piece of molding I had used to check the curves of the hull and laid it over the frame. Then, following a sudden inspiration, I moved it up to the treacherous curve at the bow. It bent like a willow as I pressed it into place.

I stood there amazed. The solution had been at hand all along. Moving around to the stern, I put one end of the molding in a clamp against the transom and bent it forward around the hull to the bow. It clung to the curve like a strand of spaghetti.

I took a one-and-a-quarter-inch-thick stringer and rushed over to my table saw. I ran it lengthwise through the saw and cut two narrow, pliable pieces. Racing back to the boat, I clamped the stringers to the ribs, one on top of the other. The split pieces fitted together easily around the curve. When I squeezed glue between the two pieces and laminated them together, the resulting stringer was the same thickness as the ones that had kept breaking, but since it was made up of two halves, it was far stronger.

The remaining stringers went on without a hitch. From this point on, my stomach began to heal. As Sally had guessed, it had all been a matter of psychological outlook.

The next challenge was the task of bending the three-eighth-inch construction-grade plywood onto the frame, to follow the curve of the stringers. Soon I began experiencing the same problems as I'd had with the stringers; on the compound curve near the bow, the plywood tended to break.

But now the solution came to me almost immediately. I took the troublesome plywood out onto the driveway and poured boiling water over it. Hauling the wood back to the boat frame, I found that while the boiling water had made it more flexible, it was still not bending the way it had to. I placed rags on top of it, heated more water, and saturated the rags. That did the trick. When I finally tightened the clamps, the wood bent willingly. Nothing could stop me now.

I sanded the hull down, filled the screw holes with putty, and covered everything with overlapping layers of fiberglass. The keel area got four extra layers for added strength. Then I pulled my little boat out into the driveway to cure in the hot July sun. By now it weighed about four hundred pounds. I propped the bow up on a kitchen chair so the air could circulate around it.

The neighbors strolled over to inspect my latest project. "It's an awfully small boat," one commented after studying it for several minutes. "Going to do anything with it?"

"Nothing in particular," I answered. "I just want to see if it's possible to build a boat this small that'll sail well."

The kids came, too, of course. Build a boat in your garage, and you are bound to attract kids, like kittens to milk. "How can you stand to have them around all the time?" one parent asked.

"They make my day," I said. It was true. Each neighborhood kid was a character, and they all loved to get involved.

"Can you find me a little piece of wood about this long?" I would ask Mike, holding up two fingers. He would rummage around happily and find just the right piece.

Freckle-faced eight-year-old Kenny, a compulsive cleaner-upper, would come running over whenever the garage door went up.

"Hi, Ger," he'd say. "Can I help?"

"Sure," I'd say. "First thing to do is clean up. It's not safe to have a lot of stuff underfoot." With the biggest broom he could find Kenny would then sweep out the entire garage.

When the time came to paint the hull, the kids begged to help.

"I don't have enough brushes," I said lamely.

"We'll get some from our dads," they chorused, and off they ran. Minutes later they were back, brushes in hand. I winced. Knowing what a beating the brushes would take, their fathers had given them the worst they had.

"Well," I said, thinking fast, "let's start with the inside." Soon they were at work sloshing white paint around the bilges. They were in their glory.

MY OWN PARENTS were still not aware of my plans. I hadn't yet thought of a suitable way to break the news. What could I say? "Guess what—I'm going to sail the North Atlantic in a ten-foot homemade boat."

One day late that summer Dad arrived unexpectedly while I was working. I let him walk around the boat on his own for a few minutes. I could tell he wasn't fooled—he knew it wasn't meant for White Bear Lake. After all, I'd been talking about an ocean voyage for years.

"How long is it?" he finally asked.

"She's a ten-footer," I replied, trying to stay calm.

There was a long silence. Would he try to discourage me? And what would he tell Mother?

At last he looked squarely at me and said, "She's going to be strong, isn't she?"

"She has to be," I replied, smiling. He understood.

Dad kept the secret, but it was inevitable that Mother would learn the truth sooner or later. On her birthday, my parents came over to our house for dinner. The moment they arrived, Mother said she wanted to see how our garden was progressing. The route to it was through the garage. She took two steps into the "boatyard" and stopped abruptly.

"That had better not be another boat," she said.

"I'm afraid it is," I admitted uneasily.

"Just be sure you don't sail it anywhere but on White Bear Lake," she warned. "It's much too small to take on the ocean."

I knew that I hadn't heard the end of it yet.

By September I was ready to launch my creation. On a beautiful fall afternoon, Dad, Sally and I loaded the little boat onto my homemade trailer and drove to a launching ramp near Tally's. This was it—the culmination of years of work.

I stepped the mast on the cabin top and hung the rudder. Then, with Sally on one side of the boat and Dad on the other, I carefully backed the trailer into the lake.

As soon as the boat's transom touched the water, my little craft began to float. But as more of the hull entered the lake, it suddenly lurched to one side. Sally clutched at the shroud and screamed. "It's rolling over! It's rolling over! Stop! Stop!"

Dad grabbed the other side. Together he and Sally were supporting the boat, which was tilting wildly.

"Better get her back on the trailer," he said.

Quickly I tightened the steel winch cable and pulled the trailer up the ramp, where we hastily unstepped the mast. I was thoroughly embarrassed. I had expected my boat to ride high on the water, for as yet I had not loaded it down with ballast. But I should have known better than to step the mast before launching. With no ballast whatsoever, the additional weight up high had made the boat top-heavy.

It had not been a very auspicious launching for a boat I intended to sail across the North Atlantic. But I had learned my lesson. Before taking it out again, we loaded it with my old exercise weights, rocks and a few bags of sand. That at least brought it down to the sailing lines.

Sally and I managed to do some sailing that fall. Sometimes we had to scrape ice and snow off the boat before we took it out. But the results of our tests were encouraging.

In October we tested the boat's largest sail, a red spinnaker—the big, almost spherical sail that billows from the masthead forward of the mast itself. Sally had just hoisted its one hundred and eighty square feet of canvas when suddenly the wind hit us. The boat heeled wildly, and in seconds we were running out of control.

"Don't panic!" I yelled at Sally as I clambered to the bow to gather in the icy sail.

"Why do I always end up with the tiller when things get desperate?" Sally wanted to know.

That was our last sail of the season. With numb fingers we took out the ballast, hauled the boat up onto the trailer, and took it home, where we stored it off to one side of the driveway. And there it remained during the winter of 1977–78, frozen into a snowbank.

But my little boat had shown real potential. Even on those blustery fall days, it had done everything I'd asked. It had handled with great authority, with an almost rocklike solidity and with good balance. As I was beginning to learn, it had a distinct personality and even a streak of stubbornness.

At first I had planned to call it *Yankee Limey*, since I'd be sailing it to England. But somehow that name didn't quite capture my feelings. For I was becoming enchanted with my creation.

"What a sweetheart you are," I'd say, patting her painted side. "What a sweet little girl."

And so I named her *Yankee Girl*.

CHAPTER 3

PREPARING FOR THE VOYAGE

 Snow draped the little boat parked beside the driveway that winter. But my preparations for the journey went on.

I was now confident that *Yankee Girl* was strong enough to survive any voyage. The six layers of plywood on the stem made her bow a virtual battering ram, and the fiberglass sheathing around the three-eighth-inch plywood gave her a hull like a walnut. Yet, despite my positive attitude, niggling doubts began to creep in.

Yankee Girl was virtually indestructible. But could she keep *me* alive? Could a ten-foot boat hold enough provisions for a trans-atlantic crossing?

I had learned from my research that the crossing would take about sixty days. That meant I'd need at least two months' worth of food, water, clothing, and other supplies. But the thirty-eight hundred miles of the Atlantic I'd be facing were notoriously fickle. A boat could lie dead in the water for days, be driven backward, even be disabled. For safety's sake, I'd have to prepare for three months at sea. If anything went wrong, it would be a long way to the next supermarket.

I began by calculating my food and water needs. Assuming that I'd be eating regularly, I'd need about five cans of food a day. I could, for example, have a can of milk and dry granola for breakfast, a can of chili and a can of corn for lunch, and canned peaches and stew for dinner. Five cans of food per day, times ninety days equaled—and here I gasped—*four hundred and fifty cans!*

I briefly considered dehydrated foods as a space-saving alternative. But they were awfully expensive. And I'd have to bring along so much water to mix them with that I wouldn't really be saving any space. I'd better take canned food.

Thinking about water made me wonder how much I'd need for drinking purposes, and I nervously began keeping track of my daily consumption. For the first few days I found I drank at least a gallon a day, which meant that I'd have to carry ninety gallons—an impossible figure.

After several days of concentrated effort, I got my consumption down to one third of a gallon a day—thirty gallons of water for the trip. For insurance I'd bring along some little cans of juice, too. But I got another shock when I totaled up the cans and containers I'd figured on so far. With its hull packed solid, I found my boat would displace more than two thousand pounds! I'd built it to be unsinkable, but there were limits. And what if it were holed and flooded or sprang a leak? Obviously, I couldn't carry flotation tanks or even foam for flotation. There wouldn't be room.

I struggled with these problems for days. Then I had an inspiration. It was so obvious I wondered why no one had thought of it before. The provisions *themselves* could serve as both ballast and flotation. I decided to try to prove my theory.

That evening Sally walked into the bathroom and found me leaning over a tubful of water, surrounded by cans of various sizes.

"Drowning cans?" she asked.

"Look at this," I said, carefully placing a small can of corn in the water. Then I sat back to watch.

"It floats!" I exclaimed triumphantly. "Now look." I dropped a can of baked beans into the tub. It promptly sank.

"You never liked beans anyway," Sally said, and I knew that she understood what I was doing.

This opened the door to a possible solution, for I now calculated that four hundred and fifty cans—if I could fit them inside the hull—would weigh only a little more than fifty pounds when submerged.

Next I did some taste testing. If I were going to be stuck in the middle of the ocean with a limited food supply, I'd better like what I brought along. I went to the store and bought single cans of everything I could imagine eating. During the next few months I devoured different brands of chili, stew, fruits, and vegetables, rating them on a scale ranging from excellent to awful. Few foods made it into the excellent category, but there were enough of them to provide the backbone of my menu.

I also began making beef jerky. An excellent source of protein, it keeps forever. I had tried many commercial products but liked none, so I finally came up with my own recipe, which involved marinating paper-thin slices of sirloin tip beef and then drying them very slowly. I tried using oven heat, but it dried out the beef too quickly. In the end, I spread the meat out on the oven racks, plugged in Sally's old hair dryer, and set it inside. The steady stream of gentle heat worked perfectly.

Beef jerky and canned goods would provide me with plenty of food. But storing water was turning out to be a problem. I tested many kinds of containers. In some the water picked up a plastic taste; in others mysterious green things began to grow. Some containers were the wrong shape or not strong enough for the journey. Then one day, while I was topping up the car battery with distilled water, the answer came. Although this water had been sitting in the garage for two years and had been opened many times, it still looked clean and clear. And I was delighted to find that it tasted as good as it looked.

That settled it: I would carry thirty gallons of distilled water in their original plastic jugs. But I'd choose only those with screw tops and test them to make sure they'd stay closed.

Then I found I could use plastic containers for many things. A lot of gear, even clothing, would go into widemouthed one-gallon food jars that I procured from the cafeteria of the high school where I was student teaching. By rolling a shirt very tightly I could reduce it to the size of a hot-dog bun. Seven rolled shirts fit neatly into one container.

In fact, my little "suitcases" could do double duty by keeping my clothing absolutely dry and by serving as flotation. A filled container weighed two or three pounds but had five or six pounds of buoyancy when placed in water. I decided to store everything I could in these plastic wonders, put them in sail bags, and lash them into various nooks inside the hull.

Each problem solved seemed to lead straight to another. I knew now where I'd keep my clothes, but I also knew I'd have no water to do laundry, and on a ten-foot boat there would be no place to hang clothes up to dry. In addition, clothing that gets wet with salt water is uncomfortable to wear. That meant that I'd probably use things only once or twice before I'd have to throw them away. So I'd need a fresh set of clothing for nearly every day of my trip, and in sufficient variety to meet all conditions.

I began to calculate: I would have to take at least forty shirts, twenty pairs of pants, thirty-five pairs of socks, six sweaters, and thirty-five sets of underwear. Somehow it would all have to fit inside the hull. But at least it wouldn't cost me much. For years Sally had accused me of never throwing anything away. Now I simply pulled out everything I'd collected—enough, I hoped, for my months at sea.

I continued to read the accounts of other voyagers. They told me what I must beware of: dehydration, sunburn, dampness, bitter cold, windburn, abrasion, loneliness, isolation, hallucinations, and fatigue that could spread as far as the eye sockets.

The more I read the more nervous I became, and I redoubled my efforts to take every conceivable precaution. Of particular concern to me was my still unproven theory of stability and buoyancy, for it was central to the success of my voyage. I already knew that my four hundred and fifty cans would weigh only about fifty pounds in the water. My thirty gallons of distilled water would weigh two hundred and forty pounds in the air but would float in salt water. Whatever gasoline I carried would provide two pounds of buoyancy per gallon when submerged, and the one-gallon containers filled with clothing and dried foods would be worth about five pounds of buoyancy each. All of this floatable ballast would make us virtually unsinkable. Yet the more than a thousand pounds the boat would carry below the waterline would give us tremendous stability.

The only things that would sink, in fact, were the tools and other equipment and the motor, and I could throw these overboard if we were flooded. In other words, if my ideas proved correct, I would have the safest boat in the world. *If.*

One day I discussed my theory with my friend Bill Mezzano. "It sounds good," he said, "but what happens when your supplies are used up?"

"I think I'll be able to replace that weight with salt water," I answered. More theory.

All winter long I made lists of items I'd need to carry. A radar reflector so I wouldn't be run down by ships. Fire extinguishers, flare guns, sea anchors. Insect repellent. A hatchet in case I ever had to break out of the cabin. Waterproof putty for repairing the hull if I had a collision. An unbelievable one hundred and eighteen batteries—Cs, AAs and twelve-volt ones for my various flashlights, strobe lights, radios, cabin lights, and the tape recorder. A scraper for barnacles, and a snorkel and mask to wear when I cleaned the bottom of the boat. But I knew that each item was important. No matter how insignificant it might seem on land, it could be crucial at sea.

And every addition meant another expense. My costs for the basic hull and sails had totaled only $688. I'd saved money by building the trailer myself and finding a four-horsepower Evinrude on sale for $300. But then I'd had to buy an outboard bracket, a fuel tank, and extra hardware. I had an antenna, but no radio yet. A few more items and I was already up to $1637. The tab for a solo transatlantic crossing was turning out to be steeper than I'd bargained for.

I STARTED WORKING on the boat again during the late spring. I repainted the bilges, built shelves, and strapped more equipment inside. By now I had definitely decided to wait a full year before embarking on my voyage. To get as much experience as possible, I would spend the summer of 1978 testing my boat on the water.

For a while I tried living on it at night. Sally and I would watch the ten o'clock news together and kiss each other good night; then I'd grab my flashlight and sleeping bag and head out to *Yankee Girl*. I'd take her out onto the lake and catch some sleep. Early next morning, bobbing about on my little boat, I'd cook breakfast. I had found a miniature butane stove that fitted neatly into a plastic dishpan, and pulling out my "galley," I'd drop two eggs into the pot, scramble them with a fork, and eat them right out of the pot. Then I rejoined Sally before it was time for us to leave for work.

I learned something new almost every day—or night. For example, my first "bed" was a four-inch foam cushion extending from transom to bow on the starboard of the boat. Although it allowed me to stretch out full length, the foam wasn't dense enough. So Sally and I took out one inch of the foam and replaced it with a firm piece of leftover carpet pad—a great improvement.

Gradually I grew accustomed to living in such a small space, and I began to love the hours I spent aboard *Yankee Girl*. Night after night, she gently rocked me to sleep, often after a moonlight sail. I found it hard to understand why people did so much sailing in the glare of the hot sun, surrounded by motorboats, fishermen, and water skiers. If they'd only wait until the stars came out, they'd find beautiful sailing. Night winds are steadier than day winds, the moon provides a soft, silvery light, and the lake is incredibly peaceful.

Another discovery I made during my romantic night sailing was that red lights would help my night vision. I covered both the compass light and a flashlight with red plastic. I was soon able to handle the boat in the inkiest blackness. I kept a white flashlight on hand, however, to shine on my sails to alert other boats of my presence.

During the nights aboard my little boat I had ample time to think. I felt a sense of urgency creeping up on me like a shadow. By the time I set sail I'd be thirty-nine. In terms of what my body could stand, I didn't have years left in which to realize my dreams.

I wondered if perhaps I should have taken some shortcuts—had someone else design or build my boat for me. Or I could have just bought a boat and modified it. But I knew I'd done what I needed to do. The time, energy, and money required so far had all been mine. The final satisfaction would be mine, too.

I wondered what unfulfilled dreams other people kept hidden inside themselves. I wanted to tell them something. Even a dream only partially experienced is better than no dream at all. And sometimes the goal itself isn't as important as the sense of personal satisfaction along the way.

BY AUGUST 1978 I had logged many hours aboard *Yankee Girl*. I now knew, especially after that memorable night in July when we weathered the near-tornado on White Bear Lake, that she handled better than I'd ever thought possible. But I still didn't know if she'd carry the half ton of provisions I'd need.

And I wasn't the only one having problems with those provisions. Our house had become an overgrown ship's store.

"Ger, I can't walk through this place any more without tripping over something," Sally said one evening that fall.

I looked around. Gear was strewn everywhere. There were radio antennas, charts, cameras, books, magazines, kites, plastic containers, clothing, and provisions. There were sea anchors, a tape recorder, jars of nails, packets of screws, ropes, cables, a paddle, a megaphone, two plastic sextants, three compasses, a massive first-aid kit, and butane cylinders for the stove.

I turned to Sally and patted her arm.

"I promise you that I will have everything out of here in a couple of months."

"I'll be glad when the mess is gone," she admitted. "But then you'll be gone, too. That's the part I won't be glad about."

I had to keep much of my gear in the house because the bitter Minnesota winter could ruin some of the more delicate pieces of equipment. But I had to decide soon where I would stow everything in the boat, so at night I'd bundle up in my down jacket and a muffler and head out to *Yankee Girl*, occasionally bringing Sally's hair dryer inside the cabin for warmth.

I had questions not only about weight and bulk but also about distribution. I'd have to store heavy items low, since they'd be my ballast. Light things could be stashed higher. My two sextants, for instance, fitted neatly into crisscrossing shock cords fastened to the ceiling of *Yankee Girl*'s cabin. There they would be both accessible and safe from the salt water, which could ruin their mirrors. They deserved to be taken good care of; along with my compass, they'd be the only navigational tools I'd have.

I spent hours trying to decide where to store such a seemingly insignificant item as a pair of scissors. Like everything else in the boat, they would have to be easily reachable. But because they were made of metal they had to be kept away from the compass or they would affect the magnetic heading. And they had to be secured somehow so they wouldn't stab me in the back if they came loose during a storm.

Finally I decided to put the scissors into a plastic drinking tumbler along with my silverware. The tumbler, in turn, would go inside the plastic dishpan that held my small butane stove and my single stainless-steel pot.

The stove took careful planning. I figured that I'd need at least sixteen cans of butane fuel for my voyage, but for safety's sake I added an extra eight. I'd have to be cautious storing them, since a rusty can leaking gas could cause a disastrous explosion. I ended up stowing the butane near the transom.

I chose many items for my trip in the hope that they'd do double duty. My homemade poncho, for example, was cut from a large piece of oilcloth in such a way that it could be used to catch rain if my supply of drinking water ever ran out. Even my plastic water containers would serve two functions. As soon as they were empty I'd fill them with sea water and use them for ballast.

As the winter drew to a close, I looked back at the work I'd done over the past months. Every successful adventure I'd read about had depended on planning and foresight far more than luck. I had thought my plan through again and again, sometimes working on it sixteen hours a day.

Now I was eager for spring. For I'd made up my mind: I would set sail in June.

IN MARCH I decided to buy some additional life insurance. I wondered if, under the circumstances, I'd qualify for extra coverage, but I thought it was worth a try.

As I filled out the application my agent had sent me, I paused at the question asking me to list unusual hobbies. Finally I wrote, "I take long voyages in small boats on the open ocean."

In a couple of weeks, my agent called me.

"Sorry," he said, "but we can't get you additional coverage without a big rate increase. You're a risk, you know."

I said nothing, but I could feel my heart thumping.

"After all," he continued, "you have a history of ulcers."

As soon as the weather permitted, I began reworking the outside of the boat. I designed a new rudder, because the old one was too hard to turn, and I stowed another sea anchor, a bigger one. Last year *Yankee Girl* had refused to lie to a small sea anchor. In a

37

thirty-miles-per-hour wind she would pass right by the anchor, lift it to one side, and start towing it. She was a stubborn little girl, and for this trait I almost started calling her *Yankee Brat*.

By April I knew that I would simply have to stop preparing and get going. My pilot charts told me that I'd have to leave June 1 in order to take advantage of the best winds.

I began packing in earnest, making sometimes painful decisions about what I'd have to leave behind. Many of these leftover items were necessary so, crossing my fingers, I started cramming them into the rear of the station wagon. I'd just have to try to fit them in later. Meanwhile I got out my road maps. It would be a long drive from Minnesota to the east coast, and I would make it alone.

Before leaving I shared three "last suppers" with Sally and some of our friends. There was only supposed to be one last supper of course, but getting packed took longer than I expected.

The first was a last pizza dinner on Friday, April 13. Any comments about that particular date went unsaid. The following Friday Sally and I went over to Barb and Gerry Beutel's house for a last spaghetti feast. I was supposed to leave on Monday, but I wasn't ready even then, so on that night everyone came over to our house for a third farewell dinner.

"This is the *last* last supper, isn't it?" Barb Beutel quipped.

Grinning, I assured her it was.

Later, as my friends were leaving, Gerry handed me a little plaque with a prayer engraved on it: *Oh Lord, thy sea is so big and my boat is so small.*

"This goes with me," I promised. Later I would hang it inside *Yankee Girl*, near the center bulkhead, where I'd see it often.

Bill Mezzano, who had believed in my project from the very beginning, also had a gift for me—a radio that could pick up both AM and shortwave signals; it had been his father's. I had spent several unsuccessful months looking for this type of radio; I knew it would be useful for direction-finding and for checking my watches.

"This radio means a lot to me," Bill said. "I don't mind lending it to you, but I want it back."

"I'll take good care of it," I promised. It was good to know he expected to see me again.

CHAPTER 4

EN ROUTE TO THE ATLANTIC

Rain pelted down on the windshield of my station wagon as I drove eastward. Behind me *Yankee Girl* was strapped down securely on my homemade trailer, her mast tied to its bed.

I was finally on my way to the Atlantic.

At seven am that morning, Wednesday, April 25—right after Sally had driven off to work—I had pulled out of the driveway. There was something comforting about the sequence of events. Sally had left for her job, and now I was leaving for mine. Our parting had even been a little businesslike.

"See you on the east coast in a few weeks," I'd said as I kissed her good-by.

"Drive carefully," she'd responded, hurrying off. Later she would join me in Virginia for a short visit after I'd finished packing and put *Yankee Girl* through some final tests.

After four months of agonizing over where to begin my journey, I'd settled on Chesapeake Bay. The customary departure point for transatlantic crossings is Cape Cod. But leaving from there would have taken me across both the New York and Boston shipping lanes, increasing my chances of being run down. I'd have been within the iceberg limit for a longer period of time, and I'd probably have encountered a number of foggy days. In addition, I'd have been farther away from the Gulf Stream than I wanted to be at the outset.

All things considered, I'd concluded that the route from Virginia would be the fastest and safest. Now I just wanted to get to Chesapeake Bay as soon as possible.

To save money while driving, I'd planned to spend the nights on an air mattress in the back of the station wagon. On my first night on the road I made the mistake of trying to sleep at a truck stop. I was awakened every couple of hours by the noise of heavy diesels. All next day I was tired, grumpy, and worried. I'd need to be rested when I arrived in Virginia. Where could I sleep undisturbed—and for free?

That night I pulled into a shopping center in Frederick, Maryland. I went into a restaurant, ate supper, and washed up in a bathroom. As I walked back to the parking lot, the thought suddenly occurred to me—Why not sleep here? At night, shopping center parking lots are as peaceful as graveyards. Pleased with my discovery, I hunkered down into my sleeping bag in the car and thought about Sally and home. About now she'd be finishing up supper. I'd be seeing her again soon, and already I could hardly wait.

In the morning I got up early and had breakfast in the car: milk, granola, and a can of peaches. Afterward I took the gear I'd thrown into the front seat to make room to lie down and put it in the back once more.

Sooner or later, everything in the car would have to fit inside *Yankee Girl*. I hadn't yet figured out how. There still were the two sea anchors—the large thirty-six-inch one and a smaller eighteen-inch one—and the two rudders, the old one and the new one. There were three sail bags, not to mention cushions, tools, paints, spare parts, charts, and bags of magazines I was sure I couldn't do without on my journey.

I knew that, once I arrived in Virginia, I'd face an ordeal of packing and repacking, unpacking and packing again. I still had nightmares of getting out onto the Atlantic, desperately needing some small item, and not having it on board.

If that happened, I would have nowhere to turn for help. No boats would follow me, no planes would fly overhead to check on me. Except for a few friends, no one would even know when I left. I only hoped that I wasn't asking too much of myself.

ALL ALONG THE ROUTE to the coast I kept meeting people who had mistaken notions about my *Yankee Girl*. I could feel myself becoming more and more defensive as I kept hearing all the derisive comments—"Does that thing *really* sail?"

At a tollbooth on the Pennsylvania Turnpike, the man inside leaned out to stare at her.

"What's that—a submarine?" he wanted to know.

"Yes, it is," I lied. With her tiny portholes and stubby cabin, *Yankee Girl* did look a bit like a submarine, and I was tired of making explanations.

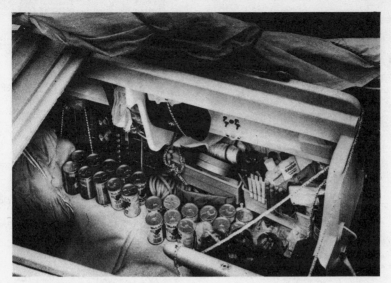

Some of the stores I crammed into the boat.

Inside *Yankee Girl*'s cabin, looking toward the bow.

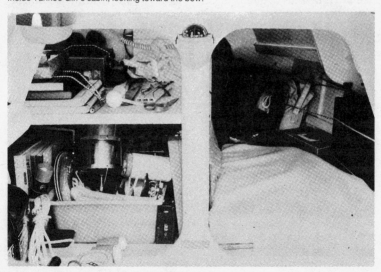

"I thought so," he said, pleased with himself.

The miles slipped by. Washington, D.C., Jamestown, Virginia, then Newport News, where there was a mariner's museum I wanted to visit. When I arrived there at eight thirty am, an old Ford pulled up alongside my car. Inside was a red-faced man wearing a baseball cap; he rolled down his window and scrutinized my boat. "You going to sail that thing across the Atlantic?" he asked.

I was amazed. This man not only knew *Yankee Girl* was a sailboat, but he also knew what I was planning to do with her.

"She's capable of it," I answered guardedly.

"Then you must have come to see the *Little One*," he said. "She's inside."

Again I was amazed. *Little One* was the boat that had belonged to the famous William Willis. I had read about them both. She was only eleven and a half feet long—a foot and a half longer than *Yankee Girl*. In her Willis had tried three times to cross the Atlantic single-handed. Twice he had been picked up at sea, but on the third voyage, in 1968, *Little One* had been spotted by a freighter only four hundred miles off the Irish coast—and Willis had not been on board. He had disappeared at sea.

And here was his boat, in a museum I had stopped at on a whim. When it opened, I was the first visitor inside. I found *Little One* in a far corner, surrounded by railings. Looking around to make sure I was alone, I climbed under a railing and peered inside her.

I could see that *Little One* had suffered a lot of damage. Her mast and boom were gone, and bare wood was exposed in several places where the fiberglass had been torn away. Her transom was battered, and part of her keel was also broken. But she had survived the Atlantic, though William Willis had not.

I stared into the cabin, transfixed. What had happened to Willis? Had he slipped overboard? Had he fallen into such a deep depression that he'd taken his own life? Why hadn't he kept a log—or, if he had, why had no one found it?

When I returned to the parking lot, *Yankee Girl's* jaunty blue and green hull was a welcome sight.

"You look great," I said, patting her side affectionately. "And I know we're going to make it."

AFTER I ARRIVED at Virginia Beach I drove around to several marinas looking for a slip where I could put in. I finally rented one of the few transient spaces available.

Since *Yankee Girl* could not be launched safely without the provisions that would make up my ballast, it was now time to get down to the business of buying food, water, and gasoline. My shopping trip took three days. I had to go to three supermarkets before I found enough distilled water. I bought four hundred and fifty cans of food, everything from asparagus to stew, chili to chicken à la king, soups to juices. I must have filled my station wagon half a dozen times.

Yankee Girl had nine compartments below the waterline. The gasoline went into the forward lockers; the food and water were distributed throughout the rest of the the boat. As I packed, unpacked and repacked my little boat, I discovered enough additional nooks and crannies to add to my original allotments of both gasoline and food. In fact, *Yankee Girl* was now carrying a total of five hundred and forty cans of food in her hull. I could last longer than ninety days at sea. I now had an eighteen-hundred-pound load on a trailer designed to carry only twelve hundred. With the springs on the trailer creaking under the strain, I drove carefully to a dry storage marina.

At this yard, launching usually involved three steps: hoisting the boat onto a forklift's sling, transferring it via forklift to an elevator, and then lowering it into the water. But the two young men assigned to the job of launching *Yankee Girl* obviously thought that, given her small size, they could skip a step or two.

"Holy mackerel," one of them said as he struggled to lift her bow. "What've you got in this thing?" With a lot of shoving and a little help from the forklift, they finally managed to get her into the sling. Then, bypassing the elevator, they lowered her directly into the water. At last *Yankee Girl* was safely launched. I jumped aboard, started the motor, and turned toward my slip.

I spent the next several days and nights aboard *Yankee Girl*, and it wasn't long before I started hearing the standard jokes and jibes. One I heard more times than I cared to count was, "Where's the rest of your boat?" By now I'd come up with an answer: "My wife and I are divorced, and she has the other half."

Some people were sincerely worried about my sleeping arrangements. Among them were Sam and Ann Murphey.

"Why don't you come and stay at our house?" asked Sam, a retired navy pilot. Ann nodded her agreement.

"I'm sleeping fine," I replied. "But there is one thing I don't have, a shower."

"You can use ours anytime," they told me, and the Murpheys soon became my close friends.

By early May I had bent on the working sails—the main and the two jibs—and stowed their bags below. The large spinnaker was secured up forward for use later on.

When I had finished loading everything but fresh foods—I'd do that just before I left—I sat back, pleased at what a splendid little oceangoing cruiser *Yankee Girl* was turning out to be. Not only was she a well designed, well planned, and well equipped little boat, she was also one of the least expensive ever launched. To date I had spent a total of $2924—all of it out of my own pocket. Most of the money added since my last cost accounting had gone for extra compasses, strobe lights, charts, and radios. I now had five radios on board.

As the day of my departure drew nearer, I started worrying about whether I'd forgotten anything important. One evening my new friends, the Murpheys, invited me to dinner, and Ann introduced a modified game of twenty questions.

"Have you got a spare can opener?" she would ask.

"Three," I'd reply after checking my mental list.

"What if your matches get wet?" Sam would inquire. "How will you light your stove?"

"They're sealed in an airtight jar, and I'll be carrying three cigarette lighters, a flint igniter, and spare flints."

We continued to play for several days, but the Murpheys never caught me with a question I couldn't answer.

THE TIME HAD COME to do some sailing with my fully loaded craft. I especially wanted to try out my new rudder. So I decided to cruise to Tangier Island, about fifty-five miles up Chesapeake Bay.

On the morning I cast off, the bay was calm—so calm, in fact, that I had to motor for the first three hours. I was determined to make Tangier in record time, so when the wind came up I sailed until two the next morning, stopping only once to wait out the ebb tide. I anchored for the rest of the night, and after a brief tour of the island I headed back down the western shore, where the winds were much stronger. Faced with five-foot waves, I had the opportunity to thoroughly test the new rudder. It proved easier to steer than the old one; all it required was finger pressure.

It rained on my way back to the marina, and that gave me the chance to check out the self-steering mechanism and my poncho. The poncho, I discovered, kept the wind out, but let the rain through. Still, all in all, I was well satisfied when I arrived back at the marina. Loaded down as she was, my tiny boat had performed beautifully.

Now, at last, it was time for Sally's visit. I had rented a rustic cabin in the woods near the beach. We'd spend a few days there relaxing together.

I met her at the airport. She was carrying her suitcase, a new poncho she'd sewn for me, and an enormous box.

"I never want to see beef jerky again for as long as I live," she said, thrusting the box at me and wrinkling her nose in disgust. In my absence she had jerked sixty pounds of raw beef down to less than twenty pounds of dried meat. The smell in the house must have been intolerable.

For the next five days we sunbathed, read, and strolled barefoot along the beach, looking for shells and watching the birds circle overhead. I caught Sally staring out at the sea more than once, but we both tried to avoid talking about my journey.

"It's nice to be alone with you," I said to her one evening as we walked through the pines behind the cabin.

"I wish it could last forever," she answered wistfully. Then, changing the subject, she said, "Your parents must have a lot of confidence in you. If they didn't, they'd be out here too."

That surprised me. I had been thinking they stayed home to give Sally and me a chance to be alone together. But their motives had been more profound. By not coming out to see me, they had been expressing their support and reassurance. I would think a lot about Sally and my parents in the lonely weeks ahead. Their love would be a constant source of strength.

My little boat, fully loaded except for perishables.

All too soon, our vacation came to an end. It was nearly the end of May, and I'd have to leave in a few days. As I drove Sally back to the airport, the atmosphere in the car grew tense. We had our final conversation at the gate.

"If you need anything, call Dad or Bill Mezzano," I said.

"I will," Sally replied evenly.

"Try to remember to keep your gas tank filled up, okay?" I asked, making an attempt at humor. She had a habit of driving around with her gas-gauge needle on empty.

"I'll be fine," she said. She was avoiding my eyes.

"I'll see you in England before you know it. We'll go to one of those old hotels by the sea and have a little holiday."

It was time for her to go, and we held each other tightly. Suddenly I felt her shoulders shaking. She was crying.

"I can't help it," she said, her voice muffled against my shoulder. "I'm just afraid that if anything happened to you. . ."

Her voice trailed off. Then she pulled away and looked down at the floor. "Ger, I wouldn't be able to make it on my own."

46

I put my arms around her again, wanting somehow to reassure her. Then I noticed a little boy in cowboy boots standing off to one side. He had obviously been staring at us.

"Someone's looking our way," I told Sally, nodding in his direction. She couldn't help but smile when she saw the expression on his chubby face.

"We'll ruin his day if we keep going on like this," I joked.

That did it. She let go of me and picked up her bag.

"I'll be waiting for you in England," she said. Then she turned and walked down the long empty corridor alone, a slim figure clutching a shoulder bag. For a moment I was tempted to join her—to go back to Minnesota, to the peace and security of home. I watched her until she was out of sight.

MY LAST DAYS in port I checked and rechecked everything on the boat. I was determined not to be caught short on anything. I bought two more grocery carts full of fruit, and sixty eggs, each of which I smeared with vaseline and replaced carefully in its carton. Shielding them from the sea air would, I hoped, help them to last longer.

I spent my last night on shore at the Murpheys', who had offered to store my car and trailer while I was gone. My friends were careful to keep me in the right frame of mind throughout the evening. When Sam loaned me a signal mirror he'd been carrying when he was shot down in Korea, he gruffly insisted, "I want this back." He knew how important psychological preparation could be to a lone sailor. In fact, all during the month of May I had kept up my mental conditioning—thinking positively and maintaining a sense of optimism. That was turning out to be just as important as any of the other preparations I'd made.

That evening I telephoned my parents and friends back home to say good-by.

"We'll be with you all the way," my mother reassured me.

"Don't get my radio wet," Bill Mezzano said.

The last person I called was Sally. She began crying almost immediately. "I need you," she kept repeating.

"Don't worry," I said. "We'll be together in England soon."

She was still crying when we hung up.

After that, I had to fight a growing depression. I knew that Sally had tried to hold back her feelings, and we had talked often about what the trip would mean to us. But everything had broken down in the end.

I slept that night at the Murpheys', for I was plagued by bad dreams. I had forgotten something; I had lost my way; I was being run down by a ship. Each time I'd rouse myself, and then the words that no one had dared to speak crowded into my mind.

There was always the possibility that I wouldn't make it.

CHAPTER 5

CASTING OFF FOR ENGLAND

 A few friends and some people from the marina were on hand when I cast off early in the morning on Friday, June 1, 1979. The day had dawned gloomy and overcast, and the leaden skies made me feel more tired than when I'd climbed out of bed.

I was at dockside by six thirty am, eager to be off and catch the tide. First, though, I had some last-minute packing to do. Somehow I stuffed two cartloads of fresh foods on board. Then I stowed my sack of books and forty back issues of *Reader's Digest*, reading material for my months at sea.

"Is there any room left for you?" a friend asked, smiling.

I paused, holding the last of five bags of grapefruit I was stuffing into the cabin. It *was* getting pretty crowded in there.

"I guess I'll just have to eat my way in," I said.

More people were gathering on the dock, watching me in silence. Although everyone had come to wish me bon voyage, they stood there now like mourners at a funeral, heads bent, hands at their sides. I had to be careful not to let their feelings affect me.

"Any last words?" someone asked. Then he looked away in embarrassment.

That did it. I handed my mooring lines to Sam. "Don't expect to hear about me for at least two weeks," I reminded him. "Don't worry—and don't ever report me missing. I may not be able to contact you until I get to the other side."

He nodded. I had given him a copy of my float plan. It listed all the information required by the Coast Guard: descriptions of my boat, myself, and the safety equipment I was carrying, and my intended route and estimated time of arrival.

I yanked on the starting cord and the Evinrude spluttered to life. As I headed out to sea, I glanced at my watch. It was seven thirty am; I was already behind schedule. I'd have to hurry to get out of the bay before the tide turned against me.

I didn't look back until I'd left the people on the dock far behind. My transatlantic crossing had begun.

A STEADY BREEZE was blowing out of the southwest as *Yankee Girl* sliced purposefully through Chesapeake Bay. Rigged under twin jibs and riding the ebb tide, she ran through the light swells easily and with grace.

I had now been on the water for about six hours. Six hours out of sixty days—if all went well. I had the satisfaction of knowing that I'd cast off on the best day of the year for such a voyage. The spring storms were over, and hurricanes usually didn't appear until late summer. If the weather followed its normal pattern, I'd have favorable winds during the weeks ahead to boost me along to England.

As the Chesapeake lighthouse sank beneath the horizon, I breathed a word of thanks for the breeze that was carrying me quickly away from the hazards of the Virginia coast.

It was then the realization finally hit home: *I was alone in a ten-foot boat facing thirty-eight hundred miles of open ocean*. I had taken every precaution I could think of; I had planned my trip meticulously. But there was one unknown that I could do nothing about: the sea itself.

Now, almost at once, the moist southwest wind died and sunlight pierced the clouds. The air became still, and *Yankee Girl*'s sails flapped idly on their lines. If I didn't do something soon, the tide would carry me back into the bay.

It was going to be a very hot day, and I was already uncomfortable. I pulled off my white wool sweater and pants and sealed them in a plastic bag. I planned to put then on again, still fresh and clean, when I reached England.

Then I pulled on a pair of shorts and buckled on my safety

harness. I would wear the harness throughout the voyage. From now on *Yankee Girl* and I would be one.

To protect myself from the sun's intense rays, I put on a long-sleeved shirt, smeared myself with suntan lotion, and then donned my sunglasses and pith helmet. Leaving the limp mainsail up for shade, I started the motor, and we were once again on our way at a steady three knots.

I was sitting on my tiller seat, sipping my first can of apple juice and enjoying the view, when I felt a stinging pain. I looked down to see a large black fly perched on my right leg. I swatted it, then noticed half a dozen more buzzing around in the cabin. Grabbing my insect repellent, I sprayed everything in sight. Then I jumped. Another fly bite.

I had expected a few stowaways, but I hadn't counted on being the only landing spot in this part of the ocean. For the next eight hours I held the tiller in one hand and the bug spray in the other, fending off flies who came from miles around to snack on me.

As I scratched my bites and sprayed, I realized how tired I really was. I hoped I'd be able to get some sleep soon. Precisely *where* I'd sleep was a problem I hadn't yet solved, though. *Yankee Girl* was stuffed full of provisions from transom to forepeak. Even the footwell, designed to allow me to sit with my feet down, was packed with extra containers of gasoline, brought on at the last minute.

Since my butane stove was meant to hang from a bracket above the footwell, I wouldn't be able to cook on it until I'd used up the extra gas. The danger of an explosion would be too great. Meanwhile I'd have to sit cross-legged—and eat cold food.

I looked up at the sky. The light was beginning to fade.

Hungry flies, a blazing sun, and lack of room to stretch had made the first day of my voyage very uncomfortable. I wondered what the night would bring and how much more discomfort I would face in the coming weeks. Then I shook my head, hard. It was far too early to be thinking like this. It was because I was so tired. I had had no real rest for thirty-six hours, and I knew from experience how dangerous this could be.

I thought of my aborted voyage five years earlier, when I had left Miami planning to sail around the world, only to realize shortly after my departure that I was so exhausted I would have to give up. I promised myself never to fall into that trap again. Yet here I was, already on the brink of exhaustion, and this trip was an even greater challenge than that earlier one had been.

I SLOWLY AWOKE AS, with each roll of the boat, the pain in my ribs increased. I had been lying in a fetal position with my head forward, my legs under the tiller, and my feet up against the transom. I sat up—and bumped my head against the bulkhead.

Groping around in the dark, I discovered the cause of my discomfort: grapefruit. In my last-minute packing, I had squeezed five bags of them into the cabin. Now they were loose and rolling everywhere. I had slept with three of them shoved against my ribs.

My first night at sea was not going according to plan. Inside *Yankee Girl's* tiny cabin, the air was stuffy and stale. Because of the condensation that occurs at night, I had closed the hatch. But the smell of gasoline had become overpowering. My head was throbbing, and I was beginning to feel nauseated.

Checking my watch, I found it was one am. I had been asleep for only three hours. Since I'd spent many nights aboard *Yankee Girl*, I'd thought sleep would come easily. But dozing off on White Bear Lake was vastly different from going to sleep on the ocean. In Minnesota I hadn't had to worry about being run over by ships. I was also suffering from a mild claustrophobia.

I slid open the hatch. The sea air felt good on my face and in my lungs. Over the undulating ocean a sliver of moon cast its pale light. I was alone with the sea, the moon, and the mist—and very aware of my terrible solitude. Then, as if to justify my fears, a set of red and green navigation lights appeared off my starboard bow. But were they headed toward me, or away? With growing anxiety I peered into the distance, trying to get a fix on the ship.

Finally I determined that we were not on a collision course. The lights were moving north. Sighing in relief, I dropped back inside the cabin and began rearranging grapefruit so I could lie down. But I soon realized I felt too ill to do anything but collapse once more on my lumpy bed.

By sunrise I was glad to get up, though it was only four thirty-five. I threw open the hatch again and stretched. After being coiled up like a spring, every muscle in my body screamed in protest.

I shivered. It was chilly at this hour. Then I became aware of something else: *there was no wind*. Nothing. Not the slightest breeze.

Precisely at that moment a voice sounded inside my head.

"Last night you didn't want wind so you could sleep. Now you want wind so you can sail. Can't you make up your mind?"

I straightened in surprise. This was happening far earlier than I'd expected. Still, it would have to be dealt with.

"You're early," I said easily.

My imaginary friend had arrived. I was prepared for the coming, knowing all along that one of the greatest dangers of my voyage would be the utter loneliness, and that in the absence of other human company I would—either subconsciously or consciously—make up a traveling companion.

The phenomenon was not at all unusual. Almost every single-hander ended up talking to himself at one time or another—and answering. But some imaginary friends were not necessarily friendly. One famous sailor, Robert Manry, came to believe he had a mischievous elf on board. Following the elf's directions to steer for a nonexistent island, Manry zigzagged around the ocean for hours. Joshua Slocum, the first great single-hander, became convinced that Christopher Columbus's pilot was beside him, urging him to turn around. Slocum gave in and only later realized he had gone miles off course.

I was determined my friend would be friendly, so I welcomed him. But I would not let him get the upper hand.

He had no name; he didn't need one. All during the crossing I would use him as a sounding board—talking to him, asking for suggestions. He would joke with me, encourage me, berate me—and, above all, allow me to establish a sort of inner equilibrium. Though he was only a fabrication, he would help to keep me alive in the weeks ahead.

Having accepted his presence, I now suddenly found I was ready to take action. I started the Evinrude and began motoring into the sunrise. By about six o'clock a slight wind had arisen. But it was coming out of the northeast: more bad news. Leaving the motor running, I quickly hoisted the jibs and the mainsail, and *Yankee Girl* veered off to the east-southeast. I would have preferred to continue due east on a course that would ultimately bring me to England, but at least we were sailing.

"Don't start complaining; you always wanted to see Africa," my imaginary friend teased.

I motor-sailed all that day and part of the night. Finally, after sixteen hours at the helm, I turned off the motor, dropped the sails, and went below.

In the dimness I tried to find something more substantial to eat than the oranges and granola bars that I had snacked on during the day. But I had not yet adjusted to the boat's constant motion, and all that my stomach would tolerate was a peanut butter and jelly sandwich.

I lay down in *Yankee Girl's* crowded cabin, determined to catch some sleep. The grapefruit hadn't become any softer.

"Why don't you eat them?" my friend suggested.

My stomach lurched.

"That's a great idea," I responded, "but who's going to clean up the mess when I get sick? You?"

He didn't answer.

That made me feel better. Apparently I would have the last word with him—once in a while.

FOR THE NEXT seventy-two hours I followed the same routine: motor-sailing for sixteen to eighteen hours during the day and getting whatever rest I could at night. The waves weren't merely swells any longer; some were five or six feet in height.

Occasionally, out of sheer frustration, I would head due east. But then *Yankee Girl* would dive down the back of one wave, bury her bow in the next, and we would shudder to a stop, as if we were running into a big wet sponge. So I would have to head south for a while, giving *Yankee Girl* time to build up momentum before turning east-southeast again and starting up the next wave. I had to battle for every mile of the way. If I let up for even a moment, the headwinds and the currents would combine to drive me back to Cape Hatteras.

Though the thermometer read sixty degrees Fahrenheit, I was very cold. To protect myself from the elements, I wore gloves and a down-filled jacket beneath all my foul-weather gear. It felt exactly as if I were sitting bundled up on a teeter-totter in a brisk wind and being sprayed with a hose.

"Don't you love cruising?" my friend asked with a tinge of irony. "Isn't it just like the sailing magazines describe it?"

"Oh, I like it a lot," I quipped. "If only some of those yachting writers could be with us now!" The thought made me smile.

By my fourth day out I was starting to get desperate. The wind continued to blow out of the northeast, and I was still perched on my tiller seat, fighting the weather for hours on end. At night the motion of the sea and the pervasive smell of gasoline combined to keep me awake. Often I came close to vomiting.

The weather seemed to be following a pattern: a strong wind during the day, squalls in the afternoon, and then, in the evening, the winds and the sea would die down. Each day the waves were higher and stronger. The squalls burst forth in groups of six to eight at a time, marching across the sea, driving the rains before them like steel-gray curtains. Each time I saw them approaching, I rushed to drop and lash the sails and I braced myself for the sixty-knot winds and sheets of lightning I was sure would follow. But the squalls would pass over, bringing only light winds and misty rain. Gradually I realized that they were very different from the squalls I'd encountered along the coast. After that I just sailed right through them without bothering to douse my sails.

Once, as a group of squalls cleared, a rainbow appeared off my port bow. Startled, I pushed back my long-billed baseball cap and stared at it.

I had seen innumerable rainbows over inland lakes and fields, but never one at sea. It arched perfectly over the churning waters, its hues brilliant and clear.

This incredible beauty was a gift I hadn't expected. Was it a sign to me that I wasn't really alone? Suddenly I was overcome by a profound sense of peace and joy, as if a hand had reached out to touch me when I most needed it.

The mood stayed with me long after the rainbow faded. Out here by myself, I was beginning to appreciate the vast disparity between my little world and the immensity of God's creation. Hour after hour, I was feeling closer to God than I ever had before.

CHAPTER 6
BATTLE TO THE GULF STREAM

 Something peculiar was happening. Whenever I pointed *Yankee Girl* toward our east-southeast heading, she buried her bow in a wall of water. The wind was shifting again. Should I head south or north? Any attempt to keep going east directly into the wind would be fruitless. At this point I was being pushed to the south, but when I tried to force *Yankee Girl* to the northeast, the wind and the waves drove me due north.

"First it was Africa, now it's Nova Scotia," my friend said gleefully. "We can always stop in Halifax and start over again."

My friend's suggestion was a distinct possibility, I thought. After four days at sea I had not yet reached the Gulf Stream. I was cold, tired, miserable, and unsure of my position, all because of these freakish weather conditions. At this time of year I wasn't supposed to be bucking easterly winds. I felt cheated.

But I gritted my teeth and reverted to my original southeasterly direction. "Better Bermuda than Nova Scotia," I told my friend.

The fifth day dawned bright and clear. The wind was down and I was glad to see the sun again, even though I was motoring right into its glare.

At about eleven thirty am the wind died completely, and the surface of the water was as flat as a billiard table. This was the moment I had been waiting for. Eagerly I shut down the outboard, dove into the cabin, and grabbed my bottle of dishwashing detergent—an all-purpose liquid that to my mind is far more effective than so-called saltwater soap.

I stripped off my long-sleeved shirt, flung my cap below, and leaned over the port side as far as I could. *Yankee Girl* responded under my weight by heeling over about a foot—enough for me to dip my hands into the ocean and splash water over my head. I was enjoying my first shampoo in five days.

I had to wash and rinse my hair three times to remove the accumulated salt and sweat, but the cool wetness felt good. Hands reaching into the Atlantic, my eyes screwed shut to keep out the salt and soapsuds, a loud *whoo-oo-oo-sh* suddenly made me jerk upright. I stared at the water in front of my boat, transfixed.

From fifteen feet away a pilot whale was looking directly at me. We locked eyes for what seemed like ages. Then, with a twist of his great dark body, he slid beneath the waves. I watched until he disappeared from view. Whales *were* beautiful—especially when they were swimming away from me and my tiny boat.

I motored along through the afternoon. Suddenly, incredibly, I saw a white triangle in the distance. With growing excitement I reached for my binoculars. It was a sail!

The prospect of meeting another sailboat, seeing a human face, talking to someone, cheered me enormously. I wasn't about to give up—not yet—but frustration, loneliness, the contrary winds, and my nausea had taken their toll. I turned up my Evinrude for more speed and steered in anticipation.

But the sailboat maintained its pace and distance. In truth, my chances of overtaking it were remote.

At about three thirty the sun was low enough for me to take a sight for longitude. I could only guess at the distance I'd covered, and I had no idea where the currents had carried me. So I carefully unshipped my primary sextant and took a shot. The fix I got— thirty-seven degrees five minutes north, seventy-two degrees twenty-five minutes west—wasn't all that encouraging. *Yankee Girl* and I had made only a hundred and sixty nautical miles since our departure. That meant that we'd been averaging thirty-two miles a day and England was still more than three thousand miles away. At that rate it would take a hundred days for the crossing—with only a ninety-day supply of food and water aboard. All I could do was hope that the Gulf Stream wasn't too far ahead.

About five the other sailboat veered off sharply to the southeast, and I suddenly felt more alone and discouraged than ever. But as night wore on a magnificent breeze came up, and that lifted my spirits. I raised my twin jibs, and soon *Yankee Girl* was ghosting along at a couple of knots. When the stars started appearing in the sky, I hoisted my strobe light to the masthead. The brilliant light reflected off the sails like a beacon. I told myself that a passing ship couldn't help but see me.

Considering the state of the sea, the weather, and my stomach, it seemed like a good time to try to eat a hot meal. Amazingly, I even felt a bit hungry. For five days I had subsisted on apples, oranges, jerky, crackers, and peanut butter and jelly sandwiches.

Because of the gasoline smell in the cabin, I was afraid to light the stove down there. So I held it on the cabin top while I heated my one-course dinner of beef stew.

"Now *this* is living," I told my friend. "Hot stew, a beautiful night, and a boat steering herself for England." That last statement was a slight exaggeration, but I didn't care.

"How about some music?" my friend asked.

"Good idea," I answered. "Will Linda Ronstadt do?"

We listened to the tape of "Blue Bayou" over and over again as the miles slid away behind us.

I SPENT THE NEXT two days motoring. When there was a wind, it was against me. In periods of calm, I held my umbrella up to protect myself from the sun. Though exhausted, I was more determined than ever to reach the Gulf Stream. At least I was over my sea sickness. From now on I'd be fine, no matter how rough it got.

Finally, after an entire afternoon of fighting winds directly out of the east, I had to quit. There wasn't much sense in wasting precious fuel beating into those head seas.

Under these conditions the best I could do was to slow my drift back toward Virginia. I dug down under my sleeping bag and clothing and pulled out my large sea anchor, a six-foot-long cone-shaped device of heavy nylon. I had experimented with it on White Bear Lake, but I had never used it in waves this high. As soon as I attached it to two hundred feet of three-eighth-inch nylon line and streamed it from her bow, *Yankee Girl* was up to her old tricks. She sailed right past it, turned downwind, and, like a puppy pulling a blanket, dragged it along behind her.

Sighing, I retrieved the anchor and put it back into its plastic bag. The only thing to do now was to heave to. Clambering onto the cabin top, I hoisted the sails. With the mainsail sheeted in tight, the jib brought across to the windward side, and the tiller hard alee, *Yankee Girl* was, for all practical purposes, "parked."

I slid the hatch closed. Secure inside my tiny, tossing cabin, I felt physically safe, but the isolation and fatigue were wearing me down.

I had spoken to no one for an entire week, and I was beginning to worry about Sally, my family, and my friends.

I had thought I'd be able to speak with an occasional ship and have it radio a message back to the Coast Guard. I knew that Sally would be checking with them; word from me would ease her mind tremendously. But though I'd tried to reach half a dozen passing ships on my VHF radio telephone, I'd never received a reply. Once a ship had passed within a quarter of a mile, and I had steered in her direction, yelling the whole time, "WXQ 9864 . . . this is the yacht *Yankee Girl* calling any ship in this area." Nothing had ever come back. The ship had simply sailed away, and I'd wondered if my radio were working. Did this mean that I wouldn't be able to count on help from other ships if I became ill or *Yankee Girl* were badly damaged? I wouldn't know until I tried again.

It was already the evening of my seventh day out, and nothing had gone as I'd planned. I had been forced to use up a third of my gasoline supply. The wind and the waves seemed determined to push me backward. And the characteristic violet-blue color of the Gulf Stream was nowhere in sight.

If conditions didn't improve, my food and water would run out long before I reached England.

"Cheer up," my friend said. "Things can't get much worse."

Silently I wondered how long it would be before they got better.

CHAPTER 7

THE FURY OF THE GATHERING EASTERLY

 Again and again *Yankee Girl* and I were lifted up on ten or twelve-foot waves, held there an instant, then dropped with a sickening lurch, while I hung on for dear life.

For two solid days the Atlantic had been a gigantic roller coaster. We were hove to, bucking an easterly wind with gales of up to thirty knots and mountainous waves that often broke right over the boat. But *Yankee Girl* seemed to be in her element. With nothing but her mainsail—twenty-three square feet, little larger than a beach towel—she was managing to stay heeled over at about thirty degrees, and stubbornly maintaining her northeasterly heading.

I had no way of knowing where we were. Perhaps we were being driven even farther away from the elusive Gulf Stream. I kept leaning over the side of the boat, checking the color of the water, but it remained leaden green. And though its temperature had been rising steadily—from sixty-three degrees off Norfolk to a present reading of seventy-four that was still not warm enough; the normal temperature of the stream was eighty-one degrees.

All told, in eight miserable days at sea I'd seen the sun only three times and had had no more than twelve hours of favorable winds. Also, I'd had no real sleep. Inside the cramped cabin, the air was hot and stuffy. I couldn't open the ventilator, because the waves breaking over the boat invariably surged in, and whenever I tried to leave the hatch open a crack, I was doused.

Toward dawn of the ninth day, bruised and fatigued, I crawled up into the bow and wedged myself in among the grapefruit and gear. The tiny pocket of air around me quickly became stale with my breathing and the smell of gasoline. For once I didn't care. At least I could lie there without being slammed around. But by late afternoon there was a gnawing in my stomach; I needed to eat something solid. I found an orange. It wasn't much, but I knew that my stomach could tolerate it. As I chewed on its last section, I reached out to rinse my hands in the sea.

The water was as warm as a bath. I checked it with the thermometer: eighty-one degrees. The Gulf Stream. At last.

THE NEXT DAY the wind continued to head us, still blowing directly out of the east. I was having trouble controlling my impatience.

"It can't last forever," my friend said.

"Can't it?" I answered testily. I was in no mood to talk. Now that I had reached the Gulf Stream, I wanted to get going.

Later that morning, when I checked the water temperature, I was shocked to discover it had dropped to seventy-eight degrees. The treacherous easterly had pushed us back out of the stream. Desperately I hoisted the mainsail and tried to sail southeast. *Yankee Girl* leaped from crest to crest, but once again we were sailing a zigzag course for nowhere.

As I sat huddled inside the cabin, the waves grew steeper and broke more frequently. I found myself staring out the portholes into green water. Finally I realized that I couldn't subject *Yankee Girl* to this beating any longer. Reluctantly, I hove to. Then, out of curiosity, I checked the water temperature.

It was eighty-one degrees. We were in the Gulf Stream again.

It seemed as if we were caught in the middle of a giant tug-of-war between the elements. The wind wanted to drive us one way, while the current wanted to carry us another. I thought about those people who claimed to have conquered the seas, or the air, or the mountains. To me, that was just talk. Human beings never conquered anything in nature; sometimes they were able to accomplish tremendous feats, but that was usually when nature was looking the other way.

I was startled out of my reverie by a loud *bla-a-a-a-at* from—incredibly—*outside* my boat. I threw open the hatch.

A fishing trawler was heading toward me across the water, her horn sounding. Frantically, I waved my arms over my head. After days of isolation I wanted desperately to talk to someone, and to get a message through to Sally and my parents.

Three burly fishermen grinned and waved back.

Diving below, I turned on my radio. "This is the yacht *Yankee Girl* calling any ship in the area."

There was no response. I repeated my call again and again, but they never answered. I stood in the open hatch and looked longingly after the trawler as she dissolved into a smudge on the horizon.

As the sky darkened, I wearily reconciled myself to another night of solitude, of being cut off from everything and everyone I valued.

I rummaged about in the forepeak and eventually I found what I was looking for: the plastic jug that contained my clean T-shirts. Hurriedly I unscrewed the cap, brought the jug up to my face, and inhaled deeply, breathing in the scents of freshly washed clothing and crisp Minnesota air.

I had escaped. I was home!

NEXT MORNING I slid the hatch open and surveyed the gray swells around me. The seas were still steep-sided, and *Yankee Girl's* bow still pounded into the waves. Hove to, she made almost no progress, but nevertheless she rose bravely to meet each new wave as if she could bluff her way to England.

I had at least to try to do some sailing today. The wind was now out of the southeast, and I felt that I might have a chance. I released the lines securing the tiller, brought the rudder over, and fell off on the starboard tack. *Yankee Girl* bore off to the north and then the northeast. But again, our forward motion was negligible. I felt like a hamster in a cage—running around and around a wheel and getting nowhere.

By now I was so tired of fighting the constant lurching of the boat that all I could do was heave to once more, lie on my bunk, and hang on. Every hour or so I peered out the inspection porthole at the endless miles of tossing water.

But once, just as I was about to lie down again, I saw a larger than ordinary patch of white—and gasped.

It was a ship! I felt the blood pounding in my temples. The mere fact that I had seen her was a miracle. If I hadn't looked out the porthole at just the right time, she would almost certainly have passed by without seeing me. I jumped to my radio.

"WXQ 9864 . . . WXQ 9864 . . . This is the yacht *Yankee Girl* calling any ship in the area. . . . Over."

Holding my breath, I waited. I was about to repeat my call when a voice with an accent came back over the airwaves.

"Is that the very little sailboat?" it asked.

"Yes!" I shouted. "And it's *wonderful* to talk to someone!"

After eleven days of not hearing another human voice, I was on the verge of tears. Finally I said, "You will never know how much I appreciate your being on channel sixteen. I've called other ships, but none of them have responded."

"We always monitor sixteen," the voice answered crisply.

I breathed deeply. This was clearly a professional crew. I soon learned that I was talking with the Dutch cargo ship *Bilderdyk* out of Amsterdam. "Can you give me a position check?" I inquired.

"Certainly." Then, after a pause, "You are at thirty-eight degrees eight minutes north latitude, sixty-four degrees fifty-five minutes west longitude."

I was elated. I wasn't far off from what I had estimated. "Thank you," I said. "Would you mind relaying a message for me?"

"Not at all."

I gave them a message for Sally and we chatted for a few minutes more. Then, as I watched from my porthole, they were gone—on their way again, hidden by the waves.

Now I did start to cry. The brief conversation had brought me back in touch with the world. Now I was alone again—alone with my aching fatigue, solitude, discomfort, and fear.

I relived that brief encounter many times throughout the night, wondering if the *Bilderdyk* had reached the US Coast Guard Station at Portsmouth, Virginia, wondering if the Coast Guard had called Sally, and wondering how she would feel.

Sally told me later about the Coast Guard officer's call. It was a beautiful summer evening in White Bear Lake, and she had been working in the rose garden when the telephone rang. She was startled at first when the officer identified himself, and she asked him to repeat the message slowly, so she could write it down. Then she ran to the den and plotted my position on a wall map.

She saw that I was only five hundred miles out and wondered what had happened. Had I been becalmed? Was I in trouble? Then she looked down at the rest of my message: "Everything is OK." She read the words over and over. Somehow they formed a connection with me, a thin thread stretching over the miles, binding us together. Sally stood there a long time. Then she walked back into the kitchen and called my mother and father.

CHAPTER 8
STORM OVER THE NORTH ATLANTIC

 After four days of gradually worsening weather the Atlantic erupted into violence. The wind had swung to the south and now blew across the Gulf Stream at speeds up to forty knots, locked in a deadly battle with the stream's current. The stream wanted to flow one way; the gale wanted to push another. Long lines of waves advanced out of the south and the east simultaneously; when they met, they crested in towers of roaring, churning foam that pounded my little boat like a giant sledgehammer. I had to listen

for them, for I could see nothing out my portholes. *Yankee Girl* was closed up like a coffin, with me inside.

I was in constant pain. I had crawled up into the bow and wedged my knees against the navigation box and my head between my first-aid kit and a sail bag. This kept me from being jerked from side to side, but I still had to brace my arm against the ceiling to keep from being slammed up and down. My muscles were sore beyond belief, and my hips were badly bruised.

Whenever I managed to fall into an exhausted sleep, I awoke almost immediately, gasping for breath. Then I would slide the hatch back a few inches, risking a faceful of water for the fresh air I so desperately needed. Water was leaking in around the closed hatch anyway, and through the nylon flap fastened around the tiller opening on the transom. Every wave that slammed against the stern sprayed the inside of the boat like a firehose. I stuffed sponges into the gaps around the tiller. I put towels around the hatch and secured it more tightly by hammering a screwdriver in on one side and jamming my ballpoint pen in on the other. These emergency measures helped—a little.

I was continually sponging out the inside of the cabin. When my sponge was saturated, I would listen for the momentary hush between the crushing waves. Then I'd unscrew the inspection port in the transom, shove the sponge out, squeeze it, yank my arm back inside, and seal up the port again.

I was using an old meat baster to bail out the bilges. I would insert it down below, pump it full of water, and then shoot the water into my portable head—the one-gallon plastic jug, complete with screw top, in which I relieved myself during these stormy conditions. When the jug was full of bilge water, I'd again pause to gauge the waves. Then I'd quickly unfasten the hatch and open it just wide enough to poke my head and shoulders out and empty the jug.

Sometimes, between waves, I'd find myself staring at the seascape. Despite pain, fatigue, and the knowledge that I was in great danger, I could not help but marvel at its fierce beauty. The ocean was streaked with foam, for the shrieking winds had literally ripped the tops off the mountainous waves. The clouds were so low that they seemed to be riding the surface of the water. But I couldn't watch long. I had to get on with the business of staying alive—and keeping my tiny boat afloat.

Once, as I was dumping another jug of bilge water, I decided to take a few seconds and resecure the fastenings on the nylon tiller flap. Too much water was still coming in around it. I bent over the side of the boat, grabbed the flap, and became so engrossed in what I was doing that I forgot to pay attention to the waves.

Suddenly there was a terrible silence. I looked up to see a solid wall of green water towering over me. It was more than seventeen feet in height—taller than my mast—and was headed right for *Yankee Girl* and her wide-open hatch.

I ducked down into the cabin and frantically slammed the hatch shut—just as the wave broke over the boat. There was no time to lock the hatch, so I braced myself against it with every ounce of my strength. It was wrenched out of my hands.

With incredible force the water poured in. I was knocked back against the bulkhead. Stunned, I felt as if I were in a horrible dream, in which everything moved in slow motion, inexorably, and there was no escape.

Somehow my adrenalin took over. Scrambling up, I tore at the hatch. Under my desperate clawing, it moved an inch at a time until finally it closed, shutting off the deluge. Then, groggily, I surveyed the cabin. What I saw nearly made me panic. There was water everywhere.

I had to get it out as quickly as I could. At first with a tin can and then with the baster, I bailed. And bailed. It was like trying to empty the ocean with a spoon.

HOURS LATER, on the brink of total exhaustion, I sat down to rest. Only then did I notice that I was sopping wet. My clothes were pasted against my body by a combination of sweat and salt water. Piece by piece, I began to peel them off. I hadn't undressed in days, and I wasn't prepared for what I saw.

I had been immersed in water for so long that my outer layer of skin had simply dissolved. As I toweled myself off, slimy masses fell away. Worse still, the skin on my groin had turned a fiery red and itched horribly. That could mean I had a fungus infection. Under the best conditions, with proper care and treatment, it took days or even weeks for this type of infection to clear up. I reached for my talcum powder and began dusting myself with both hands. For a moment, I let go of my hold on the boat.

That was my second unforgivably careless act of the day. A rogue wave (one caused by two or more waves combining forces) suddenly caught us broadside. I was thrown down violently, and my head struck the side of the cabin. My hip hit the gas tank hard enough to leave a dent in it. I lay on my back with my eyes closed, not daring to move. When I opened them, I found myself staring straight out the starboard ports. I was lying on the *side* of the cabin.

We were capsized.

Instinctively I scrambled upward, trying to get my weight on *Yankee Girl's* high side. Meanwhile, things kept falling toward me—my hand compass, foul-weather gear, bags of batteries, and more of the ubiquitous grapefruit.

When I was up, I threw all my weight on top of my bunk and pushed. "Come on, *Girl*," I pleaded. "Come on. Over." I had to right her—now. If another wave hit while we were capsized, she might roll all the way over. We would lose both our mast and rigging. Suddenly, blessedly, *Yankee Girl* popped upright. The half ton of supplies below her waterline had levered her mast out of the water.

I didn't even have time to breathe a word of thanks. I had to find out whether there was any damage on deck. I slid back the hatch and saw that the six empty gasoline containers I had lashed to the side of the cabin had been literally torn away by the force of the knockdown. So had the sea anchor. I watched helplessly as they drifted out of reach, gone forever.

The loss of the sea anchor didn't bother me that much—it was clear that *Yankee Girl* was never going to lie to it, anyway. But the gasoline containers had been part of my backup flotation system, for use if *Yankee Girl's* hull were ever damaged.

With growing anxiety, I glanced at the back of the boat. Had my little Evinrude been torn off its bracket? No—I could see it bouncing along behind the transom. Whether it worked, after the beating it had taken, was a question I wasn't ready to face.

I looked down at my hands. They were trembling. As I slipped backward into the hatch, I gripped the rails hard and gritted my teeth. More than anything, at that moment I wanted to give up—to get away, to escape. I wanted to close my eyes and open them again and be *somewhere else*—back home in Minnesota, in safety and security, with my family and friends.

I had never been so frightened in my life. I bowed my head. I would cry out to God to save me. But then, surprisingly, I found myself hesitating.

I was here of my own choosing. God had given me all the resources I needed to survive. It was up to me to use them—and not to ask for more. Instead of pleading for help, I said a prayer of thanks. I was alive, and my boat was whole.

"HEY, THERE'S a gas station!" I shouted excitedly. "That's just what we need!"

It sat like a gleaming oasis at the side of the road. I turned the wheel of my car and slowed down. At last, a gas station! After all those miles! I smiled in relief.

But as I pulled in beside the pumps, I sensed that there was something wrong. Something dreadfully, terribly wrong. . . .

I awoke with a start. My teeth were chattering, and I was lying in a pool of perspiration. There *was* something wrong—with me. I was losing control of my mind.

This had been going on for most of the night. I would fall into an exhausted sleep, and my subconscious would take over. The gas station was the latest in a series of escape routes my mind had fabricated. Earlier there had been a park, then a rest stop. But each time I had awoken, shivering, to find myself back in the boat. The thunder of the waves, the constant rocking motion, the darkness in a howling storm that wouldn't end—*these* were reality.

I stared at the luminous hands of my wristwatch—three o'clock. It would soon be dawn and still the waves kept coming, rumbling and thundering like locomotives. Suddenly one broke, slamming us sideways. I heard the noise I had been dreading.

Cr-a-a-a-ck! It came from somewhere beneath me. With growing apprehension I grabbed my flashlight and started pulling gear from the forepeak and shoving it behind me. I had to get down to the keel. Had *Yankee Girl* finally succumbed to the pressures of the storm? Was she breaking up?

I played the light on her glue lines, the point where a fracture was most likely to occur. I ran the beam down one side of her stem in the forward compartment and up the other. Nothing.

Was my mind playing tricks on me again? I searched further. No cracks; the forward bilge was dry.

But I *had* heard the sound of breaking wood! There had to be a problem *somewhere*. Perhaps a split under the keel that hadn't worked its way through to the bilge yet.

I reached for my life jacket.

"That's a first," my imaginary friend observed.

I was shocked as, suddenly, I realized what I was doing. In all the hours I'd spent aboard *Yankee Girl*, I hadn't once thought of donning my life jacket. But if *Yankee Girl* were seriously injured, if I had to survive in a swamped boat, my life jacket would keep me afloat—if I didn't die first of cold and exposure.

Methodically, instinctively, I began going through emergency procedures. I pulled out my air bags, inflated them, and tied them to both sides of the stern. Afterward I sat and stared at my EPIRB. An orange and yellow transmitter about the size of a half-gallon milk carton, my Emergency Position Indicating Radio Beacon was my final card, the one I'd hold in my hand until the very end. When—if—I switched it on, it would send out a continuous tone, which would be heard by aircraft on a monitored frequency. They in turn would report it to the Coast Guard, who would request a ship in my area to pick me up.

I shuddered. Even if I did call for help, how could anyone rescue me under these conditions? Trying to get from my boat to a towering steel ship would be more dangerous than staying aboard *Yankee Girl*. I visualized a huge black hull, looming fifty feet above me, plunging and wallowing alongside—and, with a final roll, crushing my little plywood vessel.

But what if a ship were to come along *right now* and ask, "Do you want to be brought aboard?" What would I say? And what if they said, "There's a hurricane coming—the storm is going to get a lot worse." What then?

I pondered the alternatives. On one hand, I was determined not to give up just because I was frightened and miserable. On the other, though, I wanted to act intelligently. Would it be worth the risk to stay in this storm? Or should I give up my dream, let myself be rescued by a ship, and go back home?

I shook my head. Again I was losing my grip on reality. For there was no ship. I was alone, and all I could do was hope to survive.

CHAPTER 9
OVERBOARD!

 Slowly the storm was dying. Waves were now only six to ten feet high; the wind had dropped to a more tolerable twenty knots—and, perversely, had swung around to the northwest. *Yankee Girl* bobbed downwind, moving an inch at a time, but moving.

It was June 15, the fifteenth day of my voyage, and I was impatient. I had suffered this storm long enough; I wanted to do some sailing!

I slid open the wooden hatch, breathed deeply, and smiled for the first time in days. The fresh salt air filled my lungs. But when I tried to stand up, my smile quickly changed to a grimace. My muscles and tendons, cramped for so long, simply wouldn't function. Gradually and painfully, I straightened my back and held my body erect at last.

I would have to take my foul-weather gear off soon. The fungus on my groin itched horribly, and I felt slimy everywhere beneath my clothing. But that could wait. I wanted to get the boat going.

I looked around at the foredeck. The mainsail was still secure, the twin jibs furled and strapped down. I knew that the wind would now allow me to carry some canvas, but the speed and height of the waves still intimidated me. And I would have to be careful. In order to hoist the twin jibs, I would have to go forward to the bow and release them.

Cautiously I climbed out of the hatchway, grabbed the stainless-steel shroud with one hand and the mast with the other, and finally stood upright on the cabin top.

"It's a little like standing on a trampoline during an earthquake, isn't it?" my imaginary friend asked mischievously.

"With a four-hundred-pound wrestler jumping up and down on the other end," I answered, grinning.

I spread my feet apart on the hatch cover, thankful for my safety harness and lifeline. It had been seven long days since I'd been able to see beyond our immediate vicinity; just standing on top of the boat filled me with elation. It was like coming out of solitary confinement.

Now to get to the jib. It would be tricky; with my weight up forward, *Yankee Girl* already had an uncomfortable dip to her motion. Climbing even farther forward would bury her bow. I would have to move fast. Muscles tensed, I waited for a lull between the waves. Then, glancing over my shoulder, I froze in terror.

A massive wall of water was roaring toward us. A new wave—a rogue—was crossing over the old wave system, flattening it, and suddenly I realized I had forgotten to close the hatch. Now the wave was towering over it, threatening to fill the cabin. Frantically I leaned backward with all my weight, hoping to lever the stern up.

The wave slammed into the transom, lifted the stern, and threw it sideways. I was plunged into the churning water. Gasping for breath, I watched, horror-stricken, as the deck went completely under on the port side. *Yankee Girl* was now so far over that I could see inside her cabin. If she were struck by another wave, she could roll all the way over. Then my safety line would wrap itself around her bow—and I would be trapped below the surface.

Kicking desperately, my hands clenched around the rigging, I struggled against my water-filled clothing. Then, abruptly, *Yankee Girl* righted herself—pulling me up with her. Once again she had saved me from my own carelessness. And it had all happened so quickly that I'd been in the sea only a few seconds.

I scrambled below and slammed the hatch shut behind me, thoroughly shaken. How could I have been so stupid? Standing on top of the cabin, feeling I owned the world, I had taken a chance—a dumb, unforgivable chance that had nearly cost me my life. I sat there for a long time, raging at myself.

Finally I became aware of my soggy clothing—and my pain. My raw, infected skin, irritated by its unexpected salt-water bath, burned as if it were on fire. I found a clean shirt and pants, then stripped off my wet clothes and threw them overboard, knowing that they would eventually disintegrate.

I felt better after I'd dried myself off and changed my clothing. But my pants hung loosely around my waist. In my fifteen days at sea I must have lost ten pounds.

THE NEXT MORNING dawned breezy but sunny. Overnight the wind had swung to the north-northeast—perfect for sailing due east. Best of all, the waves, having settled down at heights of four or five feet, seemed like ripples on a pond.

Still unnerved by my unexpected dunking of the day before, I went forward cautiously and hoisted the jib. With an exhilarating surge, Yankee Girl began to slice through the water. For the first time in eight days we were sailing a course for England.

The weather was so favorable I decided to let Yankee Girl steer herself. Threading the line for the starboard jib through a hole in the side of the cabin, I brought the line inside, wound it through a block, and pulled the end back to the tiller. The resulting tension was balanced out by two pieces of surgical tubing—like big rubber bands—which I connected to the tiller from the opposite side. This arrangement allowed Yankee Girl to continue moving on her present course—at least for as long as the wind direction remained fairly constant. As I was both surprised and humbled to discover, it freed her to sail both straighter and faster than she would have if I were steering her.

Reclining in the cabin, I enjoyed the sound of the waves—and the miles—rushing by. Under sail and steering herself, Yankee Girl zipped along for three days and three nights at near her maximum speed.

Slowly but surely we recuperated from the storm. I was unable to determine the source of the cracking noise I'd heard, but since the boat seemed structurally sound and there was no sea water in the bilges, eventually I stopped worrying about it.

Sometimes I listened to the radio, welcoming the company of the announcers' voices. And I began forcing myself to eat regularly. I couldn't afford to lose any more weight.

Up to now, to fix my position, I'd relied mostly on rough sightings taken while Yankee Girl was gyrating wildly through the waves. On

70

the nineteenth day of my voyage, I finally took some I considered accurate, and found that I had covered one fourth of the distance to England—more than eight hundred and twenty-five nautical miles. This was encouraging—until I realized I'd been traveling only forty-three miles per day. I was still behind schedule. But by the twenty-third day my fix indicated that I had come more than twelve hundred miles. England once again seemed a reality.

Unfortunately I still wasn't getting more than an hour of uninterrupted sleep at a time. Often I'd just be dropping off when a midnight squall would rouse me to lower the sails. And I hadn't yet found a truly comfortable position inside the cramped cabin.

One morning, as I bent over the stern to wash my red plastic cereal bowl, I dropped it. I knelt there helplessly and watched it float away. I might have been able to turn *Yankee Girl* around, go back, and retrieve it, but I was simply too tired.

At least we were now making good progress, averaging sixty nautical miles per day. Though I kept the hatch closed over me because of the spray (that wouldn't stop being a problem until the waves subsided), I was able to leave out the drop board at the stern end of the cabin and so get some fresh air. Occasionally I'd scan the horizon for ships, just in case. The Gulf Stream was carrying us slowly northward, closer to the shipping lanes, an area of very heavy traffic. I hadn't seen a ship for nearly two weeks, though. It seemed as if I had the Atlantic all to myself.

I GOT INTO THE HABIT of eating my evening meal early. I'd have my pan and spoon washed and put away in time for one of the highlights of my day: the sunset. I'd gaze at that glorious spectacle, then slink into my little cabin and slide the hatch shut.

During the next hour or so I usually listened to my tapes and sang along with Linda Ronstadt or the Powdermilk Biscuit Band, a Minnesota group. Somehow music had the power to carry me back to the pines, birches, and sparkling blue lakes of home, and I spent many evenings curled up on my bunk, dreaming about my family and friends. These flights of fantasy helped me fight off my withering loneliness. Afterward I'd sleep peacefully, rocked by my little boat's gentle motion. Every hour or so I'd wake myself and poke my head out of the hatch to look for ships, then lie down again.

71

One night, when my inner clock woke me as usual for my ship check, I started for the hatch—and stopped. I hadn't seen anything for days, and the chances that I would now, at this very minute, were slim. Besides, I was hungry. I'd eat now and check later. I turned on my small battery-powered cabin light and rummaged through my provisions for a can of peaches. Then I opened it, reached for my spoon, sat back, and started digging in.

Suddenly *Yankee Girl's* cabin was flooded by light streaming in through her portholes. For one wild moment I thought a spaceship had landed directly on top of us. I heaved the hatch open and stared in disbelief as a towering wall of steel slid by only yards away.

At least she had missed us. Trembling, I dove for my radio.

"WXQ 9864 . . . WXQ 9864 . . . This is the yacht *Yankee Girl* calling any ship in the area . . . Over."

The response came immediately.

"*Yankee Girl, Yankee Girl*, this is the *African Comet*. We were surprised to see your light."

What light? What were they talking about? "You really gave me a start," I answered. "Didn't you pick me up on radar?"

"Negative. We saw your light and tried to miss you."

Then the realization hit me. The only light they could have seen was the cabin light. I was astounded—and badly shaken. What would have happened if I'd slept five minutes more?

CHAPTER 10
DAY OF CALM

By nine am on June 29 the sun was already high over the softly undulating ocean. It was a perfect day. As I glanced at my watch, I saw my morning nap had lasted three solid hours—the longest uninterrupted rest I'd had in nearly a month.

After so many days of being tossed about by the waves I was not prepared for the almost palpable silence. No slap of the halyards against the mast, no rattle of gear in the lockers, no gurgle of water under the hull.

Slowly unkinking my body, I stared out the hatchway. The North Atlantic was in one of her rare benign moods, and she was beautiful, a gleaming blue plain extending in every direction. I had to suppress the urge to jump out of the boat and run wildly across the water. This was exactly the sort of day I'd been waiting for, and I would make the most of it.

As I scrambled my breakfast eggs, I went over my list of things to do: check the motor, lubricate the sliding hatch cover, transfer some food and fuel. Later I'd reward myself with a bath.

Immediately after washing my dishes I began working on the outboard, which during the past weeks had been hammered by hundreds of waves and occasionally immersed completely. I unscrewed the clamps and hoisted it up on the half-open hatch cover. Slipping paper towels beneath it, I unscrewed the oil plug. The trickle that flowed out was thick and clear. No sign of sea water. Replacing the plug, I swung the motor back over the stern and secured it to its bracket.

Next I removed the power head cowling. The starting mechanism and coils were corroded by rust, so I sprayed them with lubricant and wiped them clean. I also replaced the spark plugs with two new ones.

I paused to wipe beads of perspiration from my forehead and my month-old beard. The sun was getting hotter. I was starting to itch, and the idea of a bath was becoming an obsession.

As I turned to put my wrench back in the toolbox, I glanced overhead. There, like a giant white plume against the azure sky, was a jet's contrail. I stared in envy, reflecting on those two hundred or more passengers up there, merrily eating and drinking their way to London. But I found it comforting to know they were around, and I watched until the jet was out of sight. Its contrail lingered, miles above my mast; I took it as a good omen as I turned back to the motor.

I crossed my fingers and pulled the starting cord. But its recoil spring was rusted; it would not rewind. I sprayed the spring with oil and pulled again. And again. Seven pulls and it didn't even cough.

This was not good. How would I be able to avoid the ships in the calms that lay ahead? What about the English Channel with its

Secure in my safety harness, I head east for Britain.

heavy traffic and strong currents? I *had* to have power for both safety and maneuverability. I yanked the cord again.

With a rasp that was music to my ears, the little engine spluttered into life. I turned up the throttle to warm it up, then ran it for fifteen minutes at speed before turning to my next project.

I was still concerned about the strange cracking noise I'd heard during the height of the storm, even though inside I'd found no sign of damage. Perhaps the fiberglass sheathing around the hull had been harmed in some way that could eventually allow sea water to leak into the hull's plywood and cause delamination. I was also worried about the fittings that held the base of the rudder. They had taken a real beating from the breakers. I simply had to give the boat a thorough going over, and there was only one way to do it.

I searched through my gear until I found my mask and snorkel. Then I stripped off my clothing and, for the first time since the beginning of my voyage, unsnapped my safety harness. Climbing onto the cabin top, I peered into the water. I needed to know what was down there.

A foot or so below the surface little maroon and silver fish zoomed about. As I leaned over, they darted out of sight beneath the hull. Long, tubular jellyfish drifted through the water all around the boat. They appeared harmless, but would bear watching. I couldn't see any sharks, but that didn't mean there weren't any. In mid-ocean, passing vessels regularly tossed garbage overboard. Any boat, even one as tiny as mine, would draw local sharks like a dinner bell.

Satisfied that the area looked safe, I donned my mask and snorkel and jumped in with a splash. The water was surprisingly clear, and the temperature was in the comfortable seventies. I rose to the surface, took a breath, and dived under the boat. Moving along beneath the blue hull, I ran my fingers over it, looking for damage. But the bottom was as sound as it had been back in Minnesota.

Out of breath, I headed for the surface and hurriedly hauled myself back on deck. Only then did I realize I'd been so apprehensive about sharks that I hadn't even thought about the rudder fitting. I hesitated. Should I go back down to check it? Then I remembered the bath I'd been promising myself all morning. Somehow that took precedence over fear.

I reached into the cabin and brought out my bottle of dishwashing detergent. Humming aloud, I happily began sudsing myself and was soon covered in lather, ready for a rinse. I braced myself, inhaled deeply, and dived. Immediately after rising to the surface I swam to the transom step and hauled myself up, naked and dripping, to the deck.

For the second time I'd forgotten to inspect the rudder. Still filled with an eerie uncertainty about sharks, nothing now could induce me to go back in the water. I'd examine the rudder later, from the surface, using my diving mask.

I grabbed the bucket and finished rinsing myself on deck. Then I toweled myself off quickly, getting rid of the salt water before it had the chance to dry and leave a sticky residue. Next I got a cup of fresh water from one of my containers, dipped paper towels into it, and wiped off my body. Afterward I slowly trickled the rest of the water down my back and chest.

Clean at last! I felt wonderful. Refreshed. Almost civilized. As I stood naked on the deck with the hot sun beating down on me, I decided to remain in my pristine state for a while longer. Maybe the sunshine and fresh air would have a healing effect on my raw skin. By now my fungus infection was extremely painful. I donned a T-shirt and my safety harness, but that was all. Then I returned to my chores.

My next priority was sealing the nylon cover over the tiller opening. I got out my hammer and two dozen nails and nailed the flap down—permanently. It seemed such an obvious solution. My life at sea would have been a lot easier if I'd thought of that before leaving Virginia.

Next I wanted to improve my system of reefing the foresails. With a couple of lines and cleats, I devised an arrangement that allowed me to partly lower the twin jibs and secure their position from the safety of the hatchway. When I tried it out it worked perfectly. I'd never again have to endanger myself or *Yankee Girl* by going forward during a storm.

By this time the sun's rays were becoming so intense that it seemed wise to work below for a while. There were two jobs to be done: transfer gasoline to the main tank, and retrieve some of the food stored up in the bow.

To get to the forward lockers, I had to move everything in the bow to the stern. I squirmed through my gear like a mole, passing clothing, books, and cans down toward my feet as I went. Once I made it to the bow, I couldn't move back again without reversing the procedure. It all took nearly an hour.

When I was done I was dripping with perspiration from the cabin's ninety-degree heat. But at last I could relax and enjoy a leisurely lunch. I opened a can of asparagus, a can of corn, and a can of tuna, and jazzed up the tuna with salt, pepper, and fresh lemon juice. Finally—I was really splurging now—I opened a bottle of Pepsi.

"How's this for a picnic?" I asked my friend.

"Great," he replied. "We've got everything but the ants."

After lunch I decided to get moving again. I started the Evinrude, and for the rest of the afternoon we chugged steadily along while I kept a close eye on the compass. The glassy blue Atlantic was utterly empty and utterly peaceful. But it was obvious that others had been here before me. The sea was littered with Styrofoam cups, wooden crates, pillows, sheets of plastic, oil drums, and the ever present globules of crude oil.

Just after sunset the wind came up out of the southwest at about eleven to sixteen knots. I was delighted. This was what the prevailing wind should have been from the very beginning! All that night and the following day, we sailed under *Yankee Girl's* self-steering mechanism. She did the work; I read and relaxed.

It was a great way to spend my thirtieth day at sea.

"DON'T YOU WANNA. . ."
   ". . . like to . . ."
   ". . . Ger . . ."
   ". . . are you . . ."

The voices came through the sides of the boat, from somewhere out on the water. I sat very still for a moment, listening and wondering. They chattered eerily, like ghosts calling weakly from afar, always in snatches of words or phrases, never in complete sentences.

I shivered in the gathering darkness. I *knew* there was no one out there, but the strange babbling sounds still raised the hairs on the back of my neck. Was I losing my grip on reality?

". . . *Ger* . . ."

Forcing myself up, I peered out over the transom.

"Is there anybody out there?" my friend inquired.

"Not in our immediate vicinity," I answered.

Now all I heard was the burbling of the water in *Yankee Girl*'s turbulent wake. The physical act of getting up had cleared my head.

I was aware of what was happening, of course. I was alone in the middle of the ocean, and my mind was trying to create some company for me. The only real conversation going on at the moment was the one between my *Yankee Girl* and the sea.

I retreated into the cabin, got out my tape recorder, and sang along with the Ink Spots' rendition of "I Cover the Waterfront." The sound of my voice filled the tiny cabin, and I no longer felt like a castaway.

When I tired of singing, I sat in the open hatch and ate a late-night snack of canned peaches. Then I stared in fascination at the sea. The Atlantic was more beautiful than I had ever seen her. Phosphorescence, so bright that it illuminated *Yankee Girl*'s hull, spread out behind us like a trail of sequined milk, mirroring the stars overhead.

At about eleven pm, on one of my hourly inspections, I saw a ship's light off on the horizon. I scrambled to my radio, and to my surprise they responded immediately.

"Where are you?" a voice asked.

"You're bearing fifty degrees," I answered. "There's a strobe light at my masthead."

There was a pause. "We see you now," the voice said, "but not very well. Is that your only light?"

"Yes, but my boat is pretty small. Only ten feet."

"Really?" the voice asked incredulously. "How many in the crew?"

"Well, there's only room for one."

Another pause. "Can you give us a repeat on your length?" By now their curiosity was growing.

"Ten feet, and thirty days out of Norfolk, Virginia. Bound for Falmouth, England. Would you be kind enough to give me a position check?"

"It will take a couple of minutes. We'll get back to you."

I waited for what seemed like a long time, becoming increasingly nervous. I was afraid we'd get cut off as the distance between us increased, and I wanted to give them a message to relay back home. I was relieved to hear the voice once again.

"*Yankee Girl*, we make our position to be forty-one degrees forty-one minutes north, forty degrees thirty-three minutes west."

"Thank you," I said warmly. "Would it be possible to call back to the States?"

"Sorry," the voice said, sounding genuinely concerned. "Can't do. We have only code equipment." In other words, all they could do was send messages by Morse code—the old-fashioned way.

I was disappointed that I couldn't get a voice message home, but I was told they would report my position to the Coast Guard at Portsmouth, Virginia. We chatted for several minutes more, and I learned I was talking with the *Josepha*, an English cargo ship bound for the States.

Afterward I went below and plotted the position I had been given. It compared favorably with my own sights. Incredibly, I was only thirty-three miles from the halfway point. By morning I would reach the very center of the North Atlantic ocean.

But what would I do then? Head straight for Falmouth—or turn southeast toward the Azores? For some time I had been considering stopping off at these Portuguese islands. Since they lay only four hundred miles away, and we were currently making about seventy miles per day, I could get to Flores, the northernmost island, in five and one-half days. There I could stretch my aching legs, relax, talk to someone besides myself, eat something that didn't come out of a can, and call home. It was *very* tempting.

On the other hand, I didn't need any provisions or repairs, and I had just sent a message home via the *Josepha*. If I steered for Falmouth, I'd be sticking to my original plan of sailing nonstop across the Atlantic. And I'd be sailing "downhill" after tomorrow. The worst of the voyage *had* to be over.

I made up my mind. I would set my course for England.

CHAPTER 11
RACE FOR FALMOUTH

 The days that followed were, for the most part fair and sunny. The breezes were variable but favorable. And the sea, formerly an adversary, had now become my friend. I began sailing both day and night, getting bolder by the minute. On some nights I'd even sleep with the spinnaker up, a practice that would have alarmed the most experienced sailor. The large, red, balloon-shaped sail had never given me any problems, but I kept a close eye on the weather just in case.

My little girl and I continued to make astonishing progress. Our speed was exhilarating and did wonders for my spirits. On July 15 we set a record: eighty-four miles in twenty-four hours, our longest run of the voyage. After the terrors of the storm, it almost felt as if we were riding a trade-wind passage. By midmorning the sun was usually warm, and I had so little to do that I could spend hours simply reading and relaxing in the shade of my umbrella.

I took pleasure in everything—the billow of the red sail above me, the blue sky, the steady breeze, the open horizons. The sea slipped by with a pleasant gurgle, mile after mile. I especially enjoyed eating. Food was no longer something I stuffed into myself to keep my strength up; I had fun with it. On one beautiful Saturday night, under a brilliant full moon, I got out my cooking pot, put a little oil in the bottom and popped a batch of popcorn. Then I happily devoured it all, relishing my "night out".

Occasionally I had visitors. Sea birds—shearwaters and terns and storm petrels—would circle the boat, schools of fish would flash through the water around us. One morning I was awakened by a chorus of piercing, high-pitched squeals. As I looked out over the transom, I saw dozens of porpoises diving and weaving around and under the boat. They were as curious about me as I was about them. One mother brought her baby up to look at me, gently nudging it away when it passed some invisible boundary she'd drawn. From time to time others would swim near, but most of them glided ahead of the boat, somersaulting through the air.

Usually, though, I was very much alone. For weeks my life had been intertwined with *Yankee Girl* and the endless ocean. I had developed great affection for them both, but I had been at sea too long: I was eager to return to my family and friends.

There came a day when I realized that if all went well, I would see them soon. It was on Wednesday, July 18, forty-eight days into my voyage, that my calculations showed that I would be in England shortly, perhaps by the following Sunday, July 22. The only thing disturbing my eighteen-day idyll had been the fact that I'd been unable to contact anyone since June 30. Now, more than ever, I needed to reach a ship and send a message home. And, on this same Wednesday, even that worry was taken care of.

I was standing on the cabin top, looking around, when I noticed masts on the horizon. Although previous attempts at calling ships in the distance had been unsuccessful, I decided to try once more. An answer came back within moments.

"This is the *Potomac*, nine days out of Philadelphia, bound for Rotterdam." There was a pause. "We can't figure this out," the voice went on. "We can receive you fine, but we can't see you."

"I've got a big red spinnaker up," I responded, "but you won't see me because I'm below your horizon. I'm in a ten-foot boat headed for Falmouth out of Virginia."

"How long have you been at sea?" asked the voice.

"Forty-eight days. I'm making good progress. Actually, my family isn't expecting me to arrive in England so soon. They haven't heard from me in quite a while. If you can get a message back, it will really make my day."

"No problem," the voice replied.

Human contact! It meant more now than it ever had. I gave them my message, but as soon as they pulled out of range, questions began to gnaw at me. I was confident that the *Potomac* would relay my report to the Coast Guard station in Virginia, but I couldn't be sure what would happen next. Would the receiving officer get it right? Would Sally receive it soon enough to change her plans? What if she didn't arrive in England until the end of July—the time we'd originally agreed on? And what would happen when I finally reached Falmouth? To begin with, I had only about twenty-three dollars in my wallet. If Sally wasn't there to meet me, my lack of funds could quickly become embarrassing. I was dog-tired; I needed a place to rest, a place to stretch out. From the looks of things I wouldn't even be able to afford a hotel room.

And what would I do with *Yankee Girl*? How could I possibly meet the costs involved in bringing her home—the dockage, boatyard, crating, trucking, and shipping? They would add up to almost as much as I'd invested in building her.

Suddenly I felt strangely melancholy. During these past seven weeks I had accomplished a long-cherished goal. My dream was coming true. But I wasn't looking forward to stepping out on dry land with no one there to meet me. My thoughts, once again, turned to Sally and my family.

LOOKING BACK NOW, I realized that those first weeks in July—an idyll of sorts for me—were for Sally the most difficult time of all. The break in communications that came after my message was radioed back from the *Josepha* worried her deeply. And she had other worries as well—how to handle the news media.

Larry Maddry, a news reporter I'd come to know in Virginia Beach, had written an article transmitted by the Associated Press on June 12, the day after I had been sighted by the Dutch ship *Bilderdyk*.

Ever since then the wire services had been carrying stories about my progress across the Atlantic, and reporters had been calling Sally regularly.

Normally she didn't object to sharing with them any news she had. But by mid-July, when more than two weeks had passed since my last message, Sally began to detect a certain inflection in such questions as, "Are you getting concerned?" It was the reporters' polite way of asking if she was worried about the imminent possibility of becoming a widow.

Soon Sally learned to reply with the carefully rehearsed answer, "No, I'm only concerned that I won't be in England when he arrives there."

Sally told me later that she never really doubted that *Yankee Girl* and I would make it. But during this period one question was ever present in the back of her mind: Where are they? Hating the constant uncertainty, she buried herself in her work. Her co-workers helped keep her spirits up, but she was fighting intense loneliness and fear.

By the morning of Wednesday, July 18, she could stand it no longer. Instead of waiting for the Coast Guard station at Portsmouth, Virginia, to call her, as she usually did, she decided to call them. To her immense relief, the duty officer who answered said that they had been about to call her. Then he read the message, just in, from the *Potomac*. While he spoke, Sally excitedly pinpointed my position on her chart of the North Atlantic. She stared in disbelief. It seemed as if I had *jumped* across the ocean since she had last heard from me, for I was now less than four hundred and seventy-five miles from Falmouth. Suddenly she thought of all the things she must do to be in England in time to meet me—finish up at the office, get airline tickets changed, buy traveler's checks, pack. . . .

Feeling dazed, she thanked the Coast Guard officer, hung up and immediately dialed my parents to give them the news.

It wasn't until later that morning that Sally got the rest of my message—from a reporter. At about eleven am the telephone rang on her desk at work. It was Larry Maddry, the AP reporter who had been following my solo crossing. He wanted to know if Sally had talked with the Coast Guard.

"Yes," Sally replied. "Isn't it fantastic?"

"Can you make it over by Sunday?" Larry asked.

"What do you mean, *Sunday?* Where did you hear that?"

"The Coast Guard. Didn't they tell you that Gerry's estimated time of arrival is July 22?"

Sally couldn't believe what she was hearing. Then she remembered—she had been so busy plotting my position that she hadn't listened closely to all the Coast Guard officer had said. "I guess I missed that part," she confessed. Then she thanked Larry and called my parents.

The three of them talked it over and agreed. If they were going to arrive in England, five thousand miles away, before I got there on Sunday, they would have to leave Minnesota on Friday—and it was already Wednesday noon.

"Do you think we can make it?" Sally asked them.

"Of course we can," my dad told her.

CHAPTER 12

SURPRISE!

The weather began turning foul as I neared the English coast. Another worry to add to my list. This was a critical point in my journey. Success or failure hinged on the next few hours.

As I approached land, the current would divide, and I could easily be swept along in the wrong direction. If I sailed too far north, I might end up in Ireland; too far south, and I might find myself in the treacherous Bay of Biscay or on the shores of France. My small sailboat didn't have the power to fight against both adverse winds and tricky currents. And I was also low on gasoline.

It was already Monday, July 23. The day before, July 22—my estimated day of arrival at Falmouth—I'd been able to contact a ship called the *Manchester Concept* and had confirmed that I was still about a hundred and fifteen miles from Land's End, the southwestern tip of England. According to my charts, this was a heavily trafficked area: in fact, there were more freighters, tankers, liners and trawlers steaming around this part of the ocean than anywhere else in the world. It was certainly a bad place to be, with my visibility and maneuverability as limited as they were. I was also far more fatigued than I should have been on entering these dangerous waters.

All I could do was sail as fast as possible on a heading of sixty degrees magnetic. If I steered straight and wasn't carried astray by currents, this course would bring me—or so I believed—to Wolf Rock, the first point of reference guiding me to Falmouth. The trouble was, I hadn't been able to take a proper sight that morning because of the overcast sky, and I was relying on a combination of instincts and dead reckoning.

As the day wore on, the wind swung around to the west, and I set both jibs to sail at top speed. Sailing under these conditions was exhilarating and frightening; I enjoyed zipping along at four knots, but I didn't like not knowing how close we were to the rocky cliffs of the Scilly Isles.

Mist and fog shrouded the sea. As patches lifted or cleared, I sighted ship after ship, dark strangers steaming past for ports unknown. Frequently, I tried calling them, but I never received a response. It was very frustrating.

By late afternoon I was seriously concerned. I was still running steadily under twin jibs before a brisk wind and making good progress, but I still didn't know where I was. When I sighted another ship off on the horizon, I radioed her without much hope of a reply.

Suddenly I heard words emerging through the static. "*Yankee Girl. . .Yankee Girl. . .*" Faint and faraway, but they were there.

Desperately afraid of losing contact, I called again and again.

Then, like a whisper, the voice came back to me. "This is Land's End Coast Guard."

I was overjoyed. I was talking to someone on *land!* "Can you give me a bearing?" I inquired.

"Sorry, *Yankee Girl*, we don't have the equipment to do that. What is your estimated position?"

"I'm about twenty-five miles southwest of Land's End, course sixty degrees magnetic. Over."

But I couldn't understand their static-riddled reply. Finally I gave up. "Thank you, Land's End, over and out," I said.

I turned my attention to my radio direction finder. Last night I had made several unsuccessful attempts to pick up a radio beacon that could help me pinpoint my position. Today my luck was no better. I'd just have to wait for darkness, when I might see a recognizable light.

But when night came, the visibility was further reduced by rain squalls, and the impenetrable darkness made me more nervous than ever. The shipping traffic had increased; at one time I counted eight ships heading in different directions around me. Sometimes I smelled passing ships even when I couldn't see them: the reek of diesel fumes or the aromas of food and coffee would waft toward me over the water.

Since I was having difficulty seeing the white, red and green lights of these speeding leviathans through the rain and mist, I could imagine how hard it was for them to see me. To make myself more noticeable I hoisted my strobe light to the masthead, rigged the radar reflector, and occasionally shone my flashlight on the sails. I knew, though, that these precautions wouldn't help much if a ship came straight at me.

Finally, around midnight, I saw a flashing light off to the north. "This might be it, Ger," my imaginary friend exclaimed.

"Keep your fingers crossed," I answered.

Controlling my impatience, I reached into my navigation box and carefully removed my only working watch from its plastic bag. I'd kept it there for weeks to protect it. The one I'd been wearing when I left Virginia had long since stopped.

I timed the light's period at thirty seconds.

But when I consulted the lists of lights I'd brought with me, there was no mention of a thirty-second light. Something had gone wrong. I had been carried too far north.

Again I stared at that blinking light. Slowly the simple facts began to penetrate my sleep-dazed brain. What I was seeing wasn't a thirty-second light but a beacon flashing white at the end of fifteen seconds, then red after fifteen more seconds, then white again. The red had been obscured by the weather conditions. So I was looking at the light on Wolf Rock. We had made a perfect landfall!

I sailed directly toward it—and saw the red flash just before another squall moved in to obliterate it. Estimating my distance to be some ten to fourteen miles offshore, I headed for Lizard Point, where I knew I would find the Lizard light flashing—three seconds on, three seconds off—to guide me safely to Falmouth.

By this time fatigue and poor visibility were combining to confuse me. I was finding it more and more difficult to interpret the myriad lights of the ships around me and determine their course and speed, in order to stay clear of them. So although I knew where to look for the Lizard light, I only saw it once, and by the time I reached for my compass, it had disappeared again in the rain.

My only choice now was to maintain a more easterly direction and wait for daylight, when I should be able to see the cliffs.

DAWN BROKE at about four o'clock on that Tuesday, July 24, bringing with it a pea-soup fog that limited visibility to a hazardous fifty yards. I was now in the midst of the east-west shipping lane, and I had to turn my head every few seconds to listen and smell for ships. I felt as if some shadowy force had played a terrible trick on us. We had journeyed thirty-eight hundred miles across the Atlantic only to encounter a deadly fog that impaired our visibility when we needed it the most.

Finally I dropped the sails and yanked the Evinrude to life. I would have to risk using the rest of my gasoline, since I desperately needed maneuverability. With the engine at full throttle, I'd at least have a chance to scoot away if anything loomed out of the fog toward me.

"I don't like this part, Ger," my friend complained.

"Me neither," I replied.

The strong tidal currents along the coast were also making me nervous. They could easily carry *Yankee Girl* astray and toss her up on the craggy, treacherous Cornwall coast. Many sailors had lost their lives on those rocks I had altered my course to ninety degrees so I wouldn't come up windward of the Lizard. But I still didn't know how far away the rocks were.

Suddenly I raised my head and listened. Had I heard a sound? I turned off my motor and waited. It had come from a long way off, deep-throated and urgent. There it was again: the booming drone of the Lizard's foghorn! A long blast followed by a short one—morse code for the letter *N*, the Lizard's call sign.

At last I knew exactly where I was. The Lizard's horn was bearing due north; that meant I'd been pushed eastward by the current. I started up the engine again and headed at top speed directly toward the Lizard. After ten minutes I shut down the motor, listened, and took a new bearing. Then I was off again. I kept repeating this procedure until the horn was so loud I could almost feel its vibrations. But foghorns can play tricks, changing their range and direction with atmospheric conditions. So, to be on the safe side, I turned east once more.

At about nine am a miracle occurred: the fog lifted. There, spread out before me like a vision, were the jagged cliffs of Cornwall. The scene literally took my breath away.

Rising above the cliffs was the sparkling white Lizard Point lighthouse. Just beyond lay amber fields, neatly outlined by stone walls. It was a fairyland. As a faint zephyr drifted toward me, bearing the scent of new-mown hay, I realized, more than ever before, how much of a land animal I was. I loved the challenge of the sea, but I belonged to the land.

No longer worried about my fresh water supply, I washed my face and hands until they squeaked. Then I crawled forward and found the plastic bag containing the clean white sweater and slacks that I had stowed there after leaving Virginia. I put them on; then I brushed my teeth and combed my hair and beard.

"You *look* clean," my friend commented, "but I wouldn't want to be downwind of you."

I had one more job left to do. I took out my British ensign and my American flag and hoisted them both, according to flag etiquette, with the host country's emblem at the masthead. Then while I was puttering around below, tidying up the cabin, I was startled by the sound of a klaxon.

I stuck my head out the hatch and saw a boat was coming down the coast at full speed, heading directly for me. I had never been so startled in my life. All I could think about was getting out of her way. And then I saw Sally.

FROM THE MOMENT Sally and my parents had arrived in London on Sunday, they had been at the center of a major media event. A late report had confirmed that I was nearing the coast, and upon their arrival in Falmouth they found their hotel already overflowing with reporters, photographers, and TV newsmen from both British and American networks.

Throughout that evening and the next day the press had scrambled about in a frenzied competition to get a piece of the story about the lone Minnesota sailor who was still out there somewhere, battling the rough seas off the coast. Every boat in Falmouth capable of going out to meet me had been chartered, and some of the London reporters, who had reserved Falmouth's pilot boat *Link*, had invited Sally and my parents to come along as special guests.

Tuesday morning, July 24, had dawned gray and rainy. When the *Link* shoved off, about nine forty-five, visibility was down to a hundred and fifty yards. Sally stood at the rail, her face grim, while reporters jostled beside her, scanning the waters for any sign of *Yankee Girl*.

"Do you think that we'll be able to find him?" one interviewer asked Sally.

"Of course we'll find him," Sally replied confidently. "It's just a matter of *when*."

At that moment, another reporter, pointing off to starboard, shouted, "Is that it? That little blue thing over there. . .?"

Sally stared out into the mist. "Yes!" she cried. "Yes, that's *Yankee Girl!*"

Other reporters surrounded her now, holding up microphones. "Sally, how do you feel?"

But Sally didn't hear them. She was no longer conscious of anyone else. She strained forward over the rail, waiting for the tiny boat to emerge from the mist once more. "There he is!" she shouted. "Over there!"

Now the *Link* bore down on *Yankee Girl*, its klaxon sounding.

"Ahoy, *Yankee Girl!*" Sally yelled.

"But where's Gerry?" someone asked. At that instant my head popped up through the hatch.

"He has a beard," Sally noted incredulously.

"You swore he wouldn't," one of the reporters said.

"Well, he won't have it much longer."

And then the *Link* was alongside *Yankee Girl*, my little yacht bobbing like a cork in the larger boat's wake.

AFTER THAT everything happened very quickly. The pilot boat was crammed full of people—Sally, and yes, there were my parents, and reporters, photographers, crew. Everyone was smiling, shouting, asking questions. "What was the most dangerous part of your trip?" "Did you run out of food or water?" "Were you menaced by sharks or whales?"

After weeks of longing desperately to talk to someone, I was speechless. And the only people I really saw were Sally and my parents. I was choking back tears.

Finally one reporter's voice boomed out over the others. "What do you have to say after fifty-four days alone at sea?"

There was a hush. I saw microphones extended to capture my first words. "Well, I made it," I said lamely.

It wasn't the profound statement they expected, but it was the best I could come up with in my dazed state. And it wasn't *quite* true. I was still twelve miles out of Falmouth, and I would be bucking an ebb tide the whole way. I had to get going.

We waved a temporary good-by and I started my little motor. The pilot boat headed rapidly back toward port, urged on, I suspected, by reporters eager to file their stories. But soon another boat full of TV newsmen pulled up alongside. More questions. More pictures. I talked with them as I motored along, and then I heard a noise overhead.

Two Royal Navy helicopters were circling above, the crewmen leaning precariously out the doorways to wave. They were followed by several small airplanes, full of waving, smiling, picture-taking people. I waved back, mystified. Where were all these people coming from? Sooner or later, I thought, this would have to stop. But I was wrong.

I had the engine turned up full, and *Yankee Girl* was making her best speed. Even so, it was several hours before I sighted the entrance to the harbor. Meanwhile I was beginning to worry about all of the boats crowding around me. Sometimes there would be one in front of me, another alongside, a third behind me, and yet another would come out of nowhere. Everyone was shouting congratulations and questions. "Well done!" "Good show!"

As I neared the harbor, I couldn't believe my eyes. An entire flotilla of boats was streaming towards me—cruisers, sailboats, open launches, even small inflatables with outboard motors—each one racing through the water, eager to get to me first. A mass collision seemed imminent. Then, with some good-natured shouting and gesturing, my ragtag escort formed itself into a gigantic nautical parade. A navy cruiser blew its whistle in salute; other vessels echoed the greeting with their own horns, whistles, and bells.

We entered the harbor. The city of Falmouth, nestled at the foot of castle-crowned hills, seemed to rise up from the horizon to welcome me, and suddenly I knew why I had chosen this city as my goal. I was sailing into a haven that had hosted centuries of privateers, men-of-war, clippers, and many of the single-handers I had read about.

Then with a jolt I was drawn back to the present. There were people everywhere. Crowds lined the piers, quays and hillside roads. Thousands of people, all cheering and clapping. What had happened to my vision of a lonely docking?

I was wondering what to do next when the harbormaster's boat shouldered its way up to me. "Welcome to Falmouth, sir, and congratulations," the harbormaster said. "Please follow us." Maneuvering his vessel until it was directly in front of *Yankee Girl*'s bow, he cleared a path for us through the water to the mooring that had been set aside for me.

Now the clamor intensified. I stepped out of *Yankee Girl*, and was led like a sleepwalker through the crowd to the customs launch, where the entry paperwork awaited my signature.

Meanwhile, my little boat was towed away for safekeeping; otherwise, the harbormaster said, the tourists might strip her bare for souvenirs.

A launch took me to the steps of Falmouth Yacht Club. Dad and Mother and Sally were there, along with Falmouth's mayor, Olive

Sally and I make our way through the streets of Falmouth.

White, and other local dignitaries were waiting. Someone handed me a glass of champagne, and the mayor stepped forward, smiling warmly.

"We're proud to welcome you to Falmouth," she said, "a port that has played host to so many other courageous seamen."

Photographers jostled one another, and reporters shouted question after question. For a moment, as I looked at the mass of people surging toward me, I was afraid I'd find myself back in the water again.

On top of the stress of my voyage, this reception was almost too much. Suddenly I was aware that my legs felt like rubber bands and the earth seemed to be tilting crazily back and forth.

"Are you okay, Ger?" Sally asked. "Why don't you put your arm around my shoulder and lean on me?"

I held her tightly.

IT TOOK US NEARLY twenty minutes to wind our way to the Greenbank Hotel, only half a block away. People pressed forward to shake my hand, and several elderly ladies planted motherly kisses on my cheek.

At last Sally and I managed to escape the throng and climb the stairs to our large, cheery room overlooking the harbor.

I closed the door behind us, "Now," I sighed, "we can relax."

"That's what you think," Sally said. "There's another reception and a press conference in the lobby."

My face fell.

"We *have* to go down," she said apologetically. "Some of those people have been waiting for three days to see you."

"Don't I even have time for a bath?" I asked desperately.

"You've waited two months; another hour or so won't make that much difference." Her voice was firm.

Reluctantly I clumped back down the stairs. Another glass of champagne was pressed into my hand as we took our seats in the glare of the television lights.

The questions started. "Did you have any bad moments?" "Were you frightened?" "Did you ever feel like giving up?"

I did my best to answer each one, but my exhaustion must have been apparent, because finally a very proper British journalist stood up and signaled for silence. "I think Mr. Spiess deserves a rest and a slap-up meal," he said.

The others rose to their feet and applauded as we made our way to the hotel's elegant dining room. And there was the final surprise of this long, astonishing day: a banquet table covered with white linen, neatly arranged napkins, silver, china, and crystal. Sally, my parents, and I were seated at the head, flanked by the mayor and other Falmouth dignitaries.

"Would you like some water, Mr. Spiess?" a waitress asked.

I nodded. It felt odd to have people waiting on me.

"Would you rather have peas or carrots?" another asked.

"I'll have some of each, please," I heard myself saying.

"Creamed or fried potatoes?"

"Both, please."

Secretly I wished that someone would put everything on the table in front of me and be done with it. After weeks of eating out of cans, I was starved for fresh food. And it was wonderful to sit upright without having to brace myself.

As the crowning touch, we had steak for our main course. I couldn't believe how marvelous my first bite tasted. It paled, however, beside the rolls and butter. Fresh bread! Real creamery butter! I gobbled roll after roll, hoping no one would notice.

The evening passed in a blur of questions, congratulations, phone calls, and telegrams from around the world. It wasn't until two am that Sally and I were able to break away and trudge upstairs to our room.

"Now for that bath," I said.

As Sally filled the oversized pink tub with steaming water and sprinkled it with bubble bath, I peeled my clothing away from my skin. "Good heavens," she gasped, staring in disbelief at my bruises, scaling skin, and flaming red rash. "What on earth did you do to yourself out there?"

"I'll tell you later," I replied, stepping into the tub.

At first the pain was intense.

Soon, however, I could sense the warmth radiating through me, soothing my aches. I sighed in relief.

"You just can't imagine how great it feels," I told Sally.

She leaned over the tub and began shampooing my hair. I

reached up and took her soapy hands in mine. "At last we're together again, Sal," I said.

She knelt down beside me, still holding my hands. "And I'm so grateful to have you back."

I closed my eyes, supremely content.

MANY OF US grow up with dreams we never realize. We don't take time to live them, or we let others discourage us. We listen to the choruses of "Why bother?" and "What will you gain from it?" and never experience the joys of achieving goals we set for ourselves.

I believe that everyone should have a dream and strive to reach it. People's dreams can be big or small—it doesn't matter. What matters is that a dream once realized can change a person in some indefinable but vital way.

And sometimes one dream will lead to another, and another, until finally the act of dreaming becomes an endless cycle, a limitless horizon as vast as the sea itself.

ON JUNE 1, 1981 Gerry Spiess and *Yankee Girl* left Long Beach, California, to cross the Pacific Ocean. Their destination: Sydney, Australia, seventy-eight hundred miles away.

Gerry Spiess

When my college roommate introduced me to Gerry Spiess more than twenty years ago, I knew I'd met someone with a yen to travel that set him apart from our classmates. Even so, I would never have believed then where the years would take us: around Europe by camper; to the Far East by plane; to South America by sailboat.

I'm often asked why Gerry does what he does. I can only say that he has always sought to test himself, to take on the greatest challenges. His marathon sailing trips begin with the intellectual challenge of design and planning. (This is the part he likes best.) The second challenge is emotional: "psyching" himself up until he feels that the voyage will be "a piece of cake." Third is the physical challenge of getting himself in shape to "tough it out" at sea. By the time he's ready to set sail—always an exceedingly uncomfortable time for me, when it just tears me up to be around—I'm as certain as he is that everything humanly possible has been done to ensure success.

Gerry has always believed that we have been put here on earth to learn, to make the most of our God-given potential. Whatever challenge he chooses next, I have no doubt it will fully occupy our lives.

—Sally Spiess

EDITORS' NOTE: *Gerry Spiess and* Yankee Girl *sailed safely into Sydney harbour on October 31, 1981. The epic five-month voyage, which included brief stops in Hawaii, Samoa, and Fiji, earned Gerry the distinction of having crossed both the Atlantic and Pacific in the smallest craft ever. Although he plans no more solo voyages in* Yankee Girl, *another long-distance sail in a different boat is likely. His latest achievement, Gerry says, has convinced him more than ever that "you can do anything, if you really want to."*

GILDED SPLENDOUR
Rosalind Laker

DECORATIONS FROM
THE GENTLEMAN & CABINET-
MAKER'S DIRECTOR

Gilded Splendour

THE STORY OF

Thomas Chippendale

A CONDENSATION OF THE BOOK BY

ROSALIND LAKER

Illustrated by Yvonne Gilbert
Published by Eyre Methuen

Young Thomas Chippendale could work magic
with wood. His artistry shone through, whether in a
table of gleaming walnut or a chair of sturdy country oak.
One day the world would acknowledge his genius, and
his magnificent furniture would grace the most
elegant houses in England.
But when he and Isabella Woodleigh first met,
a gulf of class and circumstance stretched between them.
He was only a humble carpenter, working on the great
estate of Nostell Priory in Yorkshire, and she was an
honoured guest in the house, daughter of a distinguished
Member of Parliament.
Nonetheless a link of love and friendship was
forged between them which was to survive all manner
of scandal and separation, and was to last a lifetime.

Chapter One

She did not notice him in the sun-shadows. Yet his keen gaze followed her intently as she was borne down the steps of the great house in a specially constructed chair suspended on a pair of shafts held fore and aft by two burly menservants. It was the first outing of Isabella Woodleigh's convalescence since her arrival nearly a month ago at Nostell Priory, the country seat of the Winn family. All unaware of being observed by a stranger, she raised her oval face eagerly to the sun, her narrow hands gripping the arms of the chair as it swayed a little.

"Such a splendid day!" Her grateful exclamation in clear tones reached far in the quiet air. It was full spring in the year of 1737, but a setback to her health after the long journey to Yorkshire had kept her indoors far longer than had been expected. Now, in spite of the physical weakness that bound her to the chair, she was filled with a sense of liberation as she was carried towards the spread of lawns beyond.

Thomas Chippendale, tall, broad, and muscular, a bag of carpentry tools in his hand, had paused on an errand to watch her go by. Although he had not quite finished his seven year apprenticeship as a cabinet-maker, he had made the chair in which the girl invalid was sitting. It was a handsomely fashioned piece of furniture, no doubt of that. Never one to be modest about his own achievements, he viewed it appreciatively, noticing too that the trio looked remarkably like the figures on a Chinese lacquered cabinet, each gilded by sunshine against the myriad greens of the lush foliage and parkland. He knew the very cabinet. It was in this house, a splendid piece in that particular greenish-gold that he much preferred to the more usual black or scarlet of the pieces imported from China. The girl's flat-crowned hat with its wide brim, tied by ribbons over the muslin cap that covered her hair, added to the faintly oriental image of the little procession.

The formal gardens were now opening out around Isabella. Previously she had only glimpsed them, when, ill and exhausted, she had been lifted bodily from the carriage after reaching Nostell Priory. She had travelled the many miles from home alone with her maid, as her widowed mother and her younger sister, Sarah, had been only too thankful to bundle her off to the Winns after nursing her for many weeks. Isabella was still haunted by memories of the sickroom and the torments of a fever that the physician had thought to subdue by having all the hair clipped from her head. It was growing again, forming a pale golden cap beneath the muslin one that covered it, but until she could dress it again with some style she would continue to keep it hidden from sight.

"Just listen to the birds, Dawson," she said to the man at the front of her chair. Her mother would have disapproved of her making conversation with servants, but she was not in the habit of taking people for granted.

"Right noisy they are this mornin', mistress," Dawson agreed, nodding his grey-streaked head.

Behind Isabella and her bearers Nostell fell away beyond the greenery, but rising nearby to the north of it was the new mansion, still sheathed in scaffolding and far from completion. It was destined to be a much grander edifice than the old house, showing the influence of the sixteenth-century Venetian architect, Andrea Palladio, whose villas in the classical style of ancient Rome graced the contemporary Italian landscape and had brought about a virtual revolution in architectural design in England. Many wealthy families were rebuilding their residences in the Palladian mode, and small temples, rotundas and colonnaded orangeries were being added to family parkland in the evocation of all that was classical.

Isabella's host, Sir Rowland Winn, had seen Palladio's work at first hand during the Grand Tour, and had come home with the wealthy traveller's usual complement of works of art that needed the right setting in which to be displayed to best advantage. But far more important was that not long after his return he married the lovely Susannah Henshaw, heiress of a London lord mayor, and he wanted a truly splendid residence where the new Lady Winn could hold sway. The original plans, almost a copy of a villa that Sir Rowland had much admired, had been modified to blend more harmoniously with an English setting by an eminent young architect, James Paine, and the building taking shape had pavilions and quadrant colonnades that would be both imposing and gracious.

Meanwhile Sir Rowland continued to entertain lavishly in his present home, and had decided with his wife that Isabella Woodleigh, the daughter of a deceased political acquaintance, should be invited to Nostell to recuperate from a fever that had almost taken her life. He had an unshakeable belief in the beneficial properties of the northern Yorkshire air, and the carrying-chair had been his idea.

Isabella was brought by way of an arbour to the orangery, with its columns, balustrades, and panelled inside walls. The chair was set in a patch of sunlight, the back adjusted and the footstool drawn out into place for her comfort, and then the servants departed. Left alone, she thought she had never been more grateful for the transport that had been contrived for her than on this day. So much thought had gone into the design of the handsome chair. In a slot by the arm there was a place for her book, her needlepoint, and her draw-string purse, and the generous seat of green haircloth was broad enough to accommodate the side panniers of her dress without crushing them. She had been told that the chair had been made by the same craftsman who was engaged in making a doll's house for Lady Winn, a replica of the new house, with every piece of Nostell's furniture accurately copied in miniature and tiny wax figures of the ladies clad in copies of their own gowns. Isabella was looking forward to seeing it.

It was not long before the gentle warmth of the sun faded and the sky became cloudy and overcast. With a shiver Isabella threw aside the shawl that covered her knees and levered herself up out of the chair. It was better to walk than to sit and be chilled. She supported herself with a hand against the doorjamb, and as usual she set herself a target. She would walk twenty paces more than she had walked the previous day within the house. Resolutely she set off slowly along the path between the flowerbeds. The sheer physical effort involved brought a trembling to her knees, but she persisted, and achieved the distance for which she had aimed. It was only when she turned to go back again that she realized her mistake. It was not enough that the orangery looked alarmingly distant, but without any warning, a harmless breeze had become a rising wind, buffeting her in the face.

Already tired, every retraced step proved to be a battle for her. Then to her dismay a heavy drop of rain thudded onto the back of her hand, and another plopped onto her shoulder. Within seconds the skies had opened in a downpour.

Spurred into a supreme effort to reach shelter she tripped and fell headlong, the breath knocked out of her, her small reserve of strength quite gone. Then she was lifted up. Dawson and his companion, returning upon the change in the weather and failing to find her in the orangery, had come at a run to search for her. Wrapped up against the rain, she was borne back to Nostell, her head lolling in a faint, her face ashen.

Cossetted by her hostess, she cast off within a few days the effects of the disastrous outing. Yet the experience had completely unnerved her, and she became less and less willing to leave the sanctuary of her chair. Daily she became more and more obsessive about it, asking questions about the wood from which it was made, getting upset when she thought it had been scratched. Finally and inevitably, Isabella sent for the carpenter who had made it.

She awaited him in the library, situated at the far end of a long tunnel of rooms, which opened one into another in a glowing aura of sunshine shimmering on damask and porcelain and rich tapestries. As Thomas Chippendale appeared in the most distant doorway, she was surprised to see that his age was little more than her own. He approached with the purposeful step that comes only from the exuberance of youth and vibrant good health.

"I'm Thomas Chippendale, mistress." He bowed to her, his attitude respectful but not servile. "You wished to see me."

He had a deep, strong voice that matched his appearance. In spite of the flat Yorkshire vowels, he appeared to have dropped from his vocabulary the *thee* and *thy* of the county's dialect. He did not show any kind of countrybred awkwardness, but instead stood with quietness, obviously puzzled by the summons, a gulf of class and background stretching wide between them. He was in his working clothes, a homespun coat that reached to his knees over a buttoned waistcoat of well-worn leather. He wore his rich blue-black hair tied back at the nape of his neck, and with his arresting good looks dominated by shrewd dark brown eyes, he was a male to make any female look once, and maybe twice, before letting him pass by. More than usually vulnerable in her present state, already biased towards him because of the chair, Isabella felt her breath constrict as she answered him. "Ah, yes, indeed. It's a matter concerning this chair that you made for my sojourn here—"

"Is it no longer right for you? It can only need some minor adjustment." His tone implied a firm disbelief that anything could be wrong with his workmanship, but nevertheless he swiftly crouched down by her, letting his frowning gaze run over the chair. But the girl plucked at his sleeve.

"There's nothing *amiss* with the chair. Quite the reverse! I wanted to compliment you on your craftmanship and to thank you for all the thought taken towards my comfort in it."

He let one knee drop to the floor and rested one forearm across the other, his eyes narrowing at her. She wanted to thank him? Nobility did not know the meaning of courtesy as far as those of a lower social order were concerned. He knew what it was like to fetch and carry and haul without as much as a nod of appreciation. But to be thanked! He looked at her anew now and he realized that if she had not been so thin, lacking all the sweet curves on a woman that were such a pleasure to fondle, she might well have appealed to him. He liked hair of a fair colour, and although hers was covered by a cap, a few soft tendrils had escaped by her neck. In spite of her brittle look she was not plain, there being a compelling quality in her face. He noticed a rapid increase in the pulse in her throat under his sharp-eyed scrutiny. Her colour was rising as well, and her eyes were a remarkably clear blue.

"This is my first visit to Nostell," she confided simply. "I had feared to be a great nuisance to my host and hostess, but your chair has eliminated much of that for me."

"I merely carried out Sir Rowland's instructions," he reminded her, not unbending in any way.

"I know, but it was your own design. I was told that."

He began to see that her appreciation was quite guileless, and was led to offer further information. "The oak for it was felled in a stretch of the Wharfedale woods near Otley, where I was born."

"I've heard of Otley, although I have never been there. But then, I was never in Yorkshire until I came to Nostell."

"It's the finest county in the kingdom. My family have lived in these parts for generations, and we Chippendales have always been in some branch of the timber trade. Wheelwrights like my grandfather, carpenters like my father."

"Have you been long at Nostell?" she inquired.

"I'm reaching the end of my seven years' apprenticeship. By then I shall have qualified as a cabinet-maker." He rose to his feet and looked towards the window as if it encompassed his new horizon.

"I suppose you will soon be making furniture for the new house?"

His gaze flicked down at her. She was quite enthralled by him. Her eyes held an admiration as much for his craftsman's talents as for his personableness, of which he was very aware. If she had been in robust health he would have been sorely tempted to try his luck. None was quicker than he to take advantage of any opportunity that presented itself. But in the case of Isabella it was only possible to feel compassion for her in her sickliness. "I anticipate being elsewhere before long, mistress. My plans are my own as yet."

It was a rebuff politely stated and he saw her lower her lashes. "I'm keeping you from work, Mr. Chippendale. Good day to you."

He took up his hat, bowed, and departed. She watched him stride away as forcefully as he had come. It was not his reluctance to discuss his future that had hurt her, but the pity that she had seen in his glance. Yet it could be argued that she had no business to be caring about the attitude of a common workman. Her mother would have been the first to condemn it, but from her father, who throughout his political life had sought to better the lot of ordinary people, she had learned respect for all who toiled honestly, whatever their station in life.

She looked longingly towards the nearest window. From there it should be possible to see Thomas once more as he left the house.

With a supreme effort of her thin arms she thrust herself up out of the chair. Giddy with weakness she stumbled across to clutch at the window drapes for support as she looked out. There he was on the path! She felt her heart explode upon the pleasure of it. Then, even as he was about to disappear, he came to a halt and looked back up in the direction of the library windows. She drew aside, and then, a moment later, he was gone from view.

THOMAS SAW ISABELLA twice during the next few weeks. Neither time was she aware of his presence. On the first occasion he was in the house, assisting a fellow carpenter in an upper saloon, when from the gallery he happened to sight Isabella in the hall below. Originally the hall had been the nave of the mediaeval priory. Two rows of stone pillars still flanked it, and it was to these that she clung for support in a supreme effort to traverse the hall without aid. Guessing she would not wish to be seen at a disadvantage, he hastened away. But he had marked her courage and wished her well.

The next time he happened to be sitting on the back of a cart as it was driven out of the grounds, having seized the chance of a lift to Otley. Isabella was strolling on Sir Rowland's arm. She seemed to have overcome her infirmity, and there was a pretty look about her, even from afar. She was wearing a dress that was light-coloured and gauzy, the side panniers caught up with cherry ribbons. A cap still covered her hair and he mused over the pleasure it would be to remove it from Isabella Woodleigh's well-shaped head in a place of privacy and let her loosened hair come curling free about his hands.

He had been given some long-overdue time off from work. John Chippendale had fallen from a ladder, injuring an arm, and Thomas was going home to see how his father was progressing. During his sojourn there, he would break the news that he planned to leave Nostell before long and go to York.

York. He had been only eight years old with dialect still thick upon his tongue when he and his father had taken the wagon to that thriving city, but how well he remembered the excitement of it all—the noise of wheels over cobbles, the bawling of street hawkers, the high-pitched laughter of folk reeling from the taverns and over it all the sweet chiming of the Minster's bells. That day in York he and his father were importantly on their way to a timber yard where

John was to select some of the best wood he had ever bought, for he was to lay a whole new replacement floor in the drawing room of a grand mansion. His chest was quite expanded with the honour of it as he strutted about the yard, viewing one stack of planks and then another, unaware that at his heels young Thomas had adopted the same manly air. When the wood was finally selected there began the usual haggling over price, and Thomas, bored with the proceedings, wandered off to look into another of the high-roofed sheds. An old workman, wary of a boy's mischievous ways, came shambling forward.

"What d'thee want? Don't touch nowt, d'thee hear?"

Thomas, inhaling the good aromas that came from the expensive woods stored there, only shrugged an acknowledgment. Looking about, he recognized some walnut, which was the fashionable wood for those who could afford it. Usually, the chairs, cupboards and tables that John Chippendale made were fashioned robustly out of oak or beech or yew. But recently he had been commissioned to make a cradle of walnut and the rich sheen of the finished piece was appealing to the eye.

Moving along, the old fellow shuffling behind him, Thomas caught sight of some strangely cracked lengths of dark wood shot through with delicate cream and pinkish tones. He ran his fingers reverently over one lustrous piece of it. "What's this? It would be handsome with a good polishing."

The guardian of the wood saw the genuine interest being displayed and answered, "That's ebony."

Thomas looked astonished. "It can't be. Ebony is black."

"Not always. Some of it is a really sandy colour, but it's a devil of a wood, I'm telling thee. It has pockets of rot, so that as soon as it's felled in those mighty forests across the sea, great cracks appear and it splits into short lengths like those th'see here. That's why ebony veneers are made up of small pieces, and even then it'll vein with thread-like cracks, no matter how skilled the veneerer may be at his craft." He saw that the boy was listening attentively, and went on. "I'm telling thee, lad, we get some of the best craftsmen in England—nay, the world—coming in here to choose their woods, but I'd wager my last shilling that our York cabinet-makers are better than any."

Thomas did not doubt it. "What are those other woods?" he inquired eagerly.

"That one is satinwood, and over there is some sycamore, or harewood as it's called in the workshops. Thee can see rosewood next to it. The cabinet-makers use these fancy woods for veneers, to give a variety of shades and patterns in their work. Veneering doubles and trebles the cost of every piece of furniture where it's used, because it's a costly and lengthy process. Any furniture-maker worth his salt can polish up a solid piece to a good shine, but veneering is like the painting and powdering of a woman's face. The result must be pretty and perfect, or else nobody'll want the goods." He chortled wheezily at his own wit, but it was lost on the boy, who had gone ahead to gasp at some huge lengths that met his gaze.

"That's mahogany, from the West Indies." The old man bent towards the stack and pulled out a piece that had been split through the middle. Thomas saw that it was a section known as the crotch, where a branch grows away from a tree. The old man balanced it on his knee to show off the curling pattern that the growth of the branch had formed. "Take a good look, lad. That's what is used to get a pretty *flame* in veneer. Yes, *flame* or *curl* or *fiddleback*, or any amount of other trade names for the figuring in wood, according to whatever it happens to be. Thin layers are cut from pieces like this one for veneers to make fancy furniture at fancy prices for those who are better off in this world than thee and me."

Thomas and his new acquaintance were still talking together, when John came in search of his son. "Thomas! It's time to go."

The boy bade the old man farewell. His request for a scrap of mahogany to take home was refused bluntly, but when he had clambered up beside his father on the wagon seat, the old fellow came with a small chunk of pearwood, pale as ivory, and gave it to him, "Carve thyself something out of this," he said.

"I thank thee!" Excitedly, Thomas clutched the gift to him. Pearwood was soft and easy to fashion. He knew exactly what he would make out of it. He would carve a doll for Polly Barlow. She was seven years old, and had never had a doll in her whole life.

The wondrous day did not end there. After buying a length of lace for his mother from a pedlar, he and his father dined on beefsteak and ale, with a loaf of crusty bread, in the Blue Boar tavern. Then, in the small hours, when the journey came to an end, he stumbled, barely awake, into the cottage. His mother, who had been listening for them, came with a candle, relieved that they were safely home again. She smiled as he summed up the whole expedition. "We have the timber and York is a great city and one day I'm going back there."

She guided him by the shoulder to his bed and helped him off with his clothes. "We bought thee a present," he said. He took the lace from his coat pocket. He thought she had never looked prettier than when she draped it over her head. She leaned forward and kissed him goodnight. She had already closed the door behind her when he realized he had forgotten to tell her about the pearwood, and how he would carve a doll from it for Polly.

He could not recall exactly when Polly Barlow, with her grimy face and lank, reddish hair, had become part of his existence. His home, a sizeable thatched cottage, was in the heart of Otley, and his father's workshop was attached to the rear of the cottage, facing a yard with a stable and outhouses where the wagon and some timber were kept. An arched passageway with uneven cobbles, wide enough to take the horse and wagon, gave access to the yard from a busy street named Boroughgate, and it was not unusual for children to wander down it to gather outside the open doors of the shop to watch the two Chippendales at work, mixing foul-smelling glue or working the treadle of the pole-lathe. But Polly did not come openly to the doorway. Thomas would catch her peeping at him from the corner of the passageway or flitting away down a neighbouring alley. He knew her identity. She was one of the Barlows, a quarrelsome family with a slattern for a mother and a drunkard for a father, who occupied a damp hovel not far from the banks of the Wharfe.

Then on one bitterly cold autumn day, Thomas was alone in the workshop eating a gingerbread man his mother had baked when one of the doors creaked and opened. His mouth full, he stared as the little girl entered. In filthy rags, her nose running and her bare feet purple with cold, Polly lifted a hand out to him in wordless appeal. She wanted what was left of the gingerbread man. He held it out to her.

She devoured it like a little animal and he realized that it was a frantic hunger that had finally driven her into the workshop. When

110

she had swallowed the last morsel she crouched down and searched the sawdusty floor about her for crumbs, popping each one into her mouth. "There's no need to hunt for crumbs. I'll fetch thee some more to eat."

She said nothing, but her light brown eyes followed him as he went through a door that led into the cottage. He found his mother kneading bread dough on the kitchen table, a crusty fragrance coming from the brick oven. "May I have another gingerbread man, Mother?"

She answered automatically. "No. It would spoil thy dinner."

He was persistent. "*Please*. I don't want any dinner."

Mary Chippendale sighed wearily. "No, Thomas." Her tone was sharp because she was tired and her back ached. Miscarriages played havoc with a woman's health, and she had not recovered from her last one. "Th' must have gobbled up that gingerbread man I gave thee like a pig at a trough to come back again so soon."

Normally Thomas would have explained his reason, but he knew his mother would be aghast that he had left a member of that wayward Barlow brood in the workshop where valued items could be easily thieved. So he disputed no further, but turned thief himself, whipping half a dozen gingerbread men from a platter on a sidebench as he went out of the kitchen.

"Here th' are," he said to Polly, who squatted down to eat no less ravenously than before, her amber eyes fixed on him all the while. Already racked with guilt over taking the food, he was made more irritated by her silent and unblinking gaze. "Don't come around here any more," he ordered gruffly. "I don't like being gawped at."

"I don' gawp." She spoke through the last of the gingerbread that she had shoved into her mouth, crumbs spluttering.

He rounded on her in the relief of fury. "Yes, th' do! Why? Why?" Then to his horror he saw huge tears spill from her eyes.

"I likes thee," she gulped. "More'n anyone else."

He blushed dark crimson. "Thee don't know me. Just because I gave thee some food doesn't mean we're acquainted in any way." His exasperation grew. "If those no-good parents of thine fed thee properly th' wouldn't get such touched ideas in thy silly head." He regretted the abuse even as it was uttered, seeing hurt and hostility sear her thin face. But the damage had been done. She did not

111

answer him in words. Instead, with her eyes blazing, she threw the remaining gingerbread to the floor. Then she turned and ran from the workshop.

He hated her. Hated her and was ashamed of himself. Plagued by his conscience, he tossed and turned on his pillow that night.

The chance to make up to her came early one morning in December. She had not been near his home since that disastrous meeting, but now he saw her lingering cautiously in the yard entrance. She looked more wretched than before, but she was a welcome sight to him. "Polly!" he exclaimed warmly, running towards her.

She had been prepared for flight, but at his tone she stayed warily where she was. For no reason that the limits of a child's mind could fathom, she loved him. She liked his black, curly hair and his round cheeks like rosy apples, and the sturdy way he held himself. Her simple adoration was completely innocent. She had been witness to all kinds of brutality, knowing nothing of the gentler side of life, but deep within her a capacity for love had found an outlet.

"I'm sorry," he burst out. "I shouldn't have said the things I did. Let's be friends. Come to the back porch. Th' shall have some meat and cheese."

Fortunately he had not yet breakfasted, and he felt he had a right to give his portion away to the needy. Leaving her on the doorstep, he entered the hearth-bright kitchen. His father was already tucking into cheese and cold mutton, while his mother sliced a loaf. Thomas took a defiant breath. "Polly Barlow is outside. She's hungry, and I'm doing what the vicar said last Sunday and sharing my worldly goods." Taking advantage of their surprise at his extraordinary announcement he began to scoop food onto a plate.

"Wait a moment," his mother instructed quietly. She brushed past him and opened the kitchen door wide. "Come in, Polly. It's too cold to eat outside. I'll give thee some broth by the fire."

Thomas watched his mother tip some broth into a small cauldron. "There's no need to fuss with that. She can eat my breakfast."

"That child's poor, shrivelled stomach needs something more easy than cold meat and new bread," she replied. "Now go and find that pair of shoes th' grew out of last year, and take a pair of thy old white stockings from the ragbox at the same time."

112

He beamed. "Thank you, Mother."

Polly left the cottage an hour later, well-shod, with stockings covering her legs, and in her pocket a packet of bread and cheese for a noon-piece later. She had had the first of many meals that she was to receive at the Chippendale home.

Sometimes she visited the workshop or waited to walk with Thomas when he was sent on an errand by his father. Best of all she liked those Sunday afternoons when Thomas was freed from work. The two of them would go walking through the woods, or fish with homemade rods in the Wharfe. As for Thomas, he had become fond of Polly, who trotted after him like a devoted puppy.

More and more now he was accompanying his father with the horse and wagon to outlying houses. There would be walls to wainscot, rooms to partition, and new doors to hang. Mostly Thomas was there to learn from all that took place, but now and again there was a small task that he could do on his own. He took great pride in these achievements. Between the visit to York and the laying of the new floor he made the doll for Polly. His father showed him how to fix the arms to pivot on a nail, and his mother sewed a dress for it out of a scrap of yellow silk, with a bonnet and apron of India calico. He painted the face carefully, giving it red cheeks and a smiling mouth.

When he presented it to Polly she laughed and hugged the doll to her. "Eee! A dolly! Of my very own!" She kissed and cuddled the doll, and from that moment forth she was never without it.

Thomas liked nothing better than when work took his father and him into one of the many grand houses in the district. John, who was quite a knowledgeable man, had told his son about the London architect, Inigo Jones, who had first introduced the Palladian style into England in the previous century, that classical architecture that demanded perfect balance and symmetry. Thomas took in every tiny detail of the rooms through which they were guided. The fashion was for strong colours offset by white and gilded plasterwork, thick as whipped cream, while overhead the high ceilings were aswirl with tempestuous skies and amply proportioned gods and goddesses, the whole effect dazzling. And such furniture!

Sometimes he would hang back, letting his father and the escorting servant go ahead without him, and with luck he would not be missed for a little while. Although he gazed open-mouthed at the Italian baroque pieces set hugely against the walls, richly gilt, with heavy marble tops, it was always the English furniture that drew him. He was stunned by its beauty: there were marquetry table-tops, with their exquisite floral designs of varying woods and colours set in panels; bureaux with crisply carved friezes and legs that had lion heads carved on the knees; chairs upholstered in costly silks and embossed leathers, their strongly curved cabriole legs ending in ball-and-claw feet; and such a host of desks, chests on stands, cabinets, and bookcases, all in walnut of a quality that made Thomas catch his breath in delight.

He tried to describe to Polly all he had seen, but for one who slept on straw and lived in filth and squalor it was beyond her range of visioning. As it happened, their days of companionship were numbered. When she failed to appear at his home for almost a week Thomas became anxious that she was ill. His father went himself to make inquiries, and returned with the news that good fortune had come Polly's way. At the previous week's market her parents had lined her up with others seeking employment, and she had been taken on by someone recruiting domestic staff for a country house some miles away. Thomas was aghast. "But she is not eight years old yet."

John clapped a comforting hand down on his son's shoulder. "Don't fret, lad. Polly has been given a better home than ever she's had in her life before."

Maybe the change in her circumstances was for the best in the long run, but all that registered with Thomas was the bewilderment she would experience in alien surroundings.

About this time John decided that Thomas had reached the age to benefit from some formal education and he was duly enrolled at the local grammar school. An exceptional boy, he had learned to read, write, and cypher at a very early age. He also had the makings of a good carpenter, with an inherent feeling for wood, as well as the patience and precision needed for the craft. No need to worry that carpentry would be neglected for other studies, for Thomas could not be kept out of the workshop when he had a project in hand.

John's supposition that his son's keenness for carpentry would only be strengthened by schooling proved to be correct. More and

114

more, Thomas talked of yearning to make grand furniture for himself one day when he was a grown man. John took note, and decided he would see to it that his son had every chance to achieve that dream through an apprenticeship.

One winter's day took father and son on a journey to a large Tudor house where John was to assist in the building of an extension to the stables. Thomas was hoping at the very least to get a glimpse through the windows at whatever treasures lay within the residence. Unluckily for him there proved to be innumerable duties for a strong boy and not once did he get a chance to roam anywhere near the house. In a disgruntled mood on the journey home through the wind-swept darkness, cold and tired, he clambered over the seat into the wagon to curl up among the tarpaulin covers there. He closed his eyes but the chance of sleep lasted for only a matter of seconds. There was a rustle under another tarpaulin, and even as he jerked up, thinking it was a rat, a small hand clamped over his mouth and Polly's well-remembered voice hissed, "Don't thee make a sound, Tom Chippendale! I've run away!"

He reacted automatically to her order, pulling the tarpaulin over both their heads and answering her in an angry whisper. "Polly! I didn't know th' worked at that place! Thee gormless loon! What have thee run away for? They'll only come after thee and take thee back!"

"Not if they don't find me, they won't!" she snapped back. "I hates it." Her tone had taken on a dimension of utter despair. "Th've gotta help me, Tom." Her arms gripped him about the neck in a choking clasp as she burst into a flood of smothered tears.

He was exasperated with her. If he had any sense at all he would take her back before she was missed. But he could not betray her. She smelled sweet and clean, her hair soft and silky as it lay tumbled about his face, and quite gone was the stale stench that in the past had lingered about her. The pressure of her body was entirely pleasurable, and he could tell by her weight across his chest that she had grown since he had last seen her. "Think this over, I beg thee," he implored. "It can't be as bad as th' say."

She answered him fiercely. "If th' send me back I'll drown myself in the river, I swear it."

He was disconcerted by her vehemence. "But why?"

It was a full minute before she could bring herself to tell him. "I've been treated cruel. By the master. He's a grown man what don't like grown women, if thee know what I mean."

Thomas felt the shock chill his veins. To think that Polly had been subjected to sinful abuse filled him with a terrible shame for the whole of the male sex. "Then th' shan't go back to that place! Never! I'll keep thee safe."

He made a plan. She should be concealed in the workshop loft. His father rarely went up there, and with his mother lying abed weary from the ordeal of another miscarriage it would be easy enough to obtain food for Polly without it being missed from the pantry. The situation became wonderfully simple. It never occurred to him that Polly had not told him everything.

She remained under the tarpaulin in the wagon until Thomas and his father unhitched the horse and John went into the cottage to see his wife before crossing the street to The Carpenter's Arms. As soon as the coast was clear Thomas led Polly, carrying a small bundle of possessions, into the kitchen. For the first time he saw her in the light. Her hair, tied back with a ribbon, had enriched itself to the finest red-gold colour he had ever seen. "Thy hair is right gradely," he said admiringly in dialect. She looked pleased.

They ate supper quickly and then took extra supplies, a blanket, and a flagon of water with them into the workshop. He carried it all up the narrow ladder into the loft, she following with her bundle and a lighted lantern. "I'll be at school tomorrow," he said, "and my father will be working at home all day, so th'll have to stay up here until he goes out in the evening. Will thee mind being shut away until then?"

She came and stood close to him in the lantern light, all her devotion in her face. "No, Tom. I feel safe here."

He was deeply moved by her trust in him. Then, to his surprise she put her arms around his neck to place her soft, moist mouth on his in a kiss of strange dimensions. He was startled into an excitement that made his heart race. "I loves thee, Tom," she whispered. "And I always will." He descended the narrow flight in a daze, and at the bottom he looked back up at her. She blew him another kiss from her fingertips, her silky hair swinging in the glimmer of the lantern light.

116

The next day at school he paid little attention to his lessons. Polly couldn't stay in the loft until he was old enough to marry her and protect her from the world. If his mother had not been in her present nervous state of sickness he would have persuaded Polly to confide in her, and in normal circumstances the girl would have received the protection she deserved. But Polly's word would never be taken against that of a gentleman of quality, and moreover she came from a family associated with troublemaking. Whichever way he tried to resolve the matter he was brought around in a full circle to where he had started.

He hurried homeward, and as soon as he entered the cottage he knew that something was terribly amiss. His mother, up and dressed, was sitting in a chair by the hearth, her eyes red with weeping. His father, sternfaced, confronted him. "How long was Polly Barlow concealed in my loft?"

So his father had discovered her. It was just as well. He could now seek adult help with the matter. "Since yesterday evening. She has been greatly wronged. I hope th' weren't angry with her, Father. Any fault in this affair is mine."

"I have not seen her. I only know she was there."

Fear struck Thomas. "Where is she, then?"

"She must have panicked," John said heavily, "when she heard two representatives of the law making inquiries in the yard. Naturally I denied any knowledge of her whereabouts, not having the least suspicion of her presence. I was out of the workshop later in the morning, and when I returned I found the trapdoor open. She must have feared they would return and taken to her heels. She was caught around midday."

"She mustn't go back to that old house. It is a wicked place."

"They've not taken her there, but to the gaol at York to await trial." Thomas stared in disbelief. "The charge is theft. I heard that in her pocket she had three golden guineas stolen from her master."

Thomas turned ashen. "Polly's no thief!" But at the same time all became clear in his mind. Those guineas had been payment for her silence, and then when she ran away, the accusation of theft had been thrown after her to ensure that even if she spoke the truth, none would listen to her. He shuddered, feeling sick. "What will happen to her?" he asked fearfully.

117

John put an arm about his son, drawing him close. "I don't know, my boy. In the eyes of the law her guilt is proven already. We must hope for a lenient sentence."

Three weeks later Polly was tried with seventeen other prisoners who had been caught with stolen property. The same sentence was passed on them all. The customary verdict was death by hanging, however young the convicted prisoner, but the judge happened to decide otherwise. The need for labour in the American colonies was pressing, and the men could be put to good use there. As for the red-haired child, if she survived the voyage and all its hazards she would be sadder and wiser enough to mend her ways in bondage in a new land.

Thomas's reaction was one of relief that Polly had been spared the gallows. She had spirit and resilience, and he hoped with all his heart that fortune would stay with her.

ANOTHER YEAR and more went by. At school Thomas became a better than average scholar and he had developed a talent for drawing which gave him considerable satisfaction. He was currently making a child's chair as a birth gift for his mother in readiness for the new baby, because at last there were all the signs that she was going to reach her time. The chair was never given. Mary died giving birth to a stillborn son. It was a blow that drove the last of Thomas's childhood from him. His grief threatened to drown him. Tragically, he and his father found themselves unable to comfort each other, their mourning too individual. John took refuge in work, but Thomas sought diversion in the playing of stupid pranks that continually landed him in trouble. From being a promising pupil he became a headache to his teachers. His behaviour deteriorated even more when he learned that after only a few months as a widower his father intended to marry again. The thought of a stranger taking his mother's place so soon was more than he could bear.

John, driven to exasperation by his son's inexplicable rebelliousness, thought it would do Thomas good to have a change of surroundings. They had always talked together in happier days of securing a more advanced training for him when the time was right, so, unbeknown to Thomas, John put together some of the boy's best pieces and journeyed to Nostell Priory. There he showed them to the estate carpenter, John Harrison, a man of exceptional talents, who had made many handsome pieces of furniture.

"Hmm." Turning the pieces over, Harrison examined Thomas's work with a critical eye. With his high reputation he could afford to be selective in his choice of apprentices. He ran his hands over the back and arms of the child's chair. The proportions were good and he recognized the instinctive craftsmanship. "Let me see the lad. If he measures up I'll take him on. But," he added, "if he don't meet my mark th'll be taking him home with thee again."

To Thomas it was as if a cloud had lifted from him. He became full of talk about all he hoped to do and achieve. At the interview, Harrison soon summed him up as a suitable candidate, and gave a nod to his father.

The carpenter's shop at Nostell was at the rear of the stable buildings, and consisted of several small rooms with benches and pole-lathes. It was all remarkably familiar: the pungent aromas of wood and glue and tallow, the rows of planes in every shape and size, the racks of tools and wooden templates, the noise of tapping and hammering and sawing that continued from morning till night.

Harrison proved to be an exacting master. As one year followed another, the latent genius in Thomas, which Harrison had perceived in its embryo state, began to thrust forth under the expert training being given to him. Not that Harrison praised him. He was endlessly critical, and Thomas found himself disciplined at the least provocation with the most mundane work on the estate, such as repairing fences or mending a hen coop. Yet he felt the strength and power over wood that was developing in him.

If he needed confirmation of the special abilities that were his, it came in the sixth year of his apprenticeship when Harrison selected him above older and more experienced men to make the furniture for the doll's house that Lady Winn wanted. Cheerfully Thomas faced the mammoth task. Each tiny joint would have to be cut with the most fastidious accuracy, the carving on the bedposts and chairs and picture frames copied minutely from the originals. It was a challenge beyond all challenges. If he did well, it would prove that there was nothing he could not do in the world of cabinet-making.

James Paine, the young architect in charge of building the new Nostell, had himself designed the doll's house, and when Thomas began making it, he came along to the carpenter's shop to watch its progress. During these visits the two men, whose ages were not far apart, struck up a friendship. James liked to talk about architecture, and Thomas was enlightened on many matters of proportion and style and construction about which he had been almost totally ignorant. James also loaned Thomas books, which he read far into the night, and the range of his vision was widened to new horizons.

Now, as Thomas jogged into Otley on the back of the cart, his thoughts dwelt on the doll's house. He had become obsessed with the project, often working long after the others had gone home to their lodgings. Breaking off to make the carrying-chair for Isabella Woodleigh had set him back, but as soon as the last piece was finished he would leave. The future beckoned enticingly.

In Boroughgate, outside The Carpenter's Arms, Thomas leaped down from the back of the vehicle. With a grin of thanks he tossed the carter the price of a pint and crossed the cobbled street to the cottage that had once been his home.

Chapter Two

"Eee! It's good to see thee, lad!" Thomas's stepmother embraced him. She was a buxom, comely woman, who always had a baby in her arms or another on the way. His boyish resentment against her had long since gone. She was by nature a loving woman, doting on her husband and their offspring, and for that he liked her and was grateful that she kept his father content.

"Thee'll be wanting to see thy dear Pa right away," she declared, and began to shoo away the little ones who had gathered about them. But Thomas never came empty-handed. He stooped down to hand around sweetmeats from his pocket, and small cheeks bulged with the welcome delicacy.

John was in the workshop, overseeing a journeyman he had hired until he should be fit again. The injuries caused by the fall from the ladder were not serious, but were inconvenient, his broken left arm held by splints in a sling. But like most healthy men temporarily discommoded, he was extremely irritable with it, and by the next day Thomas's respect for his stepmother had increased considerably, for she was always quite unruffled by her husband's tetchiness.

Thomas stayed three days and would have extended his visit by two more if it had not been for the doll.

On the third evening there, he outlined his future plans, and they met with his father's approval. Then in the cheerful turmoil that ever prevailed in the household, Thomas accidentally stepped on a toy. Looking down, he saw it was Polly's doll. "Where did this come from?" he asked quietly, reaching down to pick it up. It had no clothes. There was little paint left on it.

"What? Oh, that old thing?" his stepmother said. "I found it in the loft one day when I was having a hunt around up there."

Without a word, the doll still in his hands, he went out into the peace of the moonlit yard, shutting the door behind him. He could still remember his sorrow at Polly's fate. The fact that she had forgotten the doll in her attempt at flight from the law showed the extent of her blind panic.

Where was Polly now? Was she still alive? Only the image of her red hair and her sweet mouth remained with him like misty remnants of a dream. Out of her lost innocence she had awakened him to a first realization of manhood. Since then he had taken his pleasure with any number of girls. He was strongly sensual, his physical needs as driving as the force of ambition that gave him no rest. But he had not cherished for any of his conquests the kind of tenderness that had made him want to protect Polly against the world. Perhaps it was never to come again. Except that he was tantalized by the indefinable feeling that somehow quite recently he had been touched briefly by a finger of it. But how and where?

Then it came to him, surprisingly and forcefully, that it was Isabella Woodleigh who had caught a facet of his nature that he had believed lost with the past.

As he went into the cottage the usual din of children enveloped him, his stepmother shouting to make herself heard, the baby bawling. "I'm leaving in the morning," he announced. He was going back to Nostell. And to Isabella Woodleigh.

UPON HIS RETURN he was informed by Harrison that Lady Winn had brought Miss Woodleigh to see the doll's house in his absence. Just as Thomas was cursing his luck for having missed a golden opportunity, Harrison added, "But when I told them th' weren't here, the young lady said she would like to wait until thee were present in order to ask thee some questions about it."

Thomas's face did not reveal the satisfaction that the information gave him.

Isabella came on her own the next day when he was busy at his bench making a tiny rack that would hold pewter plates in the kitchen of the doll's house. He was amazed at the change in her since their first meeting. She was still wand-slender, but there was a roundness to her arms and a swell to her bosom, and her fine, patrician face had filled out enough to erase all gauntness. But a frilled cap still covered her hair.

The taps of her heels had announced her approach, her petticoats rustling. Then came an entrancing fragrance of musk. Slowly he had turned his head and looked her full in the eyes. It was a look designed to leave her in no doubt that what he saw pleased him to the marrow of his bones.

For Isabella it had all the impact he had desired, and more. She felt an instant upsurge of delicious fear, her veins coursing with it. For him she had overcome every kind of anxiety and weakness. For him she had sought to regain speedily the looks that had brought her male admirers in the past. Her reward was in the eloquence of his gaze. Yet her strict upbringing, combined with her own natural reticence, enabled her to maintain a carapace of calm.

"Good day," she said evenly. "I have come to view the doll's house."

"Miss Woodleigh." He had risen to his feet. "I'm at your bidding."

Conventional words. Everyday politeness. And yet he imbued them with a meaning that matched the look he had given her. She

122

seized upon the diversion of admiring the little plate rack. "What patience you have!"

He turned to a box and from it took a couple of tiny pewter plates and slotted them into place for her. He then proceeded to take from careful wrappings the pieces of furniture he had completed. She exclaimed over their exquisite details, the perfection of tiny drawers that slid in and out with the smoothness of silk. "Now I will show you the house itself," he said, leading the way into another part of the workshop that was used for storage.

It was a darkish place of stone walls and floor. She was conscious of the intimate atmosphere created by their being alone there. He opened the front of the doll's house, leaving the interior revealed for her inspection. She thought it quite the best she had ever seen, each room panelled and painted, the fireplaces set in place, and a brick hearth fitted in the kitchen where the plate rack would stand. "It's all enchanting," she declared. "It almost makes me wish that I could shrink down to the size of the dolls that will live in it, and take up residence myself under its roof."

"Dismiss the thought," he insisted vehemently. The fantasy did not amuse him. He had seen the dolls, which were made of wax, and, to his eyes, had a dead look. Polly's doll had been made of living wood, which had given it some kind of forceful personality that had appealed to her. Isabella, with her youth and warmth and appealing femininity, belonged to his world where a man of flesh and blood could change her from girl to woman in his arms. He turned to close the doors across the doll's house and spread a dustcover over it.

Already the interlude was drawing to an end. "When shall I see those rooms furnished?" she asked.

"That depends on whether you will be staying at Nostell long enough to see the completion of my task."

"I have been invited to remain as long as I wish."

"If you stay to the summer's end you would see the doll's house furnished and installed at Nostell." He pulled the last corner of the dustcover into place and turned about to face her. It was to both of them as if they had been drawn closer together.

"Then I have no choice but to stay." She spoke quietly, feeling as though all power to control her life were draining from her.

His eyes narrowed at her. "It would have been disappointing if you had decided otherwise." He moved forward and stood so near to her that if she had turned an inch her shoulder would have brushed against his chest. He said, "Do you ever walk by the lake in the evening hours? When my day's work is done I sometimes go down there myself when nobody else is about."

She had not yet been out of the house on her own after dusk, but if she could evade other company that state of affairs should be quickly amended. "I may take the air there later. I cannot say for certain." It was as much as a promise as she could give him for the present.

She left then, and as she went back to the house she was held by the conviction that on this day she had somehow sealed her entire fate, and there was no escape from it.

IT WAS THREE O'CLOCK in the afternoon, the customary hour for dinner, and Isabella took her place amid the forty-odd relatives and guests at the spread of damask and crystal and silver. But she found herself unable to concentrate on the conversation. All the time her mind was busy selecting the evening hour when she might slip away.

For the rest of the day she watched the weather. Even a servant would challenge her madness if she ventured out on anything but a mild evening. And she must return for the supper hour of ten o'clock, when all would gather together between amateur theatricals, cards, or other games, for a light repast.

That evening she left the house by way of a door, and her excitement swept high. The stars were bright and, through the trees, they lay reflected in the lake like tiny lights to guide her.

She had almost reached the willows on the bank when Thomas stepped into her path so suddenly that she gave an involuntary cry. He caught her by the elbows, drawing her against him, and looked down into her face. "Forgive me for frightening you," he whispered, half smiling. "I saw you from a distance, and in my eagerness quite forgot that you could not possibly see me."

She laughed softly. "I knew it was you even as I cried out."

His clasp slid lightly along her forearms to capture her hands in his. "You do me much honour by coming here."

124

He had learned a great deal about gracious manners from observing the behaviour of the nobility towards each other, and he had the wit to see that the adding of some polish to simple good manners did no man any harm. This gently-born girl would not be allowing him to link his fingers with hers if he had not matched his approach to his good looks.

"I can stay for an hour," she said.

"Would you like to walk as far as the rotunda?"

She nodded. "I've never been there by night."

Hand in hand they began to stroll along the lakeside path. The talk flowed between them, each opening up to the other. She told him of her parents and her younger sister, and how her father, Henry Woodleigh, had risen in politics to the Walpole Cabinet. She was justly proud of him and the good he did until cut down in his prime by a seizure of the heart barely eighteen months ago. It was at her father's persuasion that Sir Robert Walpole had agreed to the withdrawal of the unpopular Excise Bill, that bitterly resented taxing of tea, coffee, and chocolate. As a result, he had received praise from his political opponents as well as from his own Whig party, and adulation from those whose hard and poverty-stricken lives would have been additionally burdened by the tax. It was no wonder that the whole country had grieved at his untimely passing. "It dealt me a blow from which, in the first shock of grief, I feared I would never recover," she admitted.

"I can understand," he said, sympathetically recalling the bereavement that had once weighed so heavily upon him.

She paused for a moment, looking into his eyes with a kind of wonder. "You know, this is the very first time I have been able to talk to anyone about my father since I lost him. It gives me the greatest comfort."

He smiled at her. "I'm pleased to know that."

She returned his smile and they continued at their leisurely pace. "We were so close, my father and I. It was only with me that he was able to relax and forget the troubles of the day." She did not add that she missed him far more than her mother did. Augusta Woodleigh, spoilt and foolish, must have won Henry with her pretty looks, because intellectually they had been poles apart. Augusta, never practical, had become in widowhood as addle-headed and improvident as a hen let out of a gate. She ran up bills as if she had quite forgotten that her husband was no longer there to pay them, and it had fallen to Isabella to discuss financial matters with the lawyers. As a result, the expensive house in London had been sold and a smaller one purchased in Bath, where Augusta could still enjoy the social pleasures that were so important to her. Just as Isabella was feeling relief that she had managed to get some order into their joint existence, she had fallen ill with the fever.

"But I've talked too much about myself," she insisted. "I want to hear about you. Tell me your earliest recollections."

He laughed. "Making pies out of sawdust and glue, and using discarded sections of wood as building blocks." He filled in details of his home and background, and by then they had reached the rotunda. It had a domed roof rising on six Ionic pillars against which a circular seat was set. On many country estates rotundas and temples provided a place for rest and often refreshment, as well as enhancing the setting. This one gleamed in the darkness, almost as if fashioned out of moonstone. Isabella sat down and rested her head back on a pillar. She thought the structure was like a miniature palace and said as much. When Thomas made no comment where he sat beside her, she turned to look at him.

"Why do you keep your hair covered?" he questioned quietly. "Caps are for matrons, not for one as young as you."

She answered hesitantly, embarrassed and shy. "It was shorn when I was ill. I'm ashamed of it being so short."

"I'm sure that it is beautiful to look upon. Let me see it."

"No!" But he leaned towards her and gently slid the cap from her head. Her hair slipped free to swing to a length about halfway down her neck. It was as he had imagined: thick and soft and gleaming. He put one silken strand to his lips. "You look lovely, Isabella," he breathed.

He meant it. He thought he had never seen a sight more beautiful than this girl. For her, his whispered words, and his action in freeing her hair, had induced her to a melting state with all resistance flown. His arms enfolded her and his mouth came down on hers with a tenderness that made her cling to him as if she would never let him go. It was all she had ever imagined a first kiss would be. For him it was a time of almost superhuman restraint, in order

127

not to startle her. The essence of her attraction for him was her unwitting ability to arouse all that he associated with a half-forgotten scrap of a girl who had loved him without stint.

THEIR TRYSTS HELD no regular pattern, for Isabella was drawn, through courtesy to her host and hostess, into various social activities at the house. But when together they were both extraordinarily content. When he confided his hopes for the future to her it was because he wanted to share them with her, not to emphasize the impossibility of any lasting involvement between them. The truth was that she was a gratifying listener, her interest total, her serene blue eyes never leaving his face as she took in all that had been said.

"As soon as I've finished the last of the furniture for the doll's house I'm leaving Nostell," he told her one evening. They had taken shelter in the orangery against a cold breeze that held a hint of rain, and it was warm there from the sun earlier in the day. "I shall go to York and widen my experience in cabinet-making there. The completion of my apprenticeship this month qualified me as a master craftsman in my own trade, but that is not enough for me. I want to study further the crafts linked to mine—the art of marquetry, for example, as well as wood-gilding and lacquering. I know none could better me at carving and at the draughtsmanship of furniture, but I cannot rest on my laurels." His dark gaze glinted with an obsessive determination. "I must be the best in all that I do, and I must be able to gauge the best that exists."

She gave him a clear look. "You aim to make your fortune one day, do you not?"

He did not deny it, his eyes amused. "By hook or by crook, Isabella."

She looked down at her hands, linking her graceful fingers. With a fortune, whatever his position in life, he could marry her. But without it, although she had a dowry, the gulf could never be bridged.

To her that gulf was never more emphasized than when she attended balls at Nostell, assemblages aglitter with jewels and powdered wigs and fine clothes. But she never failed to wish herself with Thomas. As for him, he felt no pangs of jealousy when she

128

attended these gatherings, not caring how many gentlemen she danced with, since she was destined to marry into her own stratum of society one day, and he had not the slightest aim in that direction. Yet it would have been against the whole of his sensual nature not to desire her. He was fully aware how easy it was to set her pulse throbbing with a tender caress. Inevitably the evening came when he judged the moment opportune and no longer restrained his kisses, crushing her to him in a passionate embrace. But he had a line drawn for him across which Isabella would not let him pass.

When she appeared at the usual time the following evening, there seemed, oddly, to be a new and deeper understanding between them, although why this should be he did not know. In some ways he had come to see her as his equal, and not a female to be manipulated for his own masculine ends. He began to suspect she was having an effect on his reason, for there had never been a man in all creation prepared to admit that a woman should not be subject to his domination. It never occurred to him that it might be the measure of how much she had come to mean to him. He only realized he could not win her without love, and therein lay the impasse.

The day came when he penned his letter to a cabinet-maker in York, applying for employment. Summer was dwindling, and only a few pieces for the doll's house remained to be completed. He told Isabella about the letter that evening.

"Are there no short cuts to hasten the fulfilment of your aim to set up your own business as a cabinet-maker?" she asked him.

"I dare say for those with funds in their pockets. If I had a nobleman for a father, all doors would be opened to me, but then I should not be in such a trade anyway."

"Why not? It is creative work that you do."

"I fear the world lacks your perception, Isabella."

After she had returned indoors, she pondered a possible aspect of his future that had not crossed her mind before. Artists and composers and writers were frequently taken up by wealthy benefactors who cushioned them against the financial hazards of life. Why not secure a noble patron for Thomas? Then he could obtain whatever location that he required, with ample funds for stock and equipment, and none would oppose a match between them. She truly believed he would come to a realization of love for her, and speak of it before the summer's end.

She decided that at the first suitable opportunity she would approach Sir Rowland for his patronage on Thomas's behalf, and on this satisfactory resolve she went into the drawing room, unprepared for the shock of surprise that awaited her.

In the midst of the throng of guests gathered there was her own mother. And so splendidly attired in a new dress of costly French lustrine trimmed with lace and pearls! More pearls adorned her hair, which was powdered white in the new fashion, the rolls and ringlets quite stiff with it. But before Isabella could make any move her sister appeared. "Isabella! Wherever have you been? We arrived an hour ago expecting to give you a most amiable surprise, but you were nowhere to be found." She kissed Isabella on both cheeks, then stood back appraisingly. "You are positively blooming. The air here has done you good. How do you think I look?"

Isabella saw that Sarah had acquired a distinctly adult air with her raven-black hair in a new arrangement, framing her heart-shaped face with its flashing green eyes and rosy mouth. A black beauty patch shaped like a crescent by her left eye helped to accentuate the creaminess of her complexion and the thickness of those sweeping black lashes that she had used with such effect to get her own way over any number of years. But to Isabella she appeared as endearing and difficult and demanding as ever, her very presence an immediate guarantee of the loss of all tranquillity at Nostell. "You look quite beautiful, Sarah," Isabella said.

Augusta was relieved to see that the good reports of Isabella's recovery had not been exaggerated. Unhappily, she had never quite cared for her elder daughter, unable to forget the pangs of jealousy experienced when Henry had shown a devotion to their first child that he no longer showed to her. And Isabella had always been such a serious child that Augusta felt she could be excused in favouring Sarah, who was so much like herself, and a far more entertaining young creature. Without doubt father and daughter had made a dull pair, Isabella following in Henry's footsteps after his demise by tedious talk of economies, which had been wonderfully relieved by her absence at Nostell. It was a pity that financial troubles had loomed again in a manner that could not be hidden from her elder daughter. Crushing down her inward qualms about it, she embraced Isabella with a great show of affection for the benefit of all those gathered in the salon.

"Sweetest child! You are looking so well again! When Lady Winn wrote to say she had persuaded you to spend the rest of the summer at Nostell, I decided to take advantage of her invitation to join you, and here we are!" She flung out her hands prettily, her head thrown back on her white neck.

Isabella did not know why she should feel so ill at ease that her mother and sister had descended upon Nostell. Lady Winn was obviously delighted that they had come. It just seemed odd that Augusta should suddenly take it into her head to travel to Yorkshire. In a state of considerable disquiet Isabella took her place with everyone else at the supper table.

She was not kept long in suspense. Later, in her mother's bedchamber, the whole sorry tale was poured out to her. Augusta wrung her hands in misery, while Isabella listened, scarcely able to credit that so much disaster should have befallen her mother and sister in the space of a single summer. Augusta, seeing the look of Henry in her daughter's face, began to turn defiant and aggressive, determined to assert herself. "I have considered the difficulties and have found a solution, although I must swear you to secrecy. Not a word to Sarah on any account. Not a word!"

Isabella, hearing what the solution was to be, made vehement protest on Sarah's behalf, all to no avail. She was left with the unhappy conviction that Augusta was taking a savagely vengeful delight in the fate she had planned for her younger daughter.

SARAH WAS BORED and disappointed, a potentially dangerous state of affairs. She had hoped to find a stimulating gathering at Nostell, but the company proved to be singularly dull. The Winn relatives were either elderly or devoted robustly to the pleasures of the saddle and the gaming table, or were married, with a host of children. At sixteen Sarah was not far removed from the oldest of them but in loss of innocence she was far advanced.

Like a prowling young cat Sarah looked about for some diversion, someone to coquette with or to encourage to bolder encounters. At times her nubile young body longed to feel again secret caresses and

131

intimacies. After Isabella had been packed off to Nostell, a distant cousin, Matthias Hammond, had come to visit them, a big, handsome fellow with a deal of charm and silken manners. Augusta made much of him, greatly pleased to have such a dashing escort for herself and Sarah. It never crossed her mind that behind her back he had set about seducing her daughter. The whole experience was altogether satisfying to both seducer and seduced, and their lovemaking might have continued indefinitely if Augusta had not suddenly become suspicious. He vanished without trace the same day, having charged everything in her name. Augusta, with bills of her own, became almost demented. In panic, they had left Bath, flight being the immediate means of keeping the creditors at bay.

The morning after their arrival at Nostell, Sarah had expected some reproof for her indiscreet behaviour from Isabella, knowing that their mother would have revealed all, and she thought it would be fun to shock her sister with a few pertinent details. But the subject was not brought up. Instead, Isabella sat with furrowed brow at a bureau, totting up figures and studying bills. She was hoping that by the profitable disposal of the house at Bath and all their assets, to spare Sarah what amounted to being sold to the highest bidder in the marriage market.

When she presented her findings to Augusta they were ill-received. "Sell everything?" her mother gasped. "Where should we live? How should we manage?"

"Quite adequately, in a small house," Isabella replied firmly. "But no longer in society. I could teach, with Sarah to assist me. There would be no carriage, no servants—"

"What would my acquaintances say?" Augusta interrupted hysterically. "We should be disgraced! Do you imagine that I would suffer such indignities for the sake of a wanton daughter who has done nothing to deserve such a sacrifice?"

"Surely you don't want to see her married to such a man as Nathaniel Trench, a widower more than twice her age, for whom she has no liking at all. I cannot bear to see Sarah made a scapegoat. The bills of Mathias Hammond amount to small change beside the enormous sums that you have run up for new dresses, jewels, a sedan chair—"

"Stop it! Be silent!" Augusta beat her clenched fists against her

132

skirt as she paced up and down. "I cannot live without the necessities of life, and I will not endure criticism from you! If your father had provided properly for me I should never have come to this predicament. Naturally I would prefer to see Sarah wed to a younger man, but none can match the Trench fortune. Nathaniel is so ardent that he spoke some while ago to your father and, more recently, persistently to me."

"I am sure my father turned him away."

Augusta ignored the accurate supposition. "I know well that Nathaniel will agree to any settlement I require from him. Sarah is to be our salvation from penury, and should be thankful for it."

"She will not see it in that light," Isabella warned.

"Pish! You and Sarah have always known that you would marry the husbands selected for you. It may be that she will come to care for a man prepared to give her anything her heart desires. If not, she may look elsewhere for affection once she has been wed a while. In sophisticated circles this is entirely acceptable."

"If Nathaniel is as obsessed with her as he appears to be, he would make a jealous and possessive husband. I remember hearing that his late wife was barely seen after their marriage."

Augusta stamped her foot in an outburst of rage. "She fell into sickly health! Now he is to go into politics he will need a wife of charm and beauty to appear with him in public. Put your fears away, Isabella. I tell you all will be well."

Isabella made a last desperate appeal. "I implore you, please do not condemn Sarah to this marriage."

Augusta turned away. "It is too late," she declared. "I have already written to Nathaniel, and he is due here very soon. To enter politics he needs the support and backing of such landed gentlemen as Sir Rowland, and is visiting throughout the county."

Augusta's greedy thoughts were already racing ahead to the size of the settlement that would be hers, a house in London, an income for life, nothing stinted. Then, when all was signed and sealed, the news would be broken to Sarah, who would have no choice but to abide by the decision. At all costs she must get Sarah safely wed and her own future secured before there was any risk again of scandal. She would not be sorry when all responsibility for the minx was taken from her hands.

Isabella went from the room, forced to accept that nothing would turn Augusta from the decision made. With all her heart she pitied her lovely, wayward sister.

IF SARAH HAD BEEN less bored at Nostell she might never have noticed that Isabella frequently absented herself before the supper hour. When questioned, Isabella was evasive, inadvertently quickening Sarah's interest. Surely she was not keeping assignations with one of the married men in the company? No, not Isabella! To satisfy her curiosity, Sarah set her maid to spy on her sister. The report was interesting. Isabella sometimes met an unknown man down by the lake.

"You'll keep your own counsel on this matter, Amy," Sarah admonished her maid.

The woman answered quietly. "There's no need to warn me about gossip, mistress." Amy Wallace had no liking for her young mistress, but she valued the position that she held, and intended to do nothing that would jeopardize it.

Sarah did not have to ponder long over the identity of the mystery man. Going out of her room, she met Lady Winn, who greeted her with a smile. "My doll's house has been brought from the carpenter's shop. I am on my way to see it. Accompany me, do."

Side by side they went downstairs and across the hall towards an anteroom. Sarah, looking ahead into the room, could see her sister engaged in conversation with a tall workman of formidable physique. Something in Isabella's rapt expression seared a shaft of comprehension into Sarah's brain. So *this* was he! No wonder Isabella met him in secret. Oh, what fun it would be to tease her demure, straitlaced sister about such an unexpected choice of male companionship.

Deliberately Sarah dawdled, letting Lady Winn go before her into the room, in order to view unobserved the black-haired fellow who had ensnared her sister. Something in Sarah rasped and grated. What a waste of an undeniably splendid male on her virtuous sister. Because in spite of his rough attire his appearance was altogether pleasing, his voice firm and assured. Then he happened to turn his head and see her.

She recognized what lay behind the look that snapped into his

134

eyes. She had seen it burn in men's stares before, and it gave her an exultant sense of power over the opposite sex, knowing that she possessed a magnetism to entice whomever she wished to her. Her green eyes gave him back a look that was provocative and wholly challenging. Then almost in the same moment she swept forward, exclaiming as she went, "What a fine doll's house! Who has made it, pray?"

"That honour has been mine," he said, with an edge to his words.

"Indeed? What is your name, my man?" She saw his jaw tighten at the arrogance in her tone and knew a thrill of almost unbearable excitement. She inclined her head in acknowledgement as he told her, and then she deliberately turned her narrow back to join in conversation with her hostess and Isabella. But the game was on.

Within an hour Amy had been dispatched to discover all she could about Thomas Chippendale, his hours of work, his place of abode, and where on the estate he was most likely to be found. The information delivered, Sarah began to plot a scheme. Whatever lovesick relationship existed between Thomas and Isabella she would soon nip in the bud, and she salved her not-too-troubled conscience with the thought that it would most certainly be for Isabella's own good in the long run. As for herself, it was not sentiment but excitement and danger she desired.

She went at once to the stable yard, where she had a horse saddled up for her. Bidding the groom be gone, she went to the doorway of the carpenter's shop and stood framed against the sun, the scarlet of the plume in her tricorn hat echoed in the piping of her riding habit. "I need assistance," she announced imperiously. Then she pointed her riding crop at Thomas. "You! Yes, you will do."

He went out into the yard after her. All she wanted was to be assisted into the saddle, and he linked his hands to make a step for her. When she was seated she looked down into his angry face, her eyes twinkling mischievously.

"I'm not a stable lad," he informed her forcefully.

"You're extremely ungallant," she replied, treating him to her ravishing smile. "Was it such a hard task to assist me?"

His eyes narrowed. "No," he said uncompromisingly, "but never use that tone of voice to me again."

Her eyebrows lifted. "What makes you think I'll ever address you again?"

He could have replied. He had a deal of home truths that he could say to her, but it was neither the time nor the place. Instead, he let a hard glint of mockery at her wiles show through. "If you needed assistance into the saddle, you will surely need a helping hand to dismount again."

"I dare say I shall. Be here in the yard when I return. If you *please*, Mr. Chippendale." Laughing, she rode away.

His lips twitched close to a smile as he went back to work. He was in the yard taking a midday break in the sun when she returned, and he forestalled the groom who would have helped her dismount. Looking down at him from the saddle, she was full of smiles, and put both hands on his shoulders as he reached to support her. She slid down slowly against him, her high spirits seeming to pass from her body into his. For a few more seconds he held her, each of them affected dizzily by the other's physical nearness.

After she had gone, he found it impossible to dismiss her from his thoughts. He simmered with resentment and a sharp desire to meet the challenge he had seen in her eyes.

At dinner Isabella could not help noticing that Sarah looked undeniably self-satisfied, and that her glances across the table had a triumphant flash to them, an indication since childhood that Sarah felt she had scored over her elder sister. Isabella was puzzled and wary. Was it possible that she was so transparently in love that Sarah suspected it simply from seeing her in the same room with Thomas that morning? If that was the case, why then had it not melted Thomas into the words she longed to hear from him?

NO MEETING WITH THOMAS had ever seemed as sweet as theirs that evening. He hugged her and swung her around as soon as she appeared, eager to tell her that a place of employment awaited him in York at the cabinet-makers of his choice. She listened happily, thinking how even more excited he would be when she had spoken to Sir Rowland on his behalf with regard to patronage.

Then, when all was harmony to her, her head resting against Thomas's shoulder as they sat together in the orangery, her peace of mind was suddenly shattered. A trifle too casually he began to inquire about her sister. How old was she? Was she to stay long at Nostell? Isabella was gripped by an ungovernable fear as he said amiably, "Did she tell you that she rode a very spirited horse today and rode it well?"

"You saw her in the saddle?"

"She took off across the park from the stable yard."

Isabella recognized her sister's tactics. When Sarah had wished to ride on previous days a horse had been brought to the door of the house, which was customary when guests took to the saddle. Isabella tried to suppress her qualms, but the joy of their tryst had evaporated for her. She wondered if Sarah had already thrust herself between them.

In that she was mistaken. It was a fact that Thomas had been able to think of little else but Sarah all day, almost as if a heated poison had seeped into his blood. But she was a trollop in his estimation, and when the chance came he would use her like one. He would have preferred her not to be related to Isabella, but in his male mind, a promiscuous female such as Sarah was entirely divorced from his deeper feelings for the woman for whom he truly cared. Unfortunately for Isabella, she lacked security in her relationship with Thomas. If her alarm had had the effect of releasing at last the full force of her pent-up passion, she could have driven all thought of Sarah from Thomas's mind and brought him to the fullness of love. But instead, her fear had a constricting effect, making her less responsive than usual, more reserved.

He was not insensitive to her withdrawal, but he put his own interpretation on it. The end of their time together was in sight and she, sensible and dignified girl that she was, was winding down their romantic friendship. He was resigned to it and yet he would miss her, having come close at times to trying to define some kind of future for them together. And he knew a keen disappointment for what had never been between them. But perhaps it was as well. Having once possessed her, he might never have been able to let her go from him.

As they made their way back to the house, they passed through the rose arbour. He plucked a rose for her as he had done many times before. Usually, he would tuck it in her hair or into the bosom of her dress. This evening he handed it to her by the stem, matching

137

his seriousness to hers. The bloom was as silvery white as the moonlight. She bowed her head, scarcely able to see for the tears in her eyes, because this evening more than any other it hurt that the rose had never once been the crimson colour of love.

Then out of the pain her spirit rallied. The summer was not over quite yet. Some time was left to strengthen all that had drawn them together in the first place. She raised her face to his. "Until tomorrow if all is well," she said as she always did.

Then each held the other as if the hour of final parting were already upon them, no telling how long their deep kiss would have lasted if a door out to the terrace had not opened and voices disturbed their solitude. She broke away and hastened into the house.

Through no fault of his, Thomas was not at the orangery or at the lake the following evening, and Isabella waited in vain. He had been dispatched by Harrison that morning to travel a considerable distance to judge the quality of some mahogany that had been put up for sale and, if all it was reputed to be, to make an offer for it on the estate's behalf. He had just set out when Sarah came to the stable yard and saw him riding away in the distance. Wheeling her horse about she rode after him.

He heard the overtaking hooves but kept his horse to the same steady trot. She drew level with him breathlessly. "What chance! To think we should meet on the road."

"Good day to you, mistress." His tone was dry.

She matched the pace of her mount to his. "Whither are you bound, Mr. Chippendale?"

"On business for the estate of Nostell."

"How important you sound!" she taunted wickedly. "Is it far?"

"Southeast of Wakefield. I reckon to cover thirty miles before the day is out."

"I shall accompany you," she announced impishly.

"You have not been invited," he pointed out, although far from averse to the prospect of having her with him to enliven the journey.

Her dimples twinkled. "I invite myself."

"It will be long after nightfall before I return."

"Fiddle-de-dee!" she retorted. "I am bored with Nostell, and it will be agreeable to have an outing."

"And create a hue and cry all over the county when your absence is noticed?" He did not intend to allow that to happen. "They would think you had taken a fall somewhere, and send search parties out looking for you and your horse."

"Let them look!" she retaliated. "It will make everyone glad to see me when I do return."

He saw she meant it. It sickened him that she would get a malicious satisfaction out of the anxiety and trouble she caused. Angrily he reined in, grabbing her reins at the same time, their horses jostling against each other. "If you come with me," he stated fiercely, "you will send a message back from the next cottage we come to that you are not without escort and protection, and that there is no cause for concern. I will not let there be any doubt about your safety."

She glowered, not at all pleased at being ordered about. Then she said pithily, "*Am* I safe with you?"

"As safe as you wish to be," he gave back arrogantly.

The thrust and parry of their verbal exchange was as satisfactory to her as it was to him, liking or disliking of each other not coming into it. She bitterly resented the fact that momentarily he had gained the upper hand, and he considered her devious and shallow-natured, but the sexual pull between them was a vibrating force. With a show of indifference she gave a curt nod. "I will send word. It matters not one iota either way to me."

The set of her mouth was far from sweet as they rode on along the country road. He should pay for his high handedness towards her before the day was out. When they reached a clay and wattle dwelling, the woman there summoned one of her young sons from potato-digging to bear the message. Sarah instructed the lad and gave him a silver coin for his trouble. Then she launched once more into coquetry, bantering with Thomas, and he played along with her flirtatiousness. The knowledge of the inevitable outcome of their undeclared battle seemed to charge the atmosphere around them.

They had not gone more than a few miles when she made the first move, complaining of the heat and arguing that they find a tree-shaded road to follow instead of their route through harvested cornfields. When he replied that there were woods further on, and he would not be diverted, she pouted provocatively. A little later she took an interminable time choosing the choicest plums for refreshment from a basket of fruit put out for sale by a cottage gate. When he protested at the delay she only made a teasing face at him, then, as if to make amends, leaned across to hold a luscious-looking plum in front of him. "Do taste it," she urged persuasively.

He steadied her wrist with his hand and bit into the plum, only to have the rottenness she had concealed from him burst into foul-tasting brown juice in his mouth and spill down the front of his coat.

"Pah!" He spat it out furiously while she threw back her head in peals of laughter.

They stopped by a wayside stream where Thomas washed the stickiness from his hands before removing his coat to sponge it clean. After he had done so, he blocked her path deliberately, resolved that she should not get away lightly with her mischief. "The bitter taste of that plum is still in my mouth. You shall remedy that for me."

She looked up at him through her lashes and an anticipatory shiver went through her. "I know of only one balm in such a case." She took his face lightly between her hands, swaying against him as his arms clasped her, and put her lips to his. The moment ignited like a torch to thatch. Not even she had expected such an onslaught of passion, her mouth devoured and devouring, as he bore her back against the trunk of an oak. With a supreme effort she wrenched free. "You presume too much! Remember your place, *cabinet-maker!*" She poured such amused scorn on the title that meant so much to him that rage and lust became indistinguishable as he watched her return to where they had tethered the horses. He drew a deep breath to ease the seething of his blood, and with a face dark as thunder he snatched up his coat, tossed it over one shoulder, and followed her across the grass.

It was a relief to get away from her when they arrived at their destination, a sizeable market town set about a square, she to pass her time in the bow-fronted shops, he to see the merchant who was offering the wood for sale. When he viewed the stack of mahogany, dense and dark, he recognized it instantly as being the best of its kind to come out of Jamaica.

Thomas had been entrusted with the purchase because of an innate business sense that enabled him to drive a hard bargain without appearing at first to hold the upper hand. On this occasion the deal took some time, but when the agreement was signed and sealed, he emerged from the merchant's premises with a feeling of intense well-being. He had obtained the mahogany at far less than its market value. With a swagger he strolled across the cobbled square to The Hare and Hounds, a large coaching inn where he had arranged to meet Sarah.

He found her in one of the parlours away from the taproom. She was tapping her foot impatiently, and sprang up at his approach. "Such news! I have learned that there is a country fair on an alternative road that we can take back to Nostell. It will only add two or three miles to the journey. Nobody will be anxious about me due to the message you so wisely persuaded me to send, and I have never been to a fair. Say we may go, Tom!"

He was not taken in by her flattery over the message, but as it happened, he liked a fair, and since he had done so well in the purchase of the wood, a little celebration would be in order. He was reminded that Isabella would wait in vain for him that evening, but even if he had set off for Nostell this minute he would never get there in time.

It was already dusk when they saw the fair in the distance, the blaze of torches silhouetting the trees. In the clear air they could hear the clash of cymbals, the boom of drums, the shouts and shrieks, and the occasional roar of a wild animal. Leaving their horses at a nearby inn, Thomas and Sarah joined a stream of people bound in the same direction. The jester colours of the fair burst upon their gaze in the striped booths and fluttering pennants, and pungent aromas filled the air from roasting meat, boiling caramel, gingerbread, sweetmeats and spices. They took some refreshment, slices cut for them from an ox sizzling on a great spit, and they ate the meat on trenchers of thick black bread that sopped up the meat juices. Sarah shared a tankard of ale with him and was so merry afterwards that he might have thought her inebriated if it had not been clear that it was freedom itself that had gone to her head. Refinement left her. She wanted to go into every booth they came to, no sideshow of a two-headed calf or a shrunken mermaid too grim for her gleeful appreciation.

On the swings they soared together towards the stars and back again, Thomas laughing with her when they topped the greatest height, she completely unafraid and urging him on, while her hair swung and whirled like finest silk about her wildly excited face.

When the ride was over she elbowed her way through the crowd as she spied the next diversion. "Look, Tom! Oh, look! I have never seen a pantomime!" Sarah was pointing ahead to a large theatrical booth hung with an eye-catching banner. *The True and Ancient Account of Dick Whittington, thrice Lord Mayor of London. A Grand Pantomime as performed before His Gracious Majesty, King George II*. Thomas thought it highly unlikely that the dour monarch had ever been to a fairground production, but he was no less eager than Sarah to take a look at the pantomime.

They managed to get two seats on a bench that ensured a good view, and the show proved to be splendid entertainment, having everything from romance and chivalry to the bawdiest of comedy. Sarah was entranced, her whole face radiant. She had been to the theatre before, but only to classical productions deemed fit for innocent girls, and she had never seen anything like the riotous abandon of the fairground players.

When all ended well, with Dick Whittington triumphant as Lord Mayor and reunited with his true love, Sarah was still under the pantomime's spell. Outside in the night air, heedless of the crowd, she flung her arms passionately about Thomas's neck, her eyes fired to a dark green. "Now, Tom!" she hissed exultantly through her teeth. "Now!"

He bore her with him away from the lights of the fair into the darkness. They ran down a slope, and through a copse to a meadow on the far side. Then he seized her in his arms and they savaged each other with their kissing. In the grass, her riding jacket flung aside, his coat sent flying, she writhed against him, and her rapturous cries were soon lost in his burying mouth. Only the noise of the fair throbbed and jangled in the distance.

SHE STIRRED FIRST. Smoothing out the tangle of her skirts, she looked in the direction of the fair, able to see the tint of its torches against the sky. "Let us stay with the fair, Tom." Her voice was husky with longing. "We could cut ourselves free this night from all we have ever known and follow the fair to the ends of the earth."

142

Lazily he sat up. "How should we live?" he asked, humouring her indulgently.

"We could join the theatre players. You could be stage carpenter and I could sing and act."

"Such a life would be purgatory to me," he answered with all honesty. "Knocking boards together and making sham furnishings. Oh, no." He shook his head as if to drive away the whole appalling concept of it, and stood up.

She reacted tempestuously to his statement, springing to her feet. "I hate you, Tom Chippendale!" she screeched. "I hate you! Do you hear me?" She flew at him to scratch and kick and bite.

He seized her wrists, struggling with her until she was trapped within his arms. When she became limp through exhaustion he took a deep breath and released her. "Now," he said firmly, "we shall return to Nostell."

She made no move, her head hanging. He picked up her jacket and found his coat. Then he stood in front of her and took hold of her lightly by the arm. "Come, Sarah. It is time to go."

She raised her head slowly, her narrowed eyes hard and glittering. Then she spat full in his face, stalking past him with an air of frantic desperation.

They did not speak to each other on the way back to Nostell. When they rode into the stables, she dismounted at once and without as much as a glance at him, hurried away.

In spite of the lateness of the hour, gaming was still taking place in one of the drawing rooms, and dancing in another. She entered by the side door that she knew Isabella used for coming and going in evening hours, and went straight upstairs. She found her maid waiting for her. "Amy!" she snapped. "I trust the message I sent here this morning was duly delivered. Was there any concern when I failed to return for supper?"

"No, mistress. It was assumed you were with the Gower family since an open invitation to ride with them was given yesterday in your mother's hearing."

"That's a mercy. After I have bathed and made ready for bed you shall inform my mother that I have returned and have fallen asleep already, but I will see my sister when she retires to her room."

Amy could judge her young mistress's moods and could tell that

144

the present one was vicious. Sometimes a calming down could be achieved through quiet talking. As she helped Sarah to disrobe she said blandly, "Sir Rowland returned today and he brought a gentleman with him. The new arrival is known to you. Mr. Nathaniel Trench."

Sarah barely listened, too wrapped up in her own intentions. It merely registered with her that there was one more dreary personage to avoid in the company at Nostell. Nathaniel was abhorrent to her, from his foul breath to his conceited pomposity.

Isabella was in bed and about to blow out the candle when her sister came into her room. "Could you not sleep?" she inquired sympathetically and patted the bedcover. "Come and sit down and tell me about your day with the Gowers."

Sarah remained by the door for a moment. Then she crossed to the bed. "I was not with the Gowers," she said with venom. "I was with Tom Chippendale." Then she told all, only keeping back her plea to remain at the fair and the subsequent quarrel. When Isabella tried to cover her ears in an attempt to escape the graphic descriptions, Sarah wrenched her hands away. When Isabella lay huddled and weeping, Sarah went back to her own room.

NATHANIEL TRENCH was well pleased that his intention to make Sarah his bride had met with Sir Rowland's full approval. To marry one of Henry Woodleigh's daughters was to establish a link with that respected name in the Whig party, and at this time, Nathaniel needed all the staunch political support that he could gain. Lady Winn was in favour of the match, too. She knew from Augusta of their newly impoverished circumstances, and she was thankful that at least one of the widow's daughters was to be successfully married.

Nathaniel had risen early the morning after his arrival to make his immediate wishes known to Augusta, and she had received him while still in bed like any grand lady holding a levée. At the sight of her, so befrilled and becurled, he marvelled that she could get so much paint on her face at such a tender hour of the day. After an exchange of greetings he took the chair placed ready for him. It cracked alarmingly under his weight, for he was a thick-set, bull-necked man with a portly shape that came from a gross appetite. "I want the marriage to be held as soon as possible," he informed

Augusta abruptly. Since he was dealing in what amounted to a business arrangement, he saw no reason to honey his words. "Three weeks at the most. Is that understood?"

"Yes, yes. Whatever you say." She rolled her eyes up blissfully, and fluttered her hands, refusing for the sake of her vanity to accept the conversation at his level. "All the world loves a lover, and your romantic eagerness will cut such a dash."

His heavy florid features retained a severe expression. He had never had a romantic notion in his life. This avaricious woman was selling her daughter to him and lining her own pockets, no matter how much she tried to cloak the transaction, and he despised her for her hypocrisy. "You will prepare your daughter for the formal proposal that I shall make to her this evening," he continued in the same businesslike tones. "As you know, there is to be a dancing party tomorrow evening. I intend to prevail upon Sir Rowland to make the official announcement of the betrothal after the supper."

He left the room then, took his hat and cane and went for a walk before breakfast. He wanted to take a look at the new Nostell that was being built and viewed the handsome Palladian façade appraisingly. He had not the least desire to change his own home in any way, and if Sarah proved to be no better at running a house than his first wife had been it would be of no consequence. All he wanted was that she should be decorative and pleasing and faithful, the third virtue being the most important since a man must be certain that his sons, particularly his heir, were of his own flesh and blood.

He had first seen Sarah when she was thirteen, already dazzling with her black hair and milky skin and emerald eyes, and had spoken there and then to her father. He had been given short shrift by Henry Woodleigh, but after Woodleigh's death, Nathaniel found Augusta more than amenable to him as a suitor, and it did not take him long to discover her deteriorating financial situation. As he agreed to her grasping and mercenary terms, he thought that on the whole it was not much to pay for the renewal of youth and virility that he sought to gain through a union with the bewitching Sarah.

Nathaniel's decision to enter politics was by no means a long-standing ambition. At the age of twenty-two he had been recalled from the Grand Tour upon the sudden death of his father, and he had spent the next decade putting to rights the mistakes and

146

ignorance of the past in the running of the great estate that he had inherited. He turfed out incompetent tenant farmers, brought in new methods of cultivation, bought prime bulls to revitalize the herds, and made land that had long lain fallow into fertile fields.

He had married for convenience. By the time everything he surveyed had fallen into a well-organized pattern, his wife had died. It was then that he met Henry Woodleigh and his wife and daughters. He could pinpoint the dawning of his parliamentary ambition to the snub he had received from Woodleigh over his offer for Sarah, soon becoming obsessed with a vengeful resolve to outshine that high-handed politician in his own sphere.

Nathaniel was only too aware of his sensitivity to insult. As a boy, he had taken too much derision from his father to endure now the slightest offence from any source without being aroused to a kind of madness. He knew his tenants feared him, and he could be sure of the vote of those among them who were freeholders and thus enfranchised. But those votes were not enough. He had to win the goodwill of Whig gentlemen of influence, such as Sir Rowland. With the daughter of the esteemed Henry Woodleigh as his bride, he was confident of enough reflected glory to win over those powerful landowners whose support was still in the balance.

He was out of earshot in the afternoon when in Isabella's presence, shut away in a bedchamber, Augusta broke the news to Sarah that he was soon to be her bridegroom, and he did not hear the terrible scream that threatened to shatter the windows.

Augusta had chosen a time when almost everybody in the house would be out on social excursions, anticipating some argument, although never such a scream. Then stillness and silence, which after such a wild outburst of sound, was almost eerie. Sarah had shrunk into herself with shock, standing huddled with her arms thrown wretchedly over her head. Augusta took a deep breath and plunged into the rest of what she had to say. "As a responsible parent it is my duty to see that you make the best possible marriage, and without a dowry no family of any consequence would consider you a suitable prospect. Nathaniel, out of his devotion, is prepared to overlook this matter. Indeed, he has signed a contract for a marriage settlement of generous proportions. As if all that were not enough, Nathaniel gave me a most generous advance on the settlement several months ago." Twisting her hands, she expected some reaction. Yet Sarah still did not move. It was Isabella who swung about to regard her with cold surprise.

"How much did Nathaniel advance you, Mother?"

Augusta blinked defiantly. "I prefer not to say."

"Where did it all go, then?"

She snapped, "If you must know, I lost most of it at gaming. Deep play is all the fashion these days."

Isabella passed a weary hand across her eyes. She had not slept during the night, her own private anguish almost too much to bear, and the present ordeal was taking its toll on her.

"In any case, the matter is of no consequence. The sum I lost is a mere fraction of what will be forthcoming to us when Sarah is wed."

At this point Sarah lowered her arms slowly even as she raised her tormented face. "I shall never marry him. Never!"

Augusta fought down a rising panic. "You must marry him, I tell you. If I sold everything down to the clothes on our backs I could not offset that advance paid to me. And if I broke the agreement I, and you, should be sent to prison for embezzlement. So which is it to be? Incarceration in prison or marriage to Nathaniel Trench?"

At this Sarah became quite crazed. Isabella and Augusta had to struggle with her to prevent her injuring herself in her hysteria of horror. She finally collapsed in exhaustion across the bed and lay there weeping helplessly. Augusta, in tears herself, sank down onto a chaise longue. Isabella, white and trembling from the ordeal, sat on the bed and pulled a blanket over her shocked and shivering sister. All three made no other move, each seeking to recover her strength, until Amy brought in a tray of tea and a small decanter of brandy with which to lace it.

Sarah needed some persuasion to sit up and drink her tea, although when she did, it had a soothing effect on her. Isabella also felt calmer. Only Augusta became cheerful, seeing that the day was hers. Sarah had capitulated.

Isabella went out in the park. She needed to adjust to the dashing of all her hopes that had been brought about by Sarah's revelation of what had happened at the fair. She had suffered pain and anger and despair in equal measure. As she wandered by the lake she derided her foolishness for imagining that there could ever be love between

148

Thomas and her. He had never offered more than affection and friendship. He played no tricks and told no lies, curbing his passionate advances with great self-control when she made it obvious that she was incapable of easy surrender.

Ahead of her lay the orangery. She paused, letting the sweetest of her memories return. For the rest of her life she would remember Nostell and the unrequited love that she had known there. If all was still as it had been, she would have come here again this night. In a way it was in the orangery that her brief romance with Thomas had had its beginnings, in the thankfulness for the skills that had gone into the making of the carrying-chair. And she had been forewarned under that same roof that all was changing when he had first mentioned Sarah by name. Turning her gaze away from that place of joy and heartache, she returned to the house.

Half an hour later she went to keep an appointment she had made the day before with Sir Rowland. He was awaiting her in a small music room, and he thought her a pretty sight in her blue patterned muslin, with twists of ribbon in her hair which had grown into luxuriance over the past weeks. If he had been Nathaniel Trench he would have chosen her before her sister, but every man to his own taste. "You said yesterday that you had a matter of the utmost importance to discuss with me," he said when they were seated. "How may I be of assistance?"

"I seek your patronage, Sir Rowland," she said quietly. "For a young man truly deserving of it, an artist in his own field."

Sir Rowland regarded her kindly. "If you truly believe you have found a promising artist on my estate, I will take a look at his paintings and judge for myself."

"He is not an artist in oils, but in wood. I am asking you to become a benefactor to a cabinet-maker, Thomas Chippendale, he who made the exquisite furniture for the doll's house."

Sir Rowland's expression was one of incredulity. "You wish me to give my patronage to a maker of furniture?"

Her reply was swift. "A beautiful piece of furniture is as much a work of art as anything that hangs on a wall."

He was firm. "I disagree. Furnishings, however splendidly made, are the work of skilled craftsmen, not of genius. Therein lies the insurmountable difference."

149

"We each hold our own opinion on that point," she said, refusing to concede. "You have seen for yourself what he can do now. Only think what the future might bring forth."

Sir Rowland smiled patiently. "You do not know the ways of the world yet, my child. Every man is born into his own station in life, and it would be a grievous sin on my part to single Chippendale out. Let him prove the quality of his work in the years ahead and then perhaps I shall be prepared to commission a table or a chair or two from him for my new Nostell. There! Does that please you?" He saw that she was looking down at her hands in disappointment. "I commend your concern for others less fortunate than yourself, my dear," he continued gently. "You are your father's daughter, Isabella. He would have been proud of you."

Their interview was at an end. Sir Rowland went from the room, leaving her alone. She sat very still, her eyes tight shut. She had failed. At the end of everything she had done nothing for the man she loved. He would go from Nostell unchanged by having known her. Only her life would never be the same.

It was early evening when Sarah came face to face with Nathaniel. No trace remained in her face of the stormy tears and she was calm as she accompanied her mother into the salon. Isabella had declined to join them, deciding to retire early. Sarah came close to experiencing a twinge of pity for her sister. Yet she did not regret that outburst of venom against Tom to Isabella the previous night. Vicious though it had been, it could not have happened at a better time or more to her advantage.

Thomas, waiting in vain for Isabella to meet him by the light of the stars, could be instrumental in a subtle scheme she had devised on the strength of all her mother had let fall about the nature of the man she was expected to marry.

Nathaniel noted Sarah's downcast lashes and shy demeanour, which boded well for their future union. He knew that she had the makings of a frivolous piece if not subjected early to the authority of a strict husband who could mould her into a respectful and obedient wife. His first spouse had been older than Sarah when they wed, her will already set, and although he had broken it eventually, he did not intend to go through that time-wasting process again. With a smile that revealed his discoloured teeth he said, "We meet again,

150

my dear." His bow had a flourish. "Your servant and your swain."

She curtsied in a rustle of primrose silk, her lashes sweeping upwards to give him the full benefit of her marvellous eyes. "An honour indeed, sir." Her reply was soft as a purr.

He offered his arm in a courtly fashion, leaned towards her. "I have your mother's consent to an audience alone with you later this evening. I suggest the library. We can be certain of no interruption there."

She did not care where they met as long as it was in a setting and at an hour suitable to her plan. Yes, the library would do. Tilting her head engagingly, she whispered agreement, adding a request as to the manner and time of their appointment. "That is how it shall be," he promised heartily, willing enough to indulge her modest fancy.

In the orangery Thomas waited for Isabella. As the minutes went by with no sign of her, there drummed at him the certainty that all was over anyway. Summer was at an end, and with it everything that had beguiled its balmy hours. He moved to the window. A chill rain blinked against the glass panes.

A movement from the direction of the house caught his eye and he opened the door to call eagerly through the rain. "Isabella!"

The figure in the cape came to an abrupt standstill. "Tom! It is I! Sarah!"

He went to meet her, irritated that in spite of his dislike of her he should experience a surge of excitement at her proximity. "What has brought you to this place?" he questioned tersely.

"I had to speak with you."

"How did you know my whereabouts?" He was suspicious and wary, inwardly damning the racing of his blood.

"Who else but my sister would be able to guide me to you at this hour? You must come with me to the house." She beckoned urgently. "It is a matter of life and death!"

Anxiety gripped him. "Is something amiss with Isabella?"

"Quick!" she cried. "Or else it may be too late!" Already she had turned back towards the house. He hesitated no longer, setting off at a speed after her.

At the terrace, she opened the glass-paned door into the library. He entered and looked about quickly as Sarah bolted the door behind them. There was no sign of Isabella. In the great hearth a fire of crackling logs cast a rosy glow that picked out the embossed gilt lettering here and there on the leather-bound books that lined the walls, and a twin-branched candlestick held a pair of lighted candles on a table.

There came a swish of damask as Sarah let the drapes fall across the glass doors. "There!" she said, discarding her hooded cape. "Nobody can chance to see us from the terrace."

Roughly he caught her by the wrist, jerking her towards him. "Tell me the truth!" he ordered. "Isabella had nothing to do with your fetching me into this house, did she?"

She ignored his question, snatching off his hat by the brim, and casting it aside. "Remove your wet cloak," she urged. "All I have to say cannot be said in two minutes."

"I want the truth!" He was in no mood for any evasiveness, and captured her other wrist. He expected a struggle but she did not attempt to pull free. She answered him with a sad little sigh. "I did discover by chance that you and Isabella met at the orangery, so in that sense she was my guide to you there."

"You are a devious creature!"

"Do not judge me until you have heard me out." Her eyes were serious and full of appeal. "Since you saw me yesterday such misfortune has befallen me that my brain is quite addled. I need your help, Tom, and I simply thought the library a safe place in which to talk. Before coming in search of you I took the precaution of locking the inside double doors to prevent any intrusion."

Slowly he released her wrists. Still reluctant to trust her, he said grimly, "I'll check that lock." The double doors proved to be securely fastened, the key on the inside. When he turned, she was close to the fireplace, looking into the flames. Through being out in the rain her hair had been disturbed, tendrils hanging bewitchingly on either side of her face, and she seemed unaware that a loosened satin ribbon had caused her dress to slip from one smooth shoulder. He did not believe that any man could have remained impervious to her allure. She reached out a hand blindly to him, and when he took it, she turned eyes on him that were asparkle with tears.

"I know we did not part on the best of terms yesterday, Tom," she admitted with regret, "but I was hurt and angry. I choose to remember how blissful the rest of the day was for me."

"I'm not one to sustain hostility when there is no need. If you mean what you say, we shall let bygones be bygones. Now let me hear whatever it is you have to tell."

She withdrew her hand from his and sank down to her knees by the hearth. "It is terrible," she moaned. "An elderly man named Nathaniel Trench wants to marry me, and my heartless mother has agreed. I loathe him! I'm mad with despair."

So that was it, he thought pityingly. He crouched down beside her, putting a comforting arm about her shoulders. "How then did you think I might help you?"

She raised her taut face to his. "Let me take shelter in your home at Otley," she implored. "For a week or two—it would not have to be longer, because Nathaniel Trench is a man of such conceit that he would not want a runaway bride."

The naiveté of her request was touching. But Thomas shook his head. "It is highly unlikely that you would not be traced within a day or two. In any case, my father once had a brush with the law through unwittingly sheltering a runaway and would now bar the door to King George himself."

"Then I am lost!" She flung her arms about his neck, and her lips, moist and parted, came within an inch of his. As the library clock struck half-past nine with a tinkling chime, her face took on a look of desperation as if the hour of her marital doom was almost upon her. "Dearest Tom! Before all joy in life is taken from me, let me know once more how love should be."

He thought her mad to invite danger of every kind at such a time, and took her by the shoulders to put her firmly from him. At that moment she lunged at him with the force of a tigress, bowling him over. He made to wrench her from him and they rolled over together; then in the last of the few seconds in which the whole tempestuous struggle took place, he was suddenly and thoroughly enlightened. The ring of a closing trap was in the small sound of a turning doorknob.

In her bedchamber Isabella had been trying to read. But she found her eyes travelling down the page with no awareness of what was printed there. Finally she put the book aside and went to the window, looking out at the blackness of the night. She was certain that Thomas would be there in the orangery, and when she did not come he would suppose some social engagement had prevented her. Then, when night after night went by, he would soon guess that she had gained some inkling of his dalliance with her sister, and their friendship would be tainted by it and thus crumble away in an ugly fashion. How much better if she went to him and said farewell on the happiness of the past summer weeks, with nothing to spoil memories of their time together. She drew in her breath. She would go at once.

With her cape about her shoulders she went swiftly down the stairs. Sounds of merriment came from the main part of the house, but she followed her usual route through the wing of rooms that opened into each other. When she came to the last one, the library, she passed by its double doors, making for a corridor that ran parallel to it with a way out to the terrace at the end of it. Then, too late, she saw she was not alone in the passageway.

By the light of a wall sconce no more than three yards from her, Nathaniel, in a powdered wig, was preening himself in front of a gilt-framed looking glass. She drew back quickly into a recessed alcove, unable for the moment to advance or retreat. To be seen in outdoor attire with such pelting rain outside would cause questions later. She held her breath in suspense as he regarded himself again, brushing some wig powder from his shoulders. Then with a swagger he turned towards a recessed door that led into the library. It was one that Isabella knew to be covered on the other side with a façade of books, to blend in with the rest of the volume-packed walls, and impossible to discern from within the library unless one knew it was there.

He swung open the door and was illumined in silhouette for her by the candlelight from within. She saw his features turn into a congested mask of rage. He roared one word. "Strumpet!"

There was confusion within the library where the candlelight was instantly doused. As Nathaniel charged into the room he was met with a blow that sent him reeling back into the corridor to crash to the floor. Isabella, taking advantage of the unexpected furore, sped away. She gave no immediate thought to the possible identity of the couple whom Nathaniel had apparently interrupted in amorous pursuits and it was not until she reached the seclusion of her own bedchamber that it came to her. She clapped a hand across her

154

mouth in dismay. This was the evening that Nathaniel was to propose formally to Sarah. His preening before the looking glass took on its full meaning. "Mercy! No!" she exclaimed aloud.

She went from the bedchamber and ran back along the gallery, relieved to see that the hall below was still deserted, the long wing having insulated the fracas in the library from the festivities in the main room. Then she heard heavy footsteps coming from the direction of the library and Nathaniel came stalking into view, a bloodstained handkerchief held to his nose. At the sight of her he came to a halt. "Fetch your mother to the library!" he thundered. Then he turned on his heel and went striding back again.

Isabella found Augusta playing whist, but upon hearing that her presence was required in the library, she bustled happily off with Isabella, entirely misconstruing the reason for the summons. "Mother," Isabella stated soberly as they hurried along. "Something has gone seriously awry with your plans."

Augusta gave a screech. "What has that ungrateful wretch done? Has she refused him after all?"

In the library they found Nathaniel alone with Sarah, a padding held to his nose. Sarah, her expression one of nervous triumph, sat in a wing-chair, her hair in a state of disarray. For the second time Augusta misread the situation. "Sir! Have you dared to take liberties with my daughter?"

He almost exploded. "No, madam!" he roared. "She has betrayed me. There will be no marriage. I came to the library at her special directions only to discover her in the arms of an unknown rascal, who had the temerity to strike me!"

"Then we must find this dreadful fellow who took advantage of my defenceless girl."

"Bah! You are as stupid as you are greedy, madam! She was a willing partner!"

Augusta sat down weakly in the nearest chair. No marriage. No fortune. Only disgrace and the certainty of prison for herself when it came out that she could not repay the advance. She groaned, putting a hand to her head.

Isabella, numbed by all she had heard, still clung to the faint hope that it was not Thomas who had been here this night. Out of a personal abhorrence of gossip and scandal, she spoke up in quiet tones. "Does any of this have to go beyond these four walls? As yet nobody else knows that anything is amiss here." She looked directly at Nathaniel. "Somehow I will repay the money that is outstanding on the marriage settlement. All I ask is that you grant me time."

In spite of the angry turbulence of his mood, Nathaniel was impressed by her integrity and dignity, but that in no way influenced him towards leniency. "You ask far too great a favour of me," he answered heavily.

Sarah sprang to her feet with a look of disdain. "A favour? Fiddle-de-dee! It is *you* who have severed the marriage contract. Therefore my mother is free of any obligation to return whatever monies she has already received." She raised a mocking eyebrow at Isabella. "And you, my dear sister, did you imagine that I had not thought of everything before my lover took me in his arms this night?"

Augusta sat bolt upright in her chair and clapped her palms together. "You clever, clever girl!"

Isabella, unable to keep patience with her foolish mother's chameleon moods, turned her face away despairingly. By chance her glance fell on a man's hat half hidden under the library desk. She recognized it instantly.

"On the contrary, madam," Nathaniel barked, glowering at Augusta. "If you read again the terms on which that sum of money was given to you, you will see that you were only absolved from repayment *if the marriage took place*. Since wedlock is not to be, you have a month in which honourably to reimburse me. Good night, Mrs. Woodleigh, and farewell."

Her wailing and pleas for mercy followed him as he left the library, degrading her still further in his eyes. In his room his valet put a cold compress on his nose to reduce the swelling and he reclined on the bed, a glass of brandy in his hand, to view the horrendous events that had taken place. That little vixen had spurned him by the most despicable method imaginable. And who had his assailant been? It had all happened so quickly, the fellow having the wit to send crashing the only lighted candle in the room, and then to rush forward like a huge black shadow to deal him the most excruciating blow. And Sarah had laughed as the stranger departed with all speed. It was obvious that the culprit did not wish to be known and for his part Nathaniel wanted no scandal to sully his political aims. He feared he would have nightmares for months ahead over how near he had come to disaster. But Sarah should pay for her insult! He would see her clapped into a debtors' prison with her detestable mother.

When all the house was asleep Isabella returned to the library. She took Thomas's hat and burned it in the red-gold embers of the fire so that no evidence of his visit should remain in the house. It seemed to her that the last of her dreams turned into ashes with it.

IN THE MORNING Nostell was abustle with preparations for the dancing party. Less formal than a ball, it was a light-hearted opportunity for those in the Winns' circle to make their partings until summer came again. Most people were having their town houses made ready for their winter return, and Sir Rowland and his wife would soon depart for their London residence too, leaving Nostell closed up.

A bell clanged distantly through the house, announcing that it was nine thirty and the hour for breakfast. Isabella went down to the breakfast parlour where smallish tables were covered with damask, each set out with a silver tea kettle, jugs of fresh cream, and fruit in porcelain bowls. The long sidetables were loaded with dishes of meat, poultry, fish and game, pies and kedgerees, cakes and scones—gluttony being as socially acceptable as drunkenness for those of the male sex. Nathaniel was already seated, and he was making a start on a gargantuan portion of lark pie, a white napkin tucked under his chin. As Isabella was making her way to a vacant place he looked up from his plate, shoved in another mouthful of pie, and watched her until she came within earshot.

"Miss Woodleigh!" he said. "There is a place opposite me."

She hesitated, taken aback as much by his ungracious bark at her as by his facial appearance. His nose was swollen to twice its size, the bruise having spread to black both eyes. "I prefer to sit elsewhere," she said pointedly, and would have moved on if his next words had not halted her.

"I wanted to advise you against any thought of taking your mother and sister on a Channel crossing to France," he stated sardonically.

She felt the colour drain from her face. Flight to France, often a last resort for those unable to escape their creditors in any other

157

way, was the course she had decided upon to gain time. "Sit down," he ordered brusquely. "You look nigh to fainting." As she sat down unwillingly Nathaniel spoke again. "You strike me as one who would listen to reason. Do not contemplate any foolish attempt to save those two devious creatures to whom it is your misfortune to be related, or else you might find yourself in chains with them. You do not deserve to be party to embezzlement. The crime of your mother and sister is not yours."

"Then again I ask you to grant me time," she implored. "If it takes me the rest of my days, you shall be repaid."

He looked at her, his expression impossible to read. "Sit with me until I have finished breakfast. I am promising nothing, but if you show patience it may encourage me to a degree of clemency."

She endured for nearly two hours. Such was his greed that his lips became besmeared with grease and the white napkin was soon soiled with drops of gravy. When he was finished he sat back with a sigh of satisfaction, wiped his lips, and belched deeply. "Now," he said, "we shall find a quiet corner to go over some details. I have decided to set an interest on the money outstanding to me at a rate that you should be able to meet."

She bit into her lower lip on a gush of trembling relief. Provided she was given enough leeway for ultimate payment, all should be well. Why then did she fear it was too good to be true?

THAT EVENING the dancing party was a huge success. Indoors all was music and gaiety, the dresses of the women in the soft meadow colours that were so fashionable, the men in richer, darker hues of blue and crimson and green and gold. Out of doors it was cold and windy. Whirling leaves blew across the lawns, some lodging against Thomas's high boots as he stood a few yards from the windows, watching the dancing within. He had come out of curiosity, out of a cynical astonishment that what had happened in the library was kept from the knowledge of anyone else in the house, except most surely Isabella and her mother. If a whisper of the occurrence had leaked out elsewhere he would have heard gossip in the servants' hall that day, having been in and out with everybody else commandeered to help with the evening's preparations. He had also taken advantage of the running to and fro to get into the library to

158

search for his hat. He spotted almost at once the blackened buckle of his hat band in the ashes of the fireplace. Had Sarah destroyed the evidence that might have traced his identity? He writhed yet with outrage that she had manipulated him for her own vicious aim. All he had worked and slaved for at Nostell would have been forfeit if he had been identified.

He scanned the dancers. Sarah flitted by, but he gave her no glance. In these last hours before he left Nostell it was Isabella he wanted to see. Why? Did he expect to read some sign in her face that he had not lost all chance of meeting her just once more?

There she was! Not far from the other side of the glass. Yet he felt a tremendous distance from her. Like a little wax doll that had come to life, she was all smiles for her partner, pale arms and bosom rising from the long-bodiced dress of honeysuckle shades. Nothing of the Isabella he had known was there in that figure dancing gracefully around the floor. Never again would she come running to him. He walked away from the lighted windows into the blustery darkness and did not look back.

Early next morning the doll's house stood on view for all at Nostell, an acknowledged masterpiece, fully furnished and peopled by the dolls that were to live in it. But Isabella did not go to view it until late evening when she could be alone. She knew that Thomas would have gone from Nostell that day for his task was at an end. She had never thought that when the day came she would be thankful that no farewells had been said. It would have been more than she could have borne if he had asked her about her forthcoming marriage that had been announced to all after supper at the dancing party.

Nathaniel had been frank with her. He wanted a Woodleigh bride for political reasons, and since his first choice had been a mistake, he would take her instead. "But I will not coerce you into marrying me," he had said. "You have a choice."

She was held stiff by shock, her throat tight and dry. "But no mercy will be shown to my mother unless I become your wife."

"It is not a question of mercy, only of justice. I am prepared to allow your mother the same settlement and terms that would have been granted if Sarah had become my bride, which means that the present debt to me would be changed back into an advance on the agreed sum. Only one proviso would be added to a new contract, that in the matter of Sarah's dowry. On that score I intend that any marriage should take place only after my permission had been given, the dowry being withheld from her until she has been taught the error of her ways under strict supervision in a seminary for not less than a year."

That was minor indeed in comparison to the fate that otherwise awaited her sister. For herself, she felt she knew what it must be like to look into the mouth of hell, her one and precious life set on a course beyond her control. Nathaniel had said she had a choice, but in reality she had none. She could no more put herself before those for whom she was responsible than her father could have done. As if from far away she had heard her own voice answering the suitor for whom she felt nothing, and whose whole appearance and personality were repugnant to her. "I will marry you, Nathaniel."

He had kissed her hand, but not her lips, for which she had been thankful. She hoped it was a sign that he was not a demonstrative man. Now she touched the doll's house, resting her fingertips lightly on the pewter plates in the rack that Thomas had made. She wished him well in York. And she believed the day would come when the name of Chippendale would mean more than that of a doll's house maker.

Chapter Three

In the din and clatter of the workshop Thomas continued with the mundane task of fashioning a simple tabletop, resentment simmering in him. Six months in York and he had been given no chance to work on anything of importance, although some very fine pieces were constructed in the main workshops. He was confined to an outlying building with some thirty craftsmen and a number of apprentices but with no chance to observe the specialized crafts performed by hands of long experience. Simple, everyday furniture was produced under his particular roof, and it appeared to have a ready market. Thomas had twice made application to Richard Wood, his employer, for transfer to the main workshops, but had been refused. Wood was a hard-headed Yorkshireman, a cabinet-maker of renown who promoted in his own time and not before. He made it plain to Thomas that a third request might easily result in dismissal. Thomas resigned himself to a degree of patience and made his work more interesting by discovering how he could produce a piece in less time while experimenting with recipes for the making of a glue that would be stronger and less evil-smelling than any other he had used.

He was able to experiment with glue-making in his own room without giving offence to anyone because a far greater stench often rose from the gutters outside. His accommodation was in the Shambles, where butchers sold their meat as they had done since mediaeval times and cast their rubbish into the street. If Thomas could have afforded a better location he would have taken it, but his wages were small. Now and again he bought cheaply a piece of wood from the workshop until he had gathered enough to make a table and chairs and a few other items of furniture for his own use. All of it was in Yorkshire oak, simple and functional with a rich polish that brought out the beauty of the wood. He was prouder of it than anything he had ever made before.

Winter went by and spring came. For five nights of every working week he usually arrived home too late to do little more than eat his supper and fall into bed. On Saturday nights when Wood's premises closed at an earlier hour, he would go out with some friends he had made, young and lusty bachelors like himself, and they visited ale houses, played cards, attended cockfights and bull-baitings, and above all flirted with pretty girls.

One Saturday morning Thomas was contemplating the pleasures awaiting him that evening, when a sudden uproar ensued outside the workshop that sent everyone running into the yard. Wood came from his office too.

"What is going on here?" he bellowed at the foreman.

Angrily the man faced his master. "This apprentice failed to remember the most basic rule and took wood from the wrong section of a stack, bringin' about a slide. The result lies there before thine eyes."

All looked in the direction in which he was pointing. It was disaster indeed. Recently a dozen walnut chairs had been sent to the premises for the seats to be re-caned. It was a handsome old set, much prized by the owner for its rich carving. All the chairs had been taken into the shed except the last one. As it was about to be fetched the apprentice had inadvertently shifted the wood stack, and it had collapsed across the chair, smashing it to splinters.

"Dear God!" Wood exclaimed, aghast. "Not one of *those* chairs! I know them to be irreplaceable." He stooped to pick up what had once been part of a chair leg, then looked up. "Get this timber restacked and sweep away the remains of the chair. It will do no good to let it lie there." He returned to his office, wondering how he should break the news to his client.

As Thomas went back to his bench a plan was forming in his mind. It would involve a tremendous amount of risk, but it was better to stake his craftmanship on one great gaming throw than to stultify at the mundane work allotted to him.

At the close of the day he went out of the gates with everyone else. Two hours later he returned in the darkness over the wall, a packet of food and a flagon of ale in a satchel over his shoulder, and picked the padlock to get back into his workshop. He toiled all night, snatched a couple of hours' sleep at dawn, then worked again through Sunday. Then he removed all evidence that his workbench had been in use, relocked the padlocks, and went back over the wall, leaving twelve antique chairs in the shed where previously only eleven had been.

The working day had not been in full swing for very long before the hubbub started, the foreman being summoned to the shed, his master hurrying there at a run. Thomas smiled to himself.

During the morning the mystery of the twelfth chair remained unsolved, and Thomas waited until midday before going to the office and enlightening his employer.

"I can scarce believe it!" Wood sprang up from his seat at his desk and led the way with swift strides to the shed. There he cleared everyone out and shut the door so that he and Thomas were alone. "Now! Show me how it was done!"

"I took a leg from this chair," Thomas said, tapping the first one in the row, "and then a toprail from the next, and another leg from its neighbour." Down the row he went, explaining how he had taken a vital piece from each chair, replacing the missing part with one of his own handiwork until he was able to make the twelfth chair from a collection of pieces. Though Wood examined each chair carefully, he could not discern the new piece without having it re-identified for him. In all his years as a cabinet-maker he had never seen such work from a craftsman. He sat down on the twelfth chair as if to get his breath.

"Th' have done well," he said severely. "Th' saved me from paying considerable compensation, to say nothing of preventing the loss of a valued customer." With thumb and forefinger he rubbed his chin thoughtfully. "Th' asked me a while ago about working in the main building. I daresay a place can be found for thee after all. Tomorrow there is an order for a harewood card table that I will allow thee to fulfil."

The card table proved to be a turning point. The client was so pleased with it that he came back to order a matching games table, which Thomas made with an inlaid chess board in contrasting woods, and a specially designed drawer that could be drawn out and slotted into the top for play. All his life he was to be fascinated by the challenge of design in fashioning wood for practical as well as aesthetic purposes. He was in his element.

More fine work followed. His wages went up. He moved into better accommodation, and spent much of his spare time drawing and designing. He rarely saw his previous drinking companions, because they had become ensnared by betrothals, and one by a hastily conducted marriage. Thomas resolved not to be trapped into wedlock until he had fully established himself as a businessman in his own right. He was already looking beyond York to the day when he could go to London, the heart of the furniture trade.

Once he thought he saw Isabella going into a shop, but he proved to be mistaken. He knew of her marriage to Trench from the good people with whom he had lived as an apprentice, and who liked to send him all news. He concluded that Isabella had been compelled by circumstances to step into her sister's shoes. He had been disturbed by this turn of events, and the trick of vision that had made him think it was Isabella in the street brought back memories of her with impact. But the incident was forgotten again as soon as he re-entered Wood's premises and resumed his work.

Sarah had not been at Isabella's marriage. A dour-faced couple had taken her away to a seminary in Dorset where convent-like rules were observed. Augusta had spared her younger daughter no sympathy, only exulting that all had turned out so admirably after all. Meanwhile Lady Winn had made sure that the wedding should be exactly the same for Isabella as it would have been for Sarah.

Her wedding gown had a deep square neckline, sleeves tight to the elbow where a foam of frills burst forth, and a wide skirt supported on either side by hoops. The material was champagne-coloured silk with gauzy panniers shot with gilt threads, and a milliner created a pleated hat of the same silk, with ribbons that floated down the bride's back. With her golden hair dressed with a single love-lock on the shoulder, Isabella shimmered like pure candleflame in the soft greys of her September wedding day. Hundreds of guests crowded into the parish church and afterwards at Nostell the banqueting and dancing went on until dawn. Nathaniel's austere nature did much to quell the ribaldry that so often prevailed at wedding celebrations, for which Isabella was intensely thankful. Lady Winn helped her to prepare for bed, and kissed her affectionately before leaving her on her own in the huge fourposter. Then the door of the dressing closet opened and Nathaniel came to her. She never allowed herself to remember anything of her wedding night beyond that point. It was the only way by which she could face the rest of her life with Nathaniel.

They left Nostell a week later. Amy, bereft of a mistress after Sarah's banishment, elected to accompany Isabella. The destination of the newly-weds was another Whig household that had invited a visit from Nathaniel, and Christmas was spent in the home of a most jovial gentleman, William Marwell, and his wife and grown-up family of six sons and a daughter. Lorinda and her twin brother, Owen, at the age of nineteen were not quite two years older than Isabella. Try as she would, it was beyond Isabella's power to like her husband. They had nothing in common except an interest in politics, thin comfort for a young and warm-hearted woman. So, with so much young company in the house, and others of the same age gathered in from neighbouring houses for parties, this was the merriest of times for Isabella. Nathaniel found so much exuberance wearisome and avoided it as much as possible. Certainly it was a good thing that he was not present when in the midst of a hectic game Owen caught her in his arms and crushed her to him. "A kiss for a forfeit!" he demanded jubilantly. And he kissed her most soundly under the mistletoe.

There had surged through her then an anguished remembering aroused by the strength and hardness of his body, his firm-lipped mouth, and in the magnetism that draws youth to youth.

It was a sad day for Isabella when Nathaniel decided to return home, but leaving was made easier for her by Nathaniel's high good humour. He had been given the assurance of William Marwell's powerful political patronage. And Isabella looked forward to settling under a roof that she could think of as her own. Nathaniel had talked about the house and its wide lands that lay within easy distance of York, but she never suspected that he might have omitted one detail that would affect her whole attitude to living at Trench Hall. Thus she came there late one afternoon on a sombre day, totally unprepared for what she would find.

The lush parkland stretched on either side of the carriage as far as the eye could see, and when finally the Hall loomed up ahead, Isabella was struck by its splendour. Built in Elizabethan times, its Yorkshire limestone burned with rose and purple tints, and the gaunt, unspoilt lines of it towered in masses of carved masonry and in the glint and sparkle of the many mullioned windows.

The entire household staff had formed lines on either side of the wide stone steps of the entrance, the footmen matched in height and build in their immaculate dove-grey livery, and the maidservants in dark print dresses with snowy mob-caps and aprons. Isabella looked to the right and to the left as she went up the steps, smiling along the lines of servants' faces, some of the maids blushing and smiling in return. But she was not aware of the question in silent glances exchanged between them when she had gone into the house. How much did she *know* about what awaited her in Trench Hall?

In the Great Hall Isabella stood gazing about her with pleasure. Furniture of good English oak was enhanced by panelled walls, and the principal staircase with ornamented balusters rose majestically to the upper floors. All was conscientiously cared for; no dust or cobwebs or any other sign of neglect to be seen. In spite of that, there was a faint and peculiar mustiness in the air which the lavender arranged in pewter containers failed to quell. Isabella supposed that with windows opened it should soon be dispelled.

"What think you of Trench Hall?" Nathaniel asked.

"It's a beautiful house!" she exclaimed warmly.

"May I show you to your rooms, madam?" The housekeeper, whose name was Mrs. Finley, came forward and bobbed a curtsy.

"Yes, do." Isabella was shown into the wing that was by tradition allotted to the mistress of Trench Hall and into a bedchamber which held a fourposter with carved posts thick as tree-trunks and wide enough to have slept six in comfort. She went straight to one of the mullioned windows and saw below her an Elizabethan garden of small flowerbeds laid out in geometrical patterns.

Behind her in the room, Amy, who had been making a tour of inspection in preparation to unpacking, gave an exclamation of distaste. "Ah! Whose underlinen is this, Mrs. Finley?"

The housekeeper coloured uncomfortably to see that the maid had pulled out a drawer in which the offending garments lay. "Mercy me! Those should have been removed with the rest of the clothes." And she ran to scoop them up.

"To whom do those articles belong, Mrs. Finley?" Isabella repeated Amy's question.

The housekeeper drew breath uneasily. "To Mr. Trench's late wife, madam."

Isabella gasped. "But she has been dead for over six years. Do you mean that her possessions have remained in these rooms ever since?"

"Yes, madam." She hurried away, the linen in her arms.

Isabella spoke thoughtfully to Amy. "Those garments were not at all yellowed with storage, were they?"

Amy answered without hesitation, "I'd say it wasn't long since they were laundered. I can always tell freshly tubbed clothes."

Isabella's face revealed her astonishment. "How strange!" She

166

shivered. It was quite eerie to have displaced so abruptly a predecessor whose sway had continued indirectly in the house until this very day.

After Isabella had bathed and changed into a striped silk dress she decided to do a little exploring before joining Nathaniel in the small dining parlour. Candlelight glowed everywhere, and each room that she went through had a fire burning in it. Opening one door, Isabella found herself in the Long Gallery, a place for walking, particularly by ladies, when the weather was bad. She wandered along it, filled with admiration at the scenes of the Creation painted on the curved ceiling. She left the Long Gallery by way of the far door and came to another part of the house. Again the stale odour prevailed, and it was even stronger than it had been in the Great Hall. She hesitated, trying to locate its origins, and was drawn to a pair of ceiling-high double doors ornately carved.

As soon as she had entered she realized by the rich screens and superb tapestries that she was in the Great Chamber, which would have been the centre of all hospitality in the days of her husband's ancestors. A portrait of Walter Trench, who built the house, had pride of place above the huge stone mantel, and Isabella, about to cross the wide room to take a closer look at it, was halted by the unexpected presence of a woman seated in a high-backed chair facing the fire. It appeared that she had not heard Isabella come through the doors behind her. The embroidered satin skirt spread about the chair gleamed carnation red, and denoted that the visitor had come in her best attire.

"I bid you good evening, madam," Isabella said, not wishing to startle the lady with a sudden appearance. Still there was no movement. Advancing, Isabella could see that the visitor wore a wig of curling brown hair adorned with pearls. She came around the chair to face the occupant, saying, "I am Mrs. Trench, madam." Then her voice strangled in her throat as she looked into the mummified face of the creature sitting there with claw-like hands resting on the chair arms. From that dreadful form emanated the perfumed odour of whatever unguent had been used long ago to embalm the body of Nathaniel's first wife.

Isabella did not scream. She only stood as if transfixed by the spasms of horror that ran through her. The glass eyes that shone in the parchment-coloured face seemed alive, catching the flickering light of the flames and giving the illusion of staring back at her.

That is where Nathaniel found Isabella when he came in search of her. He strode down the room to her, irritated more than concerned. "I intended you to see Henrietta after we had dined. Whatever possessed you to come in here?" He touched Isabella's arm. She turned to look at him with eyes so dilated that he was seized with fear that she had lost her wits. He was used to Henrietta's mummified presence, and even the servants had adjusted to its being dressed and shod at all times. Too late he realized he should have prepared Isabella for a chance encounter. "Pull yourself together," he ordered in a shout, for he had no idea how to console. "Good God! There is nothing to harm you here. I am the only person whom Henrietta ever harmed. She tried to run away from me. From *me!* That is why she sits there. There is no more running away for her, not even to the grave!"

Isabella tried to speak, but instead slipped to the floor in a faint. He was only just in time to break the worst of her fall.

THE COUNTRY went to the polls three months later. It was a period of free entertainment for the man in the street, with rousing speeches, fights between rival supporters, and riots that flared up at the least provocation. Thomas thoroughly enjoyed himself, and was particularly keen to see the Whig candidate whose nose he had bloodied in the library at Nostell.

On the day of the election itself, a Friday, Thomas was engaged in making an ornamental chest of drawers of the type known as a commode, double doors concealing the drawers within. If he had had a vote he would have been allowed time off from work to go to the nearest polling station, where barrels of free ale had been set up and vast amounts of food made ready at the expense of the candidates as inducements to the favour of the voters. All night the city streets were alive with the noise of singing and brawling as people passed the time until the results should be known.

The name of the successful candidate was announced late on Saturday. Thomas finished work in time to reach the crowded square where Trench was acknowledging the acclaim from the steps of the Mansion House backed by all the chief local dignitaries.

Thomas edged his way through to a tall tree, clambered up to a stout branch, and secured an excellent view.

With that big, hard-featured face set on a neck as short as if compressed by the weight that it carried, Nathaniel Trench bore his huge frame with a pompous air. It sickened Thomas to think of Isabella wed to such grossness.

Every man present waved his hat, except Thomas. Then the dignitaries parted for Isabella to come through and take her place at her husband's side. Another wave of cheering went up. Isabella, smiling and waving, was a sight to gladden any eye, in a velvet coat the colour of a sunset and a huge-brimmed hat adorned by a nodding white plume. Thomas concentrated on her lovely face. Again he sensed an immeasurable distance between them as he had from the darkness outside the windows of Nostell on the night of the dancing party. Yet he wanted to read in her features some indication of whether she was happy. But her face gave nothing away.

Isabella had looked for Thomas, but she had not seen him. It had become her custom to watch for him whenever she was in York. Now she mocked herself a little for imagining that she would be able to pick him out from all those hundreds of people even if he had been somewhere in their midst.

A banquet was held in celebration of her husband's victory, and when it was over, although the hour was extremely late, they drove home. Isabella experienced the sinking sensation in the pit of her stomach that always assailed her when she had to return to Trench Hall. She could not think of that beautiful house as a home. She could only see it as a mausoleum for a poor creature denied Christian burial for the simple fault of damaging a husband's terrible pride.

Gradually she had pieced together the story of Nathaniel's first wife. Henrietta had been twenty-eight at the time of the marriage. She had a dowry, and lands adjacent to the estate of Trench Hall, which made her a suitable choice as far as Nathaniel was concerned. No doubt she had thought that as wife to Nathaniel she would at last come into her own as lady of a great house, with all the social pleasures that were generally involved. But he showed little or no hospitality to neighbours, and she discovered that he wanted nothing more from her than an heir. After a time her loneliness and despair, coupled with the increasing certainty that she was barren, brought about a nervous collapse. She could no longer endure living under the same roof with Nathaniel and went back to her father's house. He refused to take her in. She had no choice but to return to Nathaniel, but she pined and sickened and died soon afterwards. Nathaniel never pardoned her for her attempted desertion or for making him the subject of hostile gossip in the neighbourhood. Although Isabella pleaded with him to let Henrietta be put to rest, he would not relent.

It was dawn when the coach turned in through the gates of Trench Hall. Nathaniel did not look at the letters awaiting him until he had slept for several hours. Then, the first he opened was from the seminary, informing him that Sarah Woodleigh had run away and disappeared without trace.

Chapter Four

It took Thomas another three years before he was able to move from York to London, but he had gained experience that was to stand him in good stead all his life. He showed an exceptional talent at marquetry, which was the process of two veneers being put together and then the chosen pattern or motif cut out to appear as delicate as a painting in variegated wood colours. He became so expert in gilding and carving his furniture that Richard Wood's clients began to ask for him by name.

When Thomas had saved enough money to give him a modest start in London, he notified his master of his intention to leave. They parted on good terms, promising to keep in touch.

Thomas left York by stagecoach on a hot June morning. The oak pieces he had made for himself would follow on a wagon when he had secured an address. He looked about in farewell at the city that he had come to know so well. He would never sever his links with York, any more than he could lose his beginnings in the simple, rustic furniture of the Otley workshop. York had become his city, wherein his craftsmanship had come into its own.

The journey to London took four days, and he arrived on the morning of his twenty-fourth natal day. He felt no strangeness, being well used to the bustle of city life, and when pimps and touts and other rogues tried to waylay him on the streets, he thought himself lucky not to be a gormless lad fresh from home, but an astute, down-to-earth Yorkshireman who had rubbed shoulders with people from all walks of life. Nevertheless he found London exciting, the busy river as crammed with water-traffic as the streets were with wheeled conveyances. His first task was to find himself a workshop in the vicinity of Long Acre, the cabinet-makers' district. He located one on the humblest fringe of the area in a squalid court amid a sprawl of narrow streets. It was not a site that would attract custom locally, and no carriage of distinction would be risked going through it except at a swift pace with a whip at the ready, and a cocked pistol too. But it was all he could afford. With time he would move to something better.

His premises had a sizeable room on the ground floor with workbenches, and a hearth where a good fire could be stacked high when needed. On the upper floor were two small rooms for living. Thomas hung out the sign of a chair that denoted his trade, but by morning it was gone, probably stolen to fuel a cooking pot somewhere. He painted his sign on the wall instead.

Ready at last to seek work, he put into a satchel some carefully wrapped miniature examples of his best craftsmanship and went out to conquer London. By the end of the day nothing had come his way. He thought he knew why. None of the cabinet-makers believed the miniatures to be totally his own work, thinking other craftsmen had been involved in the intricate gilding and carving. Well, tomorrow he would take simpler pieces.

It was a wise move. A cabinet-maker gave him an order for a picture frame, not an auspicious start, but the frame was made and duly delivered, the carved motif of such a high standard that the

172

man looked at it once, twice, and then again, thinking his eyes were deceiving him. He gave Thomas more work in a pair of chairs, then a bookcase. Sub-contracts began to come in from other quarters. He took on six journeymen and an apprentice, and turned no work away. He slaved as hard as his workmen. When veneering, which was a hot and exhausting process, he did not spare himself. The stacked fire gave out a great heat to warm the pieces of wood suspended by chains in front of it. Then he and the apprentice would swing the heated piece over to the central bench and lower it onto the thin veneer that lay there ready glued. As the glue sizzled, Thomas and his workers threw themselves across the wood, beating and thumping it into a smooth contact with the veneer, every second counting, every muscle brought into play until the job was done. Thomas often thought, when a veneered surface had been subsequently polished to a satin-like shine, that it was doubtful if the future owner of the piece would ever have the least idea what sweaty, strength-wrenching effort went into the making of it.

He had almost no money to spare, but what he did have he put to full advantage. The theatres had plenty of cheap seats, bawdy-houses flourished to suit every pocket, and a modest bet was accepted as quickly as those of a thousand guineas at cock-matches and bear-baitings. He had a full choice of London's pleasure gardens, Ranelagh and Vauxhall being the best, and if he wished to drink well he could find taverns in almost every street in the city. A Bow Street gin shop displayed a sign that read *Drunk for a Penny, Dead Drunk for tuppence, Straw free*, but he had not yet been so helpless in his cups that he had needed to sleep it off on free straw in a gin shop's yard. There were also the coffee houses, centres of talk where one could exchange gossip or commercial information, all for the price of a cup of that fragrant beverage. It had come about that men of certain professions or trades would congregate at a coffee house that they had made their own. It was Old Slaughter's in St. Martin's Lane that was the coffee house of the cabinet-makers, and it was there that Thomas made many useful contacts. It was at Old Slaughter's that he met Matthias Darly, an engraver and drawing teacher. A bluff, jovial, red-faced man who wore an outmoded periwig, Darly was able to spot real talent when he saw it, and took Thomas as a pupil for a short period of instruction. What he learned from Darly was comparable to the final polish put to a piece of completed furniture, and Thomas's drawings soon held a professional glitter. His friendship with Darly was to continue long after the lessons had come to an end.

He had been in London almost a year when he went one warm May evening across the river to Vauxhall Gardens, dressed up in his best clothes. His one extravagance had been the dark blue velvet coat and knee-breeches which he wore with a ruby silk waistcoat, a tricorn hat, and buckled shoes. No wig for him, but his own hair, black and unpowdered, tied back at the nape of his neck with a crisp bow. Women always looked at him, but never more than when he dandified himself in this grand attire. Among Vauxhall's trees and flowerbeds, its grottoes and trellised walks and ornamental archways, there were centres of lively entertainment and innumerable eating-places, and always there was the sound of music drifting from one direction or another. Vauxhall was usually thronged with people, those of every class mingling together, and it was here that Thomas saw Sarah.

At first he did not realize it was she. His eye was caught by a stunning creature with a white bosom almost pouring out of her bodice, and a huge hat of emerald green as vivid as her eyes. Then he heard her laugh, and for a second he was back in the library at Nostell, all the attendant loathing of her making his flesh crawl. She was in the company of about twenty flashily dressed men and women, sitting at a long table on the terrace of a minareted eating-place. Consumed by curiosity in spite of himself, he took a table in a shadowed alcove and ordered a glass of wine. He studied her from his vantage point.

He could see that time had both enhanced and tarnished her beauty, leaving a full perfection that had no need of so much artifice of rouge and white complexion paint. She must have found the excitement in life that she had craved on that night of the fair, but it appeared to have taken its toll, for there was a toughness about her.

She seemed totally enamoured of the fellow at her side, handsome as Apollo, who now and again nuzzled her ear with some whispered comment. Her actions as well as his were all indefinably emphasized. Then it came to Thomas that they were actors and actresses! He knew the signs, the laughing, talking, and posturing in

174

a manner that was slightly larger than life. Thomas signalled to the waiter. "At which theatre do those actors and actresses perform?" he inquired.

"No theatre, sir. They are from a travelling company hired for the season to put on plays and light comedies nightly in the grotto. Very popular they are, too."

Thomas decided he would see a performance. He drained his glass and rose to leave. As he made for the steps, a quick footstep followed in his wake. "La! I thought so! It's the cabinet-maker! Would you leave without speaking to me, Tom?"

He came to a halt with a sigh. Half turning, he looked up at Sarah. She stood at the head of the steps, her amused eyes mocking him. "That was my intention, Sarah."

"Shame on you, Tom! In this life one must learn to let bygones be bygones." She came down the steps to him, her every movement sinuous.

"I seem to remember you said something similar to me once before, and it had dire results," he stated coldly.

She giggled, unrebuffed. "I have no trick up my sleeve this evening, I swear it. Come, Tom, be agreeable. I want to know what brings you to London. Are you working at your craft in the city?"

"I am."

"Surely you are eager to know about all my adventures since I was banished from Nostell?"

"No." His tone was blunt.

She tilted her flawless face up to his mischievously. "Why then were you staring at me from the alcove table?" Her perceptive taunt made him flush angrily, and he would have moved away from her if she had not caught her arm into his. "Tom! Tom! Let me at least give you news of Isabella."

She had him there. He hesitated, and then stood still. Sarah's companions came down the flight, she explaining to them that she had met an old friend and she would follow after in a few minutes. Apollo looked sharply at Thomas, dislike and jealousy flickering in the golden-lashed eyes, and spoke only to Sarah. "Do not delay too long, my love."

"Never fear, beloved," she replied, blowing him a kiss. Then she gave Thomas a sideways glance. "Will you walk with me as far as the grotto? I'm appearing there in a production of *The Provok'd Wife*. So you see, I have attained the ambition to appear on the stage that was ignited in me that night at the fair."

"I cannot imagine that an actress in the family pleases your brother-in-law," Thomas remarked drily as they set off.

She was still holding on to his arm, leaning sensuously against him. "I have not seen Nathaniel or Isabella since I was sent away from Nostell. I'm known as Sarah Loveday and few others know my real name. As for my mother, she disowned me when I ran away from the institution where Nathaniel had me incarcerated. I made several attempts to escape, but I was always caught. Then a regiment came to town, and the soldiers were billeted on local families as they always are. The lodgekeeper and his wife had a spare room, and a sergeant was put up there, a married man considered to be trustworthy." She smiled a catlike smile. "But a sergeant is only a man in a scarlet coat. I soon had him besotted enough to help me escape. I left those hateful grounds in a drummer boy's uniform, and nobody was any the wiser."

"What happened then?"

"The sergeant hid me among the camp-followers who always stay with any regiment, and when the regiment moved on, I went as well." She flung her head back lightheartedly. "I had such merriment after all those months of being shut away. My sergeant was good to me. He gave me all the money he had, and it was just enough for me to take a stagecoach to York where I intended to see Isabella without Nathaniel's knowledge."

"That was a risk."

"I was cautious. I went to the servants' quarters, saying I was Isabella's former maid who had called to see her, but she and Nathaniel had left for London. I did not know what to do or where to go, so I made the excuse that I was with child and not well enough to leave. The housekeeper let me stay on for a while, and it was during my stay that I discovered from servants' talk the unhappy time my sister was having."

Then Thomas heard the full story of Isabella's sacrifice. He faced Sarah angrily. "It was a mercy that Isabella was absent. If she had been discovered helping you, God alone knows what punishment her husband would have vented on her."

"I know! I know! But what was I to do?" Her gaze shifted momentarily away from his hard stare but then she smiled. "I helped myself to some of Isabella's dresses and left a note in her jewel case to explain the absence of a few rings before making a formal farewell to the housekeeper."

"You have heard from Isabella since?" he asked.

"No. She has never known my whereabouts, or that her clothes and jewellery changed my luck. I met a gentleman who had theatrical connections and arranged for me to have some training with an old, retired actress. Now I have leading roles opposite Sebastian Searle, with whom you saw me at the table."

"Tell me more of Isabella."

"She is not a widow," she jibed maliciously, "if that is what you hope to hear. Nor does she take lovers," she continued in the same barbed tones. "Isabella has become one of the most brilliant hostesses in London, but she remains tediously faithful to Nathaniel. How deeply do you still harbour affection for her? Enough to think that you before all others would do better with her now than you did at Nostell?"

Hate exploded within him. He seized Sarah and shook her. "Be silent about Isabella! I hope you and I never meet again!"

He left her gasping and went from the grounds, determined to avoid returning until Sarah was gone from Vauxhall.

Several more months went by. Thomas chafed constantly at having to accept prices far lower for the furniture that he made than the seller of it would receive from the clients. When work orders overwhelmed his small shop, he sub-contracted in turn to gilders and marqueteers and veneerers, choosing only the best, because he could not have tolerated less than his own high standards going out under his name. But the best craftsmen demanded the best payment, and often he made little profit on a finished piece. The only consolation was that he was building a reputation with fellow cabinet-makers of high repute.

It was hard to be patient when one was fiercely ambitious, but gradually conditions improved. In the year of 1745, Thomas took on more journeymen after moving into larger premises in the same street as the little church of St. Paul's, Covent Garden, which brought him well into the cabinet-makers' realm. Many had come to

177

admire unstintingly his furniture drawings, and he had been asked so often to supply them that he gradually found himself becoming a professional designer as well as a furniture-maker. It was a sideline that he enjoyed, carrying out the drawings in pen and ink, with a grey or brown or richly coloured wash, and it was financially rewarding.

Then the kernel of an idea began to form in his mind. How rewarding it would be to create a pattern book full of inventive, beautiful, and practical designs, not only for the trade, but for architects and for persons of quality to choose whatever they required when planning and decorating a new home. The one great obstacle to this splendid scheme was money. The cost of publishing a book with hundreds of engravings would be tremendous. Yet if it could be done he was convinced it would put his name on everybody's lips. The more he thought about the book, the more he longed to see his dream come to fruition.

It was on a spring morning in 1746 that a gleaming carriage with a full complement of liveried coachman and grooms drew up outside his workshop, and a gentleman, bewigged, tricorn-hatted, and wearing a crimson coat trimmed with gold lace, stepped out. Thomas came out to greet him.

"Good day to you, sir. May I be of assistance?"

The gentleman looked him up and down, taking him for one of his own workmen. I will speak with Mr. Chippendale."

"I am he."

"Are you, by gad!" A quizzing glass was raised, magnifying the brown eye that regarded Thomas through it.

Thomas's jaw clenched at the familiar arrogance, but he merely bowed and showed the newcomer into the workshop. He would say nothing to drive away his own first client of quality. "May I ask your name, sir?"

"I'm Lord Burlington."

If he had announced himself to be King George II himself Thomas would have been no more jubilant. Lord Burlington was a nobleman-architect, and Thomas recalled an order for a library table that he had fulfilled for him on Richard Wood's premises. "You do me great honour, my lord. What was it you required?"

"A sidetable specially made to fit into a recess at my London

178

house. I have a piece made by you and have always liked it. So I have a mind that you should make this for me as well."

Thomas was never to forget the pride with which he entered the name of his own first client of importance in his order book. He went to view the room concerned at Burlington House in Piccadilly and to measure the recess before he drew the design. When he presented the finished drawing to Lord Burlington for approval, he had added to enhance the sidetable a girandole on the wall above it, an oval looking glass that held double candle branches on either side and three more at the base. Lord Burlington saw how effective the *ensemble* would be, and ordered both.

Thomas carved the frame of the girandole in a floral festoon, afterwards gilded, which he repeated in the ornament of the sidetable, and it was with justifiable pride that he delivered it to the house. There he supervised the hanging of the girandole and the sliding of the sidetable into the recess, where it fitted like a hand in a glove.

Lord Burlington came to view the result. "Splendid, by gad! Truly splendid!"

Thomas returned to his workshop certain that more orders would come in from clients of quality as soon as the *ensemble* had been seen and admired. But nothing happened. He sent in his account once, and again a second time. When no payment was forthcoming he went back to Burlington House. The bill? Oh, that would be paid one day, the housekeeper told him. No need to worry about it. Thomas had already settled his debts to fellow craftsmen for supplying the mirror for the girandole, had paid for the rosewood and satinwood and gold leaf used in the making of the sidetable, and he felt a considerable draught in his pocket. He welcomed the humbler customers who came into the workshop and paid solid cash for their small purchases.

Then, unexpectedly, a lady named Mrs. Dorrington came into his workshop one day. She was sharp-featured and keen-eyed, intent on securing a bargain. She wanted a sofa and eight chairs *en suite* for which she would supply the light blue silk that she had recently purchased abroad. He guessed that she had obtained estimates elsewhere, and made his price a little higher. She blinked, having expected it to be half as much, but he judged her to be the type to boast of the expense to her acquaintances if it was high. And he wanted her to talk about the furniture if he made it for her, for that was the best advertisement. "You are vastly expensive," she said scathingly, "for a cabinet-maker unknown to any by name."

"My furniture speaks for me, madam."

No doubt of that, she thought, glancing at an exquisite pair of corner commodes. Avarice for his skill warred with her parsimonious nature, and avarice won. "I agree to your price," she said at last, "but I expect to have the best sofa and chairs in the whole of London for it."

"They will be the best in the whole of the kingdom, madam."

Thomas made the frames of the sofa and chairs, but subcontracted to an upholsterer named James Rannie for the silk work and padding. Rannie had a thriving business and was renowned for his fine upholstery.

The results were dazzling. "We've done a fine job between us, Mr. Chippendale," Rannie said when they stood side by side to survey the finished work. It was certainly true. Thomas had crested the curved back of the sofa with a gilded scallop shell, the oval backs of the chairs were similarly adorned, and the blue upholstery was taut and smooth.

"I agree, Mr. Rannie," Thomas replied.

Rannie gave Thomas a speculative glance. "You should stop hiding your light under a bushel, which in your case is letting other cabinet-makers sell your work to their own profit. You should only take orders that come direct to you from a client."

"That is my aim," Thomas answered readily, "and had I the financial wherewithal I would move my workshop to more prominent premises where I could attract the notice of quality folk. Needless to say, that is quite out of the question at the present time."

Older than Thomas, Rannie felt it would not go amiss to hand on some good advice. "Haven't you thought of marriage, Mr. Chippendale? It wouldn't be difficult for a young fellow like yourself to get a bride with some money of her own that you could put to good use."

Thomas smiled, shaking his head firmly. "I've no thought of marrying for a long time to come."

There were no more immediate results following the delivery of the blue silk sofa and chairs than there had been with Lord Burlington's sidetable until one day Mrs. Dorrington's daughter-in-law placed an order with Thomas for an even grander sofa with chairs *en suite*, the upholstery to be in peacock brocade. About the same time Lord Burlington settled his long-overdue account, and decided that he must have some new bookcases. A decided trickle of important new business had begun to seep through to swell Thomas's order books.

He returned one day from visiting a client to find a message left in his absence that he should call with drawings of dining-room furniture at an address in elegant Soho Square. The house he sought was an imposing rosy-bricked mansion. He was admitted, and shown through to a drawing room which was deserted. He stood looking about him, able to tell that the heavy, gilded furniture with its encrusted acanthus leaves and goddess heads was by William Kent and, in his opinion, thoroughly outmoded. More acanthus formed the frame around a huge chimney glass. Even as he looked towards it, there moved into its reflection the figure of a young woman, who paused in the open doorway behind him. His skin tightened with astonishment. He had recognized her instantly.

"Isabella!" He swung about to face her as she came towards him, radiant and smiling, her hands outstretched to his.

"Thomas! Thomas! Whoever thought we should meet again? I refrained from leaving my name at your workshop to give you this surprise!"

"A most joyous one indeed!" He caught her fingers in his own, smiling broadly with her in mutual pleasure at this unexpected reunion. She had matured exquisitely from girl to woman, the bloom of her innocence having given way to a polished poise and confidence.

"How well you look!" she declared. "London surely suits you. Have you been long in the city? Oh, there is so much I want to hear from you."

"First, tell me how you discovered my workshop," he said.

"Mrs. Dorrington told me her handsome sofa and chairs had been made by a Mr. Chippendale. I imagined you to be still in York."

"I saw you there at the time of the election in '39 when your husband won the Whig seat." Reminded of that violent skirmish he

181

had had with Trench, he raised his eyebrows in wary inquiry at her.

She understood immediately, and gave a little shake of her head in reassurance. "Nathaniel never knew the identity of the man in the library at Nostell."

"You must have despised me when the whole sordid story reached your ears."

Briefly her fingertips settled on his lips in a touch light as a butterfly's, showing he had no need to speak of it now. "I only remember the happy times at Nostell."

"Do you ever see Sarah?"

Her expression saddened. "No. Once she visited Trench Hall, but Nathaniel and I were not there. Fortunately he never knew about it. He is not a forgiving man."

"Sarah is an actress," he said. "I met her by chance nearly three years ago at Vauxhall."

"You saw her! Oh, tell me all that you know."

They sat together on the sofa while he told her of Sarah's misadventures. Afterwards they talked of themselves, Isabella describing her life as a politician's wife, he recounting how he had established himself as a cabinet-maker. Tea was served to them, and still they talked. It came out that Nathaniel did not spare himself in his political life and his health was suffering. "It is as if he is driven by a kind of madness," she explained. She glanced about the room and gestured with her hand. "This house is leased to us, and has been since we came to London, but Nathaniel has decided to buy a residence in Arlington Street. For me it will be a home that I may furnish to my own taste, which is why it was my pleasure to invite you here, both as an old friend and as one who will make me some beautiful furniture for its many rooms."

It was an order of proportions that dazed him.

"I'm honoured, Isabella."

She smiled, seeing how pleased he was, and asked to see the drawings he had brought. He spread them on a sidetable, the better for her to study them. They were still in discussion over the design of the dining chairs when there came the sounds of someone arriving in the house. Isabella put a hand on Thomas's arm. "That's Nathaniel! What has brought him home from the Commons at this hour? I must find out."

182

She left him alone in the drawing room. Thomas could not help but overhear the conversation in the hall between her husband and her. Nathaniel declared himself to be unwell, saying he would rest by the fire while she sent for the doctor. When he came into the room, leaning heavily on a footman's arm, grey beneath the purple veining of his face, he frowned to see a stranger in the room. Isabella said at once, "This is Mr. Chippendale, the cabinet-maker whom I mentioned to you."

Thomas bowed conventionally. Nathaniel gave a nod and allowed his massive frame to be propelled by the footman into the chair, where he sat down heavily. Isabella herself brought forward a footstool for him. "I thank you for coming, Mr. Chippendale. You will not forget the other designs for furniture in the new house?"

"No, madam. I shall present them with pleasure."

She did not watch him go, but busied herself looking after her husband. Dr. Stoops arrived and escorted the patient up to bed before bleeding him. Afterwards, outside the bedchamber door, he advised Isabella that Nathaniel had been overworking, something she already knew, and that he must rest for at least a week. "I will instruct Mr. Redshaw, the apothecary, to make up some special powders that should disperse the discomfort in the patient's chest."

Isabella returned to Nathaniel's bedside and found him sleeping, so she went downstairs. Thomas's drawings still lay spread out on the table. She touched them, her whole body stiff with repressed emotion. It had not occurred to her that after almost seven years she would experience again that extraordinary rush of joy at the sight of him. Only by denying love had she been able to come to terms with her marriage. Her failure to give Nathaniel an heir had made him as intolerant of her as of anyone else who crossed his will. She was now merely a useful appendage to his parliamentary aims, and only by shutting away her heart had she been able to prevent herself from hating the man she had married. How then could she endure her existence if Thomas destroyed her defences once and for all?

Her reverie was interrupted by the butler informing her that the apothecary's daughter had arrived with the powders. "Show Miss Redshaw in," she said.

Isabella had befriended Catherine some two years ago. The girl's father, in order to show respect to such an important customer, would only entrust the delivery of Nathaniel's physic to a member of his own family, and it was on one such visit that Catherine, normally a calm, sensible girl, appeared pale and fraught, not far from tears. Isabella invited her to sit down, pouring her a glass of cordial. Being a sympathetic listener, Isabella found nothing unusual in an opening of the heart by the girl to her.

Catherine's beloved was a Royal Navy sea-officer. She had met George Andrews, tall and dashing in his gold-buttoned, dark blue coat, after his ship docked at Greenwich and he called in at her father's shop for a potion to banish a searing headpain after celebrating his return to home shores the previous night. Catherine was behind the counter that day, and gave him a distillation of marigolds. Before the week was out they were seeing each other at every available moment, arousing her parents' disapproval. As happens so often in such cases, their opposition only served to strengthen their daughter's devotion to George Andrews, the snatched meetings and smuggled love messages adding to the excitement and desperation of the romance. But the Redshaws were adamant. George Andrews sailed with his ship, and then fate settled the matter once and for all. In the Bay of Biscay an enemy vessel was engaged in the continuing war against France. During the battle George suffered fatal injuries and he was buried at sea.

Catherine became a wraith of her former self. It was due largely to Isabella's visiting her, inviting her to the house, and taking her for drives in the country that she began to revive. She took up the threads of her life again, but with a new seriousness. It was as if all that had been lighthearted in Catherine Redshaw lay somewhere in the depths of a dark green sea.

Now Isabella greeted her as she entered the room. "Thank you for coming so promptly, Catherine."

"How is Mr. Trench, Isabella?"

"It is difficult to say. He is sleeping now, but I must wake him to begin giving him the medicinal powders you have brought."

Catherine went upstairs with Isabella to help. She was a tall, willowy girl with a handspan waist and thick, silky chestnut hair. She was the only one of five daughters unmarried and still living at home. If she had been born male she would have followed in her father's footsteps by becoming a qualified apothecary. He had taught her a great deal, and she had read his many books on anatomy and botany. She could prepare and blend, decoct or grind, all the ingredients that went into remedies for every ailment, whether goat's dung, oil of earthworms, bulls' testicles, or any other such items. It was no wonder that her mother thought it indelicate that she should work in the dispensary. Nevertheless it came as a devastating blow to her when her father, at his wife's instigation, took one of his sons-in-law, Lewis Wickham, as a partner in the business. Lewis's skills were far less than her own, and she was outraged to find herself relegated entirely to making deliveries.

Upstairs, Nathaniel was still sleeping. Isabella awakened him gently and Catherine deftly tipped the powder on his tongue and gave him a quick sip of water to swallow the bitterness down. She had a flair for nursing and saw now that her ability might be put to good use for Isabella. "Would you like me to assist you in the nursing of your husband?" she asked when they had left the bedchamber again. "It will be hard on you if you try to manage alone."

Isabella closed her eyes briefly in gratitude. "I should be so glad if you would. You shall take my carriage home and fetch whatever you need."

Catherine returned with her belongings to take the first turn at the bedside that night, allowing Isabella to get some sleep.

The two friends cared for the patient, sharing hours in the sickroom. Catherine's efficiency was beyond price. Dr. Stoops came twice daily, more anxious about the ailing politician than he cared to show. Fortunately the chest pains subsided, and Nathaniel became increasingly querulous and demanding, which was a good sign, and by the end of the second week he was sitting up in bed.

During the third week, when Nathaniel had begun to take a few shaky steps with the aid of a stick, Thomas came again to Soho Square with a second batch of drawings. Isabella was dazzled by the beautiful designs, particularly by the bedchamber furniture for her own use in a glorious japanned green with sprays of gilded blossoms. The canopied bed was hung with damask caught up into drapings by silken tasselled cords. "I would like to go through the house with you," Thomas said to her. "There are several matters that we should discuss."

"I will meet you there tomorrow at noon." Suddenly she felt the colour flood her face, aware that his eyes were holding hers, and she could tell that he was also remembering when they had made such arrangements to meet during a summer that was not so very long ago. The resurgence of love, which she had tried so hard to combat, gushed into her heart. She looked down, fearing he had glimpsed too much in her eyes, and she sought swiftly to amend the situation.

"I never thought I should become your patroness," she said, "though I did once ask Sir Rowland to be your patron, to finance you during the years when you would have been establishing yourself as the artist in wood that you are."

"You asked him that for me?" he breathed incredulously.

It was not having the effect she had intended. "It is as well that my request was not granted. You have made your own way. I had no right to try to interfere in your life."

"You of all people had every right."

She could feel his gaze warm and soft upon her. Like his breath. Like the first beginnings of his kisses, which she had tried to put from her memory. All in vain. "The right I have now is to praise your furniture to others when it is completed," she said, appearing composed. "I will say farewell until tomorrow."

Entirely for her own sake Isabella took Catherine with her to Arlington Street at the appointed time. On no account would she allow her feelings to get the better of her, and in the presence of a third person that could not possibly happen. They arrived a little early. The house was of graceful proportions, the rooms large, with some very fine fireplaces and ceilings. They completed a preliminary circuit and then sat down on a window seat in the sun to wait.

Thomas arrived on the stroke of noon, his footsteps echoing hollowly in the emptiness of the hall. Isabella called to him. "I'm in here, Mr. Chippendale." She would not use his Christian name in front of Catherine.

She saw as he came into the room that he was taken aback not to find her alone. Regret, sharp as pain, blended with a dreadful thankfulness that she had brought Catherine. She rose to her feet, making the introductions as she did so. It was difficult for her momentarily to look into his face and see whatever might lie in his eyes. Disappointment? Even anger that she should have wilfully cast aside a golden opportunity? Side by side they went from the room and began a slow and careful tour of the house, he showing her how and where he thought certain pieces of furniture should stand. Catherine followed in their wake, listening for a while then becoming bored. She was pleased when Isabella was ready to leave, and was first out of the house to the waiting carriage.

A month later Catherine returned to her father's house. Nathaniel had made what could be called a recovery since he was able to move about the house and take walks in the garden, but in reality he was still an invalid. He decided to leave his trustworthy steward in charge regarding the new house, and to spend some quiet months in recuperation in Yorkshire.

Isabella had never been more loath to leave London or to face the prospect of weeks and weeks without seeing Thomas. Worst of all, it had never been more difficult for her to bear her husband's boorishness. It was no relief to arrive at Trench Hall. She was so haunted by the presence of Henrietta that her only escape was to be in the park as much as possible, and she would ride for hours out across the moors.

Frequently now they took their meals in almost total silence, Nathaniel's attitude towards her having become so unmistakably hostile that in his moroseness he would often not answer her when she spoke to him. She excused him by reason of his ailing condition. He was no longer capable of giving her a child, and she had failed him in the days of his potency. Without an heir Trench Hall and all its lands, being entailed, would go to a distant cousin with whom Nathaniel had had a violent quarrel many years earlier. She could guess the torment it was for him that all he had built up should one day go to an old enemy.

She had retired to bed one night and had fallen asleep when the sound of her door opening awakened her. The room became threaded with candlelight as Nathaniel approached carrying a branched candlestick in his hand. His face was flushed to a sinister purple tinge. "What is wrong, Nathaniel?" she asked with concern.

He plodded across to the nearest chair and collapsed heavily into it, puffing and gasping, hardly able to draw breath. With a shaking hand he fumbled in his capacious pocket to take out one of the powders that he found necessary to keep with him constantly, and

Isabella threw off her bedclothes to go to him, calling to her maid for help.

By the time Amy bustled in, Isabella was standing with her arm against the wall, her face buried in the crook of it. She was weeping. "He's dead!" she gasped. "Nathaniel is dead."

Amy rang to summon servants. As there came the sounds of the house stirring, she hastened across to Isabella's robe that lay across a chair, and then went to her with it. All the time she talked to her distressed mistress. "You must come into the next room. Mr. Trench is not a pretty sight."

Isabella moaned at the sight of Nathaniel's grotesquely distorted face as he sat with his head hanging back and his mouth gaping. Pulling herself free of Amy's support she went across and mercifully closed his staring eyes.

A week later Nathaniel and Henrietta were laid to rest in the Trench tomb. Augusta Woodleigh arrived from Bath in time for the funeral, and Isabella guessed correctly that her purpose was to hear the terms of the will. Apart from a few minor bequests, Nathaniel left the bulk of his vast fortune to Isabella. As for his mother-in-law, it was stipulated that the same conditions laid down in his lifetime should continue after his death, not an extra penny to come to her. In addition he banned her from ever residing in any house owned by his wife. Augusta was livid. She departed immediately in a terrible huff.

Nathaniel's distant cousin, Edward Trench, to whom the house and estate were entailed, came to view his new property. He proved to be a kindly, charitable man who had completely forgotten the quarrel about which Nathaniel had held such a bitter grudge for so many years. Although he was most anxious that Isabella feel no haste to move out, she and Amy travelled back to London in time to spend Christmas at Arlington Street.

THE HOUSE was ready, with fires dancing in every fireplace, servants installed, and all the furnishings in place. In spite of the gloom of the day, the sky being dark with snowclouds, there was warmth and light in every corner, and Isabella ran from room to room in sheer delight.

All the walls were panelled with silk or damask, the colours soft

188

green or gold, amber, ivory, or palest coral. Chandeliers poured from ceilings encrusted with white plasterwork, carpets lay underfoot in pastel hues, and everywhere stood Thomas's beautiful furniture. She ran her palms reverently over the exquisite marquetry that graced two handsome pier tables, and her fingers tripped along the gilded backs of sofas and chairs. Upstairs in her bedchamber she caught her breath at the splendour that was there. Against walls covered with Chinese ivory silk glowed Thomas's japanned furniture in a rich apple-green. But it was the bed that held pride of place, more exotic and spectacular than she had been able to visualize from Thomas's design. The head was elaborately carved and gilded and it complemented the huge, domed canopy topped by moulded cherubs. The green japanned posts were hidden by the loops and swags and drapery of matching damask threaded with gold and adorned with fringe and tassels.

With delight she moved to the bed and lay back across its coverlet. Under the canopy above her head, silk in a lighter shade shirred out from the head of a cherub centred there. It was a lovers' bed. A bed for passion and sweet dreams. A bed in which the true joy of marriage could achieve its ultimate fulfilment. She closed her eyes, her lashes quivering. Here she would lie with Thomas. Here she would draw from him the love that she had come to believe had only been withheld from her through circumstances. She had not been on her own with him since their meeting in the Soho house, but that should change.

She sprang up again and raced downstairs. Taking up a pen and paper she wrote that she had arrived home—how gladly she could write the word *home* and mean it truly—and invited him to take supper with her that evening. She did not doubt that he would come eagerly.

Amy had unpacked her scents, oils and other cosmetics by the time she sat down in front of the dressing-table mirror. She did not put much paint on her face, using it to enhance and not disguise. With her hair dressed and a final dab of scent applied here and there, she let Amy help her into a dress of topaz-coloured silk embroidered with roses, singing to herself under her breath.

Amy cleared her throat. "Madam," she said uncomfortably. "There is something you should know."

Isabella caught the note of doom in the maid's voice, and it was as though a cold and invisible fog had suddenly swirled into the room. Her singing faded. "What should I know?" she asked quietly.

Amy swallowed. "I heard it when I was downstairs a few minutes ago. Mr. Chippendale is betrothed. To Miss Catherine Redshaw."

There was a long pause. Then Isabella answered her almost inaudibly. "You did right to tell me, Amy. I will be ready with my congratulations. Leave me now. I will wait here until my visitor arrives."

Isabella remained quite motionless at her dressing table until she heard Thomas arrive. Then in a rustle of silk she went downstairs to him. She felt as drained and lifeless as if she had at last become one of the stiff-limbed wax dolls that peopled the doll's house at faraway Nostell.

THOMAS HAD LOOKED at Catherine and loved her and wanted her for his own from the moment he first saw her beside Isabella on the window seat in the house in Arlington Street. Yet he had gone there that day with a very different aim in mind, believing Isabella would be his at last. He experienced a bitter sense of disappointment at not finding her alone. It was almost as if he saw in Catherine a release from the frustrations heaped on him by the evasive Isabella.

But Catherine had shown no interest in him then. Her greeting was conventional, her gaze indifferent, her smile distant. He was not used to being thus passed over, and it all added to her attraction.

He began to devise some plan of action by which he might see her again, but it did not prove necessary. A few days after Isabella and her husband had departed to York, Catherine came to his workshop. She missed at home the convenience she had had at Soho Square of a table at her bedside and he showed her some simple, inexpensive pieces, with drawers, that were made-up stock. When she selected one, he promised that it should be delivered that same evening.

He took the table himself to the shop in Tyburn Lane. The Redshaws lived above the shop and it was Catherine who admitted him through a side door and led him up a narrow staircase into a large parlour where her mother sat stitching at an embroidery

190

frame. Some mild conversation took place, with comments on the weather. Then he unpacked the table and Catherine regarded it with satisfaction. "Is it not just what I need for the side of my bed, Mother?" she declared.

"Does the drawer slide easily?" Mrs. Redshaw asked.

"Perfectly," Catherine replied, demonstrating it.

Then Thomas seized his chance. "What an oversight!" he exclaimed with dismay. "The drawer has not been lined. I will take it away with me and return it to you myself tomorrow evening if you will be at home."

"Yes, I will," she replied.

He departed with the drawer and lined it himself with the expensive, marbled paper that he kept exclusively for drawers of more costly commodes. Mrs. Redshaw was not at home when he returned to Tyburn Lane the following evening and Catherine offered him tea. She appeared to enjoy the talk they shared over books they had both read, and when he was about to take his leave he asked her if she would accompany him to Ranelagh pleasure gardens the next evening. She gave him one of her veiled and distant glances, but to his relief she accepted. It was the beginning of his courtship.

Like many experienced and worldly men in love for the first time, he was besotted with her. Her enigmatic containment gave her a mystery that had him spellbound, her whole being a challenge to him of depths to be discovered and conquered.

As soon as it became obvious to her parents that he was courting their daughter he was made unwelcome at the house. But Catherine met him outside instead. A changed person from the pliant girl who had once obeyed her parents' commands, she would make her own decision as to whether or not to marry Thomas when he asked her.

Catherine would not indeed have minded remaining a spinster if she could have continued in the dispensary but the shop had become forbidden territory to her. Lewis had used her absence at Isabella's to install a male assistant of his own choice, leaving no room for her. She might even have settled for a domestic future at home if a happy atmosphere had prevailed, but her mother was a querulous woman, impossible to please.

So she accepted Thomas. He loved her, and she had the upper

hand on that score. She admired him for being the highly competitive man that he was in the business world, and finally no normal woman harbouring a liking, if nothing deeper, for a particularly fine-looking man could have remained indifferent to his kisses and his protestations of love for her. After weighing up everything carefully, she agreed to become his wife.

The marriage took place on a May morning, in the presence of family and friends. Mrs. Redshaw, accepting defeat, was determined that none should say that Catherine's wedding day was less grand than those of her other daughters. So there was feasting and dancing that would go on all through the night. None saw the bride and groom slip away during a merry romp except Isabella. Catherine gave her a swift embrace on the landing before running off down the stairs to join Thomas at the carriage.

Isabella remained on the landing until the sound of the carriage wheels faded away. Then she sighed deeply and pressed her fingertips to her closed eyes. She had not known how she would get through this day, but she had done it.

By the time the bridal couple were missed, they had reached the sanctuary of their home, the rooms at the rear of Thomas's workshop. "I love you, my beautiful Catherine," he murmured tenderly as he drew her to him in love.

FOR THE FIRST WEEKS of their marriage all went well. Catherine's feelings for Thomas developed from liking to affection, if not to love. Their living quarters were humble, but adequate for a struggling cabinet-maker with no cash to spare, their bedchamber and the parlour being furnished mostly with rejects from the workshop. The only pieces of any mark were the oaken table and chairs, the desk and bookcase Thomas had made for himself in York. But they were simple, basic pieces for all their fine workmanship, and although he had said that he would never part with them she had decided that when she had a home of her own of which she could feel proud, those pieces should be relegated to an inconspicuous corner.

Thomas dealt with all the work orders himself, but had a clerk to do the books. When the clerk had to be dismissed for pilfering only a week before the wedding, Catherine seized the chance. She offered to keep the ledgers as she had done on occasion for her father and this was agreed as a temporary measure. The day after she had become Mrs. Thomas Chippendale, she settled herself in the office.

She soon discovered the work was as interesting as anything she had done before. In no time at all she had made herself familiar with locks, keys, mouldings, gold leaf sheets, and all else that comprised the cabinet-maker's craft.

She had been Thomas's wife for three months and was at work in the office one morning when she felt her stomach lurch and turn. She clapped her hand over her mouth, her whole frame racked by spasm after spasm. When the attack had passed, a terrible suspicion assailed her. No! No! No! She wanted children, but not yet. Not when life had become interesting again with so many ideas of her own developing in her mind as to how she might become more influential in her husband's business.

To her annoyance Thomas was not in the least surprised when she announced that she was with child. Moreover, he was proud and pleased. "But it is too soon for me," she protested vehemently. The prospect of having to withdraw even temporarily from a re-established foothold in a masculine world was galling to her. "I was looking forward to taking a far more active part in the business. Is it not exasperating for me to be handicapped, first by pregnancy, and then by a babe to suckle night and day?"

His eyes narrowed at her. "How can you be so foolish? Since when has the care of a child been less than the best that any woman can do for the world in which we live? I did not marry you to be my business partner. I married you to be my loving wife and the mother of my children and the keeper of my home."

She was enraged. "Home?" she flung back at him. "What sort of home is this to bring a child into? A parlour with furniture fit for a bonfire. Even the door of our home opens from that yard into a passage through which your workmen tramp all day, dragging wood-shavings and dirt on their boots. Have you any idea how often I must take a broom to that flagged floor?"

He was stunned by her tirade and answered her coldly. "I did not realize you had taken such a dislike to our abode. One day you shall have all your heart desires. In the meantime, conditions here shall be made more tolerable for you."

That night they made up their quarrel. There was forgiveness on both sides, but no change of attitude, each being as stubborn as the other.

Within a few days Thomas had hired a clerk for the office. As for the passage, an apprentice was assigned to keeping it swept. In addition, Thomas replaced some of the furniture in the parlour with better pieces from the stockroom.

When the attacks of nausea passed, Catherine continued to ail. At times she lacked the will to do anything but drag herself to the sofa and lie there all day, her energy having quite deserted her. Then Isabella went to see her. Isabella was preparing for a journey abroad, and she had come this day to call before setting out. Her house in London had proved to be too full of reminders of Thomas for her to find peace of mind there, no matter how much she kept up a social whirl to occupy her thoughts. On her travels she hoped to readjust completely to a life without Thomas, and to be able to see him after her return without the pangs of yearning that were such agony to endure.

At the door Isabella was taken aback by Catherine's wan appearance. "How kind of you to come when you are so busy at this time of departure. How fine you look! That stylish dress! You are a breath of the outside world. I feel sometimes that I shall die of boredom cooped up in these rooms day after day."

"Neither you nor I shall be bored this day except by the clacking of our own tongues!" Isabella spoke jestingly to hide the deep concern that she felt for Catherine's condition. Then as they took seats opposite each other, to her dismay Catherine burst into tears. "My dear! What is it?"

"Nothing. It is just so wonderful to have you here. You don't know how much I have needed to talk to a good friend who would not preach at me."

"Why should anyone do that?" Isabella asked.

Catherine took a deep breath. "Because I loathe being with child. There! Am I not the most unnatural mother-to-be that ever lived? My mother and sisters think so."

Isabella thought quickly how she should answer. She snapped her fingers casually. "Pssh! What is wrong about not wanting to feel ill or uncomfortable for nine months? How thoughtless of Mother Nature

194

not to arrange for gestation in a woman to last only twenty-four hours! Twelve would have been even better!"

Catherine managed a faint smile. "If that were the case I could have carried on with the work I was doing for Thomas without any trouble arising from it." Then she confided the splendid plans she had made for her future in the business and the answer that Thomas had given her regarding the role he had allotted to her in their marriage. Isabella could foresee endless strife ahead for this union between Thomas and his wife unless a compromise was reached. As Catherine talked on in a continued outpouring of dissatisfaction, it was almost as if she had made work a substitute for love. But why, why? Unless she did not love Thomas as he so obviously loved her. The thought chilled Isabella.

But Catherine was her friend and must be aided in any way possible. If her state of mind could be eased, then it should follow that her health would similarly improve. Somehow to widen her horizon beyond these four walls that she regarded as a cage was the first step.

"I only wish that a little of your time of waiting for your baby could be diverted to my good use in London while I'm on my travels," Isabella said with perfect truth.

"What do you mean?" Catherine looked puzzled.

"I dearly need someone I can trust to keep charge of my house in my absence. I have a steward to ensure order and protection, but a friend's personal visits would be something quite different."

"I could go there on my good days," Catherine volunteered.

"Would you? Oh, it would mean so much to me." Isabella was entirely sincere. "You can rest when you get to the house, and my library is full of books—still unlisted, I'm afraid—and you could read or take home whatever catches your interest."

"I will do it," Catherine promised. "And you? Shall you be home in April before I'm brought to bed?"

"I cannot say. If the winter roads permit, I plan to travel to Italy."

"May I ask you a great favour? Would you be godmother to our firstborn? Thomas and I would be greatly honoured. If you should not be home in time for the baptism, one of my sisters could stand as proxy for you."

Isabella felt herself blanch. Fate was decreeing that her life and

195

Thomas's should be inextricably linked until the end of their days through a child yet to be born. It was as if, however hard she tried to run from him, it was only to find that a circular path had brought her back to him again. She answered huskily, "I will be godmother to your child."

Chapter Five

A week after her visit to the Chippendales' home Isabella departed for the Continent. All her life she was to remember her time in Italy. Its mellow colours and tarnished splendours, the spectacle of teeming life in the streets and piazzas, all were like an animated tapestry being unfolded especially for her.

She was in Venice when she received some letters from home. One of them was from Catherine. Thomas, coming upon his wife writing it, had leaned down to plant a kiss on the nape of her neck, then perched on the edge of the table, the better to see her. To his relief she had overcome her earlier resentment about the baby, and often he would hear her singing to herself.

"I'm writing to Isabella," she said by way of explanation. "I want her to know that all is well at her home."

"How could it be otherwise when you have it under constant surveillance?" he said teasingly.

She made a little face at him. "Would you have me neglect my promised duty to a kind friend?"

"Not at all. Yet I cannot believe that she expected you to spend as many hours there as you do here. How do you pass the time?"

She looked away from him, avoiding his gaze. "It's an elegant house. I like being in it," she replied evasively.

196

He reached out and took her by the shoulders, looking down into her face. "I'm thankful to see you content. But one day you shall have all you lack now under your own roof." He kissed her soft lips before leaving her on her own to finish the letter.

She frowned briefly, thinking of how she really spent her time at Arlington Street. Isabella would approve, although Thomas would not, thinking she had deliberately flouted his wishes by taking on a clerical task every bit as demanding as his bookkeeping had been. She had almost completed the cataloguing of the several hundred books in Isabella's library.

Three weeks later he caught her redhanded at it. He had called in to take her home, the afternoon being late. How long he had been standing in the open doorway of the library watching her work she had no idea.

It made his heart contract painfully to see the fear and defiance in her face. Did she think him such an ogre that a role must be played for his benefit? At best Catherine did not open up her innermost thoughts to him, always holding back something of herself. Although for him this added to her allure, it was a portent of disaster for living together in harmony.

She spoke first in a quavering voice that tore at him. "Please try to understand," she implored. "I cannot endure to be idle. Just consider how my humour has improved since I became engaged in this work, and with it my health. Weigh all this up and let me complete my task."

After a moment or two he said, "But what comes afterwards? When your task is done, time will lie heavily on your hands again." He paused, coming to a decision. "Instead, I would take it as a great favour if you should help me at home in the preparation of a book. I have long wished to publish my designs for furniture—a selection in the Gothic, Chinese, and modern taste. I have the title quite decided. *The Gentleman and Cabinet-Maker's Director*. What do you say, Catherine? Will you be my right hand in this venture?"

Her eyes shining, she gasped, "Yes, Thomas! Oh, yes."

In the weeks that followed Catherine became absorbed in sorting through the hundreds of designs that Thomas had drawn over a number of years. Whenever Thomas had time to spare he gave a hand, and they worked in happiness together. Hundreds of letters

would have to be written to summon up subscribers to offset the mighty cost of publication. The copper-plate engravings alone, done by Matthias Darly, would cost two pounds each. But Thomas was determined that *The Gentleman and Cabinet-Maker's Director* should win a place alongside the great architectural books of the day.

Isabella read the news from Catherine of all that was taking place, and immediately she wrote to ask that her name head the list of subscribers. She thought what pleasure it would be to own a book of Thomas's splendid drawings.

From Venice Isabella had gone to Rome, and winter had given way to spring before she came to Florence, a glittering white and russet city set like a jewel in the Tuscan hills lush with vineyards and olive groves and flowers everywhere. She had secured a large and palatial villa for her sojourn in Florence with the aid of an English diplomat, Sir Horace Mann.

In Florence, there was a large number of English residents, some there for their health, others with commercial interests or attached to the embassy, and almost all entertained a steady stream of visiting fellow countrymen. In no time at all Isabella found herself with many invitations, one to a masquerade the evening after her arrival. She wore a white panniered dress dripping with crystal beads, a black satin mask and a charming Venetian tricorn hat of black velvet.

It was a dazzling occasion, held at Sir Horace's residence. Isabella was soon singled out by her striking attire, but since there was no unmasking until midnight, her identity would remain a secret until then with everyone except the host. She was therefore surprised when he brought a tall man in a gold mask across the ballroom floor to her and said, "My dear lady, I present to you a gentleman who has pierced your disguise. He works closely with me in the service of our King, which is how he happened to hear of your coming to Florence. I am to have no peace until he and his sister have drawn you into their own company for supper. Such impatience! I made one stipulation. You must guess his identity before granting him that privilege."

Isabella smiled in puzzlement at the stranger whose eyes twinkled through the slits of the mask. His squarish chin was slightly cleft, but it was impossible to tell the colour of his hair since it was powdered white as fashion decreed for grand occasions. "I have to confess myself baffled," she admitted. "Am I allowed a clue?"

"None!" her host replied jovially. "Now, madam! Shall you take the risk and talk to him in an attempt to solve the mystery?"

Isabella laughed. "Gladly," she endorsed.

"Then I leave you to each other."

"I'm honoured, Isabella," the stranger said. He escorted her away from the ballroom into one of the mosaic-floored corridors. "I was watching for you from the moment this evening began, eager to renew our acquaintanceship."

She knew him. Oh, yes! It had been a long, long time, but in speaking to her his voice brought back a flood of happy memories of a Christmas in Yorkshire and of garlands of winter evergreens, and the mistletoe under which he had once kissed her in the frivolity of the moment. She gave him a dazzling smile of pure joy. "Owen! Owen Marwell! I do declare!"

He flung back his head and laughed heartily. "Well done! I cannot have changed so much after all." He whisked off his mask.

There burst from her an involuntary cry for the loss of sweet, young years. "Why did that Christmas at your father's house ever have to end? I have never spent a happier one since."

"It stands out in my memory, too. Naturally I did not know then that it would be the last one I should spend there, but shortly afterwards I joined the Diplomatic Service and have thus been engaged in foreign parts ever since."

"Sir Horace mentioned your sister. When am I to see Lorinda again?"

"Any moment now." He glanced around him. "She and her husband, Claude Pargeter, are here tonight. I told them to find us in the drawing room. We had better go along now, for if we are sighted without our masks we'll be liable for forfeits that will be less agreeable than the one I once claimed from you!"

So he remembered! Willingly she let him catch her by the elbow, and like runaway children they sped down the corridor to a room at the far end. When they were safely inside he shut the door after them and leaned against it, amused to see that she was breathless and excited as she collapsed onto a sofa. "This is how it was that Christmas," she laughed. "Full of hilarious games and wild chases. Have you not grown up at all, Owen Marwell?"

He twisted his mouth wryly. "Too much, I fear."

The shift in his mood encompassed her. "So it has been with me," she said soberly. He came and sat turned towards her on the sofa. "Have you been long in Italy?" she asked.

"Nearly seven years. What made you decide to set out on your travels?"

"Does one have to have a reason beyond a desire to see foreign places?"

"No. It is simply unusual for a women to undertake such a tour without the escort of husband, father, or brother."

"Since I'm a widow and have no close male relative, do you consider that I should have stayed at home?"

He shook his head. "No. Forgive me—but I have my reasons. My wife and son were murdered by brigands four years ago when travelling from Milan to join me here in Florence."

Her face was stricken. "My dear Owen. What a tragedy!" Impulsively she reached out her hand and put it on his arm to convey all the sympathy that could not be put into words. "I wish I had known her."

He looked at her with a faint smile. "You did. Or, at least, you met her at our house at Cawood."

Isabella searched her memory. "Yes, I do remember her. She danced more with you than with anyone else."

"That was Nesta." Then he hesitated, eyeing Isabella reflectively before he spoke again. "She did not speak to me for two days after the night I kissed you. I thought you beautiful then. I find you still lovelier now."

She made no answer. Many men paid her such compliments. At twenty-nine, with her looks at their zenith, she was pursued more fervently than she had ever been in her younger days. "If you will allow me, Isabella, I hope to make your sojourn one that you will remember with as much happiness as you found at Cawood."

She looked up into his face, her eyes warming. "That is most kind, Owen. It should not be difficult to match that wintertime in Yorkshire with the magic of a Florentine spring to aid us."

"Then let us make a beginning," he said, half smiling.

They moved towards each other. He put his hands on her narrow waist and drew her close to him. Her response to his kiss was one of unexpectedly deep delight. They drew apart reluctantly. She was left with a sweet exhilaration of spirit.

The door burst open and Lorinda came sweeping into the room in a frenzied rustling of mimosa silk, her discarded mask trailing ribbons in her hands, her husband in her wake. She gave an excited squeal at the sight of Isabella, and they embraced, both talking at once. Her husband, Claude, had a shy manner and little conversation, well content to let his wife hold the floor. Isabella liked him and thought he had kind eyes.

Before long Isabella began to believe that in Florence she had found everything for which she had left her native shores. She danced, went to the theatre, listened to grand concerts, and danced again. And since Owen was her constant companion it was inevitable and to her great joy that she felt herself being drawn irrevocably to the time when they should make love.

The moment when it came was sweetly unexpected. They had ridden out from Florence into the sun-drenched countryside, and had come to the ruins of an ancient villa. Leaving the horses tethered, they entered the ruins hand in hand. A natural spring had been ingeniously channelled through an ornamental spout to cascade into a pool of green marble, and the water was clean and pure.

Isabella wandered around the edge of the pool, and when she reached wide steps leading down into it, she put her hands to her bodice and began to unfasten it. When she had removed all her clothing, except a knee-length chemise that wafted transparently against her, she went down into the water.

He disrobed completely and slid down into the pool to swim across to her. They swam together, limbs entwining, and then he put his arm about her shoulders to guide her towards the steps. They emerged from the pool and she came into his arms like another Aphrodite.

It was the new beginning for which she had yearned. With every shared kiss and loving murmur, her heart was being released from old shadows as freely as her body had shed its covering. "I love you," he whispered against her lips, her hair, her flesh. And she echoed his words with a force that almost stopped his heart and hers in the full perfection of love.

THOMAS STOOD with his hands on his hips, grimly surveying the smashed mirror being uncrated in the yard after its return to the workshop. He was enraged that such an expensive item should have arrived cracked at its destination. It was insured, as were all his goods sent out any distance, but the greatest harm lay in the displeasure and disappointment of the customer. In the steady building up of his business it was essential to generate goodwill.

With a sigh Thomas started towards his office to instruct his clerk to make out an insurance claim. Before he could reach it, he saw Catherine coming from the building with some haste. One look at her taut, bone-white face told him why she was searching. "Get back indoors," he said reassuringly, supporting her elbow to aid her. "I'll call in the neighbourwoman and send for the midwife."

The rest of the day was the longest he had ever known. As hour after hour went by a stark look came into his eyes as his young wife's half strangled cries penetrated the closed windows of the room where she lay. To add to his misery, the women would not let him in to see her or to give her some loving word of encouragement.

Not long before midnight Catherine began to scream. Long, terrible screams that rang through his head until he thought he would go crazy with despair. Then with a final great cry, she gave forth his child.

A boy. He had a son! A *son!* Three weeks later, on the twenty-third day of April in that year of 1749, the Chippendales took their son to the neighbouring church of St. Paul's, and there he was baptized Thomas. One of his baptismal gifts was an engraved box of Italian silver from his godmother, for whom one of his aunts had stood proxy.

TOMMY WAS A STRONG and healthy baby, and after the first few weeks he rarely disturbed his parents once he was in his cradle for the night, enabling Catherine to devote many evening hours to writing letters to possible subscribers for *The Gentleman and Cabinet-Maker's Director*.

Thomas's business was flourishing. It would have been no hardship to rent a good-size house for them, but the truth was that it suited him to live on the workshop premises. All along he had hoped to move business and living quarters together when the time was ripe. But when Tommy was barely nine months old Catherine was already two months gone with child again. She could not be expected to start rearing a second infant in these cramped rooms. So a house was found in Conduit Court, Long Acre, a mere stone's throw from the workshop. Catherine was so thankful to move into her new home that she did not mind that their furnishings were still modest. Already Thomas was talking as if they would not be long in Conduit Court and this did not displease her. Any future changes would be a sign of progress.

ISABELLA WAS presently having her portrait painted by the most eminent artist in Florence. She was keeping the sittings a secret from Owen, planning to make it her gift to him on their wedding day. But as the weeks went by Owen never once broached the subject of marriage. He was ardent, always talking of their love in terms of the rest of their lives, but the question she longed to hear was never forthcoming.

The day came when she knew the outcome must be settled once and for all. She waited until evening. They sat down to supper at the candlelit table on the terrace of his residence that overlooked the garden. As always, he was loving and attentive, preferring to dismiss the servants and wait on her himself. But now she found it impossible to relax. Later, when they strolled through the garden in the warm autumn night, he eased the way for what she had to tell him. "You have been so quiet this evening," he said thoughtfully. "What is troubling you?"

"The time has come for me to leave Florence," she replied in a choked voice. "I plan to leave at the end of the week."

"Shall you go back to England?"

She was sick with disappointment that he had made no protest. "That is my destination."

"Then we'll meet again in London."

Hope soared in her. "Oh, when? When?"

He turned and cupped his hand against her cheek, looking down into her eyes. "I cannot say when it will be. It depends how long my duties keep me in Italy. I'm needed here in more ways than you could understand. I wish I could ask you to remain with me in this city, but I have to let you go."

"For mercy's sake," she cried in despair. "Did you make some lover's vow to Nesta that no other woman should ever take her place?"

"No," he exclaimed, gathering her to him. "Nesta has never been a barrier between us. I look forward to the day when nothing shall part us ever again. In the meantime I ask you to never doubt that I love you and always will."

She sagged against him in a half-swoon of despair. It would be easier to die than live out time not knowing how long it would be before they met again. Then his next words, although spoken with love and tenderness, only served to increase her anguish.

"This then is our last night together. I must leave for the Court of Rome in the morning. When I return to Florence you will be gone."

It was a night of loving that surpassed her wildest dreams. She was his—heart, soul, and body, completely and utterly his, even more than he knew or guessed. At dawn he left, and when she awoke he was many miles on the road to Rome.

On the eve of her departure from Florence, Isabella said farewell to Lorinda and Claude. Lorinda was full of plans for visiting Isabella in London and with arms linked, the two young women went down the steps to the courtyard where Claude was waiting by the carriage. Suddenly Isabella came to a standstill and faced Owen's sister directly. "Why?" she demanded brokenly, having no need to say more.

Lorinda put a consoling hand over Isabella's. "Give my brother time. In any case, whatever happens, things will change."

"What things?" Isabella inquired quickly. "Please explain."

Lorinda gulped, overcome with confusion, seeking some way to answer. Then the words came in a rush, almost as if on the surge of inspiration.

"My brother would never let the world brand him as a fortune-hunter, and you are possessed of a great fortune. How could Owen offer marriage when he has almost no money of his own?"

So that was it. For a few dreadful moments it was as if Lorinda had had some dark secret to keep from her. Instead it was all perfectly simple. She released a long, slow sigh.

Isabella waved until their carriage was out of sight, and then light-heartedly went inside. "I have changed my mind about leaving," she informed Amy gaily. "Florence may claim me for a long time yet."

"Forgive me, madam," Amy replied crisply. "Is that wise?"

Isabella gave her a keen glance. As yet, Amy was the only one who shared a secret about her condition that not even Owen suspected. "I appreciate your concern. Have no fear. Much has been explained to me."

Amy continued to have doubts, for she had heard disquieting things on the servants' grapevine about her mistress's lover, but it was not her business to interfere. Isabella was convinced that the problem of her wealth could be easily eliminated. She was filled with eagerness to see Owen again.

Early on the morning of his return, Isabella arrived at his villa as his baggage was beginning to be unloaded. She sped past the busy servants into the cool marble hall that she had thought never to enter again. She heard his voice on the terrace overlooking the garden and ran towards it. The terrace doors were standing wide. She came to an abrupt halt as if suddenly transfixed by the sight held in framework there. It was a perfect domestic scene.

Seated at the table laid for breakfast was a woman in a silk and lace boudoir robe. A Florentine woman with huge, dark eyes, masses of black hair, and a skin with a golden bloom. Owen had just kissed her on the lips. Two little black-haired boys were clamouring for his attention, and laughing, he turned and swung the first boy high in the air. Then he saw her.

His gaze hardened as he put down the boy. He said something briefly to the woman and stepped inside and closed the doors to the terrace. Isabella was perfectly still, the only movement about her in the aspen-shiver of the pearl ear-drops that she wore. "Why are you here?" he asked gravely.

"Your sister tried to placate me with some invented tale of how my fortune stood between us. So I came back. I had decided on a way by which that impasse might be solved. I had not the faintest notion that she had lied to me."

"She did not lie, although if that was all that kept us apart I would have spoken frankly of it. As it is, she did not tell you the other side of it."

"Who is the woman on the terrace? Is she your wife?"

"No. Her name is Maria Corradini. She is another man's wife."

"The children? Are they yours?"

"No. But I care for them as if they were my own."

She fought against a strangling sensation in her throat. "No sooner am I gone than this Corradini woman is reinstated in your affections. Is this the pattern of your life in Florence?"

"Isabella!" His eyes darkened at her accusation. "Do not judge me so swiftly. It is not through choice."

Her initial shock was turning to anger and an unbearable heartache. "How you must love this woman!"

"I have a deep affection for her. She came into my life after I lost Nesta and my own son. She gave me consolation and love."

"So you have formed a lasting liaison on the strength of a harlot's accomplishments." Her bitterness made bile in her mouth.

"You defame her, Isabella. I take all the blame. She is a noblewoman who had nothing to taint her good name before I took advantage of her loneliness in a need to assuage my own."

Isabella caught her breath on a sudden revelation of memory. "I recall her surname now. Did I not hear that her husband was imprisoned by the Grand Duke himself?"

"That is correct. Corradini was charged with treason and incarcerated for ten years. At least Maria can pay for him to have every comfort possible for a man in a cell; good food, medical attention."

"A salve for her conscience, no doubt!"

Owen looked grim. "I tell you again she is blameless. You have been in Italy long enough to know that the most cruel punishments for crime are not yet outmoded here. Men's spines are broken on the *cavelletto*, and for little more than a misdemeanour, unfortunate beings are strung up by their arms to be witnessed by those with a liking for such spectacle." A shiver of abhorrence went through her.

"I tell you that Corradini was tortured in such a way. Now his mind is quite gone. If I have helped to ease Maria's burden by caring for her and her sons I have not the least regret. My only sorrow is that it has brought about a breach between us."

207

Nothing he said could drive out her own sense of hurt and betrayal. "I can understand how you and she were drawn together," she said, "but why should you take her back into your house if you love me as you say you do?"

"I did not take her back. She lives here."

For a few seconds the full significance of what he had said did not dawn on her. "You mean that she was here—all the time we—?" Her cheeks became completely devoid of colour.

"This villa is spacious. One wing is an entire apartment."

It was like some awful game of truth revealed without mercy. Owen came closer and took her by the shoulders, but she flung herself back from him. "Do not touch me!"

His face tautened. "Isabella, I did *not* go from your arms to hers and back again. There was only you."

She shuddered convulsively. "She was *here*."

"I could not turn her out. Not even for you, Isabella. The stark truth is that without me she would kill herself."

She stared at him in tormented disbelief. "Then you have made your choice, Owen. Everything is over between us."

She turned and left the house, giving no backward glance. At her own villa she found Amy waiting for her. "We are leaving at once, Amy. At once! I want to get home!" She put her clenched fists to her temples in desperation. "Dear God! Let me get home!"

Amy watched her run past and up the stairs, thinking that she could have pulled the one string that would take Owen Marwell away from any number of fancy women. But Isabella Trench would not coerce for love.

They left within the hour. It was to be a long and tiring journey, the need to be safely home drumming at Isabella with increasing urgency. But it was a lost cause. In a village thirty miles south of Genoa, in a loft room, which was the only accommodation available, Isabella miscarried in terrible distress the longed-for child that had been conceived in past halcyon days.

WHEN ISABELLA returned to London, she had been away two years. Much had happened in her absence. The new heir to the throne was a boy who would one day be George III. London itself was spreading out at a remarkable speed, and the prosperity of its trade and commerce, the splendour of its new buildings, gave it a throb and vitality that made Isabella realize how much she had missed it while away.

Her first outing was to visit the Chippendales and see her godson. A second boy, named Edward, had been born to them, giving them two children within fifteen months. As soon as Isabella arrived at Conduit Court, Thomas came to meet her, hurrying with hands outstretched. "My dear Isabella! Welcome home again."

She was not prepared for the effect that seeing him again would have on her. It had been her belief that Owen had made her whole heart his own, but she realized with a pang that her rock-like love for Thomas had endured throughout the great passion for another. What she felt for him was calmer now, and yet as she put her hands into his, she knew a sense of belonging that nothing could sever.

"Ah. I see my son and heir has come to meet you," Thomas said, a proud smile curling his mouth.

Advancing towards them was a strong-looking toddler with round apple cheeks and black hair. Isabella stooped and held out her arms to him. He regarded her gravely with eyes as dark as his father's, and then shyly came to her. She scooped him up in a rush of love.

Chapter Six

Catherine sat on a window seat looking out listlessly at Somerset Court. She was in mourning for little Edward, who had failed to reach his second natal day. Once she would have thought herself a queen to live at this new address, the house far more elegant than their previous home in Conduit Court, but to her it was just a place of walls and a roof, simply because little Edward had died there.

Fortunately, it now seemed that they were likely to move again. Only this morning Thomas had gone to take possession of some property in St. Martin's Lane, which would allow their home to be adjacent again to his workshops, for he was a man who would live, breathe, eat, and sleep with his work if it were possible. At times she had wished he would remove his bed there and give her complete respite from his ardent lovemaking.

For herself, she could find no way of escaping from the numbness of soul and body that afflicted her after Edward was born. From the moment she had heard his first weak cry, it was as if all else but a powerful maternal love was struck from her. When the battle for his life had been lost she sat for hours with her hands idle in her lap and grief heavy in her heart. Thomas had tried to involve her in the drafting of notices and advertisements for *The Director*, which would be a masterpiece when eventually it appeared. Its glorious designs were free of any of the heavy ornamentation of the past, and acanthus was pruned as rigorously as if cut back by a meticulous gardener. Instead, each drawing rioted in the elegant splendour of Rococo or Gothic or Chinoiserie, which could not fail to make a most tremendous impact on anyone even remotely knowledgeable about fashion in furniture. She had struggled to pen what Thomas required of her, only to collapse in desperate sobbing for the baby she had lost.

As Thomas came into St. Martin's Lane his wife was not on his mind. Her listlessness worried him enormously, but whenever he left his house, all personal problems remained there. If not, his work and their livelihood would have suffered. In his pocket were the keys to the property that was now his, a block of three houses with yards and outbuildings to the rear, which were the sixtieth, sixty-first, and sixty-second buildings facing St. Martin's Lane. There were a number of prosperous businesses on the fashionable thoroughfare, displaying in their bow windows everything from clocks and Chelsea porcelain to befeathered hats and the choicest of fruits. Being also at the heart of the furniture trade, it seemed to Thomas to be the ideal site from which he could expect to become widely known and greatly acclaimed.

The yard and outbuildings which had been used by a builder had been vacated, as were two of the three houses. He planned to make

210

his home in No. 60. No. 61 was already fitted out as a shop where customers could select from stock or study patterns and place their orders, and No. 62 was to be the residence of his newly acquired partner, James Rannie, who had put up some of the money necessary for expansion, and was to come in on the soft furnishings side. But No. 60 had remained locked and barred, the tenant, a widow named Anne Davis, refusing to admit him. She was in arrears with the rent and had taken fright, no doubt believing that she was to be arrested for debt. He did not blame anyone for dreading the filth and squalor of a debtors' prison but since the property was now his, the widow today was to be forcibly evicted.

As he approached No. 60 he saw the two bailiffs, both big, burly men, awaiting him at the door. "Good day to you, sir," the first man said. "Morgan is my name, and this 'ere is Wickham. We'll ask the tenant for admission on the hour, and if the door ain't opened prompt, then in we go."

"I want no violence," Thomas stipulated sternly. "The widow has a young daughter, and they are both to be treated with respect."

Morgan eyed him cynically, then he gave his companion a sharp nod and Wickham's huge fist hammered with a force that made the door shake. Neither man gave time for the bolt to be drawn back, one smashing a boot home against the door, the other thundering in to the sound of a scream of fright somewhere in the house. Thomas rushed in after them and in a large and completely bare room Anne Davis, a poorly clad, sickly-looking woman, stood cowering with her terrified, copper-haired daughter of about nine years clutched to her.

"Don't 'arm us, I beg you," the woman implored, her lips quivering with apprehension.

Morgan snarled at her. "That depends on 'ow you behave. Where's your furniture?"

"I 'ave none. It is all sold. Every stick of it."

"We'll see!" He and his companion went off to take a look for themselves, and the widow, trying to soothe her daughter by stroking her hair, faced Thomas fearfully. "You're Mr. Chippendale. I've seen you several times. Do not ask me for the money that I got for selling the furniture. It 'as gone on keeping me and Elizabeth alive. Now we 'ave nowhere to go." She gulped nervously. "What is to 'appen to us?"

"Nothing as far as I'm concerned, madam," he replied stiffly. "I would simply be obliged if you would vacate my property."

"No, Mamma, no," the girl wailed, pressing herself against her mother. "I won't leave our 'ome. I won't!" Then she withdrew from her mother's arms and turned to face him with huge grey eyes aswim with tears, and tendrils of her rich-coloured hair clinging in strands to her damp cheeks. "I've seen what 'appens to people without 'omes. Please don't turn us out, sir. *Please*."

To Thomas it was as if echoes from the past were drumming in his ears. He could have been a boy again in the Otley workshop. This child did not resemble Polly, but there was something about the eyes, the hair, and in the stubborn refusal to give up fighting that for a matter of seconds made Elizabeth Davis become Polly to him. He looked from her to her mother. "How did you come to live here in the first place?"

"My 'usband was foreman to the builder that 'ad the workshops until there was an accident. 'E had a terrible fall and was never able to work again. I nursed 'im till 'e died, and by then most of our money 'ad gone."

Thomas drew from his pocket a notebook and pencil. "You have to go from this house, I cannot change that. But I'll give you a letter to take with you to an address in Arlington Street where I know you will find domestic employment and be given a roof over your head."

The girl reacted instantly, hugging her mother in a speechless expression of relief at this timely deliverance. Thomas wrote a few words of explanation to Isabella. She would understand that Catherine in her present state could not be troubled by the settling in of two new servants. He handed the note to Anne Davis. "My most 'eartfelt thanks. Mr. Chippendale," the woman mumbled, still dazed.

He went to the front door with her. "Good day, Mrs. Davis," he said. "Good day, Elizabeth."

The girl had hung back in her mother's wake, and now she rushed forward to snatch up his hand and kiss it, looking up into his face with such dazzling gratitude that he was quite taken aback. Then she ran out into the street to her mother's side.

212

The bailiffs were soon gone and he began to inspect the house. All the rooms were a good size and well proportioned, although there was none of the refinement of detail that he would add to it. He decided to have new fireplaces and he would enlarge doorways and create and ornament alcoves with delicate mouldings as well as carry out a number of other improvements.

He left the house by a back door that led into the extensive cobbled yard and began to stroll the length of it. Two-storeyed buildings stood on either side and at the far end was another building, three-storeyed this time. He went into each in turn, to check that nothing was amiss. Tomorrow work should begin on clearing out rubbish left by the builder, and also the muck left by the homeless and destitute who had taken advantage of the empty buildings for night shelter. It was probably glimpses of these ragged sleeping creatures that had added to little Elizabeth Davis's terror of leaving the security of a home.

As he was about to leave the building that was to be the upholsterers' shop he shook his head at the sight of the ashes of a fire. It was fortunate the place had not burned down. Then something about a bundle in a dark corner made him pause and stare. Was it a body? He went towards the bundle and saw a long tangle of black hair. The woman was lying face downwards on some straw, with more straw pulled over her emaciated form. He pushed it aside to feel for a pulse in her neck. She was not dead. The pulse was faint, but it was there. He turned her over and put an arm under her shoulders, smoothing away the hair that had fallen across her face. Then, in spite of the dirt and the sores about her closed eyes and her mouth, he recognized her instantly.

"Sarah!" There was no response. He quickly carried her out into the Lane and summoned a hackney coach. It did not take long to reach Arlington Street.

Isabella, seeing him there with the woman limp in his arms, the long, black hair hanging dusty with straw, gave a stunned gasp of recognition.

"She's alive," he said at once, "but very ill."

Instantly Isabella sent for the doctor and ran herself to lead the way up to a bedchamber. Thomas put Sarah carefully down, and when two maids arrived to give assistance, Isabella went out to the landing with Thomas. For the second time that day he was given a look of overwhelming gratitude. "You found my sister, Thomas. I'll be for ever in your debt." Impulsively she kissed him lightly on the lips. It was a moment of unexpected sweetness for both of them.

For several weeks Sarah hovered between life and death. But Isabella's constant nursing and the best of nourishment gradually restored her strength to the point where she could sit out of bed for short spells at a time. Isabella summoned Augusta, who made the journey to London and stayed nearby with acquaintances. At first Sarah had only recognized her mother by voice. Her whole face had become disfigured by the mercurial paint she had used over the years, a fate common to many who ignored the warnings of doctors that expiration through the use of cosmetics was a legitimate entry on a death certificate. Sarah, whose own skin had suffered through an excess of painting, groaned at the sight in a handglass of her sunken eyes and pock-marked cheeks in a face as white as the pillows against which she was propped.

"I've become a hag. My face is more pox-pitted than ever from that scourge that changed my whole life."

It had been a sad and harrowing experience for her. Fêted and praised by audiences, usually on excitingly tempestuous terms with fellow stage-players, she had believed herself loved by her leading actor of long standing, Sebastian Searle, and had loved him to the extent of which she was capable. Then they had arrived in Norwich to open in a week's run of *The Beaux' Stratagem* and she suddenly collapsed.

She felt better once she was lying down in their lodgings, going to sleep almost at once. They slept late. He rose from the bed first and drew back the curtains, letting in the sunshine and turning to look towards her. Then disgust and revulsion swept over his face at the sight of the first blisters of the dreaded smallpox on her visage. Powerless to lift her aching head from the pillow, she watched with pure fright and disbelief as he threw on his clothes, snatched all his belongings together, and dashed from the room, deserting her in her most urgent hour of need. When the landlady discovered that the travelling players had left the city with all speed, abandoning their responsibilities, her husband and another man came, each taking up an end of the sheet on which Sarah was lying, to carry her

214

to the steps of a parsonage. Nursed there by an old woman who had survived smallpox, which was known not to strike a second time, she was turned out to fend for herself as soon as she was able to stand weakly on her feet.

The landlady at the lodgings declared that the actor had returned to take all her possessions away, which Sarah knew to be a lie, and she had been given only charity clothes and a shilling from the church poorbox to help her on her way. With the coin in her pocket she set out for London, hoping for work in one of the theatres there.

On the road she was given a lift now and again on a wagon or cart by a decent countryman, but she became weaker daily, her shoes wearing through and her clothes almost always damp from sleeping under hedges and in byres and grain sheds. By the time she reached London she was so ill with a fever of the lungs that she could hardly reason. Remembering that her sister had once lived in Soho Square, she managed to make her way there, going agonizingly from house to house asking for Mrs. Isabella Trench. She drew a blank at all the houses except one. There an elderly butler told her he recalled a mention that Mrs. Trench was in Italy or France or some such foreign land.

The information was long out of date, but Sarah in her ignorance was left completely at a loss. Now she had nowhere to go and no one to whom she could turn.

All she could do in her exhausted state was to follow others into niches of shelter for the night, lying curled up in stinking darkness where rats scuttled. She could just remember the premises in St. Martin's Lane where, shivering with cold, instinctively she had burrowed into some straw. After that she remembered nothing until she found herself in a clean, soft bed at Arlington Street.

As her strength gradually returned it was matched by increasing envious resentment. Her sister had fashionable clothes and sumptuous furnishings and all the other touches that came from wealth. Isabella had also regained an association with Tom Chippendale, although it was presumably on a platonic level. Nevertheless, it seemed to Sarah that her sister had far more than a fair share of life's abundance.

Sarah refused to see anybody socially before she deemed her appearance fit, calling in women who had set themselves up as counsellors on beauty, wanting to know how best to fill the pox-pits on her cheek and to restore the bloom to her skin. Each left her with phials of beautifying water and pots of paints—all of which Isabella paid for. New dresses were ordered also, and she played like a child for hours with the bolts of silk, satin, velvet, and lace unrolled for her inspection. Sarah, who knew that nothing flattered her more than a glorious green to enhance her eyes, wore a new dress in that shade, with her black hair dressed high, on the day that Thomas and Catherine had been invited to dine.

She waited upstairs until she heard them arrive. Then, with her actress instincts timing the exact moment, she made her entrance, pausing just inside the room with a theatrical swirl of her fan. She saw Thomas rise to his feet with a darkening of colour. She knew she had always excited him, no matter how much he disliked her. As for his wife, who was dressed depressingly in black, Sarah had an impression of a drawn face, a firm carriage of head, and long, pretty hands. So this was the woman who had outweighed all the others in Tom's favours. Sarah smiled as presentations were made, and then turned to the man she had wanted savagely, won briefly, and lost again. "Dearest Tom! You saved my life. I'm for ever in your debt. If only you would tell me how I might at least repay you one sweet portion."

She was mocking and inviting him at the same time. She had not changed her ways. "Just seeing you alive and well is repayment enough."

She laughed, head thrown back, emphasizing the expanse of bosom. Catherine, watching her, was embarrassed by her flaunting, and although there was plenty of lively discussion throughout dinner, Catherine was quiet on the whole and took little part. She saw that Thomas drank far more than usual. She noticed, when there was a reference to Nostell, that all three of them skirted it with talk of something else. For the first time she caught a faint, unguarded glow of fondness in Isabella's eyes whenever she looked at Thomas. As for Sarah, there was enticement in her every glance.

Later, as Thomas drove Catherine home in the phaeton he had acquired, she kept a hostile silence the whole way. He had been too merry with wine to notice that she, his wife, had been at an

216

unhappy loss the whole evening, her heart still raw with pain. Irrational and illogical though it might be, she wanted him to solace her, not only for a lost child, but for a lost sweetheart about whose existence he had never been told.

At Somerset Court she went straight up to their bedchamber, and she was in bed by the time Thomas had seen to the horse and come reeling up the stairs himself. His merriness was quite unabated and he sang and whistled as he undressed.

Lifting the bedclothes he slid in beside her, unaware that her nerves were at screaming pitch. "My sweeting," he murmured, kissing her. "I love you more than there is depth to the sea or height in the sky."

It was natural to him to adore her with words. He thought her completely beautiful and never failed to tell her so. Yet these days she chose to withdraw within herself, deliberately isolating her whole being in the very circle of his arms. In his present wine-rosy state he was oblivious of all but his joy in her, not hearing or noticing her struggling protest as he made love to her until she began to sob uncontrollably.

He was completely sobered by her reaction, and there was a terrible look of bitterness in his eyes. He sat up slowly. "You have stopped loving me, Catherine," he said, stark hurt in his voice. "Or did you ever love me? I think I have known the truth for a considerable time, but could not bring myself to accept it." She, unable to bear his disillusionment, buried her face in the crook of her arm, still sobbing. She felt him go from the bed.

He was gone from the house when she came down to breakfast. He returned home to dine at six o'clock, and it was to all appearances as if nothing untoward had happened between them. It was not until the meal was finished that he made it clear that circumstances had changed a great deal. "Over half the rooms are ready for occupation now at No. 60. Today I have set up a truckle-bed there. I'll dine here each evening, and then Tommy will not miss me. When all has been completed at our new home, you may move in whenever you please."

He was giving her leeway as well as himself, a respite in which there would be either healing or a complete severance. "As you wish, Thomas," she replied austerely.

IT WAS CHRISTMAS, more than ten weeks later, before she went to live at No. 60. Most of the furniture had been removed there and installed the day before. Snow was falling heavily when she and Tommy arrived and as they alighted from the equipage she picked Tommy up in her arms and, holding him close, ascended the narrow front steps to the door. One of the maidservants, who had gone ahead with the last of the furniture, opened it for her.

"Mr. Chippendale is in the yard, madam. He asked to be told the moment you arrived."

"No, wait. I should like to walk around on my own first. Take Tommy to the kitchen and keep him amused for a while."

"Yes, madam." The maidservant took her mistress's cloak and hat away before taking Tommy by the hand along the passage and down to the basement kitchen. A fragrant aroma of hot gingerbread wafted out as the baize-lined door was opened and closed. The cook was already baking.

Catherine looked about the hall. All was light and airy, the coolness of ivory walls offset by the rich red-brown of the polished floor, and above a sidetable Thomas had hung one of his large, gilded girandoles, the foliated sprays holding tall candles. In the large drawing room, the one in which Thomas had first seen the widow and child who were now servants in Isabella's household, the walls were hung with blue and gold silk. To the furniture that had graced her drawing room at Somerset Square Thomas had added a truly magnificent rosewood pier table, its marquetry designs in harmony with the delicately shaded carpet and the white plaster-work of the ceiling.

She went into the other downstairs rooms, an eating parlour, a morning room, and the last a place of retreat for Thomas where he could work at peace, away from the interruptions of the office he had in one of the outbuildings. His books lined all four of its walls, making a dark background for his York furniture.

Upstairs were two bedchambers larger than the other rooms, one having a new fourposter, the other containing the fateful marriage bed. One of Thomas's books on the bedside table showed that he had slept there the previous night. The choice was hers. She could take the old bed or the new.

She was on the main landing again when she heard Thomas call

218

her name from the hall. She went to the head of the stairs and he looked up at her. The first thing he noticed was that in spite of her grave and serious air she was not in mourning. Her warm winter dress reminded him of ripe summer strawberries as she descended the stairs. "I have something to tell you," she said. She went past him into the drawing room, and as if cold, she drew close to the fire. "I am with child again."

There was no sound in the room except the ticking of the clock and the whisper of the flames. He knew this third child must have been conceived on the night that had been so dreadful to both of them. He said quietly, "It is out of darkness that light comes. This babe is blameless and will be welcomed by me."

She began to shake. She pressed both hands over her eyes, tears dropping like crystals from between her fingers. He could not stand by without putting his arms about her. At his touch she threw herself against him, her face buried in his shoulder. He did not know if she wept for herself, for the unwanted pregnancy, or for the yoke of a marriage that was hard on her.

When she became calmer she drew away. "I must go and do some unpacking."

He stayed her. "Wait a moment, do. What made you decide to discard your mourning clothes?"

"It is right to look to the future in this house, not the past. We must hope that all will be well with the child that is to come." He watched her go, listening to the sound of her footsteps as she entered the bedchamber above. It was the bedchamber where he slept. So they were to make a new beginning as husband and wife. Was such a process ever possible when only one partner loved the other? At least they would try.

WHEN AUGUST CAME Catherine gave birth to a daughter and it was fitting that this baby girl should bear her name. Conceived in misery, it was as if little Cathy intended to atone by being the happiest and most enchanting baby anyone could wish for. Both Catherine and Thomas doted on her. Although they had been unable to bridge the strained relationship between themselves in spite of effort on both sides, at least they were joined in mutual devotion to their daughter.

Little Thomas, now four years old, had already made up his mind to be a cabinet-maker, and went daily into the workshops with his father. The boy even had a collection of drawings that only he could recognize as designs for furniture. "They're goin' to be in my *Di'ector*," he would say seriously, ignoring the laughter that he caused.

The publication day of Thomas's book would be the twenty-third of March in the year of 1754. His list of subscribers held some of the most noble names in the land. Many were patrons, others interested in the book for its own sake, the name of Thomas Chippendale having gained an extraordinary momentum in a comparatively short time. He was particularly pleased that his former master, Richard Wood of York, had ordered three copies.

With his larger premises now, and an increase in his work force, he was able to supply curtains, carpets, wallpaper, chandeliers, mirrors, and all else needed in the decorating and furnishing of houses great and small. Still, in no way did he scorn the humbler customer, for in the shop he or she would find a showroom giving a wide choice of goods at a range of prices.

He had just finished furnishing a town house for Sarah at Isabella's expense, and it had been a most disagreeable task. The bonhomie falsely created by wine on that evening at Isabella's had never been revived, though every time they met Sarah would tease and tantalize, knowing full well that he was not immune to her attraction. If previous experience had not taught him that an encounter with Sarah was akin to opening Pandora's box, he might have been sorely tempted to take advantage of the opportunities she offered. He had little enough at home to keep him from straying if he had been so inclined. Catherine was dutiful to him, and that was all that could be said, although she who had harboured such resentment against her first pregnancy, had become the most maternal and possessive of mothers.

Sarah's house was at the corner of Southampton Street, a district where other actors and actresses resided and within convenient reach of the theatres. Sarah had recently been taken on at the Haymarket Theatre, and although her roles were minor ones, she was jubilant at being back on the stage. Today he was to see that all was finally as she wished at her new residence.

She had often found fault with his designs, glowered at the silks and brocades in all her favourite shades, and finally had tossed everything aside, demanding to see something worth considering next time. Thomas would never have returned if he had not realized how much Isabella must be longing for Sarah to have her own establishment.

During the past months, Isabella had not lost any true friends through her sister's outrageous behaviour, but they had endured much out of loyalty on her behalf. As an actress, Sarah had been too long in a world of emotions larger than life to conform to anything less hectic, her irrepressible exhibitionism sometimes startling the most liberal-minded in Isabella's sophisticated circle.

Lorinda and Claude Pargeter were two loyal friends who put up with Sarah's ill manners for Isabella's sake when they came to London. Although it brought heartache, she was always glad to hear news of Owen. He was now at the Court of Naples and had not been back to England since Isabella's departure from Italy. But he never failed to send her his most courteous regards, which she duly accepted and returned via Lorinda's next letter to him.

The Pargeters happened to be staying at Arlington Street when Sarah borrowed without asking and lost most carelessly a gold locket set with pearls that had been a gift from Owen. Isabella, who treasured it above all else, had difficulty in concealing her deep distress when the loss was discovered. The next day Lorinda seized a chance to speak to her. "I have something to ask you, and it is of great concern to me. Would you permit my brother to write to you?"

"Has that request come from Owen himself?"

"No, not directly. I happen to be able to read between the lines of his letters when he asks for word of you."

Isabella regarded her friend steadily. "Is Signora Corradini still his companion?"

Lorinda's cheeks flooded with embarrassed crimson. "That lady's home is in Florence, not Naples."

"Is her husband still alive?"

"No. He died some time ago."

"Then she has nothing to stop her residing where she pleases."

The reply came with impatience. "How can you be so harsh

towards a man you love? I saw your stricken face when the pendant that he gave you was lost."

"I treasure it only for its association with the past. You are simply making romantic and mistaken suppositions. Owen had a valid choice when I was in Florence."

"But he and Signora Corradini had no plans to marry."

"How can you be sure?"

Lorinda took a deep breath. "Would it make any difference if I told you that in his last letter Owen wrote that Signora Corradini is to wed someone else very shortly?"

Isabella's gaze did not falter, although her cheeks hollowed. "None at all," she replied succinctly. Then her voice took on a softer note. "He gave me the happiest hours of my life. It is simply that the knife of his deception went too deeply into me."

The two women looked at each other across the table, Lorinda's face crumpling with disappointment. They spoke no more of Owen Marwell, but Isabella's anguish and the sheer hungry yearning for him was as it had ever been.

It was not long afterwards that, with Sarah on the stage again, Isabella resolved that there should be no risk of her ever wandering penniless again. She made a financial arrangement on Sarah's behalf, with an income allotted to her so as to ensure a lifetime security that might otherwise have been gambled away. Sarah, who would have preferred the income without any strings attached, showed no gratitude, and Isabella had expected none. It was enough that the house in Arlington Street would be free at last of her disruptive presence.

WHEN *THE DIRECTOR* was published it became an immediate success. Thomas was acclaimed as being a fine artist and an ingenious author and artificer who had changed the whole face of design. He found himself swept forward on a high crest of fame that threw ripples far and wide. Orders for furniture flowed into the office in St. Martin's Lane from every part of the country, and Thomas's financial outlay became enormous. His premises were a veritable treasure house, not only of glorious woods, but of jasper, marble, ormolu, hand-painted Oriental wallpapers, lacquered panels, tapestries, rich Spitalfields silks, and expensive mirrors. He cut costs wherever he could. He was an astute businessman through and through. But the smooth running of his affairs was constantly disrupted by the failure of the wealthy to pay what they owed him promptly. Thomas always wrote himself to important patrons, penning letters that were suitably servile while at the same time pressing strongly for payment. Still, it was often his misfortune that a number of large outstanding accounts, amounting to thousands of pounds, would coincide, reducing him almost to penury for the time being.

That same year of 1754 saw the arrival of a second daughter, Mary. Although she was as dear to him as his other two children, little Cathy remained the giver of a special sunshine in his life. Warmly affectionate, she followed him about, eager to be picked up and set upon his shoulder. When work took Thomas far afield, which it did more and more, he found it was little Cathy he missed more than anyone else. His wife was always too occupied with nursery matters to spare any thought to his going away, and she had never once been at the door to welcome him back. They had drifted into a colourless existence, and although he had become resigned to the situation, it nevertheless saddened him.

NORMALLY THOMAS SLEPT heavily, so that when Catherine began to shake his shoulder vigorously one night, he had to stir from deepest slumber before he grasped what she was saying. "Fire! Thomas, wake up! There's a fire! In the workshops!"

He hurled himself from the bed, threw on some clothes and clattered down the stairs. Fire was the great dread of every citizen in London, but to a cabinet-maker with rooms full of furniture and stacks of wood, the threat was that in seconds the whole premises would become a blazing torch.

He gave the firebell a violent pull on its rope before he raced towards the far end of the yard where the three-storied block was ablaze. Behind him Rannie's house came to life, as did neighbouring residences. There would be no shortage of helping hands, and there would be need for every one of them. He snatched two fire buckets from a row on the wall and filled them from the horse trough before kicking open the door and plunging into the smoke and the heat.

Catherine had hastily dressed the three children and herself, and took them across the Lane to a neighbour's house where they were taken in. Returning to the scene of the fire, she rolled up her sleeves as she ran into the smoke-filled yard where sparks from the burning building were showering down like red-gold stars. There were two sweating men on each pump handle, and it was the same at the well. She joined the nearest bucket-chain and passed buckets along until it seemed her arms must be pulled from their sockets. Finally, with her strength completely gone, she let a bucket drop. Somebody took her by the shoulders and led her to a seat by the wall. "Take a rest now, Mrs. Chippendale."

She saw it was one of the elderly workmen, and his grey hair was singed. She sat down thankfully, and looked about her. The fire having become completely out of control, effort was being concentrated on the workshops near the burning building. On the highest roof of one already afire a man was balanced precariously, taking up buckets from those on a ladder. Catherine rose to her feet in horror. It was Thomas. One slip, and he could plunge into the flames he was trying so desperately to douse. "Merciful Saviour!" she breathed, "Don't let him fall!"

Then there swept through her a terrible realization of what life would be to her without him. A love such as she had never known existed gushed out of her heart, sweeping away the girlish dreams of what might have been with a man long gone. For the first time she saw how little she had appreciated her husband-lover. "Thomas!" The cry broke from her throat. Springing forward, she began to shoulder her way through the busy groups in her path, her dilated eyes fixed on the man on the roof. She got close enough to feel the heat like a furnace before Rannie himself grabbed and held her, hauling her back out of danger. "No, no, Mrs. Chippendale! This is no place for you!"

Then she stood as though transfixed, never taking her gaze from her husband. Others jostled her as they went about the business of fire-fighting, and still she stood there until dawn began to tint the sky and the flames to die down to no more than greyish plumes of smoke. She saw Thomas move to a ladder and descend, his face tired and blackened, and swiftly she darted to him. She would have thrown herself into his arms except that he, totally unused to any demonstration of affection from her, reacted automatically by

224

reaching out to grip her shoulders, while he scanned her face with concern. "Are you quite unharmed? And the children?"

"Safe. Quite safe." She swallowed hard. She wanted to bare her love to him and the words would not come.

"Good. Go back into the house now," he advised, giving her shoulder a hurried pat. "The fire is under control." He left her at a run and she stared bleakly after him. The moment was lost, probably for ever.

IT TOOK A WHILE to assess all the damage caused by the fire. Insurance would cover the rebuilding of the burned-out shell of what had been the cabinet-making section, but Thomas had lost many valuable pieces of furniture, water had stained or destroyed other items, and smoke had blackened bolts of fine fabric in the upholsterers' shop. It all added to the financial troubles that already beset him.

The smell of smoke in the house persisted for weeks, even though Catherine saw to the laundering of every curtain and bed-hanging and cushion, and had the whole place washed and polished from cellar to attic. She was pregnant again and was much troubled by a cough.

A third daughter was born and baptized with the name of Ann. In August of the following year another baby girl came and was named Dorothy. Twelve months later, a male child was baptized Edward after the little brother who had left such a lamented gap seven years ago in the family circle, which now numbered six offspring. Still Cathy continued to reign as the apple of her father's eye. It was she who always watched for his homecomings, even late at night leaping from her bed at the first roll of carriage wheels and in her nightgown running out of the door into the yard with fair hair flying. He would snatch her up and kiss her cheek, and be hugged in turn, thinking himself the most blessed of men to have such a daughter.

Isabella had bought a country house at Chiswick, not far from London and Thomas had supplied the furniture. It was not large, its wooded grounds a few acres, but she had become very fond of it and the house was usually filled with guests in summertime. One morning she returned from an exhilarating ride with a number of her guests to be told that a gentleman awaited her in the

226

drawing room. "His name?" she questioned, while the rest of the party went past her to the room where refreshment awaited them.

"Mr. Marwell, madam."

She thought her heart had stopped. Almost automatically she removed her hat, gave her hair a few touches to tidy some stray tendrils, and entered the drawing room.

Owen was standing in the middle of the room. He bowed to her. "I'm honoured that you would see me," he said, staring keenly at her as she approached. "I took hope from your acceptance of my compliments sent through Lorinda."

"There is no one with whom I'm not on speaking terms," she replied with restraint. "How are you, Owen?"

"In good health. And you? You look radiant from your ride." He spoke easily, as if only days instead of years had passed since they last met. Yet for her too much time of heartache lay between, and seeing him again she knew that she had not forgiven him for any of it. "Do sit down. What brings you back to England?"

He took a seat beside her on one of the sofas. "I have completed my duties in Italy and am spending a time in England before going on to the American Colonies where I am to take up a diplomatic post in New York."

"Have you been to the Palace?"

"I present myself there tomorrow afternoon. A ship brought me to London from Naples at dawn this morning. I went to Arlington Street, only to be told you were at Chiswick." He smiled, seeming to take the whole matter lightly, although the significance of her house being his first place of call was not lost on her.

"Should you wish to stay overnight before returning to London, that could be easily arranged. Would that fit in with your plans?"

"To perfection. From London I go north to Yorkshire. My parents are old and I shall visit them before leaving the country again by ship from Bristol."

Isabella smouldered. He had come back into her life then with no more intention than to disrupt it briefly with a stirring up of memories. For the rest of the day she managed to avoid being alone with him, and when supper was done she would have joined in the charades if he had not seized her firmly by the wrist and drawn her aside. "Where can we talk without disturbance?" he demanded.

She led the way stiffly to the music room. But when she would have sat down, Owen prevented her by holding her arms, making her face him, his expression urgent. "You have allowed me scarcely a minute of your time since we met this morning."

She disengaged herself and drew back a step. "I think you have forgotten the terms on which we parted. Nothing has changed since then."

"Nothing *has* changed. I still love you as I did in Florence, and I have been told that you have taken no other man into your life."

Her displeasure showed in her eyes. "Your sister had no right to send you reports on my personal life."

"No reports, only answers to my persistent questions. She knew how much it meant to me that you had retained your freedom."

Her gaze on him was cool. "I understand that you recovered yours some little while ago."

He answered her steadily. "I had never lost it. Maria Corradini never had any thought of marrying me, or I her. Before you and I met, Maria had made three attempts on her life, each time after she had visited her husband in prison. If I had withdrawn my protection from her, she would have made an end to herself sooner or later. That was why there was no question of my deserting her, not even though I loved you then as now."

Isabella shook her head in pity. "It was a tragic situation, but you had no right to involve me in a purposeless love."

"It was not without purpose to me. I saw the future as being ours. I knew that when Corradini died, the dreadful pattern of Maria's despair would end. Six months after I moved to Naples a blessed end came to his torment and to hers. Immediately it was as if a cloak had fallen from her and she took up the threads of her long-neglected life."

"Are you telling me that she did not love you after all?"

"No. But she loved no man as she had loved her husband. For myself, I do not deny that I loved her once, but never, never as I love you. Will you not soften your heart and consider a new beginning?"

She had to look away from his demanding gaze. It had been her secret longing that one day all would be as it had once been between them. The tragedy was that now that the time had come, she could

228

not find forgiveness for him in her heart. "I have built up my life into a full existence that has no need of new beginnings."

"I do not believe that. You simply need more time to consider all that I have said. I want you to come with me to Cawood. Could you leave with me tomorrow?"

"No, that's out of the question." She felt almost panic-stricken, as if the pull and power of love might be her undoing.

"Then I shall not leave Chiswick." He looked thoroughly determined. "I will stay here until I leave for America."

She was filled with dismay. "But your parents—"

"Say you will come to Cawood then."

"Very well." Anger rose in the confusion of her emotions. "Do not raise your hopes that anything will come of it. I cannot forget or forgive because all my trust in you has gone!"

He put his hand over hers. "In the years to come I will prove to you that I can be worthy of your trust. You and I knew love as few can know it. It is still ours. Do not fight me, Isabella. I will not lose you now."

She saw he was going to kiss her and an involuntary tremor went through her. He clasped her hard in an embrace and locked her in a kiss of such passion that she thought she must die of it. It was as if her whole being was in rebellion against her mind. His fingertips stroked a wayward tendril of her hair back from her forehead. "Leave with me tomorrow?" he implored.

"I cannot. But I shall join you there for the last few days."

He took her face between his hands. "Come prepared to travel on to Bristol and sail with me. Use the week we are apart to send your packed boxes straight to the ship. We can be married before we leave Cawood."

If only he had asked her in Florence when she carried his child, how gladly she would have accepted him. Now she said, "I cannot make any hasty decisions. You must not expect it of me."

He had to be content with that reply, for they bade each other both goodnight and farewell in the presence of company, giving him no chance to speak any more with her on private matters, and next morning he left before the rest of the house was astir.

By the end of the week her guests had departed, and she herself left Chiswick to travel with Amy in attendance to Yorkshire. It necessitated overnight stays at hostelries, and a spell of wet weather hampered the speed of their carriage. Late in the evening of the second day, there were still many miles to cover before Cawood was reached. The coachman drew up in the courtyard of The Fox and Hounds, and Isabella took her supper alone in a private eating parlour. To retire she had to pass along a hallway through which the taproom could be viewed. It was crowded and thick with smoke, the atmosphere jovial. She had just reached the stairs when the taproom door opened and a man stumbled in, his voice demanding attention. "Landlord! Do you have a room for the night?"

It was Thomas! Even as she turned, the landlord made his reply. "My apologies, sir. Every room is taken."

"Then I want a bottle of brandy and a private corner in which to drink it. You have that, don't you?" It was the voice of a man exhausted almost beyond the point of endurance.

"I fear the private parlours are taken."

Isabella had edged her way through to the bar where the conversation was being exchanged. "Bring the brandy through to my eating parlour, landlord. He is welcome to share it with me."

Thomas turned in a kind of crazed disbelief at finding her there, his face stark. She slipped an arm through his and led him away to the private room. "Are you ill?" she inquired anxiously.

He did not answer her, his throat working, a nerve throbbing at one corner of his mouth, as he sank down on the wallbench in the small panelled room. "It's little Cathy," he said hoarsely. "I was in York on business when a message was brought to me that I must return to London immediately. My darling child is dead." His head bowed slowly and he burst into the most despairing sobs that she had ever heard. It caught her heart and tears flowed from her own eyes for him in his awful grief and for the loss to the world of the lovely, enchanting little girl who had brought such light and laughter into the house in St. Martin's Lane.

The brandy came and she poured some into the goblet, but for the time being she could do no more than sit down beside him and put an arm about his shoulders. When the first onslaught of his grief subsided she put the goblet into his hand, and obediently he lifted it and drank in gulps. Although his sobbing had ended, tears continued to run down his face. "I have never been more thankful to see a dear, familiar face than I was in the taproom," he said huskily. "How am I to bear this loss, Isabella? She was dearer to me than life itself." Then he managed to relate how the accident had occurred. "I was due home after a few days in York, but my departure was delayed. Cathy, watching out for me at home, heard wheels late at night and thought I had returned. Outside the house she was killed instantly by a cart being driven by a drunken workman coming back into the yard after making a delivery."

There were no words of comfort adequate for the moment. Only by being there and letting her presence keep at bay his present personal loneliness could she be of any help at all. "Come up to my room, Thomas," Isabella insisted firmly. The bed was wide enough to sleep four people, and he could have one side of it while she had the other.

By drawing the bed curtains of the fourposter, she was able to undress in privacy in one half of the room while he discarded his top clothes in the other, then slid in between the sheets. They lay at a chaste distance from each other. She thought he should sleep well through sheer physical and mental weariness. For herself, the emotional toll of lamentation had had the same effect, and she was already slipping into unconsciousness.

She did not know why she awoke. Looking around, she saw Thomas sitting on the edge of the bed, his back towards her, his whole posture one of abject despair and desolation. Slowly she sat up, pushing back the fall of her shining hair. "My dear, dear friend," she said softly. He turned to look towards her, his face wrenched by distress into a stage mask of tragedy. She thought her heart must break for him. "Have you not slept?"

He shook his head. "Every time I close my eyes I see my daughter's face, and I am utterly bereft."

She gave no verbal reply. Instead she held out her arms to him. He came to her and buried his face against her, and she held him close, soothing him with gentle phrases. Then, in the warmth and darkness and softness of that feather bed, she let him make love to her. They spoke no word to each other, perfect communication in the silence between them, and afterwards he slept in her arms.

Early next morning they parted company in the courtyard of the hostelry. What had happened between them would never be referred to by either of them again. He kissed her hand before she took her seat in her carriage. "God speed you," she said to him.

"May He watch over you," he replied, his eyes holding hers. Then her equipage rolled away.

By the time Isabella reached Cawood, her bitterness against Owen was quite gone, melted away in Thomas's arms. She had discovered for herself how love and loyalties could be shared in exceptional circumstances, and it had totally freed her from all resentment against him.

Owen came hurrying out of the house to meet her as soon as she arrived, and taking both her hands in his, he looked lovingly into her eyes. "All is well, is it not? You are to marry me."

She nodded emotionally. The long, hard path with all its pain and sorrow was at an end. "I will be your wife, Owen."

The Marwell family gathered for a betrothal party the next evening, and there was great rejoicing, with the marriage date fixed at the local parish church. During the evening Isabella slipped away from the merry company for a few minutes to be alone. It was about this time that Thomas would be arriving home. All her thoughts were with him. She hoped that in spirit she was helping to sustain and strengthen him.

WHEN THOMAS REACHED his house in St. Martin's Lane young Tom was there on the pavement. The boy flung arms about him, and both of them embraced in silent commiseration with each other. When they drew apart Thomas put a hand on the young shoulder, pretending not to notice the tremulous lower lip. "Tell me how your mother is."

"Very poorly, sir. And very strange since Cathy was—was—"

"Say no more now. We will speak again later."

Thomas went into the house. How silent it seemed. The rest of the children were all in bed. He had never noticed the stillness with Cathy hugging his neck and full of chatter. He went to the drawing room where the little closed white coffin lay on a draped bier with a single candle burning.

How long he stayed there he did not know. Twice young Tom came to the threshold of the room and went again. Finally Thomas turned to go. Picking up a lighted candlestick in the hall he went

232

upstairs in search of Catherine. She was not in their bedchamber, nor anywhere else on that floor, and he mounted the stairs to the next one, passing the servants' quarters and looking up the last flight which led to a door into the attic.

The attic door creaked as he pushed it open. He had to duck his head to avoid the huge, low rafters, as he tried to see into the countless dark corners. Then the candlelight fell on her. She was in nightgown only, crouched in the farthest corner with her arms over her head, her hair hanging in strands down her back. A terrible fear that she had quite lost her wits afflicted him. "Catherine!" He knelt and gathered her to him.

"Cathy's going is my punishment for having loved her more than the rest of our children," she moaned brokenly.

"No, that is not why she was taken from us. All blame is due entirely to my not coming home when expected."

"No!" She became frantic, clinging to him. "Never think that! Don't carry that burden until the end of your days. My grief is driving me mad already. Add no more to it."

"Do you mean it would hurt you more to know that guilt about her death plagued me?"

"Yes! I've been such a poor wife to you and caused you such misery! You must have no more to bear than you have now!"

He sought to quiet her violent agitation. "None could fault you as a wife, Catherine. You have cared for the children and for me and for our home as no other woman could have."

"But I've never told you that I love you, Thomas! And I have! All these years! I've wanted to tell you a thousand times and have never been able to." He closed his eyes on this new shaft of pain that she had unwittingly inflicted. He saw how the years had been wasted, years that could have been rich in all that gave meaning to life between a loving man and woman. Instead she had left it too late to tell him. His love for her had faded a long while ago in the climate of her apparent indifference.

"Come now," he said quietly, "I'll take you downstairs."

The funeral took place the next day at St. Martin's-in-the-Fields. Afterwards Cathy was laid to rest in the churchyard beside the baby brother whom she had never known. To Thomas that small plot was the most hallowed place in all of London.

Chapter Seven

After Isabella and Owen were married at Cawood, a diplomatic matter necessitated his presence in London for a while before leaving England, giving Isabella time to sell her London and Chiswick houses, and to decide which pieces of furniture to take with her. Thomas was given a list, and he arranged for it all. Isabella also gave him a special order for a new piece. She wanted a secretaire of Wharfedale oak, something of Yorkshire to take with her. Thomas was pleased and honoured, and he surprised his workmen by appearing in the cabinet-makers' shop to do the work himself. The upper stage of it was fitted with small drawers and letter-holes, and he had included a secret drawer, something most people liked to have for private papers. But he added another to it, most cunningly hidden. When Isabella expressed her delight in the secretaire, he did not tell her of its special secret. The evening before the secretaire was due to be crated, he released the second secret drawer with a touch of his fingertips. Then in it he laid a crimson rose. It was the rose he might have plucked for her long ago at Nostell. She might never find it, but it was there. Next morning the secretaire was wrapped and crated with the utmost care.

Isabella wanted to take Amy with her, but Amy had flatly refused to consider the move. "No, madam," she stated dogmatically, "I made up my mind when we returned from the Continent never to set foot outside dear old England again." Surprisingly, young Elizabeth Davis, who at fifteen had grown into a strapping girl, straight-backed and full-bosomed, with a sensible outlook on life, had also declined to go. She wanted to stay in London.

Isabella promised to secure another place for her before she left, feeling a special responsibility for the girl that Thomas had brought as a homeless waif to her house. Mrs. Davis had died long since and the Chippendale home seemed a natural choice for Elizabeth's re-employment. When Isabella informed Elizabeth of this arrangement, she could scarcely believe her ears. "Is it true?" she said. "Could such good fortune really be mine?" She had never ceased to respect and admire Mr. Chippendale. To be under his roof, waiting on him and his wife and children, would make sheer pleasure out of her daily work.

Elizabeth had moved in and slipped into the routine of the household by the time Isabella went to say farewell to the Chippendale family. She was unaware that Catherine, for reasons of her own, was withdrawing from all her women friends. The truth was that since the declaration of her love she had become extraordinarily possessive towards Thomas, not liking any other woman to be near him. Nevertheless, this did not stop Thomas from embracing Isabella when she made her parting. Young Tom presented her with a handsomely polished trinket chest which he had made himself. Isabella had always loved the boy, and was touched by the presentation.

"I'll treasure it for evermore," she expressed warmly.

Four months later Isabella's first letter came. She and Owen had a grand mansion in New York on the Hudson River. Her impressions of the New World were vivid and exciting, bringing a breath of alien air in the closely written lines. She noted that there was some minor unrest in the American Colonies, although nobody appeared to challenge seriously the right of the British Government to legislate, thus ensuring law and order.

After two years in New York the Marwells moved to Boston and it was from there a year later that Isabella wrote to say that she and her husband's dearest wish had come true. She had been safely delivered of a daughter, a lovely, healthy baby, whom they had named Verity. Catherine paused when she read this news. Her own son, born to her after Isabella's departure for America, had lived only a few weeks, coinciding with the return of a troublesome cough that had bothered her at intervals in the past. The following year another male child had lived an even shorter time, she herself almost dying at his birth. There must be no more pregnancies. It was only through rest that her coughing could be kept at bay. She, who had always been so busy and active, was compelled to spend some hours of every day on a sofa. She now had time for reading again, and books were a great solace to her, except when Thomas was away from home. Then nothing could keep her calm, plagued as she was by jealousy.

But she was not alone in being relieved at each homecoming. Apart from his children, there was another in the house who missed him, for Elizabeth, come to full womanhood, loved him with a maturing of the innocent hero-worship of her childhood. Once he came upon her in the drawing room stealing a look at the latest edition of *The Director*, which by now had been reprinted twice. She could neither read nor write, but the wonderful pictures fascinated her, and she stood absorbed, turning the pages reverently. She did not hear him approach. "What do you think of the designs?" he asked.

She started violently. "Forgive me, sir. I had no right to pry or waste my time."

He caught an echo of some reprimand from Catherine. "Nobody pries into a book, Elizabeth. The whole purpose is that it should give pleasure. Answer my question now."

She was blushing furiously. "I think the furniture pictures are very fine. All of them."

"Which would you choose for yourself if the choice were yours?"

"None, sir," she replied.

"None?" He raised an eyebrow in amusement. "Have I not yet designed a piece to meet your standard of perfection?"

"Oh, it's not that! No, indeed. But I should not be at home with all that gilt and splendour. I don't mean I'm not at home in your house, sir. But I'd be quite overwhelmed to find myself with all these beautiful things on my own."

He chuckled, a twinkle in his eye. "I will tell you something, Elizabeth. I believe I should be, too." Still grinning at his little joke, he went from the room. She was left more steeped in love than ever. He had revealed to her that they were kindred spirits, he sharing a preference with her for simple surroundings.

Thomas's now widespread fame had resulted in his being elected to the newly formed Society of Arts, which was a great honour for him. He had been a member of the Society for just over two years when his partner, James Rannie, died. It had not been an ideal business arrangement, Rannie being far too set in his ways, and Thomas decided against taking a new partner. It was not that he needed money any less but he was staking everything on a stroke of good fortune that had come his way. At the Society of Arts he had met a brilliant architect at that time taking London by storm, who was prepared to put a massive amount of work his way. Ten years younger than Thomas, the architect was Robert Adam.

Robert and his brother, James, had set up their practice in London at St. James's Place, and Robert soon emerged as the dominant figure. In a particular neo-classical style that was to become his own, he changed the façades of mansions, added wings, and altered interiors structurally to give a whole new gracious look to the halls and rooms. He created deeply coved ceilings and spread them and the walls with Italian stucco in the pastel shades that made his work so delicate in appearance, sometimes inserting roundels and panels painted with scenes by distinguished artists. Floors of marble or specially woven carpets would echo the circular designs of ceilings, as would the carved motifs on the marble fireplaces, all executed in perfect symmetry. Robert Adam designed his own furniture to harmonize completely with his neo-classical interiors, but he lacked the technical knowledge of cabinet-making and needed a craftsman who could execute his sketches. In Thomas Chippendale he found a man completely in tune with his ideals.

In 1765 Thomas travelled north to Yorkshire in the company of Robert who had been summoned to Nostell by its new owner. The Sir Rowland Winn in whose employ Thomas had served his apprenticeship had died, and now his son, young Sir Rowland, wanted the most fashionable architect of the day to make alterations to the house that Thomas still thought of as the "new" Nostell. For Thomas it was a nostalgic return to the place of his youth. Of the old Nostell there was no sign, nor could he see a sign of the old orangery or the rotunda.

"To you, Mr. Chippendale, I entrust the refurnishing of the entire house," Sir Rowland said formally. Thomas was honoured. It was the kind of commission he most enjoyed. He would design pieces for Nostell that would delight the eye with their beauty for evermore.

One day Sir Rowland found him looking at the doll's house. "My late mother treasured it," the young man remarked, "and for that reason it will always be revered. I would say it is the best and most ambitious apprentice piece ever completed."

With this praise ringing in his ears Thomas returned to London. Young Tom gave a whoop of pleasure at hearing the good news of the commission. At sixteen Tom had the good looks and sparkling eyes that made the girls simper together whenever he was near. He was no less hardworking than his father, and Thomas's earliest hopes for him were being fulfilled. The lad had the skills of cabinet-making in his very bones.

At present he was doing a stint in the veneering shop. Catherine did not allow him indoors until he had bathed in the outhouse and put on the clean clothes laid out for him by Elizabeth. He liked Elizabeth, and it amused him to tease her, making her blush by asking if her current swain had kissed her yet, or when was she to be wed. She always took his leg-pulling in good part, and sometimes gave him back some spirited taunt that put him in his place and made him laugh. Being five years older than he, she thought of him as a child, for all his height and young male bravado. She tried not to blush at his good-natured tomfoolery, but the colour ran along her cheekbones at the least provocation.

She had had five proposals of marriage. Two were from workmen in Mr. Chippendale's yard, young fellows who would have made reliable husbands, but she had turned down both of them. The others she had refused as well. There could be, of course, one exception. But he was more than double her age, married to her mistress, and did not even notice that she was grown up.

It was a great day for her when she found herself included with the family to view the wonderful library table that had been made for Nostell. Even Mrs. Chippendale, who was far from well, joined the procession of family servants across the yard to the workshop where it stood. There Thomas withdrew from the library table the specially made leather cover for its protection and stood back. Catherine spoke for them all in a spontaneous exclamation of praise. "It's superb!"

Even Elizabeth could see that it was a most eloquent master-piece. Made of deeply-hued mahogany, it was wide and long

enough to accommodate the opening out of huge folio volumes, its ornament rich and yet restrained, with carved festoons, corner trusses embellished with lion masks, the whole supported on powerful lion paws.

Thomas's obvious pride in the table touched Elizabeth, and when the others left the workshop, Elizabeth lingered on. "May I offer my own special compliments on this grand table, sir?" she said. "I'm sure Sir Rowland will be pleased with it."

"I thank you, Elizabeth. He will be. It is without doubt the most handsome library table ever made anywhere."

She saw no conceit in a statement of truth. It *was* beyond compare. "You are a great artist, sir."

She was expressing her feelings of love for him without being aware of it. He, with his mind elsewhere, neither saw nor heard that there was anything below the surface. But someone else did. Catherine had returned unnoticed to the workshop door, her eyes glittering with suspicion, to investigate why the maid had remained in the workshop. She had been watching Elizabeth carefully, and if she had still harboured any doubts about the girl's devotion to her husband, they would have been banished now. Catherine's voice rasped forth on a note of fury. "Get back to the house at once, you lazy creature! How dare you dally here!"

Elizabeth, overcome with dismay, darted away. Thomas regarded his wife with a frown. "Was it necessary to be quite so harsh with the girl, Catherine? It was natural that she should wish to look her fill at this library table."

She was further inflamed by his words. "She is an ignorant, illiterate wench, incapable of a finer appreciation of things."

"I disagree. An inability to read or write does not dull the eye to beauty."

"And a literate man's eye is not blind to a comely form! Especially when his wife can no longer be as she would to him!"

Thomas sighed inwardly, more than used to his wife's tirades. "My dear Catherine, I have more to think about than the shape of servant girls. My creditors are dunning me left, right, and centre, and I need some ready cash urgently. I can tell you that unless Sir Rowland proves mightily different from the rest of his well-bred kind, not a farthing will be forthcoming for this costly piece until it has been safely delivered to Nostell and installed there for several months."

"Don't keep changing the subject!" she shrieked. "I'm talking to you about other women in your life!"

"Catherine," he said in steely tones. "Take your accusations about Elizabeth away with you into the house."

"Is the company of your wife so tiresome to you?"

"I simply wish to be left to get on with my work."

"You did not say that to *her!*" She flew at him in her rage and caught her side with such force against the lion-headed truss of the table that she lost her balance and fell heavily to the floor. He rushed to her, but after one terrible gasp for air she began to cough ferociously, spasm after spasm racing through her. The attack subsided, and picking her up in his arms, he carried her into the house. Twelve-year-old Mary helped put her to bed, and he went downstairs to meet the doctor, whom young Tom had fetched.

Exhausted, Catherine nevertheless seized the chance to glance at the handkerchief she had kept clasped tight in her hand since the coughing bout. It was as she had feared. It was pinpointed with specks of blood.

If the doctor had had his way, Catherine would have remained bedridden for her convalescence, but she feared complete invalidism, and almost from the first day put her legs to the floor and took a few steps, if only to collapse on the sofa by the window. She seemed to improve and get stronger again. For a while everything went well, and she and Thomas resumed a close relationship.

At this time Isabella wrote to her, anxious over several matters. So much had changed since she and her husband had first gone to the Colonies, the atmosphere being quite charged at times with a spirit of rebellion. With all her heart she hoped that trouble could be averted. She also inquired after her mother.

Catherine, lying on the sofa alone in her room, read the letter with interest. She had been wanting to get rid of Elizabeth for a long time, and Isabella had all unwittingly given her the means to do so.

Catherine rang the bell by her sofa. Elizabeth answered the summons. "I have heard from Mrs. Marwell," Catherine said, lifting the letter from her lap and giving it a little wave. "She has a special message in it that concerns you."

Elizabeth smiled with pleasure. "I'm honoured, madam."

"Mrs. Marwell's mother, Mrs. Augusta Woodleigh, who resides at Bath, has not been well recently and is in the most urgent need of a capable housekeeper to take charge. Knowing your character, Mrs. Marwell thinks that you would be the ideal choice if I can spare you."

Elizabeth stood stricken. "Go to Bath, madam?" she said huskily. "Oh, no. I could not. I don't want to go so far away."

"So far away from what? Or from whom?"

Elizabeth looked down at her hands. "I have always thought of this house as my home. It was where I was born, nine years before Mr. Chippendale bought the property. I can't endure the thought of leaving it or your family, madam."

"Tush! Nobody should stay in the same rut for ever. Apart from anything else, could you in all conscience refuse this request from a lady who took you and your mother in when you were homeless? Come, come, Elizabeth. What do you say?"

Her hands clenched together until the knuckles showed white. Catherine watched her without pity. Slowly Elizabeth raised her head, her eyes gleaming with unshed tears. "I will go to Bath. You are right, madam. My duty lies there."

Elizabeth almost ran from the room. Catherine smiled triumphantly. The house would be rid of that conniving baggage at last! Sooner or later the wretched girl would have taken advantage of Thomas's susceptibility. He was too passionate a man to live like a monk simply because he could no longer share his sickly wife's bed.

Abruptly she began to cough and a spot of blood appeared at the corner of her lips. With a courage she had not known she possessed, she had long since come to terms with the dreadful knowledge that there was no cure for the consumption that had laid such a hold on her.

When Mary came to her room later, Catherine dictated a letter to her, informing Augusta Woodleigh of her new housekeeper. Mary went to post the letter, and Catherine knew an enormous sense of relief. It quite revived her.

Thomas came home from Wiltshire, and departed again for Yorkshire four weeks later without ever noticing that Elizabeth was absent. Admittedly it had been a hectic time for him. He was supplying the Earl of Harewood with the most sumptuous furniture for Harewood House, an imposing mansion designed and decorated by Robert Adam, and much was involved. Then, to his jubilation, there was work with royal connections to be done, sofas and chairs and footstools *en suite* for the Duke of Gloucester. In spite of all that, Thomas was going through another financial crisis. On paper he was possessed of a fortune, but his coffers were again virtually empty. Lord Harewood owed him thousands of pounds for work done and goods supplied, coinciding with other large, unsettled accounts.

Thomas knew what he must do. When James Rannie died, an accountant named Haig had wanted to buy into the business and manage the financial side of it. Thomas, having made up his mind never to have a partner again, had turned him down. But Haig, who had remained interested in the business, had the necessary cash and credit to help in this crisis. Thomas now asked him to become his partner, and Haig agreed.

When the day came that Catherine could no longer rise from her bed, she knew a tremendous relief. The pain and effort of struggling to keep on her feet were over. She could lie in her comfortable bed, and with less strain on her body there was less coughing, at least for the time being. Her children had never been dearer to her, and they came to her with smiles and anxious eyes. Thomas was forever at her bedside. He tried to involve her in all that was happening in his work now, not wanting her to feel left out. She particularly wanted to see the very large and very rich "Diana and Minerva" commode, the dressing table being made for the state bedchamber at Harewood House. It was one of the most expensive pieces that Thomas had ever made. Over seven feet long, it was inlaid with satinwood, harewood, kingwood, and ivory, and had gained its name in the workshops from the two pictorial roundels on its doors, depicting the two goddesses with their emblems. The drawers were enclosed by a graceful recessed door, the marquetry so delicate as to appear to have been painted instead of exquisitely fashioned out of contrasting light and dark woods.

There was no question of Catherine's being carried down to the workshops to see it. She was far too weak, and any contact with cool air would set off the cough that tore at her so mercilessly. Thomas therefore had the commode taken into the yard on a fine day, and he carried Catherine to a window from where she could see it. Mary put a shawl about her shoulders in preparation, while Ann and Dorothy brought her slippers for her feet that they had put to warm earlier in the August sun. When Thomas picked her up, he almost wept at her lightness. It was like holding a frail little bird in his arms. But in the yard below young Tom stood at one end of the commode and Edward at the other, both waving to her. Behind them stood the little group of workmen who had borne out the commode, and they smiled and nodded and made little bows as Catherine gave them a special wave of thanks.

"It's the most beautiful piece you've ever made, Thomas," she breathed, still gazing her fill. "I cannot see clearly enough from here, but does either of the goddesses look a little like me?"

"They both do," Thomas answered her. "I took your profile for Minerva and your full face for Diana."

She looked up at him from his arms with her eyes full of love. "My dear husband," she said huskily.

He smiled down at her, his throat working. "My dearest wife," he whispered.

That night she died, with his arms still around her. Catherine, the woman whom he had loved with a young man's passion, drifted from in the mundane trials of marriage, and at the end had loved again with a gentleness of the heart that had bound them closer than they had been in all their years together.

Thomas found his antidote to grief in hard work, and such splendour came from his brain and from his pen that even he could see that he was riding the peak of his creative genius. Yet his particular joy was that he was gaining a fierce rival in his own son. Thomas the Younger, as he was now known, was beginning to make his mark on the world of cabinet-making. Yet Thomas the Elder still harboured his own little conceit. He had been the first to publish a great book of furniture designs. Imitators had followed in his wake, but he was still the undisputed master.

He had been a widower for three years when late one night he heard the thump of marching feet, the clops of hooves, and the rumble of wagon wheels, and he went to the front door to look out. They were not the first soldiers, muskets on their shoulders, to march down St. Martin's Lane on their way to ships. The War of Rebellion in the American Colonies was proving to be more serious than anyone had supposed. Thomas's thoughts went to Isabella. There had been no letters for a long time. He hoped that she and her husband were safe. She lingered in his mind as he closed the door, coughing as the cool night air troubled his chest.

Chapter Eight

It was a cold January morning in 1777 when Isabella, with her daughter, Verity, at her side, stood on the pavement and looked again upon the Chippendale premises in St. Martin's Lane. It was as busy as it had always been and the house at Number 60 was neat, trim, and well-kept.

Isabella had been happy and content during her years abroad, and desperately saddened when everything was disrupted. Now, when it was all to late, Owen had been summoned home by the King to offer guidelines as to how the situation might yet be saved. He was at St. James's Palace at this very minute, much aged by years of tireless work on his country's behalf, and facing honourable retirement. Soon he and Isabella would travel north to Yorkshire and live once more in a part of England that was dear to them both.

Isabella and Verity passed under the sign of the gilded chair and entered the covered wagonway. The girl was much like her father in facial looks, but she had her mother's fair complexion and golden hair. She wore a plumed hat with a wide brim that swept up flatteringly from the face, a modified version of her mother's, and beneath their cloaks both wore dresses of fashionable simplicity that had replaced the stiffer, panniered modes of recent years, and were soft and flattering. In the yard they were met by a din of hammering and sawing and whirling lathe wheels, and the smell of sawdust and glue. Almost at once a tall, broad-shouldered young man with an air of authority and a confident step came from the office to meet them, and gave a gentlemanly bow. "Good day, ladies. My name is Chippendale. How may I be of assistance to you?"

Isabella would have known Thomas's son even if he had not given his name. She said, "I have come to commend the excellent workmanship that you put into a trinket box for me a long time ago."

His eyes were narrowing at her smilingly. "I do believe you must be my godmother."

"I am, Tom, and this is my daughter, Verity."

He ushered them both into the drawing room of the house and made them most welcome. "Where is your father?" Isabella asked, a little throb in her voice. Tom's reply astonished her.

"He is not here. He has taken a house in Kensington and has virtually retired. Apart from a backlog of his designs and commissions, I am designing everything that leaves the workshop."

"Is your father not in good health?"

"It is my belief that he worked himself to a standstill. After years of travelling and working to all hours, he seemed to decide overnight that the time had come for him to hand everything over to me. He said if he went on living on the spot I should never be my own master, and so he moved away."

"I should like to go and see him," Isabella said.

"I know how glad he will be to see you. In truth, I believe time must hang heavy on his hands."

The next day she drove alone to Kensington. When her carriage passed a notice of a Drury Lane play, she was reminded of her sister. Before arriving in London, Owen and Isabella had visited her mother's house at Bath, where Augusta had died a few months before. To Isabella's dismay she found that Sarah had stripped the house of all items of value, sold the rest, and dismissed the servants. She had taken no heed of their loyal service or where they might find other employment.

Thomas's residence proved to be a modest, unpretentious house in a terrace on one side of a square. Isabella observed that the steps up to the porch had not been cleaned for several days. The

246

manservant who opened the door was elderly, and his dark brown livery was grease-stained. "Is your master at home?" she inquired.

"No, madam. 'E's over there." A grubby finger pointed to the garden in the middle of the square. She saw between the trees the figure of a man strolling leisurely along.

Her cloak billowed out as she hastened down the steps and across the road towards him. "Thomas!" she called. "Thomas!"

He turned and such pleasure swept into his face that to her it was as if time had rolled back and once again her feet were flying across the lawns to meet him by the lake at Nostell. "Isabella!" He rushed to meet her, and caught her outstretched hands in his. "Where have you sprung from, my dear girl? What a wonderful surprise." He kissed her hand and her cheek and embraced her.

Girl! He had called her a girl, and she would be fifty-eight on her next birthday. "Tom told me where to find you," she explained. He looked somewhat gaunter in the face, but to her eyes he had really changed very little since she had last seen him. In all her life she had never met another man with such splendid, onyx-black eyes. She loved him still, not as she loved Owen, who was the passion of her life, but Thomas occupied a niche in her heart from which he could never be dislodged.

"Come into the house," he said, giving her his arm. "You shall stay and dine with me. There is so much I want to hear from you."

If she had been taken aback by the slovenliness of the servant, it was nothing to the astonishment she felt when she entered the house. She had expected to see it gleaming with furniture of rich woods, glowing with silken upholstery, and dazzling with ormolu and finely chased silver and rich mirrors. Instead, against the simple, white panelled walls of the drawing room, there stood the pieces of furniture that she knew he had made in his young days at York. On either side of the fireplace was a concession to comfort: two of his large, comfortable chairs, the intricately pierced mahogany backs flaring outward pleasingly, taken from a design in *The Director* that would be ever associated with him.

He had taken her cloak from her and she shivered for there was little warmth from the smoking fire in the grate. "You're cold," he said with concern. "Come and sit by the fire. I'll have the flames roaring up the chimney in a few moments."

247

He thrust logs into the fire, and soon the room was bright and warm from the blaze. He poured a glass of ruby wine for her, and with another glass for himself, he sat back in the chair opposite her. They exchanged all news, both eager to hear everything that happened to the other over the years. Then Isabella returned to the subject of her time in America. "We had to leave all our possessions behind. Everything will be auctioned, as the goods of other loyalists have been, but at least the secretaire of Wharfedale oak that you made me is ensured of a good home."

Watching her, he wondered if she had ever found the rose, dried and faded by time, in the secret drawer within a secret drawer. He did not think she had. There was nothing in her eyes to give the knowledge away.

"How is that to be?" he asked.

"I gave it to my maidservant, who will treasure it always. Her husband removed it from the house only an hour before the confiscation order was carried out. She is an Englishwoman who was transported to the Colonies for theft when she was only a child. After serving her twenty years as a bond-servant, she married a gardener, also of British stock, and the two of them came eventually into our employ. Have you not guessed her identity? Her maiden name was Barlow. Polly Barlow from Otley, a childhood companion of yours, Thomas."

He closed his eyes at the memory of that stricken waif. "Polly," he repeated ruminatively. "Well, well. I once carved her a doll out of a piece of pearwood."

"So she told me. When she knew you had made the furniture in our house, none could have taken greater care of it. As for the secretaire, the knowledge that it was made from oaks that grew where she had once lived made it a link with Yorkshire for her as it had been for me. Once I found her kneeling by it, her cheek pressed to its side, sobbing with homesickness. Yet, when she and her husband could have come away with us, they decided to stay. Both feel they belong to the new country, as do their children. Polly wanted me to tell you that the secretaire of Wharfedale oak will never go out of her family, but will be handed down from generation to generation for evermore."

It was a good fate for a good piece of furniture. He was more than pleased. If Polly ever found the rose it would not go amiss. She had been the sweetheart of his boyhood.

When eventually he and Isabella sat down to dine it was not an appetizing meal that was set before them. The roast was burned and tough, the vegetables cooked to a mash. "I fear old Robert is no chef, Isabella," Thomas said.

She had decided that the time had come for plain speaking. "Neither is he able to keep this house clean. Why do you employ him?"

"He was one of my first workmen years ago when I had my business near St. Paul's Church. I found him down on his luck shortly before I moved and it seemed a sensible means by which to provide him with a home and myself with a servant."

Shaking her head, she smiled at him. "You should have relegated him to simple chores and taken on a housekeeper."

He smiled back at her. "I need very little these days. I have my books, I amuse myself sketching and I go riding or strolling wherever the mood takes me."

She put her hand over his on the table. "Are you not lonely?" she asked very seriously.

He twisted his lips wryly. "If you want to know if I miss my busy life, I do. But I had had my fill of the crawling obsequiousness expected of a tradesman dealing with the nobility and the gentry. So Tom is now the Chippendale of *Chippendale and Haig*. Commissions are pouring in to him as they did to me. I took the right step at the right time. In that respect I have no regrets whatever."

She parted from him with the promise that she would see him again when she was next in London. Both knew it could be months and months before their paths crossed again.

After watching her out of sight he went back into the house with a renewed sense of the loneliness that dogged his days. One week and then another went by with no lessening of the heaviness of its yoke, made more unendurable by a sweet contact with the past.

When almost three weeks had gone by since seeing Isabella, he had another visitor. Reading by the fire, he heard old Robert's creaky voice speaking to someone at the threshold, and then a tap came on the drawing-room door. Then a well-built, upright woman of about thirty years old came into the room, her copper-red hair making a fine blaze of colour against the upswept brim of her dark hat, her clothes neat and of good quality. "Good day, Mr. Chippendale," she said. "Mrs. Owen Marwell sent me to be your housekeeper. I'm Elizabeth Davis."

Astonished, he rose to his feet. "Yes, I remember you, of course. It has been some years since you left my house in St. Martin's Lane. We both have a considerate friend in Mrs. Marwell."

"Then I may stay?"

"Yes, indeed. You are more than welcome in this house."

"Good. I have brought all my possessions with me."

Elizabeth seemed surprised and pleased with the spacious quarters she was given upstairs. Thomas bade old Robert light a fire for her, and later he heard that she had had fires lit in all the other rooms to banish a chilly dampness from the house. It was certainly the first time a cosy atmosphere had prevailed overall.

At dinnertime he found that she had unearthed some spotless damask for the table, and the first course was a Yorkshire pudding, crisp and golden and high-risen, the best he had tasted since his childhood. How on earth London-born Elizabeth had learned to make such a pudding he could not imagine. He congratulated her, and saw that she had not lost her habit of blushing.

That evening he wrote to Isabella and thanked her for her thoughtfulness, telling her that Elizabeth had taken charge completely. He did not add what a pleasure it was to him, ever a sensual man, to again behold the graceful movements of a well-shaped woman. The house no longer seemed empty to him. Within a few short hours Elizabeth, by her delightfully feminine presence, had turned it into a home.

He had had no ulterior motive when he had given her the bedchamber opposite his across the landing, but as the days went by he began to look contemplatively across at it whenever he retired for the night, tantalized by her alluring proximity. The night came when he went to her room. The door was not locked. She was in her nightgown, brushing her long hair before a mirror, and he caught his breath at the magnificent red-gold flow of it. Slowly she turned her head to look at him, and she spoke in a husky whisper, a lovely blush in her cheeks, her grey eyes misty with love. "I've been waiting for you, Mr. Chippendale. All my life I've waited only for you."

She had spoken the truth. That night he knew a great rebirth in the joy of living and in the wonder of love.

Elizabeth's happiness overwhelmed her. All her life she would be grateful to Mrs. Marwell for taking the trouble to search her out after she had been turned out of the late Mrs. Woodleigh's house by the other daughter. To crown her own pure bliss was the knowledge that she was making her darling man happy.

They had been lovers for five months when one night, with Thomas's arms about her, she saw his dark, penetrating gaze upon her. "You are with child, Elizabeth," he said.

She bit her lower lip. It had been her aim to keep the secret from him as long as possible. No man wanted a bastard, least of all a man in his years of retirement. "Say no angry word to me, I beg you. I will keep the babe out of your way and never let it be a trouble to you. I confess I have longed for a child of yours, but it shall be my responsibility alone and if you wish to send me away I will go."

"Send you away?" he exclaimed in astonishment. "I'm going to marry you!" She stared at him, sure that her ears had deceived her, and then, as he drew her to him, she flung her arms about his neck, laughing and crying in her joy.

They were married on the 5th August in that year of 1777 at Fulham Parish Church. Elizabeth, painfully embarrassed by her own illiteracy, signed the register with a cross beside Thomas's flourishing signature. When she put down the pen he took up her hand and kissed it, banishing her sense of discomfiture with the love she saw in his gaze. She had no kin of her own to attend her at the wedding, but his children came, all well pleased with the match. Only Tom had reservations, but that was because he alone out of the family knew that his father had had another reason for retirement. Thomas was in the early grip of consumption.

"My felicitations, dear Stepmother," Tom said smilingly when he kissed the bride.

She held the young man's eyes for a few serious moments, and spoke only for his ears while all around them the merry chatter flowed. "Do not fear, Tom. I will take care of him."

"I thank you, Elizabeth." He pressed her fingers in his. So she knew. He could only pray that with her strength and wisdom she would prolong his father's life for many years to come.

251

It was Tom who sent news of the marriage to Isabella. She was staying at Nostell Priory when she read it, and she looked about the beautiful state bedchamber that the correspondent's father had created. The walls were hung with a hand-painted, Chinese paper covered with every kind of exotic bird in wonderful hues of green and blue and clearest pink, and the green and gold japanned furniture gleamed richly in the light of the tall windows. She had slept that night in the jewel-like, domed bed, and now she was sitting in one of the green and gold chairs by the window. She lowered the letter to her lap and sat back, setting her elbow on the arm of the chair, her chin cupped in her hand. Although her gaze rested on the view of the park through the window, she was not aware of it. Instead, she was delighting in the good news she had received, and calling to mind images of Thomas's wonderful work that she had seen during short sojourns in many houses over the past weeks.

Miles away to the south, in London, Elizabeth sat in the shade on a garden seat at the Kensington house, watching Thomas at work. He had taken his toolbox out of storage and was making a cradle for the baby that was to come. It was simply shaped, which was what she wanted, but Thomas being the man he was, it had to have the quality that he gave all his pieces. The result would be a little masterpiece.

She glanced happily towards the house, thinking of all the items of solid plain furniture that made it such a haven for her. In her opinion they showed more of Thomas's own thumbprint than any of the splendid pieces that graced great mansions throughout the land. Looking back again towards her husband, she saw he had taken a brief rest from his work and was watching her in his turn. She blew him a kiss from her fingertips and he smiled, taking up his plane again to continue his task. In her heart she knew why he never wearied of gazing at her, which was why she spent every minute near him. Yet it was with hope and courage that she looked to the future. There was no adversity that love could not conquer.

Rosalind Laker

A vivacious and charming woman, Rosalind Laker obviously relishes her work. In order to write *Gilded Splendour* she followed in Chippendale's footsteps—from Otley in West Yorkshire to St. Martin's Lane in London, to great country houses like Nostell Priory where his beautiful furniture still stands. She also combed through mountains of documents, church registers and public records. "And I loved doing it," she says. "Very little is known about the personal life of this great cabinet maker," Miss Laker goes on to explain, "and so I worked like a detective, gathering clues to his character."

Her sleuthing paid off. She found, for example, that Chippendale was in dire need of money at the time he married Catherine, who had no dowry whatever. "I concluded," says the author, "that he *must* have married for love." Other interesting facts turned up too, as bit by bit she built the framework of her story. One was an account of a man who, like Nathaniel Trench, kept the mummified corpse of his first wife ensconced in his home. "Imagine!" Miss Laker exclaims. "When he brought his second wife home, there it was!"

An abiding interest in history and a love for things old have become the hallmarks of this author. *Banners of Silk*, an earlier Condensed Books selection, was based on the life of Charles Worth, the famous French couturier, and her next story, already taking shape, again harks back in time. She has decided to write about the great Art Nouveau jewellery-makers of the late 19th century, and she has seized the opportunity to travel widely, collecting the vivid detail that makes her books so popular. Once she has done this, she likes to settle down to write at her home in West Sussex, where she lives with her Norwegian husband.

THE DAM
Robert Byrne

THE
DAM

A CONDENSATION OF THE BOOK BY
ROBERT BYRNE

PUBLISHED BY ATHENEUM, NEW YORK
ILLUSTRATED BY SANFORD KOSSIN

Theodore Roshek, president of a prestigious Los Angeles engineering firm, sat at his desk and turned a gaze of unnerving intensity on the young man before him, his newest employee.

"Kramer, tell me if I've got this straight. You have no practical experience except for a few summers' work with the highway department in Kansas. You've never been involved in the design or construction of a dam. Yet you think you can sit in an office five hundred miles from a dam you've never seen and understand it better than men with lifetimes of experience who are sitting on top of it. . . ."

With this tirade ringing in his ears, Phil Kramer begins a desperate eleventh-hour attempt to convince complacent dam authorities, the police, and the sleepy little town of Sutterton that the Sierra Canyon Dam is about to collapse; that it will happen in a matter of days . . . or hours.

PART ONE: The Fear
Chapter 1

Five years after its completion, Sierra Canyon Dam, at eight hundred and twenty-five feet the highest dam in the United States and the highest earth and rock dam in the world, was subjected to a series of minor earthquakes. Seismograph needles in northern California trembled at eight twenty a.m., when the first of twenty-nine foreshocks was recorded. The main tremor, which struck five hours later, had a magnitude of 5.5 on the Richter scale and rattled dishes over an area of two hundred square miles. The rolling motion lasted for seven seconds and was disconcerting mainly to people who were indoors at the time. Most of those outdoors ascribed the quiver to the passing of trains or trucks. Fishermen and water-skiers on Earl Warren Lake behind the dam noticed nothing.

The only terror was reported by a hiker crossing a hillside five miles southwest of the dam, the epicenter of the quake. He was thrown off his feet by the heaving ground and grabbed handfuls of grass to keep from rolling down the slope. "It was like trying to hang on to a raft in rough water," he told a reporter from the Sacramento *Bee*. "A crack opened up in the ground and I could see the sides rubbing together."

The crack delineated a previously unknown rift in the surface rock, now called Parker's Fault after the hiker who first saw it. The fault ran in a northeasterly direction and could be traced for nearly half a mile. Geologists found that the ground had shifted six inches horizontally and three inches vertically. According to a study made by the United States Geological Survey, there was a possibility that Parker's Fault ran under Sierra Canyon Dam.

259

Despite the scarcity of measurable damage, the earthquake made headlines in Caspar, Butte, Sutter, and Yuba counties. At Rio Oso, a thousand turkeys panicked in a pen, and three hundred were so seriously wounded in stampedes that they had to be slaughtered. A woman in a Roseville supermarket had a toe broken by a collapsing display of canned peaches. With so little hard news to go on, newspapers had to run editorials on what might have happened had the quake been bigger.

One thing that might have happened was a failure of the dam, a thought that crossed the mind of Wilson Hartley, chief of police of Sutterton, a town of sixty-five hundred on the Sierra Canyon River downstream from the dam. As the local officer in charge of public safety, it was up to Hartley to supervise the evacuation of Suttertonians in case of a disaster. In his files was an Inundation Map furnished by the Office of Emergency Planning in Sacramento. It was required of the owner of every large dam to confront the possibility of failure and to make estimates of the resulting flood. The map showed how high the flood crest would be and how long it would take to reach key points downstream. Such information was valuable to communities with time to react, but in Sutterton it was good only for morbid jokes. The flood Hartley and his staff would face would be five hundred feet deep and would be upon them in minutes.

When the quake hit, Hartley was at his desk. He put his pen down and stared at the office window, which had begun shaking noisily. His first thought was that Mitchell Brothers had set off a blast at their quarry, but when the window continued to tremble he rose to his feet, trying not to imagine the worst.

A policeman appeared in his doorway. "Did you feel that? We just had an earthquake."

"And now we might get a bath," Hartley answered.

They moved to the window. Half a mile away, looming above the trees of an intervening hill, the dam was almost unimaginably massive, higher than an eight-story building, more voluminous than Grand Coulee and Hoover dams combined. Only the knife-like straightness of its mile-and-a-half-long crest, outlined sharply against the sky, identified it as man-made. Its vast downstream face was like a prairie tilted at thirty degrees.

"Looks tight as a drum," Hartley said.

"The mountains will cave in before the dam goes. They built that one to last."

"Well, that's what the engineers say."

As they turned away from the window, the overhead light flickered and went out.

FOUR DAYS after the earthquake, a Pan American flight from London landed at Los Angeles. Among those waiting for the passengers was a newspaper reporter with notebook in hand. The reporter watched with interest as the man he was after appeared in the doorway of the plane. Shrugging off the assistance of a stewardess and wielding his aluminum crutches expertly, the man maneuvered himself into a waiting wheelchair. Theodore Roshek, president of the international engineering firm of Roshek, Bolen & Benedetz, Inc., was easy to recognize, and not just because of his handicap. His thin, hawklike face was always topped by a gray felt hat with an unfashionably wide brim. Full black eyebrows, which contrasted with his white hair, gave his deep-set blue eyes an unnerving intensity. He sat leaning slightly forward in the wheelchair, as if he were a commander at the bridge of a warship. It occurred to the reporter that if Roshek could walk, it would be with the stride of a man crossing a room to punch someone in the nose.

The interview was conducted as the wheelchair was pushed by an airport official to the street, where a limousine was waiting.

"Excuse me, sir, I'm Jim Oliver of the Los Angeles *Times*."

"My deepest sympathy," Roshek said, not turning his head. "I read the *Herald-Examiner* myself. Now *there* is a paper."

"Your firm designed Sierra Canyon Dam. . . ."

"Right. We also have a twenty-year contract to monitor performance. It's probably the safest dam ever built."

Oliver, a short man, had to walk as fast as he could to keep up with the wheelchair. He explained that the *Times* was doing a background piece on the earthquake.

For the first time Roshek looked at him. "The earthquake? Are you just getting around to that? Newspapers dealt with news when I was your age. I'd rather talk about something more current. Do you think the Dodgers will ever score again?"

261

"We tried to reach you in London."

Roshek turned away. "I was busy. I thought you were calling about a subscription."

"Did the earthquake cause you any concern?"

"Yes. I have a summer place below the dam. The fireplace may be cracked."

"You don't think the public was in danger?"

"No. Well, yes. The public is always in danger. Did you get here by car? Have you no regard at all for your safety? Fifty thousand people were killed last year in this country by cars."

"The fact remains that an earthquake took place next to the world's highest dam."

"The world's highest earth and rock embankment. Several concrete arches are higher. Grande Dixence in Switzerland is nine hundred and thirty-two feet. Nurek, if the Russians ever finish it, will be over a thousand. A scrupulous regard for accuracy, that's what I like about the press."

"Is Sierra Canyon Dam earthquake-proof?"

"Earthquake-resistant. Nothing is earthquake-proof. The little shake last week was five point five on the Richter and was centered five miles from the dam. The dam is designed to take six point five at five miles. There hasn't been a quake that big in that neck of the woods for a hundred thousand years."

"The little shake, as you call it, shut down the power plant for forty-five minutes."

"That was the result of too much of a good thing. There are hundreds of sensors in the dam and power plant. The rotating shafts of the turbine generators are three feet in diameter, and if they quiver more than a couple of millimeters, everything shuts down automatically until the situation can be assessed. You don't take chances with million-dollar generators, nor with dams."

"But isn't it true that the contractors who built the dam may not have followed your specifications in every detail?"

"Who gave you that question, the Sierra Club? The dam was built as designed. I made sure of it by spending three years on the site watching every move the contractor made. I wanted to make sure the thing would never help you sell papers by falling apart. This is my car, so I will say good-by. Sorry I didn't give you a better story.

If you are determined to write about the threat to the public from dams, you'll have to go outside California. California has a whole department that does nothing but worry about dams. Most states have no inspection system at all. I'm telling you God's truth! It is a scandal, my boy, that deserves the attention of your fine paper. Drive carefully!"

THE SIX WATER DISTRICTS that jointly owned Sierra Canyon Dam convened a panel of engineers to determine if the earthquake "had in any way compromised the structural integrity of the dam." While no structural damage was found, almost a third of the measuring and recording devices that had been implanted during its construction were put out of service by the tremor. This was not considered serious, because the remainder still left the dam the most extensively instrumented in the world. It was found not to be practical to replace the severed wires and tubing that led from sensors in the embankment to the banks of dials in the inspection galleries.

Inspection and drainage tunnels were contained within a concrete core block that ran like a spine through the embankment at foundation level. The shocks sustained by the dam opened construction joints in the core, allowing brown water to flow into the tunnels in the weeks following the earthquake. This caused concern, but a program of grouting—the injection through drilled holes of a mixture of sand, water, and quick-setting cement—eventually eliminated the flow. The temporary crisis was not made public.

The following spring, as a safety precaution, the reservoir was filled at a slow rate and its elevation was held to twenty feet below maximum. It was not until the fifth year after the quake that the lake reached capacity. On May 19, for only the second time in the ten-year life of the dam, water poured over the concrete spillway on the right abutment, providing a sensational display for tourists. A three-inch-deep sheet of water flowed in shimmering waves down the thousand-foot-long chute, ending in an explosion of spray. No one who heard the roar, who felt the cold wind and mist, or who photographed the rainbows will ever forget it.

On May 22 the water gliding into the spillway reached a depth of eleven inches, a historic high. It was also particularly wet in the lowermost drainage and inspection tunnels, which rested on bedrock eight hundred and twenty-five feet below the crest of the dam. Water stood an inch deep on the walkways, the most inspector Chuck Duncan had ever had to wade through on his weekly rounds. Water was trickling, dripping, and flowing from every drainage hole, crack and crevice, running down the endless flights of concrete stairs in a series of miniature waterfalls. There was more water than usual, but not so much more that Duncan was moved to make a note of it. The tunnels were always sloppy when the lake was high, and the form he had to fill out with meter readings provided no space for editorial comments from a beginning-level technician.

Duncan hated the eerie lower tunnels. He hated the long descent, the stale air, the dampness, and the tomblike silence. The overhead light bulbs were too widely spaced to alleviate the gloom, forcing him to depend on a flashlight. How was a person with just two hands supposed to write on a clipboard while holding a flashlight? Worst of all was knowing that the full weight of the dam and the lake was directly overhead—thinking about that sometimes made sweat form on his back, despite the cold.

A heavy steel door marked the entrance to Gallery D, a hundred-foot-long side tunnel that housed many of the dam's monitoring instruments. It was hard to open because settling had twisted the jamb out of alignment. With his clipboard tucked under his arm, Duncan used both hands to wrench the door free.

Standing before the bank of dials at the end of Gallery D was like standing in a rainstorm. Grinding his teeth and shivering, Duncan quickly jotted down figures for the dials he could see and made educated guesses for a few that were obscured by falling water. What the heavy seepage and the meter readings revealed about the dam was for other people to decide. His only concern was filling in all the blanks on the form, and getting out. Once back on the surface, he would take a break, light a cigarette, and think about his upcoming Friday-night date with Carla.

Chapter 2

After only three weeks in southern California, the newest employee of Roshek, Bolen & Benedetz, Inc., found himself in a position that struck him as extraordinary—lying on a shag rug in Santa Monica. A

264

month earlier Phil Kramer had been mowing a lawn in Wichita, Kansas. "Just because you got your degree," his mother had said, "doesn't mean you don't have to cut the grass." Each time he pushed the clattering machine past the porch, he stopped to read the framed document propped against the steps:

The Regents of
THE UNIVERSITY OF KANSAS
have conferred upon
PHILIP JAMES KRAMER
the degree of
DOCTOR OF PHILOSOPHY
CIVIL ENGINEERING

How he loved that piece of paper! Invested in it were seven years he had thought would never end. And now, miraculously, he was in a young woman's apartment two blocks from the Pacific Ocean. He wasn't exactly sure what was going to happen. What Janet *said* was going to happen was a massage.

"You've taken me to two expensive restaurants," she said. "You fixed my car. Now I'm going to do something for you. I'm going to give you my class A deluxe body massage. Lie down on the rug in front of the fire while I change into my masseuse outfit."

He walked to the rug and hesitated. What if she was kidding?

"Don't be bashful," she said. "You'll love it."

He waited face down on the rug, resting his chin on the backs of his hands, feeling the glow of the fire. What struck him as so extraordinary was that this was only their third evening together. He was shy, especially with women. As a youth, his premature height and unmanageable red hair had made him feel ungainly and even absurd. In college he was still unsure of himself. Too tall and nervous, with a sprinkling of freckles across his nose that undermined his credibility. He had learned to live with the harsh truth that any girl who went for him would probably be known for her brains.

He had met Janet Sandifer at a weekend seminar on new computer languages. He glanced at her several times during coffee breaks, but he didn't have the courage to start a conversation until she smiled at him. She had a trim, compact figure and a face that held his eyes like a magnet. She was three years out of UCLA, where she had earned a dual degree in computer science and mathematics. She now worked as a computer systems analyst for a firm that designed and manufactured scientific instruments.

Phil closed his eyes and smiled. Things certainly were going well for him. It was a wonderful feeling to be finished with school. Lingering in his ears were words of praise from the faculty for his dissertation on computer prediction of dam failures. He had landed a job with one of the world's most highly regarded engineering firms. The only thing that had gone wrong recently was the crazy response that the Roshek, Bolen & Benedetz computers had made when he tried his failure-prediction program on the Sierra Canyon Dam. Readouts indicated that the dam was about to burst like a water-filled balloon, which meant that there was something wrong with the computers, the dam, or the program. The computers were in robust health; the dam was of a universally revered design. So the disease had to be in the program. He would describe it to Janet. She might be able to spot some flaws.

She was kneeling beside him now, dressed in a kind of Japanese robe. "You have to understand," she said, "that I'm not trying to seduce you. I'm just giving you a massage. Close your eyes."

She pressed her fingers into the muscles of his neck and urged him to relax. "You're as tight as a coiled spring. Haven't you ever been massaged before?"

"Massage isn't too big in Kansas."

She scratched his scalp, molded his shoulders with the heels of her hands. Pressing hard, she slowly pushed her fingertips from his neck down to the small of his back.

"It feels unbelievably good," Phil said. "I don't know how much of this pleasure I can take. I feel selfish just lying here."

"I am giving you a gift. You are supposed to enjoy it."

After she said that, it was easy.

THE LOS ANGELES headquarters of Roshek, Bolen & Benedetz occupied three floors of the Tishman Tower on Wilshire Boulevard. There were a hundred employees on each floor, over half of them engineers, who worked at drafting tables in a central area surrounded by offices.

266

On Thursday, May 28, Phil Kramer was at work an hour early, sitting at a terminal, feeding his remodeled dam-failure program into a computer. The revision was the result of five evenings of collaboration with Janet. She knew nothing about dams, but she knew how to forge a chain of logic and how to ask questions that made him alter some of his numerical assumptions. It was she who suggested that the original mathematical model was too small and simple to be applicable to Sierra Canyon. The model had to be expanded to accommodate the sheer size of the structure and the greater-than-average volume of data provided. Their work together had resulted in a program tailor-made for Sierra Canyon.

When he had completed his preliminary operations, Phil opened a copy of the latest inspector's report from the dam. The Gallery D meter readings had been taken three weeks earlier, when the surface of the reservoir was five feet below the spillway at the crest of the dam. He fed the data into the system, and then instructed the computer to estimate the dam's condition under his "best-case" assumptions. Four minutes later, columns of figures appeared on the screen. These identified each ten-thousand-cubic-yard block of the dam that showed above-normal seepage, pressure, settlement, or shift. Twenty blocks came on the screen under the heading "Exceed values predicted in design." Five were labeled "Critical. Conduct visual inspection."

Phil pursed his lips and shook his head, wondering if he should junk the program and start from scratch. Apparently it was even more skewed than before. He asked the computer to calculate the "worst case." This time forty-seven blocks appeared under "Exceed values . . ." and twelve were called "Critical." The characters faded and were replaced with the command "Take immediate action." Phil asked for displays of the critical cross sections. As triangular images came on the screen, moving dotted lines indicated the plane of maximum weakness—in each case it was at the lowest elevation, apparently between the embankment and the foundation rock.

A new message appeared on the screen: "Garbage coming out? Don't cry. Recheck garbage going in." It was one of the messages Phil had included in the program to relieve the tedium.

When he phoned Janet at work, she greeted him cheerfully. "How is everything at Colossal Engineering?"

"Wonderful. According to the giant brain, our finest dam is dissolving in forty-seven places at once. Janet, the results are worse than before. I don't think anything's wrong with the logic. My initial assumptions must be too pessimistic."

"I can't help you there. Why don't you explain it to old what's-his-name—Roshek? He could probably spot the flaw in a second."

Phil laughed. "You must want to get me killed. That guy scares me to death. You should see the way he swings through here in the morning on his crutches. I swear, just with a glance, that man can knock a guy right off his stool."

"You've got to talk to somebody."

"Should I call the senior partners together and tell them that according to my calculations Sierra Canyon Dam is on its way to Sacramento? They would fall on the floor laughing. I'm fresh out of college. I'm not supposed to act as if I know anything."

"You're too bashful. And you've got an ingenious program. Don't you have a boss you could talk to?"

"I suppose I could go to Herman Bolen, who interviewed me before I was hired. A nice guy, but a little on the pompous side."

"Talk to Bolen. If the dam collapses tomorrow, you don't want to have to say that you knew it was going to but were too embarrassed to mention it."

Phil spent the rest of the morning trying to summon up courage to ask Bolen's secretary to make an appointment. Twice he put his hand on the phone but withdrew it in the face of dreadful visions. "Are you crazy?" Bolen might rage. "I have better things to do than talk to children about their hallucinations." Another possibility was that Bolen would fire him on the spot for not devoting a hundred percent of his attention to his assigned work.

Phil was part of a four-man team designing a rock-fill dam for an agricultural development in Brazil. Most of his time was spent double-checking the drawings and computations of others, but he was sure that if he applied himself, he would be given more responsibility. Already there was a possibility that he would accompany the team leader to the jobsite later in the year. A junket to Brazil! There would have been no chance of that had he joined one of Wichita's small consulting firms.

He put his hand on the phone again. Bolen might be impressed with a new employee who looked beyond his immediate assignment. Phil thought of various pieces of advice his father had given him on how to succeed in the business world. If you have a problem you can't solve, take it to someone who can, and make sure your facts are right. Phil frowned. His facts were three weeks old. He'd better get the latest meter readings. He picked up the phone and put in a call to Sierra Canyon.

HERMAN BOLEN had the second largest office in the company. The left side of his desk resembled the instrument panel of his private plane. At the touch of a button he could summon his secretary, ring fifty phones around the world, get a stock quotation, or rotate the louvers outside the windows.

He didn't mind being number two in the firm when number one was Theodore Roshek. Roshek was a brilliant engineer with an inhuman capacity for work; he deserved his larger share of the profits. Herman Bolen was, in fact, grateful to the older man. If Roshek hadn't taken a chance on him years ago, he would probably still be a drudge in the Bureau of Reclamation. As it was, thanks to Roshek and hard work, he was now enjoying considerable power and prestige. He was making more money than he ever dreamed he would, and he had played a role in some of the century's most notable engineering achievements: Iraqi Integrated Refineries, the Alaska pipeline, the Sinai canal, Sierra Canyon Dam.

He worked well with Roshek, whose normal manner was harsh and cutting. Bolen's was soft and fatherly. He smoothed the feathers that Roshek ruffled. Not that life was perfect. Bolen mourned the retreat of his hair and the advance of his waistline. His pear-shaped body was gaining weight relentlessly—the current rate, according to his desk-top calculator, was approximately 0.897 pounds per month. *Reading* about dieting was obviously not enough. Now he touched a button, and instantly appearing on a small glass screen was the time to a hundredth of a second in twelve zones. In Los Angeles it was 5:06:34.14 p.m. Time to call it a day.

There was a light knock on his door, followed by the gray head of his secretary. "That young Mr. Kramer from downstairs is here to see you," she said.

"Oh, yes. Send him in."

Kramer, the lad who had just come aboard. Bolen had recommended that he be hired. Likable young fellow, and well mannered. Just the kind of raw material the firm was looking for.

Kramer was thanking him for his time with a trace of awkwardness as he sat down on the edge of a chair. "You said that if I ever had any trouble, I should feel free to come to you."

Bolen smiled in a friendly fashion. The boy had to be put at ease. "I said that and I meant it. I know how hard it is to come right out of college into a huge organization. The shock of the real world, eh?" He chuckled, mirth that wasn't shared by his young visitor, who sat staring at him, frowning. Bolen joined his hands and leaned forward. "Now, what seems to be the problem?"

"Well, Mr. Bolen, yes, there is a problem. I think that one of the firm's structures . . . that is, according to some computer modeling I've been doing . . . Sir, I think that Sierra Canyon Dam is, or *could* be, and I might be wrong, and I'm hoping you can show that I'm off base in thinking that the dam, well, is . . ."

"Mr. Kramer, just lay out the problem in an orderly manner. Sierra Canyon Dam is what?"

Phil began again. "In graduate school I worked out a computer program to analyze embankment dams, with the goal of detecting conditions that might precede . . . um, failures. It's a mathematical model built up of data from ten dams on pore pressure, settlement rates, seepage under various hydrostatic loads, and so on. There's a built-in comparison with dams that failed, which I got from studying Baldwin Hills and Teton."

"I remember reading about it on your résumé. Nice work for a student. Imaginative." What was Kramer working up to?

"I use not just the *amount* of pressure, seepage, settlement, and movement in different parts of the embankment, but their *relationship* to each other and, most important, the *rate of change* of the values as the reservoir rises."

Bolen nodded and tried to adopt an expression that would convey both sympathy and a slight impatience.

"Mr. Bolen, in my own time I've been trying my program on Sierra Canyon. What happens is that"—he paused—"the dam, according to the model, is not . . . is not doing too well."

Bolen smiled faintly. "Now, really, Mr. Kramer . . ."

270

"It sounds ridiculous, I know, and when I made this appointment I was intending to ask your advice on revising the program. But this afternoon I began to wonder if I'm not on to something."

"Oh?" Bolen was beginning to regard the young engineer in a less flattering light. He was clever, but somewhat immature.

"I had been using readings from three weeks ago, when the lake was five feet from the top. This afternoon I used values from last Friday, May 22, when the water was eleven inches deep going over the spillway. The computer showed that . . . that . . ."

"That the dam is failing?"

Phil exhaled. "All the way from the maximum transverse section to the right abutment."

While Bolen searched for a remark that was suitably sarcastic without being contemptuous, he asked how Phil got Friday's figures.

"I called the dam," Phil said.

"You *what?*"

"I talked to the man in charge of maintenance and inspection. A Mr. Jeffers. The lake is higher now than it's ever been."

"You called Jeffers? And told him you were with R. B. and B.?"

"Yes, sir. I asked him if there was excess seepage in Gallery D. He said the inspector hadn't mentioned anything. I asked about the meters that weren't registering, and I was surprised to learn that in the earthquake five years ago—"

"I've heard enough." Bolen raised his voice slightly and lifted his hand for silence. "This is a serious matter. Something must be done and I'm not sure what."

"Well, the spillway gates could be opened to start lowering the reservoir, and a special inspection could be made of—"

"I don't mean the dam," Bolen said, practically shouting. "I mean *you!* Something should be done about *you.*" Surprised at his own vehemence, he lowered his voice. "The failure we need concern ourselves with here is your loss of perspective. Have you ever even *seen* Sierra Canyon Dam? Have you ever worked on the design or construction of a dam of any kind? . . . I thought not." Bolen studied the young man, whose cheeks were turning red. He couldn't help feeling sympathy for him. He was sincere. He probably expected to be complimented for his efforts. Bolen adopted his well-practiced soothing manner and said, "I want you to attend to the duties for which you were hired. Don't use the computers for anything not authorized. Don't mention what you've done to anybody, or, I can assure you, you'll be the butt of jokes for years to come. Above all, don't call the site again. Leave the dam in the hands of those of us who have lived with it since its beginning. All right? Agreed?"

Kramer gestured with his hands, then let them fall helplessly to his lap. "The readouts scared me," he said in a soft voice. "I still think an inspector should be sent down to Gallery D. The readings there are high by anybody's standards."

"You have the courage of your convictions, I'll give you that, even if they are wrong." Bolen waved vaguely toward the door to indicate that the meeting was over. As Kramer struggled to his feet and headed toward the door, Bolen stopped him with a final comment designed to cheer him up. "I won't mention this to Mr. Roshek. It will just be between the two of us."

Kramer nodded and closed the door behind him.

Thirty minutes later, after checking the Sierra Canyon report himself, Bolen touched a button on his console. A phone rang five hundred miles away in an underground powerhouse.

"Jeffers here."

"Herman Bolen. I was afraid you'd be gone for the day."

"Hello, Herman! Hey, we work day and night up here in the mountains. Not like you city slickers."

"I'll trade places anytime. You breathe this air for a while. Larry, did you get a call from our Mr. Kramer this afternoon?"

"Yeah, what was that about? He seemed all excited, especially when he found out that a lot of the instruments haven't worked since the quake."

"You volunteered that?"

"I mentioned it in passing. I figured a man in the company would already know. I called Roshek to find out what was up, and the girl put my call through to him in Washington! I didn't mean to bother him there. He didn't know Kramer and seemed a little riled up about the whole thing."

Bolen had been doodling on a scratch pad. The lead broke when he heard about the call to Roshek. "Thanks a lot," he said. "He's difficult enough when he's happy."

Jeffers laughed. "Sorry about that. Did Roshek call you?"

"No, but I'm sure he will. Kramer is a young engineer we just hired. We gave him a research job to do. We didn't intend for him to start phoning around the country." He chuckled to give the impression that the affair was trivial. "But in looking at some figures he rounded up, I see that drainage in Gallery D is a little on the high side. Wouldn't you say?"

"Up from last year, maybe, but not much."

"My thought is that the dam is under maximum stress for the first time in years. Larry, I want you to make a visual check of Gallery D. Personally."

Jeffers moaned. "Herman, do you know what a drag it is to go down there? Two hundred steps! Duncan was down there last Friday, anyway."

"Duncan can't bring your wealth of experience to the task. Go yourself, Larry, and call me back and describe what you see."

"You mean go tonight? I'm bushed."

"Yes, I mean tonight. If anything needs attention, it should be taken care of right away, the reservoir elevation being what it is. If by some miracle young Kramer has hit on something, we don't want him coming around later saying I told you so."

Jeffers sighed. "Okay, boss. I'll phone you tomorrow."

Chapter 3

Barry Clampett introduced himself to Roshek and apologized for the inconvenient hour. "When the President heard you were in town for the engineering convention," Clampett said, "he thought it would be a good idea to arrange a meeting. First let me relay his regrets at his inability to be here."

"When the President of the United States issues an invitation," Roshek said, putting aside his crutches and settling into a chair, "a man doesn't think whether it comes at a convenient hour."

It was nine o'clock and the sky was dark. Through the windows Roshek could see lights burning in other government buildings. The Washington Monument, gleaming under floodlights, could be made out through the trees.

Roshek eyed the man opposite him. Bland. Slick. An unblinking gaze. "What's up?" Roshek asked. "I know you've been running a security check on me. Friends have told me they've been questioned by FBI agents."

"I hope they haven't been too obtrusive."

"I just wonder if it's necessary. My firm has done a lot of work for the military over the years. I must have every kind of clearance in the book."

"Except one. The kind required for a man who may enter the public eye."

The public eye? Roshek had heard rumors that he was being considered for some kind of an appointment, but had dismissed them as poppycock.

Clampett opened a folder on his desk. "What we need to know has to do with things of a personal nature. Things that could embarrass the administration if unearthed by the opposition." He removed a sheet from the folder and studied it. "Theodore Richard Roshek. Born May 22, 1919. Graduated MIT 1939. Worked for Bureau of Reclamation on dam design and construction, served with distinction in World War II with the Army Corps of Engineers. Married Stella Robinson 1946. No children. Formed own consulting firm 1947, now ranked by *Engineering News-Record* as the twelfth largest in the country. Partial use of legs due to misdiagnosed polio in 1953."

"I hope you didn't pay too much for that information. Most of it is in *Who's Who in Engineering.*"

Clampett smiled, then asked, "Do you have a personal bank account of more than a thousand dollars in any foreign country?"

"I wish I did."

"Have you ever taken a loan from or made a loan to a person or company with connections to organized crime?"

"Of course not! What are you driving at?"

Clampett stubbed out his cigarette and fixed his gaze on the man across from him.. "The President is thinking about forming a Department of Technology. This would require a major reorganization. The Bureau of Reclamation, the civilian functions of the Corps of Engineers, Transportation, Environment, Energy, a dozen research-funding programs, all would be put under one umbrella. We need a man to put in charge, and you, Mr. Roshek, are one of a

274

handful of engineers and scientists being considered. The title would be Secretary of Technology."

Roshek listened with growing astonishment. A Cabinet post! He had never seriously considered such a possibility. Being in charge of federal funding for science and technology, settling policy and priorities would give him tremendous power.

"Your corporation," Clampett went on, "would have to be turned over to your partners for a period of time, with your shares held in trust to avoid overt conflict of interest."

"Oh, yes, of course." Roshek thought about his partners. Bolen in his estimation was a man who always finished second. Benedetz was a paper shuffler with the outlook of a bookkeeper. But the two of them could probably run the firm for a while without doing irreparable damage.

"Your qualifications are superb," Clampett said. "You have a reputation as a man of imagination at the conceptual stage, conservatism at the execution stage. Your designs are noted for strength as well as aesthetics. These things can be sold."

"Sold?"

"To voters. To Congress. Your public image, presented through the media, would be of an experienced man of backbone and integrity." He permitted himself another small smile. "You see, Mr. Roshek, in matters like these, image is as important as substance if you are to survive the Senate confirmation hearings."

As Clampett continued talking, Roshek's mind was racing. Putting his shares in the corporation in a temporary trust would cost him nothing. Foreign governments would love to do business with a firm whose de facto head was a member of the United States Cabinet. When his term was over, the lines of influence he would have established would give him the inside track on contracts beyond counting.

"Mr. Roshek," Clampett said, "do you gamble?"

"An occasional game of poker with friends. Small stakes."

"Have you ever been drunk?"

"Not since V-J Day. For heaven's sake—"

"These are the areas our great free press will dig into once your name is brought forward. We have no interest in your secret vices, unless they can't be *kept* secret. Is your marriage solid?"

Roshek tightened his lips. "Is my marriage solid! Now that makes me laugh! How long have I been married to Stella? A hundred and fifty years?"

"Thirty-five." Clampett closed the folder and pushed it to one side. "Is there anything else we should know about? Anything that might be used against us . . . and you? Think hard."

"Let's see . . . No, I believe we've covered everything." Eleanor hadn't been mentioned. Surely the snoops had found out about her, but he wasn't going to volunteer her name.

Clampett fastened his unwavering gaze on Roshek. "In the past year," he said, "you have been seeing quite a bit of a Miss Eleanor James in San Francisco."

"That's none of your business."

"It is if you want your name in nomination for one of the most important positions ever created in the federal government."

"All right, I'll tell you. I've developed an interest in ballet in the last five years. I contribute money to the San Francisco Ballet, and I know the staff. Eleanor James is a dancer. She wants to start her own studio, but she needs financing. I've met her several times to discuss a loan. End of story."

"I see. The meetings take place at such San Francisco restaurants as the Blue Fox, the St. Tropez, and La Bourgogne."

"Listen, this girl is the most wonderful thing that ever happened to me. I'm not giving her up."

"We are merely suggesting discretion. Public restaurants are hardly the place for a married man under consideration for high government office to conduct business meetings with an attractive, unmarried woman thirty years his junior. Don't you agree?" Clampett rose and extended his hand. "Will you accept the nomination if it's offered? . . . Good. You'll be hearing from us."

THE TWISTING, twenty-mile-long groove that the Sierra Canyon River has worn through the foothills northeast of Sacramento is too narrow for most of its length for more than a county road and a string of cabins. Twelve miles upstream from the mouth of the canyon, the valley widens enough to accommodate the treelined streets of Sutterton. In the nineteenth century, Sutterton was a quiet village that flourished under successive waves of prospectors, miners, loggers, and railroad builders. By the 1930s it had subsided into little more than a point of departure for fishermen and hunters.

In the 1960s Sutterton was assaulted by a new wave of invaders: geologists, surveyors, soil analysts, hydrographers, and civil engineers, looking for the best site for a dam of record-breaking size. Close on their heels came representatives of the Corps of Engineers, the Bureau of Land Management, the California Division of Highways, and other local, county, state, and federal agencies that claimed jurisdiction over parts of the project.

The owners of the project, the Combined Water Districts, assigned the preparation of plans and supervision of construction of the dam to the engineering firm of Roshek, Bolen & Benedetz, Inc. A year before the design was completed R. B. & B. awarded two preliminary contracts: the driving of a diversion tunnel to carry the river around the site, and the excavation of a cavern in which the powerhouse would be built.

The fifteen-foot-diameter diversion tunnel entered the mountainside at river level and emerged four thousand feet downstream. The diversion of the river into the finished tunnel was witnessed by hundreds of people. The feat was accomplished in the fall, when the river flow was a tenth of what it reached during the annual spring flood. At a signal, a fleet of trucks and bulldozers dumped load after load of rock into the river, building the banks on each side toward each other until the channel was pinched off. The water rose quickly, but before it could overtop the barrier and wash it away, it found the opening of the tunnel. Cheers were heard in the canyon when the water first entered the tunnel and again when it emerged from the downstream portal.

After the river was diverted, work began on the foundation of the dam. Scrapers, power shovels, and bulldozers stripped away topsoil from one side of the canyon to the other, then excavated a trench two thousand feet long, five hundred feet wide, and a hundred and fifty feet deep. Cracks in the foundation rock were sealed by pumping grout under pressure into hundred-foot-deep drilled holes. A concrete core block eighty feet high and a hundred and fifty feet wide was built along the bottom of the trench. Inside this core were drainage and inspection tunnels, reached by stairs leading down from the underground powerhouse.

When the foundation work was finished, the dam took shape rapidly. Fifty scrapers and trucks shuttled twenty hours a day between the site and nearby quarries. Impervious clay was placed in the center, while earth and rock, in precisely specified zones, were placed on either side. The material was spread into foot-deep layers and packed down by rollers.

In the year following the awarding of the two-hundred-million-dollar contract for construction of the dam, the population of Sutterton had doubled, and it doubled again in the second year. The newcomers were specialists in such things as concrete production, heavy-equipment operation, steel erection, and earth-moving. For nearly four years the residents of Sutterton were jolted by explosions and coated with dust, but few complained. The dam was putting the town on the map. New gas stations, car lots, realty offices, souvenir shops, and trailer parks sprang up like weeds. The highway south of town eventually was lined with every fast-food franchise known to man, plus one that was invented on the spot: Dorothy's Damburgers.

A popular form of entertainment was watching construction from the overlooks on the hillsides, one of which was equipped with bleachers and loudspeakers. According to a statement broadcast every hour, the dam required placement of enough material to duplicate the Pyramid of Cheops thirty times over.

"Although Sierra Canyon is not a concrete dam," the voice intoned, "a million cubic yards of concrete are required for the core block, the powerhouse foundations, the spillway, the intake and outlet works, and a highway across the top—enough to build a sidewalk from San Francisco to New York and back, with some left over. The lake that will form behind the dam will at its maximum elevation have an area equal to eighteen thousand seven hundred and seventy-five football fields.

"The chimneylike structure you see under construction just upstream from the dam will be eight hundred and forty-five feet high, with its top twenty feet above the surface of the lake. It is the ventilation intake tower, which among other things will provide emergency ingress and egress for powerhouse personnel. Inside will be a massive vertical pipe leading to the powerhouse turbines. Water will be admitted through remotely controlled gates at ten

278

elevations. The Combined Water Districts hope you enjoy your visit and ask you not to throw garbage over the guardrails."

Sidewalk superintendents at the site became familiar with a certain blue pickup truck. The driver was the project's chief designer, Theodore Roshek, who had taken it upon himself to make sure the contractor followed every line of fine print in the specifications. Construction crews learned that it was useless to try to cut even the smallest corner, because Roshek would wave his crutches, turn red, and threaten to shut the job down. He was always on the move, in his pickup or on foot, despite the discomfort he felt when walking over rough ground. Each week he spent three days in Los Angeles tending to his consulting firm and four days at the dam.

During those four days, it was agreed by the project's seventeen hundred and sixty workmen, he succeeded in making life miserable for everybody.

When the dam was completed, a platform draped with bunting was set up in front of the town hall and a dedication ceremony was held, featuring oratory, high-school bands, and barbecued chicken. Several of the speakers mentioned Roshek. The contractor said that the engineer's nit-picking, his refusal to negotiate even trivial points, had resulted in an overall loss of four million dollars for his company. The audience laughed. Contractors were always claiming to lose money. The laughter changed to applause when he added that the result of "that SOB's meanness" was the best-built dam in the history of the world.

LAWRENCE JEFFERS was a happy soul, given to whistling while he worked and talking to himself. Chief of maintenance at Sierra Canyon Dam was a job that suited him perfectly. He loved the friendly foothills of the mother lode country, he loved fishing in the lake behind the dam, and, yes, he loved the dam.

It was after ten p.m. when Jeffers nosed his pickup truck into the powerhouse access tunnel at the foot of the dam. Lights strung on utility poles on each side outlined the constant left curve of the roadway as it descended into the mountainside. Jeffers honked his horn every few seconds in case a vehicle was coming up the slope, but at this hour the powerhouse operator was probably the only one on duty. Jeffers would say hello on the way out, but first he wanted to get the trip to Gallery D over with.

Three hundred feet from the portal, the tunnel opened into a cavern of solid rock that was big enough to house the state capitol building. Jeffers turned his truck down a steep ramp to the floor below the generator deck. He had a lot of walking to do and wanted to get as close as he could to the drainage galleries. At the bottom of the ramp his headlights fell on the six massive turbines, each one taking the thrust of three thousand cubic feet of water per second. At the center of each was a rotating steel shaft that led to a generator one floor above. The generators turned out a hundred and forty thousand kilowatts each and could meet the peak demands of a city of more than a million people. The facts came readily to Jeffers' mind—he had been reciting them for years to visitors ranging from senators to school kids. As he drove slowly over the steel decking alongside the turbines, he could hear their electrical hum, but so perfectly were the massive rotors balanced, there was no vibration.

He parked behind the sixth turbine, at the end of the chamber, put on his mud-splattered hard hat, went up a flight of steel steps, and pulled open a steel door marked DANGER, NO ADMITTANCE. Inside was a rack of flashlights. He picked one and set out through a dimly lit, eight-foot-diameter tunnel that seemed to recede into infinity.

Thank goodness he had worn his boots, he thought, for there was water everywhere: seeping through hairline cracks in the tunnel lining, falling in misty veils from construction joints, running out of drainage holes drilled through the concrete to keep pressure from building up. The trough alongside the walkway was full of water moving swiftly toward the next catch basin, where pumps would lift it into pipes for discharge downstream. Jeffers pulled his jacket tightly around him; the air was cold as well as damp.

Soon he was so far from the powerhouse that the only sounds to be heard were the soft dripping and trickling of seepage water and his own footsteps. The tunnel took a sharp bend downward. Jeffers stood at the top of the long flight of stairs and probed ahead with his flashlight. Two hundred steps without a single landing to break the monotony. "Let's go," he muttered, beginning the descent. "You need the exercise."

Jeffers didn't give a thought to the lake over his head, a lake that constantly probed for points of weakness in the dam, that pushed against it relentlessly and with crushing force. Neither did he worry about the water percolating into the tunnel on every side. All dams leaked, and seepage water was no threat—unless it suddenly increased, or was muddy, or was coming in under pressure. It was simply a nuisance that had to be drained away.

What Jeffers was thinking about was an article he had read that evening about electric cars. Oh, how the public loved the idea of electric cars—or was it only the newspapers? Drive an electric car a hundred miles at forty miles an hour, then plug it in for twelve' hours. While you sit on a curb and read a book! Yes, but it doesn't pollute the air, the posy pluckers say. Like hell it doesn't! To recharge it, there has to be a generating plant somewhere burning all that nice Arab oil. What you're doing with electric cars is moving pollution from tailpipes to a smokestack. In the meantime California was headed for a terrible energy crunch, Jeffers said to himself, and not ten years down the pike, either. Right now! What California needs is *power!*

He stopped and examined the tunnel walls, streaked where seepage had left mineral deposits. The top of a fuse box was carrying a four-inch-deep buildup of rust-colored sludge. He resumed the downward trek. A soreness was beginning to grow in his upper legs. The climb back out was going to be murder.

"Hydro power is best, you don't have to be a genius to see that." He talked out loud, imagining a sea of faces from the chamber of commerce nodding in agreement. "It's cheap, it's clean, it gives you flood control as well as water for irrigation and recreation. So why aren't we building a hundred dams? I'll tell you why, my fellow Americans. Because the Sierra Club and the Friends of the Earth and the Environmental Defense Fund don't want us to. Don't flood the valley, they say. Don't spoil the wild river. . . . Now, my friends, I like wild rivers. But I like electricity, too!"

He had reached the bottom of the stairs. He looked at his boots and saw that he was standing in six inches of water. He checked the three electric pumps in a side chamber. Two of them weren't working. Jeffers opened the metal door of a wall box; two circuit breakers had tripped and cut the current. Probably overheated, he

reasoned, as he clicked them back into position and heard the motors hum to life. They have to work around the clock when the lake is high; maybe a couple more pumps should be put in. Anyway, the gallery should be dry again in a day or two.

He pushed deeper into the tunnel. Stopping before a bank of dials, he positioned the flashlight to light them up and began jotting numbers into a notebook. Water was falling from the crown of the tunnel almost like rain, and he had to watch where he held the notebook to keep it from getting drenched. Several of the readings were higher than he ever remembered seeing them, Jeffers had to admit. New cracks must have opened up—grouting might be needed to seal them.

Fully a third of the meters were out of order, most of them victims of the earthquake five years earlier. Plastic tubes that led to sensors in the embankment had been pinched off or split by settling, or the meters themselves had corroded or worn out. So a few meters were on the fritz. Big deal! In the old days, Jeffers thought, we didn't need piezometers and strain gauges and all the rest, and the dams we built then are still standing.

Sure was wet, though. Duncan should have said something. The trouble with Duncan was that he went too much by the book. Fill in the numbers, that's all he cared about. Awful wet. It was going to be interesting to see Gallery D. If it was as bad as it was here, he would have to tell Bolen to take corrective measures.

He tried to open the Gallery D door. The knob wouldn't turn. He grabbed it with both hands and applied his full strength to it. By hunching his shoulders and squeezing as hard as he could he managed to turn the knob slowly all the way to the right.

The steel door exploded open with the force of a cannon, sending Jeffers sprawling backward to the floor. Instantly tons of water landed on him, sweeping him down the tunnel in a flood of wild brown water. Over and over he tumbled, his knees and elbows and head knocking against the walkway and walls as the torrent rushed over him.

With growing speed the water leaped two hundred feet down the bore until it struck the concrete stairs. Jeffers, unconscious and three feet below the surface, opened his mouth spasmodically and inhaled.

Chapter 4

A White House limousine took Theodore Roshek back to his hotel, where an alert bell captain was at his service with a wheelchair. He was trundled into an elevator and taken up to his floor.

"Here we are, sir."

Roshek struggled to his feet and arranged himself on his crutches; then the bell captain escorted him to his room.

Roshek crossed to the far side of the room and sat on the bed. If he had glanced into the adjoining room of his suite, he would have seen a line of light under the bathroom door. He had accompanied his wife to the airport earlier in the evening and assumed she was on her way to Los Angeles. She had planned to stay with him in Washington until tomorrow, but that morning, with uncharacteristic suddenness, she had decided to return home on the next available plane. She didn't explain why.

He picked up the phone, shaking his head at the impossibility of understanding his wife. There were advantages in having her gone. One was that he could call Eleanor from the comfort of his room instead of from a booth in the lobby.

How happy Eleanor would be when she heard that he might be chosen for a Cabinet post. He heard the phone ring at the other end and tried to imagine her walking across the room, the poise, the exquisite balance she brought to every gesture. He summoned up the image of her oval face, the black hair drawn tightly back, the alabaster skin, the subtle gray-green of her eyes. . . .

"Hello? Eleanor? It's Ted. How are you, darling? Yes, I'm fine, and missing you terribly. I have some incredible news. . . ."

When she heard her husband's voice, Stella Roshek leaned toward the bathroom mirror and finished redoing her makeup. Satisfied that no signs remained of the tears that had earlier reddened her eyes and streaked her cheeks, she took a deep breath and opened the door. She was going to have to confront him and she might as well do it now.

PHIL LIGHTLY traced with his fingertips the outline of Janet's ears, eyes, and mouth. "Back in Kansas a woman as beautiful as you would set off riots in the streets," he said as he kissed her.

"I'm not beautiful," she whispered. "I'm cute. I'm a cute person who likes you very much."

Phil put his hand over his eyes. "Why can't I stay with you day and night? Why does life have to include lectures from Bolen and appointments to get chewed out by Roshek?"

"How did Roshek get involved? You said Bolen wasn't going to tell him."

"I called a guy named Jeffers at the dam. He called Roshek and asked who I was. Roshek had no idea, but he told Bolen to have me in his office the minute he gets in from the airport."

Janet thought for a moment, then said, "Roshek might want to compliment you for your concern about public safety."

"What he wants to do is jump up and down on my face. Apparently he's mad as hell. Even Bolen sounded scared. He called me at home after work today and lectured me on how to act with the old man. He told me not to defend myself if I valued my job. I guess I'll just let my natural cowardice shine through."

Janet laughed. "I think I know why I like you so much. Because you treat me like an intellectual equal, which I am. Because you are considerate and gentle and sensuous. You have no idea how many toads I've gone out with. Don't laugh! In the last year—"

"I don't want to hear about it! I've got enough on my mind without your lovers."

"That's just it. There aren't any."

"Good. Now let's find out how liberated you really are. I want you to pat me on the head and tell me everything will be all right." He nestled his head on her shoulder and closed his eyes.

"Poor *baby*," she said, patting his head. "Everything is going to be *all right*. That nasty old Mr. Roshek won't hurt you. If he says something that makes you cry, you can always move in here and go on welfare."

"You are wonderful, Janet."

LANGUOROUSLY Eleanor James extended her arm to the bedside table and lowered the telephone receiver into its cradle. She laced her fingers across her stomach and raised her left leg in the air, foot extended, until it pointed directly at the ceiling. The leg was long and straight, thin but steely strong.

"It feels good to stretch after being cooped up in the car." Her voice was small, like a child's.

"I gather that was old hatchet face?" said the young man lying beside her, raising his leg until it matched hers.

"Yes. He's going to get some sort of government job. I wasn't really listening."

"Does he call every day?"

"Of course. He loves me. That's what you do when you love somebody." Slowly she bent her left leg until the knee touched her chin while lifting her right leg to full vertical extension.

"How long are you going to string him along?"

"Until I get the money."

"Then what? Cut him off just like that?"

She watched her legs with satisfaction. "Oh, I don't know. There are advantages to being adored by a rich old man. He buys me jewelry. Change the record, would you, sweetheart? I get awfully tired of Ravel." He got up and strode over to the record player. She watched his dancer's body, the broad shoulders, the small waist. When he returned to the bed, she lowered her legs and sat up.

"Why, Russell Stone," she asked with a coy smile, "are you jealous of an old man?"

He shook his head. "I just don't see how you can do it. The whole thing is sick."

"I want a studio of my own and he can give it to me. Besides, he can be very sweet." She looked past him to the windows, to the trees, to the canyon walls on the other side of the river. "He treats me as if I were a fantastic work of art. He said that next to me the greatest structure he ever designed was like a mud pie."

"I give him credit for finding the key to you: flattery."

She looked at him with round eyes. "Oh, Russell, you shouldn't make fun of a man whose hospitality you are enjoying."

"Without his knowledge." He looked around. Through an open door he could see the enormous fireplace and the parquet floor of the living room. "It's weird, not hearing traffic noises. I get the creeps when I'm not in the city."

"We're hardly roughing it. This is probably the most elaborate home in the whole valley. It even has a name, Creekwood, that's listed on county maps."

286

"Fancy place, all right. Still, I don't see how I am going to stand it up here for two whole days."

Eleanor got up. "Let's take a walk by the river and fill our lungs with mountain air. You might like it." She caught his hand and pulled him to his feet.

The river was well worth seeing. At the Sierra Canyon power-house ten miles upstream, the maximum amount of water was being released to generate electricity during the evening hours of peak demand. The river was close to overflowing its banks as it surged down the canyon. It was an invigorating spectacle.

"WHAT HAPPENED, Stella? Did you miss the plane?"

Roshek put the phone aside and watched his wife take a chair facing the bed. Her movements were controlled, as if rehearsed, and her eyes were full of a quiet strength he had never seen before. Had she overheard the whole conversation with Eleanor?

"I let the plane take off without me," she said. "I've been waiting for you in the sitting room, watching it get dark."

Roshek made an effort to smile. "You scared the daylights out of me!" Then with concern, "Are you all right?"

"I'm fine. Wonderful, in fact, because I have finally made a decision about something that has made me miserable for years. I came back to tell you. Tomorrow I am going to file for divorce."

"Oh, now, Stella, for heaven's sake! What brought this on? You're upset about something. I'm sure if we talk about it . . ."

She shook her head. "That you should have to ask . . . I suppose that's what brought it on. You're so self-centered, Theodore, so sunk in yourself and your work, that you are completely unaware of how profoundly you've insulted me."

"Eavesdropping on my phone calls, that's what brought it on. In your mind you've twisted something innocent into—"

"Nothing about Eleanor James is innocent," she cut in sharply. "Oh yes, I've known from the beginning. I was at those cast parties in San Francisco, remember, when we first met her. I saw how she played up to you, how you fawned on her. For months you talked about her and found excuses to make trips to San Francisco. Then suddenly you stopped the talking, but not the trips." She turned away and fought to retain control.

Roshek tightened his lips, then said, "On an assumption like that you want to end a marriage that has lasted—"

"You've been seen together!" she said, facing him. "Friends have told me. Don't say how innocent you are. I heard you on the phone. I'm not deaf. I'm not stupid."

It would be worse than futile, Roshek realized, to try to defend himself—the effort might send Stella into the lobby in hysterics. But he would have to do something to change her mind about a divorce, at least delay the filing until after the Senate confirmation hearings. There were also financial consequences, should Stella claim half of his interest in the company as her share of community property.

"Maybe I have been a fool," he forced himself to say. "But, Stella, my feelings for her don't match my feelings for *you*."

She waved her hand and made a sound of contempt. "You have no feelings for me. Not as a wife. I'm your social secretary. I cater for your business dinners. You think of me as one of your employees, that's all. Well, Theodore, employees can quit. That's exactly what I'm going to do."

"You are getting all worked up over nothing. Eleanor James means absolutely nothing to me! Surely we haven't come to divorce. Not after all we've been through together."

He looked at his wife, who sat facing him with unwavering composure. The possibility that she would yield to tears was plainly remote. "You are a very handsome woman, Stella." A very handsome woman who could get a court order freezing community property, thus destroying the company's financial flexibility. "I haven't paid as much attention to you as you deserve. I've been working too hard, trying to lift the firm into the greatness we seem close to achieving. Eleanor has distracted me, made me behave, I see it now, like a fool. Please forgive me."

"No, Theodore, you can't manipulate me anymore. It's over. Nothing you say can make me forget the pain you've given me. How your eyes lit up when Eleanor James smiled at you! You probably think of her the way you think of engineering designs. I've heard the phrase a hundred times: a beautiful combination of form and function. You said that about Sacramento's new sewage treatment plant. Graceful lines, you said. Do you tell Eleanor James she is more beautiful than any sewage plant? Is that what you whisper to her when she is caressing your wallet?" She rose and put her hand on the doorknob.

"Stella, sit down! We've got to talk this out."

"Don't raise your voice. You don't frighten me anymore. You did once, did you know that? You are so sure of yourself, so used to holding hoops for people to jump through. I never knew quite where I was going, so I followed you and helped you pursue your goal, which, as I understand it, is to become the richest engineer who ever walked the earth. Well, my life isn't over yet. I'm going to the airport. Good-by."

"Stella . . ." Roshek got to his feet and took several awkward steps toward her before his legs buckled. He hung on to a chair to keep from falling to the floor. He grimaced. "Help me. . . ."

She stood in the doorway looking at him sadly. "I never thought I'd see you resort to that," she said. "If you need help, I suggest you call the front desk."

Chapter 5

A battered green Volkswagen with a plastic daisy atop its antenna pulled into a parking space behind the Center for Holistic Fitness in Berkeley, California. A slightly built man with a thin beard and wearing faded blue jeans got out and walked around the one-story cement-block building to the front door.

The receptionist was impressed when he gave her his name. "Dr. Dulotte is expecting you," she said with a smile. "I'll let him know you're here."

Scattered on a low table were sports and health magazines. The man saw his own photograph on the cover of Western *Strider*. KENT SPAIN WINS AGAIN, the banner caption read. "See page 32 for his quick-energy tips."

"Won't you have a seat?" the receptionist asked. "The doctor might be a few minutes."

"No, thanks. Sitting is bad for your lumbar."

He walked around the waiting room, studying framed testimonials from satisfied patients. The Center for Holistic Fitness was a medical-mystical smorgasbord catering to a broad range of physical achievers and those wishing to be. The building directory showed that appointments could be made with a general practitioner, a nutritionist, a physical therapist, a behavioral psychologist, a hypnotist, an acupuncturist, a foot reflexologist, and a Buddhist priest. The brainchild of David Dulotte, a doctor-businessman who was more businessman than doctor, the center was under constant scrutiny by divisions of the state government and the American Medical Association. No one on the staff cared what the AMA thought, because none of them were members.

Dr. Dulotte now appeared. He was an enthusiastic, dapper, portly man with steel-rimmed glasses, and he pumped Kent Spain's hand vigorously as he guided him into his office.

"Good to see you again, Kent! Have a chair!" He sat behind his cluttered desk and spread his arms. "What do you think of our little establishment?"

"You sure cover all the bases."

Dulotte chuckled appreciatively. "We give our patients a more complete workup than any hospital in the state. We do thermography, plethysmography, Doppler ultrasound. We stare into their eyeballs—that's iridology. We are the only place in the western states that does moxibustion. Sit down, will you?"

"I was sitting in the car. Just what is moxibustion?"

Dulotte clapped his hands with glee. "I love it! It's the very latest thing from ancient China. A jogger comes in with, say, a pain in the hip. Where it hurts, we put a little pile of wormwood leaves along with some secret herbs and spices—I don't know what exactly—and set it on fire! People say it helps! I think what happens is they get so distracted by the pain of the blister, they forget about the original complaint."

"You're a quack, Doc. A regular Donald Duck."

"There are gray areas," Dulotte said with a shrug. "Our policy is to give the customer what he wants, provided it can't be proved harmful. What customers want these days is hooey from the Orient, so I'm importing everything I can lay my hands on."

From a cooler beside his desk Dulotte took a tall green bottle and poured a murky liquid into two glasses. "Try this," he said. "Mineral water from Szechwan province. Sold a ton of it already at ten bucks a quart. Here's to your decision to turn pro!"

Spain took a sip and made a face. "A laugh, isn't it? A marathon runner turning pro? I'll be lucky if I make bus fare."

"You'll be surprised at how much you can make. Endorsements are big business. Of course, it depends on what you endorse."

"On the phone you said if I gave your shoes credit for winning a race, you'd give me twenty-five hundred bucks, right? I'll do it. I'm thirty-three years old and I'm not getting any faster."

Dulotte smiled benignly. "Your problems are over if you do what I tell you. What kind of shape are you in?"

"Not the shape I was in a year ago. I'm only doing sixty miles a week. I used to do a minimum of a hundred."

"Can you win tomorrow's marathon? Tommy Ryan is in it."

"Yeah? He can be tough. My money is on him."

"And my money is on you." Dulotte glanced at his watch. "At about this time tomorrow morning you'll be crossing the finish line in front of the Sutterton town hall. On Monday, if you will sign a personal services contract I have for you, you can be in the bank of your choice with a check for ten thousand dollars."

"Cut it out. You can't make that kind of money off me."

"Oh, yes, I can. Look, what if you were to turn in your lifetime best mark tomorrow? While wearing and eating and drinking products made by Jog-Tech, which happens to be my Hong Kong manufacturing subsidiary?"

Kent Spain began pacing in front of Dulotte's desk. "How am I going to run my best time? By prayer? By magic?"

"No. By cheating." Dulotte let the word sink in as Spain put his hands on the desk and stared at him. "You get ten thousand bucks for starters. If you can learn to talk, you can make twice that on the lecture circuit even after I take fifteen percent."

Spain collapsed in a chair. "Ten thousand! What's the plan?"

Dulotte unfolded a map and traced a line. "The race starts here, follows a highway, then a fire road, then a trail through a forest. What you have to do is run five-minute miles for the first fifteen miles. Ryan will be trying for five seven or five eight."

Spain looked worried. "I'll burn myself out. I'll have to crawl the last eleven miles."

"No, you won't. Look at the map." He tapped a spot with his forefinger. "The trail comes out of the woods right here, goes across the top of Sierra Canyon Dam, and back into the woods on the other side. After that is a long switchback through heavy timber, downhill all the way. You'll be taking that stretch on a bicycle, old buddy, catching your breath and whistling."

"A *bicycle!*"

"A bicycle. It's in the bushes waiting for you. Watch for a T-shirt tied to a limb. Make sure you are the first to get there. There isn't another aid station until mile nineteen."

Spain was out of his chair again, pacing back and forth. "It won't work," he said. "There's no *way*. If somebody clocks me at the dam, the monitor at mile nineteen will figure out later that something is haywire. You're nuts, Doc."

"Which brings us to the real beauty of the concept. I am the monitor at mile nineteen."

Spain stopped and stared. "You?"

"Me." Dulotte resumed tracing a line on the map. "You'll be ten or fifteen minutes ahead of the field. After dumping the bike you can catch your breath for five minutes."

"I hate sitting down."

"Walk, then. The course comes out of the woods here at the county fairground. Trot the rest of the way as fast as you can. You'll be on a highway with people cheering you on. You will break the tape"—he tapped the map with triumphant finality—"in downtown Sutterton, the new champion of the Mother Lode Marathon, with an amazing new lifetime record, achieved while festooned with Jog-Tech gimmicks."

Spain watched the doctor empty the contents of a drawer onto the desk. There were a pair of ribbed rubber heel caps to provide "greater lift", a digital pedometer, a microelectronic pulsimeter that recorded pulse rate, blood pressure, temperature, and electrolytic balance. "This hot item," Dulotte said of the pulsimeter, "goes for four hundred bucks."

Spain protested. "But all that junk must weigh at least ten pounds!"

"A little over a pound. You can manage. After the race you will say that your performance was the result of being able to keep track of your body functions, scientifically adjusting your pace. You will also say that you trained on our home treadmill—another four-hundred-

292

dollar item—while drinking our vegetable-vitamin-almond consommé."

"I feel sick," Kent said.

"We will make a killing. Sign here."

JUST BEFORE LUNCH Herman Bolen phoned Sierra Canyon and was told by an engineer in the powerhouse control room that Lawrence Jeffers had not yet made an appearance that day.

"He might have gone to Sacramento and forgot to tell us," the engineer said, trying to be helpful.

"You're probably right. Have him call me when he comes in."

Odd, Bolen thought. Not like Jeffers to leave his whereabouts unknown. Surely he would have phoned early this morning before leaving for wherever he was going. A trip to Sacramento—yes, that was probably it. Or a dental appointment. Still . . . he might have fallen down that accursedly long flight of stairs and broken a leg or a hip. He might have had a heart attack.

Come, come, Bolen chided himself, you are overdramatizing. If Jeffers were still inside the dam, someone at the site would have noticed his car in the parking lot. You would look pretty foolish if you launched a manhunt for a man who might stroll into his office at any moment.

Bolen looked at his calendar. There was a meeting that afternoon at Southern California Edison about the plan to enlarge Sequoia Dam. If it dragged on, he would excuse himself at some point and make a phone call. If Jeffers still hadn't reported in, he would make a few discreet inquiries.

ALONE IN HIS OFFICE, Theodore Roshek closed his eyes and touched his temples. For the first time in years he had a relentless headache. He hadn't slept well the night before in his Washington hotel room. The flight to Los Angeles this morning had hit rough air which had made it impossible to think about anything except the plane shaking itself apart.

At least he had had a small success with Stella. He phoned her from the airport and got her to agree not to see an attorney until they could discuss their problems that night. He would play on her sympathies, and if that didn't work, he would break her down, make her fold up and cry, the way he had on previous occasions when they had argued.

He thought of the small gun he carried in his attaché case for protection. She knew it was there, and if their emotions boiled over, one of them might grab for it. Unlikely, but nevertheless . . . He snapped the case open and removed the weapon, turning the cold steel over in his hand. The safety was on, but it still felt ominous and deadly.

A red light flashed on his intercom. He depressed a lever and heard his secretary's voice. "Mr. Bolen wants to know if you'll be going to the Southern Cal Edison conference."

Roshek put the gun in a drawer and felt glad to be rid of it. "I'll try to get there in an hour or so. After I talk to young Kramer, I want Jules Wertheimer on the phone. Set that up, please."

He broke the connection and jotted down a list of questions to ask Wertheimer, the only lawyer he knew whom he trusted completely. Could Stella freeze community property, thus depriving the company of its freedom of action? Were there enough assets in the estate to satisfy her rights without giving her any part of the company? Wertheimer would know.

The more he thought, the angrier he got. She could have the Beverly Hills house, the Sierra Canyon house, the art, the stocks, the insurance, everything, but not the business. He would hang on to full control, no matter what the divorce laws said.

His secretary came on the intercom again. "Mr. Kramer is here to see you."

PHIL CROSSED the carpeting and sat down tentatively on a leather chair in front of Roshek's massive mahogany desk. Good Lord, Phil thought when he saw the old man's face. He looks as if he's going to spring at my throat! What's he so mad about?

"Kramer, tell me if I've got this straight," Roshek began. "You have no practical experience except for a few summers' work with the highway department in Kansas. You've never been involved in the design or construction of a dam. Yet you think you can sit in an office five hundred miles from a dam you've never seen and understand it better than men with lifetimes of experience who are sitting on top of it. Is that right?"

Phil stared, speechless. Was Roshek kidding? He crossed and uncrossed his legs. "No," he managed to say, "that's not right at all. You've put the worst possible interpretation—"

"Furthermore, you had the audacity to call the chief maintenance engineer on the site and lead him to believe that headquarters people think his dam is failing. I don't need a greenhorn employee casting doubts about one of our structures. What you have been doing amounts to a whispering campaign against your own employer."

Keeping his voice calm, Phil tried to make his point. "Mr. Roshek, the computer data clearly indicate to me that some sort of investigation is called for."

"You're not an engineer. Not yet. Not by a long shot."

"I'm not a licensed engineer, true. In California you need five years' professional experience after graduation before you can apply. I have a doctorate in—"

"An engineer is more than a man with a diploma and five years' experience. True engineering involves a man's personality, the way he respects the materials he works with, his sense of history and the future, his integrity."

Phil thought, He's not listening to a word I say! He's using me to practice some sort of commencement address.

"Most important," Roshek went on, "is maturity. A sense of proportion. Judgment. You could have caused a panic. What if word leaked out that we were worried about the safety of the nation's highest dam? Rumors start flying, newspapers pick them up, politicians demand an investigation, environmentalists charge a cover-up. . . . I've seen it happen. Over nothing. Because a smart college student gets excited over drivel in a computer."

Phil felt his cheeks turning red. He knew he should let Roshek's tirade run its course, but he hated distortions and being accused of something he didn't do.

"Sir, I didn't say to Mr. Jeffers that I thought the dam was failing. I did tell Mr. Bolen, in private, that my computer model indicated something was wrong. . . ." Phil let his voice trail off because his words were being ignored. Roshek's eyes were wandering around the room, resting on the photographs of his projects, and he was reciting their names like a litany.

"Sinai, Maracaibo, San Luis, Alyeska. These tremendous developments are as sound as the day they were built." He gestured toward a glass display case in which was a scale model of Sierra Canyon Dam, complete with tiny trees on the abutments and a center stripe on the road across its crest. "Not one of the structures this company has had a hand in has ever suffered a failure of any kind. Durability like that is a result of skill, hard work, intuition, and uncompromising insistence on quality every step of the way. When a design philosophy like that is brought to bear, structures don't fail."

Did Roshek really believe that? Phil wondered. That if a skilled engineer did his best, nothing could go wrong? The proposition was absurd.

Roshek gazed with a kind of rapture at the display case. "Sierra Canyon Dam, about which you have developed such a lunatic obsession, is an engineering landmark. It represents an unprecedented effort to ensure safety, from the thoroughness of the geophysical investigations right through to the ongoing system of inspection and maintenance. I insisted on the most extensive network of sensors ever implanted in a dam."

"Half of those sensors don't work anymore."

Roshek pushed his swivel chair away from his desk and glowered at Phil. "I've spent too much time on this already. I will tell you just one thing. Stop concerning yourself with the dam. If you want to fool around with schoolboy computer models, use your own computers and your own time. That's all. You can go."

Phil did not rise from his chair. "Mr. Roshek," he said, "in my defense I could point out that—"

Roshek cut him off. "What do you mean, in your defense? This is not a trial. I pay your salary and so you do whatever I want you to do. I'm telling you to drop Sierra Canyon Dam. You should read the Code of Ethics of the American Society of Civil Engineers. Point number two is that engineers should perform services only in their areas of competence."

"I know the Code of Ethics, too," Phil said half to himself. "Point number one is that engineers should put the safety, health, and welfare of the public above everything else."

"What? What did you say?"

Phil stood up, his cheeks hot and his heart pumping. "I don't deserve to be treated like a child," he said in a loud voice. "In the past few weeks I've been closer to that dam than you. It's true that extensive foundation borings were made before construction, but the earthquake five years ago may have changed everything. The dam leaked so badly after the quake, two million dollars had to be spent to plug up cracks. The reservoir was filled this spring fifty percent faster than you yourself recommended that it should be."

Roshek was so astounded by the outburst that he couldn't find his voice. His mouth opened and closed and his eyebrows rose.

Phil tore a sheet of paper from a notebook and dropped it on the desk. "Here are the latest seepage figures from Gallery D. In every case they are higher than you said they should be when you wrote the original specifications. Somebody should go down right now and take a look. Next week may be too late."

Roshek crumpled the sheet into a ball and hurled it against the wall. He found his voice, and it was loud. "I don't need you to tell me how to look after a dam! Your sophomoric opinions are more irrelevant now than they were before, because you are fired! Get out! If you are at your desk this afternoon, I'll have you arrested for trespassing!"

Phil tried to slam the door on the way out, but hydraulic hinges made it impossible.

JANET SANDIFER could hardly recognize the voice on the telephone. "Is that you, Phil?" she asked, smiling and frowning at the same time. "You sound funny. Is that a jukebox I hear?"

"That's a jukebox, all right. I'm at a bar on Figueroa Street doing some research. I'm trying to find out if it is possible to drink fifty bottles of beer and still hold a pool cue."

"What are you talking about?"

"They have one of those little coin-operated pool tables here, and I'm locked into a big eight-ball shoot-out. I'm two dollars ahead. I haven't played pool in years! I must be naturally gifted."

"What about Roshek? Did you talk to him?"

"Roshek? You mean the distinguished engineer? Yes, I talked to him. Did I *talk* to him! Janet, it was the weirdest thing I've ever been through. I'm not kidding, somebody should rush him to a

psychiatrist. He called me a sophomoric greenhorn who was trying to wreck his company. He said if he saw me around there again, he'd arrest me for trespassing. It was unbelievable!"

"Phil, wait a minute. Are you saying you got yourself fired?"

"Yes. Roshek went after me as if I were an axe murderer. The most unbelievable part was that I tried to defend myself. Good old shy Phil Kramer, arguing like the sophomore he said I was."

"Oh, Phil, I'm so sorry. I know how much you liked your job. Maybe he'll take you back when he cools off."

"I'll refuse! Work for him again? Not a chance. I'm going to be a professional pool player, a hustler going from town to town. You can be my sidekick. It'll be a wonderful life, Janet! Just the two of us, alone together on the open road!"

"I have a better idea. Come over tonight. I'll thaw something for dinner and later I'll pat your head."

"It's a deal."

At two p.m. Phil called Janet again. "I've changed my mind," he said. "I'm not going to become a pool hustler. I'm three dollars behind and I think the dude I've been playing with is a shark. Janet, I want a rain check on tonight. I'm going to drive to the dam. I can make it in seven or eight hours. I want to see Sierra Canyon for myself and try to get into the drainage galleries. What can they do to me for making one last effort to prove something is wrong? I'm already fired."

"I liked your first idea better."

IN THE MIDDLE of the afternoon Herman Bolen excused himself from the Southern Cal Edison conference room and made a phone call. Again he was told that Jeffers had not been heard from.

"Is Chuck Duncan around?" The young inspector could be sent into the lower gallery to see if anything was amiss.

"Chuck is gone for the day," the powerhouse engineer said. "Should I try to track him down?"

"No, that won't be necessary. Just make sure Mr. Jeffers gives me a jingle when he gets in."

Bolen returned to the conference room and resumed his seat next to Roshek. He had a hard time keeping his mind on the subject under discussion: the cheapest way to enlarge Sequoia Dam. Like

299

Bolen, Roshek had contributed little to the discussion beyond a few wise looks and noncommittal shrugs. He sat oddly subdued; his eyes were closed, and he was rubbing his forehead.

By the time the meeting was over, traffic on the Hollywood Freeway had eased. Bolen had no trouble maneuvering his Mercedes 300SD into the fast lane. He would drop Roshek off at his home in Beverly Hills, then return to the office to clean up some paperwork before the weekend. One thing he would do was solve the Jeffers problem, even if it meant calling hospitals.

Strapped into the seat beside him was Theodore Roshek, who used the seat belt only when riding with Bolen, as a way of showing disapproval of his partner's driving habits. "Your image usually suggests prudence and propriety," Roshek had once told Bolen, "but behind the wheel of a car you become as idiotic as a teenager." Bolen could have pointed out that Roshek's image could stand improving as well. The gray felt hat he wore made him look like something out of an old Humphrey Bogart movie.

"How did your chat with Kramer go?" Bolen asked by way of making conversation. "Impressive young man, don't you think? Still a little wet behind the ears."

Roshek, preoccupied, turned his gaze back to Bolen. "The chat with Kramer? That went very well. I fired him." Noticing the dismay that came over Bolen's face, he added, "I know he was a favorite of yours. But he had the nerve to tell me how to run my business. Never saw such impertinence in my life."

Bolen looked straight ahead for a full minute before speaking. "He wasn't a favorite of mine, particularly," he said, using a casual tone. "It's just that I felt he was intelligent and he might develop into a valuable employee." He wondered if he should try to get Roshek to rescind his action, at least until the situation at the dam could be evaluated. If emergency measures had to be taken, it would be disastrous if the press learned that the man who first tried to sound an alarm had been fired for his trouble. "Was it really necessary to let him go?" Bolen ventured.

"It was either that," Roshek replied calmly, "or turn the company over to him to run his way. He started in on his ridiculous computer model, and before I knew it, he was raising his voice to me. He should have known I wouldn't tolerate that."

Roshek squirmed in discomfort as Bolen, with a burst of acceleration, knifed his way over to the right lane and took the Santa Monica Boulevard exit westbound. "I rather liked Kramer's enthusiasm," Bolen said. "What I'm thinking is—"

"We have more important matters to discuss. You and Benedetz might have to run the business for the next few years."

With that abrupt announcement, Roshek began a summary of his meeting with the President's aide. He brushed aside Bolen's congratulations. "There must not be any negative publicity about the firm. There must not be a juicy divorce between Stella and me, which is my main problem at the moment."

"Good heavens, Theodore! Stella wants a divorce?"

"Keep your eyes on the road. Yes, she dumped that on me last night in Washington. Tonight I get one last chance to talk her out of it. If she makes allegations that I have to answer in court, then my chances of getting the appointment will be zero. I can't let her ruin me and the company. I *won't* let her."

The Mercedes made several turns along streets lined with forty-foot-high palm trees. Roshek's home was in the Spanish style, with thick walls, a red tile roof, and a broad lawn. The car glided up the curved driveway and stopped at the front door.

"Wait until you see I'm inside," Roshek said. "Stella might have changed the locks. Just get the chair out of the car. How the Sam Hill do you unhook these seats belts?"

Bolen reached over and depressed the release catch. "You never were very good with small mechanical devices, were you, Theodore? Unless a thing has at least five hundred moving parts or is worth ten million dollars, it doesn't engage your attention."

"Then why haven't I paid more attention to my wife? She might cost me ten million dollars. Of course, she has only one moving part. Her mouth."

After Bolen removed the collapsible wheelchair from the back seat, he decided to risk bringing up the subject of Kramer and the dam one last time. "Did you by any chance take a look at the seepage figures Kramer compiled?"

"He handed me a sheet of paper," Roshek said, getting into the chair. "I crumpled it up."

Bolen shook his head gravely. "Seepage is high. I called Jeffers and asked him to take a look around in the lower galleries. I expect him to call in a report any minute."

Roshek looked up at Bolen with mild exasperation. "Herman, whose side are you on, mine or that kid's?"

"I'm on your side and the firm's side," Bolen said, keeping his voice low. "But it may be that new leaks have sprung up that call for grouting, overhauling the drainage system, lowering the reservoir, or whatever. We can take corrective action quietly, provided we don't have a disgruntled ex-employee running around shooting his mouth off. As you said, we don't need bad publicity."

Roshek sagged. "As if I didn't have enough on my mind."

"Suppose I tell him you are willing to give him another chance? I'll assign him to the London office. Six months from now we'll terminate him when it won't seem connected with trouble at the dam . . . if there is any trouble."

"Good. I like it. Just don't mention his name around me again. Now, excuse me, I have an appointment with my loving wife."

Bolen returned to the driver's seat. He watched Roshek wheel himself to the door and try his key. When the door swung open, Roshek turned and mouthed the words, "Wish me luck." Bolen waved reassuringly, then coasted down the driveway to the street.

Driving east toward the freeway, he planned the actions he would take when he reached the office. He would phone Kramer and tell him "the good news." He would track down Jeffers, wherever he might be. Finally, he would permit himself thirty minutes—not a minute more!—of daydreaming about what it would be like to control the company in Roshek's absence.

PART TWO:The Race
Chapter 6

Seventy miles an hour was the most Phil's aging Mustang would do without shuddering uncontrollably. He held it at that speed and drove with both hands clamped on the wheel, leaning forward in an unconscious effort to urge the car beyond its limits. He read every road sign on Interstate 5 and studied the region he was passing through. He had often heard his father talk about California's Central Valley as one of the world's greatest displays of engineering achievement.

Phil's father, Carl Kramer, had been road superintendent of Sedgwick County, a job that carried considerable prestige around Wichita. Phil had both loved and admired his father, a man whose interests ranged far beyond the duties of a county engineer. He was a serious student of the history of engineering, and both Kansas and Kansas State had asked him to join their engineering faculties. But he had turned them down, confining his professional ambitions to his son. When he died, Phil was in his first year of graduate school. "Keep up the good work," his father had written in his last letter. "You've got something extra and there's no telling how far you can go." He said things like that so often that Phil sometimes almost believed him.

Phil looked toward the east, where a thin haze obscured the horizon. Behind that haze were the Sierra Nevada, where more major dams had been built than anywhere else on earth. Mammoth Pool Dam, Wishon, Don Pedro, Camanche—dams that generated power, controlled floods, created recreational lakes, slaked the thirst of San Francisco and Los Angeles, and supplied irrigation that had transformed a desert into a fantastic engine of agricultural production.

Surrounded by so much engineering history, Phil wondered if maybe he qualified for some sort of record book himself. He was possibly the most presumptuous, reckless, plainly ridiculous young engineer in the world. Here he was driving through a wonderland of famous projects, headed for one of the most famous of all, to prove that it was a grave threat to public safety. Phil Kramer, a greenhorn from Wichita, Kansas. What a joke!

Once he got to the dam, what then? He still hadn't made up his mind what he would do if the people in charge laughed at him and slammed doors in his face. Maybe the whole trip was a mistake. He was acting emotionally, out of anger at getting fired. He should have stayed calm and thought things over.

He was passing Sacramento. Through the car window he could see rays of the setting sun glinting off the dome of the capitol building. If he were going to turn back or spend a night in a motel, this would be a good place to stop. There was an off ramp coming up on the right. He let it go by, stepped on the gas, and swung over to the fast lane. "I am calm," he said aloud. "I *have* thought things over." By pushing on to Sutterton, now only an hour and a half away, the worst that could happen was that he would be proved wrong. "When you feel you are right about something," his father had told him more than once, "stick to your guns, come hell or high water."

Hell or high water. If his theory was right, there would likely be plenty of both.

WILSON HARTLEY, Sutterton's chief of police, wiped spaghetti sauce from his chin and took the phone from his wife. It was Karsh, the night sergeant. "Sorry to bother you at home, Chief, but I got a guy on hold who wants to talk to you personally. He alleges that his name is Herman Bolen and that he is calling from Roshek, Bolen and Benedetz in Los Angeles."

"Put him through, Karsh." Hartley recognized the name of the engineering firm in charge of the dam.

"I don't know if you remember me," Bolen said when he was on the line. "We met during the dedication ceremony ten years ago."

Hartley didn't remember. "Yes, of course. How are you?"

"Fine, thank you. Mr. Hartley, a matter has come up that has to be handled with some discretion. I'm sure you know Lawrence Jeffers, our maintenance chief at the dam."

"Larry? Sure. I go deer hunting with him every year. Is he in some kind of trouble?"

"I'll come right to the point. He's been missing all day. I talked to him twenty-four hours ago and haven't been able to locate him since. What worries me is that he promised to call me first thing this morning. Now, maybe I'm worried over nothing. For all I know, he's visiting a sick friend and simply forgot to call."

"You want me to take a look around? Make a few inquiries?"

"Exactly. But I don't want to alarm anybody unnecessarily. To be quite frank, I don't want to embarrass myself or him by searching for a man who may not be lost."

"I get the picture. I'll swing by his house and see if his pickup is in the garage and I'll call on a few of his friends. If I don't find him, I'll call the Highway Patrol and the hospitals. Give me a phone number and I'll call you back."

"Thanks very much, Mr. Hartley."

Next, Bolen tried to reach Phil Kramer by phone. Failing, he stared absently at a pile of papers on his desk, wondering what to do if Hartley failed to find a trace of Jeffers. If that happened, he would have to send somebody into the drainage gallery to look for him, even if it meant admitting that he had ordered Jeffers to make a night inspection.

PHIL DROVE SLOWLY down Sutterton's Main Street, unable to take his eyes off the dark, looming wall of the dam that filled half the night sky. He hardly noticed the floodlit town hall, the Wagon Wheel Saloon, the banner stretched across the street announcing the Third Annual Mother Lode Marathon. The road across the dam's crest was marked by lights, and to take in the entire glowing line Phil had to put his face close to the windshield. The dam was so overpoweringly huge, it was hard to accept it as man-made, hard to imagine the lake behind it. The dam was a mountain. And yet, towering over a town it miniaturized, it was intense and sullen and alien, threatening in a way the surrounding mountains were not.

A few blocks from the downtown district, Main Street reverted to a country road, passed through a grove of pines, and climbed to the top of the canyon. On a promontory above the dam was an overlook where the teenage occupants of half a dozen cars were listening to music and ignoring the view. Phil parked and walked to the railing, stretching his arms and legs. It was ten thirty—he had made it from Los Angeles in just over eight hours.

The cool breeze off the lake carried the scent of evergreens and was sweet relief after the heat of the Central Valley. The only sounds were the strains of rock music from the parked cars and the distant roar of the spillway water plunging into the river a thousand feet below. To Phil's right was the shining black expanse of the lake, its surface divided by a trail of reflected moonlight, its shoreline defined by low, furrowed hills, with the snowy peaks of the High Sierra in the distance. Breaking through the surface of the lake directly below the overlook was a doughnutlike circle of concrete that Phil knew was the top of the intake tower. Slightly to the left and only barely higher than the water was the crest of the dam. On the valley floor below the dam was a brightly lit rectangle that was the electrical switchyard. Farther to the left, Sutterton was a sprinkle of pinpoint lights.

Gazing at the dam, Phil began to appreciate how foolish he must have looked to Roshek and Bolen. Studying a mathematical model and drawings of a dam was one thing; confronting the reality was another. The dam was so magnificent, so *permanent*. It spanned the canyon gracefully and seemed to resist the weight of the lake with ease, anchored so solidly that no force on earth could dislodge it. The computer images and columns of figures that had struck Phil as so significant suddenly seemed irrelevant, meaningless marks on paper. Once again Phil had half a notion to drive back to Los Angeles before making a bigger fool of himself than he already had.

On the other hand . . . the seepage figures were not irrelevant. The dam looked sleek and powerful on the outside, but deep within its bowels, if the meter readings were correct, were possibly fatal flaws. The dam was colossal and enormously strong, but so was the lake.

He climbed into his car and headed down the hill. He reminded himself that he had begun to overcome his shyness. He had found the nerve to make himself heard, to introduce himself to a beautiful woman, to talk back to an elder. He would not allow himself to be driven back into his shell by a mere *dam*.

HERMAN BOLEN was in the study of his home in Westwood, a phone pressed to his ear. "Yes, Mr. Hartley. I appreciate the trouble you've taken. Please call me at any time of night should something turn up later."

He replaced the receiver on its hook. So Jeffers was nowhere to be found. He was not with friends or neighbors. He was not in a Sutterton bar. His pickup had not been in an accident of which the Highway Patrol was aware. He was not in a hospital or a jail. Where was he, then? Was he still inside the dam?

Before Bolen could decide on the next step, the phone rang again. It was Officer Baker of the Beverly Hills police.

"I'm calling from the home of Mr. and Mrs. Theodore Roshek," the voice said. "The Rosheks have been involved in a dispute. Could we put Mr. Roshek in your care for the night? Tomorrow we will know whether Mrs. Roshek wants to press charges."

"Good heavens . . . I'll be there in fifteen minutes."

PHIL DECIDED to present his case to Lawrence Jeffers. Let the veteran maintenance engineer decide whether there was anything to get excited about. But Jeffers wasn't answering his phone. He wasn't answering his doorbell, either.

Plan B was set in motion. From a phone booth Phil started in on the eleven Duncans listed in the directory. "I'm trying to reach Chuck Duncan," he explained to the woman who answered his fifth call. "He works at the dam. Have I the right number?"

"Sure have. I'm his mother. Chuck went off with Carla and Burt and the Peterson girl."

"Do you expect him home soon?"

"Not hardly on Friday night." She laughed with a twang that reminded Phil of his aunt Lorene in Topeka. "Try the Wagon Wheel on Main Street. They go there and stay till all hours."

"Main Street. Thank you, Mrs. Duncan."

It was country and western disco night at the Wagon Wheel. Women as well as men were dressed as if they were at a rodeo, and they were singing, dancing, and shouting.

Phil wedged his way to the bar and managed to attract the attention of the bartender, a large, unpleasant-looking man. "Do you know Chuck Duncan?" Phil shouted over the din. "Is he here?"

The bartender peered over the heads of the dancers. "He's in the corner booth. The blond kid with the stupid expression."

Phil picked his way between crowded tables to a party of four: Duncan and, if Phil remembered correctly the words of Mrs. Duncan, Carla, Burt, and the Peterson girl.

"Are you Chuck Duncan?" Phil asked the blond youth.

The young man turned and tried to focus his eyes. "Speaking."

Aside from the effect alcohol was having on his mind, Duncan appeared to be no more than nineteen years old. Hardly a person you would entrust with your fears about the structural integrity of the world's highest embankment. "My name is Kramer. I'm with Roshek, Bolen and Benedetz. Could I talk to you?"

"What?"

"Could I talk to you? The music is so loud I can't hear myself think."

"Great, isn't it?"

"Let's go outside. It'll just take a minute." He took Duncan by the arm and gently urged him to his feet. The young inspector yielded, mumbling, and let himself be guided through a side door.

"Let's make this fast," Duncan said when they were outside. "Burt is going to move in on Carla, I know he will. He's done it to me before." The cool night air and the effort of walking seemed to bring him out of his trance.

"Don't worry," Phil said reassuringly. "He's on the wrong side of the table. Look, I don't want to take up any more of your time than I have to. Where can I find Lawrence Jeffers?"

Duncan sat on the fender of a car and crossed his arms. "Beats me," he said. "He didn't show up for work today. The big bosses in L.A. are looking for him, I hear. Did they send you?"

"Nobody sent me. I . . . I'm one of the guys that looks over those meter readings. I want to get a look at the drainage galleries."

Duncan grimaced and shook his head. "You don't want to see the drainage galleries."

"I don't? Why not? It would give me a feel for what those numbers mean."

"You don't want to see the drainage galleries because it is an extreme pain in the rear end. You climb down two hundred steps. Then you climb back up two hundred steps. It's dark. It's wet. It's the total pits. You want to get a feel for it? Stand under a cold shower in the dark with your clothes on, then climb up and down the stairs of a fifteen-story building. That'll give you a feel for it." Duncan chuckled, pleased with the image.

"It's that bad, is it?"

"I deserve a raise for taking readings down there. Last time I thought I was going to drown."

"A lot of water comes in?"

"A lot of water. This year is the worst. I bet we pump more out of Gallery D alone than goes through the turbines."

Phil took a notebook from his shirt pocket, flipped it open, and scribbled a few words. "I had no idea it was so bad. I definitely will recommend you for a raise. On your last report there was a whole bank of meters you didn't include. Why was that?"

"I took the readings, but Jeffers told me to leave them out. They were goofy, he said. Some were zero, some were off the high end. Every year more of those meters go out of whack and we quit reading them. They're not necessary, anyway. Guys who work on other dams around here don't have to climb down holes and read meters. Listen, I better get back inside."

"Wait a minute," Phil said, putting a hand on Duncan's shoulder. "Those readings from the broken meters, where are they?"

"In the trunk of my car."

"Where's your car?"

"I'm sitting on it. You think I'd sit on a car that wasn't mine? Some of those guys in the saloon are *mean*."

While Phil looked on, Duncan opened the trunk and sorted through a box of envelopes.

"I still want to go into the dam," Phil said. "If Jeffers isn't back tomorrow, will you take me?"

"No way. Saturday's my day off. First thing in the morning I'm going to the middle of the lake with my fishing gear."

"How about taking me right now?"

Duncan looked at Phil in amazement. "Man, you got to be crazy," he said, slamming the trunk and handing over an envelope. "I wouldn't go into that hole in the middle of the night for a million bucks. I'm going back into the bar and peel Burt's hands off Carla. Nice to meet you."

Phil followed him along the wooden plank sidewalk. "Could I go into the galleries alone?"

"Sure, if you could get past Newt Withers. He'll look you over on closed-circuit TV, and if he doesn't like what he sees, he won't raise the door. Something wrong?"

"No. Just curious, that's all. You're right—it's crazy to take a tour tonight. Thanks for the information, Chuck. Good luck with Carla."

In a phone booth a few minutes later, Phil heard the long-distance operator's reedy voice say, "I have a collect call for Janet Sandifer from Philip Kramer. Will you accept the charges?"

"Yes, Operator, but he's got a lot of guts."

"Janet! I'm calling from my command post in the heart of downtown Sutterton. Am I interrupting anything?"

"Only a shower. I'm dripping wet. How are things going?"

"I struck pay dirt, as they used to say around here in 1849, in the form of the meter reader whose figures we've been using. From what he told me, I'm surer than ever that all hell's about to break loose. I told him I would recommend him for a raise."

Janet laughed. "Your recommendation will sure carry weight."

"He gave me a list of readings that weren't in the last report. I know you have a terminal in your office with dial-up ports. Have you got keys to get in? . . . Okay, here's what I want you to do. Get down to your office. Feed the new figures into the program. I'll give you the phone number of the R. B. and B. computer and the password that will give you access. Then I'll call you when you get back to find out what the new readings mean."

"Phil, it's almost midnight! And I could get arrested!"

"So could I. If the computer shows what I think it will, I'm going to try to break into the dam. I'll get a motel room now and study the plans while you do your job. Got a pencil? I'll give you the figures."

Janet sighed. "Okay," she said. "Fire away."

Chapter 7

They drove for several minutes without speaking. Roshek was staring straight ahead, and Bolen was struck by the uncharacteristic aura of confusion and defeat that surrounded him. "Do you want to tell me what happened?" Bolen asked gently.

Roshek wet his lips and swallowed before replying. "I can't recall everything," he said in a distant voice.

After a pause Bolen ventured a comment. "The police implied that you struck her and that she ran from the house."

Roshek took a deep, ragged breath. "We were sitting in the living room. We talked about our life together. Pros and cons. It was like compiling a feasibility study. We both tried to be calm, but after an hour or two we more or less cracked."

Bolen turned into his driveway, shut off the engine, and looked at Roshek, who was still staring straight ahead.

"I didn't know either of us was capable of such hostility," Roshek said, speaking in a monotone. He rubbed his temples. "I remember feeling outraged at the way she rejected my offer, a generous settlement if she would delay filing. We raised our voices. Insults

310

came. I remember throwing a wineglass against the wall. I didn't throw it at her. I definitely did not." He lifted his head and looked at Bolen, astonished at his own words. "She ordered me out of the house, Herman. I refused to go. She ran to a phone and asked the operator for the police. I lost control of myself. I lunged across the room, shouting at her." He turned away and sighed again, deeply. "I lifted a crutch, trying to knock the telephone receiver from her hand. I believe I hit  her on the wrist. Yes, that must be it. She screamed."

Bolen studied him. Roshek's face was twisted as if he were in pain. "Let's go inside," Bolen said. "We'll have a brandy and talk."

"I don't remember her running out of the house," Roshek went on. "I fell into a chair and sat like a zombie until the police came."

Bolen got the wheelchair out of the back seat and helped Roshek into it. "The police were very understanding," Bolen said as he pushed Roshek to the house. "They saw the importance of keeping the matter private. I'll talk to Stella in the morning. If she doesn't press charges, the whole thing will be dropped."

In the foyer, Bolen's wife told him that two phone calls had come for him while he was gone. One gentleman didn't leave his name; the other, a Newt Withers at the Sierra Canyon powerhouse, wanted a return call.

JANET SANDIFER, alone in a shadowy sea of deserted desks and typewriters, opened her notebook and dialed the number Phil had given her. A steady tone indicated that she had reached the Roshek computer. She pressed the telephone into a cradle on top of a terminal housing. A row of letters and numbers silently appeared in green on the cathode-ray tube, followed by:

311

Roshek, Bolen & Benedetz
HQ   Technical bank
Please identify

Her fingers moved deftly over the keyboard. One by one, letters appeared on the screen:

Philip Kramer   RB&B
Hydro Design Section

When she pressed the Enter key, the words vanished and were replaced with:

PASSWORD

Carefully Janet typed:

Grand Coulee

The machine responded immediately:

INCORRECT
Try again

"Whoops," Janet said after looking more closely at her notes. She had capitalized the wrong letters. She entered:

gRand cOulee

Again the machine responded. Within seconds the screen was filled with program titles. She moved the little cursor to the seventh item on the list, the Kramer Dam-Failure Model. At the touch of the Enter key the screen displayed a message:

CONGRATULATIONS
You have reached the amazing Kramer Dam Model

Janet worked as fast as she could. She was breaking the law, and she didn't want to spend all night doing it.

Add new values
Meter bank 9 Gallery D Sierra Canyon Dam

Janet fed in Phil's columns of new figures. She instructed the computer to evaluate the condition of the dam under the most optimistic assumptions.

312

> BEST CASE
> Begin lowering reservoir
> Make visual inspection Galleries C & D

She jotted down the response, then bent over the keyboard and made another request:

> WORST CASE
> Evaluate   Instruct

The response came on the screen five minutes later, and she couldn't help smiling. Phil had told her what he had put in the program to indicate a failing dam that was beyond salvation:

> RUN FOR YOUR LIVES!

When Janet got back to her apartment, it was after one a.m. and her phone was ringing. It was Phil. "I'm calling from the beautiful Damview Motel in Sutterton, California, Gateway to a Mountain Wonderland," he said cheerfully. "If you project the plane of the surface of Earl Warren Lake in a southwesterly direction, I am under seven hundred feet of water."

"Sounds like a good spot to be. Your computer suggests that you run for your life."

"Did you ask for the most likely points of failure?"

"Yes. Got a pencil?"

After writing down the numbers, Phil read them back to her to make sure he had them right. "Sounds like the contact between the fill and bedrock. Water must have found a way through the grout curtain under Gallery D. I've been studying the plans, and if I can get into the dam, I'm sure I can find the place."

"What's next?"

"I'll call Bolen. He should be interested to know that the inspector who reads the meters in the lower galleries says he needs scuba gear. Maybe Bolen will authorize me to inspect them."

"What if he tells you to mind your own business?"

"I'll make an inspection anyway. If I can't bluff my way in, I might go down the intake tower. There's a little elevator, a man cage, inside. The problem would be getting to it—the tower sticks up twenty feet above the water. I was thinking of stealing a yacht."

Janet groaned. "This is sounding worse and worse. You'll get thrown in jail if you don't kill yourself first."

"Why not look on the bright side? You are an attractive woman who will have no trouble finding yourself another engineer."

"Don't make me laugh. I learn from my mistakes."

PHIL TURNED ONTO THE powerhouse access road and immediately hit the brakes: both lanes were blocked by a double-chain link gate. "Duncan didn't mention this," he muttered.

He left the car with the headlights on and the engine running to examine the obstacle. The padlock on the gate looked impregnable, and the chain would withstand a week of hacksawing. The good news was that there were no electrical connections on the gate or adjoining fence, which meant that if he could force it open, alarms wouldn't go off up and down the Pacific Coast.

He returned to the car and sat behind the wheel, pondering. Climbing the fence and walking to the tunnel portal would be no problem, but that is hardly the way an inspector from the Occupational Safety and Health Administration would arrive, and it was an OSHA representative he had decided to impersonate. Picking the lock with a piece of wire would take too long. He had to act fast if he was going to exploit Bolen's absence—his wife had said on the phone that he would return home within the hour.

Phil lifted his eyes from the gate to the massive bulk of the dam looming in the background, bathed in faint light from a moon that now was high in the sky. The longer he gazed at it the more uncomfortable he felt. It was so big! An enormous jungle cat, sleek and muscular, crouched in the canyon, its back arched against the force of the lake. Phil felt like a gnat in comparison.

He put the car in reverse and slowly backed away. "What I need," he said aloud, "is a way to get this car past that gate. Something subtle and sophisticated." A hundred and fifty feet from the gate he stopped, checked his seat belt. Bracing himself, he let out the clutch. Tires squealed. The car shot forward.

A speed of forty miles an hour proved sufficient to break the gate apart, cave in the car's grille, and smash one headlight. The nice thing about driving an old car, Phil thought, is that a few more scratches don't make any difference.

314

Half a mile down the road, set into the base of a vertical wall of rock, a steel hangar door marked the mouth of the powerhouse access tunnel. Next to it was a concrete panel with a microphone and a loudspeaker. Phil, a roll of plans under his arm, walked over and pushed a large black button. A red light went on and a voice came over the loudspeaker: "Control room."

"Mr. Withers?" Phil asked crisply.

"This is Withers."

"I'm Charles Robinson of the Occupational Safety and Health Administration." It was the biggest lie Phil Kramer had told in his life. When the state of Kansas was admitted to the Union in 1861, Charles Robinson was elected governor. "I trust you've been expecting me," he added.

"What did you say your name was? Robinson?"

"Mr. Withers," Phil said with mock impatience, "didn't Mr. Jeffers or Mr. Bolen tell you that there might be an OSHA night inspection this weekend?"

"Nobody told me. May I ask how you got through the gate?"

Phil raised his voice slightly. "With a key that Herman Bolen gave me today in Los Angeles. Your communications seem less than adequate. It makes me wonder what else might be."

Withers said defensively, "My standing orders—"

"Excuse me, I don't mean to blame you for the failure of others to keep you informed. Here's what I want you to do—call Jeffers and Bolen at their homes right now. They will give you the okay to let me in. If they don't, I'll have to file a report with Washington as well as with the State Division of Dam Safety."

"Yes, sir. I'll do that right away."

The loudspeaker fell silent. With luck, Phil thought, Bolen won't be home yet and nobody will answer Jeffers' phone. Withers will be on the spot and will probably yield.

After several minutes two floodlights went on, illuminating Phil like a singer on a stage. "Would you stand in the center of the platform?" Withers asked over the loudspeaker.

Squinting, Phil noticed a camera housing on the rock wall five feet above his head. He saw the lens retract slightly to put him in focus.

"May I ask what the cylinder is you are carrying?"

315

"This? A set of plans of the dam's instrumentation and inspection tunnels." Phil unrolled them, realizing that Withers wanted to make sure he wasn't concealing a rifle or a bomb. He held the sheets toward the camera. "You can see the Roshek company seal in the lower corner," he said.

"I see it. If you are carrying any metal, an alarm will sound in the Sutterton police station when you go through the detector. I'm going to raise the door high enough for you, Mr. Robinson, but not for your car. You'll have to walk down the tunnel."

There was a rumble as the ponderous door rolled upward. It stopped a few feet above the pavement. Phil ducked inside and heard it thunder shut behind him with reverberating finality.

"THIS IS Herman Bolen speaking."

"Oh, yes. Newt Withers here. Thanks for returning my call. I had a question and I couldn't locate Mr. Jeffers."

"I must say I was surprised to get the message that you called, Withers, because I was about to phone the powerhouse myself. I have to tell you that I'm a little worried about what might have happened to our Mr. Jeffers. I'm afraid that he's had some sort of accident in the lower tunnels. When I talked to him last night, he told me he was thinking of checking a few meters before going to bed. No reason to get excited," Bolen added quickly when he heard Withers' low whistle. "This is just supposition on my part."

"If he was in the dam, wouldn't his truck be here? I didn't see it in the lot when I came in."

"Good point. Still, I'd like somebody to take a look below."

"Well, the OSHA inspector said that he was going to check Gallery D. That was about twenty minutes ago. . . . When he gets back, I'll—"

"What OSHA inspector?"

"Robinson. The one you gave the key to the gate to. The reason I called you was to make sure he had authorization."

"I don't know any OSHA inspector. My key is in my desk."

Withers moaned. "He said he was here to make a night inspection and that you knew all about it. He even had a set of R. B. and B. plans of the tunnels. Should I call the cops?"

"He had a set of plans? What did he look like?"

316

"Tall guy, young, maybe six feet two. Reddish hair."

Bolen cursed quietly. "Call the police. Your OSHA inspector sounds like Phil Kramer, an engineer Roshek fired about twelve hours ago. He is absolutely convinced that the dam is going to fail. He's possessed by the idea, which is why we let him go."

"Is he violent? Mr. Bolen, I'm in here alone."

"As far as I know, he is rational except when it comes to the dam. Unless I miss my guess, he's going to want you to declare an emergency. He's never been inside a dam, and when he sees how much leakage there is, he'll think it's about to bust."

"I hope the cops can get here before he gets back."

"Withers, I want the police to restrain him and keep him from going to the newspapers until I get there. I'll come up by noon tomorrow. Let's keep this quiet if we can."

PHIL SQUEEZED PAST the pickup truck parked behind the sixth turbine. Was there a workman in the tunnels, despite the hour? He sprinted up the steel stairs and pulled open the door marked DANGER, NO ADMITTANCE. He grabbed a flashlight from the rack and headed down the tunnel at a half-trot. He couldn't help smiling over his success in bluffing Withers.

The tunnel was better suited to screams of fear than to smiles of satisfaction. It was no bigger than the culverts under his father's county roads, poorly lit, and so wet he had already ruined his shoes. Casting his flashlight onto the swiftly flowing rivulet in the gutter along the walkway he wondered what it was going to be like a hundred and fifty feet lower.

The air was stale, and the tunnel seemed to get smaller the deeper he advanced, although he knew that was just his imagination. He felt a touch of claustrophobia, not enough to make him turn back but enough to make him feel that the fear would surface if he let it. He pushed on, each footstep making a splashing sound. At an intersection with a cross tunnel, he unrolled the plans. The sight of the technical drawings with dimensions, cross sections, and explanatory notes, helped him keep his intellect in control. There was nothing to be afraid of, the drawings seemed to say. You aren't lost. Straight ahead is the way to the base of the intake shaft. To the left, that's where you want to go.

The side tunnel was definitely smaller, no more than seven feet in diameter. I can see why Duncan hates to come in here, Phil thought. If I really were an OSHA inspector, I'd raise hell about these tunnels—not enough light, terrible air, treacherous footing. Seepage water should come in through the collector pipes instead of through cracks in the walls. This is some mess.

Phil stopped at a stairwell that descended at a steep angle. His flashlight beam had little effect on the gloom below. He stood very still and listened.

Water was trickling around him, but the faint sound that held his attention was deeper and stronger, like that of a waterfall plunging into a pool. He started down.

AFTER SAYING good night, Herman Bolen waited in the hall outside the guest room to see if Roshek would go to sleep. When the slit of light under the door went out, Bolen sighed in relief. He went downstairs to his den and dialed the powerhouse.

It was amazing how complicated life had suddenly become. One of the company's most reliable employees was inexplicably missing. Roshek announced that he might abdicate his throne for a few years, then proceeded to terrorize his wife and get evicted from his own house by the police. Now this thing with Kramer.

"This is Bolen again," he said when Withers answered. "Any developments?"

"The cops are on their way. Kramer is still down in the hole."

"Don't let him in the control room. If he throws a fit in there, he could do a lot of damage. I've been thinking. Kramer was particularly upset about what he regarded as excessive seepage in Gallery D. Can you tell me about conditions there?"

"Gallery D? There are a few remote-reading pore-pressure sensors. I think they're out of order. The readings never change. The current drain for that reach of the electrical network . . . let's see, looks like about a third of normal. I would guess two of the three pumps aren't working."

"Two pumps out? That means there might be a few inches of water on the tunnel floor. Kramer will think the lake is coming in. Don't let him scare you."

"I understand."

AT THE BOTTOM of the steps, Phil found himself in darkness, standing in water to his thighs. Don't get excited, he told himself, just because the lights are out and the pumps aren't working. The situation was hardly normal, but there was no proof that a catastrophe was pending. He wanted proof. Leaving the roll of plans on a dry step, he waded toward the sound of surging water. Fifty feet from the steps, he found a vigorous upwelling of water from beneath the surface. He groped with one foot to try to determine if it was erupting from a broken pressure pipe, but the force of the jet knocked his foot aside and into a submerged object covered with cloth that was snagged on the wall. It yielded as he pushed past.

Deeper in the tunnel, Phil flashed his light on a half-open steel door marked GALLERY D. There, he knew, he would find the proof he needed. The fantastic amount of water demonstrated beyond argument that the drainage, pumping, and monitoring procedures that Roshek was so proud of were inadequate. Further, the computer program, while perhaps far from foolproof, had at least revealed that *something* was haywire.

The passageway behind the Gallery D door descended gradually, and after eighty feet Phil was in water up to his chest. He stopped, and shone his light ahead, wondering how much farther he had to go to reach the meter bank. Twenty feet away he saw a shimmering horizontal band that made his mouth open and his flesh crawl: a sheet of water was jetting from one wall of the tunnel to the other from a jagged crack. The volume of water grew as he watched it, and he saw several small pieces of concrete at the base of the stream scoured loose and shot across the tunnel with the force of bullets.

"That's not seepage or a broken pipe," he said, taking several backward steps and trying to swallow. "That's a *breach.*"

He turned and waded toward the main tunnel as fast as he could, aware for the first time how slippery the footing was. Slippery? Holding the flashlight aloft, he lowered the other hand to the walkway, submerging his head and shoulders. He scraped his palm along the concrete and brought it to the surface. The flashlight confirmed his suspicion: his cupped hand was filled with clay. The incoming water was carrying with it part of the embankment. He poured the clay into his shirt pocket and fastened the button. Ten feet away, sudden waves of water in the main tunnel began closing the door to Gallery D. With a desperate lunge he jammed his arms into the narrowing gap and forced himself through the door. He no longer was worried about verifying a theory. All that mattered now was escaping with his life.

Gasping, he pushed toward the steps. Blocking his way was the submerged fountain, gushing upward now with ten times its earlier force and sending a boiling mass of water against the tunnel crown. Phil plunged wildly forward and into the cold, stiffened arms of Lawrence Jeffers.

THEODORE ROSHEK couldn't sleep. He fumbled in the darkness for the bedside lamp and the telephone. He would call Eleanor. Just hearing her voice would make him feel better. Unfortunately there was a busy signal when he dialed Creekwood, his house on the Sierra Canyon River. She had probably turned in for the night and, as usual, had taken the phone off the hook.

He put his head on the pillow and lay staring at the ceiling.

Chapter 8

When the jet of water in the tunnel floor erupted into a fully-fledged geyser, the increased force dislodged the snagged body of Jeffers and rotated it upward in a grotesque cartwheel. Phil caught a flash of glassy eyes that were frozen in an expression of terror even greater than his own. Phil hurled himself backward in fright, dropping the flashlight. His hoarse shout was stopped by the water that closed over his head as he fell. When he regained his footing, he was in total darkness. He waded toward the sound of the upsurging water, again encountering the body, which was blocking his way. Taking a deep breath and ducking beneath the surface, Phil drove up the slope, pushing the dead man ahead of him as a way of keeping his balance. Once past the jet, the water level came to his waist—a foot higher than it had been on his way in.

At the base of the steps he saw faint lights far above him. Thank God, he thought. He began the climb, pulling the ungainly body behind him. But after advancing twenty feet he released his grip and sat down, gasping for breath. He tried to clear his thoughts. What was the point of risking his life to retrieve a corpse? He felt a coldness growing in his legs and wondered if he were going into shock. Peering down through the semidarkness, he saw that the silently rising water was creeping over his feet, calves, and knees. He rolled over and clambered up the steps on all fours.

WITHERS CURSED his own stupidity. Why did I let that guy in? But how was I supposed to know he was a phony? He knew all the right things to say. Anybody would have done what I did.

There were four closed-circuit television screens mounted on the wall. One displayed the access tunnel entrance and parking area, one the electrical switchyard, one the generator deck, and one the turbine deck. Withers trained camera four on the door leading to the inspection galleries. He hoped the police would appear first.

A buzzer sounded on the hot-line phone to Pacific Gas & Electric's Power Control Center in Oakland, from which the power grid in northern California was monitored.

"Sierra Canyon," Withers said into the phone.

"Power Control Center. Rancho Seco may have to cut back in a few hours. We'll need an extra twenty megawatts from you during the morning peak. I guess you can handle that?"

"No problem," Withers replied. Just then, on the fourth television screen, he saw Kramer burst through the door and drape himself over a steel railing. He was gulping air like a beached fish, his shoulders heaving. Was he sick? Withers couldn't tell.

The voice from Power Control Center went on. "Checking our printouts on Sierra Canyon. There seems to be a frequency fluctuation during the last thirty minutes or so. What do you indicate?"

"Look, I'm awful busy right now. I'll call you back."

"At three in the morning you're busy?"

"I got a slight problem here. I'll explain later."

Withers hung up, staring at the monitor. Kramer's clothes looked wet, his eyes were wide, and his mouth was hanging open. "Oh, no," Withers whispered. "A pipe must have burst and hit him with spray. He looks like he's flipped his lid completely." As he watched, Kramer closed his mouth and swallowed with difficulty, glancing behind him as if he were being pursued. Then he lunged down the short flight of steps to the turbine deck, out of the camera's view.

Withers swiveled toward the windows that lined one wall of the control room. The apparition that now appeared on the other side of the windows was like something out of a bad dream. Kramer's clothes were soaked and torn, and the expression on his face was that of a man who had only a tenuous connection with reality. He ran drunkenly across the tiled floor, skidded to a stop, and pressed his hands against the glass. The voice Withers heard over the intercom was high-pitched and breathless.

"The dam is failing! Sound the alarm!"

Withers nodded sympathetically but did not move.

"Can you hear me? The lake is breaking into the tunnels. . . . We've got to warn the town. . . ." Kramer looked wildly around, then hurled himself to the end of the windows and tried to open the control-room door. "Unlock the door! The dam is failing!"

Withers leaned close to a microphone on the counter. "Yes, I can hear you," he said. "I can't open the door. It's against regulations." He concentrated on presenting an unruffled appearance, even though beads of sweat were forming on his forehead.

"To hell with regulations!" Kramer shouted. "This is an emergency! We've got to get out of here. . . . Are you crazy?"

"Calm down, Mr. Kramer. You're all excited."

"Sure I'm excited! We've got to get on the phone. . . ." He frowned. "How did you know my name was Kramer?"

Withers hesitated, hoping he hadn't made another terrible error. "I talked with Herman Bolen. He identified you."

"Get him on the phone! When I tell him what I've seen . . . Call him! Call anybody! You dummy! Do something!"

"Mr. Bolen will be here at noon. You can talk to him then."

Kramer shook his fists. "By noon the dam may not be here! Sutterton may not be here! You'll be floating around in the middle of San Francisco Bay. *The . . . dam . . . is . . . failing.*" He rolled his eyes in disbelief at the lack of effect the words had on Withers. Whirling around, he saw the row of offices on the opposite wall of the lobby. He ran from one to another, trying telephones, throwing them aside when he couldn't get a dial tone.

"Those phones are dead," Withers said. "The switchboard is turned off at five. Mr. Kramer, you've got to get hold of yourself." Where the hell were the cops?

Kramer tightened his fists and walked back to the control-room

windows. "You think I'm a raving lunatic, don't you?" he said. "Bolen told you that I wasn't to be taken seriously, is that it?"

"If the dam was failing, the instruments would—"

"The instruments are out of order! Ask Duncan, he'll tell you. I *know* the dam is failing. With my own eyes I have . . ." Kramer slapped both hands over his face, digging his fingernails into his forehead in frustration. Withers stood up, studying him, hoping he was about to succumb to some sort of seizure.

Kramer lowered his hands. The men stared at each other through double panes of bulletproof glass. "I am not a crackpot," Kramer said, making precise gestures. His voice and face had become utterly calm. "I was just down in the lower drainage galleries. The lake is breaking in under pressure even as we stand here having this friendly discussion. I saw two breaches. Each is bringing water in at maybe ten thousand gallons a minute. I'm sure you realize, Mr. Withers, as an engineer, that water coming in under pressure is—how shall I put it?—bad news."

"I . . . I'm not an engineer."

"I am. I have a Ph.D. in civil engineering. My special interest, as luck would have it, is the prediction of dam failures. One thing you learn when you pursue such an interest is that leakage under pressure is a poor sign. Another poor sign is the presence of clay, which shows that the core is being scoured away by the water under pressure, to which I have just alluded." He dipped a hand into his shirt pocket and extended it toward Withers. "See? I scooped this up from the lower gallery. From under four feet of water. That's clay from the core. What this means—pressure, clay, rapid increase in flow—is that the dam is failing. That's it in a nutshell!" He smiled as if pleased at finding words that even the dumbest child could comprehend. "Now, Mr. Withers, what should two intelligent adults do when confronted with a failing dam?" His voice began to rise. *"Get on the phone!"*

"I'm not an expert on hydraulics."

"I am an expert on hydraulics!" Phil shouted. "You idiot! We may have hours or we may have minutes. This dam may be ready to split open like a watermelon dropped from a truck." Phil pounded his fists against the windows. "One man is dead already! You want to stay here? Fine. Then open the outside door so I can get out.

324

Otherwise I'm going to grab a crowbar and tear this place apart."

Withers was sweating profusely. "What man is dead?" he asked. Could Jeffers have had an accident in the inspection gallery?

"How should I know? The guy whose truck is parked behind the turbines, I guess. He landed right on my head!"

"What did he look like?"

"He looked terrible! He looked dead!" Phil lifted his eyes to the television screens. "Hey, did you call the cops?"

Withers turned to the monitors and saw a policeman's face on the screen. "Newt? This is Lee Simon. You okay? What's going on?"

Withers spoke into a second microphone. "I'm okay, Lee. I'll raise the door. Come up to the control room."

"You got a trespasser?"

"Yes. He's on the control-room deck."

"Is he armed?"

Withers looked at Kramer, who was holding the sides of his head as if to contain an explosion. "I don't think so."

"You've got to be out of your mind," Phil said, edging away. "We'll all drown."

"Look, Kramer," said Withers. "Stay cool and everything will be fine." Then he cursed when he saw Kramer run for the stairs to the lower decks. "Where do you think you're going?" he shouted into the microphone.

Within minutes officers John Colla and Lee Simon were standing in the control-room lobby awaiting further instructions.

"See those stairs?" Withers said. "Two flights down is the turbine deck. Go to the end of the chamber and you'll see a steel door. I saw him go through there on the monitor." His attention was caught by a red light flashing on an instrument panel to his left. "Wait a minute. He's in the elevator."

Although Withers had never been in it, he knew there was a man cage inside the walls of the intake tower. He should have realized that Kramer would be aware of it. The red light showed that it was in use, and a dial showed that the cage was at the seven-hundred-foot level and rising steadily. With a slight smile, Withers reversed a switch labeled OVERRIDE. The arrow stopped and began to swing slowly to the left. It would take the cage about five minutes to return to the bottom of the shaft. Withers ran toward the stairs.

"Come on," he shouted, waving for the policemen to follow him. "He's trapped in an elevator. We've got him now!"

The footsteps of the three men as they ran down the steps masked a faint throbbing vibration in the hum made by the generators. In the control room, a series of lights went on, indicating a drop in frequency, then went out as circuits were short-circuited by water.

THE ELEVATOR was really an open framework on a three-foot-square platform. A waist-high grillwork fence shielded the passenger from the concrete walls of the shaft. One of these walls was covered with water pipes, ventilation ducts, and bundled electrical conduits; another, in a two-foot-deep vertical inset, carried a steel ladder that ran the full height of the tower.

As the cage rose, Phil reviewed in his mind the drawings of the tower he had studied at the motel. At the top, a flight of stairs led to a hatch cover. Once he got past that, he would be outside, twenty feet above the lake and about two hundred feet from shore. With enough of a head start, he could swim there and sound an alarm before Withers figured out where he was.

With a lurch the cage stopped moving. Phil's first thought was that the water had risen high enough to short out the generators . . . but no, the lights in the shaft were still on.

When the cage began to descend, Phil guessed that Withers had discovered where he was and was using some emergency hookup to bring the elevator down. He climbed to the top of the railing, caught hold of one of the ladder rungs, and stepped out of the cage. Then he began climbing. The rungs were so wet from water trickling down the walls that he had trouble keeping his footing, but he kept his eyes fixed on the light above him.

After several minutes Phil reached the top landing and stepped off the ladder through an opening in the concrete wall. He ran up the stairs, pushed open the hatch cover, and climbed outside. He was now on the outer rim of the tower. The moon was still bathing the valley in light and casting a trail across the water. The sky was full of stars and there wasn't a trace of movement or sound in the surrounding forests. It was a scene of such tranquillity that Phil began to wonder if his brain were playing tricks on him. Had he simply imagined what he had just been through?

If I'm nuts, he thought, they can lock me up. If I'm not, I'd better get a move on. He placed his car ignition key in the right side of his mouth between his cheek and his gum. In the left side he put two dimes he had in his pocket—they would be handy if he could find a phone booth. He removed his shoes, socks, shirt, and slacks and folded them in a neat pile. Then he turned and leaped off the edge of the concrete, pinching his nose shut with one hand. The shock of the cold water gave him new energy, and he pulled for shore with clean, strong strokes.

HERMAN BOLEN lay on his side in bed, scowling into the telephone. "He told you he saw a dead body?"

"It must be Jeffers," Withers said. "When I went to the elevator, I saw his truck behind the last turbine."

Bolen lay stunned. Jeffers! Dead! Or was he? "Is there a body or not?" he said suddenly. "Didn't you go down to make sure?"

"Things have been so hectic I haven't had a chance."

"Send somebody else, then! Call Cooper and Riggs. Damn it, Withers! I want somebody to go *now!* What else did Kramer say?"

"He said water was jetting in all over the place and bringing the dam with it. He dug some dirt out of his shirt pocket, as if that was supposed to prove something."

"Good Lord!"

"I didn't let that bother me because you told me he was going to say the dam was failing. My dials showed two pumps out, so I knew water was accumulating. When he saw a dead body, I figure he got hysterical. You should have seen him—he's definitely psycho."

"For everybody's sake, Withers, I hope he was hallucinating. What's your version of the way things are?"

"Looks like all three pumps are out now in the lower gallery. The remote sensors in Gallery D have shorted out, too. My guess is that Gallery D is flooded."

"Wonderful," Bolen said with heavy sarcasm. "And Kramer? You say the police have him cornered?"

"They saw him run across the road by the left overlook, wearing nothing but his shorts. He's hiding in the Mitchell Brothers' construction yard. They'll have him in a few minutes."

"Get hold of Leonard Mitchell and give him the job of pumping

327

out the lower tunnels. I'm going to leave Beverly Hills now." He looked at his bedside clock—it was five thirty. "I can be there in three hours. I'll take my own plane and land on the dam."

Bolen hung up and began dressing hurriedly. "When Theodore wakes up," he said to his wife, "tell him I had to go to Sierra Canyon and I'll call him as soon as I can."

In the guest bedroom, Roshek carefully replaced the receiver of the extension phone. He stared into the darkness, his jaw muscles tense and his lips pressed into a thin line.

AFTER SCALING the rocky slope from the lake to the road, Phil stood shivering, wondering which way to turn. Sutterton was a mile downhill to the right. The overlook was closer, up the road to the left, but he didn't recall seeing a pay phone there. Across the road were fuel and water tanks and what appeared to be an asphalt plant. Against the night sky he could see wires fanning out to several corrugated metal buildings from a nearby pole. One could be a telephone line. He trotted across the road.

Just before he reached the shadows on the other side, a car rounded a curve. For an instant Phil was caught in the beam of the headlights. He sprinted between two parked tractors and tried the door of the largest building. It was locked. He ran to the rear of the building and saw a row of windows hinged at the top. He broke one out with a rock, and as he climbed carefully inside, he heard the car slide to a stop in the gravel. The crackle of a two-way radio confirmed his fears. "Suspect in construction yard on Sterling Road. Maybe inside one of the buildings. Send everybody up here."

Phil hugged himself in the cold, his eyes gradually becoming accustomed to the darkness. Looming over him were the shapes of two earth-moving trucks, with tires eight feet high and cabs that could be reached only by the built-in ladders. What appeared at first to be a man standing against the wall turned out to be a pair of white coveralls on a hanger. As he put them on, a second car arrived outside, and a third.

"No shooting," he heard an authoritative voice say. "There's fuel tanks all over the place and maybe dynamite, too."

"Yes," Phil whispered, groping across the floor, "let's have no shooting. The suspect hates shooting."

In a momentary flash of headlights Phil saw a desk and on the desk was a phone. He raised the receiver and heard a dial tone. Sixty seconds later Janet Sandifer was on the line.

"Phil, it's five thirty in the morning! Where are you? Did you get in the dam?"

"Getting in was easy, getting out wasn't. The cops are after me. The dam is failing, water is pouring into the tunnels under pressure. You've got to sound the alarm. . . ."

"What?"

"I'm cornered in a garage and about to be arrested for trespassing or something. Tell everybody the dam is failing. Call the towns downstream, call the sheriff. The state has some sort of disaster office. . . . Call that."

"The dam is failing? You mean right now? Can't the cops see it's failing?"

"There's nothing to see unless you know where to look. Water is probably oozing out of the downstream face where the computer said it would, but nobody will listen. Janet, this is the only phone call I'll be able to make. There's still time to evacuate the town. You've got to believe me. I know I'm right. You've got to do what you can . . . please, please!"

"I believe you. I'll do what I can. How much I can accomplish from Santa Monica, I don't know, but I'll do my best. Phil? I'm worried. About you. Don't take any more chances. Okay?"

Phil closed his eyes in relief. "Whew! I knew I could count on you. I've got to hang up. Good luck!"

"Don't take any more chances! Promise?"

"There's just one more stunt I can try. Then I'm through. Then it's up to you."

Chapter 9

When Chief Hartley arrived at the construction yard, a patrolman apprised him of the situation. Prints of bare feet had been found leading to the rear of the main building, where a pane of glass had been broken. "I'll see if I can talk him out," Hartley said, crouching behind his car with several aides and raising a bullhorn to his mouth. "This is Wilson Hartley," his voice boomed through the still night air. "Sutterton Chief of Police. You might as well give yourself up, Mr. Kramer. Just stroll through the door with your hands up and you won't be hurt."

"Promise not to shoot?" came a call from within the building.

Hartley widened his eyes at the deputy next to him. "We don't shoot trespassers in Caspar County," he said into the horn.

"Good," was the muffled reply, "because I don't have a gun."

"If you can get them talking, set up communications," Hartley whispered to the deputy, "they usually won't do anything crazy."

"I heard that," said the voice from the building. "Communication works both ways. Get a policeman talking and he usually won't do anything crazy, either. How do you like police work?"

Hartley frowned at the bullhorn and flicked the switch on the handle several times. "We can talk about that later," he replied.

"I know we can talk later," said the voice, "but we should talk now. The dam is failing, did anybody tell you? I am a civil engineer. University of Kansas. You and your men should be waking up the town instead of terrorizing an engineer who is trying to do everybody a favor and whom you can't help liking once you get past his shyness that is a carryover from his childhood."

"Oh, boy," Hartley whispered, "this guy is a real fruitcake."

"The reason I am talking," said the voice, "is that I'm stalling for time. I'm checking out a few things in here. There, I'm ready now. See the garage door? I'm going to push a button that opens it. Then I'm coming out. I mean, coming *out*."

The door rolled to one side with a rumble. Hartley peered into the building and was startled by the sight of two headlights winking on. There was the roar of a diesel engine, and a fifteen-ton dump truck leaped into view. Before anyone could react, the truck was out of the yard and turning left on the highway.

A deputy raised a rifle. "No shooting," Hartley commanded, jumping into his car. "He won't get far in that thing."

Hartley stepped hard on the gas and took off in a cloud of flying gravel. He turned on his roof lights and siren and overtook the truck in less than a minute. As he tried to pass, the truck swerved right, onto the narrow road that crossed the dam. "Where does he think he's going?" Hartley said, cramping the wheel hard right into the turn. "He'll never make the curves on the other side."

The deputy beside him had rolled down his window. "Let me take his tires out, boss."

Hartley pursed his lips in indecision. "Well, okay, go ahead. . . . Wait, he's stopping! He's raising the dump—" The police chief slammed on the brakes and his car skidded to a stop with its nose under the tail of the truck.

Before the two policemen could open their doors, the car was jolted violently as tons of crushed rock slid out of the upraised dump and crashed on the hood. By the time they had crawled out of the rear windows, the truck was lumbering away, its upraised dump outlined against a graying sky.

PHIL STOPPED the truck when he saw the numbers 50+00 stenciled on the concrete shoulder of the crest road. According to the figures Janet had relayed to him at the motel, the most likely point of failure on the downstream face was just past this marker. He climbed down the cab's ladder, dressed in the white coveralls and a pair of rubber boots he had found in the garage. The sound of an approaching siren told him that a police car had gotten around the pile of rock.

He walked over to the guardrail and looked down at the face of the dam, which angled at a two-to-one slope into the shadows and the thundering mists far below. At the base of the dam on the other side of the river was the powerhouse parking lot. There were half a dozen cars there now, including his own beloved jalopy. His tongue touched the ignition key—still wedged between his cheek and gum.

The crest of the dam was a thousand and fifty feet above sea level, the predicted failure point at three hundred and seventy-five feet. Phil swung himself over the guardrail, hung for a moment from the edge of the road platform, then dropped five feet to the top of the slope. Above him he heard a car stop. He clambered as quickly as he could down the face of the dam, which was composed of rough chunks of quarried rock.

"Get back up here," a voice shouted. "Stop or I'll shoot!" Two policemen were looking down at him from twenty feet above.

"You wouldn't shoot a harmless, unarmed engineer," Phil shouted. "Aren't you going to follow me? I want to show you where the dam is leaking. Then you'll know I'm not nuts."

"Son of a gun. John, send some men to the bottom of the dam. I'll chase him down. You stay here in case he doubles back."

The policeman vaulted the rail and shouted at the figure scuttling below him. "If you make me climb all the way down this lousy dam, I'll wring your neck when I catch you."

There was no answer.

POWER CONTROL CENTER was on the line again. "Rancho Seco has to cut back more than we thought," the dispatcher said. "We need forty extra megawatts, not the twenty we asked for earlier."

"No sweat," Withers said. "We got plenty of water here."

Riggs and Cooper, two R. B. & B. engineers, had arrived and let themselves into the control room. Withers covered the mouthpiece with his hand and told them that Herman Bolen was on his way. "He wants the lower galleries inspected. Look for a dead body. The kid we had in here said he saw one. Could be Jeffers." Riggs and Cooper left for the tunnels on the run.

"Okay," Withers said into the phone. "Forty megawatts? You want it in a lump?"

"Feed half onto the line in thirty minutes and the rest thirty minutes later. Are you having some kind of trouble up there? You said you were going to call me back and you never did."

"Trouble? No trouble. Well, actually we had a little trouble with an ex-employee. He's gone now and everything is quiet." Withers looked at one of the television screens. A thin line was coming from the half-open door at the end of the turbine deck, a sparkling line like a piece of tinsel. Was that water?

"Good," said the dispatcher. "One other thing. We definitely have a frequency problem in the foothills sector of the grid. Could be Sierra Canyon, could be one of the automatic plants downstream. What do you show? Give me your readings."

Withers swiveled to the right and glanced at the bank of frequency meters. All arrows were on zero.

"What the hell—"

"Beg pardon?"

Withers was half out of his chair, leaning toward the dials. "I can't quite see them from here. I'll call you back."

He hung up and ran to the generator meter bank. He tapped the glass dial coverings and gave the panel housing a rap with his hand. Nothing flickered. "That stupid lunatic," he said. "He must have tripped the circuit breakers." Cursing, he made a series of connections to find out how much of the system was affected. The overhead lights dimmed, then came on brightly as a backup diesel-electric generator in the next room coughed into life. On the television monitor behind him, the silver strand emerging from the turbine-deck doorway grew into a small waterfall that bubbled down the short flight of steps. Through the windows he saw Riggs running toward him waving his arms.

PHIL STOOD on a rock and slowly turned in a circle. As closely as he could estimate, he was standing on the coordinates that the computer indicated as the likeliest point of failure. But there was no leak. The sky was light enough now to enable him to examine the face of the dam for a hundred feet in every direction. It was as dry as Death Valley.

"Well, so much for mathematical models," Phil said, glancing at the policemen working their way toward him. He sat down, put his arms wearily on his knees, and hung his head. The hours spent running up and down stairs and ladders, swimming across the lake and climbing down the dam were having their effect.

The policeman from above arrived first. He stood for a moment catching his breath and looking at Phil with an expression of revulsion. He said, "I'm Officer Lee Simon and I place you under arrest. I caution you that any statement you make can be used against you, and sure as hell will if I have anything to say about it. Couldn't you give yourself up at the top instead of making me climb all the way down here?"

Phil looked up. "I made you climb down to show you the leak in the dam. As you can see, there is no leak, which puts me in . . . an unfortunate light. There is an old proverb in the computer industry: 'Garbage in, garbage out.' What that means is—"

Hands landed on his shoulders. There were three policemen now, the arrivals breathing hard and looking unfriendly. "See these?" the first policeman said. "Handcuffs. See this? A nightstick. Put out your hands so I can snap on the cuffs or I will introduce the stick to your head."

"Well put," Phil said, "but handcuffs won't be needed. I give up. I'm sorry I put you to so much trouble."

"I'll bet you are," the policeman said, locking Phil's wrists together. "Let's go." Phil was pulled to his feet. He winced at the pain in his calves and thighs.

At the bottom of the dam they filed along a path formed by the juncture between the embankment and the natural hillside.

"Looking at the dam in the dawn light," Phil said, "you'd never guess it was about to burst apart, would you? Fact is, the dam is hemorrhaging. The lake is pouring into the inspection galleries right now. Sooner or later it's going to find its way to the downstream face. Start counting minutes then."

"Would you knock it off, kid? You're going to jail. You can talk about the dam to all the new friends you'll meet there." The policeman leading the way warned the others of a muddy patch ahead.

"You can't put me in jail," Phil said in a voice edged with alarm. "I'm a first offender. I didn't cause any damage."

"No damage, eh?" said the policeman behind him. "You totaled the chief's cruiser by burying it in rocks, that's all."

"It was an accident. I pushed the wrong button. I was trying to turn on the radio."

"There's more water than when we came up," said the policeman in the lead, jumping over a rivulet.

Phil stopped walking. He looked down at his boots, which were partly sunk in mud. Crossing the path ahead was a shallow stream of brown water several feet wide. He traced its course with his eyes to the point where it emerged from the rock on the dam's face, and his expression changed from desolation to triumph. "Wait a minute! This is the leak!" He jumped in the air. "Hallelujah, the dam is failing! I *told* you!" The smile left his face. "The dam *is* failing!" he said in an awed whisper.

He was grabbed by both arms and pushed forward roughly. "Springwater," one of the policemen said. "Lots of springs in the hills this time of year."

"This is no hill, this is a dam," Phil said as he was hustled along the path. "Springwater is clear, this is muddy. The leak is going to get bigger and bigger until there'll be no stopping it. . . . We've got to tell the authorities. . . ."

334

"We are the authorities."

They had arrived at a group of waiting police cars. Phil was thrown into a back seat. "The town has to be evacuated!" he yelled. "Can't you see that? Are you completely stupid?" He instantly regretted using the word stupid.

Officer Simon shouldered his way into the car and twisted the end of his nightstick against Phil's upper lip. "Either you apologize for what you just said or I'll give you some purple knobs."

"I am sincerely sorry for what I just said."

Simon glowered, then backed out of the car and slammed the door. Phil turned his face into the upholstery and made no sound during the ten-minute drive to the local jail. His misery derived not only from his failure to convince anyone that a disaster was impending; when Officer Simon twisted his nightstick under his nose, Phil had swallowed his car key and twenty cents.

JANET SANDIFER SAT DOWN at the phone and positioned two pencils alongside a sheet of paper on which she had made a list of the agencies she would call. First was the state of California. She dialed a number and a female voice came on the line. "Directory assistance for what city?"

"Probably Sacramento. I want to report a dam disaster. An impending dam disaster."

"How do you spell that?"

"How about *d* for disaster? Doesn't the state have something called a disaster office?"

"Emergency."

"That's it! I've got an emergency to report. A big dam is failing and I can't find out who should be told."

"Let's see. The Office of Emergency Services."

"Marvelous!" Janet dialed the number she was given.

There was a buzz, followed by a deep voice that was clipped and all business. "Emergency Services. Hawkins."

"I'm calling to report that Sierra Canyon Dam has been breached. Sutterton should be evacuated at once."

"Are you calling from the dam?"

"No, Santa Monica."

"Is this the Southern California Disaster Center?"

335

"I sometimes think of myself in those terms. At the moment I'm a private citizen trying to warn you about a leaking dam."

"All dams leak, lady. You're a long way from Sierra Canyon. You had a vivid dream, is that it?"

Janet inhaled and exhaled between clenched teeth before replying. "An engineer at the dam called me. He told me water was breaking into the drainage galleries and that it was only a matter of time before it found its way through the embankment."

"Funny he didn't call us. Or the police."

"He didn't call the police because— Everybody up there has his hands full, don't you see? The engineer only had time for one call, so he asked me to sound the alarm."

"Sorry, that's not how it's done. I'm not going to order an evacuation at the suggestion of a housewife in Santa Monica who didn't sleep well. I think you're a practical joker and I ask you nicely to get off the line."

"You mean you won't do anything? What's the Office of Emergency Services for? Wait till the newspapers hear about this!"

Janet slammed the receiver down, cursing the state of California, the Office of Emergency Services, and the cruel gods that had brought Phil Kramer into her life. After several minutes of raging, she dialed the next number on the list. While listening to the ringing signal, she decided to try a slightly different tack; the plain truth was apparently not persuasive enough.

WITHERS WATCHED Riggs run past the control-room windows, fumbling with his keys. The phone rang and Withers answered it automatically. It was Leonard Mitchell, the contractor.

"Yes, Mr. Mitchell. Would you hang on a second?"

Riggs burst into the room, gasping. "Water is pouring from the gallery entrance . . . running into the turbine wells. Got to shut everything down. . . ." He ran to the master panel and started throwing switches.

Withers leaped up after him and grabbed his arm. "What are you doing? We can't shut down. . . . I've got to feed in forty megawatts—"

"Water . . ." Riggs pointed at one of the television monitors. "I hope we can save the generators."

336

When Withers looked at the screen, it was his turn to gasp. Water a foot deep was surging through the doorway to the floor of the turbine deck. As he watched, stunned, a warning horn began to sound rhythmically. "Where's Cooper?" he shouted.

"Still in the tunnels to see if he can find where the water's coming from."

Withers swallowed. "The dam is failing. That's what Kramer said."

"Look," Riggs said sharply. "Water is coming in, that's all we know. We've got to shut the place down and find the problem."

Withers nodded and picked up the phone. "Mr. Mitchell? We need some pumps. Got any at your yard?"

"A few small ones. Did I hear that the dam is failing?"

"No, no, nothing is wrong with the dam. We think three of our pumps stopped at the same time. . . . The horn? A warning that something is wrong in the drainage system. We've got water coming in at about ten cubic feet a second. Can you handle that?"

"I'll round up some men and equipment and be right over. I'll have to bill this at weekend labor rates, you know."

"Just keep records. And Mr. Mitchell, keep this under your hat till we know what we're up against. We don't want a panic."

Withers hung up and showed Riggs the banks of inoperative gauges. Everything relating to sections of the embankment below the generator deck was dead.

"No way of telling what's going on," Riggs said, grimacing. "Water must have shorted everything out."

They were interrupted by Cooper, who was red-faced and drenched. "I got as far as the center-line intersection," he said, collapsing into a chair. "Lights went out, so I came back. Couldn't tell where the water was coming from."

"I'll bet the kid did something in the intake tower," Riggs said. "Maybe he opened a bulkhead door and let the lake in."

"That might be it," Cooper said, nodding. Then he asked, "Can you stop the horn? It's driving me nuts."

Withers cut the horn circuit. A heavy silence settled over the control room. With power production stopped and the generators stilled, there was not even the customary electrical hum. "Well," he said, looking at the other two men, "do you think we should tell the police we've got a crisis on our hands?"

"Not yet," Riggs said. "Maybe with Mitchell's pumps we can dry everything up and keep the whole thing quiet."

"How are we going to keep it quiet," Cooper said, "when we've shut the plant down? I think we should assume the worst."

"Why don't you call Bolen?" Riggs suggested. "Ask him what we should do."

"He's in his plane on his way here to take charge."

Riggs walked to the door. "Turn on the phones in the offices. I'll see if air communications in Oakland can reach Bolen."

While Riggs was out of the room, Cooper suggested to Withers, "I think we should start lowering the reservoir now."

"There's two feet of water going over the top already. Dropping the gates would cause a good-size flood all by itself. It would take out Sutterton's Main Street Bridge, for starters. Let's see what Bolen says. If we can't get him, then we'll decide."

Cooper jumped to his feet and strode to the door. "I'm not going to sit here twiddling my thumbs. I'll drive around and look things over. If I see anything that isn't a hundred percent normal, I'm sounding an alarm, whether you guys want me to or not."

The phone rang. Withers answered it while waving good-by to Cooper. On the line was Bill Hawkins of the Office of Emergency Services to Sacramento.

Hawkins said with a trace of amusement in his voice, "We just had a call from a woman in Santa Monica who said that the dam you have there is busting up. Now where do you suppose she got an idea like that? . . . Hello?"

"A woman from where said what?"

"A woman from Santa Monica said poor old Sierra Canyon Dam is on its last legs. A friend of hers called her and told her that water was coming in on all sides. Just a crackpot, eh?"

Withers whistled. "Kramer must have gotten to a phone. . . ."

"Come again?"

"We had a nut up here a while ago and had to call the cops on him. He must have a friend who's trying to make us look bad."

"So everything's okay? Water is not coming in on all sides?"

"No, just into the powerhouse."

"Just into the powerhouse. Water is coming into the power-house." Hawkins repeated the words slowly, as if examining them.

338

"We've got a flow that may not be normal. We've shut down."

"If you've shut the plant down, it sure as hell is not normal."

"We are having a problem, but we don't think it is serious. Excuse me. I've got a call on the other line."

On the other line was an irate dispatcher from Power Control Center.

"What's wrong up there? Are you ready to start feeding in the extra power? Why didn't you call us back with those readings?"

"I was just going to. Say, about that extra power. We've got some percolation—well, more than percolation—coming into the turbine bays and we've had to shut down the plant."

"You've *what?* You're kidding! Tell me you're kidding!"

Withers hung up and took the next call.

"Newt? This is Luby Pelletier over at the Butte County Disaster Office. How is everything up your way this fine day?"

"Wonderful, Luby, terrific. Say, would you mind—"

"The dam isn't falling apart, is it? We just got a weird call from a woman in Santa Monica—"

"God! She must be calling everybody in the state!"

"You know her? She said she was a psychic who just had a vision of Sierra Canyon disappearing and swarms of people running naked into the woods. Came to her in a flash of light, she said. I could hardly keep from laughing."

"Look, Luby, we do have a small problem." Withers kept his eyes on the television screen. The flow into the turbine deck seemed to be increasing. "As a matter of fact, Luby, I'm awful busy. We may have to evacuate the town. I'll call you later."

As Withers took the next call—the phone rang the instant he hung up—Riggs shouted to him over the intercom that Bolen's plane had been located over Fresno. Withers acknowledged the news, then heard Lee Simon on the phone.

"Your friend Kramer led us on a merry chase," the policeman said, "but we've got him under lock and key now. Say, Newt, we saw a wet spot at the bottom of the dam a while ago. About a hundred yards from the riverbank on the north side. Kramer got all excited when he saw it, but he gets excited about everything."

"A wet spot?" Goose bumps advanced across Withers' shoulders. "Is it just a spot, or is there a flow of water?"

"Sort of a trickle. Like you see in the gutter when somebody up the block is washing a car. Think it means anything?"

"Cooper is in his car right now. I'll call him on the radio and have him take a look. Lee, I got a horrible feeling we've got big trouble. I'll call you back."

Withers got Cooper on the radio and directed him to a vantage point next to the switchyard. Withers' phone was ringing again. "Powerhouse. Withers speaking."

"This is the news desk of the Sacramento *Bee*. We're tracking down a rumor that Sierra Canyon Dam has been mined by former members of the Iranian secret police. Our source says the blasts will go off in thirty minutes and Sutterton should be evacuated."

"Is your source a woman in Santa Monica?"

"You know her? Anything to what she says?"

"I'll call you back."

Cooper's voice came over the radio loudspeaker, announcing that he had arrived at the overlook.

Withers leaned into his microphone. "Can you see the toe of the slope on the north side? See anything odd? A trickle of water, about a hundred yards up from the riverbank?"

"That's a quarter of a mile away. Let me put the binoculars on it."

In the silence that followed, Withers drummed his fist against the counter top at a rate that matched his heartbeat. He glanced at the wall clock: seven ten. Riggs came into the control room and began to report on the conversation he had just had with Bolen, then froze at the sound of Cooper's voice on the radio:

"A boil-out . . . Must be five hundred or a thousand cubic feet a second . . . We've lost her, we've lost the whole damn thing, Newt. The dam is a goner."

PART THREE: The Failure
Chapter 10

Herman Bolen pushed back his Eddie Rickenbacker goggles and scarf and fanned his perspiring face. The heat in the cockpit remained constant. Through the window he gazed dully at the

340

blanket of fog that filled the Central Valley. The sun was above the Sierra Nevadas now and the reflected light was blinding.

To take his mind off his discomfort, he tried to calculate his precise position: ground speed, wind speed, bearing. He was somewhere around Fresno and he was seized with the wish to be elsewhere, anywhere but in his sickeningly expensive toy five thousand feet above Fresno.

Five years—five years!—he had spent designing and building a personal airplane, and still it wasn't right. It was, in fact, a torture chamber. The chair, the cockpit, the whole plane had been designed around his body—but his body, now a pear-shaped blob, had drifted far beyond its original specifications. You can let the seams out of a suit, he thought, but not out of a plane.

A voice came over his radio. "Aircraft N97307, this is Oakland Center. Can you read me?"

Bolen picked up his microphone. "Oakland Center, I read you."

"We have a call from Sierra Canyon Dam."

"Can you patch through a direct line?"

"No, but I can relay both sides of the conversation."

Bolen hesitated. If there was an emergency, did he want everyone at Oakland Center to know about it? "Tell them to call me on the telephone through the mobile operator."

Bolen looked at his watch. It had to be something serious if they couldn't wait another forty-five minutes for him to get there.

At seven o'clock a buzzer sounded on his instrument panel. "This is Burt Riggs, Mr. Bolen, at Sierra Canyon. We—"

"Did you find Jeffers? Did you check Gallery D?"

"We couldn't reach Gallery D. Water is flowing out of the access tunnel into the turbine wells. It may be that the lower galleries are flooded. Jeffers might have got caught down there."

Bolen listened to the description of the incoming water, the inoperative meters, the plant shutdown. Then before Riggs could finish, he cut him off. "Have you told the police Sutterton has to be evacuated?"

"No, we thought we'd better let you decide that."

"Riggs, how much evidence do you need? Listen to me. I think the core block has been breached. What you do in the next few minutes could save a thousand lives. Call the police, the county

disaster headquarters. Tell them there's a possibility we could lose the dam. Bypass as much water as you can around the turbines directly into the outlet works. Drop the spillway gates."

"Withers says that will cause pretty heavy flooding—"

"I don't care what Withers says! Do what I tell you!"

"Yes, sir. Mr. Bolen, I can see the television monitors and it looks like a Mitchell Brothers crew has arrived with pumps."

"If you can get rid of the water faster than it's coming in, fine— that will let you into the tunnels to find the source. Maybe we'll find a leak that can be plugged. But if the embankment is breached, it's probably all over."

DAPPER DR. DULOTTE eased his station wagon around the huge truck that was inexplicably parked on top of the dam. Before reaching the far side, he had to slow down to follow the hand signals of a policeman. A wrecker was extracting a police car from a pile of gravel.

"What happened, Officer?" he said, rolling down a window.

"No stopping," the policeman replied curtly, waving him on.

The road left the dam. Dulotte nodded in satisfaction when he saw the arrows and signs marking the marathon's route. It was seven twenty. The race would start at eight, and an hour or so after that, if

342

everything went according to plan, Kent Spain would be the first to cross the dam and disappear into the woods, the scent of money driving him on.

Dulotte parked where the trail turned into the woods. From the back of the station wagon he dragged a three-wheeled pushcart called the Dulotte Trail-Barrow. Into it he loaded a collapsible table and chair, four five-gallon bottles of water, a clipboard, a stopwatch, a first-aid kit, and a crate of oranges. Ten minutes later he was striding briskly through the woods, pushing the cart ahead of him.

The T-shirt was still on the branch, where he had put it a few days ago. Behind the bushes was the bicycle, ready to go. Dulotte strode on, humming "The Impossible Dream."

PHIL KRAMER clamped his hands around the bars of his cell door. A short distance away Sergeant Jim Martinez sat at his desk, doing paperwork.

"Let me out of here!" Phil shouted, rattling the door. "This is an emergency! Let us all out! Every minute counts!"

"Shut up," somebody said behind him.

Phil looked over his shoulder. There were four cots in the cell, three of them filled with blanket-covered lumps. "I will not shut up," he said, addressing the cots. "I am trying to save your necks as well as mine." He turned back to Martinez. "Maybe you weren't paying attention, so I will run through it again. I am a world-renowned authority on dam failures. Ask anybody. I have just finished inspecting Sierra Canyon Dam. That's the one you can see out the window, Sergeant, if you'd care to look."

"Shut up," the voice behind him said again.

"Listen, everybody," Phil said, rattling the door again. "The dam is failing. I saw it with my own eyes. A leak has started on the downstream face. That means that a great big lake is going to come crashing down on our heads, because once water finds its way through an embankment, you can kiss it good-by. That's what happened to Baldwin Hills in 1963 and Teton in 1976."

From an adjoining cell, "Hey, Martinez, can't you do something about this guy? There are people here with serious hangovers."

Sergeant Martinez sighed and got to his feet. He walked down the corridor and studied Phil, standing just beyond arm's reach.

"This is an emergency," Phil said to him. "We'll be trapped in here like rats. You've got to get us out and yourself as well."

There was a crash that made Phil turn around. A giant of a man with a tangle of long blond hair had risen from one of the cots, knocking it over. He took two strides and dropped a huge hand on Phil's chest, gathered the front of his coveralls, and lifted him off the floor. His breath smelled of garlic, tobacco, beer, stale air, and feedlots. "I told you to shut up," he said.

"Put him down, Haystack," Martinez said. "I'll handle this."

The man called Haystack glared at Phil, then released him.

The phone on Martinez' desk rang.

"Kramer, I'm going to answer the phone," Martinez said. "When I get back, unless you have stopped talking, I'm going to say a certain code word that makes Haystack go wild. Think about it."

Martinez walked back to his desk and picked up the phone. Phil watched the expression on his face change as he said, "Yeah? It is? Now? You mean everybody? Are you sure? Right. Okay." He hung up slowly.

"What is it?" Phil shouted. "What's happening?"

Martinez ran his fingers through his hair. "They think the dam might go," he said. "A school bus is on its way to pick us up." He pushed a button that set off an ear-shattering alarm bell.

Phil grinned at his cell mate. "Pack your bags, Haystack. We're getting out of this joint."

THE BEGINNING of the Mother Lode Marathon was an elbow-to-elbow mêlée. At the crack of the starter's pistol, nearly fifteen hundred people surged forward, a colorful swarm of arms, legs, and bobbing heads. Kent Spain was in the group of fifty top-seeded runners given priority positions at the front, but once the race was under way, he felt just as engulfed by humanity as he would have in the rear with the weekenders, school kids, and geriatrics.

The first couple of miles were more like a steeplechase than a cross-country run, a process of jumping over barking dogs, dodging dropouts, and watching for chances to pass scores of puffing laggards. But by the three-mile mark, the runners were strung out in single file about fifteen feet apart. Kent guessed there were at least a dozen ahead of him. In the next twelve miles he would have to pass every one of them, for if Dulotte's plan was to work, he would have to be first across the dam.

Only two runners figured to be trouble—Tom Ryan, immediately ahead of him, and Nabih Yousri of Ethiopia, a world-class marathoner who had entered at the last minute. If Yousri was following his usual strategy, Kent thought, he was probably in the lead, his bald black head glistening in the sun like a polished eight ball. His policy was to start fast and hang on to win. Passing him would take a maximum effort.

Ryan was a different kind of runner, a crafty calculator with a great finishing kick. With steady effort, Kent pulled up on Ryan's heels and said, "Honk, honk."

Ryan, unworried, moved to the left and glanced at Spain as he went by. "What's the hurry? You'll burn out."

"Maybe." In the next seven miles Kent passed ten runners who were showing the effects of the blistering early pace. It was a pace far faster than he himself had ever taken, and he felt twinges in his calves and an ominous tightness in his midsection.

At the ten-mile mark was Cardiac Hill, a mile-long grade that led to a ridge overlooking Earl Warren Lake. Kent spent a few seconds at the checkpoint and aid station at the bottom of the grade. As he sponged off his face and neck, he asked the man behind the table how many were ahead of him.

"Four. Yousri's in the lead, a minute and a half ahead."

"I'm going to catch him," said Kent. He drained a paper cup of water while picking up speed and entering the woods, where the trail rose cruelly through tall trees. He drove his legs hard, setting up a tempo better suited to a sprint than a marathon.

"You can do it, old buddy," he said, addressing his body in a strained whisper. "Come through for me just once more. I know it's tough, then we'll take a long rest, just the two of us. No, don't tell me to stop, think of the money. Push, push, push. . . ."

Five hundred yards from the top of the slope he had passed everybody but Yousri, who was still not in sight. Kent concentrated on breaking through "the wall", that half-physical, half-psychological barrier that stood in the way of a peak performance. Never before had he encountered the wall so early in a race. His calves were red-hot pokers and his stomach a mass of cables stretched to the breaking point. He kept on going. The secret was to ignore his body until it gave up sending pain signals and unlocked its secret stores of energy.

"Push, push, push," he muttered, his teeth and fists clenched. "Money, money, money, money."

Behind him he heard footsteps. He turned for a backward glance and saw a blond teenager approaching at what seemed to be fifty miles an hour, with only a faint trace of sweat on his face. On his chest was the number 1027, which meant that he was unrated. Kent drove himself forward, but the kid drew even.

"Excuse me, sir," 1027 said, scarcely breathing hard, "where's Cardiac Hill?"

Kent Spain's face was a mixture of agony and loathing. "At the top . . . of this slope . . . the trail swings left . . . through a field of ferns. Half a mile more . . . that's the start of Cardiac Hill." It was hard to talk. He couldn't seem to get air into his lungs.

"Thanks a lot," the teenager said, pulling away. He looked back and added, "Hang in there, old-timer."

Minutes later Kent labored to the top of the ridge and followed the trail to the right. The area called Fern Gardens was on his left, and on a hillside beyond it he could see 1027 striding along a path that Kent knew led only to an abandoned ranger station.

Feeling pleasure for the first time since the race began, Kent let out his own stride. As he rounded a curve, he almost stumbled over Yousri, who was down on one knee tying his shoe. The African jumped up and bounded away, his sinewy legs flicking like licorice whips. Kent shifted into higher gear, and lashing himself with the fury of a madman, he gradually closed the gap.

Yousri wouldn't yield the right-of-way. When Kent tried to pass on the right, Yousri moved to the right. When Kent moved left, Yousri moved left.

"Let me pass, damn it," said Kent.

"No pass," Yousri said. "Not right for you. You poop out."

"Let me by!"

The black man's reply was to quicken his pace. Kent Spain, teeth clenched, matched him step for step. For two hundred yards they ran a draining duel, knowing that if they kept it up for long, they would collapse. Then Kent fastened his eyes on the shoes ahead of

346

him. Timing his move nicely, he leaned forward and slapped one sideways so that it caught on the back of the opposite ankle. The great Nabih Yousri crashed to the ground in an explosion of twigs, pebbles, and incomprehensible curses.

At last, at mile thirteen, Kent Spain was in the lead. He was running downhill now, through a hillside of scrub oak and manzanita·toward the crest of the dam. In a few minutes he would emerge from the woods at the right overlook ... provided he hadn't overexerted himself. He felt dizzy. The ground was undulating like the floor of a fun house. A roaring filled his ears, and he was sucking and blowing air like a steam locomotive.

A PERSISTENT knocking woke Theodore Roshek. The door opened and Mrs. Bolen put her head into the room. "Theodore? There's a call for you from Sierra Canyon. A Mr.Withers."

Roshek picked up the bedside phone and listened to Withers with disbelief and rising alarm. "How much water is coming through? Have you seen it yourself?"

"No, but one of our engineers estimates it at a thousand second-feet." Withers hesitated, then added, "He thinks the dam is lost. I thought I better call you. Your wife told me where you were."

Roshek exploded. "Are you bulldozing rock into the breach? Have you dropped the spillway gates? Have you told the police?"

"We've dropped the gates and the police are evacuating the town, but as for bulldozers, nobody here knows what to do. Mr. Bolen is on his way. We think Mr. Jeffers is dead."

"Where's Kramer?"

"In jail. Locked up."

"Unlock him."

"Unlock him?"

"Who else around here knows more about what's going on than he does? Maybe he has some smart ideas."

Roshek hung up and dialed Creekwood. Eleanor was in danger. If the unthinkable happened . . . Was it possible? Images of dams that had failed crowded into his mind—Saint Francis and Baldwin Hills in California alone, Malpassant in France, Vega de Tera in Spain, Teton in Idaho. The catastrophes were as vivid to him as the anguish suffered by the engineers responsible. "Acts of God," "standard industry practice," "inescapable unknowns"—these phrases came up over and over in the inquiries that followed every disaster. Certainly nature was capable of dreadful surprises. Yet Roshek couldn't help feeling that if a man paid enough attention to detail, then— A busy signal told him that Eleanor still had the phone off the hook.

Could Sierra Canyon Dam fail? Was the contempt he held for designers of inadequate structures to be applied to himself? Would the name of Theodore Roshek be attached forever not to dreams but to nightmares?

With the dam destroyed, Eleanor would be even more important to him than she was now. She would make life worth living. He would go to her and warn her of the danger.

He dialed Carlos Hallon, the corporation's pilot. If the dam held for at least an hour and a half—a conservative estimate in view of the density of the embankment and the massive concrete core block— then there was time to reach Eleanor before—

"Carlos? We've got an emergency in northern California. Is the Lear ready to go? Also arrange for a helicopter to meet us at the Yuba City airport to take me to Sierra Canyon Dam."

PLUMP, gray-haired, and sweet-faced, Elizabeth Lehmann looked more like a spokesperson for a line of frozen pies than the county disaster control officer, but such she was and proud of it. When the emergency call came, she threw off her robe and hurriedly put on black slacks, a blue blouse, and a black jacket. If the dam did fail, she might not get home for days and she didn't want to look like a frump.

Now she would find out if all those practice sessions paid off. Once a month she had forced grumbling local officials to spend an afternoon in the disaster office reacting to hypothetical atomic explosions, chemical spills, earthquakes, train wrecks, and terrorist attacks. In the opinion of the penny-pinching county supervisors, planning for disasters was a waste of money, because God in His wisdom doesn't announce which disaster He is going to unleash, or when. But Elizabeth Lehmann had managed to get enough money to put the county's radio equipment into a van that could be moved quickly to wherever it would function most efficiently. She was proud of her command car, equipped with a two-way radio, medical supplies, and a "resource file" that listed the location of everything from doctors to sandbags.

At least this is happening on a weekend, she thought, as she ran down the porch steps. No school kids to contend with.

Her command car wasn't there. The driveway was empty and so was the garage. She clutched her head when she remembered that the car was at the office. The previous week the board of supervisors had decided that employees could no longer take county vehicles home. In other words, from now on, disasters would have to occur during regular office hours.

Elizabeth ran into the street and looked both ways for help. In a weedy yard two doors away knelt Norman Kingwell polishing his motorcycle. Kingwell was a teenage good-for-nothing to whom she had not spoken for two years, not since the day he turned fifteen and removed his muffler. She ran toward him, waving. "Crank that beauty up, Norm," she called. "You are taking me for a ride."

WITH ONE HAND on the tiller, Chuck Duncan guided his small, flat-bottomed boat out of the secluded inlet. There was little wind so early in the morning and the surface of the water was smooth. Duncan set a course for the widest part of the lake, five miles above the dam. When he got there, he would cut the motor and begin a lazy day of drinking beer, fishing, and drifting wherever the current took him.

Chapter 11

The four steel trusses crossed the river on piers of quarried granite. At the approach closest to town was a concrete monument inscribed MAIN STREET BRIDGE, SUTTERTON, A.D. 1933. A school bus filled with prisoners from the town jail stopped beside it. "Holy Toledo," said the driver. "Look at the river!"

Water had crept to within two feet of the roadway and was rising. Policemen were everywhere, setting up barricades across the approach, and the air was filled with flashing lights and the sounds of sirens and radio static. Wilson Hartley emerged from a car and waited for the bus driver to open his window.

"Where to now, Chief?"

"The high-school gym in Sterling City. Take route one ninety-one. You got Phil Kramer in there?"

"I'm Kramer," Phil said, pushing his way to the front of the bus. A guard stepped aside to let him out. Phil found himself shaking hands with a silver-haired policeman with a familiar voice.

"Wilson Hartley, Chief of Police. We should have listened to you last night. All charges against you are dropped. We need your help. They tell me that until the bigwigs get here, you know more about what's going on than anybody. For starters we need an estimate on how long the dam is going to hold."

Phil shook his head in amazement, then tried to adopt a professional manner. "I'll have to see how much worse the leak has become. Can you take me to the powerhouse parking lot?"

He was interrupted by a loud popping and grinding noise. All eyes turned. The river had reached the bridge roadway, and its force had broken the connection between the two center spans and the pier on which they rested. The entire bridge began shuddering. At that moment a motorcycle hurtled onto the far end.

"Look at that fool," someone shouted. "He'll never make it!"

Several inches of water were flowing across the second span. The motorcycle crossed the pavement like a speedboat, sending waves to each side. The bridge lurched, almost upending the bike, but with a thrust of his leg the driver managed to keep his balance. When he reached solid ground, he swerved to a stop.

"Are you out of your mind?" Hartley shouted. "Didn't you see the roadblock on the other side?"

Norman Kingwell looked at the chief with a half-smile. "The devil made me do it," he said, jabbing a thumb over his shoulder.

The disaster-control officer climbed off the seat behind Norman Kingwell. "Whew!" she said. "That was invigorating!"

"Mrs. Lehmann!"

"It's okay, Wilson. I ordered him to take me across. I've got to get my car. There goes the bridge. . . ."

Water was boiling over the railing and sidewalk. With a deep, wrenching sound, the two center spans of the bridge folded in slow motion, pulling the side spans after them and rolling under the water. Within one minute everything was out of sight.

Elizabeth Lehmann got back on the motorcycle behind her teenage chauffeur. "I've got to move the radio van to high ground," she said to Hartley. "Would the right overlook be safe?"

Hartley looked at Phil, who assured them both that the right overlook, being on solid rock, was perfect.

Mrs. Lehmann turned her attention to Phil. "And you are . . . ?"

"For the time being," Hartley said, "he's the technical expert in charge of this event. Anything he says goes."

"The right overlook it is, then. Let's go, Norman." The woman threw her arms around Kingwell as he took off with a roar.

WITHIN MINUTES Phil Kramer stood with a group of men at the powerhouse parking lot scanning the lower reaches of the dam with binoculars. The boil-out was a torrent now, flowing from a hole thirty feet in diameter. Phil handed the glasses to the man next to him, contractor Leonard Mitchell.

"I talked to Roshek a while ago," Withers offered. "He said maybe the flow could be pinched off by dumping rock on it."

Phil dismissed the suggestion with a shake of his head. "Too late for that. The dam is going to fail, no matter what."

"How long have we got?" Officer Lee Simon wanted to know. "We've got a town to evacuate."

"The embankment is three quarters of a mile thick at the base," Phil said, "so it's going to take a while. The hole is going to keep caving in until a notch is cut all the way to the crest. That's when the lake will come shouldering through in a big wave."

"How long in minutes?" Simon insisted.

"I'd just be guessing. But where we're standing could be under hundreds of feet of water in as little as forty-five minutes."

"Forty-five minutes! We'll never be able to knock on every door in town. We'll be lucky to cover the streets with a sound truck." Simon reached into his car for the radio microphone.

"Suppose I keep an eye on the breach and keep giving you updated estimates?" Phil suggested.

"Good idea. We'll put you on the overlook with the radio van."

"I'll take you in my pickup," Mitchell said to Phil.

Minutes later Mitchell swung off the county road onto the top of the dam, the crest road stretching ahead of them like a taut white

352

ribbon. "Look!" the contractor said, pointing through the windshield. "Some fool is trying to land a plane on the dam."

Phil followed Mitchell's gaze and saw a small plane approaching the crest road. The plane lost altitude, rose to clear the truck Phil had abandoned in the night, then touched down smoothly. "I hope he sees the gravel," Phil said.

"What gravel?"

"I stole one of your trucks last night, and to slow down the police I dumped a load of gravel on the road."

Mitchell squinted at Phil. "You stole one of my trucks?"

"Well, I borrowed it."

The bright red plane was taxiing toward them when the landing gear hit the gravel. The tail flipped upward, the fuselage balanced on its nose for a second, then toppled over on its back.

By the time Phil and Mitchell got there, two highway patrolmen were cutting the pilot out of his seat belt, from which he was suspended upside-down. "I'm all right," said the pilot, but clearly he wasn't. A large contusion showed on his forehead. As he was revolved into a sitting position, his lips drew away from his teeth in pain and his eyes shut tight.

When the pilot was right side up, Phil recognized him. "Mr. Bolen!" He clambered out of the truck. "Am I glad to see you!"

Bolen forced an eye open and looked at Phil. "Do I know you?"

"I'm Phil Kramer. Roshek fired me yesterday, remember?"

"Kramer," Bolen said, "I'll apologize later for yesterday. Right now you've got to listen. Block this road except for emergency vehicles. When the breach reaches elevation seven five five, get everybody off the dam, because it will go fast then."

By now more cars had arrived. A man behind the wheel of a van volunteered to take Bolen to the right overlook, where a medical tent was being set up. Phil and Mitchell helped Bolen to his feet. While they walked him to the van across the highway, Mitchell said, "There must be some way to save the dam. Suppose we dump rock into the lake over the point the water's getting in? I've got a loaded barge at the quarry dock that could be towed into position in half an hour."

"Useless," Bolen said. "In about half an hour a whirlpool will be forming. You'd lose the barge and everybody on it. Too late now."

353

As he was helped into the van, he turned his head away to hide the tears that were leaking from his eyes.

"We'll drag your plane off the dam," Phil said. "We'll save that, at least."

Bolen lifted his hand weakly. "Forget the plane. I'm too old to fly. Dump it over the side to clear the road." He motioned for Phil to lean close. "If Roshek shows up, keep an eye on him. This may be more than he can take."

Phil nodded. "I'll do that."

THE SMALL TWO-SEATER helicopter skimmed the treetops ten miles below the dam. Roshek pointed to the green lawn surrounding Creekwood, and the pilot made a slight course correction.

The river didn't look good . . . already out of its banks and dotted with driftwood. Roshek hoped Eleanor had heard the news and was gone by now. If not, he would tell the pilot to lift her to safety, then come back for him. If the wave arrived in the meantime, too bad. Better she survive than he. He was old and falling apart fast. His career, which just days before had been on the verge of reaching unprecedented heights, was falling apart as well.

The house came into view. The car in the driveway wasn't Eleanor's. If he wasn't mistaken, it belonged to Russell Stone, the dancer she had been living with when he had come into her life. Good Lord, Roshek thought. Surely they aren't in the house together, not after she had sworn she was through with him. Stone must have come alone—she had loaned him the key.

"Hover," Roshek shouted to the pilot as they approached the house.

The front door opened. A slim, well-muscled young man stepped onto the porch. It was Stone, all right, and Roshek felt a rush of anger. He didn't like the idea of a rival spending the night at Creekwood, even with Eleanor's permission.

A woman appeared in the shadowed doorway. "Don't let it be Eleanor," Roshek whispered. "Please, please."

But it was Eleanor, dressed in the silk pajamas he had given her for Christmas. She glided into the sunlight and slipped an arm around Stone's waist. He put an arm around her shoulder and pulled her close as they stared at the helicopter together. Roshek

354

saw her hand move to shield her eyes, like a bird rising to a limb. Even her simplest gestures were so graceful that he—

"Up," he said to the pilot, pointing upward. "Take her up."

As the helicopter soared up, Roshek was seized by convulsive sobs. He buried his face in a handkerchief.

"Hey," the pilot said, "you all right?" Roshek nodded, blew his nose noisily, and took several deep breaths.

The helicopter tilted slightly and swooped forward toward the northeast. In the distance, Earl Warren Lake tapered to a narrow finger above Sutterton, where a tiny brown patch that was the dam held it back like a cork in a bottle.

THE RIGHT OVERLOOK WAS A two-acre flat area a hundred feet above the crest of the dam. Phil, with a two-way radio and a pair of binoculars, established himself at the outermost point, where two reaches of guardrail met atop a rock outcropping shaped like a ship's prow. It was a spectacular vantage point. At the far side of the river was the electrical switchyard and the powerhouse, which had now been evacuated. To Phil's left a deep green river swept smoothly downward over the lowered spillway gates. At the bottom the torrent dissolved into a continuous explosion of spray.

Just beyond the spillway, near the bottom of the embankment, a circular area a hundred yards in diameter was glistening with moisture. The lower edge was a ragged gash thirty yards long, from which brown water was cascading steadily down the hill.

Holding his radio close to his mouth, Phil reported on the progress of the failure: "Upper edge of breach now at elevation five hundred. Volume of flow has doubled in the last five minutes. Estimate main collapse in thirty-five minutes."

The lower sections of Sutterton were being nibbled away by the rising river. Through binoculars Phil watched a dozen houses twisted off their foundations, upended, and smashed to pieces. He felt like a spotter in a war, relaying battle information to generals at field headquarters behind the lines.

Headquarters in this case was just a few feet away, for the overlook had been transformed into a kind of seat of government. First came cars carrying the chief of police, the fire chief, and the head of the local Red Cross. Highway patrolmen kept one area clear for helicopters bringing officials from Sacramento, though the first helicopter to arrive carried a television news crew. Behind the radio van that bristled with antennae, Mrs. Lehmann kept a steady stream of information flowing to communities downstream. Her voice had a hard edge to it, and Phil could hear almost every word she said over the cacophony of roaring water, vehicle engines, shouts, and loudspeaker static. She was obviously attacking her job with tremendous energy and effectiveness. To a remark from Wilson Hartley that she seemed almost to be enjoying what she was doing, Phil heard her reply, "I'll cry if it will help any."

At that moment Phil turned and found himself looking into the lens of a television minicamera. Next to the cameraman was a man in a tan sports jacket speaking earnestly into a microphone. "On your screen is Phil Kramer, the heroic young engineer who spent the night sounding the alarm. As I understand it," the reporter said, "water will come out faster and faster until the valley is flooded, is that it?" He thrust the microphone in Phil's face.

"No. In about half an hour a wall of water will go down the valley like a bulldozer."

"Traveling fifty or a hundred miles an hour? What a spectacle that will be for our cameras."

"It might go a hundred down a straight canal, but this valley has twists and turns. Turbulence and the load the water will pick up will cut the speed down to ten or fifteen miles an hour. Now, if you'll excuse me . . ." Phil turned and scanned the lake through binoculars. "I think I see a boat," he said into his radio. "Right side, about a quarter-mile from the spillway. He must have missed the warnings. Is there a helicopter that can get out there?"

Wilson Hartley put his hand on Phil's shoulder. "Did I hear you say the flood would move at ten or fifteen miles an hour?"

"Just a guess, but I can't imagine it going much faster."

"A man could drive down the canyon a lot faster than that to make sure everybody has been moved out. I'll take our best car, the one we use to track down speeders."

Phil stared at the policeman. "Are you serious? I don't know for sure how fast the water will go. It might—"

Hartley turned away. "You just keep talking into that microphone so I know how much time I've got."

A clap of thunder pulled Phil's attention to the dam. In the circular saturated area a tremendous geyser exploded upward, and viscous brown water gushed out like blood from a wound.

"A major blowout," Phil reported excitedly. "Flow spurting at what looks like full pressure. Won't be long now, maybe twenty minutes. Anybody still in town should get out fast."

On the surface of the lake three hundred yards from the spillway, a column of bubbles broke the surface and a circle of water began to revolve slowly around it.

FROM ROSHEK'S helicopter the town, the lake, and the dam presented a scene of picture-postcard splendor. Only by close observation was it possible to see the lines of cars fleeing Sutterton on every available road. The lake sparkled in the sun, and the foothills rolled away toward the snowy high country, like a rumpled green blanket. Looming ever larger as the helicopter approached was the dam, a colossal wall that swept from one side of the valley to the other. On its left side, like a silver bracelet on a suntanned arm, was the spillway, and beside it, half as high and twice as wide, was an ugly, seething mass of brown water. Roshek stared at the great structure sprawled beneath him, broken and bleeding, and tears came again to his eyes.

When the helicopter landed and the rotor stopped, he did not move. The door opened, and he felt himself lifted to the ground. Men surrounded him, but their words came to him as from a great distance. He put his arms automatically into his crutches, walked to a guardrail, and looked over the edge.

A powerful tide of water, green and glassy, was hurtling down the concrete spillway in perfect laminar flow, gradually changing to white turbulence exactly as the formulas and tests predicted it would. It was beautiful and hypnotic, a photograph in an engineering textbook. Beyond, where there should have been nothing but the smooth, tawny flank of the embankment being warmed by the sun, was a raging brown beast from a nightmare, roaring, and gnawing a fatal cavity in one of the man-made wonders of the world.

It's all wrong, Roshek thought. Through no fault of his, Sierra Canyon Dam was unraveling before his eyes. Forces of nature were at work. There was nothing he could do. He imagined the hands of

357

an insolent young ballet dancer caressing Eleanor James, but what was that to him? Eleanor was out of his life now, and soon the dam would be as well.

Wind tugged at his clothes. His hat was snatched from his head and catapulted into the air like a clay pigeon. Roshek watched it soar high in the sky, then fall in a long arc, spinning, shrinking in size until it became a hard-to-follow dot against the river that was cascading down the face of the dam.

He let his crutches clatter to the ground. To keep from falling, he closed his fingers around the guardrail. If it weren't for his withered legs, he could have hurdled it in an instant.

He became aware then of a voice that sounded familiar, and he turned slowly to his right. Ten feet away, a man in white coveralls peered through binoculars and held a radio to his lips. "I can see a whirlpool forming in the lake," the man was saying, "about three hundred yards northeast of the spillway. Top of breach now at seven hundred feet."

Roshek stared, trying to place the man. What was it about the sight of him that stirred such hatred in his heart? He worked his way along the guardrail to get closer.

"Main break only ten minutes or so away," the man said into his radio. "I see people standing on the rim of the canyon below town, where the river bends. They may be goners if they stay there. When the wave hits that hillside, it might surge all the way to the top."

The man turned, lowering the radio and binoculars. "Mr. Roshek!" he said in astonishment.

"It's Kramer, isn't it?" Roshek said in a quavering voice. "You were incredibly lucky. It was a chance in a billion that the dam would fail and you would blunder in when you did." The roar of the water was so loud he had to raise his voice to be heard. "Your idiotic computer program had nothing to do with it. . . . Sheer stupid luck." He took hold of Kramer's shoulder. "Before you came, there was no problem. You made this happen—yes, sabotage—to prove your crazy theory, to tear me down. . . ."

Roshek felt a strong hand on his arm. He turned and saw a man with his head wrapped in bandages who was shouting his name. "Can't you hear me?" he was saying.

358

It was Herman Bolen. Roshek evaluated the situation coldly. If I don't answer him, he reasoned, he will think I've lost my mind. "Of course I can hear you, Herman. What happened to your head?"

Before Bolen could answer, there was a deep, rolling thunder as a great triangular block of the embankment gave way and sank into the water surging beneath it. The lake seemed to leap into the slot that now reached from the bottom of the slope to within a few yards of the crest, fighting its way through with awesome frenzy. Directly above the breach, the crest roadway began to sag.

Roshek turned away. "Where are my crutches?" When they were handed to him, he swung himself toward his helicopter. "I don't want to watch," he said to Bolen, who had to hurry to keep pace. "I'm not a masochist. I'm going back to Los Angeles."

Bolen helped him climb into the passenger's seat. "Are you sure you are . . . Will you be—"

"I'm perfectly all right, Herman. We'll have a talk when you get back to Los Angeles." Roshek concentrated on smiling reassuringly as he lifted Bolen's hand off the door.

The helicopter took off and veered away toward the southwest. Roshek twisted in his seat for a last glimpse of the ravaged dam. The breach now dwarfed the spillway. Tens of thousands of tons of water per second were pouring through in a flood that was like a slice of Niagara Falls and three times higher. He watched in spite of himself until a mountainside mercifully obstructed his view.

Chapter 12

Three times Chuck Duncan pulled the cord and three times the outboard motor failed to start. The boat had drifted much more quickly than usual toward the dam, which was now only a quarter of a mile away. Not that he thought he was in any danger. There were trash racks on the lake side of the gates—large steel grilles—that retained debris so that it wouldn't damage the spillway, and a hundred feet from the dam was a long string of logs chained together to prevent boats from running aground on the embankment. But Duncan didn't like being so close to the dam. He saw enough of it during the week.

He tried again to start the motor—this time it caught. He swung the boat around and set a course for the center of the lake. He drained a can of beer, held it over the side until it filled with water, then leaned over to watch it sink. The can faded from view after a few feet. Weird. He had never seen the water so murky in this part of the lake, where it was eight hundred feet deep. Something must be stirring up the sediment.

He sat up and looked around. A man was standing on the crest of the dam, waving his arms. Duncan waved back. The right overlook was full of cars and trucks. What was that all about? Maybe something to do with the marathon. He noticed that he was even closer to the right side of the dam than before, and he moved the throttle to full open. He kept his eyes on a fixed onshore point to check his progress—he was *still* losing ground.

He shifted in his seat and looked toward the spillway. For the first time he became aware of a muffled roar. Usually on the lake it wasn't possible to hear the water at the bottom of the spillway, because the dam acted as a sound barrier. They must have lowered the spillway gates during the night, he thought. He had visions of his boat being drawn against the trash racks and held like a stick of wood on a sewer grating. If that happened, he would have to be lifted out with a crane.

He saw a helicopter leave the overlook and disappear to the southwest. A minute later another helicopter rose from the same point and headed toward him. His boat was picking up speed and the tiller angle had no effect on his direction. Then he noticed a depression in the water about a hundred yards away, a depression around which a large section of the lake was revolving. "Some kind of eddy," Duncan said aloud, watching with rising fear as he was swung in a wide circle; a minute later he was ten yards closer to the center. His motor was now useless against the quickening spiral current. After two more revolutions the boat was angled steeply downward. It was as if the surface of the water were a rubber membrane that was being pulled down from below.

Whirlpool! The word dropped into his mind like a snake. In a panic he saw that he had been drawn so far beneath the surrounding surface of the lake that he could no longer see the dam or the shore. His boat spun in ever-tightening circles. The helicopter appeared above him, hovering, the pilot gesturing for him to try to grab one of

the landing runners. The boat made two twisting passes beneath it. Both times Duncan, kneeling on the seat, reached as high as he could but missed the connection. As the boat careened around the banked curve for a third approach, Duncan rose unsteadily to a crouching position, vowing he would catch hold even if he had to leap upward to do it.

He never got the chance. Striking a half-submerged log, the boat upended and Duncan was pitched into the center of the vortex, where he was instantly sucked out of sight.

The helicopter lingered, turning slowly before lifting away.

KENT SPAIN felt nauseated and dizzy, and he wondered how much longer he could last. Staggering out of the woods onto the right overlook, he nearly knocked over a fat man with a bandaged head. He threaded his way through sawhorse barricades so ineptly placed that they hindered his progress rather than guided it. There were a lot of spectators, but they didn't greet him with the spontaneous cheer usually given to the runner in the lead. Several people shouted when they saw him; others were looking in the wrong direction.

Reaching the pavement of the road across the dam and ducking under a chain that somebody had stupidly stretched across it, he saw a cop waiting with a hand extended. Kent had no intention of stopping for a handshake, and he sidestepped and slipped from the cop's grasp, marveling at the general thickheadedness of the human race. Now the cop was chasing him and shouting words he couldn't hear because of the head-splitting roar that filled his ears. Legs churning, Kent left the cop behind.

A few minutes earlier, coming down the mountainside to the dam, the trees had shimmered and the ground undulated like a flag in the wind. He had heard roaring then, but nothing like the thunder that filled his skull now. The road here was quivering and at one point seemed to sink beneath his feet. Stop for a minute, an inner voice told him; wait for the roaring and quivering to go away. No! He would keep going. Perseverance was the mark of a champion.

Now there were people at the other end of the dam, too, clutching at him as he ran by and shouting things he couldn't decipher. But soon he was alone again among the trees, jogging determinedly along a trail that followed a side canyon. At the far end of a long switchback Dulotte would be waiting. Kent was beginning to feel a little better, and he kept his eyes open for the white cloth that marked the hidden bicycle. His breathing was not as ragged as it had been coming across the dam. The roar had diminished and the ground had almost come to rest. The cool breeze felt good.

He stopped when he saw a Center for Holistic Fitness T-shirt dangling from a limb. He parted the bushes and the bike was there, gleaming and beautiful. He dragged it into the open and bounced it several times before climbing aboard.

WHEN DULOTTE saw the bike coming, he stepped from behind his table. Kent skidded to a stop. "Not so fast," Dulotte said with a smile. "At this rate you'll break the world record by ten minutes. How are you holding up?"

"I feel terrific. How far ahead of the field am I?"

"I don't know. Back in this canyon there's nothing but static on the radio. Did you use the pedometer, the pulsimeter, the—"

"No, all that stuff broke down a couple of miles out."

"Well, nobody will ever know. Leave the bike here and jog the rest of the way. Your time has to be in the realm of reason."

Kent got off the bike and pushed it into the weeds. "Anything you say, Doc." He helped himself to a peeled orange. As he trotted away he looked over his shoulder and waved. "So long," he said. "See you Monday at the Bank of America."

OFFICER JOHN COLLA SPED through the side streets of Sutterton with his siren wailing, stopping at every third house to tell anybody he could find to warn the neighbors, then head for high ground. Most of the houses were already empty, thanks in part to a plane that had been flying above the town broadcasting the evacuation order over a public-address system.

When he heard Kramer's radio report that the dam's major break was estimated at five minutes away, Colla abandoned his efforts and took one of the roads leading to the tablelands above the town. He was satisfied that Sutterton was almost entirely empty. He would be surprised if more than a dozen people were unaccounted for when the flood was over.

At the edge of town he stepped on his brakes. Two kids not more than ten years old were sitting quietly in a tree. "What are you kids doing?" he shouted out of his window.

"The dam is breaking," one of them called down. "We can watch the water from here."

Colla got out of his car and ordered them down. "Where are your mom and dad? In the house?"

"Dad's divorced," the older of the boys said, working his way to the ground. "Mom's upstairs fixing her nails."

"Hasn't she heard the sirens and bells and airplanes?"

"She said it was awful noisy today."

Colla fired two shots in the air. A woman's face appeared in an upstairs window. "The dam is failing!" Colla shouted. "I'll wait thirty seconds for you, then I'm getting the boys out of here."

The woman raised her eyes and looked across the rooftops toward the dam. What she saw made her mouth fall open. She was running down the frontwalk twenty seconds later, a cat under each arm and purses swinging from both elbows.

"Look out!" an excited voice on the radio was shouting. "Here it comes!"

FROM PHIL'S vantage point it looked like the end of the world. With deep-throated booms and crashes, great chunks of the dam fell into the breach, until a ragged V-shaped notch had been opened to the top. The lake, with an unobstructed path to a level a thousand feet lower, pushed forward like a massive tide, and the lower section of the breach, where brown water was still erupting like lava from a volcano, was obliterated by hundreds of thousands of tons of white water from above. The concrete spillway sagged sideways and was torn apart from the top down, one ponderous block after another. Phil stepped backward instinctively, fearing that the rock abutment on which he was standing might be the next to go. He had intended to continue describing the scene before him, but he had lost the power to speak, so stunned was he by the unleashed reservoir smashing through the dam.

The ground beneath his feet shuddered as a section a thousand feet wide and four thousand feet thick at the base detached itself from the rest of the embankment. Fully a third of the dam, thirty million cubic yards of material, began to edge downstream as a unit. As it moved, it slowly lost its shape, sinking and spreading like a pile of mud under the seething mass of water.

A river wider than the Columbia pushed through the opening. A quarter-mile downstream, the flood from the first break was overtaken by a veritable avalanche of new water hundreds of feet deeper. In minutes Sutterton was obliterated by a fury that rolled over the town, at fifty miles an hour. When it struck the hillside below the town, where the river and the canyon turned right, a mighty sheet of water surged up the slope like the crash of surf against a seawall.

When the wave fell back into the main flood, the slope had been swept clean of trees, topsoil, houses . . . and sightseers.

KENT SPAIN was feeling fine, striding along and breathing free. And smiling. Only a mile more to the Sutterton town hall, where he would break the tape for a stunning new Mother-Lode-Marathon record. The big bucks, the fame, the cars, the clothes, the women would be his. Downhill the rest of the way, along a hill above the town, down a steep gravel road to the city limits, then up Main Street, waving to the cheering throngs.

A helicopter clattered overhead, the fourth he had seen since crossing the dam. Sure a lot of hoopla for a relatively obscure cross-country run, he thought. Rounding a corner, he saw people standing in the pathway, on the grassy slope above the pathway, and on the ridge in the distance, people in clusters with their backs toward him.

"Keep this lane clear!" he shouted, sidestepping through the strangely silent crowd. "There's a race on! Let me through."

"Stupid fool," he heard a man say.

Responding with curses, Kent left the path and picked his way along the hillside to get around the congestion. When he saw what they were looking at, he stopped in confusion. He was on the edge of an inland sea. Where he expected to find the gravel road that descended into town, there was only water—water that stretched to the hills on the opposite side of the valley a mile and a half away.

"Where am I?" he shouted. "I must have made a wrong turn. Where's Sutterton? Which way do I go? Are you people deaf?"

A woman raised her arm and pointed toward the center of the lake, where floating debris revealed a swift current. "There is Sutterton," she said. "The dam broke. Everything is gone."

Kent turned in a slow circle as the truth of the woman's words sank into his brain like a deadening gas. The desolation on the faces around him made it clear that the loss he had suffered was trivial compared to theirs.

Near him, sitting on the grass, were a man and a woman and three children, all sobbing quietly. Beginning to sob himself, Kent Spain sat down and lowered his face into his hands. Sitting was bad for the lumbar, but he didn't care anymore.

FORTY-FIVE MINUTES after the destruction of Sutterton, Police Chief Wilson Hartley was ten miles below the dam, careering down the county road in his police cruiser. He had stopped and pounded on the doors of at least thirty cottages, house trailers, and camper trucks, sending their occupants scampering up hillsides to safety. No telling how many others hadn't heard the warnings he broadcast over and over on the car's public-address loudspeaker.

The advance of the water was being monitored from helicopters and relayed to the communications van. Hartley heard Mrs. Lehmann report that the wave had just hit the fish hatchery at Castle Rock. The hatchery was a mile and a half upstream from where Hartley now was.

He braked to a stop at the driveway leading to Creekwood, Roshek's imposing summer home. He debated with himself whether he had time enough to check it out—he was between five and eight minutes ahead of the wave. Two miles downstream, just across the bridge, were three different roads he could take to high ground. He had seen Roshek arrive and leave the overlook in a helicopter, so chances were the old man had made sure there was nobody at the house, but still . . . With his siren turned to high, he headed into the Creekwood driveway.

A man and a woman who obviously had heard him coming were watching him from the porch. "The dam has broken!" Hartley shouted, stopping at the bottom of the porch steps. "A flood

366

hundreds of feet deep will be here in minutes." He cut the siren, and it was possible to hear a faint, distant rumble. Hartley pointed upstream. "That's the flood coming down the canyon now. Look, you can see the dust it's raising. Run up the hill to the top. It's your best chance. Good luck!"

Hartley made a hard U-turn on the lawn, pausing for a few seconds to watch the frightened pair running up the grassy slope behind the house. Then he floored the accelerator and shot down the driveway, confident that he had saved two more lives; now he would concentrate on saving his own.

The two miles to the mouth of the canyon he took at seventy miles an hour. Just before the road crossed the river and intersected with a road to high ground, he had to slam on the brakes. Four cars were stopped ahead of him. The Sierra Canyon River, out of its banks and carrying a heavy load of flotsam, had taken out the bridge. Hartley got slowly out of his car, staring at the gap in the road. There was no way he could climb to safety on foot, for this part of the valley was lined with nearly vertical cliffs. Drivers from the other cars ran to him, shouting questions. He raised his hand for silence. "There's a Forest Service fire road half a mile upstream," he said. "Follow me."

Driving up the canyon in the face of a steady head wind, Hartley saw in his rearview mirror the caravan of cars following him. What he saw through the windshield made it plain that they were all on a journey of futility. Above the trees was a cloud of dust that turned the morning brightness into ominous gloom.

The fire road was little more than a wide dirt path, blocked to hot-rodders by a horizontal steel beam that was hinged to a post and padlocked at the other end. Hartley ran to the barricade and shattered the lock with two shots from his revolver. As he climbed back into the car, wind whipped his clothes and hurled dirt and pine needles with such force that he had to close his eyes to keep from being blinded. A continuous and growing roar told him the wave was no more than half a mile away.

The car lurched forward, the wheels bouncing over ruts and scattered rocks. The high-powered V-8 engine enabled Hartley to leave the other vehicles far behind, but he wasn't thinking about them. He didn't glance in the mirror, afraid that he might see the source of the thunder that had grown so loud it blotted out every other sound. A slight splash of water struck the windshield.

The fire road rose steeply up the slope of the side canyon, and Hartley plunged recklessly ahead. Even though one tire had gone flat and the oil pan had been lost to rocks, he kept the accelerator floored. To his left, far above on the opposite slope, he could see a diagonal line—that, he knew, was the fire road after it had rounded a switchback at the end of the canyon. If he could reach that elevation, he would be safe.

With stunning speed the opposite slope turned white. A sheet of foam swept over it as if a bucket of soapy water had been dashed against a wall. At the same time a river several feet deep surged uphill around and under the car, sliding it ahead. The engine died. Within seconds a powerful backwash streamed over the hood and roof, turning the car until it was facing downhill. Water boiled over the windows.

Hartley set the emergency brake and waited. The car was totally submerged and water was squirting through crevices in the floor, the dashboard, and the doors. He wondered if this was the worst of it. Maybe the flood would subside before the car filled with water. Maybe . . . He felt a current dislodge the car and give it several gentle shoves along the ground, like a box being nudged by a giant paw.

A tremendous force lifted the car, revolved it slowly end over end, and dropped it on its side to the ground. Hartley was dazed when his head struck the doorhandle, but his reasoning powers continued to function with eerie coolness. Two windows were broken and water was jetting against him. An air bubble will form near the rear window, he told himself. If the car stays where it is, I can last for an hour, maybe more. The water will have dropped by then. If I run out of air, I'll push myself through a window and swim to the surface.

The car was picked up again and pulled swiftly into the canyon. With a profound sense of hopelessness, Hartley realized he was caught up in the flood's main current. The car was rolling over and over and quickly filling with water. When Hartley felt the coldness on his face, he held his breath. There was no sense of panic. He was simply a boy again, on a carnival ride, being drawn with delicious

368

anticipation to the top of the roller coaster, ready for the big plunge that would make the girls scream and the boys hang on to their caps.

Suddenly the car was hit by a counterforce that sent it straight down. Along with a thousand other pieces of debris, it was hurled against the canyon floor from a height of two hundred feet, crushed to a fourth of its original size, then rolled along like a wad of paper on a windswept street. Again the car was drawn upward by circular currents in the flood wave and propelled downstream through the mouth of the canyon. The second time the car dropped, it was driven like a stake into the loam of the Sacramento River. In the following three hours, as the tide rolled over it with decreasing energy, it was buried under thirty feet of silt.

IT WAS TWELVE MILES FROM the dam to the mouth of the canyon, where the Sierra Canyon River emerged from the foothills and meandered through the flatlands of the upper Central Valley to a confluence with the Sacramento River at the town of Omohundro. The flood fought its way down the canyon like a lengthening serpent, surging from one side to another. In the hour it took the flood to reach the canyon mouth, it picked up so much debris that only half of it was water—the rest was dam-embankment material, topsoil, trees, bridges, houses, farm animals, and at least fifty miles of wiring and fences.

Those who saw the advance of the wave from hilltops were later to describe it in a variety of ways.

"The first thing I saw was the dust cloud," said Kitty Sprague, a Forest Service trail worker. "I thought it was smoke, and radioed that a huge fire had broken out. A few minutes later I saw the flood, like a rolling mountain of water pushing a city dump. The front of it was half hidden by mist, but I could see whole houses being tossed around."

Evelyn Hayes, state assemblywoman from Sausalito, was camping with a group of Girl Scouts above the mouth of the canyon. "The odd thing was that it was such a beautiful day," she told the Sacramento *Bee*. "One would expect the end of the world to come with thunderclouds and lightning. That's what I thought, that Armageddon had arrived. The devastation was taking place on a scale that seemed beyond anything human beings could be responsible for. We watched the flood come out of the canyon and fan out across orchards and fields like a stain growing on a piece of cloth. When it reached Omohundro, the houses got pushed together as if somebody were sweeping toys into a pile. Then they got folded under and we couldn't see them anymore."

Tim Hanson, an operatic tenor who lived in Omohundro, told his story on national television hookups from his hospital bed in Chico. "I didn't hear the warnings because I was in a soundproof booth I built in my bedroom so I can rehearse without the neighbors calling the police. When I felt the house shaking, I left the booth and looked out the window. Three blocks away a tumbling wall of rubbish was coming toward me, knocking down trees and houses.

"I ran up to the attic and climbed through a skylight to the roof. I sat with my arms around the chimney and watched the houses down the street get crunched one after the other. A couple of miles away I could see water pouring from Sierra Canyon like syrup from a pitcher. When my house got hit, it started rolling over, with me climbing to stay on the high side, like lumberjacks do on logs in a river. The noise was terrific, the roll of a thousand drums with the sound of trees and boards splitting. I ended up getting swirled downstream hanging on to a piece of an outside wall. Finally I got snagged in some bushes and people with ropes helped me to solid ground."

The San Francisco *Chronicle* quoted a retired army colonel named Tom Stewart, who had witnessed the destruction of Sutterton. "When the water subsided, the valley was nothing but wet bedrock. Everything had been shaved off clean as a whistle, including building foundations. I drove north along what used to be the edge of the lake, expecting to see the town around every turn. All I saw were mud flats, and fish flopping around."

WHEN ROSHEK arrived in Los Angeles in his company's private jet, the press was waiting. A swarming pack of reporters and cameramen extended microphones, fired flashbulbs, and shouted questions, but the engineer ignored them. His face was as hawklike as ever, but his chin was close to his chest instead of defiantly thrust forward. His body didn't seem to fill up his clothes. He looked like a man returning from a long stay in a hospital.

At the curbside, when Roshek was being helped into his limousine, a reporter elbowed his way to the front. "I'm Jim Oliver," he said. "I interviewed you five years ago when an earthquake hit close to the dam. Remember? The Los Angeles *Times*."

Roshek didn't look at him. "I read the Anaheim *Shopper* myself. Now *there* is a paper."

Oliver straightened up and stepped back. Roshek had said something similar to him five years before, but it wasn't the same this time. The line was delivered mechanically, as if Roshek were playing a role that was expected of him.

Roshek's limousine rolled ten feet and stopped. The driver got out. "Jim Oliver of the Los Angeles *Times*?" Oliver raised his hand, and the driver motioned him into the car.

"Thanks very much for singling me out," Oliver said to Roshek when the limousine was under way again. "I can understand why you might not want to talk to the press right now."

Roshek waved his hand to indicate that pleasantries were unnecessary. Oliver noticed that his suit was flecked with mud and that he wasn't wearing his hat.

"I singled you out because I remember that last article you wrote about dams. It was the least ridiculous piece I've seen in a newspaper on an engineering subject. Newspapers should—"

"Did you see the dam fail?" The question stopped Roshek. His mouth closed and his eyes drifted into the distance. "Could you tell me how it made you feel?" Oliver persisted.

"My feelings aren't important," Roshek said in a quiet unemotional voice. "I have a message to give to the American people. That's why you're here."

"The American people will want to know why the dam failed."

A shadow of pain crossed Roshek's face. "The dam failed because of me. Because I thought it couldn't. I believed that nothing I designed could fail. I accept part of the blame for what has happened. At the same time, though, God is partly to blame for providing misleading geophysical data."

Oliver eyed the man slumped in the corner of the seat, wondering if he were losing his grip on reality. "I'm afraid I—"

"I didn't know the fault was there," Roshek said. "The one that caused the earthquake five years ago. We had brown water coming

371

into the lower galleries on that occasion, did you know that? No, because we kept it quiet. We thought the problem was minor and corrected it. It's obvious now we were wrong. You are probably looking for a villain for your story, an incompetent designer, a contractor using substandard materials, a corrupt politician pushing through a pork-barrel project that made no sense. It's not that simple. The dam made a lot of sense. If there is a villain, it is the unknown, which we can never eliminate entirely. What we didn't know destroyed us."

Oliver looked up from his notebook. "You say an earthquake weakened the foundation. You thought you fixed it. The weakness reappeared five years later and wasn't noticed because . . . Why? Aren't there instruments in the dam that—"

"It wasn't noticed because of an incredible string of human and mechanical breakdowns," Roshek said, his voice getting louder. "Instruments failed, gave wrong readings, weren't read. As if that wasn't enough, we had a nincompoop of a control-room operator who didn't grasp what was happening until it was too late." Roshek's eyes were flashing, and he was opening and closing his fists in frustration. "Another terrible thing is that this happened in California, which has the best system of dam-safety regulations in the world, regulations I fought for. . . ."

Roshek turned his face to the window. Oliver then asked the engineer if it was true that a young employee of his spent the night fruitlessly trying to sound an alarm.

"If you can't have a villain, you want a hero—is that it?"

"I'm only trying to verify rumors I've heard."

"A young employee," Roshek said with distaste, "tried to sound an alarm that would have been sounded anyway. No, I take that back. Because I detest Kramer doesn't mean I should run him down. What he did was remarkable. Ask somebody else. I can't be objective."

"Is it true," asked Oliver, "that you fired him for telling you the dam was in trouble and that you had him jailed when he tried to prove he was right?"

Roshek's response was explosive. "It's also true I had him released from jail when I knew he was right. And when I saw him a few hours ago, I had the urge to kill him. Why? Because the greatest

372

engineering structure ever built was failing. Because an arrogant young puppy who has contributed *nothing* to building this nation—absolutely nothing—is to be idolized, while I . . . My life and my career are wrecked." He clapped a hand over his eyes and bared his teeth as if trying to withstand a terrible pain.

The limousine now swung off the Harbor Freeway at the Wilshire exit. When Roshek spoke again, he was calm. "Kramer is still with our firm and we have big plans for him."

"I don't imagine you want me to write that you had an urge to kill him."

"Write what you want about me. If you want to trivialize your story with personalities, go ahead. Gossip may be what the American people want, but it's not what they need."

"What is it they need? What is it you want me to tell them?"

Roshek leaned toward Oliver and spoke with great earnestness. "The American people need safe dams. There are nine thousand dams in this country that would cause extensive damage if they failed, and a third of them don't meet modern safety standards. It's like having three thousand bombs waiting to go off. There are states where a real-estate developer or a farmer can build a dam without even applying for a permit! Without hiring an engineer to design it! When it's built, there is no requirement for periodic inspections. Not more than thirty states have even half-decent regulations backed up by adequate enforcement. How many people are going to have to be killed?"

The limousine pulled up in front of Roshek's office building.

"I care about dams, you see," Roshek said. "When one fails, it is a reflection on engineers. There will be a big clamor now about dam safety, but it will die down as it did after the failure of Teton in Idaho. Don't let it fade! Keep beating the drums! Make the states and the federal government face up to their responsibilities before there's a worse disaster than this one."

"That's a big order. I'm just a reporter and feature writer."

"Promise me you'll do what you can."

"I'll do what I can. It sounds like a worthy campaign. But I can't imagine things are quite as bad as you say."

"They are."

On the sidewalk, Roshek made a show of being his old self,

shaking the reporter's hand with vigor. Oliver watched through the building's glass doors as Roshek wheeled himself to the elevators. He was surprised to realize that he liked the sharp-edged old man. He felt he almost understood him. He felt something else as well— that he would never see him again.

Chapter 13

At Sierra Canyon, Phil Kramer took a last look. Above the damsite, in deeply fissured beds of sediment, meandered a placid Sierra Canyon River, sparkling in the noon sunshine. On the far side of the canyon was the apparently undamaged intake tower, rising from the mud like an elevator shaft without its skyscraper. All that was left of the dam was a section of the embankment extending about a thousand feet from the opposite abutment.

He turned when he heard his name, and saw the television reporter in the tan sports coat.

"Everybody agrees you are the key to this story," the man said, "so we'd like an interview."

Phil walked slowly away from the railing and sat down on the bumper of a truck. "I don't want to be interviewed. I need a couple of days of sleep." He hung his head and closed his eyes. "My legs are killing me. My back is killing me. I feel sick. My car is gone. I'm hungry. I want to go home."

"If you could just tell me . . . Hello? Are you asleep?"

Phil looked up. "Say, are you the guys with the helicopter?"

"Yes. We call it the Telecopter."

"Tell you what. I'll give you an interview if you'll do me a favor. See that intake tower over there? My shoes and watch and clothes are up on top in a neat little pile."

The reporter eyed him narrowly. "On top of the tower? How did they get there?"

"That will emerge during the interview. I also want you to take me to a phone so I can call Santa Monica and ask a certain special someone for a date, whose name will also emerge during the interview."

"Mr. Kramer, I don't know if you're joking, but I can't give you a ride in the Telecopter. Crew only. I could lose my job."

Phil shrugged. "Okay. I'll give the interview to someone else."

The reporter cursed under his breath. He pointed at the helicopter. "Get in," he said.

"I CAME IN as soon as I heard the news."

"Thank you, Margaret," Roshek said. "I knew I could count on you." It looked to him as if his secretary had powdered her face to cover the traces of tears.

"You have a ton of messages. Everybody under the sun has been trying to reach you, including your wife."

"Tell them I'm in a meeting. I don't want to be disturbed."

Roshek locked his office door behind him and shifted himself into the swivel chair behind his desk. A touch of a button turned on the television next to the door. The three network channels were presenting flood coverage, and he lingered for a minute or two on each one. The Sacramento River was out of its banks and the capital was bracing itself for water at least five feet above flood stage. Suisun Bay, San Pablo Bay, and the northern half of San Francisco Bay were expected to turn brown for a day or two, but marine biologists did not foresee a major fish kill. Sutterton and Omohundro were thought to have been evacuated in time. Most homes in Sierra Canyon were also emptied, thanks in part to a still-missing policeman who raced down the valley one step ahead of the wave. Fifty-six people were known dead and twice that many were missing. The governor credited the amazingly low death toll to well-organized emergency service programs in the affected counties.

Roshek turned off the set. Eleanor . . . Had she survived? Well, it didn't make any difference.

He turned on his recorder and dictated a long memo to Herman Bolen, giving him suggestions on how to act as president of the corporation. Roshek urged his colleague to assure all clients that the failure of the dam had nothing to do with design deficiencies. He also advised Bolen to pay a personal visit to every major client, particularly those with whom contract negotiations were under way.

"With regard to Kramer," Roshek said, speaking crisply into the microphone, "it is essential that he remain with the firm. For him to join a competitor would have a devastating effect on our image. He is going to get a great deal of media attention, and by giving him a promotion, the corporation can share in any acclaim he gets. Offer him fifty thousand a year if you have to.

"As you know, Herman, I regard Kramer as a presumptuous twerp who just happened to be in the right place at the right time. Seeing him in a position of prestige would make me sick. Fortunately I'm leaving.

"You're a good man, Herman. Best wishes."

Roshek picked up his fountain pen. On a sheet of company stationery he wrote:

I, Theodore Roshek, being of sound mind, as unlikely as that may seem to some, declare this to be my Last Will and Testament, and hereby revoke all other wills previously made by me. I direct that my just debts be paid and that my entire estate be given to my faithful wife, Stella, who deserved better treatment from me than she got in the last few years.

I do not wish any part of my estate to go to Eleanor James of San Francisco, who in my previous will was provided for so generously and foolishly. To my wife I want to say I'm sorry.

Roshek signed and dated the sheet. Next he dictated a letter to his attorney:

Dear Jules: Enclosed with this letter is a handwritten will. I trust you to make sure the terms are carried out and that my previous will, drawn up against your advice, is junked. If Eleanor survived the flood, she may contest my cutting her off by claiming that I am not mentally competent, as evidenced by my suicide. I assure you I am not off my rocker by any reasonable definition. On the contrary, taking my life now will save everybody a lot of grief and pain, especially myself.

It's been nice knowing you, Jules. If you want to remember me, insult somebody who deserves it.

Roshek turned the television set on again. While listening to "updates on the disaster", he removed the gun from the drawer and made sure it was loaded.

There were five bullets.

"Coming in the next hour," the newscaster said, "will be an

376

exclusive interview with Philip Kramer, the heroic engineer who is credited with saving the population of Sutterton, plus the story of two ballet dancers who had close calls but lived to tell about it, and a replay of some of the most incredible film footage ever taken. Now we take you to the Cal Tech campus, where our Linda Fong is talking to engineering professor Clark Kirchner. Linda?"

Roshek arranged every article on his desk so that the edges were parallel with each other. A photo of Eleanor went into the wastebasket, a photo of Stella was turned face down.

A moustachioed man on the screen was holding forth on the design of Sierra Canyon Dam. "I maintain that the slope of the upstream face, considering the materials used, was at least ten percent too steep. This was the highest embankment dam in the world and should not have been used to test progressive design theories that—"

The bullet entered the center of the screen, which imploded with a vacuum pop and a shower of glass needles. The next bullet shattered the glass that covered a painting of the dam.

Roshek heard Margaret scream. She had been his secretary for twenty years. He had never heard her scream before.

On the right side of the office was a framed cross-sectional view of the underground powerhouse. The third bullet smashed its glass into a thousand pieces. Men were shouting outside his office now, trying to force his door open. Roshek knew they would never get to him in time. The glass case that housed the scale model of the dam collapsed with a satisfying crash.

One bullet left. Roshek positioned the muzzle against his right temple, adjusting the angle so that the bullet would strike squarely. This had to be a suicide, not attempted suicide. No more failures. Sierra Canyon Dam was enough for one life.

He pulled the trigger without hesitation.

PHIL TELEPHONED JANET FROM a booth in Chico. A group of television and newspaper reporters waited nearby, anxious to resume questioning him.

"Phil, is that you?" Janet answered before the first ring was completed. "I'm so glad to hear your voice! I saw you on television a few minutes ago and you looked exhausted."

"That's probably because I'm exhausted. I feel like a washrag that's been wrung out and thrown in a corner."

"I'm so proud of you! What you did was fantastic!"

"You weren't so bad yourself. The guys in the control room said they got phone calls from all kinds of agencies asking about a crazy woman in Santa Monica."

"I had to act crazy to get anybody to take me seriously. When I acted serious, they thought I was crazy."

"Whatever you did worked. You sure stirred everybody up."

"What are you going to do now? When am I going to see you?"

"Soon as I get a few hours' sleep, I'm getting on the first plane headed in your direction. I'm going to wrap my arms around you and stay that way for a month. After that, give me a desk somewhere and let me sit in peace adding and subtracting numbers."

"For Roshek, Bolen and Benedetz?"

Phil laughed dryly. "I'm not thinking about a job right now. I'm thinking about sleep and I'm thinking about you. I don't ever want to be more than five minutes away from you again. Excuse me for going all mushy, but that's how I feel."

"You're a sweetheart, you know that? Do you mind if I call you sweetheart? And darling? And honey?"

"Music in my ears."

Robert Byrne

Not only is Robert Byrne an accomplished editor, journalist, and novelist, but he also happens to be a champion pool player and a civil engineer. Born and brought up in Dubuque, Iowa, and a 1954 graduate of the University of Colorado School of Engineering, he trained as an engineer with the city of San Francisco before he joined the editorial staff of a trade journal, *Western Construction*. He has been writing professionally ever since and is the author of *Byrne's Standard Book of Pool and Billiards*, which is considered the definitive work on these games.

As a technical journalist, Byrne wrote numerous articles about dams and visited more than two dozen sites while they were under construction. "The Sierra Canyon Dam in this novel does not exist, of course," says the author. "But it does have some of the design features of the Oroville Dam, north of Sacramento—the underground inspection tunnel, the heavy instrumentation, the big meter bank, and the fact that it is the highest dam in the country. These similarities, however, were adopted for my convenience only. Oroville Dam is as safe as it can be.

"At the present time," continues Byrne, "there is no computer method for predicting dam failures. However, you can study indicators from previous dam failures, and when there is a sudden change in meter readings, that can tip you off." He also notes that "embankment dams like the Oroville are so massive that they are not really damaged by an earth tremor; they're like mountains—they just shake and don't crack. That is, unless they're situated on an undiscovered fault in the earth, as is the dam in my novel."

Robert Byrne lives in Marin County outside San Francisco and is now at work on a book about how to execute trick shots in pool and billiards. Then, because he is interested in improving the public image of engineers, he expects to write another novel with an engineer as hero.

STALKING POINT
Duncan Kyle

STALKING POINT

a condensation of the book by

DUNCAN KYLE

Illustrated by Tony Coles

Published by Collins

*"You are a German airman, sworn to fight for
your country. Once, long ago, you disgraced
your uniform and your service. Now you have a
chance to restore yourself to pride and honour ...
to strike a blow for Fatherland and Führer."*

For twenty years freelance pilot Ernie Miller
had lived an uneventful but contented life as an
American citizen. Suddenly, as a result of just
one rash act, his shameful past was revealed for
what it was, exposing him to the pincer-like grip
of two men with a bold plan they believed
could win the war for Germany.

It all began with a chance remark, led to
threats, blackmail and terror, and turned at last
to desperate hide-and-seek in the night sky.
Only his old friend and fellow pilot from England,
Alec Ross, had any chance of persuading
Miller to abandon the operation—even if
it meant risking his own career.

Prologue: November 1918

Bars on the high window turned the small room into a cell; in peacetime, when the building near Mézières in the Ardennes was a school, they had protected only a storeroom. In deference to Zoll's commissioned rank, the door was left unlocked. Officers were imprisoned within the honour code. Escape was not contemplated; though one form of escape was encouraged in cases like Zoll's and had actually been offered immediately he had landed his aeroplane. With the time still well short of noon, he sat on the hard bed in his quarters, in the room he had left only two hours earlier with hopes bright and excitement rising. Tears now streamed down his cheeks.

The door opened and the adjutant, Schwarz, entered: small, rotund and jolly when he had welcomed Zoll to the mess a week earlier, but stiff and grim-faced now. Against the wall stood the table on which Zoll kept his shaving things. Schwarz placed something else on it and turned to speak. "Thirty minutes. You may wish to write. Have you paper?"

Zoll nodded, not yet comprehending.

"One letter. I suggest you do not delay." As Schwarz left, Zoll wiped his eyes with the back of his hand and saw the pistol Schwarz had put on the table. He picked it up and broke it open: a single round. Everything seemed to contract within him. So *this* was all that remained: time to write a letter; time to blow his brains out. He closed the pistol with a click and reached for the writing case his mother had given him.

He'd written to her only yesterday, reporting the excitement of the first two patrols, the joy of Max von Kleist as leader, the beauty of the high heavens with the front far below. "We seem," he'd written, "to have cleared the skies in this sector."

Zoll dipped his pen in the ink vial. "Darling Mutti, I have disgraced . . ." He paused, then forced himself on: " . . .myself and our family. When you receive this I shall be . . ." He stared at the paper, tears flooding his eyes, and the pen shook as the words appeared. "I shall be dead." What else? No explanation: that would read like an excuse and there was no excusing what he had done. "It was a moment I do not understand, and that is all I can say. I am bitterly ashamed. Please tell Father how deeply I grieve that I have brought this disgrace to our name. Goodbye." Then: "Your loving son . . ."

He put the letter in an envelope, addressed it, rested it against his clock, picked up the pistol. Here, at the table? Or on the bed? Where did a man blow his brains out? There would be a mess; he must consider the servant who would have to clean. So, not the bed. Blood would soak. . . . He took the pistol more firmly in his hand and slipped off the safety catch.

Now.

As he began to rise, the belt carrier in his tunic caught on the cracked crosspiece of the chairback, lifting it off the floor. It had happened before. He put his left hand behind his back to shift the awkwardly dangling chair, but somehow became further entangled. The pistol fired and the bullet embedded itself in the table.

He was still staring at it, aghast, when the door opened and Schwarz entered, pistol in hand. Zoll turned, the chair still hanging absurdly from his tunic. He said dazedly, "It just went off. Please— another bullet? It was an accident."

Schwarz was icily contemptuous. "Bullets are not to be wasted." He called out and Kleber entered. "This officer is under close arrest," Schwarz told him. "Remain here with him. He will go before a field court as soon as one can be convened."

The previous evening Kleber and Zoll had drunk wine together, members of the same cheerful group in the mess. Zoll begged again for a bullet and was ignored; Kleber only stared at him. He could read the thoughts in Kleber's mind. *Max von Kleist is dead. You had your chance to make the only possible gesture of atonement, and you failed there, too. The consequence is disgrace not only to yourself and your family, but to the squadron: to all of us.*

Finally Zoll ceased to ask and lay on the bed. In the silence he could hear the guns.

IT TOOK TWO DAYS to arrange the court-martial. Now, as Zoll stood waiting in the little storeroom, officers were assembling in the hall.

Zoll lit another cigarette and flexed his shoulders to ease the ache of tension, then crossed to the window and looked out at the walled square. A horse-drawn cart stood at the gate and two soldiers unloaded a crate, setting it down and lifting the lid. It was a long crate and he wondered what it contained. Nothing very heavy, not the way they handled it.

Zoll swallowed, suddenly comprehending. The thing was a coffin! For *him*. He couldn't take his eyes off the yawning box.

The door opened. A voice asked formally, "Unterleutnant Zoll?"

"Yes, sir." Zoll turned and came to attention.

"The court is ready. Follow me."

He marched, rigid and determined. He had failed twice and would not fail again! When they lifted him into that box, they would lift the body of a man who, if nothing else, had died bravely. He marched head up, between the escorts, down the short stone-flagged corridor and into the hall, where he halted with precision.

". . . you are charged with cowardice in the face of the enemy."

In the moment's pause before the prosecuting officer rose, he heard quite distinctly the boom of a field gun.

". . . Unterleutnant Zoll was flying number three in a flight of three aeroplanes on patrol over the front line. The flight was attacked by enemy fighters and . . ."

Zoll only half-listened, remembering. The patrol had been his third: a bright autumn morning, clear and cold, and before they took off Von Kleist had clapped him on the shoulder encouragingly. "We'll have to find some action for you this time. Give you something to tell your father about."

"Yes, sir." Von Kleist was a tremendous hero: thirty-two kills.

What a man to follow! The whole war was a shambles now, and defeat in prospect, but among the fliers morale remained high and Zoll was young enough to believe in miracles.

They'd been airborne for half an hour in a sky dotted with bright puffs of cumulus which today hung oddly low. And that was where the Sopwiths had been lurking: crafty, experienced and up-sun, masked by light and vapour, roaring down through their concealment to the attack, emerging so close, so *shockingly* close. . . .

An officer entered the hall, a full colonel of infantry, a man recognizably cast in the same mould as his father.

"Herr Oberst, please describe what you saw."

"Certainly, President. I observed the attack through field glasses. The three aircraft were flying in arrowhead formation and I was concerned for them because a few minutes earlier I had seen a group of enemy aircraft at somewhat greater height and circling."

"You were already watching when the attack took place?"

"Yes. As I had feared the enemy aircraft appeared suddenly. There was no means by which any warning could have been given . . ."

But *you* saw them coming, Zoll thought. I *didn't!*

". . . they began firing at once, at close range."

Zoll had heard nothing, seen nothing, until the first small impacts, the punches through the wing fabric. He'd glanced back, seen in horror how close the Sopwith was, seen the muzzle flashes and panicked, thrusting the stick forward, snatching at the throttle, seeking safety beneath Von Kleist like a child ducking behind its mother's skirts.

". . . the aeroplane at the rear of the formation dived at once beneath the leader's machine which was thus immediately opened to the attack and shot down. The left-hand rear aeroplane, number two in the formation, turned to face the enemy and was shot down very quickly, only a few seconds later."

"And the remaining one—the defendant's machine?"

"Ran."

He'd scarcely known what he was doing, just that Von Kleist was gone in a rapid, slicing sideslip of smoke and flame and that there was cloud above. He'd swung up at it with two Sopwiths chattering at his tail, almost insane with fear. Reaching the cloud as more

388

bullets stitched his wing, he flew tight circles until his fuel tank was almost empty.

"You continued watching, Herr Oberst?"

"I did. The enemy waited, patrolling the cloud. Then they must have tired of it, or perhaps they were short of fuel. After ten minutes or so they flew off. I saw the defendant returning to base half an hour after the original engagement."

"You have experience of fighter aircraft tactics?"

"Not as a flier, no. But I have observed a great many dogfights in the last four years."

"Have you seen events similar to this one?"

"No."

"How do you interpret what you saw?"

"As an act of gross cowardice and dereliction of duty."

Did the defending officer wish to question the witness? He glanced at Zoll. Shook his head. The colonel's evidence as to fact was wholly accurate, the opinion correct.

Soon, now. Zoll had asked the defending officer not to speak in extenuation, but he had refused. It was his duty to speak.

"I beg the court to take note of the fact that the defendant is a young, inexperienced pilot; that he was in action for the first time. His cowardice, if such it was, was a momentary thing, fear occasioned by a first surprise exposure to the enemy fire. The defendant is deeply ashamed . . ."

And guilty, Zoll thought.

" . . . not only of his own action and the result of it, but of the dishonour he brings upon his family. His father is an officer of distinction, several times decorated. I beg the court to deal mercifully with Unterleutnant Zoll."

Zoll could imagine his father's face. Disbelief, then that pale fury, then . . . nothing. His father would not understand.

He was marched out, leaving the court to consider. He had barely time to smoke half a cigarette before he was sent for.

"The court finds the defendant guilty of cowardice in the face of the enemy." The president then addressed himself to Zoll. "The charge allows only one sentence: that of death by firing squad. Sentence to be carried out immediately upon confirmation by the responsible officer at field headquarters."

Zoll said nothing. He rose, was marched back to the storeroom. In the distance the rumble of guns continued, a sound abruptly overlaid by the roar of a motorcycle engine just outside.

"Hear that?" Kleber said unkindly. "A dispatch rider is taking the finding to field headquarters for confirmation. When it is signed he will return immediately."

Zoll swallowed and looked away. In what time remained, self-control was the only thing of any importance and Kleber knew that. Yet his tone had been provocative, not compassionate.

Zoll said, "I have no wish to talk," and glanced at Kleber with what hauteur he could muster. The growl of the motorcycle disappeared into the distance.

Kleber remained silent, but Zoll could sense his urge to speak. Finally it could not be contained. "There is news," he said.

"Of no interest to me."

"The armistice. All firing will cease at eleven. In one hour and a quarter the war ends."

And I won't see it, Zoll thought. He'd wondered why the court had sat so early in the morning, at eight o'clock. Now he knew. It was a determination to finish him while hostilities continued: *that* was the reason for the dispatch rider, for the immediate carrying out of the sentence. And, he thought, the reason for Kleber's attitude. Germany was defeated: Kleber hated the humiliation and was finding satisfaction in Zoll's own, far greater humiliation.

He smoked cigarette after cigarette. There was sweat on his forehead and under his arms but he felt cold and tight and controlled within. Would it hurt a little, a great deal, or not at all? He would discover soon. Where was the dispatch rider? He listened hard. Silence in the room; gunfire in the distance, but no engine. His own heartbeat was almost drowning the guns, hammering in his ears, pulsing at his temple. He was very thirsty but damned if he'd ask for water.

The guns stopped, though it was moments before he understood that it had happened. The war was finished. He warned himself not to admit hope: there *was* no hope. He was under sentence of a field court-martial: death by firing squad: immediate.

It was after twelve before Zoll was taken before the court again. There was fury in the faces behind the table.

"In view of the cessation of hostilities," the president said bitterly, "it has been decided that sentence of death cannot now be carried out. The general officer commanding has reduced the sentence to imprisonment for life. You will be taken at once to the military prison . . ."

Zoll scarcely heard the rest. He was so braced for death that its removal left him nothing. He didn't know, couldn't think, whether he was glad or sorry. A lifetime in prison faced him: was that really preferable to death?

IT WAS NOT. Conditions in the gaol were appalling. He was confined in a crowded, ancient, damp fortress full of cockroaches and bed-bugs, eating food fit only for swill.

He would have killed himself, but the prison authorities, careless of every other aspect of welfare, were obsessive about the prevention of suicide. Zoll had no shoelaces, no braces, no belt. Shaving was done with a safety razor.

He was allowed to write and receive one letter a month. The first letter was to his father. It said simply that there was an urgent family matter which required discussion. His father did not reply. A month later he wrote to his mother, begging her to persuade his father to make one visit.

Oberst Zoll came. He had always been austere and remote; now, as he sat opposite his son, separated from him by the rusting wire of the screen in the visiting room, he regarded the young man with a cold and manifest contempt. "Well?"

Zoll felt himself shiver. "You are to have a grandchild."

The colonel blinked once. "Illegitimate?"

"No. We married in . . ."

He was cut off. "The girl's address?" His father took out the small pad he always kept in his tunic pocket.

Zoll gave it. "You must help her. I can't."

"Do not presume. I am aware of my duty. I have this to say: you will not communicate again with any member of the family. You are disowned. You have violated every part of the code by which we have lived. As far as I am concerned, you no longer exist." He rose, waited while the warder opened the door, and strode out.

Zoll almost vomited. He sat for a few seconds, his forehead shiny with sweat, seeking to control his stomach. Then the warder yelled "Move!" and he was returned to his cell. Yet he could understand his father's attitude.

But now Anneliese would be cared for. His father had never shirked a responsibility in his life. But God, *how* things had changed for them! The young officer, full of promise; charming, pretty Anneliese, daughter of a Lutheran pastor now dead, whose life was spent dutifully looking after an invalid, demanding mother. They were frantically in love, but marriage was forbidden for him as a junior officer.

Still, they did marry. A young pastor, more liberal than most, and persuaded by Anneliese, performed the ceremony. They were young and confident and no problems seemed insuperable. When the war ended, as one day it must, they would find their way.

When she had written to say she was pregnant, he'd been delighted. He sent her what money was in his cheque account and promised to arrange to withdraw a rather larger sum, an inheritance from his grandmother, which was in a savings account at home in Hanover.

But there hadn't been time. In every sense those damned Sopwiths had moved too fast for him. Now Anneliese was pregnant, the wife of a man disgraced and in prison, stigmatized for life. And the child, when it came, would carry the stigma, too.

The months passed. He hoped for news of Anneliese's confinement. His father certainly wouldn't let him know, but his mother might, or his sister. They didn't. Nor did Anneliese: which mystified him until he decided it must be a condition of his father's support.

In 1921 an amnesty was declared for certain categories of prisoner and Zoll, to his astonishment, found himself outside the fortress gate with a few marks in his pocket given to him by a charity for discharged prisoners. He used it to travel by train to Hanover, where he extracted his inheritance from the bank, took a dingy room in a lodging house and began covertly to watch his old home. There could be no question of approaching his father, but he hoped that some womanly softness of heart would allow his mother or sister to tell him about the child.

He saw his father come out and walk purposefully away, and at

392

half past ten his sister emerged, a shopping basket on her arm. He'd tried to watch discreetly, but she made straight for him.

"Go away, Ernst," she said bitterly.

"Tell me about the child."

She was like their father: forbidding, self-contained Gretel. "He is no concern of yours."

A *son!* "He's all right? And Anneliese?"

"Go away. I will not be seen speaking to you, Ernst. Not because I fear my father, but because I am ashamed of *you*."

"I'll go. But I have responsibilities, a son and a wife."

"She will not hear your name spoken."

"I don't believe you."

Gretel's blue eyes were hostile. "Perhaps you *should* be told what you have done. Mother's health is in ruins. Your wife and her mother and her child live in the house. Two invalids and a child must be supported on your father's pension which is very small."

"Take the money Grandmother left me."

"Do you imagine we would *touch* it? You're not only a coward, you're a fool. If you have money, use it to go to some other country." She paused. "*If* you are certain you can live with yourself."

He tried once more. "At least let me help. I'll find work . . ."

"No."

"Then I'll speak to Anneliese. She'll see the sense—"

Gretel said coldly, "Anneliese *detests* being the wife of a—"

"I don't believe you! Gretel, *please*."

She said, "I will do this, and only this. On condition that you go, and stay, abroad, you may send me an address and I will inform you of those things you should know."

She turned and walked away. Had she lied about Anneliese? No, Gretel never lied. But he had to be sure. He would wait here until the chance came to speak to his wife.

For two days, hanging about miserably in the rain, he waited. When, on the third morning, she finally came out alone, Zoll could instantly see the difference in her. The joy that had been in her face was there no more; she looked drab and serious.

He crossed the road towards her. "Anneliese."

She stopped, expressionless, stared at him for a moment, and then, with deliberation, spat in his face.

393

One: January 1941

There was one ship burning below them: also, to judge from the inky pall of smoke disfiguring the horizon, a tanker was on fire ahead. The convoy stretched wide over the water, with two corvettes and a destroyer dashing hither and yon like sheepdogs. Nothing the aircraft could do—the Liberator was a transport, and in any case had no fuel to spare.

Ross wrapped his greatcoat tighter round himself and slumped in his hard, metal-and-canvas seat, wishing he were piloting instead of sitting; wishing too that he had some idea where he was going and why.

There was urgency involved, that much was certain. Yesterday morning he'd been whipped over from Belfast at five minutes' notice, given his orders and told where to board the Liberator. "You'll receive further orders at Montreal," he'd been told by the transport officer. Apart from that there'd been nothing: nothing except a puzzling verbal check that he was the same Alexander Ross who'd been a senior captain with Pacific Airlines.

"Yes," he'd replied, and wanted to add that he was a senior captain turned into a dogsbody. He'd gone back home to Britain from America after the invasion of Poland with the idea that his experience would be useful in the war. Yet all the thousands of flying hours seemed to indicate only that he was too old. Ross had spent a year and a quarter doing random Air Ministry work; making himself useful without ever feeling he was doing a solid job.

Hours later at Montreal, Ross saw a couple of Hudsons leaving on the long journey across the Atlantic. Lonely work, he thought, but at least they knew where they were going.

"Captain Ross," he said in the onward transportation office. "You have orders for me?" An envelope was handed to him, and he found he was soon due aboard an aircraft bound for Vancouver. Further orders there.

He groaned inwardly. The whole continent to cross. "Can't you tell me more? What do I do in Vancouver?"

"Further orders waiting. It says that, doesn't it?"

THE HOURS CRAWLED BY. He was unshaven and cold, yet still sticky with sweat in places, grubby and uncomfortable. They stopped once to refuel, but there wasn't time for anything else. Across the prairies, up over the Rockies, grinding out the miles: by the time he reached Vancouver, Ross could hear his beard rasp against his coat every time he moved his head.

Now there were more orders. He was to change into the civilian clothes he'd been ordered to bring, then report to the Boeing assembly plant. Later, when he found himself in a Consolidated PBY taking off and heading south, over the border into the United States, he bellowed into the pilot's ear, "Where the hell are we going?"

The pilot turned his head. "Under orders not to say, Captain Ross."

Ross swore softly. What the hell was this damned secrecy about? This wasn't Europe, wasn't a war zone. This was the United States, very much at peace.

It was fifty-two hours, almost to the minute, after he'd taken off from Britain that the amphibian began to let down. He'd identified the route by then: no mistaking the California coastline, the mountains. They were headed for some part of the Los Angeles area.

The amphibian came in at Long Beach, bumped once quite hard, slowed and began to taxi. As it stopped, the flight engineer came back from his cramped, cold position halfway along the crawl-tunnel, lifted the hatch and put the ladder in place.

"OK, Captain Ross. We're here. If you'd like to climb down I'll hand you your bag."

Ross climbed. "OK," he said tiredly, "solve the mystery for me. Where am I going?"

"Won't be more than a moment, sir."

"For God's *sake!*"

A big, new, two-storey white building lay directly ahead, on the other side of the airfield's perimeter track. A red windsock flew from a flagpole, red and white lettering.

It couldn't be!

But it was. Ross saw a familiar bulky figure with carroty hair come bustling out of the entrance, hand outstretched. Ed Martingale.

Ed had moved factories again: always bigger and better: more and more radios for aircraft. How many times a millionaire now? Ross had known him a long time.

"Alec, how are you?"

"Tired," Ross said. "And irritable. And wondering just what stupid games are being played here." He looked balefully at Martingale.

"Not a game, Alec," Martingale said. "You're needed here."

"You've said that before. The answer's still the same. I am *not* going to work for you. I have a boss already."

"Not to work *for* me." Martingale held the door open for him. "Round to the right, there, then straight through."

Ross entered a big, comfortable office. "Shower first?" Martingale asked him. "Or breakfast, or the story?"

"The story," Ross said, then changed his mind. He'd waited this long; half an hour more didn't matter. "No," he said, "the story last."

"Wise man. You always were, Alec. That's why you're here. What d'you want? Ham, eggs, toast, that kind of thing?"

"You can load the plate with a shovel," Ross said. "Over in Britain we get two eggs a week."

Martingale's private bathroom had all the gadgets. The needle spray in the shower blasted hot water at him from every angle, up, down and sideways. He came out feeling half-better, then ploughed his way in silence through a hefty breakfast, lit a cigarette, poured another cup of coffee, and said, "Now tell me."

Martingale said, "Did you say you get two eggs a week over there?"

"That's right. So?"

"Well, I don't know about eggs, but maybe they go over in convoys, too. A lot of other things do, that's sure."

"Come on, Ed. You can do it in two words. What is it?"

"Sub-hunting," Martingale said.

"Me?"

"That's right."

"I know nothing about it, Ed. If you brought me over—"

"New equipment," Martingale said. "We're building and installing, but we're at a very early development stage. Now: I have the

396

best radio research team in the United States right here, at least *I* think so. I need the right man in charge of the flying."

"Ed, I'm not a technician! There must be a thousand people in California who can do the job as well as I can."

"There's nobody I'm as sure of as I am of you."

"That's insanity."

"OK, it's insanity. You know the way I do things, Alec. Maybe it's insane and always has been. But it works."

Ross nodded. Eleven years ago Martingale had started out with a wooden shack and an ambition to build aircraft radios. The theory had been that flying was changing, that air-to-air and air-to-ground would get more and more important with every passing month. The set, Martingale insisted, was only half the battle. The other half was operator confidence, and above all, reliability. He'd built a fortune in a decade—and a reputation for the best radio equipment flying.

Ross said, "I'm listening."

"OK. Just this and you can get some sleep. We've got a six-month development programme and I want the best man I know in charge of flying because that's the way to get ahead fastest. Well, you're the best I know. Also—no, listen—also, you won't be working for *me*. Not on my payroll, anyway. You'll continue to be paid by your own people, the British. And when the job's over, you go right back where you came from. That's a promise. OK?"

"I suppose so." Ross said, "What do I actually do?"

Martingale grinned. "Long hours of precision flying. I want a man who can fly ten hours at a hundred and fifty feet if necessary, and then ten more at two-fifty next day. I *know* you can do it."

Ross yawned. "And in any case, I haven't any option?"

"Not much."

"OK. Sold to the gentleman in the rumpled suit. Where do I sleep?"

"I have a bedroom right here. Sleep now and then we'll have dinner tonight."

Dinner was an enormous steak with salad and a bottle of first-class Californian wine, followed by coffee and a swift run-down from Martingale on the new, more scientific approach to submarine-hunting, and the terrifying rate of loss of merchant shipping on

North Atlantic convoy routes. Recalling the two ships he'd seen, Ross took the point. "Can it be done?"

"That's what we've got to find out. Now, Alec," Martingale said, "we're going to have two planes fitted out, both Cansos—that's the Canadian version of the PBY-5, the one you call the Catalina in Britain. You'll be in overall command of flying operations. We'll work first of all right here. But after a while, and I hope pretty soon, we're going to move the whole outfit to the Royal Canadian Air Force field at Kingston, Ontario. Like I said, there'll be two Cansos, and we need a master pilot for the other. And I want you to do the recruiting. You need another pilot, somebody you have faith in, somebody you've already flown with."

"That's all very well, Ed, but people have jobs already."

"Nothing that can't be fixed. Choose somebody from Pacific, for instance, and we'll set it up so he goes back there with no loss of seniority, pension rights or anything else."

"Start in the morning?"

"I can stand the delay. Just."

Ross slept again, showered, and went to work. He had a strong feeling of unreality, partly from disorientation and the long flight, and partly from the freedom he'd been given. It was hardly the first time he'd looked for a pilot for a special job, but he had never done so on the terms Martingale set out: find the man and strong-arm him into the project!

Ross began to write down names, conjuring up in his mind a picture of the man, of his record, his flying style. In an hour he had nine names; all of them good men he'd be more than happy to fly with, in whose company he could live comfortably for the promised six months. He started with the name at the head of the list: his first, automatic choice. He buzzed the secretary Martingale had assigned to him and said, "Get me John McCartney. Last I heard he was with Eastern. They'll know where he is."

Eastern knew all right. Jocko McCartney had joined the RCAF and was now in Britain. Well, he could get him back, probably, if necessary. Ross chewed his pencil. No point in bringing Jocko back if somebody like Ernie Miller was available: Miller was good, an old friend, too; intelligent and possessed of enormous stamina.

"See if you can find me a man called Ernie Miller. He's freelance;

the aviation board ought to have his address. He was in San Francisco last time I heard from him."

The board had Miller's number. Ross put the call through. "Ernie? Alec Ross. I'm in Long Beach and I'd like to see you if you're fit and still flying. Can you get down here pretty soon? Say, today or tomorrow?"

THE SPLUTTERING ROARS drew him to the window and he glimpsed a small, unfamiliar plane doing a tight roll before it vanished beyond his field of vision. He smiled but didn't make the connection.

"Mr. Miller to see you, Captain Ross."

He went out. "Hello, Ernie. It's been a long time."

"Too long. Hi, Alec." Miller was waiting in the outer office, feet planted slightly apart, wearing creased trousers and an old flying jacket, with a flying helmet crumpled in his hand.

As they shook hands, Ross said, "That was you, wasn't it, Ernie? Just now—howling by my window?"

Miller laughed. "Well, you did ask if I was still flying."

"And you really felt the need to demonstrate to *me?*"

Miller smiled. "Hell, I'm forty-two, Alec. What I thought was—at my age he'll be wondering. People start slipping. I haven't yet, but people do. So do you take my word for it, or do I have to show you?"

Ross clapped him on the shoulder. "With you, I'll take the demonstration. I can do with a little fun."

"OK." Miller handed him the helmet. "Put this on. I have another."

"How's Dot—beautiful as ever?"

"She said to give you a smacking kiss," Miller said. "You want it now?"

"Thanks, but I'll collect in person. She doing any flying?"

Miller shook his head, as he led the way out. "My fault. One day I'll swap the aerobat for something she can handle."

In the aircraft park four hundred yards away, twenty or thirty assorted planes stood.

Ross said, "Which?"

"Over there. She's black." Miller pointed. To Ross the plane appeared to consist of a massive radial engine, a three-blade prop and a pair of very short, stubby wings.

He said, "Who built *that*?"

"Me, with a little help. Dot did the needlework. Get in."

He flung the little black biplane savagely round the sky. Three times the G-forces blacked Ross out briefly as Miller pushed the stressed aerobatic special to the limit, diving into loops, then rolling off the top. He put it through the whole repertoire. At forty-two he could certainly still fly.

Miller brought her in like a zephyr, then turned his head as the engined died and yelled back: "Did I pass?"

Ross nodded. He felt a tiny bit dizzy as he climbed down, but contrived not to show it. As they walked back towards Martingale's white-painted industrial palace, he said, "The job's yours if you want it, Ernie. There's only one hurdle; it's a hush-hush project. You'll have to talk to Ed Martingale. And to the navy. They're in on it, too."

"My life's an open book. Ed knows that. Can you tell me about the job?"

"Not yet—when and if you've been cleared. You brought your papers with you?"

"Yeah, I got all the papers."

"Right. We'll do it as fast as possible. One thing, Ernie, though. Will you be able to move house? Here, first. Then onward—can't tell you where, but for about six months."

"Why not? It's only a furnished let."

"There's Dot," Ross said, but he knew the answer.

"Whither I go, she goes. You know Dot."

A year later it probably wouldn't have happened: by then there were vetting procedures, a centralized and functioning security apparatus. The armed forces already applied such checks to their own men, but Miller wasn't one of their own men. He was presented as the personal choice of Captain Ross, whose own credentials were already established.

Miller stayed overnight to await interview by Commanders Briggs and Lenahan, the two navy liaison officers assigned to Martingale Corporation. When he appeared before them next morning, Briggs accepted the proffered papers, looked at the birth certificate and said in a tone of surprise, "You were born in Paraguay, I see?"

"That's right. My father was a trader there."

"So you had the choice of citizenship?"

"Until I was twenty-one," Miller said. "Then I became an American. It didn't seem like a difficult choice, not to me." He could feel himself sweating. "Came up here in 'twenty-eight, after my father died."

"And you've been here ever since?"

"All in the records," Miller said. But it wasn't. He wondered often exactly what *was* in the records. Not the truth, certainly.

Lenahan was going through the passport. "Mexico and Canada. What were those trips?"

Miller said, "I've always been a freelance flier. Sometimes I'd have to make a trip north or a trip south, that's all." He smiled, and fancied he could smell his own fear.

"You certainly have a lot of air time."

"Nearly seventeen thousand hours." Plus some, Miller thought. God, if they knew how he'd got those precious papers! And if they knew the trouble he was in!

IN 1926, in the Paraguayan capital, Asunción, Ernst Zoll had encountered an elderly American expatriate, one Dean Miller, who ran a small and doubtful import business.

Zoll's excellent English, learned as a child when his father was assistant military attaché in London, had particularly pleased Dean Miller. The old man liked to speak English to him and particularly relished Zoll's vowel sounds. "*Carstle*," he would chortle, "and *grarss* and *barth?* That the way they talk over there?" Old Man Miller was usually drunk in the evenings, but good enough company and Zoll often stayed at his home whenever he was in Asunción. One evening he noticed a photograph he hadn't seen before: Dean Miller with his arm round a young man's shoulders. "Your son?"

"Was." Tears appeared in the old man's eyes. "They killed him—some Brazilians I was crazy enough to trade with. They'd things they wanted to sell me. Hot as hell the stuff was, a consignment of refrigerators. They wanted more than it was worth, so I sent Mike down the river to Parana to beat them down. Never saw him again. Then one of them came up to see me and I said I wasn't talking

402

because my son was doing the talking on the other side of the border."

Dean Miller paused. "Know what he said? He gave a kind of little grin, and he said, 'What son? You have no son.' So then I knew. I never heard nothing more, not in fourteen years."

Days had passed before the thought came, and then, carefully, a question or two at a time, he learned more about the son. Mike Miller had dual nationality and opted at twenty-one to become a citizen of the United States.

"So he travelled on a US passport?"

"Sure. Had it with him. Bastards sold it, I'll just bet. US passport's a valuable thing to some people."

"Was Mike's disappearance ever reported?"

"Sure, but they weren't interested. I'd no proof and I could hardly say why I thought he'd been killed. So they just thought it was a boy left home and his dad wanted him back, that's all."

"No death certificate?"

"Nope."

Next morning he was lying in his bed, looking at the fly-speckled ceiling, when the old man came in carrying a worn envelope tied round with string. "Just recalled," he said, "what we was talking about last night. Seems to me you was maybe interested in these." He tossed the envelope on the bed.

All were there: registration of birth, correspondence regarding dual nationality, confirmation of the choice, citizenship papers. Everything. Including copies of photographs submitted with the passport application: pictures of a roundish, unformed face. Height and weight were less than his own.

He'd lain there thinking: *no death ever recorded!* In America, on good papers, he'd be more secure than he'd ever been anywhere else. Could he get work there? Certainly he could.

Later that day Dean Miller gave him a sideways look. "Reckon there's anything of value there?"

"Could be, for the right man."

The eventual price had been a criminal act: a Paraguayan city politician, who had offended against the régime, was to be flown out of the country. The papers were safely in his pocket as he landed in Brazil. Six months later Zoll had his shiny new passport and a new identity and was heading north: young Miller, returning to his native land. He reasoned that the fact that the passport had been issued was proof that there had been no other application in the same name. Of course, the old man could be wrong; the son *might* simply have left home, be living in some other country. Confronted with somebody who'd known Mike Miller, he'd be finished. Unlikely, yes—but it was an Achilles' heel, however small . . .

"I see your name is Michael," Commander Lenahan was saying. "Yet people call you Ernie. How's that?"

He said, this time with perfect truth, "I've been called Ernie most of my life. Stuck with it, I guess."

"I know what you mean," Lenahan said, smiling. "I have a nickname myself, not that I'm going to talk about it!"

Now Miller knew he was *in*. A few moments later the two officers were wishing him luck on Project Cull.

He went at once to Ross's office. "What's Cull?"

"If you know the name they passed you. This thing is highly technical, Ernie. Anything you don't follow, you'll have to ask Ed Martingale. We're going chasing imaginary submarines. Come with me." They rode across the airfield in a white pick-up. Ross halted beside the familiar shape of a Canso. "Had anything to do with these ships?"

"No. Just seen them go by."

"Tons of lift, that's the important thing. You'll get flying instruction over at Consolidated. Meantime . . ."

"What's *that?*" Miller pointed.

"What's it look like?" A huge metal ring was fixed to the amphibian, encircling it from just forward of the nose almost to the point where the fuselage lifted towards the tail.

Miller pursed his lips. "Search me. A mine detector?"

"You're warm. But it's on a big scale."

"It'll pick up a sub?"

"Whoa," Ross said. "Let's not get too far ahead of ourselves. What we're really talking about is the earth's magnetic field. It's fairly regular, as you probably know. You can map it with a magnetometer, right?"

"Yes."

"Put a large body of ferrous metal down anywhere and you get

404

variations in the magnetic field. Well, it seems that's true of the ocean, too. And subs are built of steel."

Miller looked doubtfully at the big amphibian. "Sounds fine. Does it work?"

"Not yet. But we hope it will."

"Funny," Miller said. "I was expecting some form of radar."

"It'll be part of the package: radar's going in too. The idea is to get everything in combination, make a systematic thing of it. The radar pulse goes out, you wait, back it comes. Time gives distance. You can tell something's there because the pulses bounce back. Trouble is, at the moment, we don't know which direction they're coming from. Say you're at two thousand feet with a thirty-mile horizon. Anything on the surface will send radar pulses back, but you still don't know where the object is, only that it's there. Maybe the sub's on the surface, charging batteries. The crew hear an aircraft and crash dive, so radar stops registering."

"And you bring in the magnetometer?"

"If you can find out where to look. Martingale reasons that if two aircraft fly parallel, thirty miles or so apart, and they *both* get a bleep on radar, then it's probably in between them. And there'll be two magnetometers for the second phase, the hunt. The thinking's good here. But whether it will work in practice is another thing."

MILLER TOOK the little black biplane back home to San Francisco with his head in a whirl, and not just from the technicalities he'd had to absorb. A large part of it was a sudden access of hope. Two words had been spoken: the first was *secret*, the second *Canada*.

On this secret project in Canada he'd be out of reach, for six whole months, of the bastard who now had him gripped in pincers. That ought to give him time to work out how to disappear permanently. God, but what a fool he'd been to write that letter!

Two

The man who held the pincers, and to whom Miller's letter had been delivered, was a minor functionary at the office of the German Consul-General in San Francisco. Baldur von Galen was twenty-four years old, partially crippled, and deeply bitter at his situation.

Shortly after the invasion of Poland, Von Galen had completed his training as a bomber pilot. Leaving their graduation party late at night, and awash with champagne, Von Galen and two other newly-commissioned *Luftwaffe* officers were returning to their quarters, arms linked and voices raised in song, when a motorcycle, coming too fast round a corner, skidded into them. One of the young men was killed, one left unscathed; the bone in Von Galen's right thigh was fractured in three places and in addition his head struck the road so hard as to cause a small fracture of the skull.

There was no question of flying again. He walked, but with a limp, and the skull fracture gave him a degree of tunnel vision. At first Von Galen had believed that the influence of his maternal uncle, Ernst Wilhelm Bohle, Minister of State at the Reich Foreign Office, could help. Bohle tried to intercede but found that the armed forces actively resisted interference from the Party.

Bohle couldn't help. Von Galen didn't believe him—and nagged. His mother nagged too, and between them they pestered Bohle to the point where, out of sheer irritation, he acted to get Von Galen not just out of his hair, but out of the way. Thus Von Galen found himself appointed an officer of the *Auslandorganisazion* and sent to man its office in San Francisco.

And in that city he was busily making a nuisance of himself, hoping that the consul would become so infuriated as to send him home. To that end Von Galen had been using his car, an eight-cylinder, black Horch coupé, as a battering ram.

Patrolman McInerny saw the black blur, blunt-bonneted and supercharged, tearing along Market Street at half past six on a Sunday morning, and set off in pursuit. The Horch shot two red lights, swung up the steep hill towards the Coit Tower, then spin-turned on screeching tyres to come bounding down again, treating the hill like a series of ski jumps.

The patrol car hung on grimly, just in sight all the time. Finally, in Sixth Street, the Horch was there at the kerb, by the newspaper building.

McInerny climbed out of his car, slammed the door and went purposefully over to the Horch. The driver sat relaxed behind the wheel, airily lighting a cigarette.

"Driver's licence, please."

A languid hand took something from a jacket pocket and held it out, and the driver said, in slightly-accented English, "Examine it, and—what's that American expression?—vamoose!"

"I don't need to. I know what it is, it's a diplomatic passport." It was McInerny's turn to smile. "We have a request from the German consul to impound the car on sight. Better get into the patrol car."

Von Galen stared at him, but decided not to argue. He would save his wrath for Wiedemann, the consul, who would soon know better than to interfere with the nephew of the Minister of State.

When he was driven back to the office, however, Wiedemann had a surprise for him. A few days earlier there had been an article in the *San Francisco Chronicle*, which had condemned the activities of a "young German diplomat who, under the protection of diplomatic immunity, chooses to use our streets as a racetrack. He ill serves the interests of his country." Wiedemann had sent it to Bohle and Bohle had now replied. He handed the signal to Von Galen.

"Inform my nephew that any further breach of proper diplomatic conduct will result in his transfer, not back to the Reich, as he may imagine, but to the coldest, dullest, most uncomfortable backwater I can find for him."

"Why," Von Galen demanded furiously, "won't they just let me *fight?*"

"Because you're not fit. You must learn to serve Germany in other ways. Do your job."

"My job! Nursemaid to Germans living abroad. To the pathetic American Nazi organizations! They're comically ineffectual."

Wiedemann remained patient. "You're a fool, Von Galen," he said. "I have a certain sympathy because you want to fight and you can't. That's bad luck. But you'll have to learn to fight behind a desk, or accept the consequences. How *is* your vision?"

"Improving."

"Then let's see if another six months helps. Settle down and do your work. It's February now. Have another medical test in August. If, by then, there is further improvement, I will support your application to go back."

"What about my car?" Von Galen asked.

"That will depend upon your performance."

The letter was in his in-tray, part of a backlog he had allowed to accumulate. The *Auslandsorganisazion*'s job seemed to Von Galen to consist largely, though not exclusively, of welfare work: handling requests to trace families who had moved.

There were several of them now in his in-tray. He sorted through them resentfully. The letter went through with the others into the out-tray, and he had marked it: "Forward as instructed." Miller would have escaped if Karen Hanzer, Von Galen's secretary, had been less alert.

IT HAD BEGUN with Dot calling through from the kitchen of their little apartment, "Weather forecast, honey."

Miller switched on the radio receiver, saw where it was tuned and called back: "If you're going to listen to all that stuff, retune the set afterwards, will you!"

"Sorry, dear."

He turned the dials and by the time the set warmed, heard only the last words of the forecast. Dot came through, drying her hands, and kissed his cheek. "I won't do it again, promise."

He swatted at her backside and missed, and she said, laughing, "You're slowing down, kiddo."

Miller grinned and began hunting for the Air Corps forecast. He caught the words ". . . fight over the Chann . . ." from some station, and tuned back.

". . . third sortie that day," a voice was saying, "and of course we were all a little tired, but when we saw a flight of British Hurricanes below we were tired no longer."

Miller frowned. What the hell was *this* station? It was German propaganda, but well done.

He learned gradually, listening hard because the short-wave transmission surged and faded, that the voice belonged to a young German fighter pilot flying ME 109s. His description of the fight was plain and modest. The German fighters had had height and surprise on their side. They lost one, the British two.

". . . I saw my friend go down. An hour before we had been drinking coffee. It might have been me, but it was Joachim and I avenged him. He died for Germany and I was proud of him."

"You have been listening," said an announcer's voice, "to

408

Leutnant Heinz Zoll, a *Luftwaffe* fighter pilot. Last week Leutnant Zoll received, from the hands of Reichsmarschall Herman Goering, the Iron Cross First Class. Heroism runs in the family. He is the grandson of a colonel of infantry who won the same decoration in 1915. This is Deutschlandsender on bands . . ."

Miller rose, switched off the set and stumbled to the bathroom.

"What was that you were listening to?" Dot asked, when he came out a few minutes later with some degree of self-control.

"Description of an air fight, that's all."

Lying next to her that night, snug in their double bed, he listened enviously to the regularity of her breathing. His own mind turned over and over, trying to absorb the extraordinary fact that it was his own son's voice he had heard, and that his son was a *hero*, a fighter ace! His own *son* had received the Iron Cross.

A cataract of emotions roared through his head: intense pride, astonishment, above all shame. The announcer had made a point of family heroism; but between the two heroes lay the unmentionable generation: the Zoll convicted of cowardice. *Him.*

Why hadn't Gretel written? Because it was *good* news. Gretel had written three times over the years, but only with news of death: his mother, his uncle, his godfather.

God, but he wished he could tell Dot. Could he? He turned his head to look at her in the dimness, sleeping with all the peace in the world. The best thing that had happened to him in his whole life was meeting Dot. The day swam into his mind, as it often did: he'd come into a dirt airfield in Oklahoma one day, with the canvas shredding on his wing, and taxied over to the tin hangar needing canvas and skilled hands and expecting to find none of them. And Dot had come out. She took one look, laughed and said, "So that's what a wing structure looks like underneath."

"Can you fix it?"

"I think so." And she'd done it fast and beautifully.

He'd watched with amazement and pleasure: the more so because she wasn't just skilled, she was the prettiest girl he'd seen in a long time; and, as it turned out, the nicest.

He couldn't tell her about this, though. He'd do anything for Dot except tell her that he was German, and that their marriage was bigamous. That would destroy her.

But he couldn't do *nothing*, couldn't fail to acknowledge that the son he'd never seen had fulfilled his own dreams. In the end, he climbed out of bed and went into the spare bedroom and wrote the letter, hoping that maybe the radio station would send it on.

"WE JUST FORWARD IT?" Karen Hanzer asked Von Galen. "You think that's enough?" She looked at him hopefully.

"It's what my notation says." Von Galen looked at her sourly. She was a strongly built blonde, with braided hair wound tightly round her head; he thought she looked like something off a *Hitlermädel* poster.

"I know. But it's interesting, isn't it, that—?"

"This Consulate is, in part, a post office, Fräulein. Let's make it an efficient one."

She said quickly, "There's no address on this letter. Let's at least find out who he is?"

"I imagine we can find out by opening the enclosure."

"I have your permission?"

"Do as you damned well like, Fräulein."

She steamed the letter open.

Dear Heinz,

I heard you on the radio the other day and was very proud. You will probably be surprised to hear from me. If my name has been mentioned, I'm sure it cannot have been in any affectionate way. All the same, you may be interested that your father is alive and that he's a pilot like you.

I have lived in America for many years and flown dozens of aircraft, and I doubt very much whether I'm quite the same man I was when the events you may have heard of took place in 1918.

Listening to you, I envied you. You're everything I once hoped to be, and hearing your voice brought a lump to my throat. If you feel able to write to me—even a few words—it would be generous.

My congratulations on your Iron Cross. I can't tell you how proud of you I feel!

Ernst Zoll

Karen thought for a few moments. San Francisco postmark, no

telephone listing, the only address a post-office box number: he was concealing something. She sat at her typewriter and wrote:

Dear Herr Zoll,
    There is a letter for you, here at the Consul-General's office, if you wish to call and collect it.

She signed the letter with Von Galen's name; if Zoll did turn up, she'd learn of it before Von Galen did.

Karen Hanzer was ambitious to become something more than a secretary. Being intuitively certain that Herr Wiedemann had an intelligence role in addition to his consular duties, she was busily bringing herself to his notice. She found it exciting to prise reluctant Germans out of their comfortable hiding-places, to remind them sharply of their responsibilities, and to draw them eventually to Herr Wiedemann's attention.

Von GALEN was wondering how many of these damned receptions he would have to attend before Wiedemann condescended to return his car. He stood looking out from the terrace over the lights of the city and the velvet black of the bay: he and Joseph O'Hara, the only men present, were at the house of Bridget Mahoney, a member of the Women's Committee to Keep the United States out of War— another of the groups which talked a great deal and did little. It frequently seemed to Von Galen that their pro-German stances came from anything but pro-German feeling. Mrs. Mahoney was a case in point. She was Irish, bitterly anti-British, and about as interested in Germany's triumphant rise as she was in last year's hat.

"Ten minutes more," Von Galen said, gulping his cognac.

O'Hara laughed. "I'll come with you." He was a tall young man, bespectacled and earnest-looking. "I'm only here because she's been nagging me for weeks." Mrs. Mahoney apparently knew his mother. Then, leaning on the terrace rail, O'Hara said, "I'll never understand why you people stopped."

Von Galen knew what he meant: they'd been talking about it over dinner. Why hadn't Herr Hitler invaded Britain last year, when he had the chance?

"I'm as bad as the old biddies in there," O'Hara continued. "I want to see the British *smashed*. I'm Boston-Irish and my anti-British feeling's hereditary."

"But if you hate them so much," Von Galen said, "do something about it. Isn't there an Irish Republican Army? Or there's a small Irish volunteer unit attached to the *Wehrmacht*. Join one or the other."

"I have pronounced astigmatism and a prolapsed spinal disc," O'Hara said. "I couldn't even drill with a rifle, let alone shoot straight. If I could, I know who I'd shoot."

"Who?" Von Galen asked, a little wearily. Another minute or two and he'd leave.

"Roosevelt."

Von Galen glanced at him. "Why?"

"He's going to take the United States into the war—*and* on the British side. That's why."

"His removal would be useful. Pity about your eyes." Von Galen put down his glass. "Good night."

But the next words halted him. "Oh, I *am* going to get him," O'Hara said. "Somebody's got to stop him. Might as well be me."

Von Galen frowned. Was this man drunk, or what? "Why are you telling *me?* I have an official position here—possibly a duty to report what you say. Germany and the United States are not at war."

"Not yet. Want to bet they won't be inside a year?"

No, he didn't *appear* to be drunk; nor from his demeanour was he a braggart. All Von Galen knew was that O'Hara came from a rich Boston-Irish family, and that he was standing here threatening to murder the President of the United States. The thing was unreal.

"If you killed him, what do you suppose would happen afterwards?"

"OK, I can tell you what would happen," O'Hara said levelly. "There's nobody to take his place, and with Roosevelt gone, the influence would shift straightaway to people who would break their goddam backs to keep America out—like Senator Taft and Joe Kennedy. You people could take your time over Britain, and Britain wouldn't have American arms."

"Very tempting."

"Just one thing. Hands off Ireland."

"I doubt very much," Von Galen said, "whether the Führer would be interested in Ireland."

"That's right, he wouldn't. He's only interested now because U-boat bases in the southwest would be strategically vital in the war against Britain."

"Yes, well . . ." Von Galen nodded. "It's all very interesting." This time he *would* go. He began to turn away.

Then O'Hara startled him again. "There's a chance of getting Churchill too. He's meeting Roosevelt."

"How do you know?"

"That," O'Hara said, "needs explaining. Want to hear?"

"I suppose I'd better," Von Galen said, amused. "This should probably be reported to Berlin."

"Don't make fun of it. I'm serious."

"I see you are." This would be either the intelligence coup of the century, Von Galen thought, or half an hour wasted; with very heavy odds on waste. "Tell me."

"No. Not here. I'm at the Bedford Hotel. Come and have dinner with me tomorrow night."

"All right."

HAVING USED Von Galen's name once without his knowing it, Karen Hanzer did not hesitate to do so again: she inscribed it on the request to *Luftwaffe* Records Office for information on the father of the heroic Leutnant Heinz Zoll. She had marked the inquiry Most Urgent and *Luftwaffe* Records helpfully replied by signal. In a mere nine days Fräulein Hanzer had the information.

She read the signal and smiled to herself. It was now only a matter of waiting for the fly to walk into the spider's parlour, and the fly arrived in early February, its coming signalled by a call from the public counter.

"A man here to see Herr Von Galen," the counter clerk reported. "Won't give his name. Says he had a letter."

Her heart thumped pleasurably. "Ask him to wait," she said. "Then, in five minutes, tell him that Herr Von Galen isn't here today."

She looked out of the window. Fog so shrouded the city that the higher buildings seemed to be pillars supporting a vast blanket of cotton wool. Misty tendrils drifted down into the streets, carrying rain with them.

Karen Hanzer was well prepared. She slipped on her blue raincoat, picked up her umbrella and went down the stairs. She looked through the glass panel in the door of the reception area. Only one person sat waiting: a man in his early forties. She left by the side door and darted across the road.

When the man came out, he stood for a moment or two on the pavement, then turned up his coat collar and walked away.

HE HADN'T LIKED the whole thing. From the moment he'd had the letter he'd thought it strange. If his son had replied, the letter ought to have gone direct to his PO box. But the temptation of something actually *there* had been too much to resist.

Now he stood on the pavement outside, turned up the collar of his coat against the persistent rain, and looked around.

If they'd opened the letter to his son, they'd know he was a pilot. If the newspapers were to be believed, a lot of people of German origin were having pressure put on them. Probably just newspaper talk, most of it, but recruiting *was* going on, no doubt about that. He'd heard of a guy at Lockheed who'd been told he ought to be back in Germany fighting for the Fatherland and that if he didn't volunteer there could be trouble.

Yes, he'd known, but still he'd come here. He'd felt reasonably secure because there wasn't any way they could know his identity, and he hadn't told the clerk anything. But now the thought struck him that all it needed was somebody to follow him home. Would they go that far? If anybody did follow, he decided, they'd have to follow a hell of a long way. He turned and began walking.

Half an hour later he was crossing Union Square, heading west, then climbing, feeling the pull by now on his leg muscles. Several times he'd glanced back, without spotting anybody consistently behind him. The streets were quieter than usual; people were staying indoors out of the rain. He turned left along California Street, walked a few blocks, then took another left into Taylor and began running down the hill, finally dodged into the big tobacco emporium and stood panting for a minute while the assistant politely waited for him to get his breath back and buy something.

Karen almost lost him when he began running, hesitating too long, then having to run faster herself, feeling conspicuous and too far back. By the corner of Geary he was out of sight and she stood in confusion, looking around anxiously, then heaving a sigh of relief as he came out of a shop and quickly began pounding up the hill again. She put up her umbrella and followed. The rain was darkening her coat and the umbrella shielded her face. She was wet and uncomfortable, but pleased with herself. There could be no doubt this man had something to hide!

At Washington Street he caught the streetcar, scrambling aboard as it moved off, and she was very lucky indeed: a cab was just halting and she pushed in front of the elderly man who'd hailed it, telling the taxi-driver to stay behind the streetcar because she'd seen an old friend board it.

The man stayed aboard right the way down to the terminal; but she'd paid the driver in advance, got out quickly and watched from across the street as he hurried away down Market. Now she crossed too, watching him from the other side. She was shivering, wet to the skin, but she felt she couldn't lose him now.

HE'D SPOTTED NOBODY. Half an hour ago he'd seen a man a hundred yards or so back, ploughing on through the rain, but next time he looked there was no sign. Then there'd been a woman in blue going faster than most girls would walk and seeming to stay with him. He'd wondered sharply about her but then she'd gone. Now, though he couldn't be sure, it didn't *seem* as though anybody was following. And he was drenched. It was time to go home.

As he cut up Leavenworth, then along Pine, the rain stopped and a few minutes later the sun found a break in the cloud and the streets glittered. It seemed like a signal and he felt a lot happier, confident now that even if he had been followed, he'd shaken off whoever it had been. Just before he reached the apartment block he looked around again, then circled the block once before he went in.

She'd seen him glance up at the building, pause, then turn, and there was something in his manner, some relaxation of his posture which seemed to suggest that he was home. And she'd been right. She watched as he went up the steps of the apartment building, and waited twenty wet minutes before she went in. She was becoming good at this work, she thought to herself, and it gave her *great* satisfaction. No German had the right to hide away with his country at war.

"YOU SHOULD HAVE joined the Gestapo, Fräulein," Von Galen said bad-temperedly. That morning he had received a letter from his uncle, giving instructions that the Horch should be sold and replaced with a smaller, cheaper vehicle more appropriate to his status.

Karen Hanzer stood dripping on his carpet and said defensively, "At training school we were instructed always to be on the look-out for people who might be useful to the Fatherland. I now have a full dossier on this man." She held it out to him.

He put it at the side of his desk. "Go change your clothes before you get pneumonia." She went obediently. Herr Wiedemann would hear about this before long.

Von Galen resumed his study of the automobile advertising in the *San Francisco Chronicle*. The thought of parting with the Horch dismayed him, and when he finally read Karen Hanzer's small dossier he was feeling thoroughly spiteful. Zoll, or Miller, or whatever his name was, provided a tailor-made target for idle venom. He reached for the telephone, then thought better of it. Leave it a few hours; the shock would be greater.

It was.

Miller, at the phone in the hallway, felt his face go stiff. He glanced at the sitting-room door, checking it was closed. "Sorry, you have the wrong—"

"I don't think so, Mr. Zoll."

"Who *is* this?"

"I think we ought to talk about our mutual interests."

Miller said despairingly, "Look, I told you, you have the wrong—"

"We could, for example, talk about your marriage. In an hour I shall be in the restaurant beside the Pickwick Hotel, eating baked clams. Greet me as 'Jack'."

Miller was trembling as he hung up. How in *hell* had he been traced? He'd always been terrified of something like this; now it had happened.

He made himself smile at his wife. "I'm taking a walk, Dot."

She looked up. "Fine, honey." She caught sight of his face. "Are you OK?"

"Touch of indigestion, that's all."

VON GALEN SAID, a little more loudly than was necessary, "The baked clams, I think." A number of men, solitary drinkers, sat at the bar on the other side of the room. One of them would be Zoll—which?

He enjoyed the meal. As he was finishing, a voice said, "Jack?"

Von Galen raised his head. "Good evening." He picked up his bill, left a tip on the table and crossed to the cash desk, Zoll following. "Shall we talk as we walk?"

Outside, Zoll was predictably belligerent. "What in hell *is* all this?"

"It must be clear to you. I am able to address you as Zoll, so I know about your past. I was able to telephone you, therefore I know about your present." Sidelong he watched the man. Visibly, in those few seconds, all remaining hope died.

Zoll said, "Have you spoken to my wife?"

"Your bigamous wife. Your real wife, Anneliese Zoll, still lives in Hanover with your father and your sister."

"It was the letter?"

"Yes. Foolish of you." Von Galen found he was rather enjoying himself. He'd thought Fräulein Hanzer's enthusiasm childish, but there was satisfaction in applying pressure like this. "It's perfectly understandable, of course. When a coward like you has a son like yours—it is bound to inspire complex emotions."

"Who are you? What do you want?" Zoll demanded.

"You could say," Von Galen said, "that I am your country. Germany is at war and all kinds of people may prove useful. Even cowards."

Zoll was abject now.

Von Galen said, "I know everything important about you, but there are a few gaps. I know that you are still flying aeroplanes, but not what they are. That might be interesting."

"It's *spying!*"

"I know what it is. By the way, I think it's a mistake to call you Zoll. Who knows, we might encounter someone who knows you as Miller. How, by the way, did you pick that name?"

NOW MILLER was at Long Beach, working hard. He had had three weeks to plan after his meeting with Ross. He was amazed that Von Galen hadn't called him again, hadn't demanded information on the work he had just started doing—that was important enough! But he hadn't. He knew that when the project moved to Canada he'd have the only opportunity he was ever likely to be given to disappear from Von Galen's surveillance. To do it he had to cut everything clean—go, and leave no trace.

He made arrangements to sell his aerobatic biplane and paid all the bills for the apartment. He was confident he could manage things with Dot. She was accustomed to fast moves, had made them all their married life, regarded them as a challenge. The way they lived, a move meant packing a few suitcases and calling a cab.

The days passed, but the fear did not. All it would take was one phone call to the apartment: Dot would cheerfully hand out the number of the hotel he was using in Long Beach, and he dared not warn her.

Three

Von Galen entered Joseph O'Hara's suite at the Bedford and looked around him in astonishment. The place was like an operations room: two big blackboards on easels, maps spread on the floor, books lying open. The long curtains were drawn.

"You seem extraordinarily well prepared," Von Galen said.

"You think I'm crazy, don't you?"

"Ambitious."

O'Hara looked at him closely. "Don't worry. I intend to wipe that smirk off your face. I do my research. Example: you are not just a third secretary: you are the nephew of Ernst Wilhelm Bohle who, in addition to being Minister of State at the Reich Foreign Office, is an honorary major-general of the SS."

"What does all this prove?"

"That there's a lot of information around. For example, on the third of January Franklin Roosevelt decided to send Harry L. Hopkins to London to talk to Churchill. You remember?"

"Yes."

"Remember anything else?"

Von Galen felt irritated. There was more than a touch of the schoolroom about this. "Hopkins and Churchill are supposed to have got on well together. It was announced shortly afterwards that war material would be supplied—"

"Right! Does the name Wendell Wilkie ring any bells?"

Von Galen sighed. "He was the defeated candidate in the presidential election."

O'Hara said, "He went to London too, in the same month, with a message from Roosevelt. A poem by Longfellow, part of it, anyway."

"Poetry!"

"Listen. It goes like this: 'Dear Churchill, I think this verse applies to your people as it does to us:

> "Sail on, O ship of State,
> Sail on, O Union strong and great,
> Humanity with all its fears,
> With all its hopes of future years,
> Is hanging breathless on thy fate."'

"You're trying," Von Galen said incredulously, "to draw some conclusion from that?"

"Let's look at it. It's emotional. Roosevelt's putting his arm round Churchill's shoulder and saying, 'We're worried about you, but you can rely on us.'

"Let me offer you a simple statement," O'Hara continued. "Those two are the big men of the English-speaking world. They're moving closer to an alliance. They're going to want to meet and when they do Roosevelt will be consorting with Germany's legitimate enemy. You people have every right in the world to attack with everything you've got. Turn the pair of them into ground beef."

There was something infuriating in the young American's certitude. Von Galen said, "If they *do* meet—no one will know where, until it's over. If it's here in America any attack within a neutral country would not be legitimate."

"They won't meet here. They can't."

"Why not?"

"Practicalities," O'Hara said, "and protocol."

419

"Rubbish," Von Galen said, rising. "This is adolescent day-dreaming. I really see no purpose in listening."

O'Hara blinked at him through his heavy glasses. "Keep your eyes and ears open. Think about what I said. And you, my friend, will be back, believe me."

ERNIE WASN'T supposed to be home for the weekend, but he arrived Saturday night, having hitched a ride on an Air Corps plane to Oakland. He looked tired and under strain, and on the Sunday morning Dot let him sleep and slipped out to the food market. Ernie liked steak for Sunday breakfast, so steak he'd get.

As she reached the store, a girl was going in, wheeling a small baby in a big perambulator, having trouble with the swing doors. "Here, let me hold it," Dot said.

The girl smiled. "Thanks. I am not used to this yet."

Dot looked into the pram. "He's beautiful."

"Thank you."

They chatted as they waited to be served. It emerged that the girl and her husband were Norwegian and that he was a ship's officer on a regular run between the West Coast and Yokohama. She'd come out to marry him a year earlier and now, with Norway occupied, was stuck in San Francisco.

"So you see, here I am and here I must stay. It's lonely sometimes with only me and the baby. Georg, my husband, does not get back so often."

"I'm alone a lot myself so I know that feeling. Listen, why don't we have a cup of coffee one day?"

"Oh—I would like that *very* much."

"No trouble. A real pleasure, in fact." Dot ripped a page from her shopping notebook. "Here's my address and number—it's just a couple of blocks away. Why not bring that little fella to see me tomorrow? I'm Dot—short for Dorothy."

"My name is Karen."

As Dot walked away Karen Hanzer began to push the pram back towards its owner's apartment. The baby was the son of a commercial officer at the Consulate, whose mother was only too delighted to let somebody else wheel him up and down San Francisco's demanding terrain. There would be no problem borrowing him again.

THE MOVE NORTH from Long Beach to Kingston, at the northeastern tip of Lake Ontario, was scheduled for March 15. Miller collared Ed Martingale in the hangar washroom. "I hate to ask, Ed, but there's not much for me to do in the next few days. I know it's not in the contract—"

"Got a problem?"

"Well, Dot seems kind of low. Been alone a lot. I'd like to give her a little break before the work starts."

Martingale began to wash his hands. "We'll be five days or more bolting Canso Ring Two down. I don't see why not. Thinking of anywhere special?"

"Palm Springs, maybe."

"Good idea. I'll tell Alec I okayed it. Call your wife."

On the phone he said to her: "How'd you like a surprise?"

"What kind?"

"The nice kind. How about closing the apartment up and getting on the train down here? I miss you."

"Ernie, there's things to *do!* Give me a couple of days."

"It'll cost you." Me too, he thought, if you don't move fast!

"What'll it cost me?"

"A few days in Palm Springs."

She whistled. "But there's the rent to settle. Electricity."

"I settled them all."

"Ernie!" She was delighted. It was going to work!

He said, "Tell you what. I've ten bucks say you can't make the afternoon train. Leaves at four thirty."

"You lose."

"We'll stay in Los Angeles tonight, head out tomorrow."

421

"Hasta la vista, pal. I got things to do."

His hands were sweating as he hung up. She'd had plenty of practice at the quick move, but even for Dot this was short notice.

VON GALEN HAD virtually forgotten about Joseph O'Hara. For two weeks he had not thought either about the man himself or about the absurdities of his notion. Then, on a Sunday morning, he was relaxing in his bath with the radio playing in the living room. He had left it on to hear the final few minutes of a concert and when it ended the announcer intoned: "We go now to Father Coughlin at the Shrine of the Little Flower in Royal Oak, Michigan. . . ."

Coughlin, an Irish-American priest, was thought by many people to be Germany's most potent friend in America. He was a phenomenon. Having got into broadcasting in its earliest days, he had built himself an audience of millions.

Von Galen listened with growing surprise. The broadcast was a total contrast to anything else he'd heard on the pap-filled airways of America. Coughlin ended:

"You will say: but did I not support Franklin Roosevelt? To that I plead guilty. When millions of Americans were unemployed, he was creating work and nobody spoke for him more loudly than I.

"But things change, my friends. It is said that power corrupts. It *has* corrupted the President of these United States. He no longer looks inward at the troubles that afflict this nation. His attention is elsewhere. He listens to the voice of the Anti-Christ.

"And who, my friends, *is* the Anti-Christ? I will tell you, for he *is* a man. His name is Winston Churchill. He is a man whose deep and disgusting dream is to tempt America, to persuade America, in the end to *force* America into war!

"Did Roosevelt promise that no American boy would die defending foreign soil? You know he did. Will he say it again? No.

"Instead he sends his friend Hopkins to talk to the Anti-Christ, to ask what is now *required* from America. It is even said that Hopkins was given the task of arranging a meeting, of bringing *our* President, whose task is to *defend* America, to a table with the man who wants America at war.

"Let a great shout rise, a shout so loud that Churchill will hear and tremble: America must stay at peace!"

By that time, Von Galen was lying in cooling water and thinking hard. It was one thing for Joseph O'Hara to postulate a meeting; quite another for Coughlin, who was notoriously well-informed. He'd thought O'Hara mad. But was he?

Then, on March 19, something occurred which again set Von Galen thinking: Roosevelt set off on the yacht *Potomac* for a fishing cruise in the Bahamas. On the following day, political correspondents were speculating that the fishing trip was a cover for some other activity of greater importance. One writer, in the *Washington Post*, even mentioned Churchill, and pointed out that the Bahamas were British possessions, governed by the Duke of Windsor, brother of the King.

Suddenly Von Galen had a vision: a white yacht on a calm blue sea, two men at a table, one smoking a cigar, the other with a cigarette in a long stalk holder—and then a single fiery blast. And after it, no Churchill to oppose the Führer: no Roosevelt to march America towards conflict. It would do no harm, he thought, to listen once more to O'Hara.

INFURIATINGLY, O'Hara gave a little chortle of triumph on the telephone. "Sure, come on over."

"Before I do, there are two questions to be answered. Otherwise the visit is pointless."

"I know what you're going to say—you want to know *where* and you want to know *when*."

"Precisely."

"That," O'Hara said, "has to be worked out."

When Von Galen walked into the suite, O'Hara was holding a newspaper. "I'm going to make a few predictions," he smiled. "First, a question for you. FDR is fifty-nine, and crippled by polio. What does he do for relaxation?"

"Apparently he goes fishing."

"Right. He likes warm weather. What do you know about Churchill? *His* age, *his* idea of fun?"

"He's older. Late sixties. I believe he paints."

"Absolutely. Yes, he does paint. He goes off into the sunshine and he paints in Madeira and in Morocco."

"You're saying they'll meet in a warm climate?"

"Yes, I am."

"You may have a point," Von Galen said grudgingly.

"I have more than one. Roosevelt won't go to Europe because if he goes there he's in danger. Churchill must therefore come here, and when those two get together they'll want a little comfort. That by itself puts big limits on the available places."

Von Galen shook his head. "You're in a dream world."

"Stay with me." O'Hara picked up a map, unrolled and spread it out. "Look at this. We've already eliminated all of Europe and a hell of a lot of North America. What we have left is South America and the Caribbean."

"What is wrong," Von Galen said, "with Washington?"

"Listen, this meeting *has* to be kept secret! They aren't going to want the entire American press speculating on what they're talking about. They don't want big demonstrations outside the White House. No, believe me, they're going to choose somewhere quiet and comfortable. They *could* have been cruising round the Bahamas the last few days, maybe Bermuda."

"What exactly are you suggesting I do?"

"Tell Berlin."

"Look, there is nothing to *tell* Berlin except that an American of my acquaintance has a theory."

"What's wrong with theory? What the hell was *Mein Kampf* but theory? Do you imagine Germany's not looking for ways to kill Churchill and keep America out of the war?" O'Hara sighed. "I understand how you feel. I've lived with this for quite a while. You haven't. But maybe there's some information we can get out of *your* mind. Give me a few minutes more."

"I really see no purpose."

"Please. You're in the foreign service. You know about protocol. Tell me what protocol governs any meeting between Roosevelt and Churchill, remembering that one is a Head of State and the other isn't."

"It's not my department. I don't know."

"Who greets who and where? I think, for instance, that protocol is one reason we can rule out Canada. If they met there, they'd be stuck with the Canadian Prime Minister, and they wouldn't want him. But they couldn't *not* invite him—that'd be a hell of a snub!"

424

"Yet Canada," Von Galen said, his eyes on the map, "is by far the nearest point in North America to—"

"Ah," O'Hara said. "Got you interested!"

MEETING DOT, Miller said, "I was wrong about Palm Springs." Her face fell. "We're going to Flagstaff instead." He grinned and held the tickets up for her to see. "Tonight we're at the Hollywood-Roosevelt Hotel. Maybe you'll see Cary Grant. Then tomorrow first thing we're on the train."

She was hugging him when the porter came alongside with the barrow. He counted. Seven suitcases and a packing case. "Which of these goes with us?"

"These two. The rest send ahead. Oh, Ernie, was I in a *rush*."

He kissed her. "Nobody else could do it, kid. Here's your ten bucks."

They were in Flagstaff, Arizona, by the following evening. Miller was breathing more easily. After almost a month of feeling like a rabbit with its foot in a snare, he felt a free man again. The rail tickets ran clear through to Kingston, via Chicago and Toronto; but they stayed in the warm for three days, then did the travelling in a long two-and-a-half-day burst.

Ross was waiting for them at Kingston. He'd flown Canso Ring One up from Long Beach the previous day, and been busy checking arrangements. Now he picked Dot up, swung her round and said, "Did you ever think about a nice little white house with a picket fence?"

"Did I!"

He put her down and held out a bunch of keys. "You've got it. Not precisely prime waterfront property, but you can see Lake Ontario." He had a blue Royal Canadian Air Force car outside, complete with driver. Twenty minutes later, Dot was moving purposefully from room to room.

"That's a great girl," Ross said. "She really is."

"Absolutely right," Miller agreed. "Matter of good judgment."

Ross pulled a rueful face. "My wife was the most expensive mistake I made in my life." He'd married a leggy Californian blonde nine years earlier; she'd taken him for every cent he had and was still doing so. "I should have met Dot first."

Miller said smugly, "She'd still have married me."

"I heard that." Dot put her head round the door. "And I'm not as sure as you are. You never gave me a house like this."

They began work on April 1. A series of metal buoys had been sunk in Lake Ontario, of different sizes and moored at varying depths. Initially they were trying simply to locate them with the equipment. A ship on the surface produced frantic blips and major variations as the Canso flew over. But the Mark One Eyeball could spot a ship below the surface too. By fine-tuning the design and operation, they were seeking to increase the depth at which a sub might be found.

They were embarked on weeks of flying. Miller and Ross and their crews flew endless hours, working out optimum heights and improving search patterns. They were long, dull days, and improvement was slow—far slower than any of them had hoped.

Dot saw the lines of weariness deepen around Ernie's eyes, yet he remained unusually steady-humoured: no bouts of sudden enthusiasm, no sinkings into depression. Miller was, in fact, enjoying himself in a job that might have been made for him. His idea of happiness was to fly all night after he'd flown all day, then eat one of Dot's lovingly prepared meals, chat with her for an hour or two while she knitted or sewed, then sleep, preparatory to flying some more.

By far the best thing of all—he'd escaped! From the moment of arrival he'd been praying that the quick exit from the San Francisco apartment had shaken Von Galen loose, but scarcely willing to believe it. Now days were lengthening into weeks without the smallest indication that the German knew where he was. Not only that: money was steadily going into the bank. At the end of the six months, when this contract was up, he'd have enough, with a bit of luck, to go to Mexico, farther still out of the German's range.

Four

In truth, Miller could scarcely have been further from Von Galen's thoughts. To Von Galen's vast annoyance, O'Hara's idea had taken root in his head and now wouldn't go away. Twice he found himself day-dreaming: seeing again a big white yacht exploding on a blue sea. He told himself repeatedly that O'Hara was wildly impractical. Yet the idea stayed with him. To annoy him further, a word entered his consciousness, a stupid word he could do without. *Destiny.* The Führer believed in destiny. Well, *he* didn't. And yet—the accident that had cut out his flying; the posting to America; the meeting with O'Hara; what was all that?

Not destiny. Just a chain of circumstances.

More to try to exorcise the troublesome notion than to forward it, he began to read, and to study; to draw up a list of possible meeting places that was so long it would demonstrate the fatuity of the entire concept. Soon he had a list of more than seventy.

Yet, as he continued reading, he came across mention of naval and air bases. Under the terms of the Lend-Lease Act of the previous year America had handed over fifty ageing destroyers to the British in exchange for the right to lease bases in eight territories: British Guiana, Bermuda, Newfoundland, the Bahamas, Jamaica, St. Lucia, Trinidad and Antigua.

Protocol, he thought. Those bases *would* technically be American territory on British soil: and of the eight, seven were in the warm climate O'Hara swore would be chosen.

To forward all this nonsense formally to Berlin, or even give it to Wiedemann would be insane. But there might be another way to get rid of it: a letter to Bohle, his uncle. "I have met a young Irish-American with a curious idea which might amuse you, particularly since you've met Churchill." Yes, that was one way. Bohle *had* met him, three or four years earlier, in London. "Could you imagine that Churchill would act so predictably?" And then set out the whole plan. Then he would have passed the whole stupid business onward and upward, and would himself cease to be involved. He'd do that!

· "What the devil have you been doing?" Consul Wiedemann demanded when he called Von Galen into his office several days later. "For you," he said, handing him a long signal. "And it is marked 'Most Secret—Addressee to Decipher'."

Thoroughly puzzled, Von Galen took the day's cipher sheets into his office and set to work. Bohle had obviously taken him seriously. He had called some kind of gathering of naval and air experts and put the possibility to them!

427

I must tell you [the signal read], that there was general agreement that such a meeting is likely. I congratulate you on your perspicacity in recognizing the possibilities in a piece of thinking which at first seems unpromising. There must be no delay in following-up. Travel forthwith to the Embassy in Washington. Instructions already sent to provide any assistance you need. Every effort must be made to determine place, and date, at whatever risk.

Von Galen's letter had provided Bohle with more than a moment's interest. At the time of Roosevelt's fishing trip, Bohle too had thought it might be a cover for something else. He had said so, but Ribbentrop, his superior at the Foreign Ministry, had pooh-poohed the idea and it had withered on the vine.

Now, he had reflected, it was perhaps worth cultivation. Bohle knew a great deal about Winston Churchill, had met and talked with him, and was certain that Churchill would love nothing better than to play political chess with a man of Roosevelt's quality. Churchill saw himself as a figure in history, a manipulator of great events, and would see a journey across the hostile Atlantic as high adventure.

Also, nothing was more likely to trigger such a meeting than the now-imminent attack upon Russia. When that took place Churchill and Roosevelt would have a great deal to talk about. If he, Bohle, postulated a meeting and forecast where it would happen, he could collect kudos when, inevitably, it did!

His actions, however, accorded more with a bureaucrat's determination to advance his career than with a military opportunist's to attack. Bohle, in fact, was merely assembling a file. Already it contained Von Galen's letter and the minutes of a conference he had convened at his house in Wannsee to discuss it. Now a further piece of evidence lay on his desk: a letter from one of the participants in the Wannsee meeting, a psychologist from Berlin University. The letter made two points:

There is a significant coincidence in the careers of Churchill and Roosevelt. Twice Churchill has been First Lord of the Admiralty—in charge of the Royal Navy. He appears to have a deep sentimental interest in naval affairs, evidenced by the clothing he often wears. The same seems true of Roosevelt. He held the post of Assistant

Secretary of the Navy from 1913 onwards and in 1918 had already resigned to become a serving officer, but the Armistice then came. He is credited, within those years, with having successfully transformed the American Navy. It is probable that he, too, therefore has sentimental feelings about the navy.

This, I suggest, may have the effect of biasing both men towards travel by sea rather than by air, and towards a meeting at sea, or at least aboard ship.

Here was his opportunity to involve the *Kriegsmarine*!

Bohle made an appointment to visit U-Boat Command at Wilhelmshaven and talk to Admiral Dönitz.

Dönitz was polite, puzzled, manifestly busy. "What can I do for you, Minister?"

Bohle told him, compressing it, admitting the difficulties.

"That's all you have, these few theories?"

"Yes, at this stage."

"Well, I understand the attractions of a great coup, none better. It would give me intense pleasure to blow Churchill into a million pieces. But I am fighting a war in the Atlantic and I have not enough boats for it. You seem to be suggesting a permanent watch on half a dozen different places. That would be quite impossible."

"What *would* you need to act?" Bohle asked.

"More than you are likely to get. A date, a place, a target."

"Admiral, it's not likely I will be able to offer a certainty. What degree of probability would you accept?"

Dönitz smiled. "When *you* feel certain, I'll consider it."

Bohle rose. "You'll tell me, will you, if anything occurs which might have a bearing?"

"Yes, of course."

On his return to Berlin, Bohle involved another old sea dog. This particular admiral was no longer connected with the harsh practicalities of naval warfare: Admiral Canaris controlled the intelligence service, the *Abwehr*. Canaris was busy deciding on the final details of the invasion of Russia, but Bohle finally contrived to chat with him over a glass of champagne in his office. Canaris liked champagne, and sipped appreciatively as Bohle began to outline the scheme. Then he said, "It's a pretty bubble, you know. Chase it and it will burst. I agree they may meet, but if they do the secrecy and the protective cordon will be impenetrable."

Bohle said, "Both have long-standing naval associations. Don't you think they'd meet at sea, for instance?"

"Oh, it's beguiling enough," Canaris smiled, toying with his glass. "You could, for instance, work backwards. Think of the propaganda value afterwards—to *them*, I mean—the vast barrage of publicity. Churchill the bulldog under the guns, Roosevelt the cripple in a bosun's chair. If they're together on a Sunday, a religious service on deck and those two old hypocrites singing naval hymns. You couldn't match *that* on land. *Ergo*: they will meet at sea. The whole thing sounds delightful. But suppose you did succeed in finding out in advance? Suppose the *Kriegsmarine* were to attack—and fail. What have you *then*, Herr Bohle? You'd have made Roosevelt and Churchill yet bigger heroes and turned American public opinion against us even more strongly."

"All the same," Bohle said, "the possibility may exist. Will you help?"

"How can I?"

"You have people in Britain. Anything you hear of Churchill's movements may be indicative. Will you let me know?"

Canaris put down his glass. "Anything *I* hear is invariably in the past tense. But yes, if I do, I'll tell you. Meantime, take an old man's advice—don't spend too much time on it."

VON GALEN was emptying his desk, preparing to move to Washington, when Karen Hanzer came in with his cup of coffee. Glancing up absently to thank her, he saw she was also carrying an opened brown-paper parcel. "What's that?"

She was smirking. "An item of clothing for a baby," she said. "It's called a matinée jacket. It's hand-knitted."

"Really."

"You may be interested to know where it came from, Herr Von Galen."

"Where?"

She told him it had been knitted by Zoll's wife, who had moved to Canada on account of her husband's new job. Von Galen was not much impressed, and Fräulein Hanzer decided she was quite glad

430

he was going. He was too indolent, and appeared to have no dedication at all.

An hour later he left the German Consul-General's office in San Francisco for the last time and was driven to the airport. O'Hara would be on his way to the Bahamas now. It must be very pleasant, he thought, to have O'Hara's advantages. When, the night before, he'd told him of the reaction from Berlin, O'Hara had been predictably enthusiastic, only too anxious to assist.

He'd said, "But what about your work here?"

"I'm the boss's son, remember. I do as I like!" O'Hara had simply dictated a wire to his office for morning delivery, saying that he was going away, perhaps for a few weeks. "Now—what d'you want me to do?"

"The Bahamas," Von Galen said. "Roosevelt's been there once. Nobody'll think it odd if he goes there again. We need to find out—"

"How'd you like me to *go* there?"

"Well, certainly, if you can."

"Sure I can," O'Hara said. It was his private conviction that it was in those islands that Churchill and Roosevelt would find it most convenient to hold their inevitable meeting. The ex-King, now Duke of Windsor and governor of the islands, had standing enough to greet a president, but could not expect to participate in discussions between Roosevelt and the Prime Minister.

"Let me see, who do I know there? Yeah, I know some people." O'Hara laughed with sudden pleasure. "Baldur, we're going to get those bastards—I feel it in my bones!"

Von Galen was a good deal less sure.

TRAVELLING NORTH, two days later, O'Hara brooded over the recent conversation he had had over dinner with Sir Harry Oakes, who was perhaps the most influential of all Bahamian citizens and a friend of O'Hara's father. The moonlit evening had been beautifully balmy and Sir Harry had been in a mood for indiscretion. It seemed that Churchill was now out of patience with the royal couple.

"Why? I thought he supported them very strongly."

"So he did. But he thinks the Duke should be back in England, lending support, not skulking in a tropical paradise. But the Duke won't go. Can you guess why?"

431

"No."

"Because they won't agree to make his wife a royal duchess. So nobody would have to curtsy to her."

"Is it really true?"

"Well, it's what the Duke told me. He says he hardly hears from Winston now, and when he does the letter's short and ratty. I suppose the truth is that he's an embarrassment nowadays."

An embarrassment nowadays. Would that really matter? Churchill would be likely to avoid any additional burdens—after all, Churchill had a choice. But O'Hara was deeply aware that it was an uncertain conclusion.

He was still fretting when, with the train halted at Raleigh, North Carolina, he stepped off to stretch his legs and buy fresh reading matter. It was while he was reading a story in *Time* magazine about, of all things, fish, that his feelings about the Bahamas as a rendezvous at last crystallized. The article about the troubles certain fishermen were experiencing seemed suddenly to be a bright signpost, pointing directly. It was in those fishermen's waters that the whales would appear. There the whale hunt must take place.

When he met Von Galen on his return, he explained why he was sure the meeting would not take place in the Bahamas. Then he grinned, and added, "On the other hand, I reckon I have the *real* answer. I know where it's going to be."

"Where?"

The grin widened. "The one place we didn't really think about seriously. It isn't warm and sunny. But I'll bet you a thousand bucks they'll be there inside a month or two."

Five

Newfoundland.

Von Galen stared warily at the word. He'd gone into the Embassy registry, written it on a pad and begun to answer the questions it raised. Now, against his will, he felt excitement growing in him, and surprise, too: that he was turning quickly from sceptic to believer and couldn't explain why.

Question: was there an American base in Newfoundland? The

island was a British colony and the United States undoubtedly had a treaty right to lease such a base, but had they actually done so?

He found the answer: they had. Not one base, but *two!*

Now the list of advantages from both British and American viewpoints grew steadily. First, Newfoundland was the nearest point to Europe in the whole of North America. Secondly, it had an American *air* base. Thirdly, it had an American *naval* base. *And both were United States territory on British soil!* Fourthly, in addition to being the closest point to Britain, Newfoundland was easy to reach from the eastern seaboard of the United States. Fifthly, it was a vast empty landscape of deep sheltered bays and excellent harbours, where nobody except a few fishermen would see anything.

And *lastly*, Von Galen noted, lastly but most important of all, there was Newfoundland's freedom from the bedevilling toils of protocol. No Duke of Windsor, no Canadian Prime Minister, no complications at all.

Six reasons *for*. But—what were the reasons against?

He laboured, playing devil's advocate to the limit of his capacity, and could find only the climate. Yet this was June. Reference books quickly told him that summer temperatures in Newfoundland were actually pleasant.

Von Galen took a sheet of paper and began to write his signal to Bohle, setting out his points carefully, saving his trump card till the end. "Finally, there is the political status of Newfoundland. In 1934, owing to the collapse of the market for Newfoundland fish, the island ceased to be self-governing. It is now governed by a commission appointed by the British Crown. It is therefore a colony: it is *British*, not Canadian territory."

When he'd finished, he went out to tell O'Hara. "I have reported to my superiors," he said, as they walked across the grass by the Washington Memorial. "They'll want verification."

"How *can* we verify, Baldur? I mean—"

"We have to try. Those two men are going to meet, and *we* know it's going to be in Newfoundland, probably on a ship. Very well. Somewhere up there something will exist. A clue, an indication. It may be small but it's vital! You will have to go there to find the thing that's missing—one solid piece of evidence."

"Me—to Newfoundland?"

It was odd, Von Galen thought, how control had changed hands. It was O'Hara's scheme no longer, but *his*. One way or another he'd see that it did *not* finish up in some wastepaper-basket in Berlin!

JOSEPH O'HARA stood alone at a bar of the Newfoundland Hotel, a glass of beer untouched in front of him. The trip to Newfoundland was proving futile. After three days in St. John's not only did he seem to be getting nowhere, he was also beginning to feel awkwardly conspicuous: an aimless American civilian all too obviously doing nothing in a place which bustled with the activity of war. He had made only two contacts. The first was a banker with whom O'Hara Trust Co. had very occasional dealings. O'Hara had devised a thin cover: he was prospecting—after the war Newfoundland would become increasingly important in trans-Atlantic aviation, and O'Hara Trust Co. wanted to be in on the ground floor. The banker was professionally welcoming, but looked puzzled and barely hid his surprise at Joe O'Hara's presence.

The second contact seemed to have even less potential. The previous evening in the hotel lobby, a noisy crowd of navy ensigns heading for the exit had included Simmonds, an old schoolfellow, who'd paused briefly and said, "It *is* Joe? Hey, let's have a drink tomorrow if you're here."

O'Hara was waiting for Simmonds now. The bar was almost empty, and he stared into his beer glass to avoid looking round the room.

"Hello, Joe!" Simmonds was beside him. "What are you doing in this God-forsaken spot?" O'Hara told his story as convincingly as he could and stoically prepared himself for an hour of "whatever-happened-to-so-and-so?"

"Join you fellas?" Another officer stood beside them.

"Recognize him?" Simmonds asked, smiling.

"Hey, now. No games. Just introduce us," the officer said.

O'Hara thought he *did* recognize him. "Just a minute . . ."

"Let's just stop this, huh?" The young man held out his hand. "I'm John. I don't use the other half in public."

"Joe O'Hara. From Boston." Hell, yes. He knew *now*! Somehow he controlled his astonishment.

"What are you doing here, Mr. O'Hara?"

"In theory, a little business. In practice, very little. You?"

"As you see, serving Uncle Sam." He laughed. "The rest is dark and devious and you're not allowed to ask."

"Am I allowed to ask if you'll have a beer?" O'Hara waved for the barman. As he waited to be served, he could see the young officer's reflection in the mirror behind the bar. It would wipe the smug smile off your damned face, he thought savagely, if you knew what I'm planning for that crook of a father of yours.

After a minute or two the officer excused himself to join another group. He was serving, Simmonds said, in a US destroyer on escort duty in the North Atlantic. "This place is going to turn from a British colony to an American one. And two of *them*—jeepers, but the writing's on the wall for the Newfies!"

"Two?" O'Hara said. "You don't mean his father—"

"Hell, no. John's brother. He's up at the airfield at Gander."

When O'Hara met Von Galen again, he could barely contain himself. "Have I got something for you!" he said. "It clinches the whole deal. Guess who I met up there?"

Von Galen said irritably, "We're not playing games."

"Sorry. Well, he's a naval officer, and his name . . ."

Von Galen at once returned to the Embassy. He had had almost nothing by way of encouragement from Germany, but nobody could ignore *this*: not Bohle, not Dönitz. O'Hara said it was the clincher and so it ought to be.

THE STARBOARD ENGINE of Canso Ring One had given trouble on and off for more than a week. Now, with the replacement fitted, she was ready for testing. It was early on a bright Sunday morning when Ross took her up to swing out over the lake, Miller acting as co-pilot and flight engineer. At five hundred feet Ross spotted a sailboat brightly ablaze on the water below. He brought the Canso round to circle the boat.

"What d'you make of it?"

"Two people in the water," Miller said.

"Bet it was bottle gas in the bilges," Ross diagnosed, "and some idiot dropped a match."

"No life jackets."

"Sunday people," Ross said. "They're all the same."

"I don't see any other boats, Alec."

Ross looked down. "Hell!" he said. The boat was burning fiercely, the two swimmers detached from it. "We'll have to pick 'em up. Thank God for smooth water!" He swung away, turned the Canso into the wind, kissed the flying boat down and taxied towards the swimmers. Miller had moved to the hatch, and was clipping the ladder in place, waiting for Ross to turn and bring the sailboat into view. The swimmers were clearly in distress, mouths wide and arms flailing.

Getting them aboard wasn't too hard, but Miller got soaked and had no spare clothes. The two in the water had badly burned hands and arms, and were exhausted.

"Hospital," Ross said.

Miller nodded. "Where—Kingston?"

"Toronto'd be better. Hour and twenty maybe. Ambulance can meet us if we radio ahead."

Miller applied acriflavine and gauze to the burns, talking soothingly. "God, we'd have drowned!" one of the swimmers said. He was in his sixties, grey-haired and wearing expensive leisure clothes. "We're in your debt, mister."

"All in the day's work," Miller said. He thought: *How would it be if I sent you a little bill? What's your life worth? Enough to get me to Mexico and keep me for a couple of years?*

Instead, he said, "We'll go straight to Toronto. You'll be in good hands soon."

They took the swimmers to Toronto. But that wasn't the end of it. One of the yachtsmen was interviewed by a correspondent of the *San Francisco Examiner*, who chased up additional personal details on the two pilots and wrote up the story of the rescue.

On June 21, 1941, Germany made its *blitzkrieg* attack on Russia. Von Galen was thunderstruck by the news. As he stared for the thousandth time at a map of the North Atlantic, his head awhirl with the knowledge of the fighting, of Churchill's prompt declaration that "any enemy of Nazi Germany will be our ally", the thought struck him with, it seemed, the elemental force of the *blitz* itself, that now Churchill and Roosevelt *must* come together. And when they did they must be killed. Both of them.

His eye ran over the map once more. Distance, he thought: distance was the curse. Newfoundland and Washington were too far from the scene of battle. If U-Boat Command were *here*, they'd see it, would see how easy it could be. Or if not U-Boats, the *Luftwaffe*.

He stopped and his eyes moved to the window, staring out unseeing as his mind raced. All along, he'd thought of *naval* attack. Newfoundland—anywhere this side of the Atlantic—was out of range of the *Luftwaffe*.

But it wasn't out of range, was it? *Not for an aircraft setting out from America! Air* attack! The very last thing that would be expected. Launched from the least likely direction!

He closed his eyes and tried to tighten his mind. Germany had friends, here in the United States, and he, Baldur von Galen, intended to harness them. The knowledge throbbed in him that now, at last, he could fight again—and could even be the engineer of a triumph of German arms. He'd show them what youth and vision could achieve. If the proper strike force was not prepared to act, then others *must!* It was the old men who were at fault. But the Führer's young men knew how to fight—and to die if necessary!

He knew exactly what he needed: three things, and the first was already under way; he found an angry satisfaction in having used Bohle's *Auslandsorganisazion* as the tool.

Six

Contemptuous of bureaucracy as he was, Von Galen now became grateful for its detail and precision. There were tens of thousands of *Auslandsorganisazion* cards at the Washington bureau, cross-indexed by profession, by location, even by age group.

Quickly he had several cards: within twenty minutes one which tempted him greatly; that of Richard Metzhagen, a mining engineer living in West Virginia. He picked up the telephone and rang his number.

"I want to inquire about fly-fishing," Von Galen said, using Metzhagen's phone code clearance.

"So, I get my husband." Metzhagen's wife still had a thick accent; somehow the fact was reassuring.

Soon a man's voice said, "Fly-fishing?"

"Can we meet and discuss it?"

VON GALEN took a train from Union Station to meet Metzhagen at a town called Winchester. Metzhagen was a smallish, quiet man in his early fifties, with a pipe in the corner of his mouth, and a studious air. He saw Von Galen's identifying copy of *Field and Stream* and nodded. Von Galen climbed into the man's elderly Buick.

"Do I get to know who you are?"

"Not yet. I simply want to ask you a question. Would you be able to construct a bomb?"

"A bomb?" There was no surprise. Metzhagen was driving calmly, eyes on the road. "What does it have to blow—concrete, steel, what?"

"I was thinking of an aerial bomb."

"Aerial, huh?" Metzhagen drove along in silence, turning off at last into an empty picnic place in the woods outside the town. Then he said, "It's not my field. You need aerodynamic casings. That's factory work."

Von Galen's optimism fell away. "I should have realized."

"Hold it, son. Maybe I can figure out something." Metzhagen applied a match to his pipe. "An aerial bomb has to drop accurately, that's no problem. What kind of height?"

"Difficult to say. Probably low." Von Galen felt increasingly foolish. He was talking to an expert technician, a man who needed data, and he had none.

"You'd have to have some kind of bomb bay, release mechanism," Metzhagen was saying.

"Yes, I see that now. I'll have to consider it more carefully. Perhaps I could come and see you again?"

"Any time. I'm real sorry to disappoint you—but an aerial bomb just isn't my field. Explosives are. Think whether some kind of static charge won't do the job."

"I will give it more thought. Thank you."

Metzhagen took his pipe out of his mouth and said quietly, "Heil Hitler."

Von Galen blinked. The words struck a strange note in this peaceful place. "Heil Hitler," he said.

WIEDEMANN, Von Galen's erstwhile superior in San Francisco, was in Washington for a briefing, and Von Galen telephoned him to suggest dinner. Their conversation was inevitably somewhat formal and only towards the end, when a good deal of wine had been drunk, did Von Galen allow it to become more personal. "By the way," he said, "what happened to that pilot—the one who wanted a letter sent to his son?"

"I have him." Wiedemann chuckled and poured himself a second glass of old *Weinbrand*.

"He's working for you?"

"Not yet." Wiedemann sniffed at the brandy. "But he will. He tried to run away. But Karen Hanzer kept in touch with his wife. A good girl, that. And then there was this." Wiedemann took out his wallet and passed over a newspaper cutting. "Read it." He was much amused.

As Von Galen read about the rescue of the two men from the sailboat, Wiedemann said, "You see, it's all there. He's flying PBY flying boats in Ontario. The American press is wonderful. They tell us everything. They even mention a 'government project'. Quite soon Herr Zoll will get an unpleasant surprise."

"So you know precisely where he is?"

"I have his address." Wiedemann sipped the *Weinbrand*. "In Kingston." He paused, frowning. "Why so interested?"

"If you remember, I dealt with his letter."

"So you did, so you did."

When Wiedemann went off to bed, Von Galen made himself busy. He visited the Embassy's registry, and within a few minutes he found the necessary reference books. As Wiedemann had remarked, the press really *was* very helpful.

"THERE WAS A phone call," Dot said when Ernie got home. "Hung up when I answered. Could it be that burglar?"

The Kingston newspaper had recently carried stories about a thief who telephoned to check a house was empty before breaking in.

"It'll just be a wrong number, Dot," Miller said. "We haven't a damn thing worth stealing!"

"I suppose." She sounded doubtful.

He was drinking coffee and smoking his second cigarette when the phone rang again. "It'll be Alec, honey. I'll get it."

But it wasn't Alec. A slightly accented voice said, "It was interesting to hear of your rescue exploit, Herr Zoll."

His heart seemed to stop. Desperately he said, "You have the wrong—"

"You will meet me in half an hour at the foot of Brock Street, at the waterfront, Herr Zoll."

"Look—"

"Be there. Do not make me remind you of your position."

Miller hung up. His brain was racing madly. Was there time to run? Where to? His money was in the bank! He couldn't run, not tonight. Tomorrow, maybe, he could withdraw the cash, take the car, drive clear through to Mexico. But what about Dot? Half an hour, the voice had said, and the threat had been clear; he'd just have to go.

He half-opened the door. "I have to go out for a while, honey."

"OK," Dot said. "Just make sure you're here when the burglar breaks in."

Brock Street ran down to the deserted lake shore. Miller parked at the top and walked down the short, steep hill. His eyes swept the seemingly empty hill, then moved to the water, as it lapped softly at the piers of the jetty, and with a sudden, grinding sense of hopelessness he saw himself jumping, sinking. . . . The temptation was almost overwhelming.

Then a footstep. He swung round. A man in a raincoat had appeared from the shadows and was approaching, limping. "There are better things than that," the man said, halting seven or eight yards away. Miller felt black rage erupt suddenly inside him. He knew who the man was, the limp gave him away. *Von* something, the supercilious little bastard in San Francisco who'd sent him the letter. He took a sudden step forward. If he *killed* this guy . . .

"Don't be a fool," the voice said, so contemptuously that Miller hesitated, then stopped. "Do you think I'm the only one who knows about you?"

No, Miller thought dully, he wouldn't be the only one. He said, "Can't you leave me alone?"

"To work against us—why would we do that? Herr Zoll, there is work to be done." He limped off up the hill, turning his head after a moment. "Come."

Miller glanced again, almost with longing, at the smooth water, then moved reluctantly, leadenly, up the hill. The man did not speak for a while. For Miller the silence was unbearable.

"Look, Mr. Von—" he burst out.

"Applejack. You will call me Applejack. It's a drink, I believe. Useful as a codename."

"What the hell do you *want?*"

"Not what you imagine. I'm not interested in this 'government project' of yours."

Miller was astonished. "What, then?"

Silence extending, and only their footfalls in the quiet night. Now Applejack said, "One flight, a very important one, for Germany. You have a chance to atone for your disgrace."

"What *is* this flight?"

"When the time comes, you will know."

"And after that—I mean, what happens?"

Applejack seemed to hesitate for a moment. "I will not trouble you afterwards. You have my word. Now, Mr. Miller, there are two things. You must rent a small storeroom here, best of all a garage with a strong lock. Secondly, you will instruct me in the duties of a flight engineer on the aircraft you fly."

"The Canso? Hell, you can't use that—it's—!"

"You *will* instruct me. We will spend tomorrow—"

"I can't, not tomorrow! There's a man coming. He's—he'd expect me there. It would look bad."

"Very well. Sunday."

"May be bad, too."

"Sunday," Applejack said firmly. "Now go."

Miller went back to his car. He drove home badly, his mind

442

whirling. A single flight in the Canso—carrying something, must be, otherwise why the need for a store? He couldn't possibly get away with that—take the Canso and the whole world blew apart!

But what was it Von—he couldn't remember the damn name!— what was it Applejack had said? *"I will not trouble you afterwards."* And he'd given his word, too—for what *that* was worth.

What if he took the car tomorrow and drove through Toronto and over the border at Niagara Falls, then just kept heading south till he got to Mexico? No, he'd be stopped. Ed Martingale was coming in, and if Miller didn't show at the field they'd phone home, Dot would say he'd left in his car, and they'd call the cops in case there'd been an accident. A pilot on a secret project would be looked for pretty hard. He'd be stopped at the border, if not before—no doubt about it.

One flight, he thought. Then abruptly the hair on his neck prickled as comprehension came.

VON GALEN watched him drive away, well satisfied. He had no doubt that Miller would do as he was told. Miller might wriggle, but there were too many holds upon him to allow him to run away again.

Von Galen had crossed the border at Niagara Falls and travelled via Toronto to Kingston by rail. He travelled on an Argentine passport, obtained for him by a helpful South American diplomat in Washington. Even after the German invasion of Russia the South Americans had remained discreetly sympathetic to German interests. Now he caught the night train back to Toronto: he had a fancy to see the Falls, and a day to spare. Next day he stood for a while on the observation terrace on the Canadian side, watching the vast, endless, hurtling torrent of Niagara.

Later, when he had returned to Toronto and was looking for a restaurant in which to eat, he chanced to pass a store which sold central-heating equipment. Von Galen stopped, struck by an idea. If he was careful in his choice of words, he could now tell Metzhagen exactly what he needed. . . .

ON SUNDAY MORNING, Ernie phoned Ross to say he had gut ache and that he was taking a day off. Soon, with Applejack beside him, he was driving out of town, westward, into empty country. On the bench seat between them lay the pilot's notes for the Canso.

It was a long day of technical talk, mainly in English, sometimes in German, when Applejack's English wasn't quite up to it. At the end Miller said, "Well, that's the theory."

Applejack nodded. "I have it. Now give me the keys to the garage. You are not even to go near."

Miller handed over the keys.

"And now," Applejack said, "I have to go back. When I telephone it will always be at nine o'clock at night. Make sure you answer."

As soon as he arrived in Washington the next day he was on the phone to Metzhagen, asking anxiously about progress. The answer was more than satisfactory.

Now he had everything he needed. It meant an almost immediate return to Kingston, and this one would be tricky. But when it was over, he'd be ready to *act*.

THE PLYWOOD packing case sat in the back of Metzhagen's pick-up. Stencilled red lettering on the wood said, "Domestic water boiler. Soft copper. Ballards are best."

"There's a consignment going over from Oswego to Toronto," Metzhagen said. "I fixed it with a couple of men in the Bund. This one gets offloaded on shore by tender. Night's good and dark."

Von Galen climbed into the passenger seat. "The whole bomb is complete?"

"Yup. All there, except the fulminate sticks. They're under my seat, gift-wrapped in cotton wool and candy-stripe paper. We're going to drive good and slow."

It was a long drive, and an almost silent one. Metzhagen kept the pick-up at a steady forty as they wound north, driving watchfully. They stopped for a brief meal at a roadside diner near Shenandoah, Pennsylvania, then pushed on past Scranton and up to the border with New York State, and on north.

Just beyond the little town of Cortland a policeman unexpectedly appeared in front of them, arm upraised, and Metzhagen stopped and wound down the window.

"OK. Let me see your driver's licence."

Metzhagen took it from the pocket of his checked shirt. "Something wrong?"

444

The cop looked at the licence. "Where you going?"

"Oswego."

"Where you from?"

"Washington."

"That right?" The cop walked round the truck and they heard the thumps as he kicked at the tyres.

"He's bored, I reckon," Metzhagen said softly. "Don't worry about it."

The cop was at the window again. "What's your load?"

"A water boiler," Metzhagen said. "The order's here if you want to see it. Is something wrong here, Officer?"

The cop didn't reply for a moment. Then, "Metzhagen," he said. "Sounds like a German name."

"My grandad, that was. Me, I was born in Charlestown."

Metzhagen's calm was not shared by Von Galen, and the cop's next question further increased his unease.

"Who's your passenger?"

"Just a friend," Metzhagen said.

The policeman ambled over to the passenger window. "Can you identify yourself?" he asked Von Galen.

"Certainly." Von Galen had both passports with him: German diplomatic, and the other, his Argentine one. He handed the Argentine passport across.

"Carrying your passport—you going somewhere?"

"Kingston," Von Galen said. "I have a sister there."

"You're from Argentina?" the cop said.

"Yes."

"Me, I'm a Polack. Came to the US when I was a baby." The cop added deliberately, "Germans sure kicked hell out of Poland."

Von Galen felt sick. The cop seemed to *know*.

Metzhagen said, "Sure hope we don't get mixed in it."

"Hmm." The cop was palpably hostile now. He said, "Took you a hell of a time to stop. We better check your brakes."

"They're OK," Metzhagen said.

"We're still gonna check. I'm gonna go down the road and when I signal you hit those brakes, right?" He left them, got into his car and drove two or three hundred yards, then halted.

Metzhagen said quietly to Von Galen, "He's really looking for

445

trouble, God knows why! We can't take chances with the fulminate. Take the box and walk along behind. And for God's sake be careful!"

Von Galen reached carefully beneath the seat and eased out the small box. "He's guessed I'm German."

"You're from Argentina, son. Passport says so."

Von Galen climbed down, holding the package gingerly, and watched the truck start up and move slowly off. It accelerated towards the cop, and stopped abruptly. By the time Von Galen reached it, Metzhagen was out of the cab, unfastening the canvas cover that protected the load. Three hundred pounds of dynamite, packed and sealed for export. The cop looked at the seal and shrugged. Then he turned to Von Galen, "What's in the package?"

"A present for my sister. A piece of china."

"That's why you got out and carried it, right?"

"I didn't want anything to happen to it."

"Can I put this cover back?" Metzhagen asked.

"Go ahead." The cop was still staring at Von Galen. "Got the receipt?"

"No, I don't think so." He could feel the colour mounting in his face. "Threw it away, I think."

"Maybe I ought to take a look."

Metzhagen said, "Aw c'mon, Officer, it's just a little present for his sister. He had it gift-wrapped."

"Won't make no difference to the Canadian customs," the cop said. "Let's see inside it, fella."

"Aw, Christ," Metzhagen said. "We've done nothing, we're just on our way to Oswego."

"Don't know about that. Seems to me there's something a little suspicious here. OK, lean on the bonnet, the both of you." The cop was unfastening the leather cover on his revolver holster.

Metzhagen obeyed, spreading arms and legs.

"Do as he says," he whispered to Von Galen. "We've done nothing. What could he find?"

But there *was* something. Metzhagen didn't know that Von Galen's German passport was in his jacket pocket. Heart thudding with anxiety, Von Galen put the package on the ground and leaned.

Von Galen felt the hands on him, under his armpits, across his chest and his back, down each leg in turn, then the inside pocket of his jacket, actually touching the diplomatic passport. He felt himself trembling.

The cop must have felt it also, for the hand lingered before it withdrew. Von Galen felt the passport snag on the lining as it came out, and he tried to whirl fast, but the leaned-over position was designed to counter just such a move.

The cop was standing back from them now, his revolver out, his eyes flicking from the passport to Von Galen. He read the words softly: "Deutsches Reich . . ." in a tone of surprise turning to satisfaction. "What's *this?*"

Von Galen said stiffly, "It is a diplomatic passport, as you can see. I am under its protection according to—"

The cop interrupted him. "Your pal ain't, though, I'll bet." The cop was grinning openly now.

"Oh boy, I just *knew!* A pair of Germans with a little cargo for Canada. I wonder what we're gonna *find* in there. We'll sort this thing out at headquarters. Get in the truck and turn it around."

As they climbed in, Metzhagen whispered, "I'll try to run him down." He put the pick-up into gear, gunned the engine, glanced round, and swore. The cop was beside them, and there was no way to catch him any kind of blow.

The little green-and-white parcel lay at the roadside where Von Galen had left it, and the cop was walking towards it, standing for a moment and looking down at it.

They didn't hear the cop say to himself, "China—from Germany maybe!" But they saw him draw his foot, saw the vicious little kick at the parcel and felt the explosion that plastered him all over the grass verge.

Metzhagen slammed the pick-up into gear, swung it round and drove off rapidly. "Our lucky day," he said grimly. The road was still deserted, and he drove fast; no fulminate to worry about now, and the dynamite in the copper boiler was safely inert.

They reached Oswego without further alarms, and loaded the boiler on a small lake trader with the odd name of *Ontario Turk*.

Metzhagen, having introduced Von Galen to the skipper of the *Turk*, then held out a hand and said, quietly as ever, "I'll supply more detonators, don't worry. Good luck!"

"Thank you for all you've done."

Metzhagen took the pipe from his mouth, glanced quickly round him, and murmured: "Heil Hitler."

Solemnly Von Galen returned the tribute. For a moment it seemed as weirdly out of place here as it had in the woods outside Winchester; but all the same he felt the words stir him.

Turk sailed an hour later. She made no more than eight knots and the trip to Kingston, a mere fifty-five miles away, would take most of the night. The deserted lake shore in the hours before dawn was the perfect place to unload his bomb, and by six o'clock in the morning the packing case was locked safely in the garage near the airfield. Von Galen wished he could stay with it, could remain here and wait for the signal; but that wasn't the way it would happen: when it came, it would come in Washington.

Seven

The hiatus ended on Thursday, July 31 with a morning priority signal to the German Foreign Ministry in Berlin from the German Ambassador in Turkey, Franz von Papen. Von Papen had learned that Harry Hopkins, personal envoy to Franklin Roosevelt, had just flown to Moscow. There could be no doubting Hopkins's purpose: three *Wehrmacht* army groups were tearing the guts out of an unprepared Russia and he was asking Stalin how America could help. The alliance Germany most feared could be coming into being.

Bohle spent the morning with Ribbentrop and top-echelon Foreign Ministry officials attempting to produce a swift analysis of the consequences. He returned just before lunch to his office to find that, in his absence, there had been a telephone call from Admiral Dönitz in Wilhelmshaven. He returned the call, intrigued.

"I said I would let you know if I found any pieces for your jigsaw puzzle," Dönitz said.

"And have you?"

"Possibly. A Condor reconnaissance aircraft risked a trip over the British naval base at Scapa Flow yesterday. Photographs show, among other things, that the battleship *Prince of Wales* is there. She was damaged in action and has been undergoing repairs. We did not expect her at Scapa. So the question is, *why* is she there?"

"Why shouldn't a battleship be at fleet headquarters?"

"Ignore the naval aspects, Minister. It's possible that a convoy of supplies may be being assembled for Russia. And the fact that Roosevelt's man, Hopkins, is in Moscow lends support to the convoy theory. I just thought I'd mention it."

Bohle hung up, frowning, conscious of a small frisson of excitement. After all these months, could it *possibly* be happening? He drafted a quick signal to Von Galen in Washington demanding that any further hint, no matter how slight, be instantly reported.

Twenty-four hours later, another piece of the puzzle edged forward. Like the rest, it was anything but conclusive. The phone call was from Admiral Canaris. "I wondered," he said, "how your little scheme is coming along?"

Bohle thought the word "little" unnecessarily patronizing. "Have you a contribution to make?"

"I wouldn't call it a contribution," Canaris said. "You know what intelligence is. All we do is try to piece together unrelated trifles."

"Have you something?" Bohle asked flatly.

"I don't know. In Britain they have collections for charity called flag days. Last Wednesday, Churchill was photographed buying a flag. In Downing Street."

"He can afford it."

"It seems," the Admiral went on, "that the particular flag day in question is not until the tenth. You see what I mean?"

"Thank you, Admiral," Bohle said. "I see very well."

BACK INSIDE the Embassy, Von Galen warned the duty officer to waken him if any message came, and went to bed. Lying there, he found his tumbling thoughts turning to Miller. Could he really be certain of him? Miller had cracked under pressure once before. . . .

Von Galen lay thinking. After half an hour or so an idea came. He got out of bed and prowled the darkened building for what he required. With relief he found what he sought in the top right-hand drawer of a desk in the naval attaché's office. He measured it with great care, then wrote out a detailed description. Shortly afterwards he left the building and telephoned Metzhagen from the public call office.

If Metzhagen found the request surprising, he gave no indication of it. "I can get it done. No, not myself, but there's a precision engineer I know. . . . You need a box, too?"

"Can it be done?"

"A few hours' work, that's all. I'll have the whole thing sent over to you sometime tomorrow."

Von Galen hung up, satisfied. He spent a wakeful night, and fell into weary sleep at six in the morning. Full daylight, spreading across the city, did not penetrate the heavy velvet curtains of his room and it was almost ten before he awakened. Rubbing his eyes, he drew the curtains, opened the window, hoping for air. He could see movement on the roof of the White House . . . men in uniform . . . moving to the flagpole.

As he watched, the presidential flag was lowered. No need to inquire what *that* meant. Von Galen dragged on a dressing gown and hurried to the Press department, where a bored-looking junior attaché was reading the small ads in the Sunday *Post*.

"Any news about Roosevelt?"

"He's going on holiday. Announced late last night. Details are on the wire." The attaché handed him a torn-off sheet of teleprinter roll.

Von Galen's eyes raced over the message. "Leaving today by train . . . joining *Potomac* at New London, Connecticut . . . cruising off the New England coast."

He searched with his finger on the wall map. New London? Where the hell was New London? He found it and his finger traced the route.

O'Hara! He must set O'Hara on Roosevelt's track.

Limping back upstairs to dress, he looked longingly at the phone at his bedside. But if the FBI were listening, if they caught only a hint . . . no, he daren't risk that. He hurried for the side door.

"Oh, Herr von Galen." It was one of the secretaries.

"Not now," he said.

She blinked. "But there's a message for you."

He stopped. "What message?"

"An American," she said. "He wouldn't leave his name. He said he was—" she glanced at her notebook—"off and running. Heading home first. Flying. Then by car."

Von Galen closed his eyes, trying to picture the map he'd been looking at. O'Hara's home was actually in Boston: so he was flying to Boston, then going on by car.

"Thank you, Fräulein," he said and headed for the radio room.

IT WAS MID-AFTERNOON before Bohle saw the Associated Press dispatch. His secretary hurried into his office with it. "Herr Bohle, the President has left Washington!"

He read with satisfaction. The first *hard* evidence. But he knew a moment later that in truth it wasn't; or not for anybody but him. Roosevelt was going on holiday, no more.

"Shall I try to reach Admiral Dönitz?"

He looked up at her, and shook his head. "It won't convince him any more than—" and then stopped, struck by thought. "Leave me for a while." The door closed behind her, and his eyes returned to the report. "It was announced today by the White House that . . ."

Announced. The word drummed. Only an *announcement* would convince Dönitz. Very well, an announcement there would be; several of his *Auslandsorganisazion* officers abroad had cover as newsmen.

The six o'clock Radio Berlin news began by reporting gains of Russian territory by the *Wehrmacht*. Then:

> It is reported from the Portuguese capital, Lisbon, that widespread rumours are circulating both there and in Washington that President Roosevelt has left for a meeting with the British Premier, Winston Churchill. There is informed speculation that they are to meet at sea.

Bohle smiled as he listened. When the announcer switched to another topic, he turned off the radio, and buzzed for his secretary. "*Now* get me Admiral Dönitz."

AT AN AIRFIELD near Stavanger in Norway, a long-range Focke-Wulf Condor had stood ready to take off since six o'clock in the morning, but brutal weather hammering in from the North Sea, squall after squall, had kept it on the ground. The crew, not unhappy at the delay, relaxed with coffee and cards in the crew room. The pilot, Flugleutnant Keller, was not with them. Keller was keen, a medal-hunter; his idea of fun was dead-reckoning navigation in foul weather. Keller was not, accordingly, particularly popular. He spent the waiting hours, characteristically, in the weather room, eyes on the meteorological instruments, searching for the break that would allow takeoff.

At one thirty he saw the thin band of blue down on the western horizon with low black cloud crowding ahead of it. He flung the crew-room door wide, letting in a blast of air that scattered the cards, and bellowed "*Schnell!*" in his familiar, inviting way. Within minutes the Condor was in the air and on a course a little north of west. Ahead, the crew knew, lay the usual long flight out over the Atlantic, beyond the British coast, to inspect the convoy routes, to radio any sightings that might be made to waiting U-Boats, then to continue down in a long loop to the French coast.

Tomorrow, they'd fly back again.

An hour and twenty minutes after the first turn, which had taken them over the gap between Shetland and the Faroes, the Condor banked again, dropping yet lower, to fly barely above the high-reaching wavetops; it settled on a course almost due east.

The crew wondered what the hell was going on—were they returning to base? No. Keller had an announcement to make. They would make a low-level pass directly over the fleet anchorage at Scapa Flow. The camera-gun would be used, but at low altitude its breadth of focus was small.

"It is therefore up to the sharp eyes of this crew," Keller said crisply. "What we are looking for is the battleship *Prince of Wales*. Study your recognition charts."

Privately, they groaned. Ahead lay fighters, anti-aircraft guns, radar, *and* the extra blessing of massive fire-power from whatever warships might be there.

After nearly four hours of flying through murk, Scapa lay below them, and anxious eyes searched its sheltered surface. More than a dozen ships lay at anchor: destroyers, frigates . . .

Two battleships! Almost identical. Same class.

King George the Fifth and *Prince of Wales*.

And *one* was actually moving, white water churning at her stern. Keller banked for a better look. Just in time—the moving ship was *Prince of Wales*!

Quickly he swung through a hundred-and-eighty-degree turn, climbing on full power now. Anxious eyes strained back, searching for pursuing fighters, until the black cloud closed around them.

Keller circled for two hours. Some of this storm cloud could smash his aircraft, but he had to chance that. He wanted to be sure.

At last he brought the Condor down, walking her like a fly on a ceiling along the underside of the cloud layer, flying a wide circle. From time to time, wisps of dark vapour closed over the huge plane, blanketing all vision. Suddenly the nose-gunner yelled, "She's there. Starboard, four o'clock!"

Keller took a good long look and then climbed back into cloud. In his mind now was a picture of a great battleship pointing west—and a rough sea that was quickly erasing her wake. Three destroyers screened her. Later, as he triumphantly dropped the Condor to the runway, he wondered, but dared not ask, why his orders had been to return and report, rather than to alert the U-boats.

"SAW HER AT SEA!" Bohle almost yelled. "And did *nothing?*"

Karl Dönitz was not a man given either to explanations or to the eating of humble pie. But now he was at least diplomatic. "I congratulate the Minister on a remarkable piece of foresight," he said. "It seems you may be right, and I was possibly wrong. U-Boat Command will make every effort—"

"Churchill in your sights!" Bohle said. "And *nothing!*"

"The ship was spotted by an aircraft," Dönitz said, "in bad weather conditions. They did well to find her at all."

"Can the U-boats find her," Bohle inquired bitterly, "in the bad weather? And can they attack, in the bad weather?"

"They are going to try. Churchill or not, it's a battleship we hunt now."

That night, as the storm grew rapidly worse, U-boats rose uncomfortably towards the surface and thrust antennae up into the gale to receive the nightly transmissions of U-Boat Command. Dönitz debated whether to mention Winston Churchill's probable presence on *Prince of Wales*. Such knowledge could drive brave men to suicidal heroics. But finally he decided to mention it. Dönitz knew the temptations of depth when storms were raging. The thought of Churchill would counter those temptations.

SOLDIERS WITH fixed bayonets guarded the entrance to the docks at New London throughout that late afternoon while a knot of Sunday-afternoon idlers waited at the gate. Word had got round of the impending presence of Franklin Roosevelt. O'Hara joined them, to stare at the waiting, shiny *Potomac* as the crew put a final sheen on everything. He found a reporter and a photographer from one of the local papers, disgruntled that they had no passes for the dockside. "Always the same," the reporter said. "Everything for the White House reporters. Nothing for us."

At 8.15 pm the train arrived, backing to a stop a hundred yards from *Potomac*'s gangway. From that moment they saw nothing. The pressmen, meanwhile, had been badgering the dock gatekeeper, and eventually an aide of some sort appeared to smooth things over. "Look, boys, it's a holiday," he said. "But I'll give you a tip-off. If you're in South Dartmouth tomorrow, you ought to get some nice pictures."

"South Dartmouth! That's sixty miles."

"Be worth it," they were told. Bitterly the pressmen watched *Potomac* depart down the Thames River towards salt water.

O'Hara drove his Lincoln direct to South Dartmouth. In August the holiday coast was busy, but O'Hara found a room in a private house in Tiverton, a few miles away. From a roadside diner he telephoned a house in Washington, the home of a German-American widow, Hanna Schmidt, whom Von Galen had recruited as a message-passer. "I'll be using you as a relay," he told her. "Get him a message. South Dartmouth, Massachusetts, tomorrow. I'll be there."

Next morning he was at the jetty, dressed in shirtsleeves. It was widely known that several members of the exiled Norwegian royal family were in the town, and again there was a crowd of sightseers.

Shortly before ten, *Potomac* came into view, and the little crowd buzzed with excitement when a speedboat was lowered and came roaring shorewards. Roosevelt himself could be seen at the wheel, glasses, famous grin, jaunty cigarette-holder and all.

Two little girls appeared on the yacht-club dock and climbed into the boat, then the speedboat stood on its tail in a spin-turn and raced out to sea.

Word spread that FDR had taken the Norwegian princesses

fishing. It was a long, tense day in the sunshine for O'Hara until, in the late afternoon, the speedboat once more tore into the yacht-club dock, and the princesses got out, shiny-eyed and excited. The speed-boat once more returned towards *Potomac*, and within minutes it had been hoisted aboard, and the big yacht was under way.

But where to?

"No clue as to destination," O'Hara reported by phone. "Nobody knows a goddam thing."

He found a quiet bar with a radio and a few customers. As the evening wore on, speculation began to creep into the news broadcasts. Rumours were flying round the nation's capital, it seemed, that the holiday cruise was a brilliant cover for something more momentous. There was even mention of a possible rendez-vous with Winston Churchill, but the commentators dismissed it as a piece of whimsy. At midnight, full of the beer he'd had to consume, O'Hara gave up and returned to his lodgings.

He was awake early next morning, begging the use of the landlady's radio set, telling her he was a journalism student, writing a story about the President's trip. At nine the New Bedford radio station said *Potomac* had been seen heading for the Cape Cod Canal. O'Hara, his bill already paid, raced out to his car.

FOUR HUNDRED AND FIFTY miles west of Orkney, secure in the depths, U-167 waited for the storm to abate. Because of the havoc that the storm had wrought with radio reception, she had received only a badly-scrambled signal the night before and her captain, Leutnant Griese, unaware of Churchill's possible presence, had taken her deep in search of comfort.

Now, on the morning of Tuesday, August 5, her listening equipment suddenly picked up the distant throb of engines. Griese stood over the rating as he turned the tuning wheel. "What is it?"

"Not sure, sir." The young rating was concentrating hard, good at his job. A minute or so later he turned his head. "More than one. Three, sir, I think."

Griese hesitated, torn between the temptation of targets and the unlikelihood of a successful attack in heavy seas. "Take her up. Periscope depth."

As the periscope came up, Griese gripped the handles and tried to survey the sea; but he got only glimpses. One moment the periscope's tip was metres clear of the water, the next it vanished under a huge wave. He worked slowly, trying to be sure one sector was clear before moving to the next.

There! Was that—?

He waited as the seas swept by, praying the next gap would be a clear one. Then, suddenly, as a swell lifted U-167, he saw for an unmistakable moment the low, sleek shapes of three destroyers.

"Range?" But he knew. They were more than three thousand metres off, and heading away. No chance of a shot in such heavy seas.

"Three thousand five hundred metres, sir."

Griese swore. "Down periscope." He looked at the faces turned towards him. "Three destroyers, and not a chance in hell!"

"Target impossible," Griese entered in his log. An hour later he radioed Wilhelmshaven. Perhaps somebody else would get a chance.

"TURNED BACK?" Dönitz said. "Slow the battleship down to let the escort keep up, or drop the destroyers and go on unescorted. *That's* what they've done. *Prince of Wales* is alone!"

The night's broadcast carried the news to the waiting U-boats.

IN WASHINGTON, that Wednesday, Von Galen sat restlessly by the radio set. From the half-hourly news headlines he knew *Potomac* was approaching the Cape Cod Canal. But there had been nothing from Bohle in Berlin; nothing from O'Hara either, since the call to Mrs. Schmidt the previous evening.

He could only wait and hope—and think of three hundred pounds of dynamite stored in a garage near Kingston, Ontario, and the fulminate detonators in a cotton-wool-packed box beside him.

FOR BOHLE, too, the tension grew. He felt a mild guilt at not informing Von Galen of the state of affairs. But something in Von Galen's last message, a mention of "possible alternative action" had disturbed him. This was a matter now for experience and a cool head. Karl Dönitz had both. Bohle didn't want Von Galen running round America trying to do something on his own, thereby earning for Germany further animosity from the American Government.

457

THERE IT WAS—the canal! O'Hara had known it from childhood, had passed through it several times when his father's own yacht had gone from Boston to New Bedford. He drove through the little village of Buzzards Bay and took up a position behind a disused roadside hoarding, taking out a pair of binoculars he had bought in New Bedford. *Potomac* was well out in the bay, apparently halted. Now he must wait. The yacht remained motionless until late afternoon, then moved off. Behind the hoarding, nerves shredded by something between tension and tedium, O'Hara trained his prismatics on the yacht as she entered and passed slowly along the waterway.

As she came closer, a small group of men became visible, lounging on *Potomac*'s sundeck. One of the seated figures wore the white ducks and white hat Roosevelt so often favoured. The bulky, seated figure was half-turned away, but O'Hara glimpsed the long cigarette-holder.

As the yacht drew level the figure in white turned his head a little, lifted a hand in acknowledgment of the cheerful waves of sightseers. O'Hara concentrated on holding the binoculars steady. He stared, and then, incredulously, concentrated harder. As *Potomac* moved slowly past and away, O'Hara remained rooted, glasses on the white-clad figure, praying for another turn of the head. He was rewarded moments later. And this time there was no mistake.

"You're certain?" Von Galen demanded. He had gone to Mrs. Schmidt's home to receive O'Hara's call, impatient at second-hand messages.

"No doubt at all," O'Hara said. "I could see him perfectly. Listen, I saw the full rig-out. White ducks, white hat, the glasses, the cigarette-holder. I had binoculars. It was really clear. *That man was not Roosevelt!* The rig-out was Roosevelt's, but the face wasn't."

Von Galen closed his eyes for a moment. If O'Hara was right, Roosevelt was pretending to be in one place when he was really in another. . . . This, Von Galen thought, was exactly the kind of thing he had hoped for when he sent O'Hara chasing the President to uncover some subterfuge.

"Don't doubt me," O'Hara said a little desperately. "I've known that face all my life. It wasn't him."

"Thank you. You've done well."

"And now?"

"Go back to Newfoundland. I know it's a lot to ask. But get up there as fast as you can. See what you can learn."

Von Galen hung up as Mrs. Schmidt hovered, coffeepot in hand. He still felt lingering doubt. "*Potomac* went through the Cape Cod Canal," he told her. "Somebody seems to have been impersonating Roosevelt."

"Just like the cunning old devil," she said. "He's a trickster from way, way back. It's *just* what he'd do!"

He saw the excitement in her face and was somehow convinced by it.

"You really believe that?"

"He'd absolutely *delight* in it!"

BOHLE READ Von Galen's new signal with a mixture of excitement and anger. Churchill was on his way, Roosevelt was on his way. Each with his little stratagems—the flag-buying, the impersonation—to cover departure. And the *Kriegsmarine* now, at last, on Churchill's track.

But not on Roosevelt's, damn it! Even if Dönitz succeeded in attacking *Prince of Wales* he'd still have fulfilled only *half* of Von Galen's scheme. Roosevelt would survive.

What, he wondered, had Von Galen meant by "alternative measures". Von Galen didn't even know, yet, that Churchill had left Britain.

He deserved to know that, at least. Bohle replied quickly.

> Congratulations on excellent work. Churchill believed to have sailed from Scapa Flow August 4 in battleship *Prince of Wales*, heading westward. Understand ship may have abandoned destroyer escort and sailing alone. *Kriegsmarine* ordered to attack on sight.

IT WAS NOW WEDNESDAY. Von Galen, with Bohle's new signal before him, was trying to calculate timings. At full speed, *Prince of Wales* could reach Newfoundland in five days. Roosevelt was well ahead. If he'd boarded a naval vessel as soon as *Potomac* had sailed out of sight of South Dartmouth, he could comfortably be in

Newfoundland tomorrow. True, he'd have to wait there for two days: the timing wasn't perfect. But the indications were stronger.

It *was* Newfoundland.

DOT WAS COMING through from the kitchen with a beer for Ernie when the telephone rang.

"Hello, Dot Miller speaking. That you, Alec?" Nobody answered her; she heard only the click of disconnection.

"Who was it?" Miller asked.

She shrugged. "The phantom burglar again, I guess. He just hung up."

Miller sipped his beer. A moment later the phone rang again and he rose from his chair.

"OK, I'll get it," he said, and left the room, closing the door firmly behind him. Usually Ernie gave a little grunt of protest at Alec's nightly call, Dot thought. Must mean they were doing something interesting.

She sighed, reached for a new ounce of wool, and continued work on the baby's jacket. It was always men who got the interesting things to do. Not, she thought contentedly, that she minded. Still it *was* a pity she'd had to give up her own flying; it had always been such fun. And she'd been good, too, everybody said so, though on that single sneaky trip Ernie'd given her on the Canso, one day when Alec was away, she hadn't flown well. She was rusty, and the controls were so *heavy!*

"I think it will be in the next day or two," Applejack said.

Miller said, "Saturday's my wife's birthday."

"Birthday! You talk about *birthdays?*"

"It'll look funny if—"

"I want you to work out a course," Applejack said sharply.

"Where to?"

Applejack told him. "I want to know the duration of a flight in a Canso, full fuel load. Quickly. And don't let your wife answer the phone again."

Miller put his head round the door. "Got a little work to do," he said. He went into the second bedroom of the apartment where he kept his desk and his charts and flying gear. He settled, in agitation, to the calculations.

Eight

It was Dot's birthday feast and Alec Ross, best man at their wedding and on this evening their host, was in the classically uncomfortable position of the helpless friend. He wondered if there'd been some kind of marital row; they were being polite to him and each other. In the silences, he reflected idly on a social convention that would not allow people to say, "Look, we're sorry, we'll be awful company tonight so let's forget it."

And the restaurant was no place for a party: barnlike and two-thirds empty, with hushed voices and the tables far apart.

On the wall behind Ross's head, an old pendulum clock ticked audibly and almost mesmerically. Miller thought resentfully that it shouldn't be like this. That there should be some valedictory gaiety, some show of spirit before . . .

But there couldn't be, of course. Applejack had disapproved of the party, but Miller had insisted. Things must stay normal until the last moment, and anyway it was Dot's birthday and he owed it to her.

He looked angrily at the waiter as coffee splashed into his saucer, then glanced up again at the clock. Twenty after eight. Ten minutes to go.

Alec was handing a gift-wrapped parcel to Dot, wishing her a happy birthday. Miller watched her manufacture excitement to please him, and begin to pick at the wrappings.

He thought suddenly: *What if I told them, right now, the whole thing—look, I'm not who you think I am. I'm not Ernie Miller at all, I'm Ernst Zoll, a German. In a few minutes I have to leave here to fly this damned Nazi some place for reasons I don't understand, and I'm pretty sure I won't be coming back.*

What if he said it? Dot, who could tolerate most things, could not tolerate personal treachery like his, and certainly would never forgive it. And Ross would go straight to the phone and call the cops, even if it meant his own ruin—as it would, because it was Ross who had chosen Miller, recommended him. It was Ross's duty, and Ross would do it.

Dot was laughing now, struggling with layer after layer of

wrappings. "What *is* this, Alec? I thought it was a shoebox, slippers maybe, but it keeps getting smaller."

Ross said, "Some things you have to work at," and smiled at her.

There were five minutes to go when she got to the little box and opened it and found the gold necklet.

"Alec, you shouldn't; it's so expensive! Hey, I must put it on." Miller watched the expert female fingers fasten the small catch.

Eight twenty-seven.

"Looks great," Miller said. "You're a lucky girl."

Ross asked, "What did you get from Ernie?"

"I don't know. Not yet."

Miller forced a grin, hating Applejack's idea. "Well," he said, "it's a little late, that's all." He looked at his wristwatch ostentatiously. "Matter of fact, I have a collection to make right now." His grin felt taut and false. "If you'll excuse me."

"But what *is* it?" Dot asked.

"Surprise," Miller said. He rose, turned away and left them, going straight to the car park. For a long deliberate moment, his eyes prickling, he thought of Dot, sitting there in the restaurant, waiting for her surprise. And when it came . . . Aloud, as though speaking the words would somehow help, he said, "Sorry, Dot." She was better off without him now. He forced himself to put her out of his mind.

As he drove by, he saw the pick-up truck parked by the garage. Miller drove his own car well off the road until it was screened by trees, and left it. Applejack swung open the garage doors and backed the pick-up halfway inside. "The aircraft—it's ready?"

"All gassed up."

"And you?"

"I can fly it," Miller said shortly. The more he saw of Applejack, the less he liked him. He was too cold, too intense. Miller felt a tardy rebellion flowering inside himself as together they lifted the heavy carton, loading it into the pick-up with care. Applejack secured the tailgate and got into the driving seat as Miller fastened the garage doors.

Climbing into the cab, Miller found Applejack's hand outstretched towards him. "So now we are ready," Applejack said, "and we go. Good luck."

Miller looked at the hand. "Now wait a minute," he said. "If I don't?"

Applejack stared at him. "You want to go through it all again? You will do as you are told for reasons you know."

Miller said, "I can really fix your wagon. Explosives, conspiring to steal an aircraft loaded with secret equipment. If I blow the whistle on you—"

"You will blow it on yourself. But then you know that. *You* are the spy; *you* are the possessor of another man's passport; *you* are the bigamist. Do you imagine I haven't a story ready?" There was an irritating half-smile on Applejack's face. "You want to refuse to do what is, after all, your sworn duty. Very well. Let me tell you what will happen, what the Reich can do to those who betray it. You have a father, a sister, a legal wife, all in Hanover. You have heard of the Gestapo, heard of concentration camps? You also have a woman here. What would happen to her? Do you think she is beyond our reach?"

"You wouldn't—"

"I told you I'm *prepared*," Applejack said. "If you refuse, now, it will all begin in a few hours. Arrest and interrogation, and after that . . ." The words hung for a long, chilling moment.

Miller felt sick and helpless; his mind filled with pictures of horror.

"But," Applejack went on, "there is another side. All of that is unnecessary. You are a German airman, sworn to fight for your country. Once, long ago, you disgraced your uniform and your service. Now you have a chance to restore yourself to pride and honour and patriotic duty, to strike a great blow for Fatherland and Führer."

"And I'll be dead," Miller said softly.

"Yes." A simple, uncompromising monosyllable. "Myself also. A hero's death for both of us."

Applejack produced a cigarette case and offered it, and his tone changed. "It is a matter of accepting orders, no more than that. Do you think your son ever questioned his? He *died* for the Führer."

Miller blinked. "How, when?" He now felt appalled. He hadn't even seen his son, yet there'd been such pride that Heinz was a hero. Now a *dead* hero.

"Twelve kills," Applejack said. "He got twelve. He did magnificently. Believe this—you will achieve even more." He struck a match, offered it. "And now, it is time."

Miller inhaled and said sadly, "You have me. All ways."

Applejack nodded. "All ways." He started the engine, put the pick-up into gear, and moved off. "As I said earlier, good luck."

"Target?"

"Later. When we're in the air."

"Now," Miller said harshly.

Applejack took his eyes off the road briefly, and his left hand moved to the gun, ready beside his seat. Miller was vital: without him there could be no attack. Looking at the pale face with its sheen of sweat, he was looking at a man whose only choice was of the way he died. He said, "Churchill, the British battleship *Prince of Wales*, and if we're lucky, Roosevelt too."

They drove on in silence, then Applejack said, "Valhalla."

"What?" Miller, wrapped in sadness, wasn't sure he'd heard.

"Tomorrow. In Valhalla. This son you didn't know. Maybe you'll meet him there."

"You're crazy," Miller said. Yet the crazy thought lodged in his mind, and he sat silent, thinking about it.

Applejack was saying quietly, "I was once in Japan. There they have a concept of a warrior's death in battle, deliberately chosen. They call it *Kamikaze*, the divine wind. To go with that wind is a supreme privilege."

"Is that so?" Miller had a practical question. "One thing you didn't say. How do we drop that thing back there? There's no bomb bay, no sight, no release mechanism."

"You're an intelligent man. You know there is only one . . . answer. You have known from the start."

"Yes," Miller said. "I guess I have."

MURPHY WAS THE DUTY GUARD. As the pick-up approached the wire fence Miller had hoped it would be someone he didn't know. But it was Murphy, whom he knew and liked, a big cheerful Irishman, already coming out of his guard hut as the pick-up stopped.

"Who's that?" The beam of a torch flicked over him. "Gee, it's you, Mr. Miller. Didn't expect you. You flying tonight?"

"Just got some gear here," Miller said. Why did it have to be *Murphy*?

Murphy was unlocking the gates and fastening them back. Powerless, Miller watched it happen: the gun hand coming up, the shot and Murphy going down. Six orphans, he thought savagely.

"We take him with us," Applejack said. "Help me lift him."

They laid Murphy's body in the back of the pick-up and drove towards the distinctive high-wing silhouettes of the big flying boats, with the detector rings gleaming in the

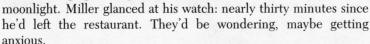

moonlight. Miller glanced at his watch: nearly thirty minutes since he'd left the restaurant. They'd be wondering, maybe getting anxious.

Applejack had a little rope sling already prepared, and together they manhandled the packing case up the metal ladder and into the Canso's belly. Abruptly Applejack spoke from the tarmac below. "Come down here."

Puzzled, Miller descended the ladder.

"Stand to attention."

"Are you crazy?"

Applejack took a small square object from his pocket, a box of some sort. The headlamps of the pick-up glinted dully on something inside as the lid was opened.

Recognition set Miller's heart hammering. Almost involuntarily his heels came together and his hands dropped to his sides, stiffening.

Applejack took a step forward, lifting the object from the box: a black and white ribbon from which hung a cross. An Iron Cross. A cross like his father's, like his son's.

"By special order from Reichsmarschall Hermann Goering," Applejack said formally. He passed the ribbon over Miller's bent head. "The Reich respects brave men. Three generations of one family. Your father will, of course, be informed of your action and this decoration. He will surely be very proud." He held out his hand. "My congratulations. Now please climb aboard."

Miller climbed the ladder in a daze. The Iron Cross!

As Applejack came up the ladder for the last time, Miller's fingers were on the small metal cross. He lowered the door and clipped the clasps into place, then turned on the overhead light. Pointing to the tunnel leading through from the belly of the plane towards the cockpit, he said, "Engineer's position halfway. On the right." He watched Von Galen move forward on hands and knees, awkward in the confined space, then stand. Only his legs were visible now.

He put out the light and crawled forward, through the familiar tunnel into the well behind the pilots' seats, then hoisted himself up into the left-hand seat, and began his checks.

He'd done it all a thousand times and the actions were almost mechanical. Miller was too good a flier, too experienced to neglect checks. His hands moved easily, confidently, and fast. Altimeters set, oil checked, gyros caged, shut-off valves open, fuel drains closed.

He could imagine Alec looking at his watch, wondering. It was a still night: Alec might even hear the engines start. And then? No doubt about it—Alec would move.

Tonight the whole routine wasn't possible, not all of it. OK. Start-up, right engine first. Fuel-booster pumps on; energize. The props turning, he counted nine blades before ignition, checking meanwhile on the hydraulic lock. OK, ignition switch *on*.

The right engine rasped, then roared. Then the left. Mixture auto rich. Fuel-booster pumps off.

After a quick engine test, he dropped the revs and put on his headset. "All OK back there?"

"I think so."

It was time to go.

He ran up the engines, watching the gauges, waiting for the magic figures. The Cyclones were almost deafening, the airframe vibrating.

Brakes off. The familiar shove in the back as the Canso accelerated up the runway. He'd always loved that feeling and he loved it now. He watched for the markers, felt the stick coming alive.

Unstick speed. And she lifted.

Canso One was in the sky, turning to swing out over the lake.

ROSS GLANCED at his watch yet again, frowning. Where in hell was Ernie? Looking up, he met Dot's eyes and her apologetic shrug.

"I just can't imagine where he's gone."

"No. It's half an—" Ross stopped, hand lifted for silence. "That's an engine starting up! Hear it?"

Head cocked, she listened. "I hear it, yes."

"Shh." He was concentrating. "There goes two. You heard the start-up? Twin Cyclones. It's a Canso."

"But not *Ernie*." Her eyes pleaded with him.

"Who else?" Ross was rising, taking out his wallet, summoning the waiter. And he was angry.

"But, Alec, he said he was coming back. With the present. He wouldn't do *this!*"

"He said he had a surprise," Ross said grimly. "Maybe this is it. Damn fool!" He was counting out banknotes.

"But Ernie *wouldn't*," she protested, near to tears.

Ross gentled his voice. "He's gone on joyrides before, Dot. You know that." He hurried her out, talking as they went. "But this time it's a government aeroplane with secret devices aboard. Come on. We're going to the airfield."

Ross drove fast and in silence through the dark. Then abruptly he said, "You had a fight today?"

She nodded miserably.

"Want to tell me what it was about?"

"Nothing, really. He's been acting strange for days."

"Like what? Hey, look!" Something dark and low roared over the road in front of them, gone in a second, masked by the roadside trees. "He's taken off. Dot, you can't even fly the thing single-handed! He must have someone with him. What in hell's he up to? *Think*, Dot."

"Oh God, I don't know!"

"What about the row you had?"

Tears were being suppressed, but he could hear them in her voice. "I said he hadn't talked to me properly for days, and he said, Don't nag me."

"Nothing else?"

"No, Alec. Really."

He turned off onto the approach to the airfield. The car park was empty. Dot said hopefully. "If his car's not here—"

But Ross had seen something. "The gates are open." He drove towards them. The guard-cabin light was on. Ross braked sharply beside it and got out. The cabin was empty.

He heard Dot's heels on the tarmac behind him. "Oh, Alec! I don't understand," she said.

Ross took her by the shoulders. "There's a radio in the other aeroplane. Get in the car. Let's see if—" He gunned the Chev forward as the doors slammed, tore across to the other plane and got out, leaving her to follow. By the time she'd reached the bottom of the ladder he had the hatch open and was climbing in, moving forward through the tunnel.

OK. Time to try. He switched to transmit: "Canso Ring Two calling Canso Ring One. Come in, please."

Dot, breathless behind him, said, "Is he answering?"

Ross shook his head and tried again.

No response. He kept trying, his mind racing as the words came out. Ernie might not hear. Ernie'd been gone ten or twelve minutes now; he'd be twenty-five miles away.

Going where? One thing was certain, Ross thought. Ernie was heading for ruin, wherever he was going, unless he could be got back on the ground quickly. He'd have to report it, and once he did so, Ernie was finished.

There was movement beside him: Dot climbing into the right-hand seat. Pity she wasn't a co-pilot. He could chance it, then; give Ernie one last, very final chance. But alone it wasn't possible, not in the Canso. Then he glanced across at her, realization hitting him. Dot *could* fly. Even had twin-engine rating. He slipped off the headphones. "Dot, have you flown in the Canso?"

She looked at him quickly, then her eyes moved away. Joyrides for wives, friends, and pretty girls were forbidden.

"Have you, Dot?"

Her eyes came back. She hesitated, then gave a little nod.

"How much?"

"I don't know, Alec. Three hours, maybe four." Then realization dawned slowly in her eyes. "I *can*, Alec."

"Can you *really?*" This could put his own career at stake. He let the radio run twenty seconds, its crackling silence making up his mind. "Get up there!"

A quick strained smile showed her gratitude, and then she was gone, into the tunnel, up to the flight engineer's position.

"OK, let's begin." Alec took a deep breath, hating this gamble he was taking. He began the sequence of checks, missing many, taking far too much for granted.

On Saturday night, August 8, 1941, two highly experienced pilots, neither of whom had previously committed that particular idiocy, ran big flying boats down the runway at Kingston, Ontario, with check lists not completed, and roared off into the night sky.

Nine

Alone in the left-hand seat of Canso Ring One, Miller took in the steady gauges. The Thousand Islands, scattered in the entrance to the St. Lawrence River where it funnelled off Lake Ontario, were behind him now.

The headphones were on the hook beside his head. Nice to fly without them. Like the old days. He'd enjoyed flying best then: with open cockpit and no controllers and the sky free to wander in, to climb and turn, or roll off a half-loop if the aeroplane could do it and if he felt like it, as he often did. No more of that, though. Canso couldn't do it.

He looked at his watch, then at the airways map on his knee pad, and the route calculations. He was half an hour airborne, flying low, under a thousand. Thirteen hours elapsed, that was the schedule, allowing for time-zone changes. All of them, including the half-hour over to Newfoundland.

On the edge of his mind the faint muttering of the headphones registered, and he ignored it. Applejack had given him solid instructions: don't call me unless it matters. And if you have to, whistle into the mike. Anything else could be ignored. He wasn't accepting instructions from any controllers, not tonight. And not again, ever, he thought. No more turn left, twenty degrees, yes sir, hold it, yes sir, thank you sir. Nothing like that.

Nothing. Not after . . . he checked his watch again. There wouldn't be a moon tomorrow. Not for him. He was mildly surprised how cool he felt about it, how easy the acceptance was.

All the same, the headphones drew him. Somebody calling. What frequency was he on, anyway? He looked at the numbers. Their own Orange channel, allocated to the project. So Alec *was* in the air!

And somebody was with him. Had to be. Who? If he'd rustled up a flight engineer, he'd been damned fast. But Alec *was* damned fast, slick, efficient. So who was with him? Half-reluctantly, half-intrigued, Miller reached for the headphones.

"Come in, Canso Ring One, Canso Ring Two calling." Repeated. Proper procedure from Alec. He listened as the call came through again and found that he was smiling to himself. Baffled, Alec? New experience for you. Call it part of life's rich pattern, and add it to all the others.

There'd certainly been plenty. In the late 'twenties and early 'thirties, flying was all new experiences: landings in rough fields, lack of instrumentation. Miller was good, and knew it; Ross just a little better, and Miller knew that too. Ross lacked the edge of daring, perhaps, he had had nothing to prove: no charges of cowardice in Alec's background. The only thing you could charge him with was over-seriousness, application.

Alone in the left-hand seat of the Canso, in the still night, with the river silver below, Miller listened with something approaching amusement at Ross's repeated, and now fainter, calls.

Betcha can't find me, Alec! he thought. And took off the headset.

MILLER DIDN'T KNOW that Ross's transmissions had already stopped. If Ernie wasn't answering, Ross told himself, it was because he didn't intend to answer. There were two radios in the Cansos and they couldn't both have gone. He didn't *want* to answer.

So how to find out where he was? Fool, he thought, and tuned the radio to Montreal control and started listening. Somebody was going to notice a pair of loose planes and start asking questions. There was military radar about.

But Montreal? That assumed east. Miller could be headed west or south. North, no; north was nowhere. Three directions, two radios. He switched to intercom and said, "OK up there, Dot?"

"Like clockwork."

"Leave it and come down here."

She was beside him in a moment. Co-pilot in a silk dress and high-heeled shoes, he thought. "Tune the radio to Rochester." He told her two frequencies. "Then to Toronto. Keep switching backwards and forwards. I'm on Montreal. If anyone asks questions about unidentified aircraft, tell me."

She nodded. "Clever."

"Obvious," Ross said. "I should have thought of it before." He flew and listened, she just listened, tuning and retuning. Neither spoke; both knew this was the only chance of finding an Ernie who didn't want to be found.

The minutes dragged by. Routine communications between aircraft and Montreal control. A DC3 in from Boston, two Hudsons leaving for Britain. No Ernie.

The controller's voice was steady, low and precise: weather, pressure, wind speed, then sharpening suddenly. "Unidentified aircraft entering Dorval control area, identify yourself."

Tensely Ross waited, heard the instruction repeated. No reply. The controller's voice took on concern: warning to all aircraft to be on look-out for an unidentified aircraft, approximate position, approximate height, the repeated demand for identification.

Was that Ernie? There were always clowns in the sky, and Ernie wouldn't be such a fool as to wander into busy airspace without . . .

"Unidentified aircraft now heading north," the controller was warning, retailing course, speed and height. The height was lower now, under a thousand, dropping to avoid the radar scan, swinging away into open spaces.

"Dorval's got an unidentified, Dot. Could be him."

"What'll happen?" she asked.

He shook his head. "They may send an aircraft up to take a look, but he's heading north. Not easy to find out there."

Fringe of Montreal control area, swinging north. Ross checked his map. Ernie nearly forty minutes ahead. He changed course, across the angle, hoping to pick up time and distance.

"Listen to Montreal, Dot. Forget Rochester. I doubt he'll cross the border. I'll try him again."

He switched to Orange channel. "Canso Ring Two calling Canso Ring One. Come in, Ring One."

THE SIGNAL wasn't strong, but Miller heard it pretty clearly, and was more than a little surprised to hear it at all. He'd expected Ross's transmissions to get fainter and vanish. Had Ross somehow picked the right direction?

He'd been worried about Alec from the start, although there was no way he could guess where he was going, or why. And there was nothing he could do to stop him, even if he found him. Still, it was smart of Alec to be even this near to getting it right. Had it been Dorval?—the radar reaching farther than he'd thought? Miller tuned the radio, listened and stayed listening. Dorval was way off now, down to the southeast, but the controller's voice came in clearly. It occurred to Miller that Ross, too, was on an unauthorized flight, and what Alec was doing would do his career no good at all. Alec was in charge of the project, and what he ought to have done was to report the disappearance of Canso Ring One and get a search going. And clearly he hadn't.

Bad luck, Alec. Sorry, Alec. What will you do?

Miller thought about it. Alec could make his own flight legitimate: call up Dorval and announce his presence. Dorval knew the Cansos, the research project. What he *couldn't* do was start asking questions about unidentified flying boats, because if he did the whole thing came out into the open: missing aircraft with secret equipment aboard, universal panic.

Yes, Alec was a gentleman. There were rules and regulations Alec wouldn't bend, and lots of them: no bending on air safety, on flying standards or anything that had to do with aeroplanes. But he was also the kind of man who'd make allowances, ignore the small private transgression so long as it didn't get in the way of important things.

Things seemed reassuringly quiet at Dorval; the controller's voice had been silent for several minutes. Miller clicked the radio back to

Orange channel, and got Ross's voice at once, anxious-sounding, a little dispirited, but still putting out the call. He clicked to intercom and spoke to Von Galen. "Ross is in the air, looking."

"Will he find us?"

"No," Miller said. "Not a chance."

There was a heater duct that was supposed to warm the small space in which Von Galen stood, but the thin stream of warm air from it seemed to be sucked instantly away in the draught that played around his body. He told himself that he was on his way to a glorious death for his Führer and his country, but that wasn't how he felt in this icy metal enclosure. Though he had been a pilot, he was unaccustomed to long-distance night-flying, the long hours of solitude and tedium.

He looked at the instruments. All steady. They had been in the air an hour and a half, and there had been nothing to do since just after takeoff. There would be nothing more for hours, apart from fuel-tank switching.

Curious, he thought, to be so helpless. He was the instigator, the organizer, the planner, of a great enterprise that might change history. He'd done it virtually alone, setting the spark to a flash of fire that would destroy Winston Churchill and, if he was lucky, even Roosevelt, too. In his mind, Von Galen tried to picture the moment. A great battleship, the aircraft approaching, diving, exploding on her decks in a huge blast of heat and fire. The thought of all that heat brought a wry twist to his mouth.

"Montreal Control. Unidentif—" The voice stopped. A pause. Then again, "Unidentified aircraft entering Montreal airspace from the west," but doubt in every syllable.

Ross swore. He could only be the faintest blip on a screen.

"Identify yourself." Still doubt, the controller unsure.

Like Miller before him, Ross failed to respond. A lifetime's habit demanded that he should, but he resisted, and pushed the Canso into a shallow dive that served a double purpose of increasing his distance from the scanner and decreasing its chance of picking him up again.

But Ross's worry was deepening. He himself was slipping further into trouble with the passing minutes. First the flight itself, unauthorized, no flight plan filed; bad enough. Now a second unforgivable act: failing to answer when directed to by a major airspace controller.

With self-reproach came self-doubt; Ross was anything but sure that Miller was up ahead, and had only Dorval's challenge to rely on. Miller could have gone anywhere; on full tanks and with strong favourable winds the Canso could even reach Ireland, or a thousand places in the United States. But it remained the only chance, if a lessening one.

"Damn it, Dot," he said angrily. "Where could he be going? Give me a place!"

But she couldn't—only a sad little shake of the head. She lived with him, spent days and nights with him and yet—nothing. No idea that he was about to steal an aircraft and set out on some crazy flight to God knows where.

Alec said, on impulse, "Seems he won't answer me—*if* he can hear. You try."

"What about the other stations?"

"It no longer matters. Unless we're with him now, we've lost him. We've come too far."

She forgot procedure, or ignored it. "Ernie, it's Dot. Come in, *please* come in." Her voice was cracking.

They waited. No response.

Ross watched her. She'd pulled herself together in the impersonal atmosphere flying demanded, but her control was slipping with the knowledge that if Ernie could hear he was deliberately ignoring her. "Ernie, *please*. Talk to me. Tell me you're all right. That's all I want to know. *Please*, Ernie!"

It's not all *I* want to know, Ross thought. I want to know where, and I want to know why. To begin with, he'd assumed that Ernie Miller was off on one of his occasional, compulsive breaks: the solo aerobatic flights that got something out of his system. But this time, he wasn't alone. And if that *was* Ernie up ahead somewhere, he wasn't playing poker with the laws of aerodynamics; this was direction flying.

Where to? Where after Montreal? North, into deserted Quebec? Northeast, along the St. Lawrence? Due east, over Maine?

"Dot, think! Any place he's mentioned. However—however un-

474

likely. If he sang 'Deep in the Heart of Texas' in his bath, tell me!"

"But he *didn't!*"

"OK, keep trying." There was nothing else to do. Without some clue somewhere, they were simply entering a void.

Dot turned to him suddenly. "Alec."

"Yes."

"Argentina?" She said it hesitantly, on a rising inflection.

"Argentina?" he said. "What about it?"

"He wrote it, Alec. He wrote that word on a pad by the phone. I was getting some paper to write a grocery list and I saw it."

"Just that—Argentina? Nothing else?"

"No. Just—oh, there was a drawing, a rough drawing."

"Of what?"

"Well—South America. That shape, you know. At least, that's what I think it was—the shape of South America. He flew there, you know, Alec, years back."

Ross knew. "He can't fly there now," he said. "Canso has long range, but not *that* long." Telephone pad, he thought. "Have you had any phone calls?"

"Only the Phantom Burglar." Dot produced a small, embarrassed laugh. "Leastways, that's what I called him. It happened a few times—phone would ring and when I answered it there was nobody there. Whoever it was just hung up."

"Did it happen to Ernie, too, or just to you?"

"Just to me, I think. I don't remember Ernie—"

"Has he had any calls?"

"Lately? Quite a lot. You usually, and some apart from that."

"Who?"

"Gee, I don't know. He didn't say."

"Dot, try to think. When the burglar called and hung up, was there ever a call immediately afterwards?"

"I'm not sure. I—yes, there was. Once I answered and whoever it was hung up and I told Ernie it was the burglar and then it rang again and Ernie said he'd get it."

"And he spoke to somebody?"

"Yes." She sat thinking. "It must have been you, Alec. He took the call in the hall, and then when he'd finished I think he said— yes, he did—he said he'd work to do for a while."

"When was it? What day?"

"Well, it was only a day or two ago. Maybe Wednesday. Around nine, as usual."

Had he called Miller on Wednesday? Dot was right that he called often, three or four nights a week. What had he done Wednesday? Ross made his mind backtrack.

Wednesday was the day he'd written the report to Martingale. Spent the whole evening on it, nonstop, finished at midnight.

He said, "It wasn't me, Dot. Listen, the thing with Argentina, when was that? You were making a shopping list. What day was it?"

"Thursday," she said promptly. "That's my market day." '

"So it was the day after the call. The day *after* he said he'd work to do?"

"Must have been. But Alec, he couldn't be going to Argentina, could he? Why would he go *there?*"

He shook his head, trying hard to think. Somebody telephones. Hangs up when Dot Miller answers. Waits. Calls again. Then Ernie has work to do. Three days later, Ernie steals a plane and vanishes.

Good God! Ross thought.

So who was with Ernie? And why were they bound for Argentina by way of the St. Lawrence River? It was absolutely crazy.

MILLER HAD SPENT nearly an hour tuned to Dorval; but after that first hesitant inquiry there had been nothing more. Alec, if it was Alec, had followed Miller's own tactic and gone away low to the north to fly round the surveillance. And Miller felt as though Alec were still there, somewhere behind, guessing, probably, that Miller was following the river.

Or maybe Alec had actually given up? Easy to find out. Miller switched to Orange channel.

And heard nothing. Good. The silence extended. One minute. Two. Then a voice, a light voice, a woman's . . . *it was Dot!* Hell, Alec had *Dot* with him!

She was faint and there was distortion, but through it all he heard her distress. "Ernie. Just *answer*, Ernie. *Please!*"

You bastard, Alec! he thought.

But he ought to have guessed. For Alec to get off the ground as fast as he had, he'd have needed somebody at once.

". . . please, Ernie."

He switched off. He'd never wanted to hurt Dot, but he couldn't have explained to her. Dot would undoubtedly have tried to stop him one way or another.

He checked his route. Quebec coming up next, northern detour again. Then rejoin the river thirty miles beyond Orleans Island. ETA at Mont Joli at 3.10 am local, six hours' elapsed flying time. Mmm. Then he'd disappear. A little more than three hours to go, and the odds were that Alec would keep coming along the river, make the same detour round Quebec City.

Would he, though? Six hours chasing a phantom. It would be a strain on anybody's determination, even Alec's. He'd get discouraged eventually, turn round and go home. Of course he would.

Yes, but Dot wouldn't. She had a very powerful streak of female never-let-go. He thought: take her home, Alec. Turn the damn Canso around and take her home. Don't put her through any more.

He switched on again, hoping they'd be gone.

"Ernie, won't you answer, *please* . . ."

He wished he could reach out, hold her, soothe her. Dot was a good woman, always had been. It wasn't easy being a flier's wife, especially with the kind of flying Miller had done; any kind of ship to any place anybody asked. Just before they were married he'd laid it all out for her: the insecurity, the dangers, the separations. And all she'd done was say, "Ernie, my dad was a flier. I know what I'm doing."

He'd traded on it, too, more than he should. Times he should have called her, and had not; times he'd left her short of money; times when he'd flown recklessly, selfishly, without a thought for her. Through all of that, she'd made nice homes in cramped apartments, looked after him and his things, endlessly thoughtful. And now . . .

"Ernie?"

What a bastard he was! It was as though all the worry in all the years had come out this one night and was concentrated in her voice. He felt tears forming, one beginning to run down his cheek, and the unbidden thought forming in his mind: would it matter? If he spoke, just once, what difference would it make?

What would he say? He felt a sudden, urgent compulsion to be honest with Dot. To tell her enough of the truth so she wouldn't spend the rest of her life trying to solve a riddle. He could say goodbye. Yes, he could do that. He could tell her he loved her.

But if he spoke, what would the consequences be? Alec would know he was up ahead, sure. But he wouldn't know where. He'd no d/f aboard and the sub-detector equipment wouldn't help.

"*Please*, Ernie!" The phrase was repeated over and over.

He forced his mind back to Alec. What could Alec deduce? *He'd know Miller wasn't coming back!* And knowing it, Alec would act, that was certain. He'd sound all the alarms, yell for the cops. He'd have to; there was no other way for him.

His mind wrestled with it. Was there a way? One transmission that wouldn't give him away. If he said, "*I love you, Dot, remember that?*" No. Not remember that. Tell her you love her. Tell Alec to take her home. Emphatic. Then switch off and maintain silence from there. To the end.

How would Alec respond to that? Sound the alarm, or follow the suggestion? Miller thought about it. Alec wouldn't do either, not straight off. He'd want more information, so he'd come right on demanding it, at least for a while. In which case, it made sense to keep Alec following. It was almost a safety precaution to lead Alec on.

But what about Applejack? If *he* had the smallest notion Miller was transmitting, he'd be down with his gun screaming murder. But he wouldn't know, would he? The flight engineer was on intercom only: the set wasn't rigged so he could hear the radio.

He went over it again in his mind. It seemed to hold water. Miller's hand moved to the mike switch, then hesitated.

Ten

Ross was tuned to Quebec, hoping for something from ground control to indicate unidentified aircraft in or approaching the area. It seemed to him that Ernie had skirted Montreal to the north, and would do the same at Quebec. He believed—made himself believe—that Miller was up ahead, even though there was no evidence beyond the unanswered challenge from Montreal.

Quebec, as Saturday night shaded into Sunday, was quiet. In his mind's eye Ross imagined the controller, feet up, coffee in hand, talking about sport or the movies, counting the hours till the change of shift.

Out of the corner of his eye he could see Dot, body hunched forward, talking with a kind of steady desperation: the few words endlessly repeated, hope dimming. Ross had always liked Dot, and he felt a deep pity for her now. She was attractive, easy to talk to, always a good listener, friendly and sympathetic. But Dot Miller was like a million others, a good wife, wrapped up in her husband. And now Ernie was somewhere in the dark limbo of the night and she was plainly terrified she'd lost him.

Miller should be close now to Quebec airspace, but Control remained silent. Below, the great river gleamed gunmetal; above, the stars were bright in a sky decorated with puffballs of cumulus; all around lay the empty night. Ross's eyes moved in instinctive patterns over the instruments; feet and hands made similarly instinctive adjustments to rudder and stick as the Canso roared on, alone in space.

Squawk! Ross came instantly alert: an RCAF transport on the airline between Quebec and Montreal was indignant. The lane had been crossed beneath him by "some damn joker with no navigation lights".

Ross listened. Control demanded to know position, height, aircraft type, heading. Figures were given, but the RCAF man couldn't be sure of any type.

Quebec was rightly angry. "Warning to all flights Quebec vicinity. Unidentified aircraft has just crossed beneath airlane . . ." Then the demand: "Identify yourself."

Ross swung north a little, listening and interpreting, faith now reinforced. The plane seen by the RCAF transport would be Ernie's, but Quebec hadn't picked him up: he'd crossed the lane on a north-easterly course, flying low. Ernie *was* rounding Quebec and would then return to the river.

"Quebec Control. Canso Ring Two. Requesting permission to enter . . ." He sensed that Dot had turned to look at him. Permission was granted, he thanked Quebec Control and signed off. At once Dot was on intercom. "What is it, Alec?"

"He's up ahead, I think," Ross said. "Flying low. Aircraft spotted a plane heading northeast. Must be him. We'll fly straight while he's on an arc, so we should catch up a little."

They flew on, over the water, past the docks and the river heights. Dot was sitting very still now, under orders not to transmit while they crossed the Quebec area. Orange channel was in a freak range, unlikely to be stumbled upon, but the world was full of people turning dials, and it was important not to let it be known that aboard Canso Ring Two, on its legitimate crossing, was a woman anxiously and colloquially calling up some other ship which clearly wasn't answering. A quarter of an hour later, with Orleans Island out of sight behind them, Ross said, "OK, Dot. Start calling."

MILLER, TUNED TO Orange channel, still had not transmitted. For an hour he had wanted to, but something had stayed his hand when he reached for the switch, and after that there had been no incoming signal. Had Alec and Dot turned back?

He checked his navigation. A little town lay due south, a thin scattering of lights on the dark earth. That would be Ste.-Ann-de-Beaupré. Fine: the river approaching; an all-but-deserted highway all the way to Mont Joli. Hazard, maybe, at Mont Joli, but after that no real obstacle. And Alec and Dot gone. Now he wouldn't ever hear her voice again.

Suddenly there was a lump in Miller's throat, equally suddenly a loud signal in his ear: Dot's voice! Mechanically he turned the volume down; half-relieved that Ring Two was there, half-apprehensive at what might happen.

"Are you there, Ernie? Ernie, please answer!"

Much closer now, no doubt about it. Must have transited direct through Quebec.

"Please, Ernie!"

The grief in her voice was almost unbearable. Miller flicked the switch to transmit, and said, "Dot," but the word stuck and he had to clear his throat before it would emerge.

"It's OK, Dot," he said.

She shouted. "Ernie!"

Ross, startled, turned to stare at her. She was smiling, her face lit with relief. He switched to Orange channel to listen.

"Ernie, are you all right?"

A pause, then: "I'm fine."

The words poured from her. "What are you *doing*, Ernie? Where are you *going?* Ernie, why didn't you *answer?*"

A pause, then Ernie spoke, flat-voiced, *very* flat-voiced. "Now listen to me. Don't try to follow. The sooner you leave me alone, the sooner it's over. I repeat, don't try to follow."

Ross cut in sharply. "Listen, Ernie. You've got to get back on the ground or you're *finished.* Return to Kingston now and we'll try to work out some story. But *you must turn back now!* Over."

"Negative. I repeat, do not follow. Over and out."

"*Ernie!*" Dot was shattered.

"Why, Ernie, why in hell?" Ross was angry now. He controlled himself, returning to something closer to formality. "I have to report, Canso Ring One. Ground must be informed. Repeat, ground will now be informed." No response.

Dot turned to him. "Alec, do we have to?"

He didn't answer. As he reached for the radio, Dot said frantically, "Ernie, I love you. If you love me—*please!*"

Ross remained still. He'd give it a few moments more. A full half-minute went by, then Ernie's voice, emotion in its gruffness. "I love you, Dot. Sure I do. But don't follow. Out."

That's final, Ross thought. He radioed: "Canso Ring Two making passage on Code G, following Canso Ring One, requesting clearance at height two zero over St. Lawrence River. This is Captain Ross, commanding."

Quickly Miller switched frequencies and listened. Code G belonged to the project, to the Cansos alone, and all controllers had notification of its priority.

Tensely Miller heard the exchange, then relaxed as he realized what it meant. Alec was protecting him still. Once Alec broke silence, it should have been to report the runaway. But he hadn't. What he'd done was to put them both temporarily in the clear. He clicked back to Orange channel. A moment later Ross's voice sounded in his earphones. "Did you hear, Ernie?"

Miller didn't reply. No more communication, he thought. I've said all there is to say.

"I've gone right down the line for you," Ross said. "I'm in as deep

481

as you are now. I've saved your goddam bacon, now it's your turn to save mine. Get the hell back to Kingston!"

Miller thought bleakly: I'm pulling them all down. This would finish Alec; Dot was in a hell of a state. . . .

And back on the air, too. For the next half-hour her voice was in his ear, pleading, cajoling, asking, endlessly insistent. Miller's hand kept wandering to the transmit/receive switch, and coming away again.

Finally he did it, the movement made almost unconsciously. "Tell Ross to take you home, Dot. This is doing no good."

She was back at once, wanting to know why. "Ernie, listen to me. Please, listen—" and then she broke off, but her fingers must have stayed pressing on transmit and Miller heard her say, "Alec, what's that? *Alec!*" Her voice disappeared on the click of the switch.

Miller blinked. There had been real alarm in her voice. Something wrong? "Come in, Dot, come in." Now it was his turn, he thought savagely. "Come *in*, Dot!"

Nothing in his headphones but a faint crackle of static. Until . . . faintly, the sound dying: "Smoke, Ernie, it's—"

Fire? was that last word "fire"?

"Your signal unclear, I say again your signal unclear. Did you say fire? Come in, please!"

No response.

Miller's brain raced. A trick? Could it be that—Alec putting out a panic message, trying to turn him in that way because he wouldn't turn for anything else?

He kept calling, with increasing anxiety. If Alec's plane was on fire, he had to do *something*. He couldn't just fly on.

His boot hitting the rudder bar, hands moving on the stick, he swung the big flying boat round. Signal strength had been very high; Canso Ring Two couldn't be far away. Miller straightened her, hauled back on the stick and began to fly back along the northern bank of the St. Lawrence; his eyes stared through the side window, searching for movement.

But the movement came beside him. He turned quickly, to see Applejack scrambling into the right-hand seat.

"What the devil are you doing?" Von Galen was yelling.

"Going back," Miller said. Crazy, but he'd forgotten about

482

Applejack. "Aircraft in trouble behind." He stared out of the window, his mind full of thoughts of Alec and Dot in a burning plane.

"No!" Applejack was shouting. "Get back on course!"

Miller ignored him, mentally counting. Ten minutes converging means sixty miles and they hadn't been that far behind, not with the signal strength—

"What aircraft? How do you know? You were told to ignore the radio."

"I got a call. Now, keep quiet, huh?"

But Von Galen couldn't keep quiet. They were on probably the most vital mission of the war, and this idiot was turning back to look for some aircraft in trouble. "I order you. Get back on course."

Miller didn't even turn his head. "Don't order me, sonny. And keep *quiet!*" He was aware of the pistol Von Galen possessed, knew it presented no threat. Von Galen was a pilot, so he said, but he couldn't fly this ship alone, not in a zillion years. He might hold her in the sky, but he'd never navigate her to Newfoundland.

As Von Galen sat fuming at his own helplessness, abruptly realization came. "Ross. That's who it is?"

A nod.

"Ignore him. We cannot *afford* this nonsense."

"He's got my wife aboard. There's a fire."

"Miller, this flight *must* go on!"

"Not till I'm sure. One way or the other."

THERE HAD BEEN a spurt of smoke, a smell of burning and not much more. Ross guessed it was a loose wire or a smashed valve, insulation material singed. He had used the extinguisher and now there was no trace even of heat, let alone fire. But the radios seemed to be out, both of them.

Switching from one frequency to another, he got nothing, not even static. Receiving on Orange channel he heard a dim hum, but that was all; there wasn't even the click as the transmit button engaged. With no radio there was no possibility of further contact with Ernie; furthermore he was now a danger to airborne traffic. He'd have to turn back.

But there remained the chance that Dot's final words had reached

Miller: that the knowledge of fire on Ring Two would bring him back.

A nudge. Dot's hand on his arm. "Alec!" She pointed to his discarded headphones. "It's Ernie!"

He slipped them on quickly, heard Miller's voice ". . . repeat, I have you in sight." So on Orange channel he could still receive! Where *was* Miller? Ross's eyes ranged the sky ahead anxiously, though he knew Ring One would not be there; Ernie would now be above and behind, in the watcher's place.

"Can you receive me?" Miller was asking. "If you can receive me, waggle your wings."

Ross hesitated, trying to work it out. If Ernie'd been watching, he'd know Ring Two was flying straight, steady and low: not an aeroplane in distress. So there was no point in trying to deceive him.

He waggled his wings.

"OK, Alec. I see you. Two questions. First, can you transmit? If not, waggle your wings."

Once more he waggled the Canso's wings.

"What's the fire situation? If it's out, waggle your wings."

Ross turned to Dot. "Get up to the observation bubble. See if you can spot him!"

"Repeat, Ring Two, if the fire is out, waggle your wings."

Once more Canso Ring Two went into the slow rocking motion that tilted first one wingtip, then the other.

Ross knew what was coming now, and it came at once. "So long, Alec," Miller said. "Go home and take Dot with you."

"What do you see, Dot?"

"Nothing." She sounded on the edge of tears. "I can't see a thing. Not a—yes, Alec! Out to the left, a thousand feet above. Oh God, he's swinging away!"

Frantically Ross swung the nose round, staring up towards the area of sky where Miller's plane might appear. Hell, Miller must be making for that cloudbank! He saw Miller then, watched him for perhaps two minutes, as Ring One rose towards the hanging whiteness, then vanished into it.

Miller was smiling a little as he headed into cloud. It was all clear now: they were safe.

He turned to Von Galen. "So let's go get Churchill."

484

BLIND, IN CLOUD, flying on instruments, Ross knew the hopelessness of it. There'd be no more sighting of Canso Ring One, and there had been an unmistakable finality to Ernie's last, "So long." Yet he was damned if he'd give up now.

Ernie wasn't flying for fun. There was a destination and there was a purpose, and though he could not for the moment imagine what either of them might be, something told him it ought to be possible to reason it out. He'd already thrown his career out of the window. No possibility, now, of trying to explain this away as some kind of test training: there were too many hours on the machine, too many infractions.

Ernie's fault, damn him. Ernie'd done it, Ernie had flown on, letting him go in deeper, ruining both of them. *But why?*

Where could the answer lie? He knew Ernie. Dot knew Ernie. Nobody on earth knew him better. He called her back to the right-hand seat. It was a contest now.

She took out a handkerchief, and mopped at her eyes. She looked shrunken, ten years older, despairing.

Ross said, "He's still going along the river. Has to be. We've three hours to Mont Joli, and we're going to use them to think!"

Eleven

Paper. He needed paper. He reached for a pencil and the log book, ripped out two pages and held them out to Dot. "We're going to list everything we know about Ernie, and then look for anything that doesn't square up."

"In his whole life? Alec, that's—"

"We've time, Dot. Get it all down on paper, where we can see it. I don't even know where he was born, for God's sake!"

"Asunción, Paraguay," she said. "It's on the wedding papers. His father was American, a small-time trader."

"Mother?"

"American too, I guess. I don't know. Not even her name. He never mentioned it."

"Write that down," Ross said. "Mother's name unknown. Where'd he go to school?"

486

In twenty minutes they had a biography of sorts. "Quite a few blanks," Ross observed.

"Not after he came to the United States," Dot said, automatically defensive where Ernie was concerned. "We know most of it after, let's see, yes—after 1928."

"When I met him."

"Some ways you know him better than me, Alec. I've only known him since 'thirty-three."

They went over the years of flying, the adventures, the business failures, lengthening the little dossier. Eventually Ross asked quietly, "Would you say he's honest?"

"Oh sure, he's honest."

"Look, we know he's been concealing something. He's been planning this thing, and somebody else is in on it. And he did it without you guessing anything was going on. I'm not being brutal, Dot, but give me a word for that."

Tightly she said, "Deception."

"That's right. Now, have there been other deceptions?"

Her hand lifted from her lap and fell back in a little gesture of defeat. "How'd I *know?* If he's been deceptive, it's worked, that's all."

"His desk—does he keep it locked?"

"Not that I know. Alec, I never go *near* it."

"Mail. Who opens the mail?"

"He opens his. I open mine."

"And when he's away? What happens then—do you open his mail in case there's something important?"

"No. I don't believe in it, Alec. It's called privacy."

He sighed. "He never gets unexplained letters?"

"Look, what happens most days is he gets out of bed and makes me coffee. Picks up the mail and brings it in with the coffee."

"So he *could*—"

"If you want to think that way. I just happen to think he doesn't."

"We have to suspect everything. He's embarked on something that's damned important to him, and there has to be a clue somewhere. Go over that list. Everything. If there's something funny, tell me. Anything."

She shook her head. "Gee, I don't know. Like what?"

"Call it discords. If anything didn't sound right."

"Well . . . you remember the wedding? It was Ernie who wanted it in church, not me. And he's never been to church since. Me, I'd have been happy with a Justice of the Peace, but Ernie wanted a Lutheran church. He even chose the hymns. And he chose the strangest hymn."

"No, Dot, I don't think—"

"You asked, Alec. We had the Wedding March and 'O Perfect Love' and—this is the funny thing—'Glorious things of Thee are spoken'. It's kind of a weird hymn at a wedding."

"Why?"

"It just *is*, Alec."

"OK. Anything else? Did you fight about things?"

"Not really. Well, just little fights, the way people do."

"You weren't exactly cooing last night."

"Oh, I told you. I was angry he hadn't bought a present and I needled him a little. That's all."

"He had a lot on his mind," Ross said. "But he didn't forget. He used the present as an excuse to leave."

"We've been over that. Look, Alec, I can't *think* of any discords. Try it on yourself. Did *you* ever fight?"

"Yes," he said, remembering. "We did, once."

"What about?"

"It was just a brawl. Bunch of us in a bar, must have been 1933, just after Prohibition ended. We got to arguing politics. I recall Ernie said Roosevelt was a Communist. We were all a little drunk."

She said, "He's not the only one who thought *that*. Plenty still do. You fought with Ernie?"

"Bar-room brawl, that's all it was. Dot, go back to that paper. The one with Argentina on it. And the map."

"It was just a sheet of a scrap pad, little eight-by-five pad, you know the kind."

"Picture it in your mind. Better still, try to draw it."

She chewed on the pencil for a moment, then wrote, and handed him the paper.

"Like that? The word written diagonally. The drawing—" He turned the paper in his hand, trying to find something, anything. "Handwriting? Not printed capitals?"

"No, handwriting. I'm pretty sure. Maybe there were numbers." She reached across and pointed with the pencil. "Yes, some numbers, I think. Right there."

"What were they? How many?"

"Like a phone number, maybe. Four, I think."

"Try to think what they were. It could be important!"

"I'm *trying*. Let me think." Her eyes closed tight. "Could it be eleven something? Oh God, I don't know!"

"Write it."

She put in two ones and two questionmarks. "I can't remember. I'm not even sure of the two ones."

Ross stared at the paper, trying to make sense of it. "There was nothing else, you're absolutely sure?"

"That's all there was."

"There's no connection. Argentina and South America, sure, they're connected. But the number? It's six thousand miles' flying time down there. So why two ones? It can't be distance. Too precise for altitude. Time? Eleven something. He'd gone by then."

She said softly, "We've nothing, Alec, have we? *Nothing!*"

"No," Ross said. Orange channel hummed in one headphone but the hum was all there'd been for two hours now. Ernie had meant that "So long" of his.

ON CANSO RING ONE, Miller had spent the last hour giving free flying lessons. Shortly after he'd headed into cloud, Von Galen had said, "Teach me to fly the Canso."

"It's not as easy as it looks, pal," Miller replied. "Not even for a bright, intelligent New German."

"It's a pity you'll never see the New Germany, Zoll. We are a great nation now, the greatest on earth. Proud, strong, victorious! Thanks to the Führer."

"Yeah." Needling Von Galen amused him. It was childish and irrational. They were going to die together, a few hours from now, Von Galen for his Führer, Miller for—what? For the Fatherland, yes. For an oath perhaps, that he'd taken long ago. But more than anything, he thought, it was shame: twenty years of living with cowardice, twenty years' knowledge that his own father wouldn't speak his name. Face it, he thought, *that's* the reason!

489

Beside him, Von Galen changed tack. "What is the time now?"

Miller glanced at his watch. "Midnight, local time."

"So today is the day we die together. Do you not think that as a condemned man I should be granted the traditional last request?"

"And yours is to fly this ship?"

"Yes."

Miller looked at him sardonically: "I know what you're thinking, pal."

"Do you?"

"Sure. You've got a gun. You're thinking that if I chicken out you can shoot me and do the job yourself."

"You 'chickened out' once before."

"I was a kid then," Miller said. "I won't fail now."

"I believe it. But it is *my* duty to establish every necessary precaution. So—you will teach me to fly this aircraft."

Miller shrugged, and thought: Why the hell not? A few hours to live: why worry about it?

"OK, we'll go down, try and get out of the clouds." He made the descent a slow one, and began the lesson one and a half hours short of Mont Joli. Von Galen turned out to be a reasonable pupil: no natural feel, but he had a mechanical competence. Miller showed him how to trim her, turn and bank, apply boost, feather the props. Then he began on the engine start-up sequence.

"Not necessary," Von Galen said.

"You're learning to fly," Miller replied. "Do it right. Anyway, it passes the time."

A quarter of an hour short of Mont Joli, Miller said, "Right, now— we go low. Real low." He took the Canso steadily down as he talked. "There's a military airport at Mont Joli, and it's more than likely they have radar. So we go right down to water level, ten, twelve feet, no more, and we stay down six miles clear of the military base to keep the sound out of their ears. Once we're past, we're OK."

"I understand."

Slowly and carefully Miller brought the Canso down towards the water. The sensations were familiar but, always, disconcerting: at height an aircraft feels as though it is suspended in space. Low, it was like being on a racetrack, with the water flashing below in a blur

490

of speed. Just once he flicked a glance at Von Galen and noted with a certain satisfaction that he was white-faced, gripping the seat arms tightly.

DOT SAID, "Is there any water? I'm thirsty."

"Should be."

"Want some?"

Ross shook his head. He was thinking about Mont Joli, whether to go down there and put out the alarm. It was what he ought to do. But what would happen if he did—what aircraft did they have there, and what chance would they have of locating Ernie? There was no visibility to speak of; it was the middle of the night, and once Ernie was clear of Mont Joli, he'd be out in the great wide spaces around the Gaspé Peninsula. The RCAF boys would have no more chance than he had. Less even.

Dot came back. "I've been thinking. Does Argentina have an air force? Look, Alec, he's going there with the Canso and all this secret stuff. Do they want what's aboard?"

"The sub-detection equipment? Why would they want that? They're not in the war. All South America's neutral." Ross went back to his own thoughts. We're approaching Mont Joli, and it's decision time, he told himself. If I go blinding ahead, they're going to pick me up, maybe scramble somebody to inspect, perhaps require me to land. Even though his clearance signal *had* gone down the line. Then there'd be long explanations and lost time. But then if he flew by he'd still be chasing Ernie into the wide blue yonder, and with even less idea where to go.

Dot said suddenly, "Alec!"

Something in her voice made him turn. "What?"

"Who'd want the anti-submarine detector? Face it, Alec! Who?"

He frowned. "Germany? That's crazy, Dot!"

"Give me one other explanation."

"Hold it!" Ross tried to grapple with the elements spinning in his mind: Ernie taking it to the Germans—*why?* No, he'd never—And what about Mont Joli? Go in there and say, "It looks as though Ernie Miller's delivering secret equipment to the Germans!" Well, they might believe him but they'd take convincing, and by then Ernie would be long gone. *If only he could radio!*

491

Ross made his decision, and pushed the stick forward.

"What are you doing?"

"I'm going to try to slip past Mont Joli," Ross said. "It may be what Ernie's doing. Probably is. So for God's sake keep your eyes open!" He levelled her off at a hundred feet, and inched lower, coming close to the northern shore.

MILLER HAD SPOTTED the mouth of the Saguenay River minutes earlier, and the lights of Tadoussac scattered on the dark shore. *Careful now!*

He said to Von Galen: "Watch for some mountains over there." Once he'd got them located . . .

"There are lights."

Miller nodded. That would be Rimouski.

"Yes, I see mountains!"

"Let me look." Hell of a thing at this height, to look away, but he risked a glance. Dim dark shapes along the horizon, with the lights up ahead.

The water tore past beneath them. Miller estimated he must be six or seven miles out of Mont Joli. Just a few minutes more. Then he could make the turn. Christ, he was low; once or twice he had fancied he'd heard the water kissing the hull, but maybe it was nerves or imagination. If he touched hard at this speed he'd cartwheel, flying boat or no flying boat. His hands were sweating on the wheel, gripping too tightly. He tried to relax as the minutes ground by.

"See the boat?" Von Galen yelled.

Oh God, he hadn't! Miller hauled back on the stick, praying, and skimmed just over it. Did I give them the kind of fright they gave me? *Concentrate!*

They must be due east of Mont Joli now. That hop over the fishing boat had taken him up to sixty, even seventy feet; had he shown up on their screens? Still, the river was widening with every mile. He gave it five more minutes, then began a slow, wide, eastward curve: he wanted a point between Mont Joli and Matane, and must judge it perfectly. Too soon and Mont Joli would spot them, if they hadn't done so already; too late and there'd be a bright flash on the hillside and it would all be over.

492

Miller corrected course again, the water still racing beneath, and the rising ground, just barely visible, tearing towards them. Some time in the next few minutes, Mr. Applejack, you're going to be looking for clean pants, he thought. He held it as late as he dared, increasing revs and boost, then hauled back on the controls. Twelve hundred feet, that was the height of the hill. God!

He watched the land rear as the Canso grabbed for height. . . .

Twelve

Ross stared anxiously ahead. He'd brought Ring Two down so low it was almost skimming the river surface. At this height the chance of spotting Miller in Ring One was infinitesimal. If he went high the chance would improve, but Mont Joli would have him.

"If you see the smallest movement, Dot, *tell me!*"

God, but this was dangerous! How soon before he dared lift the ship? Twenty-five or thirty miles—and by then Ernie could have turned anywhere.

"Watch out—a boat!" Dot said sharply.

But he'd seen it just in time to steer away.

"Come in, Ernie!" He tried to will Miller to speak, repeating the words over and over in his brain, trying to penetrate a mind that had already signed off.

And still only the hum in his ear.

Beside him, Dot sat rigid in her seat. Experienced flier though she was, this hurtling passage over water in the dark at extremely low level was wildly frightening. There was no margin: a patch of particularly cold water affecting the air above it, a slip of a hand, an engine faltering: any of them could drop the Canso suddenly and she knew that to hit water at speed was like hitting concrete. Through her headphones she could hear Ross humming softly to himself. His face was almost fierce with concentration, yet his body seemed relaxed. His hand lifted briefly. A few lights away to their right. "Matane," he said, and hauled back on the stick. "I'm going up to five thousand. For God's sake keep looking. If we don't see him now . . ." The sentence remained unfinished.

"What time is it?"

He calculated. "Three thirty-two local time."

Six hours, she thought, since Ernie'd taken off. Nearly seven since she'd last seen him, rising from the table. Oh God, why had he done it? And why choose her birthday? He'd *used* her birthday. She felt tears welling in her eyes and tried to control them.

"What made you think about Germany?" Ross said.

"I don't know. It just came into my head."

"It doesn't make any sense."

"No," Dot said, and added, hating herself, "but maybe we'd better look at it. What could he get out of it? Money?"

"He could, I suppose. But he'd be finished—with you, with America—and with flying."

"Even in Argentina?" she asked.

Ross thought about it. "I don't know. Maybe word wouldn't reach, or he's got things fixed. Maybe Argentina's pro-German."

"So he takes the Canso down there and it's handed over to the Germans. Does that make any kind of sense?"

"For God's sake, Dot, why'd he do that? Ernie's an American."

She felt her heart thud. That thing he'd been humming. That tune—it was the hymn. "Alec!"

"Mm?"

"That hymn 'Glorious things of Thee are spoken'. You've been humming it. It's *Deutschland über Alles* with different words!" Her stomach felt leaden, as though the bottom of it was sinking away.

"Dot, that's crazy!"

"Where's that list we made—now, Alec, what have we got here? Now, listen. He's born in Asunción, Paraguay. *Not* in the United States. He insists on that hymn, which just *happens* also to be the German national anthem, at our wedding. Then—yes, look! OK, it's a little thing, but he called Roosevelt a Communist."

She was staring at him, waiting for his reaction. He said, "That's not evidence, Dot."

"It's evidence all right," she said. "It's not much, but it all hangs together. You know he speaks German?"

"Ernie? I never heard him."

"I did. In Chicago one time we met some folks in a hotel. They were German. Ernie talked to them. He said he learned it when he was a kid, in Paraguay."

"Maybe he did."

"Oh, Alec, I'm his *wife!* I'm the one should be saying it's not possible! Stop resisting. He's stolen a hundred thousand dollars' worth of plane, with secret stuff aboard, and it looks like he's not coming back. Alec, for God's sake! You don't want to believe it and neither do I, but what if he's pro-German, taking that plane somewhere. Maybe he's got some kind of date with a ship—"

"An Argentine ship?"

"Any kind of a ship. He puts the Canso down on the water and they strip the equipment out. What's so impossible about that?"

"Nothing," Ross said.

"OK, Alec. What the hell do we do now?"

He sat for long moments with a face like stone. Then he said, "We have a little calculating to do."

"You calculate," she said. "Me, I have to cry." Her world was crashing; Ernie, her own husband, not just a thief, but a traitor.

MILLER WAS WATCHING the altimeter and the approaching hill, eyes flicking from one to the other. If he'd left the ascent too late there was nothing he could do now. In a couple of minutes the Canso would be either floating over the hilltop, then dropping into the Matapedia Valley, or it would be burning nicely on the slope.

He found himself grinning, jaw clenched, but grinning all the same, taking a chance for one final time and revelling in it. He said, "Enjoying your flight, sir?"

Von Galen plainly wasn't. An arm had risen involuntarily to protect his face, and his eyes were wide and staring.

"Come on, baby. You have a date with a very important man," he told the straining, vibrating Canso as she roared for height, with her engines at full throttle.

And she came on beautifully, and abruptly they were over the crest; he felt a sudden impulse to radio Alec and invite him to come and watch what happened next. Alec, if he'd continued along the river, would still be in range. He flattened the impulse and put the Canso's nose down towards the Matapedia Valley.

"That was reckless," Von Galen said harshly.

"But necessary." Miller grinned at him. "And now we're all clear ahead. Hey, did you remember to get a flask of coffee?"

CALCULATE. ROSS had spoken the word, demanding it of himself, but what was there to calculate? Whichever way he looked at it, he could still see no reason for Miller's behaviour. Ernie was American; his life was in America. So how could he have the loyalty to Germany that an action like this demanded?

Throughout the months of the project, Ernie had been an exemplary pilot, giving it everything he'd got. Was that so he could steal the Canso and its equipment at the end? It couldn't be; they weren't at the end, the anti-sub-detection equipment was not yet at optimum performance. So why hadn't Ernie waited, taken it to the Germans when all the bugs had finally been ironed out?

If it wasn't the equipment the Germans wanted, there might be something else, an entirely different imperative. What was left? A mission tied to a date. And the date was August tenth. Sunday, August tenth, nineteen forty-one.

Where? What? Why?

He and Dot sat a mere couple of feet apart: two baffled minds focusing on one man, examining him from different viewpoints. Ross knew Miller as one of his own kind: a professional pilot wedded to the air, whose thought processes and responses were essentially similar to his own. For Dot Miller he was the man whose life she shared. She thought of Miller in terms of emotional reaction, and she was looking now for something that could have pitchforked Ernie into an event as grave and as incomprehensible as this.

She'd loved Ernie more than he loved her. From the beginning she'd always known that: Ernie had two powerful emotional ties in his life, job and wife, and often the job's hold seemed the stronger. She'd never tried to fight it.

But the second place she had in his life had always been a strong one. Ernie was always glad to come home, happy to remain there until the next trip. He'd always treated her well and been considerate. He'd have liked to have children, so he said, and so would she, but children hadn't come along.

Ernie wasn't interested in politics. Such reading as he did was aviation magazines and pilots' memoirs. He'd always loved talking about flying, and appreciated having a wife who knew enough to discuss it with him. He'd theorized a lot about the *blitzkrieg*, admiring the German dedication to supremacy in the air. In her

496

mind's eye she could see him now, see the enthusiasm in the broad lines of his face as he said, "This war's all about aeroplanes, and only the Germans understand it. America doesn't. The British only half."

How long ago was that? Only a few weeks.

She'd said, "What about those British fighter pilots? And their navy? That was why Hitler didn't invade."

"Wait," he'd said. "You'll see. Those ships are vulnerable from the air. Everything is. It's just a matter of the right plane in the right place at the right time. A couple of guys in a bomber could send a thousand in a battleship clear to the bottom. With planes you can think big, Dot!"

With planes you can think big.

Suddenly urgent, she said, "Something big, Alec!"

"What?"

"Something really big. I've been thinking about it. It'll be something only a plane can do. But big!"

"I don't see—"

She cut him off. "I know it. Don't ask me how, but I do. He's not just stealing a plane." She stared at Ross, conviction in her face. "If it's Germany. If it's the war . . . Alec, what *is* going on? I don't read the papers, you do. Is there something one plane could do—one man in one plane?"

"Hell, I don't know. The war's in Europe. Three thousand miles away! He might get to Europe, but that's all. He hasn't got bombs, he couldn't attack."

"No." She paused. "Alec, that figure, the one he wrote. Eleven something. Suppose, just suppose, it's miles. Or maybe it's a time. Just work it out. Both ways. Distance and time."

He said, "Navigator's table is back there. Go ahead."

She switched on the light, got out the charts and the instrument case. She placed the point of the compass on the chart at Kingston and drew in a circle at a range of eleven hundred miles. Then another at twelve. Somewhere between those two. . . .

The first line passed through the far north of Quebec, ran through Labrador, over the Gulf of St. Lawrence, then down through Newfoundland to arc out over the Atlantic, until it met the eastern coastline of the United States far to the south.

She followed the track of the second line: the same thing, a hundred miles further on. The land between the lines consisted of uninhabited territory, almost all of it. Dot Miller stared at the chart. It showed air routes, but not too many places and the area was unfamiliar to her. She felt achingly near to something that was just beyond her comprehension. Ernie must have measured distances on an identical chart. Where-to-where, though? Kingston to *somewhere*.

Somewhere. A place. But then, it needn't be a place, not if it were a rendezvous at sea. OK, try it with time.

She put on the headphones. "Alec, where will we be at eleven local time, if we keep going?"

"Labrador. Dot, he's not going into Labrador!"

"Where else?"

"Depends on the course we take. Way out beyond Cape Breton, out over the water. We could be over Newfoundland. Down through New Brunswick we could hit Bar Harbour, Maine, even Boston."

Time and distance roughly the same, Dot thought, and no indication of which the figure referred to. She settled herself in the seat. She wasn't going to move until she knew. She didn't believe Ernie could hide this from her. Somewhere she'd find something . . .

MILLER LOOKED AT his watch, then rubbed his eyes and shook his head a little. The movement caught Von Galen's eye. "Course and speed are correct?" Von Galen asked.

"On the button. Just coming up on Campbellton. ETA at four fifty and that's when we're going to hit it."

"Give me the times for the remainder of the trip."

"Well, let's see." Miller consulted his schedule. "I estimate arrival at Sydney, Nova Scotia, at seven forty-five local time, though we don't go over, we bypass to the north. In a few minutes we cut over from the Matapedia Valley and fly down the river and out over Chaleur Bay. From then on we're over water all the way."

"You're tired," Von Galen said, almost accusingly.

"Don't worry—I'm not going to fall asleep. You?"

"Also." To Miller's surprise, he added, "And a little bored."

"Yeah? I'm enjoying this trip. Won't be making any more, might as well enjoy this one."

"You have things to interest you. I have not."

"No? Well, I can find you something. Let's get the fuel tanks in balance. Up you go."

Miller fussed, watching the gauges, getting it exactly right. There was no point, of course: Canso could get there without moving any more gas around, but, hell, it kept Applejack busy. At Campbellton he swung east. Miller said, "Be daylight soon. More to see."

"The last look."

"Yeah."

"It's very strange," Von Galen said, "to be . . . so calm. We should be excited, exhilarated, full of glory!"

"That's flying," Miller said. "Long hours of boredom, punctuated by moments of sheer terror. You have one of those coming up."

"How will you feel?"

"I have no idea," Miller said. It was true, the thing was too big to imagine.

"You have experience. . . . Do you remember how you felt—before?"

"Delicately put," Miller said. "I remember very well. They came at me and I panicked. I was very young, inexperienced and overwhelmed. Worried it'll happen again?"

"Of course," Von Galen said coolly. "And if it does, I shall know what to do. As you know."

"Just tell me," Miller said, "what makes you so damn sure *you* won't crack?"

"It would disgrace the Führer."

"Yeah. There's one other thing," Miller said. "Suppose these people—Churchill, Roosevelt—are not there at the other end."

"We discussed this. You would land somewhere. You have malfunctioning instruments and concussion. You can remember nothing, not the flight, nor the reason."

"It won't wash."

"It won't have to," Von Galen said, "because they are there. And we are going to a glorious death for Germany and the Führer!"

Miller looked again at his watch and stifled a yawn. He, too, was a little bored, and found himself looking forward to dawn: not long now, and it would be good to come out of the night into daylight. For a while. Before he went into the night again.

Thirteen

Ross was trying to think of something big, but his brain seemed tired. That was one of the traps of the time before dawn: things seemed to shut down inside his head.

As he flew further into the widening funnel mouth of the St. Lawrence, he watched the light come, dim and grey at first, then brightening. His face felt stiff, his body lethargic. He made himself think.

Something big? The Germans were still driving into Russia; U-boats seemed to be winning in the Atlantic. The detector might help a little there. Maybe Ernie *was* taking it to the Germans, even though Dot said he wasn't, out of some female instinct or another. What else? What had been in the news last night? Details of the German advance. Places with Russian names he didn't know.

There'd been something, too, about FDR. What—yes, that's right: he'd left Washington and they all wondered where he'd gone. Fishing, probably. Hold it, though . . . Ross sat up suddenly. He tried to focus his memory; there'd been speculation that he might be meeting Churchill, and if he recalled it right, Berlin radio had said so, saying it wouldn't affect the course of the war.

It couldn't be that—could it?

"Dot," he said, "if you're looking for something big . . ."

"Tell me," her voice said in his ear.

"Something on the radio news last night. Roosevelt may be meeting Churchill."

She blinked. *"May* be? You mean *now?"*

"That's the theory, but it's all speculation. FDR's disappeared from view. Nobody knows where he is."

She said harshly, "Nobody knows where Ernie is, either!" Then closed her eyes tightly, struggling to find sense somewhere in all the chaos. But she couldn't. When she opened them, the chart came into focus, but her mind was elsewhere.

"Alec, where could Roosevelt meet Churchill?"

"Any place in the world. Except—"

"Except Argentina," she said. She returned to the co-pilot's seat, the chart in her hand. "What's that mean, Alec?"

He glanced at it. "United States base."

"But isn't Newfoundland part of Canada?" she asked.

"It's a British colony, I think. The British handed over a few places in exchange for—" His voice died away. "Holy *God!* That place—you know what its name is?"

Dot Miller shook her head.

"It's Argentia." He spelled it for her. "Put the 'n' in and you've got Argentina! We *know* where he's going, Dot!"

Her first response was apologetic, shock forcing it from her. "I never heard of it. It looked like Argentina on the pad."

"Don't worry. We have it now. Measure off the distance."

She went back to the navigator's table. "It's way short of eleven hundred," she reported.

"Maybe you misread."

"I think it was two ones. I'm almost sure."

When she was back in the seat, Ross had thought of the answer. "He's flying another route."

"Why?"

"Several possibilities; most of them involve staying clear of pursuit. Hold the chart for me. Now look, he knows there's an important RCAF station at Mont Joli, and he had to get there without being challenged. So he'd plan to slip away first chance he could."

"Where would he go?"

Ross said thoughtfully, "There's a trick route the bootleggers used, running booze into Maine. Right there. You fly over the hill and drop down into the valley." Ross's finger traced the path. "The smugglers turned over New Brunswick into Maine. Ernie'd go the other way."

"It adds distance."

"Yes, it does. Around a hundred miles or a little more."

"Eleven hundred plus."

"That's right! And from here he's—yes, by the time it's light he's over water, all the way."

Silence now between them as the questions rose in their tired minds. If Ernie Miller was going to Argentia, what was his purpose? Was Roosevelt really there? Was Churchill?

Ross was trying to drag more of that broadcast out of his memory;

he'd only half-listened, his attention at the time on changing for dinner with Dot and Ernie, and the words which had been unimportant then were vital now.

Dot said, "How would Ernie know, Alec?"

"That news broadcast. They quoted German radio." He struggled to recall it. "German radio said FDR was going to meet Churchill. That's all. The big question was where FDR had gone."

"I don't see it, Alec, I really don't. Ernie hears the broadcast and steals the Canso and sets off for Argentia. That's crazy."

Ross picked the hole at once. "Where did German radio get it?"

She blinked. "I don't follow—"

"I mean *they* had a source. If Ernie's going there, he must have heard it from the *same* source."

"Oh God. If the Germans told Ernie, then he's . . . he really *is*, Alec. He's flying for them!"

Ross nodded grimly. "We have to do something now. Dot, check the distance to Argentia and to North Sydney, Nova Scotia. There's a flying-boat base there. They can radio ahead."

Back at the table she used the dividers again, calculating twice to be sure. "Four hundred to Argentia, two-eighty to North Sydney. It's forty minutes' difference, Alec, that's all. Have we that much in hand?"

No knowing, Ross thought. Ernie had started out with fifty or sixty miles' advantage, then lost it. But he himself had lost time too, flying anything but a direct route to Argentia. There was two and a half hours' flying time to Argentia now, near enough. He checked his watch. Over Anticosti Island the time zone changed. It was seven forty-five now, Atlantic Standard Time.

He said, "Argentia around ten fifteen."

"I wonder," he heard her say, "what time Ernie's planned to arrive?"

MILLER WAS LOOKING at his watch too, going over the schedule again, making an almost identical calculation.

Von Galen watched him check. "Well?"

"We're a little ahead of schedule. Tail winds pushing us along."

"You must slow down. We cannot afford to be early."

"Relax," Miller said. "It's done."

"Good. There will be only one chance, remember that."

"I know it. Listen, you didn't tell me just how you worked this thing, how it started out."

"It took a long time."

Miller knew the essence of it, but the detail surprised him. Von Galen wasn't a guy he'd choose to spend a lot of time with, but whatever else he might be, he was unusually intelligent. The ingenuity of the forecasting was breathtaking.

There was a special kind of justice, too, in the Sunday part of it. Miller distrusted politicians, and always had. There'd been a congressman once, up for re-election, who'd shaken Miller the voter's hand and said straight out that a vote for him was a vote for God! Church twice every Sunday and his snout as deep in the trough as he could push it.

Was Churchill a religious man? Was Roosevelt? He doubted it. But Applejack had them weighed up; he'd calculated their imperatives: it was the one time they'd be sure to be together, and out in the open.

"Brilliant," he said.

"A true privilege," Von Galen replied. "Think of the soldier who dies for a yard of ground. Then think of our destiny!"

Destiny. Valhalla.

Two hours to go.

ON CANSO RING TWO another mystery had been cleared up. Dot, folding the big chart in limited space, had turned it sideways, and realized that the rough shape Ernie had drawn which she'd thought was a map of South America could as easily be a sketch of Newfoundland.

The other mysteries were not, however, easy of solution. What would Ernie do when he got to Argentia? Was Sunday significant?

Ross, wide awake and ashamed of himself, said, "Let's go over it again, Dot. We have a scenario here. Churchill and Roosevelt meeting at Argentia. The Germans know it, but nobody else does. Nobody except Ernie and whoever's with him. But *he* does know. So he takes the Canso, and he flies it to Argentia. What in hell he's going to do when he gets there, I can't imagine. It's not a bomber, there are no bomb racks, no bombs, not even machineguns. But there's a plan, there has to be! He's going to be there right about the time we are. Ten fifteen. There are three things he can do, and none of them make sense. He can fly around, he can fly past, or he can land. What's he going to do, for God's sake?"

They crossed the coast somewhere south of Corner Brook with the Canso on an east-southeast heading. Two hundred and twenty-five miles to go: one and a quarter hours to find an answer. Ross began to study the chart. Argentia lay well inside a huge inlet called Placentia Bay. If Miller had flown down the Matapedia Valley and headed out via North Sydney, over the ocean, he'd come in from a little south of west. Given that Miller was behaving like a thief in the night, he'd stay low, out over the water, as long as he could.

"Dot, listen," Ross exclaimed suddenly. "Argentia will be ready with heavy defences. They'll know about the German broadcast."

"I hadn't thought—"

"What's more," he said, "anywhere Winston Churchill goes will be guarded like Fort Knox. We should have gone into North Sydney!"

"Why? I don't see why. We can land—"

"They won't let us *near*, Dot! We've no radio. If there's an air patrol we can't reply to a challenge, and they'll take us for an intruder. They'll shoot first and wonder about it a long time later."

Dot's eyes were wide. "But Alec, they'll recognize the Canso. It's not a German plane."

"It's a missing plane, don't you see! One of two missing planes. Back at Kingston they'll have put out an alert." Ross dug at his tired eyes with finger and thumb. They didn't even *know* if Churchill and Roosevelt were in Argentia. He said, "We've got to find out if they're there, and the only way is to go and look."

"But they'd shoot us down. You said so."

"Give me the chart. Let's have a good look at the place."

FIFTY MILES to the south, Canso Ring One was in cloud. Miller and Von Galen were silent now in their seats, each alone with the knowledge that they had entered the last hour of their lives. Very soon it would be time to drop down through the overcast to sea level and begin the long run in.

Miller had wondered how he'd feel. Now he knew: hands and feet felt cold and there was a sensation as though a large cold rock filled his chest and stomach. Yet he felt still and steady, surprisingly unafraid. There was a job to be done, and he made a single demand of himself: that it be done well. He wanted only to fly this mission as it should be flown, and finally show to his father and his sister that their long contempt was baseless.

A push forward with his hands, the nose tilted down, and Miller looked watchfully through the water-dotted glass, waiting to sight the sea. The last tendrils of hanging vapour vanished as the altimeter registered two thousand eight hundred feet.

"Give me the chart." He folded it, laid it across his knees, re-checked it. Very likely a long straight run to the target, long enough for counter-attack. He said, "Tell me again."

"Here." Von Galen's finger stabbed at the map. "It is the best anchorage in Newfoundland. It is secure from all wind directions. That is why they're bound to use it."

Slowly the long shape of the Burin Peninsula began to rise out of the sea, a faint, low line at first, growing thicker. There were several hills, Hare Hill the highest; thirteen hundred feet to hide behind before he burst out to attack. He couldn't distinguish it yet. But it was there. And soon. . . .

Hare Hill loomed towards Canso Ring Two. Ross, too, had come low. The only way for him to discover whether Placentia Bay had temporarily turned into one of the most important places on earth was to use his eyes.

He intended now to approach from behind the sheltering high ground, to climb sharply over the hilltop and then, as rapidly as he could, to scan the waters of the bay.

He increased boost, waited, then pulled back on the controls, lifting the throbbing Canso into her climb. Five hundred, six . . . seven . . . and the land was rising sharply. Eight.

"Look!" Dot cried, pointing.

To his right, between the hills, he saw the long, low shape of a warship: a destroyer, he thought, out on the wide mouth of the bay. One thousand—and the hilltop stark now against a grey sky. Moments to wait. . . .

The panorama of the bay was far bigger than he'd imagined: a great sweep of water and islands. His eyes ranged systematically and anxiously over it, starting in the north, sweeping southward. Ships! A *hell* of a lot of ships!

He flung the Canso round, returning to shelter on the safe side of the hill, yelling, "How many did you count?"

"I got to thirteen, Alec. You saw the big ones?"

"I saw."

"There were planes, too, out towards the sea. Flying boats."

What the hell to do now? Ross tried to work something out. Go back over the hill, perhaps. Maybe drop down on the water fast and taxi across. But the taxi would take forever, even with the Canso up on the step, skimming.

"*Alec!*" It was almost a scream. Dot pointed, her hand shaking.

A plane, low over the water, was coming towards them. He took in the characteristics; high wing, twin engines, the gleam of the ring. His stomach sank. It was Ernie.

Ross kicked at the rudder bar, tipped the Canso round in as tight a turn as it could handle and headed directly for Ring One. Too late for anything else now. Somehow Ernie must be headed off.

MILLER, PRETERNATURALLY alert, ready for surprise developments, had not been prepared for this one. In the instant of sighting, his jaw dropped in astonishment. Ross here! And with Dot aboard! He watched the plane's shape drifting down the side of the hill, making a quick turn, now heading straight for him.

Miller's hand flicked the transmit switch and he shouted, "Canso Ring Two. Urgent, Alec. Get out of here. You'll get Dot killed! Do you hear me . . ."

Von Galen, too, had by now seen the Canso, but it had taken him a vital second or two longer to identify it as Ring Two. But if his first reaction had been slow, his second was not.

As Von Galen's left hand grabbed at the stick, his right was already dragging the pistol from his pocket. It snagged briefly, but he ripped it clear, brought it round, and fired directly at Miller's head. The shot smashed Miller across the seat, to hang grotesquely in his harness. Von Galen let the pistol fall, then seized the controls with a sudden fierce delight. It was, after all, *his* plan. It was fitting that he, Baldur Von Galen, should strike the Führer's enemies down!

THEY HAD HEARD the frantic message clearly; had heard, too, the shot that ended it: the sharp crack that cut off Miller's voice. Ring One staggered briefly, then straightened.

"That was a shot!" Dot's voice rose wildly. "Alec! Ernie's been shot! *Oh God!*"

Ross didn't reply but swung round in another turn, across Ring One's approach track. There was no question now in his mind that this was an attack. What kind he didn't know and couldn't guess.

Ring One had gone by him; the warning pass in front had not diverted the flying boat a single inch from its course. Ross again flung Ring Two round. He must catch up and then overtake, get between Ring One and the target. The hill was so damn close. Would there be space? He watched Ring One begin to lift. . . .

VON GALEN hauled the handles back, hand reaching up for the throttle levers. The close pass of the other plane had shaken him; but it was just a warning pass—it would not divert him. Now, glancing left and right, Von Galen could see no sign of the other plane. It must be well behind now. He pushed the throttles right forward, then his heart lurched as he felt the momentary sag. Boost *first*, Miller had said. Damn! His hands moved frantically, bringing in boost, watching the pressure climb; the wait seemed endless.

The Canso lurched awkwardly for a moment but then lifted towards the point ahead where the hilltops rose from its ridge. And just ahead lay the two great enemies! If he was right, and he no longer questioned it, the two men would be attending Sunday morning service at sea. Together. On deck. In the same ship.

Von Galen's watch showed eleven o'clock—the timing perfect.

Ross was overhauling now. Ring One had a steeper angle of climb, therefore Ross had the greater torward speed. What *kind* of attack was intended, he wondered. Whatever kind, there was no chance of getting away with it. The whole thing was suicidal and Ernie must have known it. *Suicidal!* The word burned into his brain. No bomb racks, no bombs . . . but it wouldn't matter, *not if the Canso was loaded with explosive!*

Ross swallowed. In his mind he could now visualize the attack: the flat-out dash across the bay, the direct crash into one of the ships. Somehow the man flying now must know which ship.

507

He was closing over Ring One, his nose no more than fifteen feet above her tailplane as they cleared the tip of Hare Hill. Was there time to ride forward over Ring One, then drop—flatten it into the hilltop?

"Dot," he said, and turned his head. She looked back at him out of eyes shiny with tears. He took in the sharp irony of the party dress, the necklet he'd given her glowing gold at her throat. "There's no other way."

She said simply, "No," and turned her head away.

Ross looked down. "Here we go," he muttered, pushing at the control column, dropping Ring Two suddenly, his body tense for the impact.

But no impact came. Ring One must have dropped, too, and at the same moment. He pushed the nose down harder. If he didn't get him now . . .

He banked sharply, hoping for a sight . . . and felt a sudden, harsh juddering rack the Canso. He glanced quickly sideways. The port propeller had stopped altogether, its blades bent, and the Canso was rearing to starboard. What in *hell?*

"Alec, look!" Dot was half-standing, craning forward.

He couldn't look; he was too busy wrestling with the controls, striving to hold the Canso straight, to keep his wingtip out of the goddamned trees. "Not *now!*" he said savagely.

"But you did it, Alec. At least I think you did."

"Where?" he said, as the Canso more or less straightened up.

She pointed. Below to his left Canso Ring One was in a long dive towards the water. "I—only got a glance, but I think the prop chopped his rudder and right elevator. That's what—" She stopped. Clearly the dive was now out of control; in a moment, Ring One was going in, and going hard . . .

Beside him, Dot softly spoke Ernie's name.

Fourteen

From his look-out post high over the superstructure of the battleship *Prince of Wales*, Leading Seaman Arthur Barnes was shamelessly using his binoculars to watch the scene on deck. What a gathering of bigwigs it was! He could actually see Churchill, glasses on the tip of his nose, hymn book in hand. And there was Roosevelt, right there beside him, and all the ministers and chiefs of staff, British and American: must be enough gold braid to dress *Prince of Wales* overall.

He'd thought Roosevelt was crippled, so it had been a surprise to hear the President was coming aboard for morning service. A bosun's chair was a funny business if you didn't have control of your limbs, and not very dignified, either, for the President of the United States.

But God, if Roosevelt didn't have much in the way of legs, he certainly had plenty of guts. Barnes had watched a few minutes earlier as an American destroyer had come slowly round *Prince of Wales*'s bow, with the President on her bridge.

When she'd secured alongside, a gangway had been thrown across and he'd expected Roosevelt to be carried over, but instead the President had stood up and put his hand on the arm of a young officer—who, to Barnes's sharp eyes, looked uncannily like him— and very slowly he'd walked across the gangway. He'd come over dead upright, step by awkward step, with Churchill and the skipper waiting to greet him with the British Chiefs of Staff.

Then the band had played the anthems, and they'd walked very slowly along the quarterdeck to the chairs set out facing the guns. When Roosevelt sat down to face the two chaplains, you could see he was bloody pleased with himself. Pleased as Punch he looked!

The words of a prayer floated up to Leading Seaman Barnes's high perch. They were praying for the invaded countries, talking about the day of deliverance. Well, if this business here was anything to go by, and America really was coming into the war, that day would come a bit faster.

I'm dying for a fag, Barnes thought. And nobody's looking, not with that lot to look at. He fished the packet of Woodbines from inside his tunic, lit the cigarette and inhaled.

By gum, that was good! Yes, it was a good day all round, this one. His eyes swung, more idly than a look-out's should, round the horizon, and for a moment he thought he saw a bright flash, up above the hills far over there in the distance. Probably a plane shoving out a Verey light for some reason. Long way off, anyway. . . .

IT WAS THE purest chance that Barnes saw the explosion, and it was seen by no one else in the entire fleet, for the very natural reason that all eyes were on *Prince of Wales*.

But one other man was looking and he was not a part of any ship's company. For Joseph Patrick O'Hara, standing alone on a clifftop near the appropriately named Patrick's Harbour, it had been a morning of desperate anxiety. He'd found difficulty getting there at all, but he'd managed it on a borrowed motorcycle, riding through the night round the coast road from St. John's.

Now he did not watch the ships, which he could not see. He stood waiting for an aircraft to appear. He had young eyes, and high-quality lenses, and he glimpsed first what looked like two aircraft at the distant hilltop. Then he saw a bright flash in the water at the foot of Hare Hill.

Finally he saw a flying boat float down to a landing on the water and begin to taxi in the direction of a patrol boat which was already tearing towards it. . . .

Duncan Kyle

Duncan Kyle was born in Bradford and worked as a journalist until the publication in 1970 of his first novel, *A Cage of Ice*. The book was an instant success and it gave him the time and opportunity to fulfil his long-held ambition—to become a full-time novelist.

He aims to write a suspense thriller a year, a target he has so far achieved with considerable success. The idea for *Stalking Point* came to him while reading the memoirs of playwright Robert Sherwood, who worked as a personal secretary to Franklin D. Roosevelt during the Second World War. Mr. Kyle was intrigued by Sherwood's account of the American president's ruse to keep his meeting with Churchill, which had been arranged to discuss America's entry into the war, a secret from the world's press. As Roosevelt prepared for his journey to St. John's in Newfoundland, a man groomed to look exactly like FDR was sailing merrily along the Cape Cod Canal in the president's yacht, drawing the world's attention away from a far more important voyage. In Duncan Kyle's eyes this was "a marvellous piece of simple deception"—and an idea that he wanted to develop.

Mr. Kyle makes a point of always visiting the unusual locations described in his books, so before he started writing *Stalking Point* he took a trip to St. John's. While he was on that side of the Atlantic he wanted also to take a close look at a Canso seaplane. They are, naturally, very rare these days, and his contacts in aviation insurance had told him there were a couple in northwest Canada. Imagine his amazement, then, on arrival in St. John's when he saw six Cansos lined up on the tarmac. They are in service as water bombers for fire fighting! Duncan Kyle is deeply indebted to the kind pilot who flew him hundreds of miles in one of those Cansos, helping him to plot his hero's route across the vast Great Lakes territory.

Duncan Kyle lives in Suffolk with his Scottish wife and three children. Most of his days are taken up with reading, researching and writing—his next novel is set in Norway in World War II—but he still finds time to enjoy his other interests of travel and sport, and a Yorkshireman's fanaticism for cricket.

ALONE AGAINST THE ATLANTIC. Original full-length version © 1981 by Gerald F. Spiess and Marlin Bree. US condensed version © The Reader's Digest Association Inc. 1982. British condensed version © The Reader's Digest Association Limited 1982.

GILDED SPLENDOUR. Original full-length version © 1982 by Rosalind Laker. US condensed version © The Reader's Digest Association Inc. 1982. British condensed version © The Reader's Digest Association Limited 1982.

THE DAM. Original full-length version © 1981 by Robert Byrne. US condensed version © The Reader's Digest Association Inc. 1981. British condensed version © The Reader's Digest Association Limited 1982.

STALKING POINT. Original full-length version © 1981 by Duncan Kyle. British condensed version © The Reader's Digest Association Limited 1982.

PICTURE CREDITS: ALONE AGAINST THE ATLANTIC: Page 21 (top): Gerry Spiess; (bottom): Sally Spiess. Page 41 (top): courtesy of John H. Sheally II; (bottom): Gerry Spiess. Page 46: courtesy of John H. Sheally II. Page 74: courtesy of John H. Sheally II. Page 91: © Gerry Spiess. Page 95: © Gerry Spiess. Chapter decorations: James Alexander.